SCARLETT

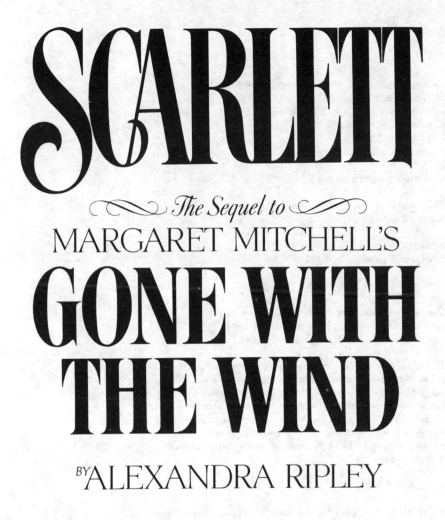

SCARLETT

The Sequel to

MARGARET MITCHELL'S

GONE WITH THE WIND

BY ALEXANDRA RIPLEY

MACMILLAN
LONDON

First published in the United Kingdom 1991 by
MACMILLAN LONDON LIMITED
a division of Pan Macmillan Publishers Limited
Cavaye Place London SW10 9PG
and Basingstoke
Associated companies throughout the world

This paperback edition published 1992

This work was first published in the United States of America by
Warner Books/New York

ISBN Hardback: 0-333-49099-1
ISBN Trade paperback: 0-333-57920-8

9 8 7 6 5 4 3 2 1

A CIP catalogue record for this book is available from the
British Library

Typeset by Crane Typesetting
Printed in England by Clays Ltd, St Ives plc

Book design by Giorgetta Bell McRee

Lost in the Dark

1

*T*his will be over soon, and then I can go home to Tara.

Scarlett O'Hara Hamilton Kennedy Butler stood alone, a few steps away from the other mourners at Melanie Wilkes' burial. It was raining, and the black-clad men and women hold black umbrellas over their heads. They leaned on one another, the women weeping, sharing shelter and grief.

Scarlett shared her umbrella with no one, nor her grief. The gusts of wind within the rain blew stinging cold wet rivulets under the umbrella, down her neck, but she was unaware of them. She felt nothing, she was numbed by loss. She would mourn later, when she could stand the pain. She held it away from her, all pain, all feeling, all thinking. Except for the words that repeated again and again in her mind, the words that promised healing from the pain to come and strength to survive until she was healed.

This will be over soon, and then I can go home to Tara.

"... ashes to ashes, dust to dust ..."

The minister's voice penetrated the shell of numbness, the words registered. No! Scarlett cried silently. Not Melly. That's not Melly's grave, it's too big, she's so tiny, her bones no bigger than a bird's. No! She can't be dead, she can't be.

Scarlett's head jerked to one side, denying the open grave, the plain pine box being lowered into it. There were small half circles sunk into the soft wood, marks of the hammers that had driven in the nails to close the lid above Melanie's gentle, loving, heart-shaped face.

No! You can't, you mustn't do this, it's raining, you can't put her there where the rain will fall on her. She feels the cold so, she mustn't be left in the cold rain. I can't watch, I can't bear it, I won't believe she's gone. She loves me, she is my friend, my only true friend. Melly loves me, she wouldn't leave me now just when I need her most.

Scarlett looked at the people surrounding the grave, and hot anger surged through her. None of them care as much as I do, none of them have lost as much as I have. No one knows how much I love her. Melly knows, though, doesn't she? She knows, I've got to believe she knows.

They'll never believe it, though. Not Mrs. Merriwether, or the Meades or the Whitings or the Elsings. Look at them, bunched up around India Wilkes and Ashley, like a flock of wet crows in their mourning clothes. They're comforting Aunt Pittypat, all right, even though everybody knows she takes on and cries her eyes out over every little thing, down to a piece of toast that gets burnt. It wouldn't enter their heads that maybe I might be needing some comforting, that I was closer to Melanie than any of them. They act as if I wasn't even here. Nobody has paid any attention to me at all. Not even Ashley. He knew I was there those awful two days after Melly died, when he needed me to manage things. They all did, even India, bleating at me like a goat. "What shall we do about the funeral, Scarlett? About the food for the callers? About the coffin? The pallbearers? The cemetery plot? The inscription on the headstone? The notice in the paper?" Now they're leaning all over each other, weeping and wailing. Well, I won't give them the satisfaction of seeing me cry all by myself with nobody to lean on. I mustn't cry. Not here. Not yet. If I start, I might never be able to stop. When I get to Tara, I can cry.

Scarlett lifted her chin, her teeth clenched to stop their chattering from the cold, to hold back the choking in her throat. This will be over soon, and then I can go home to Tara.

The jagged pieces of Scarlett's shattered life were all around her there in Atlanta's Oakland Cemetery. A tall spire of granite, gray stone streaked with gray rain, was somber memorial to the world that was gone forever, the carefree world of her youth before the War. It was the Confederate Memorial, symbol of the proud, heedless courage that had plunged the South with bright banners flying into destruction. It stood for so many lives lost, the friends of her childhood, the gallants who had begged for waltzes and kisses in the days when she had no problems greater than which wide-skirted ballgown to wear. It stood for her first husband, Charles Hamilton, Melanie's brother. It stood for the sons, brothers, husbands, fathers of all the rain-wet mourners on the small knoll where Melanie was being buried.

There were other graves, other markers. Frank Kennedy, Scarlett's second husband. And the small, terribly small, grave with the headstone that read EUGENIE VICTORIA BUTLER, and under it BONNIE. Her last child, and the most loved.

The living, as well as the dead, were all round her, but she stood apart. Half of Atlanta was there, it seemed. The crowd had overflowed the church and now it spread in a wide, uneven dark circle around the bitter slash of color in the gray rain, the open grave dug from Georgia's red clay for the body of Melanie Wilkes.

The front row of mourners held those who'd been closest to her. White and black, their faces all streaked with tears, except Scarlett's. The old coachman Uncle Peter stood with Dilcey and Cookie in a protective black triangle around Beau, Melanie's bewildered little boy.

The older generation of Atlanta were there, with the tragically few descendants that remained to them. The Meades, the Whitings, the Merriwethers, the Elsings, their daughters and sons-in-law, Hugh Elsing the only living son; Aunt Pittypat Hamilton and her brother, Uncle Henry Hamilton, their ages-old feud forgotten in mutual grief for their niece. Younger, but looking as old as the others, India Wilkes sheltered herself within the group and watched her brother, Ashley, from grief- and guilt-shadowed eyes. He stood alone, like Scarlett. He was bare-headed in the rain, unaware of the proffered shelter of umbrellas, unconscious of the cold wetness, unable to accept the finality of the minister's words or the narrow coffin being lowered into the muddy red grave.

Ashley. Tall and thin and colorless, his pale gilt hair now almost gray, his pale stricken face as empty as his staring, unseeing gray eyes. He stood erect, his stance a salute, the inheritance of his years as a gray-uniformed officer. He stood motionless, without sensation or comprehension.

Ashley. He was the center and the symbol of Scarlett's ruined life. For love of him she'd ignored the happiness that had been hers for the taking. She'd turned her back on her husband, not seeing his love for her, not admitting her love for him, because wanting Ashley was always in the way. And now Rhett was gone, his only presence here a spray of warm golden autumn flowers among all the others. She'd betrayed her only friend, scorned Melanie's stubborn loyalty and love. And now Melanie was gone. And even Scarlett's love for Ashley was gone, for she'd realized—too late —that the habit of loving him had long since replaced love itself.

She did not love him, and she never would again. But now, when she didn't want him, Ashley was hers, her legacy from Melanie. She had promised Melly she'd take care of him and of Beau, their child.

Ashley was the cause of her life's destruction. And the only thing left to her from it.

Scarlett stood apart and alone. There was only cold gray space between her and the people she knew in Atlanta, space that once Melanie had filled, keeping her from isolation and ostracism. There was only the cold wet wind beneath the umbrella in the place where Rhett should have been to shelter her with his strong broad shoulders and his love.

She held her chin high, into the wind, accepting its assault without feeling it. All her senses were concentrated on the words that were her strength and her hope.

This will be over soon, and then I can go home to Tara.

"Look at her," whispered a black-veiled lady to the companion sharing her umbrella. "Hard as nails. I heard that the whole time she was handling the funeral arrangements, she didn't even shed a tear. All business, that's Scarlett. And no heart at all."

"You know what folks say," was the answering whisper. "She has heart aplenty for Ashley Wilkes. Do you think they really did—"

The people nearby hushed them, but they were thinking the same thing. Everyone was.

The awful hollow thud of earth on wood made Scarlett clench her fists. She wanted to clap her hands over her ears, to scream, to shout—anything to shut out the terrible sound of the grave closing over Melanie. Her teeth closed painfully on her lip. She wouldn't scream, she wouldn't.

The cry that shattered the solemnity was Ashley's. "Melly . . . Mell—eee!" And again, "Mell—eee." It was the cry of a soul in torment, filled with loneliness and fear.

He stumbled towards the deep muddy pit like a man newly struck blind, his hands searching for the small, quiet creature who was all his strength. But there was nothing to hold, only the streaming silver streaks of cold rain.

Scarlett looked at Dr. Meade, India, Henry Hamilton. Why don't they do something? Why don't they stop him? He's got to be stopped!

"Mell—eee . . ."

For the love of God! He's going to break his neck, and they're all just standing there watching, gawping at him teetering on the edge of the grave.

"Ashley, stop!" she shouted. "Ashley!" She began to run, slipping and sliding on the wet grass. The umbrella she had thrown aside scudded across the ground, pushed by the wind until it was trapped in the mounds of flowers. She grabbed Ashley around the waist, tried to pull him away from the danger. He fought her.

"Ashley, don't!" Scarlett struggled against his strength. "Melly can't help you now." Her voice was harsh, to cut through Ashley's unhearing, demented grief.

He halted, and his arms dropped to his sides. He moaned softly, and then his whole body crumpled in Scarlett's supporting arms. Just when her grasp was breaking from the weight of him, Dr. Meade and India caught Ashley's limp arms to lift him erect.

"You can go now, Scarlett," said Dr. Meade. "There's no more damage left for you to do."

"But, I—" She looked at the faces around her, the eyes avid for more sensation. Then she turned and walked away through the rain. The crowd drew back as if a brush of her skirts might soil them.

They must not know that she cared, she wouldn't let them see that they could hurt her. Scarlett raised her chin defiantly, letting the rain pour down over her face and neck. Her back was straight, her shoulders square until she reached the gates of the cemetery and was out of sight. Then she grabbed one of the iron palings. She felt dizzy from exhaustion, unsteady on her feet.

Her coachman Elias ran to her, opening his umbrella to hold above her bent head. Scarlett walked to her carriage, ignoring the hand held out to help her. Inside the plush-upholstered box, she sank into a corner and pulled up the woolen lap robe. She was chilled to the bone, horrified by what she had done. How could she have shamed Ashley like that in front of everybody, when only a few nights ago she had promised Melanie that she would take care of him, protect him as Melly had always done? But what else could she have done? Let him throw himself into the grave? She had to stop him.

The carriage jolted from side to side, its high wheels sinking into the deep ruts of clay mud. Scarlett nearly fell to the floor. Her elbow hit the window frame, and a sharp pain ran up and down her arm.

It was only physical pain, she could stand that. It was the other pain —the postponed, delayed, denied shadowy pain—that she couldn't bear. Not yet, not here, not when she was all alone. She had to get to Tara, she had to. Mammy was there. Mammy would put her brown arms around her, Mammy would hold her close, cradle her head on the breast where she'd sobbed out all her childhood hurts. She could cry in Mammy's arms, cry herself empty of pain; she could rest her head on Mammy's breast, rest her wounded heart on Mammy's love. Mammy would hold her and love her, would share her pain and help her bear it.

"Hurry, Elias," said Scarlett, "hurry."

* * *

"Help me out of these wet things, Pansy," Scarlett ordered her maid. "Hurry." Her face was ghostly pale, it made her green eyes look darker, brighter, more frightening. The young black girl was clumsy with nervousness. "Hurry, I said. If you make me miss my train, I'll take a strap to you."

She couldn't do it, Pansy knew she couldn't do it. The slavery days were over, Miss Scarlett didn't own her, she could quit any time she wanted to. But the desperate, feverish glint in Scarlett's green eyes made Pansy doubt her own knowledge. Scarlett looked capable of anything.

"Pack the black wool merino, it's going to be colder," said Scarlett. She stared at the open wardrobe. Black wool, black silk, black cotton, black twill, black velvet. She could go on mourning for the rest of her days. Mourning for Bonnie still, and now mourning for Melanie. I should find something darker than black, something more mournful to wear to mourn for myself.

I won't think about that, not now. I'll go mad if I do. I'll think about it when I get to Tara. I can bear it there.

"Put on your things, Pansy. Elias is waiting. And don't you dare forget the crape armband. This is a house of mourning."

The streets that met at Five Points were a quagmire. Wagons and buggies and carriages were sunk in mud. Their drivers cursed the rain, the streets, their horses, the other drivers in their way. There was shouting and the sound of whips cracking, and the noise of people. There were always crowds of people at Five Points, people hurrying, arguing, complaining, laughing. Five Points was turbulent with life, with push, with energy. Five Points was the Atlanta Scarlett loved.

But not today. Today Five Points was in her way, Atlanta was holding her back. I've got to make that train, I'll die if I miss it, I've got to get to Mammy and Tara or I'll break down. "Elias," she yelled, "I don't care if you whip the horses to death, I don't care if you run over every single person on the street. You get to the depot." Her horses were the strongest, her coachman the most skillful, her carriage the best that money could buy. Nothing better get in her way, nothing.

She made the train with time to spare.

There was a loud burst of steam. Scarlett held her breath, listening for the first clunking revolution of the wheels that meant the train was moving.

There it was. Then another. And another. And the rattling, shaking of the car. She was on her way at last.

Everything was going to be all right. She was going home to Tara. She pictured it, sunny and bright, the white house gleaming, glistening green leaves of cape jasmine bushes studded with perfect, waxen white blossoms.

Heavy dark rain sluiced down the window beside her when the train left the station, but no matter. At Tara there'd be a fire in the living room, crackling from pine cones thrown onto the logs, and the curtains would be drawn, shutting out the rain and the darkness and the world. She'd lay her head on Mammy's soft broad bosom and tell her all the horrible things that had happened. Then she'd be able to think, to work everything out . . .

Hissing steam and squealing wheels jerked Scarlett's head upright.

Was this Jonesboro already? She must have dozed off, and no wonder, as tired as she was. She hadn't been able to sleep for two nights, even with the brandy to calm her nerves. No, the station was Rough and Ready. Still an hour to Jonesboro. At least the rain had stopped; there was even a patch of blue sky up ahead. Maybe the sun was shining at Tara. She imagined the entrance drive, the dark cedars that bordered it, then the wide green lawn and the beloved house on top of the low hill.

Scarlett sighed heavily. Her sister Suellen was the lady of the house at Tara now. Ha! Cry-baby of the house was more like it. All Suellen ever did was whine, it was all she'd ever done, ever since they were children. And she had her own children now, whiny little girls just like she used to be.

Scarlett's children were at Tara, too. Wade and Ella. She'd sent them with Prissy, their nursemaid, when she got the news that Melanie was dying. Probably she should have had them with her at Melanie's funeral. That gave all the old cats in Atlanta one more thing to gossip about, what an unnatural mother she was. Let them talk all they liked. She couldn't have gotten through those terrible days and nights after Melly's death if she'd had Wade and Ella to cope with too.

She wouldn't think about them, that's all. She was going home, to Tara and to Mammy, and she simply wouldn't let herself think about things that would upset her. Lord knows, I've got more than enough to upset me without dragging them in, too. And I'm so tired . . . Her head drooped and her eyes closed.

"Jonesboro, ma'am," said the conductor. Scarlett blinked, sat straight.

"Thank you." She looked around the car for Pansy and her valises. I'll skin that girl alive if she's wandered off to another car. Oh, if only a lady didn't have to have a companion every single time she put her foot outside her own house. I'd do so much better by myself. There she is. "Pansy. Get those valises off the rack. We're here."

Only five miles to Tara now. Soon I'll be home. Home!

Will Benteen, Suellen's husband, was waiting on the platform. It was a shock to see Will; the first few seconds were always a shock. Scarlett genuinely loved and respected Will. If she could have had a brother, like she'd always wanted, she'd wish he could be just like Will. Except for the wooden pegleg, and of course not a Cracker. It was just there was no mistaking Will for a gentleman; he was unmistakably lower class. She forgot it when she was away from him, and she forgot it after she was with him for a minute, because he was such a good, kind man. Even Mammy thought a lot of Will, and Mammy was the hardest judge in the world when it came to who was a lady or a gentleman.

"Will!" He walked toward her, in his special swinging gait. She threw her arms around his neck and hugged him fiercely.

"Oh, Will, I'm so glad to see you that I'm practically crying for joy."

Will accepted her embrace without emotion. "I'm glad to see you, too, Scarlett. It's been a long time."

"Too long. It's shameful. Almost a year."

"More like two."

Scarlett was dumbfounded. Had it been that long? No wonder her life had come to such a sorry state. Tara had always given her new life, new strength when she needed it. How could she have gone so long without it?

Will gestured to Pansy and walked toward the wagon outside the station. "We'd better get moving if we're going to beat the dark," he said. "Hope you don't mind riding rough, Scarlett. As long as I was coming to town, I figured I might as well get some supplies." The wagon was piled high with sacks and parcels.

"I don't mind at all," said Scarlett truthfully. She was going home, and anything that would take her there was fine. "Climb up on those feed sacks, Pansy."

She was as silent as Will on the long drive to Tara, drinking in the remembered quiet of the countryside, refreshing herself with it. The air was new-washed, and the afternoon sun was warm on her shoulders. She'd been right to come home. Tara would give her the sanctuary she needed, and with Mammy she'd be able to find a way to repair her ruined world. She leaned forward as they turned onto the familiar drive, smiling in anticipation.

But when the house came in sight, she let out a cry of despair. "Will, what happened?" The front of Tara was covered by vines, ugly cords hung with dead leaves; four windows had sagging shutters, two had no shutters at all.

"Nothing happened except summer, Scarlett. I do the fixing up for the house in winter when there's no crops to tend. I'll be starting on those shutters in a few more weeks. It's not October yet."

"Oh, Will, why on earth won't you let me give you some money? You could hire some help. Why, you can see the brick through the white-wash. It looks downright trashy."

Will's reply was patient. "There's no help to be had for love nor money. Those that wants work has plenty of it, and those that don't wouldn't do me no good. We make out all right, Big Sam and me. Your money ain't needed."

Scarlett bit her lip and swallowed the words she wanted to say. She had run up against Will's pride often before, and she knew that he was unbendable. He was right that the crops and the stock had to come first. Their demands couldn't be put off; a fresh coat of whitewash could. She could see the fields now, stretching out behind the house. They were weed-less, newly harrowed, and there was a faint, rich smell of the manure tilled in to prepare them for the next planting. The red earth looked warm and fertile, and she relaxed. This was the heart of Tara, the soul.

"You're right," she said to Will.

The door to the house flew open, and the porch filled with people. Suellen stood in front, holding her youngest child in her arms above the swollen belly that strained the seams of her faded cotton dress. Her shawl had fallen down over one arm. Scarlett forced a gaiety she didn't feel. "Good Lord, Will, is Suellen having another baby? You're going to have to build on some more rooms."

Will chuckled. "We're still trying for a boy." He lifted a hand in greet-ing to his wife and three daughters.

Scarlett waved too, wishing she'd thought to buy some toys to bring the children. Oh, Lord, look at all of them. Suellen was scowling. Scarlett's eyes ran over the other faces, searching out the black ones . . . Prissy was there; Wade and Ella were hiding behind her skirts . . . and Big Sam's wife, Delilah, holding the spoon she must have been stirring with . . . There was—what was her name?—oh, yes, Lutie, the Tara children's mammy. But where was Mammy? Scarlett called out to her children. "Hello, darlings, Mother's here." Then she turned back to Will, put a hand on his arm.

"Where's Mammy, Will? She's not so old that she can't come to meet me." Fear pinched the words in Scarlett's throat.

"She's sick in bed, Scarlett."

Scarlett jumped down from the still-moving wagon, stumbled, caught herself and ran to the house. "Where's Mammy?" she said to Suellen, deaf to the excited greetings of the children.

"A fine hello that is, Scarlett, but no worse than I'd expect from you.

What did you think you were doing, sending Prissy and your children here without so much as a by your leave, when you know that I've got my hands full and then some?"

Scarlett raised her hand, ready to slap her sister. "Suellen, if you don't tell me where Mammy is, I'll scream."

Prissy pulled on Scarlett's sleeve. "I knows where Mammy is, Miss Scarlett, I knows. She's powerful sick, so we fixed up that little room next the kitchen for her, the one what used to be where all the hams was hung when there was a lot of hams. It's nice and warm there, next to the chimney. She was already there when I come, so I can't exactly say we fixed up the room altogether, but I brung in a chair so as there'd be a place to sit if she wanted to get up or if there was a visitor ..."

Prissy was talking to air. Scarlett was at the door to Mammy's sickroom, holding on to the framework for support.

That ... that ... thing in the bed wasn't her Mammy. Mammy was a big woman, strong and fleshy, with warm brown skin. It had been hardly more than six months since Mammy left Atlanta, not long enough to have wasted away like this. It couldn't be. Scarlett couldn't bear it. This wasn't Mammy, she wouldn't believe it. This creature was gray and shrivelled, hardly making a rise under the faded patchwork quilts that covered it, twisted fingers moving weakly across the folds. Scarlett's skin crawled.

Then she heard Mammy's voice. Thin and halting, but Mammy's beloved, loving voice. "Now, Missy, ain't I done tole you and tole you not to set foot outside without you wears a bonnet and carries a sunshade ... Tole you and tole you ..."

"Mammy!" Scarlett fell to her knees beside the bed. "Mammy, it's Scarlett. Your Scarlett. Please don't be sick, Mammy, I can't bear it, not you." She put her head down on the bed beside the bony thin shoulders and wept stormily, like a child.

A weightless hand smoothed her bent head. "Don't cry, chile. Ain't nothing so bad that it can't be fixed."

"Everything," Scarlett wailed. "Everything's gone wrong, Mammy."

"Hush, now, it's only one cup. And you got another tea set anyhow, just as pretty. You kin still have your tea party just like Mammy promised you."

Scarlett drew back, horrified. She stared at Mammy's face and saw the shining love in the sunken eyes, eyes that did not see her.

"No," she whispered. She couldn't stand it. First Melanie, then Rhett, and now Mammy; everyone she loved had left her. It was too cruel. It couldn't be.

"Mammy," she said loudly, "Mammy, listen to me. It's Scarlett." She grabbed the edge of the mattress and tried to shake it. "Look at me," she sobbed, "me, my face. You've got to know me, Mammy. It's me, Scarlett."

Will's big hands closed around her wrists. "You don't want to do that," he said. His voice was soft, but his grip was like iron. "She's happy when she's like that, Scarlett. She's back in Savannah taking care of your mother when she was a little girl. Those were happy times for her. She was young; she was strong; she wasn't in pain. Let her be."

Scarlett struggled to get free. "But I want her to know me, Will. I never told her how much she means to me. I have to tell her."

"You'll have your chance. Lots of times she's different, knows everybody. Knows she's dying, too. These times are better. Now you come on with me. Everybody's waiting for you. Delilah listens out for Mammy from the kitchen."

Scarlett allowed Will to help her to her feet. She was numb all over, even her heart. She followed him silently to the living room. Suellen started immediately to berate her, taking up her complaints where she had left off, but Will hushed her. "Scarlett's suffered a deep blow, Sue, leave her alone." He poured whiskey into a glass and placed it in Scarlett's hand.

The whiskey helped. It burned the familiar path through her body, dulling her pain. She held out her empty glass to Will, and he poured some more whiskey into it.

"Hello, darlings," she said to her children, "come give Mother a hug." Scarlett heard her own voice; it sounded as if it belonged to someone else, but at least it was saying the right thing.

She spent all the time she could in Mammy's room, at Mammy's side. She had fastened all her hopes on the comfort of Mammy's arms around her, but now it was her strong young arms that held the dying old black woman. Scarlett lifted the wasted form to bathe Mammy, to change Mammy's linen, to help her when breathing was too hard, to coax a few spoonfuls of broth between her lips. She sang the lullabies Mammy had so often sung to her, and when Mammy talked in delirium to Scarlett's dead mother, Scarlett answered with the words she thought her mother might have said.

Sometimes Mammy's rheumy eyes recognized her, and the old woman's cracked lips smiled at the sight of her favorite. Then her quavering voice would scold Scarlett, as she had scolded her since Scarlett was a baby. "Your hair looks purely a mess, Miss Scarlett, now you go brush a hundred strokes like Mammy taught you." Or, "You ain't got no call to be wearing a frock all crumpled up like that. Go put on something fresh before folks see you." Or, "You looks pale as a ghost, Miss Scarlett. Is you putting powder on your face? Wash it off this minute."

Whatever Mammy commanded, Scarlett promised to do. There was never time enough to obey before Mammy slid back into unconsciousness, or that other world where Scarlett did not exist.

During the day and evening Suellen or Lutie or even Will would share the work of the sickroom, and Scarlett could snatch a half hour's sleep, curled in the sagging rocking chair. But at night Scarlett kept solitary vigil. She lowered the flame in the oil lamp and held Mammy's thin dry hand in hers. While the house slept and Mammy slept, she was able at last to cry, and her heartbroken tears eased her pain a little.

Once, in the small quiet hour before dawn, Mammy woke. "What for is you weeping, honey?" she whispered. "Old Mammy is ready to lay down her load and rest in the arms of the Lord. There ain't no call to take on so." Her hand stirred in Scarlett's, freed itself, stroked Scarlett's bent head. "Hush, now. Nothing's so bad as you think."

"I'm sorry," she sobbed, "I just can't stop crying."

Mammy's bent fingers pushed Scarlett's tangled hair away from her face. "Tell old Mammy what's troubling her lamb."

Scarlett looked into the old, wise, loving eyes and felt the most profound pain she had ever known. "I've done everything wrong, Mammy. I don't know how I could have made so many mistakes. I don't understand."

"Miss Scarlett, you done what you had to do. Can't nobody do more than that. The good Lord sent you some heavy burdens, and you carried them. No sense asking why they was laid on you or what it took out of you to tote them. What's done is done. Don't fret yourself now." Mammy's heavy eyelids closed over tears that glistened in the dim light, and her ragged breathing slowed in sleep.

How can I not fret? Scarlett wanted to shout. My life is ruined, and I don't know what to do. I need Rhett, and he's gone. I need you, and you're leaving me, too.

She lifted her head, wiped her tears away on her sleeve and straightened her aching shoulders. The coals in the pot-bellied stove were nearly used up, and the bucket was empty. She had to refill it, she had to feed the fire. The room was beginning to chill, and Mammy must be kept warm. Scarlett pulled the faded patchwork quilts up over Mammy's frail form, then she took the bucket out into the cold darkness of the yard. She hurried toward the coal bin, wishing she'd thought to put on a shawl.

There was no moon, only a crescent sliver lost behind a cloud. The air was heavy with night's moisture, and the few stars not hidden by clouds looked very far away and icy-brilliant. Scarlett shivered. The blackness around her seemed formless, infinite. She had rushed blindly into the center of the yard, and now she couldn't make out the familiar shapes of smokehouse and barn that should be nearby. She turned in sudden panic, looking for the white bulk of the house she'd just left. But it, too, was dark and formless. No light showed anywhere. It was as if she were lost in a bleak and unknown and silent world. Nothing was stirring in the night, not a leaf, not a feather on a bird's wing. Terror plucked at her taut nerves, and she wanted to run. But where to? Everywhere was alien darkness.

Scarlett clenched her teeth. What kind of foolishness was this? I'm at home, at Tara, and the dark cold will be gone as soon as the sun's up. She forced a laugh; the shrill unnatural sound made her jump.

They do say it's always darkest before the dawn, she thought. I reckon this is proof of it. I've got the megrims, that's all. I just won't give in to them, there's no time for that, the stove needs feeding. She put a hand out before her into the blackness and walked toward where the coal bin should be, next to the woodpile. A sunken spot made her stumble, and she fell. The bucket clattered loudly, then was lost.

Every exhausted, frightened part of her body cried out that she should give up, stay where she was, hugging the safety of the unseen ground beneath her until day came and she could see. But Mammy needed warmth. And the cheering yellow light of the flames through the isinglass windows of the stove.

Scarlett brought herself slowly to her knees and felt around her for the coal bucket. Surely there'd never been such pitch darkness before in the world. Or such wet cold night air. She was gasping for breath. Where was the bucket? Where was the dawn?

Her fingers brushed across cold metal. Scarlett scrabbled along on her knees toward it, then both hands were clasping the ridged sides of the tin coal scuttle. She sat back on her heels, holding it to her breast in a desperate embrace.

Oh Lord, I'm all turned around now. I don't even know where the house is, much less the coal bin. I'm lost in the night. She looked up frantically, searching for any light at all, but the sky was black. Even the cold distant stars had disappeared.

For a moment she wanted to cry out, to scream and scream until she woke someone in the house, someone who would light a lamp, who'd come find her and lead her home.

Her pride forbid it. Lost in her own backyard, only a few steps from the kitchen door! She'd never live down the shame of it.

She looped the bail of the scuttle over her arm and began to crawl clumsily on hands and knees across the dark earth. Sooner or later she'd run into something—the house, the woodpile, the barn, the well—and she'd get her bearings. It would be quicker to get up and walk. She wouldn't feel like such a fool, either. But she might fall again, and this time twist her ankle or something. Then she'd be helpless until someone found her. No matter what she had to do, anything was better than lying alone and helpless and lost.

Where was a wall? There had to be one here someplace, she felt as if she'd crawled halfway to Jonesboro. Panic brushed past her. Suppose the darkness never lifted, suppose she just kept on crawling and crawling forever without reaching anything?

Stop it! she told herself, stop it right now. Her throat was making strangled noises.

She struggled to her feet, made herself breathe slowly, made her mind take command of her racing heart. She was Scarlett O'Hara, she told herself. She was at Tara, and she knew every foot of the place better than she knew her own hand. So what if she couldn't see four inches in front of her? She knew what was there; all she had to do was find it.

And she'd do it on her feet, not on all fours like a baby or a dog. She lifted her chin and squared her thin shoulders. Thank God no one had seen her sprawled in the dirt or inching along over it, afraid to get up. Never in all her life had she been beaten, not by old Sherman's army, not by the worst the carpetbaggers could do. Nobody, nothing could beat her unless she let them, and then she'd deserve it. The very idea of being afraid of the dark, like some cowardly cry-baby!

I guess I let things get me down as far as a person can go, she thought with disgust, and her own scorn warmed her. I won't let it happen again, ever, no matter what comes. Once you get down all the way, the road can only go up. If I messed up my life, I'll clean up the mess. I won't lie in it.

With the coal scuttle held in front of her Scarlett walked forward with firm steps. Almost at once the tin bucket clanged against something. She laughed aloud when she smelled the sharp resinous odor of fresh cut pine. She was at the woodpile, with the coal bin immediately beside it. It was exactly where she'd set out to go.

The iron door of the stove closed on the renewed flames with a loud noise that made Mammy stir in her bed. Scarlett hurried across to pull the quilts up again. The room was cold.

Mammy squinted through her pain at Scarlett. "You got a dirty face —and hands, too," she grumbled in a weak voice.

"I know," said Scarlett, "I'll wash them right this minute." Before the old woman drifted away, Scarlett kissed her forehead. "I love you, Mammy."

"No need to tell me what I knows already." Mammy slid into sleep, escaping from pain.

"Yes there is a need," Scarlett told her. She knew Mammy couldn't hear her, but she spoke aloud anyhow, half to herself. "There's all kinds of need. I never told Melanie, and I didn't tell Rhett until it was too late. I never took the time to know I loved them, or you either. At least with you I won't make the mistake I did with them."

Scarlett stared down at the skull-like face of the dying old woman. "I love you, Mammy," she whispered. "What's going to become of me when I don't have you to love me?"

2

*P*rissy's head poked sideways around the cracked-open door to the sickroom. "Miss Scarlett, Mister Will he say for me to come sit with Mammy whilst you eat some breakfast. Delilah say you going wear yourself out with all the nursing, and she done fix you a fine big slice of ham with gravy for your grits."

"Where's the beef broth for Mammy?" Scarlett asked urgently. "Delilah knows she's supposed to bring warm broth first thing in the morning."

"I got it right here in my hand." Prissy elbowed the door open, a tray in front of her. "But Mammy's sleeping, Miss Scarlett. Do you want to shake her awake to drink her broth?"

"Just keep it covered and set the tray near the stove. I'll feed her when I get back." Scarlett felt ravenously hungry. The rich aroma of the steaming broth made her stomach cramp from emptiness.

She washed her face and hands hastily in the kitchen. Her frock was dirty, too, but it would have to do. She'd put on a clean one after she ate.

Will was just getting up from the table when Scarlett entered the dining room. Farmers couldn't waste time, especially on a day as bright and warm as the one promised by the golden early sun outside the window.

"Can I help you, Uncle Will?" Wade asked hopefully. He jumped up, almost knocking over his chair. Then he saw his mother and his face lost its eagerness. He'd have to stay at table and use his best manners, or she'd be cross. He walked slowly to hold Scarlett's chair for her.

"What lovely manners you have, Wade," Suellen cooed. "Good morning, Scarlett. Aren't you proud of your young gentleman?"

Scarlett looked blankly at Suellen, then at Wade. Good heavens, he was just a child, what on earth was Suellen being so simpering sweet about? The way she was carrying on you'd think Wade was a dancing partner to flirt with.

He was a nice-looking boy, she realized with surprise. Big for his age, too, he looked more like thirteen than not yet twelve. But Suellen wouldn't think that was so wonderful if she had to buy the clothes he kept growing out of so fast.

Good heavens! What am I going to do about Wade's clothes? Rhett always does whatever needs doing; I don't know what boys wear, or even where to shop. His wrists are hanging out of his sleeves, he probably has to have everything in a bigger size. In a hurry, too. School must be starting soon. If it hasn't already; I don't even know what the date of today is.

Scarlett sat with a thump in the chair Wade was holding. She hoped he'd be able to tell her what she needed to know. But first she'd eat breakfast. My mouth's watering so, I feel like I'm gargling. "Thank you, Wade Hampton," she said absently. The ham looked perfect, richly pink and juicy with crisply browned fat rimming it. She dropped her napkin in her lap without bothering to unfold it and picked up her knife and fork.

"Mother?" Wade said cautiously.

"Um?" Scarlett cut into the ham.

"May I please go help Uncle Will in the fields?"

Scarlett broke a cardinal rule of table manners and talked with food in her mouth. The ham was delicious. "Yes, yes, go on." Her hands were busy cutting another bite.

"Me, too," Ella piped up.

"Me, too," echoed Suellen's Susie.

"You're not invited," said Wade. "Fields are man's business. Girls stay in the house."

Susie began to cry.

"Now look what you've done!" Suellen said to Scarlett.

"Me? It's not my child making all that noise." Scarlett always meant to avoid quarrels with Suellen when she came to Tara, but the habits of a lifetime were too strong. They had begun fighting as babies and had never really stopped.

But I'm not going to let her ruin the first meal I've been hungry for in who knows how long, Scarlett said to herself, and she concentrated on swirling butter evenly through the gleaming white mound of grits on her plate. She didn't even lift her eyes when Wade followed Will out the door and Ella's wails joined Susie's.

"Hush up, both of you," Suellen said loudly.

Scarlett poured ham gravy over her grits, piled grits on a piece of ham, and speared the arrangement with her fork.

"Uncle Rhett would let me go, too," Ella sobbed.

I won't listen, thought Scarlett, I'll just close my ears and enjoy my breakfast. She put ham and grits and gravy in her mouth.

"Mother . . . Mother, when is Uncle Rhett coming to Tara?" Ella's voice was sharply piercing. Scarlett heard the words in spite of herself, and the rich food turned to sawdust in her mouth. What could she say, how could she answer Ella's question? "Never." Was that the answer? She couldn't, wouldn't believe it herself. She looked at her red-faced daughter with loathing. Ella had ruined everything. Couldn't she have left me alone at least long enough to eat my breakfast?

Ella had the ginger-colored curly hair of her father, Frank Kennedy. It stuck out around her tear-blotched face like rusted coils of wire, always escaping from the tight braids Prissy plaited, no matter how much she slicked it down with water. Ella's body was like wire, too, skinny and angular. She was older than Susie, almost seven compared to Susie's six and a half, but Susie was half a head taller already and so much heftier that she could bully Ella with impunity.

No wonder Ella wants Rhett to come, Scarlett thought. He really cares for her, and I don't. She gets on my nerves just like Frank did, and no matter how hard I try I just can't love her.

"When's Uncle Rhett coming, Mother?" Ella asked again. Scarlett pushed her chair away from the table and stood up.

"That's grown-ups' business," she said. "I'm going to see to Mammy." She couldn't bear to think about Rhett now, she'd think about all that later, when she wasn't so upset. It was more important—much more—to coax Mammy into swallowing her broth.

"Just one more little spoonful, Mammy darling, it'll make me happy."

The old woman turned her head away from the spoon. "Tired," she sighed.

"I know," said Scarlett, "I know. Go to sleep, then, I won't pester you any more." She looked down at the almost full bowl. Mammy was eating less and less every day.

"Miss Ellen . . ." Mammy called weakly.

"I'm here, Mammy," Scarlett replied. It always hurt when Mammy didn't know her, when she thought the hands that tended her so lovingly were the hands of Scarlett's mother. I shouldn't let it bother me, Scarlett told herself every time. It was always Mother who took care of the sick, not me. Mother was kind to everyone, she was an angel, she was a perfect lady. I should take it as praise to be mistook for her. I expect I'll go to hell for being jealous that Mammy loved her best . . . except that I don't much believe in hell any more . . . or heaven either.

"Miss Ellen . . ."

"I'm here, Mammy."

The old, old eyes opened half way. "You ain't Miss Ellen."

"It's Scarlett, Mammy, your very own Scarlett."

"Miss Scarlett . . . I wants Mist' Rhett. Something to say . . ."

Scarlett's teeth cut into her lip. I want him, too, she was crying silently. So much. But he's gone, Mammy. I can't give you what you want.

She saw that Mammy had slipped into a near-coma again, and she was fiercely grateful. At least Mammy was free of pain. Her own heart was aching as if it were full of knives. How she needed Rhett, especially now, with Mammy sliding ever faster down the slope to death. If he could just be here, with me, feeling the same sorrow I feel. For Rhett loved Mammy, too, and Mammy loved him. He'd never worked so hard to win anyone over in his life, Rhett said, and he'd never cared as much for anyone's opinion as he did Mammy's. He'd be broken-hearted when he learned that she was gone, he'd wish so much that he'd been able to say goodbye to her . . .

Scarlett's head lifted, her eyes widened. Of course. What a fool she was being. She looked at the wizened old woman, so small and weightless under the quilts. "Oh, Mammy, darling, thank you," she breathed. "I came to you for help, for you to make everything all right again, and you will, just the way you always did."

She found Will in the stable rubbing down the horse.

"Oh, I'm so glad to find you, Will," Scarlett said. Her green eyes were sparkling, her cheeks flushed with natural color instead of the rouge she usually wore. "Can I use the horse and buggy? I need to go to Jonesboro. Unless maybe— You weren't fixing to go to Jonesboro yourself for anything, were you?" She held her breath while she waited for his answer.

Will looked at her calmly. He understood Scarlett better than she realized. "Is there something I can do for you? If I was planning to go to Jonesboro, that is."

"Oh, Will, you are a dear, sweet thing. I'd so much rather stay with

Mammy, yet still I really need to let Rhett know about her. She's asking for him, and he's always been so fond of her, he'd never forgive himself if he let her down." She fiddled with the horse's mane. "He's in Charleston on family business; his mother can barely draw breath without asking Rhett's advice."

Scarlett looked up, saw Will's expressionless face, then looked away. She began to braid pieces of the mane, staring at her work as if it were of vital importance. "So if you'll just send a telegram, I'll give you the address. And you'd better make it from you, Will. Rhett knows how I adore Mammy. He's liable to think I was exaggerating how sick she is." She lifted her head and smiled brilliantly. "He thinks I haven't any more sense than a June bug."

Will knew that was the biggest lie of all. "I think you're right," he said slowly. "Rhett should come as soon as he can. I'll ride over right away; horseback's quicker than a rig."

Scarlett's hands relaxed. "Thank you," she said. "I have the address in my pocket."

"I'll be back in time for dinner," said Will. He lifted the saddle down from its stand. Scarlett helped him with it. She felt full of energy. She was sure Rhett would come. He could be at Tara in two days if he left Charleston as soon as he got the wire.

But Rhett didn't come in two days. Or three or four or five. Scarlett stopped listening for the sound of wheels or hoof beats on the drive. She had worn herself ragged, straining to hear. And now there was another sound that took all her attention, the horrible rasping noise that was Mammy's effort to breathe. It seemed impossible that the frail, wasted body could summon the strength needed to draw air into her lungs, push it out again. But she did, time after time, the cords on her wrinkled neck thick and quivering.

Suellen joined Scarlett's vigil. "She's my Mammy, too, Scarlett." The life-long jealousies and cruelties between them were forgotten in their joint need to help the old black woman. They brought down all the pillows in the house to prop her up, and kept the croup kettle steaming constantly. They spread butter on her cracked lips, spooned sips of water between them.

But nothing eased Mammy's struggles. She looked at them with pity. "Don't wear yo'selves out," she gasped. "Nothin' you kin do."

Scarlett put her fingers across Mammy's lips. "Hush," she begged. "Don't try to talk. Save your strength." Why, oh why, she raged silently to God, why couldn't You let her die easy, when she was wandering in the past? Why did You have to wake her up and let her suffer so? She was good all her life, always doing for other people, never anything for herself. She deserves better than this, I'll never bow my head to You again as long as I live.

But she read aloud to Mammy from the worn old Bible on the night-stand by the bed. She read the psalms, and her voice gave no sign of the pain and impious anger in her heart. When night came, Suellen lit the lamp and took over from Scarlett, reading, turning the thin pages, reading. Then Scarlett took her place. And again Suellen, until Will sent her to get some rest. "You, too, Scarlett," he said. "I'll sit with Mammy. I'm not much of a reader, but I know a lot of the Bible by heart."

"You recite then. But I'm not leaving Mammy. I can't." She sat on the floor and leaned her tired back against the wall, listening to the terrifying sounds of death.

When the first thin light of day showed at the windows, the sounds suddenly became different, each breath more noisy, longer silences between them. Scarlett scrambled to her feet. Will rose from the chair. "I'll get Suellen," he said.

Scarlett took his place beside the bed. "Do you want me to hold your hand, Mammy? Let me hold your hand."

Mammy's forehead creased with effort. "So . . . tired."

"I know, I know. Don't tire yourself more by talking."

"Wanted . . . to wait for . . . Mist' Rhett."

Scarlett swallowed. She couldn't weep now. "You don't need to hang on, Mammy. You can rest. He couldn't come." She heard hurried footsteps in the kitchen. "Suellen's on her way. And Mister Will. We'll all be here with you, darling. We all love you."

A shadow fell across the bed, and Mammy smiled.

"She wants me," said Rhett. Scarlett looked up at him, unbelieving. "Move over," he said gently. "Let me get near Mammy."

Scarlett stood, feeling the nearness of him, the bigness, the strength, the maleness, and her knees were weak. Rhett pushed past her and knelt by Mammy.

He had come. Everything was going to be all right. Scarlett knelt beside him, her shoulder touching his arm, and she was happy in the midst of her heartbreak about Mammy. He came, Rhett's here. What a fool I was to give up hope like that.

"I wants you to do something for me," Mammy was saying. Her voice sounded strong, as if she had saved her strength for this moment. Her breathing was shallow and fast, almost panting.

"Anything, Mammy," Rhett said. "I'll do anything you want."

"Bury me in my fine red silk petticoat what you gived me. See to it. I know that Lutie got her eye on it."

Rhett laughed. Scarlett was shocked. Laughter at a deathbed. Then she realized that Mammy was laughing, too, without sound.

Rhett put his hand on his heart. "I swear to you that Lutie won't even get a look at it, Mammy. I'll make sure it goes with you to Heaven."

Mammy's hand reached for him, gesturing his ear closer to her lips. "You take care of Miss Scarlett," she said. "She needs caring, and I can't do no more."

Scarlett held her breath.

"I will, Mammy," Rhett said.

"You swear it." The command was faint, but stern.

"I swear it," said Rhett. Mammy sighed quietly.

Scarlett let her breath out with a sob. "Oh, Mammy darling, thank you," she cried. "Mammy—"

"She can't hear you, Scarlett, she's gone." Rhett's big hand moved gently across Mammy's face, closing her eyes. "That's a whole world gone, an era ended," he said softly. "May she rest in peace."

"Amen," said Will from the doorway.

Rhett stood, turned. "Hello, Will, Suellen."

"Her last thought was for you, Scarlett," Suellen cried. "You were always her favorite." She began to weep loudly. Will took her in his arms, patting her back, letting his wife wail against his chest.

Scarlett ran to Rhett and held her arms up to embrace him. "I've missed you so," she said.

Rhett circled her wrists with his hands and lowered her arms to her sides. "Don't, Scarlett," he said. "Nothing's changed." His voice was quiet.

Scarlett was incapable of such restraint. "What do you mean?" she cried loudly.

Rhett winced. "Don't force me to say it again, Scarlett. You know full well what I mean."

"I don't know. I don't believe you. You can't be leaving me, not really. Not when I love you and need you so awfully. Oh, Rhett, don't just look at me that way. Why don't you put your arms around me and comfort me? You promised Mammy."

Rhett shook his head, a faint smile on his lips. "You are such a child, Scarlett. You've known me all these years, and yet, when you want to, you can forget all you've learned. It was a lie. I lied to make a dear old woman's last moments happy. Remember, my pet, I'm a scoundrel, not a gentleman."

He walked toward the door.

"Don't go, Rhett, please," Scarlett sobbed. Then she put both hands over her mouth to stop herself. She'd never be able to respect herself if she begged him again. She turned her head sharply, unable to bear the sight of him leaving. She saw the triumph in Suellen's eyes and the pity in Will's.

"He'll be back," she said, holding her head high. "He always comes back." If I say it often enough, she thought, maybe I'll believe it. Maybe it will be true.

"Always," she said. She took a deep breath. "Where's Mammy's petticoat, Suellen? I intend to see to it that she's buried in it."

Scarlett was able to stay in control of herself until the dreadful work of bathing and dressing Mammy's corpse was done. But when Will brought in the coffin, she began to shake. Without a word she fled.

She poured a half glass of whiskey from the decanter in the dining room and drank it in three burning gulps. The warmth of it ran through her exhausted body, and the shaking stopped.

I need air, she thought. I need to get out of this house, away from all of them. She could hear the frightened voices of the children in the kitchen. Her skin felt raw with nerves. She picked up her skirts and ran.

Outside the morning air was fresh and cool. Scarlett breathed deeply, tasting the freshness. A light breeze lifted the hair that clung to her sweaty neck. When had she last done her hundred strokes with the hairbrush? She couldn't remember. Mammy would be furious. Oh— She put the knuckles of her right hand into her mouth to contain her grief and stumbled through the tall grasses of the pasture, down the hill to the woods that bordered the river. The high-topped pines smelled sharply sweet; they shaded a soft thick mat of bleached needles, shed over hundreds of years. Within their shelter, Scarlett was alone, invisible from the house. She crumpled wearily onto the cushioned ground, then settled herself in a sitting position with a tree trunk at her back. She had to think; there must be some way to salvage her life from the ruins; she refused to believe different.

But she couldn't keep her mind from jumping around. She was so confused, so tired.

She'd been tired before. Worse tired than this. When she had to get to Tara from Atlanta, with the Yankee army on all sides, she hadn't let tired stop her. When she had to forage for food all over the countryside, she hadn't given up because her legs and arms felt like dead weights pulling on her. When she picked cotton until her hands were raw, when she hitched herself to the plow like she was a mule, when she had to find strength to keep going in spite of everything, she hadn't given up because she was tired. She wasn't going to give up now. It wasn't in her to give up.

She stared ahead, facing all her demons. Melanie's death . . . Mammy's death . . . Rhett's leaving her, saying that their marriage was dead.

That was the worst. Rhett going away. That was what she had to meet head-on. She heard his voice: "Nothing's changed."

It couldn't be true! But it was.

She had to find a way to get him back. She'd always been able to get any man she wanted, and Rhett was a man like any other man, wasn't he?

No, he wasn't like any other man, and that's why she wanted him. She shivered, suddenly afraid. Suppose that this time she didn't win? She had always won, one way or another. She'd always gotten what she wanted, somehow. Until now.

Above her head a bluejay cried raucously. Scarlett looked up, heard a second jeering cry. "Leave me alone," she shouted. The bird flew away, a whirr of gaudy blue.

She had to think, to remember what Rhett had said. Not this morning or last night or whenever it was that Mammy died. What did he say at our house, the night he left Atlanta? He talked on and on, explaining things. He was so calm, so horribly patient, the way you can be with people you don't care enough about to get mad at them.

Her mind seized on an almost-forgotten sentence, and she forgot her exhaustion. She had found what she needed. Yes, yes, she remembered it clearly. Rhett had offered her a divorce. Then, after her furious rejection of the offer, he had said it. Scarlett closed her eyes, hearing his voice in her head. "I'll come back often enough to keep gossip down." She smiled. She hadn't won yet, but there was a chance. A chance was enough to go on with. She stood up and picked the pine needles off her frock, out of her hair. She must look a mess.

The muddy yellow Flint River ran slowly and deeply below the ledge that held the pine woods. Scarlett looked down and threw in the handful of pine needles. They swirled away in the current. "Moving on," she murmured. "Just like me. Don't look back, what's done is done. Move on." She squinted up at the bright sky. A line of brilliant white clouds was rushing across it. They looked full of wind. It's going to get colder, she thought automatically. I'd better find something warm to wear this afternoon at the burial. She turned toward home. The sloping pasture looked steeper than she remembered. No matter. She had to get back to the house and tidy herself. She owed it to Mammy to look neat. Mammy had always fussed when she looked messy.

3

Scarlett swayed on her feet. She must have been as tired as this sometime before in her life, but she couldn't remember. She was too tired to remember.

I'm tired of funerals, I'm tired of death, I'm tired of my life falling away, a piece at a time, and leaving me all alone.

The graveyard at Tara was not very large. Mammy's grave looked big, ever so much bigger than Melly's, Scarlett thought disjointedly, but Mammy had shrivelled up so that she probably wasn't any bigger at all. She didn't need such a big grave.

The wind had a bite in it, for all that the sky was so blue and the sun so bright. Yellowed leaves skittered across the burial ground, blown by the wind. Autumn's coming, if it's not here already, she thought. I used to love the fall in the country, riding through the woods. The ground looked like it had gold on it, and the air tasted like cider. So long ago. There hasn't been a proper riding horse at Tara since Pa died.

She looked at the gravestones. Gerald O'Hara, born County Meath, Ireland. Ellen Robillard O'Hara, born Savannah, Georgia. Gerald O'Hara, Jr.—three tiny stones, all alike. The brothers she'd never known. At least Mammy was being buried here, next to "Miss Ellen," her first love, and not in the slaves' burial plot. Suellen screamed to high heaven, but I won that fight, soon as Will came in on my side. When Will puts his foot down, it stays put. Too bad he's so stiff-necked about letting me give him some money. The house looks terrible.

So does the graveyard, for that matter. Weeds all over the place, it's downright shabby. This whole funeral is downright shabby, Mammy would have hated it. That black preacher is going on and on, and he didn't even know her, I'll bet. Mammy wouldn't give the time of day to the likes of him, she was a Roman Catholic, everybody in the Robillard house was, except Grandfather, and he didn't have much say about anything, to hear Mammy tell it. We should have gotten a priest, but the closest one is in Atlanta, it would have taken days. Poor Mammy. Poor Mother, too. She died and was buried without a priest. Pa, too, but likely it didn't matter so much to him. He used to doze through the Devotions Mother led every night.

Scarlett looked at the unkempt graveyard, then over at the shabby front of the house. I'm glad Mother isn't here to see this, she thought with sudden fierce anger and pain. It would break her heart. Scarlett could—for a moment—see the tall, graceful form of her mother as clearly as if Ellen O'Hara were there among the mourners at the burial. Always impeccably groomed, her white hands busy with needlework or gloved to go out on one of her errands of mercy, always soft-voiced, always occupied with the perpetual work required to produce the orderly perfection that was life at Tara under her guidance. How did she do it? Scarlett cried silently. How did she make the world so wonderful as long as she was there? We were all so happy then. No matter what happened, Mother could make it all right. How I wish she was still here! She'd hold me close to her, and all the troubles would go away.

No, no, I don't want her to be here. It would make her so sad to see what's happened to Tara, what's happened to me. She'd be disappointed in me, and I couldn't bear that. Anything but that. I won't think about it, I mustn't. I'll think about something else—I wonder if Delilah had sense enough to fix something to feed people after the burial. Suellen wouldn't think of it, and she's too mean to spend money on a collation anyhow.

Not that it would set her back all that much—there's hardly anybody here. That black preacher looks like he could eat enough for twenty, though. If he doesn't stop going on about resting in Abraham's bosom and crossing the River Jordan, I'm going to scream. Those three scrawny women he calls a choir are the only people here who don't look twitchy from embarrassment. Some choir! Tambourines and spirituals! Mammy should have something solemn in Latin, not "Climbing Jacob's Ladder." Oh, it's all so tacky. A good thing there's almost nobody here, just Suellen and Will and me and the children and the servants. At least we all really loved Mammy and care that she's gone. Big Sam's eyes are red from crying. Look at poor old Pork, crying his eyes out, too. Why, his hair's almost white; I never think of him as old. Dilcey sure doesn't look her age, whatever that might be, she hasn't changed a bit since she first came to Tara . . .

Scarlett's exhausted, rambling mind suddenly sharpened. What were Pork and Dilcey doing here at all? They hadn't worked at Tara for years. Not since Pork became Rhett's valet and Dilcey, Pork's wife, went to Melanie's house, as Beau's mammy. How did they come to be here, at Tara? There was no way they could have learned about Mammy's death. Unless Rhett told them.

Scarlett looked over her shoulder. Had Rhett come back? There was no sign of him.

As soon as the service was over, she made a beeline for Pork. Let Will and Suellen deal with the long-winded preacher.

"It's a sad day, Miss Scarlett," Pork's eyes were still welling with tears.

"Yes, it is, Pork," she said. Mustn't rush him, she knew, or she'd never find out what she wanted to know.

Scarlett walked slowly beside the old black servant, listening to his reminiscences of "Mist' Gerald" and Mammy and the early days at Tara. She'd forgotten Pork had been with her father all that long. He'd come to Tara with Gerald when there was nothing there except a burned-out old building and fields gone to brush. Why, Pork must be seventy or more.

Little by little, she extracted the information she wanted. Rhett had gone back to Charleston, to stay. Pork had packed all of Rhett's clothes and sent them to the depot for shipping. It was his final duty as Rhett's valet, he was retired now, with a parting bonus that was big enough for him to have a place of his own anywhere he liked. "I can do for my family, too," Pork said proudly. Dilcey would never need to work again, and Prissy would have something to offer any man who wanted to marry her. "Prissy ain't no beauty, Miss Scarlett, and she's going on twenty-five years old, but with a 'heritance behind her, she can catch herself a husband easy as a young pretty girl what got no money."

Scarlett smiled and smiled and agreed with Pork that "Mist' Rhett" was a fine gentleman. Inside she was raging. That fine gentleman's generosity was making a real hash of things for her. Who was going to take care of Wade and Ella, with Prissy gone? And how the devil was she going to manage to find a good nursemaid for Beau? He'd just lost his mother, and his father was half crazy with grief, and now the only one in that house with any sense was leaving, too. She wished she could pick up and leave, too, just leave everything and everybody behind. Mother of God! I came to Tara to get some rest, to straighten out my life, and all I found was more problems to take care of. Can't I ever get any peace?

Will quietly and firmly provided Scarlett with that respite. He sent her to bed and gave orders that she wasn't to be disturbed. She slept for almost eighteen hours, and she woke with a clear plan of where to begin.

"I hope you slept well," said Suellen when Scarlett came down for breakfast. Her voice was sickeningly honeyed. "You must have been awfully tired, after all you've been through." The truce was over, now that Mammy was dead.

Scarlett's eyes glittered dangerously. She knew Suellen was thinking of the disgraceful scene she'd made, begging Rhett not to leave her. But when she answered, her words were equally sweet. "I hardly felt my head touch the pillow, and I was gone. The country air is so soothing and refreshing." You nasty thing, she added in her head. The bedroom that she still thought of as hers now belonged to Susie, Suellen's oldest child, and Scarlett had felt like a stranger. Suellen knew it, too, Scarlett was sure. But it didn't matter. She needed to stay on good terms with Suellen if she was going to carry out her plan. She smiled at her sister.

"What's so funny, Scarlett? Do I have a spot on my nose or something?"

Suellen's voice set Scarlett's teeth on edge, but she held on to her smile. "I'm sorry, Sue. I was just remembering a silly dream I had last night. I dreamt we were all children again, and that Mammy was switching my legs with a switch from the peach tree. Do you remember how much those switches stung?"

Suellen laughed. "I sure do. Lutie uses them on the girls. I can almost feel the sting on my own legs when she does."

Scarlett watched her sister's face. "I'm surprised I don't have a million scars to this day," she said. "I was such a horrid little girl. I don't know how you and Carreen could put up with me." She buttered a biscuit as if it were her only concern.

Suellen looked suspicious. "You did torment us, Scarlett. And somehow you managed to make the fights come out looking like our fault."

"I know. I was horrid. Even when we got older. I drove you and Carreen like mules when we had to pick the cotton after the Yankees stole everything."

"You nearly killed us. There we were, half dead from the typhoid, and you dragged us out of bed and sent us out in the hot sun . . ." Suellen became more animated and more vehement as she repeated grievances that she had nursed for years.

Scarlett nodded encouragement, making little noises of contrition.

How Suellen does love to complain, she thought. It's meat and drink to her. She waited until Suellen began to run down before she spoke:

"I feel so mean, and there's just nothing I can do to make up for all the bad times I put you through. I do think Will is wicked not to let me give youall any money. After all, it is for Tara."

"I've told him the same thing a hundred times," Suellen said.

I'll just bet you have, thought Scarlett. "Men are so bullheaded," she said. Then, "Oh, Suellen, I just thought of something. Do say yes, it would be such a blessing to me if you did. And Will couldn't possibly fuss about it. What if I left Ella and Wade here and sent money to you for their keep? They're so peaked from living in the city, and the country air would do them a world of good."

"I don't know, Scarlett. We're going to be awfully crowded when the baby comes." Suellen's expression was greedy, but still wary.

"I know," Scarlett crooned sympathetically. "Wade Hampton eats like a horse, too. But it would be so good for them, poor city creatures. I guess it would run about a hundred dollars a month just to feed them and buy them shoes."

She doubted that Will had a hundred dollars a year in cash money from his hard work at Tara. Suellen was speechless, she noted with satisfaction. She was sure her sister's voice would return in time to accept. I'll write a nice fat bank draft after breakfast, she thought. "These are the best biscuits I ever tasted," Scarlett said. "Could I have another?"

She was beginning to feel much better with a good sleep behind her, a good meal in her stomach, and the children taken care of. She knew she should go back to Atlanta—she still had to do something about Beau. Ashley, too; she'd promised Melanie. But she'd think about that later. She'd come to Tara for country peace and quiet, she was determined to have some before she left.

After breakfast Suellen went out to the kitchen. Probably to complain about something, Scarlett thought uncharitably. No matter. It gave her a chance to be alone and peaceful . . .

The house is so quiet. The children must be having their breakfast in the kitchen, and of course Will's long gone to the fields with Wade dogging his footsteps, just the way he used to when Will first came to Tara. Wade'll be much happier here than in Atlanta, especially with Rhett gone— No, I won't think about that now, I'll go crazy if I do. I'll just enjoy the peace and quiet, it's what I came for.

She poured herself another cup of coffee, not caring that it was only lukewarm. Sunlight through the window behind her illuminated the painting on the wall opposite, above the scarred sideboard. Will had done a grand job repairing the furniture that the Yankee soldiers had broken up, but even he couldn't remove the deep gouges they'd made with their swords. Or the bayonet wound in Grandma Robillard's portrait.

Whatever soldier had stabbed her must have been drunk, Scarlett figured, because he'd missed both the arrogant almost-sneer on Grandma's thin-nosed face and the bosoms that rounded up over her low cut gown. All he'd done was jab through her left earring, and now she looked even more interesting wearing just one.

Her mother's mother was the only ancestor who really interested Scarlett, and it frustrated her that nobody would ever tell her enough about her grandmother. Married three times, she had learned that much from her mother, but no details. And Mammy always cut off tales of life in Savannah just when they started getting interesting. There had been duels fought over Grandma, and the fashions of her day had been scandalous, with ladies deliberately wetting their thin muslin gowns so that they'd cling to their legs. And the rest of them, too, from the look of things in the portrait . . .

I should blush just from thinking the kind of things I'm thinking, Scarlett told herself. But she looked back over her shoulder at the portrait as she left the dining room. I wonder what she was really like?

The sitting room showed the signs of poverty and constant use by a young family; Scarlett could hardly recognize the velvet-covered settee where she had posed herself prettily when beaux proposed. And everything had been rearranged, too. She had to admit that Suellen had the right to fix the house to suit herself, but it rankled all the same. It wasn't really Tara this way.

She grew more and more despondent as she went from room to room. Nothing was the same. Every time she came home there were more changes, and more shabbiness. Oh, why did Will have to be so stubborn! All the furniture needed recovering, the curtains were practically rags, and you could see the floor right through the carpets. She could get new things for Tara if Will would let her. Then she wouldn't have the heartsickness of seeing the things she remembered looking so pitifully worn.

It should be mine! I'd take better care of it. Pa always said he'd leave Tara to me. But he never made a will. That's just like Pa, he never thought of tomorrow. Scarlett frowned, but she couldn't really be angry at her father. No one had ever stayed angry at Gerald O'Hara; he was like a lovable naughty child even when he was in his sixties.

The one I'm mad at—still—is Carreen. Baby sister or not, she was wrong to do what she did, and I'll never forgive her, never. She was stubborn as a mule when she made up her mind to go into the convent, and I accepted it finally. But she never told me she was going to use her one-third share of Tara as her dowry for the convent.

She should have told me! I would have found the money somehow. Then I'd have two-thirds ownership. Not the whole thing, like it should be, but at least clear control. Then I'd have some say so. Instead, I have to bite my tongue and watch while everything goes downhill and let Suellen queen it over me. It's not fair. I'm the one who saved Tara from the Yankees and the carpetbaggers. It is mine, no matter what the law says, and it'll be Wade's some day, I'll see to that, no matter what it takes.

Scarlett rested her head against the split leather covering on the old sofa in the small room from which Ellen O'Hara had quietly ruled the plantation. There seemed to be a lingering trace of her mother's lemon verbena toilet water, even after all these years. This was the peacefulness she had come to find. Never mind the changes, the shabbiness. Tara was still Tara, still home. And the heart of it was here, in Ellen's room.

A slamming door shattered the quiet.

Scarlett heard Ella and Susie coming through the hall, quarrelling about something. She had to get away, she couldn't face noise and conflict. She hurried outside. She wanted to see the fields anyhow. They were all healed, rich and red the way they'd always been.

She walked quickly across the weedy lawn and past the cow shed. She'd never get over her aversion to cows, not if she lived to be a hundred. Nasty sharp-horned things. At the edge of the first field she leaned on the fence and breathed in the rich ammonia odor of newly turned earth and manure. Funny how in the city manure was so smelly and messy, while in the country it was a farmer's perfume.

Will sure is a good farmer. He's the best thing that ever happened to Tara. No matter what I might have done, we'd never have made it if he hadn't stopped on his way home to Florida and decided to stay. He fell in love with this land the way other men fall in love with a woman. And he's not even Irish! Until Will came along I always thought only a brogue-talking Irishman like Pa could get so worked up about the land.

On the far side of the field Scarlett saw Wade helping Will and Big Sam mend a downed piece of fence. Good for him to be learning, she thought. It's his heritage. She watched the boy and the men working together for several minutes. I'd better scoot back to the house, she thought. I forgot to write that bank draft for Suellen.

Her signature on the check was characteristic of Scarlett. Clear and unembellished, with no blots, or wavering lines, like tentative writers. It was businesslike and straightforward. She looked at it for a moment before she blotted it dry, then she looked at it again.

Scarlett O'Hara Butler.

When she wrote personal notes or invitations, Scarlett followed the fashion of the day, adding complicated loops to every capital letter and finishing off with a parabola of swirls beneath her name. She did it now, on a scrap of brown wrapping paper. Then she looked back at the check she'd just written. It was dated—she'd had to ask Suellen what day it was, and she was shocked by the answer—October 11, 1873. More than three weeks since Melly's death. She'd been at Tara for twenty-two days, taking care of Mammy.

The date had other meanings, too. It was more than six months ago now that Bonnie died. Scarlett could leave off the unrelieved dull black of deep mourning. She could accept social invitations, invite people to her house. She could reenter the world.

I want to go back to Atlanta, she thought. I want some gaiety. There's been too much grieving, too much death. I need life.

She folded the check for Suellen. I miss the store, too. The account books are most likely in a fearful mess.

And Rhett will be coming to Atlanta "to keep gossip down." I've got to be there.

The only sound she could hear was the slow ticking of the clock in the hall beyond the closed door. The quiet that she'd longed for so much was now, suddenly, driving her crazy. She stood up abruptly.

I'll give Suellen her check after dinner, soon as Will goes back to the fields. Then I'll take the buggy and make a quick visit to the folks at Fairhill and Mimosa. They'd never forgive me if I didn't come by to say hello. Then tonight I'll pack my things, and tomorrow I'll take the morning train.

Home to Atlanta. Tara's not home for me any more, no matter how much I love it. It's time for me to go.

The road to Fairhill was rutted and weed grown. Scarlett remembered when it was scraped every week and sprinkled with water to keep the dust down. Time was, she thought sadly, there were at least ten plantations in visiting distance, and people coming and going all the time. Now there's only Tara left, and the Tarletons and the Fontaines. All the rest are just burnt chimneys or fallen-in walls. I really have to get back to the city. Everything in the County makes me sad. The slow old horse and the buggy's springs were almost as bad as the roads. She thought of her uphol- stered carriage and matched team, with Elias to drive them. She needed to go home to Atlanta.

The noisy cheerfulness at Fairhill snapped her out of her mood. As usual Beatrice Tarleton was full of talk about her horses, and interested in nothing else. The stables, Scarlett noticed, had a new roof. The house roof had fresh patches. Jim Tarleton looked old, his hair was white, but he'd brought in a good cotton crop with the help of his one-armed son-in-law, Hetty's husband. The other three girls were frankly old maids. "Of course we're miserably depressed about it day and night," said Miranda, and they all laughed. Scarlett didn't understand them at all. The Tarletons could laugh about anything. Maybe it was connected in some way with having red hair.

The twinge of envy she felt was nothing new. She'd always wished that she could be part of a family that was as affectionate and teasing as the Tarletons, but she stifled the envy. It was disloyal to her mother. She stayed too long—being with them was so much fun—she'd have to visit the Fontaines tomorrow. It was nearly dark when she got back to Tara. She could hear Suellen's youngest wailing for something even before she got the door open. It was definitely time to go back to Atlanta.

But there was news that changed her mind at once. Suellen scooped up the squalling child and shushed it just as Scarlett walked through the door. In spite of her bedraggled hair and misshapen body Suellen looked prettier than she ever had as a girl.

"Oh, Scarlett," she exclaimed. "There's such excitement, you'll never guess ... Hush, now, honey, you'll have a nice piece of bone with your supper and you can chew that mean old tooth right through so it won't hurt any more."

If a new tooth is the exciting news, I don't want to even try and guess, Scarlett felt like saying. But Suellen didn't give her a chance. "Tony's home!" Suellen said. "Sally Fontaine rode over to tell us; you just missed her. Tony's back! Safe and sound. We're going over to the Fontaine place for supper tomorrow night, just as soon as Will finishes with the cows. Oh, isn't it wonderful, Scarlett?" Suellen's smile was radiant. "The County's filling back up again."

Scarlett felt like hugging her sister, an impulse she'd never had before. Suellen was right. It was wonderful to have Tony back. She'd been afraid that no one would ever see him again. Now that awful memory of the last sight of him could be forgotten forever. He'd been so worn and worried— soaked to the skin, too, and shivering. Who wouldn't be cold and scared? The Yankees were right behind him and he was running for his life after he killed the black man who was mauling Sally and then the scallywag who'd egged the black fool on to go after a white woman.

Tony back home! She could hardly wait for the next afternoon. The County was returning to life.

*T*he Fontaine plantation was named Mimosa, for the grove of trees that surrounded the faded yellow stucco house. The trees' feathery pink flowers had fallen at summer's end, but the fern-like leaves were still vivid green on the boughs. They swayed like dancers in the light wind, making shifting patterns of shadow on the mottled walls of the butter-colored house. It looked warm and welcoming in the low, slanting sunlight.

Oh, I hope Tony hasn't changed too much, Scarlett thought nervously. Seven years is such a long time. Her feet dragged when Will lifted her down from the buggy. Suppose Tony looked old and tired and—well—defeated, like Ashley. It would be more than she could bear. She lagged behind Will and Suellen on the path to the door.

Then the door swung open with a bang and all her apprehension vanished. "Who's that strolling up like they were going to church? Don't you know enough to rush in and welcome a hero when he comes home?" Tony's voice was full of laughter, just the way it had always been, his hair and eyes as black as ever, his wide grin as bright and mischievous.

"Tony!" Scarlett cried. "You look just the same."

"Is that you, Scarlett? Come and give me a kiss. You, too, Suellen. You weren't generous with kisses like Scarlett in the old days, but Will must have taught you a few things after you married. I intend to kiss every female over six years old in the whole state of Georgia now that I'm back."

Suellen giggled nervously and looked at Will. A slight smile on his placid thin face granted her permission, but Tony hadn't bothered to wait for it. He grabbed her around her thickened waist and planted a smacking kiss on her lips. She was pink with confusion and pleasure when he released her. The dashing Fontaine brothers had paid Suellen little attention in the pre-War years of beaux and belles. Will put a warm, steadying arm around her shoulders.

"Scarlett, honey," Tony shouted, his arms held wide. Scarlett stepped into his embrace, hugged him tight around the neck.

"You got a lot taller in Texas," she exclaimed. Tony was laughing as he kissed her offered lips. Then he lifted his trouser leg to show them all the high-heeled boots he was wearing. Everyone got taller in Texas, he said; he wouldn't be surprised if it was a law there.

Alex Fontaine smiled over Tony's shoulder. "You'll hear more about Texas than anybody rightly needs to know," he drawled, "that is, if Tony lets you come in the house. He's forgotten about things like that. In Texas they all live around campfires under the stars instead of having walls and a roof." Alex was glowing with happiness. He looks like he'd like to hug and kiss Tony himself, thought Scarlett, and why not? They were close as two fingers on a hand the whole time they were growing up. Alex must have missed him something awful. Sudden tears pricked her eyes. Tony's exuberant return home was the first joyful event in the County since Sherman's troops had devastated the land and the lives of its people. She hardly knew how to respond to such a rush of happiness.

Alex's wife, Sally, took her by the hand when she entered the shabby living room. "I know just how you feel, Scarlett," she whispered. "We'd nearly forgot how to have fun. There's been more laughing in this house today than in the past ten years put together. We'll make the rafters ring tonight." Sally's eyes were full of tears, too.

Then the rafters began to ring. The Tarletons had arrived. "Thank heaven you're back in one piece, boy," Beatrice Tarleton greeted Tony. "You can have the pick of any one of my three girls. I've only got one grandchild, and I'm not getting any younger."

"Oh, Ma!" moaned Hetty and Camilla and Miranda Tarleton in chorus. Then they laughed. Their mother's preoccupation with breeding horses and people was too well-known in the County for them to pretend embarrassment. But Tony was blushing crimson.

Scarlett and Sally hooted.

Before the light ebbed, Beatrice Tarleton insisted on seeing the horses Tony had brought with him from Texas, and the argument about the merits of Eastern thoroughbreds versus Western mustangs raged until everyone else begged for a truce. "And a drink," said Alex. "I've even found some real whiskey for the celebration instead of 'shine."

Scarlett wished—not for the first time—that taking a drink was not a pleasure from which ladies were automatically excluded. She would have enjoyed one. Even more, she would have enjoyed talking with the men instead of being exiled to the other side of the room for women's talk of babies and household management. She had never understood or accepted the traditional segregation of the sexes. But it was the way things were done, always had been done, and she resigned herself to it. At least she could amuse herself by watching the Tarleton girls pretend that they weren't thinking along exactly the same lines as their mother: If only Tony would look their way instead of being so wrapped up in whatever the men were talking about!

"Little Joe must be thrilled half to death to have his uncle home," Hetty Tarleton was saying to Sally. Hetty could afford to ignore the men. Her fat one-armed husband was one of them.

Sally replied with details about her little boy that bored Scarlett silly. She wondered how soon they'd have supper. It couldn't be too very long; all the men were farmers and would have to be up the next morning at dawn. That meant an early end to the evening's festivities.

She was right about an early supper; the men announced that they were ready for it after only one drink. But she was wrong about the early close to the party. Everyone was enjoying it too much to let it end. Tony fascinated them with stories of his adventures. "It was hardly a week before I hooked up with the Texas Rangers," he said with a roar of laughter. "The state was under Yankee military rule, like every place else in the South, but hell—apologies, ladies—those bluecoats didn't have the first idea what to do about the Indians. The Rangers had been fighting 'em all along, and the only hope the ranchers had was that the Rangers would keep on protecting them. So that's what they did. I knew right off that I'd found my kind of people, and I joined up. It was glorious! No uniforms, no marching on an empty stomach to where some fool general wants you to go, no drilling, no sir! You jump on your horse and head out with a bunch of your fellows and go find the fighting."

Tony's black eyes sparkled with excitement. Alex's matched them. The Fontaines had always loved a good fight. And hated discipline.

"What are the Indians like?" asked one of the Tarleton girls. "Do they really torture people?"

"You don't want to hear about that," said Tony, his laughing eyes suddenly dull. Then he smiled. "They're smart as paint when it comes to fighting. The Rangers learned early on that if they were going to beat the red devils, they'd have to learn their way of doing things. Why, we can track a man or an animal across bare rock or even water, better than any hound dog. And live on spit and bleached bones if that's all there is. There's nothing can beat a Texas Ranger or get away from him."

"Show everybody your six-shooters, Tony," urged Alex.

"Aw, not now. Tomorrow, maybe, or the next day. Sally don't want me putting holes in her walls."

"I didn't say shoot them, I said show them." Alex grinned at his friends. "They've got carved ivory handles," he boasted, "and just wait till my little brother rides over to visit you on the big old Western saddle of his. It's got so much silver on it you'll half go blind from the shine of it."

Scarlett smiled. She might have known. Tony and Alex had always been the most dandified men in all North Georgia. Tony obviously hadn't changed a bit. High heels on fancy boots and silver on his saddle. She'd be willing to bet he came home with his pockets as empty as when he left on the run from the hangman. It was major foolishness to have silver saddles when the house at Mimosa really needed a new roof. But for Tony it was right. It meant that he was still Tony. And Alex was as proud of him as if he'd come with a wagon-load of gold. How she loved them, both of them! They might be left with nothing but a farm that they had to work themselves, but the Yankees hadn't beaten the Fontaines, they hadn't even been able to put a dent in them.

"Lord, wouldn't the boys have loved to prance around tall as a tree and polish silver with their bottoms," said Beatrice Tarleton. "I can see the twins now, they'd just eat it up."

Scarlett caught her breath. Why did Mrs. Tarleton have to ruin everything that way? Why ruin such a happy time by reminding everybody that almost all of their old friends were dead?

But nothing was ruined. "They wouldn't be able to keep their saddles for a week, Miss Beatrice, you know that," Alex said. "They'd either lose them in a poker game or sell them to buy champagne for a party that was running out of steam. Remember when Brent sold all the furniture in his room at the University and bought dollar cigars for all the boys who'd never tried smoking?"

"And when Stuart lost his dress suit cutting cards and had to skulk away from that cotillion wrapped in a rug?" Tony added.

"Remember when they pawned Boyd's law books?" said Jim Tarleton. "I thought you'd skin them alive, Beatrice."

"They always grew back the skin," Mrs. Tarleton said, smiling. "I tried to break their legs when they set the ice house on fire, but they ran too fast for me to catch them."

"That was the time they came over to Lovejoy and hid in our barn," said Sally. "The cows went dry for a week when the twins tried to get themselves a pail of milk to drink."

Everyone had a story about the Tarleton twins, and those stories led to others about their friends and older brothers—Lafe Munroe, Cade and

Raiford Calvert, Tom and Boyd Tarleton, Joe Fontaine—all the boys who'd never come home. The stories were the shared wealth of memory and of love, and as they were told the shadows in the corners of the room became populated with the smiling, shining youth of those who were dead but now—at last—no longer lost because they could be remembered with fond laughter instead of desperate bitterness.

The older generation wasn't forgotten, either. All those around the table had rich memories of Old Miss Fontaine, Alex and Tony's sharp-tongued, soft-hearted grandmother. And of their mother, called Young Miss until the day she died on her sixtieth birthday. Scarlett discovered that she could even share the affectionate chuckling about her father's tell-tale habit of singing Irish songs of rebellion when he had, as he put it, "taken a drop or two," and even hear her mother's kindness spoken of without the heart-break that had always before been her immediate response to the mention of Ellen O'Hara's name.

Hour after hour, long after plates were empty and the fire only embers on the hearth, still the talk went on, and the dozen survivors brought back to life all those loved ones who could not be there to welcome Tony home. It was a happy time, a healing time. The dim, flickering light of the oil lamp in the center of the table showed none of the scars of Sherman's men in the smoke-stained room and its mended furniture. The faces around the table were without lines, the clothes without patches. For these sweet moments of illusion, it was as if Mimosa was transported to a timeless place and hour where there was no pain and there had never been a War.

Many years before, Scarlett had vowed to herself that she would never look back. Remembering the halcyon pre-War days, mourning them, yearning for them would only hurt and weaken her, and she needed all her strength and determination to survive and to protect her family. But the shared memories in the dining room at Mimosa were not at all a source of weakness. They gave her courage; they were proof that good people could suffer every kind of loss and still retain the capacity for love and laughter. She was proud to be included in their number, proud to call them her friends, proud that they were what they were.

Will walked in front of the buggy on the way home, carrying a pitch pine torch and leading the horse. It was a dark night, and it was very late. Overhead the stars were bright in a cloudless sky, so bright that the quarter-moon looked almost transparently pale. The only sound was the slow clop-clop of the horse's hooves.

Suellen dozed off, but Scarlett fought her sleepiness. She didn't want the evening to end, she wanted the warm comfort and happiness of it to last forever. How strong Tony looked! And so full of life, so pleased with his funny boots, with himself, with everything. The Tarleton girls acted like a bunch of red-haired tabby kittens looking at a bowl of cream. I wonder which one will catch him. Beatrice Tarleton's sure going to see to it that one of them does!

An owl in the woods beside the road said "whoo, whoo?" and Scarlett giggled to herself.

They were more than halfway to Tara before she realized that she hadn't thought about Rhett for hours. Then melancholy and worry clamped down on her like lead weights, and she noticed for the first time that the night air was cold and her body was chilled. She pulled her shawl close around her and silently urged Will to hurry.

I don't want to think about anything, not tonight. I don't want to spoil the good time I had. Hurry, Will, it's cold and it's dark.

The next morning Scarlett and Suellen drove the children over in the wagon to Mimosa. Wade was shiny-eyed with hero worship when Tony showed off his six-guns. Even Scarlett's jaw dropped in astounded delight when Tony twirled them around his fingers in unison, sent them circling in the air, then caught them and dropped them in the holsters that hung low on his hips from a fancy silver-trimmed leather belt.

"Do they shoot, too?" Wade asked.

"Yes, sir, they do. And when you get a little older I'll teach you how to use them."

"Spin them like you do?"

"Well, sure. No sense having a six-shooter if you're not going to put it through all its tricks." Tony ruffled Wade's hair with a man-to-man rough hand. "I'll let you learn to ride Western, too, Wade Hampton. I reckon you'll be the only boy in these parts that'll know what a real saddle ought to be. But we can't start today. My brother's going to be giving me lessons in farming. See how it is—everybody's got to learn new things all the time."

Tony planted quick kisses on Suellen's and Scarlett's cheeks—the little girls got theirs on the top of their head—and then he said goodbye. "Alex is waiting for me down by the creek. Why don't you go find Sally? I think she's hanging up the wash out behind the house."

Sally acted glad to see them, but Suellen refused her invitation to stop in for a cup of coffee. "I've got to get home and do just what you're doing, Sally, we can't stay. We just didn't want to leave without saying hello." And she hurried Scarlett back to the wagon.

"I don't see why you were so rude to Sally, Suellen. Your wash could have waited while we had a cup of coffee and talked about the party."

"Scarlett, you don't know anything about keeping a farm going. If

Sally got behind on her wash, she'd be behind on everything else all day. We can't get a bunch of servants way out here in the country the way you can in Atlanta. We've got to do plenty of the work ourselves."

Scarlett bridled at the tone of her sister's voice. "I might just as well go back to Atlanta on this afternoon's train," she said crossly.

"It would make things a lot easier for all of us if you did," Suellen retorted. "You just make more work, and I need that bedroom for Susie and Ella."

Scarlett opened her mouth to argue. Then she closed it. She'd rather be in Atlanta anyhow. If Tony hadn't come home, she'd be there by now. People would be glad to see her, too. She had plenty of friends in Atlanta who had time for coffee or a game of whist or a party. She forced a smile for her children, turning her back on Suellen.

"Wade Hampton, Ella, Mother's got to go to Atlanta after dinner today. I want you to promise you'll be good and not give your Aunt Suellen any trouble, now."

Scarlett waited for the protests and the tears. But the children were too busy talking about Tony's flashing six-shooters to pay any attention to her. As soon as they reached Tara, Scarlett told Pansy to get her valise packed. That was when Ella began to cry. "Prissy's gone, and I don't know anybody here to braid my hair," she sobbed.

Scarlett resisted the impulse to slap her little girl. She couldn't stay at Tara now that she'd made up her mind to leave, she'd go crazy with nothing to do and no one to talk to. But she couldn't go without Pansy; it was unheard of for a lady to travel alone. What was she going to do? Ella wanted Pansy to stay with her. It might take days and days for Ella to get used to Lutie, little Susie's mammy. And if Ella carried on day and night, Suellen might change her mind about keeping the children at Tara.

"All right, then," Scarlett said sharply. "Stop that awful noise, Ella. I'll leave Pansy here for the rest of the week. She can teach Lutie about fixing your hair." I'll just have to hook up with some woman at the Jonesboro depot. There's bound to be somebody respectable going to Atlanta that I can share a seat with.

I'm going home on the afternoon train, and that's all there is to it. Will can drive me over and be back in plenty of time to milk his nasty old cows.

Halfway to Jonesboro, Scarlett stopped chattering brightly about Tony Fontaine's return. She was silent for a moment, then she blurted out what was preying on her mind. "Will—about Rhett—the way he left so fast, I mean—I hope Suellen's not going to go blabbing all over the County."

Will looked at her with his pale blue eyes. "Now, Scarlett, you know better than that. Family don't bad mouth family. I always figured it was a pity you couldn't seem to see the good in Suellen. It's there, but somehow it don't show itself when you come 'round. You'll just have to take my word on it. Never mind how she looks to you, Suellen'll never tell your private troubles to anybody. She don't want folks talking loose about the O'Haras any more than you do."

Scarlett relaxed a little. She trusted Will completely. His word was more certain than money in the bank. And he was wise, too. She'd never known Will to be wrong about anything—except maybe Suellen.

"You do believe he'll be back, don't you, Will?"

Will didn't have to ask who she meant. He heard the anxiety beneath her words, and he chewed quietly on the straw in the corner of his mouth while he decided how to reply. At last he said slowly, "I can't say I do, Scarlett, but I ain't the one to know. I never seen him above four or five times in my life."

She felt as if he had struck her. Then quick anger erased the pain. "You just don't understand anything at all, Will Benteen! Rhett's upset right now, but he'll get over it. He'd never do anything as low as go off and leave his wife stranded."

Will nodded. Scarlett could take it for agreement if she wanted to. But he hadn't forgotten Rhett's sardonic description of himself. He was a scoundrel. According to everything folks said, he always had been and likely always would be.

Scarlett stared at the familiar red clay road in front of her. Her jaw was set, her mind working furiously. Rhett would come back. He had to, because she wanted him to, and she always got what she wanted. All she had to do was set her mind to it.

5

The noise and push at Five Points was a tonic to Scarlett's spirit. So was the disorder on her desk at the house. She needed life and action around her after the numbing succession of deaths, and she needed work to do.

There were stacks of newspapers to be read, piles of daily business accounts from the general store she owned in the very center of Five Points, mounds of bills to be paid, and circulars to tear up and throw away. Scarlett sighed with pleasure and pulled her chair up close to the desk.

She checked the freshness of the ink in its stand and the supply of nibs for her pen. Then she lit the lamp. It would be dark long before she finished all this; maybe she'd even have her supper on a tray tonight while she worked.

She reached eagerly for the store accounts, then her hands stopped in mid-air when a large square envelope on top of the newspapers caught her eye. It was addressed simply "Scarlett," and the handwriting was Rhett's.

I won't read it now, she thought at once, it'll just get in the way of all the things I've got to do. I'm not worried about what's in it—not a bit—I just don't want to look at it now. I'll save it, she told herself, like for dessert. And she picked up a handful of ledger sheets.

But she kept losing track of the arithmetic she was doing in her head, and finally she threw the accounts down. Her fingers tore the sealed envelope open.

Believe me, Rhett's letter began, *when I say that you have my deepest sym-*

pathy in your bereavement. Mammy's death is a great loss. I am grateful that you notified me in time for me to see her before she went.

Scarlett looked up in a rage from the thick black pen strokes and spoke aloud. " 'Grateful,' my foot! So you could lie to her and to me, you varmint." She wished she could burn the letter and throw the ashes in Rhett's face, shouting the words at him. Oh, she'd get even with him for shaming her in front of Suellen and Will. No matter how long she had to wait and plan, she'd find a way somehow. He had no right to treat her that way, to treat Mammy that way, to make a sham out of her last wishes like that.

I'll burn it now, I won't even read the rest, I don't have to put my eyes to any more of his lies! Her hand fumbled for the box of matches, but when she held it, she dropped it at once. I'll die of wondering what was in it, she admitted to herself, and she lowered her head to read on.

She would find her life unaltered, Rhett stated. The household bills would be paid by his lawyers, an arrangement he had made years before, and all moneys drawn from Scarlett's bank account by check would be replaced automatically. She might want to instruct any new shops where she opened accounts about the procedure all her current shopping places used: they sent their bills directly to Rhett's lawyers. Alternatively, she could pay her bills by check, the amount being replaced in her bank.

Scarlett read all this with fascination. Anything that had to do with money always interested her, always had, since the day when she was forced by the Union Army to discover what poverty was. Money was safety, she believed. She hoarded the money she earned herself, and now, viewing Rhett's open-handed generosity, she was shocked.

What a fool he is, I could rob him blind if I wanted to. Probably his lawyers have been cooking those account books for ages, too.

Then—Rhett must be powerfully rich if he can spend without caring where it goes. I always knew he was rich. But not this rich. I wonder how much money he's got.

Then—he does still love me, this proves it. No man would ever spoil a woman the way Rhett spoiled me all these years unless he loved her to distraction, and he's going to keep on giving me everything and anything I want. He must still feel the same, or he'd rein in. Oh, I knew it! I knew it. He didn't mean all those things he said. He just didn't believe me when I told him I know now that I love him.

Scarlett held Rhett's letter to her cheek as if she were holding the hand that had written it. She'd prove it to him, prove she loved him with all her heart, and then they'd be so happy—the happiest people in the whole world!

She covered the letter with kisses before she put it carefully away in a drawer. Then she set to work on the store accounts with enthusiasm. Doing business invigorated her. When a maid tapped on the door and timidly asked about supper, Scarlett barely glanced up. "Bring me something on a tray," she said, "and light the fire in the grate." It was chilly with darkness falling, and she was hungry as a wolf.

She slept extremely well that night. The store had done well in her absence, and the supper was satisfying in her stomach. It was good to be home, especially with Rhett's letter resting safely under her pillow.

She woke and stretched luxuriously. The crackle of paper beneath her pillow made her smile. After she rang for her breakfast tray, she began to plan her day. First to the store. It must be low on stock of a lot of things; Kershaw kept the books well enough, but he didn't have the sense of a pea hen. He'd run right out of flour and sugar before he thought about refilling the kegs, and he probably hadn't ordered a speck of kerosene or so much as a stick of kindling even though it was getting colder every day.

She hadn't gotten around to the newspapers last night, either, and going to the store would save her all that boring reading. Anything worth knowing about in Atlanta she'd pick up from Kershaw and the clerks. There was nothing like a general store for collecting all the stories that were going around. People loved to talk while they were waiting for their goods to be wrapped. Why, half the time she already knew what was on the front page before the paper ever got printed; she could probably throw away the whole batch on her desk and not miss a thing.

Scarlett's smile disappeared. No, she couldn't. There'd be a piece about Melanie's burial, and she wanted to see it.

Melanie . . .

Ashley . . .

The store would have to wait. She had other obligations to see to first.

Whatever possessed me to promise Melly that I'd take care of Ashley and Beau?

But I promised. I'd best go there first. And I'd better take Pansy to make everything proper. Tongues must be wagging all over town after that scene at the graveyard. No sense adding to the gossip by seeing Ashley alone. Scarlett hurried across the thick carpet to the embroidered bell pull and jerked it savagely. Where was her breakfast?

Oh, no, Pansy was still at Tara. She'd have to take one of the other servants; that new girl, Rebecca, would do. She hoped Rebecca could help her dress without making too big a mess of it. She wanted to hurry, now, to get going and get her duty over with.

* * *

When her carriage pulled up in front of Ashley and Melanie's tiny house on Ivy Street, Scarlett saw that the mourning wreath was gone from the door, and the windows were all shuttered.

India, she thought at once. Of course. She's taken Ashley and Beau to live at Aunt Pittypat's. She must be mighty pleased with herself.

Ashley's sister India was, and always had been, Scarlett's implacable enemy. Scarlett bit her lip and considered her dilemma. She was sure that Ashley must have moved to Aunt Pitty's with Beau; it was the most sensible thing for him to do. Without Melanie, and now with Dilcey gone, there was no one to run Ashley's house or mother his son. At Pittypat's there was comfort, an orderly household, and constant affection for the little boy from women who had loved him all his life.

Two old maids, thought Scarlett with disdain. They're ready to worship anything in pants, even short pants. If only India didn't live with Aunt Pitty. Scarlett could manage Aunt Pitty. The timid old lady wouldn't dare talk back to a kitten, let alone Scarlett.

But Ashley's sister was another matter. India would just love to have a confrontation, to say nasty things in her cold, spitting voice, to show Scarlett the door.

If only she hadn't promised Melanie—but she had. "Drive me to Miss Pittypat Hamilton's," she ordered Elias. "Rebecca, you go on home. You can walk."

There would be chaperones enough at Pitty's.

India answered her knock. She looked at Scarlett's fashionable fur-trimmed mourning costume, and a tight, satisfied smile moved her lips.

Smile all you like, you old crow, thought Scarlett. India's mourning gown was unrelieved dull black crape, without so much as a button to decorate it. "I've come to see how Ashley is," she said.

"You're not welcome here," India said. She began to close the door.

Scarlett pushed against it. "India Wilkes, don't you dare slam that door in my face. I made a promise to Melly, and I'll keep it if I have to kill you to do it."

India answered by putting her shoulder to the door and resisting the pressure of Scarlett's two hands. The undignified struggle lasted for only a few seconds. Then Scarlett heard Ashley's voice.

"Is that Scarlett, India? I'd like to talk with her."

The door swung open, and Scarlett marched in, noting with pleasure that India's face was mottled with red splotches of anger.

Ashley came forward into the hallway to greet her, and Scarlett's brisk steps faltered. He looked desperately ill. Dark circles ringed his pale eyes, and deep lines ran from his nostrils to his chin. His clothes looked too big for him; his coat hung from his sagging frame like broken wings on a black bird.

Scarlett's heart turned over. She no longer loved Ashley the way she had for all those years, but he was still part of her life. There were so many shared memories, over so much time. She couldn't bear to see him in such pain. "Dear Ashley," she said gently, "come and sit down. You look tired."

They sat on a settee in Aunt Pitty's small, fussy, cluttered parlor for more than an hour. Scarlett spoke seldom. She listened while Ashley talked, repeating and interrupting himself in a confused zigzag of memories. He recounted stories of his dead wife's kindness, unselfishness, nobility, her love for Scarlett, for Beau, and for him. His voice was low and without expression, bleached by grief and hopelessness. His hand groped blindly for Scarlett's, and he grasped it with such despairing strength that her bones rubbed together painfully. She compressed her lips and let him hold on to her.

India stood in the arched doorway, a dark, still spectator.

Finally Ashley interrupted himself and turned his head from side to side like a man blinded and lost. "Scarlett, I can't go on without her," he groaned. "I can't."

Scarlett pulled her hand away. She had to break through the shell of despair that bound him, or it would kill him, she was sure. She stood and leaned down over him. "Listen to me, Ashley Wilkes," she said. "I've been listening to you pick over your sorrows all this time, and now you listen to mine. Do you think you're the only person who loved Melly and depended on her? I did, more than I knew, more than anybody knew. I expect a lot of other people did, too. But we're not going to curl up and die for it. That's what you're doing. And I'm ashamed of you.

"Melly is, too, if she's looking down from heaven. Do you have any idea what she went through to have Beau? Well, I know what she suffered, and I'm telling you it would have killed the strongest man God ever made. Now you're all he's got. Is that what you want Melly to see? That her boy is all alone, practically an orphan, because his Pa feels too sorry for himself to care about him? Do you want to break her heart, Ashley Wilkes? Because that's what you're doing." She caught his chin in her hand and forced him to look at her.

"You pull yourself together, do you hear me, Ashley? You march yourself out to the kitchen and tell the cook to fix you a hot meal. And you eat it. If it makes you throw up, eat another one. And you find your boy and take him in your arms and tell him not to be scared, that he has a father to take care of him. Then do it. Think about somebody besides yourself."

Scarlett wiped her hand on her skirt as if it were soiled by Ashley's grip. Then she walked from the room, pushing India out of the way.

As she opened the door to the porch, she could hear India: "My poor, darling Ashley. Don't pay any attention to the horrible things Scarlett said. She's a monster."

Scarlett stopped, turned. She withdrew a calling card from her purse and dropped it on a table. "I'm leaving my card for you, Aunt Pitty," she shouted, "since you're afraid to see me in person."

She slammed the door behind her.

"Just drive, Elias," she told her coachman. "Anywhere at all." She couldn't stand to stay in that house one single minute more. What was she going to do? Had she gotten through to Ashley? She'd been so mean— well, she had to be, he was being drowned in sympathy and pity—but had it done any good? Ashley adored his son, maybe he'd pull himself together for Beau's sake. "Maybe" wasn't good enough. He had to. She had to make him do it.

"Take me to Mr. Henry Hamilton's law office," she told Elias.

"Uncle Henry" was terrifying to most women, but not to Scarlett. She could understand that growing up in the same house with Aunt Pittypat had made him a misogynist. And she knew he rather liked her. He said she wasn't as silly as most women. He was her lawyer and knew how shrewd she was in her business dealings.

When she walked into his office without waiting to be announced, he put down the letter he was reading and chuckled. "Do come in, Scarlett," he said, rising to his feet. "Are you in a hurry to sue somebody?"

She paced forward and back, ignoring the chair beside his desk. "I'd like to shoot somebody," she said, "but I don't know that it would help. Isn't it true that when Charles died, he left me all his property?"

"You know it is. Stop that fidgeting and sit down. He left the warehouses near the depot that the Yankees burned. And he left some farmland outside of town that will be in town before too long, the way Atlanta has been growing."

Scarlett perched on the edge of the chair, her eyes fixed on his. "And half of Aunt Pitty's house on Peachtree Street," she said distinctly. "Didn't he leave me that, too?"

"My God, Scarlett, don't tell me you want to move in there."

"Of course not. But I want Ashley out of there. India and Aunt Pitty are going to sympathize him into his grave. He can go back to his own house. I'll find him a housekeeper."

Henry Hamilton looked at her with expressionless probing eyes. "Are you sure that's why you want him back in his own house, because he's suffering from too much sympathy?"

Scarlett bridled. "God's nightgown, Uncle Henry!" she said. "Are you turning into a scandal monger in your old age?"

"Don't show your claws to me, young lady. Settle back in that chair and listen to some hard truths. You've got maybe the best business head I ever met, but otherwise you're about as dimwitted as the village idiot."

Scarlett scowled, but she did as she was told.

"Now, about Ashley's house," said the old lawyer slowly, "it's already been sold. I drew up the papers yesterday." He held up his hand to stop Scarlett before she could speak. "I advised him to move into Pitty's and sell it. Not because of the pain of associations and memories in the house, and not because I was concerned about who was going to take care of him and the boy, although both are valid considerations. I advised him to move because he needed the money from the sale to keep his lumber business from going under."

"What do you mean? Ashley doesn't know tootle about making money, but he can't possibly go under. Builders always need lumber."

"If they're building. Just you get down off your high horse for a minute and listen, Scarlett. I know you're not interested in anything that happens in the world unless it concerns you, but there was a big financial scandal in New York a couple or three weeks ago. A speculator named Jay Cooke miscalculated, and he crashed. He took his railroad down with him, an outfit called the Northern Pacific. He took a bunch of other speculators with him, too, fellows who were in on his railroad deal and some of his other deals. When they went with him, they took down a lot of other deals they were in on, outside of Cooke's. Then the fellows who were in on their deals went down, tumbling still more deals and more fellows. Just like a house of cards. In New York they're calling it 'the Panic.' It's already spreading. I expect it'll run through the whole country before it's done."

Scarlett felt a stab of terror. "What about my store?" she cried. "And my money? Are the banks safe?"

"The one you bank in is. I've got my money there, too, so I made sure. Fact is, Atlanta's not likely to get hurt much. We're not big enough yet for any big deals, and it's the big ones that are crumbling. But business is at a standstill everywhere. People are afraid to invest in anything. That means building, too. And if nobody's building, nobody needs lumber."

Scarlett frowned. "So Ashley won't be making any money from the sawmills. I can see that. But if nobody's investing, why did his house sell so fast? Seems to me, if there's a panic, real estate prices should be the first thing to fall."

Uncle Henry grinned. "Like a stone. You're a smart one, Scarlett. That's why I told Ashley to sell while he could. Atlanta hasn't felt the Panic yet, but it'll get here soon. We've been booming for the past eight years—hell, there are more than twenty thousand people living here now—but you can't boom without bucks." He laughed mightily at his own wit.

Scarlett laughed with him, although she didn't think there was anything funny about economic collapse. She knew men like to be appreciated.

Uncle Henry's laughter stopped abruptly, like water turned off at a faucet. "So. Now Ashley's with his sister and his aunt, for good and proper reasons and according to my advice. And that doesn't suit you."

"No, sir, it doesn't suit at all. He looks awful, and they're making him worse. He's like a dead man walking. I gave him a good talking-to; tried to snap him out of the state he's in by hollering at him. But I don't know if it did any good. I know it won't stick even if it did. Not as long as he's in that house."

She looked at Uncle Henry's skeptical expression. Anger reddened her face. "I don't care what you heard or what you think, Uncle Henry. I'm not after Ashley. I made a deathbed promise to Melanie that I'd take care of him and Beau. I wish to God I hadn't, but I did."

Her outburst made Henry uncomfortable. He didn't like emotion, especially in women. "If you start crying, Scarlett, I'll have you put out."

"I'm not going to cry. I'm mad. I've got to do something, and you're no help."

Henry Hamilton leaned back in his chair. He touched his fingertips together, resting his arms on his ample stomach. It was his lawyerly look, almost judicial.

"You're the last person who can help Ashley right now, Scarlett. I told you I was going to deliver some hard truths, and that's one of them. Right or wrong—and I don't care to know which—there was a lot of speculation about you and Ashley at one time. Miss Melly stood up for you, and most people followed her lead—for love of her, mind you, not because they were especially fond of you.

"India thought the worst and said it. She put together her own little band of believers. It wasn't a pretty situation, but folks accommodated themselves, like they always do. Things could have rocked on like that forever, even after Melanie's death. Nobody really likes disruption and changes. But you couldn't leave well enough alone. Oh, no. You had to go make a spectacle of yourself at Melanie's very graveside. Throwing your arms around her husband, hauling him away from his dead wife, who a lot of people thought close to a saint."

He held up one hand. "I know what you're about to say, so don't bother to say it, Scarlett." His fingertips touched again. "Ashley was about to throw himself in the grave, maybe break his neck. I was there. I saw it. That's not the point. For such a smart girl, you don't understand the world at all.

"If Ashley had pitched himself onto the coffin, everybody would have called it 'touching.' If he killed himself doing it, they would have been real sorry, but there are rules for handling sorrow. Society needs rules, Scarlett, to hold itself together. What you did broke all the rules. You made a scene in public. You laid hands on a man who wasn't your husband. In public. You raised a ruckus that interrupted a burial, a ceremony that everybody knows the rules to. You broke up the last rites of a saint.

"There's not a lady in this town that isn't lined up on India's side right now. That means against you. You don't have a friend to your name, Scarlett. And if you have anything at all to do with Ashley, you'll fix it so that he's just as outcast as you.

"The ladies are against you. God help you, Scarlett, because I can't. When Christian ladies turn on you, you'd better not hope for Christian charity or forgiveness. It's not in them. They won't allow it in anybody else, either, especially not their menfolk. They own their men, body and soul. That's why I've always kept my distance from the misnamed 'gentle sex.'

"I wish you well, Scarlett. You know I've always liked you. That's about all I can offer, good wishes. You've made a mess of things, and I don't know how you can ever put it right."

The old lawyer stood up. "Leave Ashley where he is. Some sweet-talking little lady will come along one of these days and snap him up. Then she'll take care of him. You leave Pittypat's house the way it is, including your half. And don't stop sending money through me to pay the bills for its upkeep, the way you've always done. That'll satisfy your promise to Melanie.

"Come on. I'll escort you to your carriage."

Scarlett took his arm and walked meekly beside him. But inside, she was seething. She might have known that she'd get no help from Uncle Henry.

She had to find out for herself if what Uncle Henry said was true, if there was a financial panic, most of all, if her money was safe.

6

"Panic," Henry Hamilton called it.
The financial crisis that had begun on Wall Street in New York was spreading throughout America. Scarlett was terrified that she'd lose the money she had earned and hoarded. When she left the old lawyer's office, she went immediately to her bank. She was shaking internally when she reached the bank manager's office.

"I appreciate your concern, Mrs. Butler," he said, but Scarlett could see that he didn't at all. He resented her questioning the security of the bank, and in particular the security of the bank under his management. The longer he talked, and the more reassuring he sounded, the less Scarlett believed him.

Then, inadvertently, he set all her fears at rest. "Why, we'll not only be paying our usual dividend to stockholders," he said, "it's actually going to be a bit higher than usual." He looked at her from the corners of his eyes. "I didn't get that information until this morning myself," he said angrily. "I'd certainly like to know how your husband reached his decision to add to his stock holdings a month ago."

Scarlett felt that she might float right out of her chair with relief. If Rhett was buying bank shares, this must be the safest bank in America. He always made money when the rest of the world was falling to pieces. She didn't know how he'd found out about the bank's position, and she didn't care. It was enough for her that Rhett had confidence in it.

"He has this darling little crystal ball," she said with a giddy laugh that infuriated the manager. She felt a little drunk.

But not too light-headed to remember to convert all the cash in her lock box to gold. She could still see the elegantly engraved, worthless Confederate bonds her father had depended on. She had no faith at all in paper.

As she left the bank, she paused on the steps to enjoy the warm autumn sun and the thronged busyness of the streets in the business district. Look at all those folks rushing around—they're in a hurry because there's money to be made, not because they're afraid of anything. Uncle Henry's crazy as an old coot. There's no panic at all.

Her next stop was her store. KENNEDY'S EMPORIUM said the big gilt-lettered sign across the front of the building. It was her inheritance from her brief marriage to Frank Kennedy. That and Ella. Her pleasure in the store more than offset her disappointment in the child. The window was sparkling clean, with a satisfyingly crowded display of merchandise. Everything from shiny new axes down to shiny new dressmaker pins. She'd have to get those lengths of calico out of there, though. They'd be sun-streaked in no time at all, and then she'd have to reduce the price. Scarlett burst through the door, ready to take the hide off Willie Kershaw, the head clerk.

But in the end, there was little reason to find fault. The calico on display had arrived water-damaged in shipment and was already marked down. The mill that made it had agreed to knock two-thirds off the cost because of the damage. Kershaw had placed the orders for new stock, too, without being told, and the square heavy iron safe in the back room held neatly banded and precisely tallied stacks of bagged coins and greenbacks, the daily receipts. "I paid the underclerks, Mrs. Butler," Kershaw said nervously. "I hope that's all right. The notation is on the Saturday tallies. The boys said they couldn't manage without their week's packets. I didn't take mine out, not knowing how you wanted me to do, but I'd be mighty grateful if you could see your way clear to—"

"Of course, Willie," said Scarlett graciously, "as soon as I match the money to the account books." Kershaw had done a lot better than she expected, but that didn't mean she'd allow him to take her for a fool. When the cash balanced to the penny, she counted out his twelve dollars and seventy-five cents pay for the three weeks. She'd add an extra dollar when she paid him tomorrow for this week, she decided. He deserved a bonus for managing so well when she was away.

Also, she was planning to add to his duties. "Willie," she told him privately, "I want you to open a credit account."

Kershaw's protuberant eyes bulged. There had never been credit extended in the store after Scarlett took over its management. He listened carefully to her instructions. When she made him swear he wouldn't tell a living soul about it, he placed his hand over his heart and swore. He'd better stick to his oath, too, he thought, or Mrs. Butler would find out somehow. He was convinced Scarlett had eyes in the back of her head and could read people's minds.

Scarlett went home for dinner when she left the store. After she washed her face and hands, she started on the pile of newspapers. The account of Melanie's funeral was just what she should have expected—a minimum number of words, giving Melanie's name, birthplace, and date of death. A lady's name could be in the news three times only: at her birth, her marriage, and her death. And there must never be any details. Scarlett had written out the notice herself, and she'd added what she thought was a suitably dignified line about how tragic it was for Melanie to have died so young and how much she would be missed by her grieving family and all her friends in Atlanta. India must have taken it out, Scarlett thought irritably. If only Ashley's household was in anybody's hands except India's, life would be a lot easier.

The very next issue of the newspaper made Scarlett's palms wet with fear-sweat. The next, and the next, and the next—she turned through the pages rapidly, with mounting alarm. "Leave it on the table," she said when the maid announced dinner. The chicken breast was stuck in congealed gravy by the time she got to the table, but it didn't matter. She was too upset to eat. Uncle Henry had been right. There was a panic, and rightly so. The world of business was in desperate turmoil, even collapse. The stock market in New York had been closed for ten days after the day the reporters were calling "Black Friday," when stock prices plunged downward because everyone was selling and no one was buying. In major American cities banks were closing because their customers wanted their money, and their money was gone—invested by the banks in "safe" stocks that had become nearly worthless. Factories in industrial areas were closing at the rate of almost one every day, leaving thousands of workers without work and without money.

Uncle Henry said it couldn't happen in Atlanta, Scarlett told herself again and again. But she had to restrain her impulse to go to the bank and bring home her lock box of gold. If Rhett hadn't bought bank shares, she would have done it.

She thought about the errand she'd planned for the afternoon, wished fervently that the idea had never crossed her mind, decided that it had to be done. Even though the country was in a panic. Even more so, in fact.

Maybe she should have a tiny glass of brandy to settle her churning stomach. The decanter was right there on the sideboard. It would keep her nerves from jumping half out of her skin, too . . . No—it could be smelt on her breath, even if she ate parsley or mint leaves afterwards. She took a deep breath and got up from the table. "Run out to the carriage house and tell Elias I'm going out," she told the maid who came in response to the bell.

There was no answer to her ring at Aunt Pittypat's front door. Scarlett was sure she saw one of the lace curtains twitch at a parlor window. She twisted the bell again. There was the sound of the bell in the hall beyond the door, and a muffled sound of movement. Scarlett rang again. All was silence when the ringing faded. She waited for a count of twenty. A horse and buggy passed along the street behind her.

If anybody saw me standing here locked out, I'd never be able to look them in the face without perishing of shame, she thought. She could feel her cheeks flaming. Uncle Henry was right the whole way. She wasn't being received. All her life she had heard of people who were so scandalous that no decent person would open the door to them, but in her wildest imagination she'd never thought it could happen to her. She was Scarlett O'Hara, daughter of Ellen Robillard, of the Savannah Robillards. This couldn't be happening to her.

I'm here to do good, too, she thought with hurt bewilderment. Her eyes felt hot, a warning of tears. Then, as so often happened, she was swept by a tide of anger and outrage. Damn it all, half this house belonged to her! How dare anybody lock the door against her?

She banged on the door with her fist and rattled the doorknob, but the door was securely bolted. "I know you're in there, India Wilkes," Scarlett shouted through the keyhole. There! I hope she had her ear to it and goes deaf.

"I came to talk to you, India, and I'm not leaving until I do. I'm going to sit on the porch steps until you open that door or until Ashley comes home with his key, take your pick."

Scarlett turned and gathered up the train of her skirts. She heard the rattle of bolts behind her as she took a step, then the squeak of the hinges.

"For the love of heaven, come in," India whispered hoarsely. "You'll make us the talk of the neighborhood."

Scarlett surveyed India coolly over her shoulder. "Maybe you should come out and sit on the steps with me, India. A blind tramp might stumble by and marry you in exchange for room and board."

As soon as it was said, she wished she'd bit her tongue instead. She hadn't come to fight with India. But Ashley's sister had always been like a burr under a saddle to her, and her humiliation at the locked door rankled.

India pushed the door to. Scarlett spun and raced to stop it closing. "I apologize," she said through clenched teeth. Her angry gaze locked with India's. Finally India stepped back.

How Rhett would love this! Scarlett thought all of a sudden. In the good days of their marriage she had always told him about her triumphs in business and in the small social world of Atlanta. It made him laugh long and loud and call her his "neverending source of delight." Maybe he'd laugh again when she told him how India was puffing like a dragon that had to back down.

"What do you want?" India's voice was icy, although she was trembling with rage.

"It's mighty gracious of you to invite me to sit and take a cup of tea," Scarlett said in her best airy manner. "But I've just barely finished dinner." In fact she was hungry now. The zest for battle had pushed panic away. She hoped her stomach wouldn't make a noise, it felt as empty as a dry well.

India stationed herself against the door to the parlor. "Aunt Pitty is resting," she said.

Having the vapors is more like it, Scarlett said to herself, but this time she held her tongue. She wasn't mad at Pittypat. Besides, she'd better get on with what she'd come for. She wanted to be gone before Ashley came home.

"I don't know if you're aware of it, India, but Melly asked me on her deathbed to promise that I'd watch out for Beau and Ashley."

India's body jerked as if she'd been shot.

"Don't say a word," Scarlett warned her, "because there's nothing you can say that means anything next to Melly's practically last words."

"You'll ruin Ashley's name just like you've ruined your own. I won't have you hanging around here after him, bringing disgrace down on all of us."

"The last thing on God's green earth I want to do, India Wilkes, is spend one more minute in this house than I have to. I came to tell you that I've made arrangements at my store for you to get anything you need."

"The Wilkeses don't take charity, Scarlett."

"You simpleton, I'm not talking charity, I'm talking my promise to Melanie. You don't have any idea how quick a boy Beau's age goes through breeches and outgrows shoes. Or how much they cost. Do you want Ashley to be burdened with little worries like that when he's broken-hearted about bigger things? Or do you want Beau to be a laughingstock at school?

"I know just how much income Aunt Pitty gets. I used to live here, remember? It's just enough to keep Uncle Peter and the carriage, put a little food on the table, and pay for her smelling salts. There's a little thing called 'the Panic,' too. Half the businesses in the country are folding. Ashley's likely going to have less money coming in than ever.

"If I can swallow my pride and beat on the front door like a crazy woman, you can swallow yours and take what I'm giving. It's not your place to turn it down, because if it was only you, I'd let you starve without blinking an eye. I'm talking about Beau. And Ashley. And Melly, because I promised her what she asked.

" 'Take care of Ashley, but don't let him know it,' she said. I can't not let him know it if you won't help, India."

"How do I know that's what Melanie said?"

"Because I say so, and my word's as good as gold. No matter what you may think of me, India, you'll never find anybody to say that I ever backed down on a promise or broke my word."

India hesitated, and Scarlett knew she was winning. "You don't have to go to the store yourself," she said. "You can send a list by somebody else."

India took a deep breath. "Only for Beau's school clothes," she said grudgingly.

Scarlett kept herself from smiling. Once India saw how pleasant it was to get things for free, she'd do a lot more shopping than that. Scarlett was sure of it.

"I'll say good day, then, India. Mr. Kershaw, the head clerk, is the only one knows about this, and he won't run off at the mouth to anybody. Put his name on the outside of your list, and he'll take care of everything."

When she settled back in her carriage, Scarlett's stomach gave out an audible rumble. She smiled from ear to ear. Thank heaven it had waited.

Back home she ordered the cook to heat up her dinner and serve it again. While she waited to be called to the table she looked through the other pages of the newspapers, avoiding the stories about the Panic. There was a column she'd never bothered with before that was fascinating to her now. It contained news and gossip from Charleston, and Rhett or his mother or sister or brother might be mentioned.

They weren't, but she hadn't really expected anything. If there was anything really exciting going on in Charleston she'd learn about it from Rhett next time he came home. Being interested in his folks and the place he'd grown up would be a proof to him that she loved him, no matter what he might believe. How often, she wondered, was "often enough to keep down gossip"?

Scarlett couldn't get to sleep that night. Every time she closed her eyes she saw the wide front door of Aunt Pitty's house, closed and bolted against her. It was India's doing, she told herself. Uncle Henry couldn't possibly be right that every door in Atlanta was going to be closed.

But she hadn't thought he was right about the Panic, either. Not until she read the newspapers, and then she discovered it was even worse than he'd told her.

Insomnia was no stranger to her; she'd learned years before that two or three brandies would calm her down and help her sleep. She padded silently downstairs and to the dining room sideboard. The cut-glass decanter flashed rainbows from the light of the lamp she held in her hand.

The next morning she slept later than usual. Not because of the brandy but because, even with its aid, she'd been unable to sleep until just before dawn. She couldn't stop worrying about what Uncle Henry had said.

On her way down to the store she stopped in at Mrs. Merriwether's bakery. The clerk behind the counter looked through her and turned a deaf ear when she spoke.

She treated me like I didn't even exist, she realized with horror. As she crossed the sidewalk from the shop to her carriage, she saw Mrs. Elsing and her daughter approaching on foot. Scarlett paused, ready to smile and say hello. The two Elsing ladies stopped dead when they saw her, then, without a word or a second look, turned and walked away. Scarlett was paralyzed for a moment. Then she scurried into her carriage and hid her face in the shadowy corner of the deep enclosure. For one horrible instant she was afraid she was going to be sick all over the floor.

When Elias stopped the carriage in front of the store, Scarlett stayed in the sanctuary of her carriage. She sent Elias inside with the clerks' pay envelopes. If she got out, she might see someone she knew, someone who would cut her dead. It was unbearable even to think of it.

India Wilkes must be behind this. And after I was so generous with her, too! I won't let her get away with it, I won't. Nobody can treat me this way and get away with it.

"Go to the lumberyard," she ordered Elias when he returned. She'd tell Ashley. He'd have to do something to stop India's poison. Ashley wouldn't stand for it, he'd make India behave, and all India's friends, too.

Her already heavy heart sank even lower when she saw the lumberyard. It was too full. Stacks and stacks of pine boards were golden and sweetly resinous in the autumn sun. There wasn't a wagon to be seen, or a loader. Nobody was buying.

Scarlett wanted to cry. *Uncle Henry said this would happen, but I never thought it could be this bad. How could people not want that beautiful clean lumber?* She inhaled deeply. Fresh-cut pine was the sweetest perfume in the world to her. *Oh, how she missed the lumber business, she would never understand how she'd let Rhett trick her into selling it to*

Ashley. If she was still running it, this would never have happened. She would have sold the lumber somehow to someone. Panic touched the edge of her mind and she pushed it away. Things were awful all around, but she mustn't fuss at Ashley. She wanted him to help her.

"The yard looks wonderful!" she said brightly. "You must have the sawmill running day and night to keep such a good stock up, Ashley."

He looked up from the account books on his desk and Scarlett knew that all the cheerfulness in the world would be wasted on him. He looked no better than when she'd given him the talking-to.

He stood, tried to smile. His ingrained courtesy was stronger than his exhaustion, but his despair was greater than both.

I can't tell him anything about India, Scarlett thought, or about the business either. He's got all he can bear just making himself draw the next breath. It's like there's nothing holding him together but his clothes.

"Scarlett, dear, how kind of you to stop by. Won't you sit down?"

"Kind," is it? God's nightgown! Ashley sounds like a wind-up music box of polite things to say. No, he doesn't. He sounds like he doesn't know what's coming out of his mouth, and I reckon that's closer to the truth. Why should he care that I'm chancing whatever's left of my reputation by coming here without a chaperone? He doesn't care anything about himself —any fool could see that—why should he care anything about me? I can't sit down and make polite conversation, I can't stand it. But I have to.

"Thank you, Ashley," she said, and sat on the chair he was holding. She would force herself to stay for fifteen minutes and make empty, lively remarks about the weather, tell amusing stories about what a good time she'd had at Tara. She couldn't tell him about Mammy, it would upset him too much. Tony coming home, though, that was different. It was good news. Scarlett started to speak.

"I've been down to Tara—"

"Why did you stop me, Scarlett?" said Ashley. His voice was flat, lifeless, devoid of real questioning. Scarlett couldn't think what to say.

"Why did you stop me?" he asked again, and this time there was emotion in the words, anger, betrayal, pain. "I wanted to be in the grave. Any grave, not just Melanie's. It's the only thing I'm fit for . . . No, don't say whatever you were going to say, Scarlett. I've been comforted and boosted up by so many well-meaning people that I've heard it all a hundred times over. I expect better of you than the usual platitudes. I'll be grateful if you'll say what you must be thinking, that I'm letting the lumber business die. Your lumber business that you invested all your heart in. I'm a miserable failure, Scarlett. You know it. I know it. The whole world knows it. Why do we all have to act as though it isn't so? Blame me, why don't you?

You can't possibly find any words harsher than those I say to myself, you can't 'hurt my feelings.' God, how I hate that phrase! As if I had any feelings left to hurt. As if I could feel anything at all."

Ashley shook his head with slow, heavy swings from side to side. He was like a mortally wounded animal brought down by a pack of predators. From his throat burst one tearing sob, and he turned away. "Forgive me, Scarlett, I beg of you. I had no right to burden you with my troubles. Now I have the shame of this outburst to add to my other shames. Be merciful, my dear, and leave me. I will be grateful if you will go now."

Scarlett fled without a word.

Later she sat at her desk with all her legal records neatly stacked in front of her. It was going to be even harder to keep her promise to Melly than she'd expected. Clothing and household goods weren't nearly enough.

Ashley wouldn't lift a finger to help himself. She was going to have to make him successful whether he cooperated or not. She'd promised Melanie.

And she couldn't bear to see the business she had built go under.

Scarlett made a list of her assets.

The store, building and trade. It produced nearly a hundred a month in profits, but that would almost certainly go down some when the Panic got to Atlanta and people had no money to spend. She made a note to order more cheap goods and stop replacing luxury items like wide velvet ribbon.

The saloon on her lot near the depot. She didn't actually own it, she leased the land and building to the man who did, for thirty dollars a month. People would likely be drinking more than ever when times got hard, maybe she should raise the rent. But a few more dollars a month wouldn't be enough to bail out Ashley. She needed real money.

The gold in her safe box. She had real money, more than twenty-five thousand dollars of real money. She was a wealthy woman in her own right by most people's reckoning. But not by hers. She still didn't feel safe.

I could buy the business back from Ashley, she thought, and for a moment her mind hummed with excitement, with possibilities. Then she sighed. That wouldn't solve anything. Ashley was such a fool he'd insist on taking only what he could get on the open market, and that was hardly anything. Then, when she made a success of the business he'd feel like more of a failure than ever. No, no matter how much she would love to get her hands on that lumberyard and the sawmills, she had to make Ashley successful at it.

I just don't believe that there's no market for lumber. Panic or no

Panic, people have got to be building something, if it's only a shed for a cow or a horse.

Scarlett riffled through the stack of books and papers. She'd had an idea.

There it was, the plot of the farmland Charles Hamilton left her. The farms produced almost no income at all. What good did a couple of baskets of corn and a single bale of seedy cotton do her? Sharecropping was a waste of good land unless you had about a thousand acres and a dozen good farmers. But her hundred acres were right on the edge of Atlanta now, the way things were growing. If she could find a good builder—and they must all be feeling mighty hungry for work—she could put up a hundred gim-crack houses, maybe two hundred. Everybody who was losing money was going to have to draw in their horns and live closer to the bone. Their big houses would be the first thing to go, and they'd have to find someplace they could afford to live.

I won't make any money, but at least I won't be losing much. And I'll see to it that the builder uses only lumber from Ashley, and the best he's got, too. He'll be making money—not a fortune, but good steady income —and he'll never know it came from me. I can manage that somehow. All I need is a builder who can keep his mouth shut. And not steal too much.

The following day Scarlett drove out to give the sharecropping farmers notice to vacate.

7

"Yes, ma'am, Mrs. Butler, I'm hungry for work all right," said Joe Colleton. The builder was a short, lean man in his forties; he looked much older because his thick hair was snow white, and his face was leathered by long exposure to the sun and the weather. He was frowning, and the deep creases in his brow shadowed his dark eyes. "I need work, but not bad enough to work for you."

Scarlett almost turned on her heel to leave; she didn't have to swallow insults from some jumped-up poor white. But she needed Colleton. He was the only honest-to-the-bone builder in Atlanta; she'd learned that when she was selling lumber to them all in the boom years of rebuilding after the War. She felt like stamping her foot. It was all Melly's fault. If it hadn't been for that silly condition that Ashley mustn't know she was helping him, she could have used any builder at all because she would watch him like a hawk and oversee every part of the work herself. How she'd love to do it, too.

But she couldn't be seen to be involved. And she couldn't trust anyone except Colleton. He had to agree to take the job, she had to make him agree. She put her small hand on his arm. It looked very delicate in its tight kid glove. "Mr. Colleton, it'll break my heart if you say no to me. I need somebody very special to help me." She looked at him with appealing helplessness in her eyes. Too bad he wasn't taller. It was hard to be a frail little lady with somebody your own size. Still, it was often these banty rooster little men who were most protective of women. "I don't know what I'll do if you turn me down."

Colleton's arm stiffened. "Mrs. Butler, you sold me green lumber once, after you told me it was cured. I don't do business twice with somebody that cheats me once."

"That must have been a mistake, Mr. Colleton. I was green myself, just learning the lumber business. You remember how it was those days. The Yankees were breathing down our necks every waking minute. I was scared to death all the time." Her eyes swam in unshed tears, and her very lightly rouged lips trembled. She was a small forlorn figure. "My husband, Mr. Kennedy, was killed when the Yankees broke up a Klan meeting."

Colleton's direct, knowing gaze was disconcerting. His eyes were on a level with hers, and they were as hard as marble. Scarlett took her hand off his sleeve. What was she going to do? She couldn't fail, not in this. He had to take the job.

"I made a deathbed promise to my dearest friend, Mr. Colleton." Her tears were unplanned now. "Mrs. Wilkes asked me to help, and now I'm asking you." The whole story tumbled out—how Melanie had always sheltered Ashley ... Ashley's ineptness as a businessman ... his attempt to bury himself with his wife ... the stacks of unsold lumber ... the need for secrecy ...

Colleton held up his hand to stop her. "All right, Mrs. Butler. If it's for Mrs. Wilkes, I'll take the job." His hand dropped, extended. "I'll shake on it, you'll get the best-built houses with the best materials in them."

Scarlett put her hand in his. "Thank you," she said. She felt as if she'd scored the triumph of her life.

It was only some hours later that she remembered that she hadn't intended to use the best of everything, only the best lumber. The miserable houses were going to cost her a fortune, and out of her own hard-earned money, too. She wouldn't get any credit for helping Ashley, either. Everybody would still slam their doors in her face.

Not really everybody. I've got plenty of my own friends, and they're a lot more fun than those frumpy old Atlanta people.

Scarlett put aside the sketch Joe Colleton had made on a paper sack for her to study and approve. She'd be a lot more interested when he gave her the numbers for his estimate; what difference did it make what the houses looked like or where he put the stairs?

She took her velvet-covered visiting book from a drawer and began to make a list. She was going to give a party. A big one, with musicians and rivers of champagne and huge amounts of the best, most expensive food. Now that she was done with deep mourning, it was time to let her friends know that she could be invited to their parties, and the best way to do it was to invite them to a party of her own.

Her eye skimmed quickly past the names of Atlanta's old families. They all think I should be in deep mourning for Melly, no sense asking them. And there's no need to wrap myself in crape, either. She wasn't my sister, only my sister-in-law, and I'm not even sure that counts since Charles Hamilton was my first husband and there've been two since him.

Scarlett's shoulders slumped. Charles Hamilton had nothing to do with anything, nor did wearing crape. She was in the truest kind of mourning for Melanie; it was a perpetual weight and worry in her heart. She missed the gentle, loving friend who had been so much more important to her than she had ever realized; the world was colder and darker without Melanie. And so lonely. Scarlett had been back from the country for only two days, but she had known enough loneliness in the two nights to strike fear deep into her heart.

She could have told Melanie about Rhett leaving; Melanie was the only person she could ever confide in about such a disgraceful thing. Melly would have told her what she needed to hear, too. "Of course he'll be back, dear," she would have said, "he loves you so." Those were her very words, right before she died. "Be kind to Captain Butler, he loves you so."

Just the thought of Melanie's words made Scarlett feel better. If Melly said that Rhett loved her, then he did, it wasn't only her own wishful thinking. Scarlett shook off her gloominess, straightened her spine. She didn't have to be lonely at all. And it didn't matter if Atlanta's Old Guard never spoke to her again ever. She had plenty of friends. Why, the party list was already two pages long, and she was only up to letter L in her book.

The friends Scarlett was planning to entertain were the most flamboyant and most successful of the horde of scavengers that had descended on Georgia in the days of the Reconstruction government. Many of the original group had left when the government was ousted in 1871, but a large number stayed, to enjoy their big houses and the tremendous fortunes they had made picking the bones of the dead Confederacy. They had no temptation to go "home." Their origins were better forgotten.

Rhett had always despised them. He dubbed them "the dregs" and left the house when Scarlett gave her lavish parties. Scarlett thought he was silly, and told him so. "Rich people are ever so much more fun than poor people. Their clothes and carriages and jewels are better, and they give you better things to eat and drink when you go to their houses."

But nothing at the houses of any of her friends was nearly as elegant as the refreshments at Scarlett's parties. This one, she was determined, would be the best reception of all. She started a second list headed "Things to Remember" with a note to order ice swans for the cold foods and ten new cases of champagne. A new gown, too. She'd have to go to her dress-maker's place immediately after she left the order for the invitations at the engraver's.

Scarlett tilted her head to admire the crisp white ruffles of the Mary Stuart style cap. The point on the forehead was really very becoming. It emphasized the black arch of her eyebrows and the shining green of her eyes. Her hair looked like black silk where it tumbled in curls on each side of the ruffles. Who would ever have thought that mourning garb could be so flattering?

She turned from side to side, looking over her shoulders at her reflection in the pier glass. The jet bead trim and tassels on her black gown glittered in a very satisfactory way.

"Ordinary" mourning wasn't awful like deep mourning, there was plenty of leeway in it if you had magnolia-white skin to show in a low-cut black gown.

She walked quickly to her dressing table and touched her shoulders and throat with perfume. She'd better hurry, her guests would be arriving any minute. She could hear the musicians tuning up downstairs. Her eyes feasted on the disorderly pile of thick white cards among her silver-backed brushes and hand mirrors. Invitations had started pouring in as soon as her friends knew that she was reentering the social whirl; she was going to be busy for weeks and weeks to come. And then there'd be more invitations, and then she'd give another reception. Or maybe a dance during the Christmas season. Yes, things were going to be just fine. She was as excited as a girl who'd never been to a party before. Well, it was no wonder. It had been more than seven months since she'd been to one.

Except for Tony Fontaine's coming-home. She smiled, remembering. Darling Tony, with his high-heeled boots and silver saddle. She wished he could be at her party tonight. Wouldn't people's eyes pop right out of their heads if he did his trick of twirling his six-shooters!

She had to go—the musicians were playing in tune, it must be late.

Scarlett hurried down the red-carpeted stairs, sniffing appreciatively when she reached the scent of the hot-house flowers that filled huge vases in every room. Her eyes glowed with pleasure when she moved from room to room to check that everything was ready. All was perfection. Thank heaven Pansy was back from Tara. She was very good at making the other servants do their jobs, much better than the new butler hired to replace Pork. Scarlett took a glass of champagne from the tray the new man held out to her. At least he was good at serving, quite stylish in fact, and Scarlett did so like for things to be stylish.

Just then the doorbell sounded. She startled the manservant by smiling happily, then she moved towards the entrance hall to greet her friends.

They arrived in a steady stream for almost an hour and the house filled with the sound of loud voices, the overpowering smell of perfume and powder, the brilliant colors of silks and satins, rubies and sapphires.

Scarlett moved through the melée smiling and laughing, flirting idly with the men, accepting the fulsome compliments of the women. They were so happy to see her again, they'd missed her so much, no one's parties were as exciting as hers, no one's home as beautiful, no one's gown as fashionable, no one's hair as glossy, no one's figure as youthful, no one's complexion so perfect and creamy.

I'm having a good time. It's a wonderful party.

She glanced over the silver dishes and trays on the long polished table to see that the servants were keeping them all replenished. Quantities of food—excesses of food—were important to her, for she would never forget completely what it had been like to come so near to starvation at the end of the War. Her friend Mamie Bart caught her eye and smiled. A streak of buttery sauce from the half-eaten oyster patty in Mamie's hand had dribbled from the corner of her mouth down onto the diamond necklace around her fat neck. Scarlett turned away in disgust. Mamie was going to be big as an elephant one of these days. Thank goodness, I can eat all I want and never gain a pound.

She smiled entrancingly at Harry Connington, her friend Sylvia's husband. "You must have found some elixir, Harry, you look ten years younger than you did last time I saw you." She watched with malicious amusement as Harry sucked in his stomach. His face turned red, then faintly purple before he abandoned the effort to hold it in. Scarlett laughed aloud, then moved away.

A burst of laughter caught her attention, and she drifted towards the trio of men who were its source. She'd like very much to hear something funny, even if it was one of those jokes that ladies had to pretend not to understand.

". . . so I says to myself, 'Bill, one man's panic is another man's profit, and I know which one of those men old Bill's going to be.' "

Scarlett started to turn away. She wanted to have a good time tonight, and talking about the Panic wasn't her idea of fun. Still, maybe she'd learn something. She was smarter when she was sound asleep than Bill Weller was on his best day, she was sure of that. If he was making money out of the Panic, she wanted to know how he was doing it. Quietly she stepped closer.

". . . these dumb Southerners, they been a problem for me ever since I come down here," Bill was confessing. "You just can't do nothing with a

man who don't have natural human greed, so all the triple-your-money
bond deals and certificates for gold mines that I turned loose on them laid
a big egg. They was working harder than any nigger ever did and putting
by every nickel they earned for the next rainy day. Turned out that plenty
of 'em had a boxful of bonds and such already. From the Confederate
government." Bill's booming laugh led the laughter of the other men.

Scarlett was fuming. "Dumb Southerners" indeed! Her own darling Pa
had a boxful of Confederate bonds. So did all the good people in Clayton
County. She tried to walk away, but she was hemmed in by people behind
her who'd also been attracted by the laughter in the group around Bill
Weller. "I got the picture after a while," Weller went on. "They just didn't
put much trust in paper. Nor nothing else that I tried, neither. I sent out
medicine shows and lightning rods and all the sure-fire money-makers, but
none of them so much as struck a spark. I tell you, boys, it hurt my pride."
He made a lugubrious face, then grinned widely, showing three large gold
molars.

"I don't have to tell you that me and Lula wasn't exactly going to go
wanting if I didn't come up with something. In the good, fat days when
the Republicans had Georgia in hand, I piled up enough from those railroad
contracts the boys voted me so that we could have lived high on the hog
even if I'd been fool enough to actually go out and build the railroads. But
I like to keep my hand in, and Lula was starting to fret because I was
around the house too much, not having any business to tend to. Then—
glory be—along come the Panic, and all the Rebs grabbed their savings
out of the banks and put the money in their mattresses. Every house—
even the shacks—was a golden opportunity I just couldn't let pass me by."

"Stop your gassing, Bill, what did you come up with? I'm getting
thirsty waiting for you to finish patting yourself on the back and get to the
point." Amos Bart punctuated his impatience with a practiced spit that fell
short of its targeted spittoon.

Scarlett was feeling impatient, too. Impatient to get away.

"Keep your shirt on, Amos, I'm coming to it. What was the way to
get in those mattresses? I ain't the revival-preacher kind, I like to sit behind
my desk and let my em-ploy-ees do the hustling. That's just what I was
doing, sitting in my leather swivel chair, when I looked out my window
and saw a funeral going by. It was like lightning striking. There ain't a roof
in Georgia that don't have some dearly departed once lived under it."

Scarlett stared with horror at Bill Weller as he described the fraud that
was adding to his riches. "The mothers and widows are the easiest, and
there's more of them than anything else. They don't blink an eye when my
boys tell them that the Confederate Veterans are putting up monuments on
all the battlefields, and they empty out those mattresses quicker than you

can say 'Abe Lincoln' to pay for their boy's name to be carved in the marble." It was worse than Scarlett could have imagined.

"You sly old fox, Bill, that's pure genius!" Amos exclaimed, and the men in the group laughed more loudly than before. Scarlett felt as if she were going to be sick. Nonexistent railroads and gold mines had never concerned her, but the mothers and widows Bill Weller was cheating were her own people. He might be sending his men right now to Beatrice Tarleton, or Cathleen Calvert, or Dimity Munroe, or any other woman in Clayton County who had lost a son or a brother or a husband.

Her voice cut through the laughter like a knife. "That's the most low-down, filthy story I ever heard in my life. You disgust me, Bill Weller. All of you disgust me. What do you know about Southerners—about decent people anywhere? You've never had a decent thought or done a decent thing in all your lives!" She pushed with hands outstretched through the thunderstruck men and women who had gathered around Weller, then ran, rubbing her hands on her skirts to wipe off the stain of having touched them.

The dining room and the glittering silver dishes of elaborate food were in front of her; her gorge rose at the mixed smells of rich, greasy sauces and spattered spittoons. She saw in her mind the lamplit table at the Fontaines', the simple meal of home-cured ham and home-made corn bread and home-grown greens. She belonged with them; they were her people, not these vulgar, trashy, flashy women and men.

Scarlett turned to face Weller and his group. "Dregs!" she yelled. "That's what you are. Dregs. Get out of my house, get out of my sight, you make me sick!"

Mamie Bart made the mistake of trying to soothe her. "Come on, honey—" she said, holding out her jewelled hand.

Scarlett recoiled before she could be touched. "Especially you, you greasy sow."

"Well, I never," Mamie Bart's voice quavered. "I'm damn well not going to put up with being talked to like this. I wouldn't stay if you begged me on your knees, Scarlett Butler."

A shoving, angry stampede began, and in less than ten minutes the rooms were empty of everything except the debris left behind. Scarlett made her way through spilled food and champagne, broken plates and glasses, without looking down. She must keep her head high, the way her mother had taught her. She imagined that she was back at Tara, with a heavy volume of the Waverley novels balanced on her head, and she climbed the stairs with her back as straight as a tree, her chin perfectly perpendicular to her shoulders.

Like a lady. The way her mother had taught her. Her head was swimming and her legs trembled, but she climbed without pausing. A lady never let it show when she was tired or upset.

"High time she did that, and then some," said the cornetist. The octet had played waltzes from behind the palms for many of Scarlett's receptions.

One of the violinists spat accurately into a potted palm. "Too late, I say. Lie down with dogs, get up with fleas."

Above their heads Scarlett was lying face down on her silk-covered bed, sobbing as if her heart was broken. She had thought she was going to have such a good time.

Later that night, when the house was quiet and dark, Scarlett went downstairs for a drink to help her sleep. All evidence of the party was gone, except for the elaborate flower arrangements and the half-burned candles in the six-armed candelabra on the bare dining room table.

Scarlett lit the candles and blew out her lamp. Why should she skulk around in near-darkness like some kind of thief? It was her house, her brandy, and she could do as she pleased.

She selected a glass, took it and the decanter to the table, sat in the armchair at the head. It was her table, too.

The brandy sent a relaxing warmth through her body. Scarlett sighed. Thank God. Another drink, and my nerves should stop jumping around like they're doing. She filled the elegant little cordial glass again, tossed the brandy down her throat with a deft twist of the wrist. Mustn't hurry, she thought, pouring. It's not ladylike.

She sipped her third drink. How pretty the candlelight was, lovely golden flames reflected in the polished tabletop. The empty glass was pretty, too. Its cut facets made rainbows when she turned it in her fingers.

It was as quiet as the grave. The clink of glass against glass made her jump when she poured the brandy. That proved she needed the drink, didn't it? She was still too jumpy to sleep.

The candles burned low and the decanter slowly emptied and Scarlett's usual control over her mind and memory was loosened. This was the room where it had all begun. The table had been bare like this with only candles on it and the silver tray that held brandy decanter and glasses. Rhett was drunk. She'd never seen him really drunk like that, he could always hold his liquor. He was drunk that night, though, and cruel. He said such horrible hurting things to her, and he twisted her arm so that she cried out in pain.

But then . . . then he carried her up to her room and forced himself on her. Except that he didn't have to force her to accept him. She came alive when he handled her, when he kissed her lips and throat and body. She burned at his touch and she cried out for more and her body arched and strained to meet his again and again . . .

It couldn't be true. She must have dreamed it, but how could she have dreamed such things when she'd never dreamed they existed?

No lady would ever feel the wild wanting she had felt, no lady would do the things she had done. Scarlett tried to push her thoughts back into the crowded dark corner of her mind where she kept the unbearable and unthinkable. But she'd had too much to drink.

It did happen, her heart cried, it did. I didn't make it up.

And her mind, so carefully taught by her mother that ladies did not have animal impulses, could not control the passionate demands of her body to feel rapture and surrender again.

Scarlett's hands held her aching breasts, but hers were not the hands her body longed for. She dropped her arms onto the table in front of her, her head onto her arms. And she abandoned herself to the waves of desire and pain that made her writhe, made her call out brokenly into the empty, silent, candlelit room.

"Rhett, oh Rhett, I need you."

8

*W*inter was approaching, and Scarlett grew more frantic with every passing day. Joe Colleton had dug the hole for the cellar of the first house, but repeated rains made it impossible to pour the concrete foundations. "Mr. Wilkes would smell a rat if I bought lumber before I'm ready to frame," he said reasonably, and Scarlett knew he was right. But it made the delay no less frustrating.

Maybe the whole building idea was a mistake. Day after day the newspaper reported more disasters in the business world. There were soup kitchens and bread lines now in America's big cities because thousands more people lost their jobs every week when companies went bankrupt. Why was she risking her money now, at the worst possible time? Why had she made that fool promise to Melly? If only the cold rain would stop . . .

And the days would stop getting shorter. She could keep busy in the daytime, but darkness closed her in the empty house with only her thoughts for companions. And she didn't want to think, because she could find no answers to anything. How had she gotten into this mess? She'd never deliberately done anything to turn people against her, why were they all being so hateful? Why was it taking Rhett so long to come home? What could she do to make things better? There had to be something, she couldn't go on forever walking from room to room in the big house like a pea rattling around in an empty washtub.

She'd be glad to have Wade and Ella come home to keep her company, but Suellen had written that they were all under quarantine while one child after another went through the long itchy torture of chicken pox.

She could take up with the Barts and all their friends again. It didn't matter that she'd called Mamie a sow, her skin was as thick as a brick wall. One reason Scarlett had enjoyed having "the dregs" for friends was that she could use the rough side of her tongue on them any time she liked and they'd always come crawling back for more. *I haven't sunk to that level, thank God. I'm not going to go crawling back to them now that I know what low things they are.*

It's just that it gets dark so early and the nights are so long and I can't sleep like I ought. Things will get better when the rain stops ... when winter's over ... when Rhett comes home ...

At last the weather turned to bright, cold, sunny days with high wisps of cloud in brilliant blue skies. Colleton pumped the standing water out of the hole he'd dug, and the sharp wind dried the red Georgia clay to the hardness of brick. He ordered concrete then, and lumber to make the forms for casting the footings.

Scarlett plunged into a celebration of shopping for gifts. It was nearly Christmas. She bought dolls for Ella and each of Suellen's girls. Baby dolls for the younger ones with soft sawdust-stuffed bodies and chubby porcelain faces and hands and feet. Susie and Ella had nearly identical lady dolls with cunning leather trunks full of beautiful clothes. Wade was a problem; Scarlett never knew what to do about him. Then she remembered Tony Fontaine's promise to teach him how to twirl his six-shooters, and she bought Wade his own pair, with his initials carved in their ivory-inlaid handles. Suellen was easy—a beaded silk reticule that was too fancy to use in the country, with a twenty dollar gold piece inside it good anywhere. Will was impossible. Scarlett searched high and low before she gave up and bought him another sheepskin jacket like the one she'd given him the year before, and the year before that. *It's the thought that counts,* she told herself firmly.

She debated for a long time before she decided not to get a present for Beau. She wouldn't put it past India to send it back unopened. Besides, Beau wasn't lacking for anything, she thought bitterly. The Wilkes account at her store was mounting up every week.

She bought a gold cigar-cutter for Rhett, but she lacked the nerve to send it. Instead, she made her gifts to her two aunts in Charleston much nicer than usual. *They might tell Rhett's mother how thoughtful she was, and Mrs. Butler might tell Rhett.*

I wonder if he'll send me anything? Or bring me something? Maybe he'll come home for Christmas to keep gossip down.

The possibility was real enough to send Scarlett into a happy frenzy of decorating the house. When it was a bower of pine branches, holly, and ivy, she took the leftovers down to the store.

"We've always had the tinsel garland in the window, Mrs. Butler. No need for more than that," said Willie Kershaw.

"Don't tell me what's needed and what's not. I say wrap this pine roping around all the counters and put the holly wreath on the door. It'll make people feel Christmassy, and they'll spend more money on presents. We don't have enough little pretties for gifts. Where's that big box of oiled paper fans?"

"You told me to get it out of the way. Said we shouldn't use good shelf space for fripperies, when what people wanted was nails and wash-boards."

"You fool, that was then and this is now. Get it out."

"Well, I ain't exactly sure where I put it. That was a long time ago."

"Mother of God! Go see what that man over there wants. I'll find it myself." Scarlett stormed into the stockroom behind the selling area.

She was up on a ladder looking through the dusty piles on a top shelf when she heard the familiar voices of Mrs. Merriwether and her daughter Maybelle.

"I thought you said you'd never set foot across the threshold of Scarlett's store, Mother."

"Hush, the clerk might hear you. We've looked every place in town, and there's not a length of black velvet to be found. I can't finish my costume without it. Who ever heard of Queen Victoria wearing a colored cape?"

Scarlett frowned. What on earth were they talking about? She quietly descended the ladder and walked on tiptoe to press her ear against the wall.

"No, ma'am," she heard the clerk say. "We don't get much call for velvet."

"Just what I should have expected. Come on, Maybelle."

"As long as we're here, maybe I can find the feathers I need for my Pocahontas," Maybelle was saying.

"Nonsense. Come on. We should never have come here. Suppose someone saw us." Mrs. Merriwether's tread was heavy but rapid. She slammed the door behind her.

Scarlett climbed up the ladder again. All her Christmas spirit was gone. Someone was having a costume party, and she wasn't invited. She wished she'd let Ashley break his neck in Melanie's grave! She found the box she was looking for and threw it down to the floor, where it burst, scattering the brightly colored fans in a wide arc.

"Now you pick them up and dust off every single one of them," she ordered. "I'm going home." She'd rather die than start boo-hooing in front of her own clerks.

The day's newspaper was on the seat of her carriage. She'd been too busy with the decorations to read it as yet. And she didn't much care about reading it now, but it would hide her face from any nosy-body looking in at her. Scarlett straightened out the bend in it and opened it to the center page for "Our Charleston Letter." It was all about the Washington Race Course, newly reopened, and the upcoming Race Day in January. Scarlett skimmed over the rapturous descriptions of Race Weeks before the War, the customary Charleston claims to have had the finest, most elaborate everything, and the predictions that the races to come would equal their predecessors if not surpass them. According to the correspondent, there would be parties all day every day and a ball every night for weeks.

"And Rhett Butler at every one of them, I'll bet," Scarlett muttered. She threw the newspaper on the floor.

A front-page headline caught her eye. CARNIVAL TO CONCLUDE WITH MASQUERADE BALL. That must be what the old dragon and Maybelle were talking about, she thought. Everyone in the world except me is going to wonderful parties. She snatched the paper up again to read the article:

It can now be announced, planning and preparations being complete, that Atlanta will be graced on January 6th next with a Carnival sure to rival the magnificence of New Orleans' famous Mardi Gras. The Twelfth Night Revelers is a body lately formed by our city's leading figures from the worlds of society and business, and the instigators of this fabulous event. The King of Carnival will reign over Atlanta, attended by a Court of Noblemen. He will enter the city and transverse it on a royal float in a parade that is expected to exceed a mile in length. All the city's citizens, his subjects for the day, are invited to view the parade and marvel at its wonders. Schedule and parade route will be announced in a later edition of this newspaper.

The day-long revels will conclude at a Masked Ball for which DeGives Opera House will be transformed into a veritable Wonderland. The Revelers have distributed almost three hundred invitations to Atlanta's finest Knights and fairest Ladies. . . .

"Damn!" said Scarlett.

Then desolation took hold of her, and she began to cry like a child. It wasn't fair for Rhett to be dancing and laughing in Charleston and all her enemies in Atlanta to be having a good time while she was stuck by herself in her huge silent house. She'd never done anything bad enough to deserve such punishment.

You've never been so lily-livered that you let them make you cry, either, she told herself angrily.

Scarlett rubbed the tears away with the backs of her wrists. She wasn't going to wallow in misery. She was going to go after what she wanted. She'd go to the Ball; somehow she'd find a way.

It was not impossible to get an invitation to the Ball, it wasn't even difficult. Scarlett learned that the vaunted parade would be made up largely of decorated wagons advertising products and stores. There was a fee for participants, of course, as well as the cost of decorating the "float," but all those businesses in the parade received two invitations to the Ball. She sent Willie Kershaw with the money to enter Kennedy's Emporium in the parade.

It reinforced her belief that just about anything could be bought. Money could do anything.

"How will you decorate the wagon, Mrs. Butler?" asked Kershaw.

The question opened up a hundred possibilities.

"I'll think about it, Willie." Why, she could spend hours and hours— fill up lots of evenings—thinking about how to make all the other floats look pitiful next to hers.

She had to think about her costume for the Ball, too. What a lot of time it was going to take! She'd have to go through all her fashion magazines again, have to find out what people were wearing, have to select fabric, schedule fittings, choose a hairstyle . . .

Oh, no! She was still in ordinary mourning. Surely that didn't mean she had to wear black for a masquerade ball. She'd never been to one, she didn't know what the rules were. But the whole idea was to fool people, wasn't it? Not to look like you usually did, to be disguised. Then she definitely should not wear black. The Ball was sounding better every minute.

Scarlett hastened through her routines at the store and hurried to her dressmaker, Mrs. Marie.

The corpulent, wheezing Mrs. Marie took a sheaf of pins out of her mouth so that she could report that ladies had ordered costumes to represent Rosebud—pink ballgown trimmed with silk roses—Snowflake—white ballgown trimmed with stiffened and sequined white lace—Night—deep blue velvet with embroidered silver stars—Dawn—pink over darker pink skirted silk—Shepherdess—striped gown with lace-edged white apron—

"All right, all right," said Scarlett impatiently. "I see what they're doing. I'll let you know tomorrow what I will be."

Mrs. Marie threw up her hands. "But I won't have time to make your gown, Mrs. Butler. I've had to find two extra seamstresses as it is, and I still don't see how I'm going to finish in time ... There's just no way on earth I can add another costume to the ones I've already promised."

Scarlett dismissed the woman's refusal with a wave of her hand. She knew she could bully her into doing what she wanted. The hard part was deciding what that was.

The answer came to her when she was playing Patience while she waited for dinnertime. She peeked ahead into the deck of cards to see if she was going to get the King she needed for an empty place. No, there were two Queens before the next King. The game was not going to come out right.

A queen! Of course. She'd be able to wear a wonderful costume with a long train trimmed with white fur. And all the jewelry she wanted.

She spilled the remaining cards on the table and ran upstairs to look in her jewel case. Why, oh why had Rhett been so stingy about buying her jewelry? He bought her anything else she wanted, but the only jewelry he approved was pearls. She pulled out rope after rope, piled them on the bureau. There! Her diamond earbobs. She'd definitely wear them. And she could wear pearls in her hair as well as around her throat and wrists. What a pity that she couldn't risk wearing her emerald and diamond engagement ring. Too many people would recognize it, and if they knew who she was, they might cut her. She was counting on her costume and mask to protect her from Mrs. Merriwether and India Wilkes and the other women. She intended to have a wonderful time, to dance every dance, to be part of things again.

By January fifth, the day before Carnival, all Atlanta was gala with preparation. The mayor's office had ordered that all businesses be closed on the sixth and that all buildings on the parade route be decorated with red and white, the colors of Rex, the King of Carnival.

Scarlett thought it a terrible waste to close the store on a day when the city would be jammed with people from the country, in for the celebrations. But she hung big rosettes of ribbon in the store window and on the iron fence in front of her house, and just like everyone else she goggled at the transformation of Whitehall and Marietta streets. Banners and flags be-

decked every lamp standard and building front, making a virtual tunnel of
bright, fluttering red and white for the final leg of Rex's parade to his
throne.

I should have brought Wade and Ella in from Tara for the parade, she
thought. But they're probably still puny from the chicken pox, her mind
quickly added. And I don't have ball tickets for Suellen and Will. Besides,
I sent great piles of Christmas presents to them.

The incessant rain on the day of Carnival soothed any vestige of com-
punction about the children. They couldn't have stood out in the wet and
cold to see the parade anyway.

But she could. She wrapped herself in a warm shawl and stood on the
stone bench near the gate under a big umbrella, with a clear view over the
heads and umbrellas of the spectators on the sidewalk outside.

As promised, the parade was more than a mile long. It was a brave
and sorry spectacle. The rain had all but destroyed the medieval-court-type
costumes. Red dye had run, ostrich plumes dropped, once-dashing velvet
hats sagged over faces like dead lettuce. The marching heralds and pages
looked cold and wet, but determined; the mounted knights struggled grim-
faced with their bespattered horses to keep moving through the sucking,
slick mud. Scarlett joined in the crowd's applause for the Earl Marshal. It
was Uncle Henry Hamilton, who seemed to be the only one having a good
time. He squelched along in bare feet, carrying his shoes in one hand and
his bedraggled hat in the other, waving first one hand then the other at the
crowd and grinning from ear to ear.

She grinned herself when the Ladies of the Court rolled slowly past
in open carriages. The leaders of Atlanta society wore masks, but stoic
misery showed clearly on their faces. Maybelle Merriwether's Pocahontas
was sporting dejected feathers in her hair that dribbled water down her
cheeks and neck. Mrs. Elsing and Mrs. Whiting were easily recognized as
sodden, shivering Betsy Ross and Florence Nightingale. Mrs. Meade was a
sneezing representation of The Good Old Days in a billow of hoop-skirted
wet taffeta. Only Mrs. Merriwether was unaffected by the rain. Queen Victoria held a wide black umbrella over her dry regal head. Her velvet cape
was unspotted.

When the ladies were past, there was a long hiatus, and the spectators
began to leave. But then there was the distant sound of "Dixie." Within a
minute the crowd was cheering itself hoarse, and it kept cheering until the
band came before them, when silence fell.

It was a small band, only two drummers and two men playing pennywhistles and one man playing a sweet, high-pitched cornet. But they
were dressed in gray, with gold sashes and bright brass buttons. And in

front of them a man with one arm was holding the staff of the Confederate flag in his remaining hand. The Stars and Bars was honorably tattered, and it was being paraded again through Peachtree Street. Throats were too choked with emotion to utter cheers.

Scarlett felt tears on her cheeks, but they were not tears of defeat, they were tears of pride. Sherman's men had burned Atlanta, the Yankees had pillaged Georgia, but they hadn't been able to destroy the South. She saw tears like hers on the faces of the women, and the men, in front of her. Everyone had lowered umbrellas to stand bare-headed to honor the flag.

They stood tall and proud, exposed to the cold rain, for a long time. The band was followed by a column of Confederate veterans in the ragged butternut homespun uniforms they'd come home in. They marched to "Dixie" as if they were young men again, and the rain-soaked Southerners watching them found their voices to cheer and whistle and let out the chilling, rousing cry that was the Rebel Yell.

The cheering lasted until the veterans were out of sight. Then umbrellas swung upward and people began to leave. They'd forgotten Rex, and Twelfth Night. The high point of the parade had come and gone, leaving them wet and chilled but exalted. "Wonderful." Scarlett heard it from dozens of smiling mouths as people passed her gate.

"There's more parade to come," she said to some of them.

"Can't top 'Dixie,' can it?" they replied.

She shook her head. Even she didn't feel interested in seeing the floats, and she'd worked very hard on hers. Spent a lot of money, too, on crepe paper and tinsel that the rain must have ruined. At least she could sit down to watch now, that was something. She didn't want to tire herself out when tonight was the Masquerade Ball.

Ten endless minutes dragged by before the first float appeared. Scarlett could see why when it got near. The wagon's wheels kept getting stuck in the churned red clay mud of the street. She sighed and pulled her shawl more closely around her. *Looks like I'm in for a long wait.*

It took over an hour for the decorated wagons to make their way past her; her teeth were chattering before it was over. But at least hers was the best. The bright crepe paper flowers around the wagon's sides were soggy, but still bright. And "Kennedy's Emporium" in silver gilt tinsel shone clearly through the rain drops caught in it. The big barrels labelled "flour," "sugar," "cornmeal," "molasses," "coffee," "salt" were empty, she knew, so no damage was done there. And the tin washtubs and washboards wouldn't rust. The iron kettles were damaged anyhow; she'd glued paper flowers over the dents. The only dead loss was the wooden-handled tools.

Even the lengths of fabric that she'd draped so artistically over a stretch of chicken wire could be salvaged for the penny bargain bin.

If only anybody had waited around to see her float, she was sure they'd have been impressed.

She hunched her shoulders and made a face at the last wagon. It was surrounded by dozens of shouting, capering children. A man in a parti-colored elf costume was throwing candy right and left. Scarlett peered at the name on the sign above his head. "Rich's." Willie kept talking about this new store at Five Points. He was worried because prices were lower there and Kennedy's was losing some customers. Fiddle-dee-dee, Scarlett thought with contempt. Rich's won't stay in business long enough to do me any harm. Cutting prices and throwing away merchandise is not any way to be successful in business. I'm mighty glad I saw this. Now I can tell Willie Kershaw not to be such a fool.

She was even gladder to see the Grand Finale float behind Rich's. It was Rex's throne. There was a leak in the red-and-white striped canopy above it, and water was pouring steadily on the gilt-crowned head and cotton-batting-ermined shoulders of Dr. Meade. He looked thoroughly miserable.

"And I hope you catch double pneumonia and die," Scarlett said under her breath. Then she ran to the house for a hot bath.

Scarlett was costumed as the Queen of Hearts. She would have preferred to be the Queen of Diamonds, with a glittering paste crown and dog collar and brooches. However, then she wouldn't have been able to wear her pearls, which the jeweller had told her were "fine enough for the Queen herself." And besides she had found nice big imitation rubies to sew all around the low neck of her red velvet gown. It was so good to be wearing color!

The train of her dress was bordered with white fox. It would be ruined before the Ball was over, but no matter; it looked elegant draped over her arm to dance. She had a mysterious red satin eye mask that covered her face down to the tip of her nose, and her lips were reddened to match it. She felt very daring, and quite safe. Tonight she could dance to her heart's content without anyone knowing who she was so they could insult her. What a wonderful idea it was to have a masquerade!

Even with her mask in place Scarlett was nervous about entering the ballroom without an escort, but she needn't have been. A large group of masked revellers was entering the lobby when she stepped out of her carriage, and she joined them without comment from anyone. Once inside, she looked around her with astonishment. DeGives Opera House had been transformed almost beyond recognition. The handsome theater was now truly a convincing King's palace.

A dance floor had been built over the lower half of the auditorium, extending the large stage into a mammoth ballroom. At the far end Dr. Meade as Rex was seated on his throne, with uniformed attendants on each side, including a Royal Cup Bearer. In the center of the Dress Circle was the biggest orchestra Scarlett had ever seen, and on the floor were masses of dancers, watchers, wanderers. There was a tangible feeling of heightened gaiety, a recklessness that arose from the anonymity of being masked and disguised. As soon as she entered the room, a man in Chinese robes and a long pigtail put his silken arm around her waist and whirled her onto the dance floor. He might be a perfect stranger. It was dangerous and exciting.

The tune was a waltz, her partner a dizzying dancer. As they spun, Scarlett caught glimpses of masked Hindus, clowns, Harlequins, Pierrettes, nuns, bears, pirates, nymphs, and cardinals, all dancing as madly as she. When the music stopped, she was breathless. "Wonderful," she gasped, "it's wonderful. So many people. All Georgia must be here dancing."

"Not quite," said her partner. "Some had no invitations." He gestured upward with his thumb. Scarlett saw that the galleries were full of spectators in ordinary dress. Some were not so ordinary. Mamie Bart was there, wearing all her diamonds, surrounded by other dregs. What a good thing I didn't take up with that bunch again. They're too trashy to be invited anywhere. Scarlett had managed to forget the origin of her invitation.

The presence of an audience made the Ball seem even more desirable. She tossed her head and laughed. Her diamond earrings flashed; she could see them reflected in the Mandarin's eyes through the holes in his mask.

Then he was gone. Elbowed aside by a monk with his cowl pulled forward to shadow his masked face. Without a word, he took Scarlett's hand, then circled her waist with his arm when the orchestra struck up a lively polka.

She danced as she hadn't danced in years. She was giddy, infected by the thrilling madness of masquerade, intoxicated by the strangeness of it all, by the champagne offered on silver trays held by satin-clad pages, by the delight of being at a party again, by her unquestionable success. She was a success, and she believed she was unknown, invulnerable.

She recognized the Old Guard dowagers. They had on the same costumes they'd worn in the parade. Ashley was masked, but she knew him as soon as she saw him. He wore a mourning band around the sleeve of his black-and-white Harlequin outfit. India must have dragged him here so she'd have an escort, Scarlett thought, how mean of her. Of course she doesn't care if it's mean or not, as long as it's proper, and a man in mourning doesn't have to give up going out the way a woman does. He can put an armband on his best suit and start courting his next love before his wife's hardly cold in her grave. But anybody could tell poor Ashley hates being here. Look at the way he's all droopy in his fancy dress. Well, never you mind, dear. There'll be plenty more houses like the one Joe Colleton's building now. Come spring you'll be so busy delivering lumber that you won't have time to be sad.

As the evening wore on, the masquerade mood became even more pronounced. Some of Scarlett's admirers asked her name; one even tried to lift her mask. She deflected them with no trouble. *I haven't forgotten how to handle rambunctious boys,* she thought, smiling. *And boys is what they are, no matter what age they might be. They're even sneaking over to the corner for a little something stronger than champagne. Next thing you know, they'll start giving the Rebel Yell.*

"What are you smiling at, my Queen of Mystery?" asked the portly Cavalier who was, it seemed, doing his best to step on her feet while they danced.

"Why, at you, of course," Scarlett replied, smiling. *No, she hadn't forgotten a thing.*

When the Cavalier released her hand to the eager Mandarin who was back for the third time, Scarlett begged prettily for a chair and a glass of champagne. The Cavalier had badly bruised one of her toes.

But when her escort led her towards the sitting-out side of the room, she suddenly declared that the orchestra was playing her favorite song, and she couldn't bear not to dance.

She had seen Aunt Pittypat and Mrs. Elsing in her path. Could they have recognized her?

A mix of anger and fear dimmed the happy excitement she was feeling. She was painfully aware of her injured foot and the whiskey breath of the Mandarin.

I won't think about it now, not about Mrs. Elsing and not about my sore toe. I won't let anything spoil my fun. She tried to push the thoughts aside and gave herself over to enjoyment.

But, against her will, her eyes looked often at the sides of the ballroom and the men and women sitting or standing there.

Her eyes brushed a tall, bearded pirate who was leaning against a doorjamb, and he bowed to her. Scarlett's breath caught in her throat. She turned her head to look again. There was something . . . the air of insolence . . .

The pirate was wearing a white dress shirt and dark evening trousers.

Not a costume at all, except for the wide red silk sash tied around his waist, with two pistols tucked into it. And blue bows tied to the ends of his thick beard. His mask was a simple black one over his eyes. He wasn't anyone she knew, was he? So few men wore thick beards these days. Still, the way he was standing. And the way he seemed to be staring at her, right through the mask.

When Scarlett looked at him for the third time, he smiled, his teeth very white against his dark beard and swarthy skin. Scarlett felt faint. It was Rhett.

It couldn't be ... she must be imagining things ... No, she wasn't; she wouldn't feel this way if it was anyone else. Wasn't that just like him? Showing up at a ball that most people couldn't get invited to ... Rhett could do anything!

"Excuse me, I must go. No, really, I mean it." She pushed away from the Mandarin and ran to her husband.

Rhett bowed again. "Edward Teach at your service, ma'am."

"Who?" Did he think she hadn't recognized him?

"Edward Teach, commonly known as Blackbeard, the greatest villain that ever plowed the waters of the Atlantic." Rhett twirled a ribboned lock of the beard.

Scarlett's heart leapt. He's having fun, she thought, making those jokes of his that he knows I hardly ever understand. Just the way he used to before ... before things went bad. I mustn't put my foot wrong now. I mustn't. What would I have said, before I loved him so much?

"I'm surprised that you'd come to a ball in Atlanta when there are such big doings in your precious Charleston," she said.

There. That was just right. Not exactly mean, but not too loving, either.

Rhett's eyebrows rose in black crescents above his mask, Scarlett held her breath. He'd always done that when he was amused. She was acting just right.

"How do you come to be so informed about Charleston's social life, Scarlett?"

"I read the paper. Some silly woman keeps going on and on about some horserace."

Damn that beard. She thought he was smiling, but she couldn't really see his lips.

"I read the newspapers, too," said Rhett. "Even in Charleston it's news when an upstart country town like Atlanta decides to pretend that it's New Orleans."

New Orleans. He had taken her there for their honeymoon. Take me there again, she wanted to say, we'll start over, and everything will be different. But she mustn't say that. Not yet. Her mind leapt quickly from one memory to another. Narrow cobbled streets, tall shadowy rooms with great mirrors framed in dull gold, strange and marvellous foods . . .

"I'll admit the refreshments aren't as fancy," she said grudgingly.

Rhett chuckled. "A powerful understatement."

I'm making him laugh. I haven't heard him laugh for ages . . . too long. He must have seen the men flocking to dance with me.

"How did you know it was me?" she said. "I have a mask on."

"I only had to look for the most ostentatiously dressed woman, Scarlett. It was bound to be you."

"Oh, you . . . you skunk." She forgot that she was trying to amuse him. "You don't look exactly handsome, Rhett Butler, with that foolish beard. Might as well stick a bearskin over your face."

"It was the fullest disguise I could think of. There are a number of people in Atlanta that I'm not anxious to have recognize me too easily."

"Then why did you come? Not just to insult me, I don't suppose."

"I promised you I'd make myself visible often enough to keep down gossip, Scarlett. This was a perfect occasion."

"What good does a masked ball do? Nobody knows who anybody is."

"At midnight the masks come off. That's about four minutes from now. We'll waltz to visibility, then leave." Rhett took her in his arms, and Scarlett forgot her anger, forgot the peril of unmasking before her enemies, forgot the world. Nothing was important but that he was here and holding her.

Scarlett lay awake most of the night, struggling to understand what had happened. Everything was fine at the Ball . . . When twelve o'clock came, Dr. Meade said that everyone should take off their masks, and Rhett was laughing when he yanked off his beard, too. I'd take an oath he was enjoying himself. He kind of saluted the doctor and bowed to Mrs. Meade and then he whisked me out of there as easy as a greased pig. He didn't even notice the way people turned their backs on me, at least he didn't let on if he did. He was grinning from ear to ear.

And in the carriage coming home it was too dark to see his face, but his voice sounded fine. I didn't know what to say, but I hardly even had to think about it. He asked how things were at Tara and if his lawyer was paying my bills on time, and by the time I answered, we were home. That's when it happened. He was here, right downstairs in the hallway. Then he just said goodnight, he was tired, and went up to his dressing room.

He wasn't hateful or cold, he just said goodnight and went upstairs. What does that mean? Why did he bother to come all this way? Not just to go to a party when it's party time in Charleston. Not because it was a masquerade—he could go to Mardi Gras if he wanted to. After all, he has lots of friends in New Orleans.

He said "to keep down gossip." In a pig's eye. He started it, if anything, snatching off that silly beard the way he did.

Her mind circled back, went over the evening again and again until her head ached. Her sleep, when it came, was brief and restless. Nevertheless, she woke in good time to go down to breakfast in her most becoming dressing gown. She'd have no tray brought to her room today. Rhett always had his breakfast in the dining room.

"Up so early, my dear?" he said. "How thoughtful of you. I won't have to write a note of farewell." He tossed his napkin onto the table. "I've packed some things Pork overlooked. I'll be by for them later, on my way to the train."

Don't leave me, Scarlett's heart begged. She looked away lest he see the pleading in her eyes. "For heaven's sake finish your coffee, Rhett," she said. "I'm not going to make a scene." She went to the sideboard and poured herself some coffee, watching him in the mirror. She must be calm. Maybe then he'd stay.

He was standing, his watch open in his hand. "No time," he said. "There are some people I have to see while I'm here. I'm going to be very busy until summer, so I'll drop the word that I'm going to South America on business. No one will gossip about my absence for so long. Most people in Atlanta don't even know where South America is. You see, my dear, I'm keeping my promise to preserve the purity of your reputation." Rhett grinned malevolently, closed the watch and tucked it in its pocket. "Goodbye, Scarlett."

"Why don't you go on to South America and get lost there forever!"

When the door closed behind him, Scarlett's hand reached for the decanter of brandy. Why had she carried on like that? That wasn't how she felt at all. He'd always done that to her, goaded her into saying things she didn't mean. She should have known better than to fly off the handle that way. But he shouldn't have taunted me about my reputation. How could he have found out that I'm outcast?

She'd never been so unhappy in her whole life.

9

*L*ater Scarlett was ashamed of herself.
Drinking in the morning! Only low-life drunks did such a thing. Things
weren't so bad, really, she told herself. At least she knew now when Rhett
would be coming back. It was much too far in the future, but it was definite.
Now she wouldn't waste time wondering if today might be the day . . . or
tomorrow . . . or the day after that.

February opened with a surprising warm spell that called forth premature leaves on trees and filled the air with the scent of waking earth.
"Open all the windows," Scarlett told the servants, "and let the mustiness
out." The breeze lifting the loose tendrils of hair at her temples was delicious. Suddenly she was gripped by a terrible longing for Tara. She'd be
able to sleep there with the spring-laden wind, bringing the smell of the
warming earth into her bedroom.

But I can't go. Colleton will be able to start at least three more houses
once this weather gets the frost out of the ground, but he'll never do it
unless I nag him into it. I've never known such a picky man in all my life.
Everything has to be just so. He'll wait till the ground's warm enough to
dig to China and find no frost.

Suppose she went for just a few days? A few days wouldn't make that
much difference, would it? Scarlett remembered Ashley's pallor and dejected
slump at the Carnival Ball, and she made a small sound of disappointment.

She wouldn't be able to relax at Tara if she did go.

She sent Pansy with a message to Elias to bring the carriage around.
She had to go find Joe Colleton.

* * *

That evening, as if to reward her for doing her duty, the doorbell sounded just after darkness fell. "Scarlett, honey," Tony Fontaine called out when the butler let him in, "an old friend needs a room for the night, will you be merciful?"

"Tony!" Scarlett ran from the sitting room to embrace him.

He dropped his luggage, caught her in his arms for a hug. "Great God Almighty, Scarlett, you've done real well for yourself," he said. "I thought some fool had given me directions to a hotel when I saw this big place." He looked at the ornate chandelier, flocked velvet wallpaper, and massive gilt mirrors in the entrance hall, then grinned at her. "No wonder you married that Charlestonian instead of waiting for me. Where is Rhett? I'd like to meet the man who got my girl."

Cold fingers of fear traced Scarlett's spine. Had Suellen told the Fontaines anything? "Rhett's in South America," she said brightly, "can you imagine such a thing? Gracious peace, I thought missionaries were the only people who ever went to such an outlandish place!"

Tony laughed. "Me, too. I'm sorry to miss seeing him, but it's good luck for me. I'll have you all to myself. How about a drink for a thirsty man?"

He didn't know Rhett had left, she was sure of it. "I think a visit from you calls for champagne."

Tony said he'd welcome champagne later, but for now he wanted a good old bourbon whiskey and a bath. He could still smell cow manure on himself, he was sure.

Scarlett fixed his drink herself, then sent him upstairs with the butler as his guide to one of the extra bedrooms for guests. Thank heaven the servants lived in the house; there'd be no scandal about Tony staying as long as he liked. And she'd have a friend to talk to.

They had champagne with their supper, and Scarlett wore her pearls. Tony ate four big pieces of the chocolate cake that the cook had hurriedly made for dessert.

"Tell them to wrap up whatever's left for me to take with me," he begged. "The only thing I get hankerings for is cake with thick icing like that. I always did have a sweet tooth."

Scarlett laughed and sent the message to the kitchen. "Are you telling tales on Sally, Tony? Can't she do fancy cooking?"

"Sally? Whatever gave you that idea? She fixed a bang-up dessert every night, just for me. Alex don't have my weakness, so she can stop now."

Scarlett looked puzzled.

"You mean you didn't know?" said Tony. "I figured Suellen would have put it in a letter. I'm going back to Texas, Scarlett. I made up my mind 'round about Christmas."

They talked for hours. At first she begged him to stay, until Tony's awkward embarrassment changed into the famous Fontaine temper. "Dammit, Scarlett, be quiet! I tried, God knows I tried, but I can't stick it. So you'd better quit nagging me."

His loud voice made the prisms on the chandelier sway and tinkle.

"You could think about Alex," she persisted.

The expression on Tony's face made her stop.

His voice was quiet when he spoke. "I really did try," he said.

"I'm sorry, Tony."

"Me, too, honey. Why don't you get your fancy butler to open up another bottle, and we'll talk about something else."

"Tell me about Texas."

Tony's black eyes lit up. "There's not a fence in a hundred miles." He laughed and added, "That's because there's not much worth fencing in, unless you like dust and dried-up scrub. But you know who you are when you're on your own out there in all that emptiness. There's no past, no holding on to the scraps that are all you've got left. Everything is this minute, or maybe tomorrow, not yesterday."

He lifted his glass to her. "You're looking as pretty as a picture, Scarlett. Rhett can't be too smart, or he wouldn't leave you behind. I would make advances if I thought I could get away with it."

Scarlett tossed her head like a coquette. It was fun to play the old games. "You'd make advances at my grandmother if she was the only female around, Tony Fontaine. No lady's safe in the same room with you when you flash those black eyes and that white smile."

"Now, honey, you know that's not so. I'm the most gentlemanly fellow in the world . . . as long as the lady's not so beautiful that she makes me forget how to behave."

They bantered with skill, and delight in their skills, until the butler brought in the bottle of champagne; then they toasted each other. Scarlett was giddy enough from pleasure; she was content for Tony to finish the bottle. While he did, he told tall tales of Texas that made her laugh until her sides hurt.

"Tony, I do wish you'd stay over a while," she said when he announced he was about to fall asleep on her table. "I haven't had so much fun in ages."

"I wish I could. I like drinking and eating high on the hog with a pretty girl laughing beside me. But I've got to use this break in the weather.

I'm taking the train west tomorrow, before things ice up. It leaves pretty early. Will you have coffee with me before I go?"

"You couldn't stop me if you tried."

Elias drove them to the station in the gray light before dawn, and Scarlett waved goodbye with her handkerchief while Tony boarded the train. He was carrying a small leather satchel and a huge canvas bag with his saddle in it. When he'd thrown them up onto the platform of the coach, he turned and flourished his big Texas hat with the rattlesnakeskin band. The gesture pulled his coat open, and she could see his gunbelt and six-shooters.

At least he stuck around long enough to teach Wade how to twirl his, she thought. I hope he doesn't shoot his foot off. She blew a kiss to Tony. He held his hat like a bowl to catch it, reached in, took it out, put it in the watch pocket of his vest. Scarlett was still laughing when the train pulled out.

"Drive out to that land of mine where Mr. Colleton is working," she said to Elias. The sun would be up before they got there, and the work gang better be digging or she'd have something to say about it. Tony was right. You had to use the break in the weather.

Joe Colleton was unshakeable. "I come out like I said I would, Mrs. Butler, but it's just like I expected. The thaw don't go near deep enough to dig a cellar. It'll be another month before I can get started."

Scarlett cajoled, then she raged, but it did no good. She was still fuming with frustration a month later when Colleton's message brought her back out to the site.

She didn't see Ashley until it was too late to turn back. What am I going to tell him? I've got no call to be here, and Ashley's so smart he'd see right through any lie I might try. She was sure the hasty smile on her face looked as ghastly as she felt.

If it did, Ashley didn't seem to notice. He handed her down from her carriage with his usual ingrained courtesy. "I'm happy I didn't miss you, Scarlett; it's so good to see you. Mr. Colleton told me you might be coming, so I dallied as long as I could." He smiled ruefully. "We both know I'm not much of a businessman, my dear, so my advice isn't worth much, but I do want to say that if you do, in fact, build another store out here, you can't possibly go wrong."

What is he going on about? Oh . . . of course, I see. How clever Joe Colleton is, he's made my excuse for being here already. She turned her attention back to Ashley.

"... and I've heard that the city's very likely to run a trolley line out here to the edge of town. It's amazing, isn't it, the way Atlanta is growing?"

Ashley looked stronger. Very tired by the effort of living, but more capable of it. Scarlett wished urgently that it meant the lumber business was better. She wouldn't be able to bear it if the mills and yard died, too. And she'd never be able to forgive Ashley.

He took her hand in his and looked down at her with a worried expression on his drawn face. "You look tired, my dear. Is everything quite all right?"

She wanted to lay her head against his chest and wail that everything was awful. But she smiled. "Oh, fiddle-dee-dee, Ashley, don't be a silly. I was up too late last night at a party, that's all. You should know better than to hint to a lady that she's not looking her best." And let that get back to India and all her mean old friends, Scarlett added silently.

Ashley accepted her explanation without question. He began to tell her about Joe Colleton's houses. As if she didn't know all that, right down to the number of nails needed for each one. "They are quality construction," said Ashley. "For once, the less fortunate will be treated as well as the rich. It's something I never thought I'd see in these days of blatant opportunism. It seems that all the old values weren't lost after all. I'm honored to have a part in this. You see, Scarlett, Mr. Colleton wants me to supply the lumber."

She made an astonished face. "Why Ashley—that's wonderful!"

And it was. She was truly happy that her scheme to help Ashley was working so well. But, Scarlett thought after she talked privately with Colleton, it wasn't supposed to turn into some kind of fixation. Ashley intended to spend time at the site every day, Joe told her. She'd meant to provide Ashley with some income, not a hobby, for heaven's sake! Now she wouldn't be able to go out there at all.

Except on Sundays, when there was no work going on. The weekly trip became almost an obsession for her. She no longer thought about Ashley when she saw the clean strong lumber in the frame and rafters, then the walls and floors, as the house went up. She walked through the neat piles of materials and debris with a longing heart. How she'd love to be a part of it all, to hear the hammering, watch the shavings curl away from the planes, see the daily progress. Be busy.

I only have to hold out until summer—the words were her litany and her lifeline—then Rhett will come. I can tell him, Rhett's the only one I can tell, he's the only one who cares about me. He won't make me live like this, outcast and unhappy, once he knows how awful everything is. What went wrong? I was so sure that if I could just have enough money, I'd be safe. Now I'm rich, and I feel more afraid than ever before in my whole life.

But when summer came there was no visit by Rhett, no word from him. Scarlett hurried home from the store every morning so she'd be there if he was on the mid-day train. In the evening she wore her most becoming gown and her pearls for supper, in case he was coming some other way. The long table stretched before her gleaming with silver and heavy damask starched to a shine. It was then that she began to drink steadily—to shut out the silence while she listened for his footsteps.

She didn't think anything of it when she began having sherry in the afternoon—after all, taking a glass or two of sherry was a ladylike thing to do. And she hardly noticed when she changed from sherry to whiskey . . . or when she first needed a drink to do the store accounts because it depressed her that business was falling off so . . . or when she began leaving the food on her plate because alcohol satisfied her hunger better . . . or when she began to take a glass of brandy as soon as she got up in the morning . . .

She hardly even noticed when summer became fall.

Pansy brought the afternoon mail to the bedroom on a tray. Lately Scarlett had tried sleeping for a while after dinner. It filled up part of the empty afternoon, and it gave her some rest, a relief denied to her at night.

"You want I should bring you a pot of coffee or something, Miss Scarlett?"

"No. You go on, Pansy." Scarlett took the topmost letter and opened it. She stole quick glances at Pansy, who was picking up the clothes she had thrown on the floor. Why didn't the stupid girl get out of her room?

The letter was from Suellen. Scarlett didn't bother to take the folded pages from the envelope. She knew what it would say. More complaints about Ella's naughtiness, as if Suellen's own little girls were some kind of saints. Most of all, nasty little hints about the cost of everything and how little money Tara was making and how rich Scarlett was. Scarlett threw the letter to the floor. She couldn't stand to read it now. She'd do it tomorrow . . . Oh, thank God. Pansy was gone.

I need a drink. It's almost dark, there's nothing wrong with a drink in the evening. I'll just sip a small brandy very slowly while I finish reading the mail.

The bottle hidden behind the hatboxes was almost empty. Scarlett fumed. Damn that Pansy. If she wasn't so clever with my hair, I'd fire her tomorrow. It must have been Pansy who drank it. Or one of the other maids. I couldn't be drinking that much. I just hid the bottle there a few days ago. No matter. I'll take the letters down to the dining room. After all, what does it matter if the servants watch the level in the decanter? It's my house and my decanter and my brandy, and I can do what I choose. Where's my wrapper? There it is. Why are the buttons so stiff? It's taking forever to get it on.

Scarlett hurried downstairs and to the dining room, where she tossed her mail onto the table in a heap. She poured brandy into a glass and drank a reviving swallow at the sideboard before carrying the glass to the table and sitting in her chair. Now she'd just sip her drink while she calmly read her letters . . .

A circular for a newly arrived dentist. Pooh. Her teeth were just fine, thank you very much. Another one for milk delivery. An announcement of a new play at DeGives. Scarlett sorted irritably through the envelopes. Wasn't there any real mail? Her hand stopped when it touched a thin crackling onionskin envelope addressed in a spidery script. Aunt Eulalie. She downed the remainder of her brandy and ripped open the letter. She always hated the preachy, prissy missives from her dead mother's sister. But Aunt Eulalie lived in Charleston. She might mention Rhett. His mother was her closest friend.

Scarlett's eyes moved rapidly, squinting to make out the words. Aunt Eulalie always wrote on both sides of the thin paper, and often she "crossed" the letter, writing on the page then turning it to a right angle and writing across the previous lines. All to say a great deal about precious little.

The unseasonably warm autumn . . . she said that every year . . . Aunt Pauline having trouble with her knee . . . she'd had trouble with her knee as long as Scarlett could remember . . . a visit to Sister Mary Joseph . . . Scarlett made a face. She couldn't think of her baby sister Carreen by her religious name, even though she'd been in the convent in Charleston for eight years . . . the bake sale for the Cathedral building fund was far behind schedule because contributions were not coming in, and couldn't Scarlett— great balls of fire! She kept the roof over her aunts' heads, did she have to roof a cathedral, too? She turned the page over, frowning.

Rhett's name leapt from the tangle of criss-crossed words.

It does one's heart good to see a cherished friend like Eleanor Butler find happiness after so many sorrows. Rhett is quite his mother's gallant, and his devotion has done much to redeem him in the eyes of all those who deplored the wild ways of his younger days. It is beyond my comprehension, and also that of your Aunt Pauline, why you insist on maintaining your unaccountable preoccupation with trade when you have no need to remain associated with the store. I have deplored your actions in this regard on many past occasions, and you have never heeded my pleas that you abandon a course of action so unsuitable to a lady. I therefore ceased to refer to it some years ago. But now, when it is keeping you from your proper place by the side of your husband, I feel it my duty to once again allude to the distasteful matter.

Scarlett threw the letter onto the table. So that was the story that Rhett was handing out! That she wouldn't leave the store and go to Charleston with him. What a blackhearted liar he was! She'd begged him to take her with him when he left. How dare he spread such slander? She'd have some choice words to say to Mister Rhett Butler when he came home.

She strode to the sideboard, splashed brandy into her glass. Some fell onto the gleaming wooden surface. A swipe with her sleeve mopped it up. He'd probably deny it, the skunk. Well, she'd shake Aunt Eulalie's letter in his face. Let's see him call his mother's best friend a liar!

Suddenly her rage left her, and she felt cold. She knew what he'd say: "Would you rather I told the truth? That I left you because living with you was intolerable?"

The shame of it. Anything was better than that. Even the loneliness while she waited for him to come home. Her hand lifted the glass to her lips, and she drank deep.

The movement caught her eye, reflected in the mirror above the sideboard. Slowly Scarlett lowered her hand and set the glass down. She looked into her own eyes. They widened in shock at what they saw. She hadn't really looked at herself for months, and she couldn't believe that pale, thin, sunken-eyed woman had anything to do with her. Why, her hair looked as if it hadn't been washed for weeks!

What had happened to her?

Her hand reached automatically for the decanter, providing the answer. Scarlett pulled her hand away, and she saw that it was shaking.

"Oh, my God," she whispered. She clutched the edge of the sideboard for support and stared at her reflection. "Fool!" she said. Her eyes closed and tears slid slowly down her cheeks, but she brushed them away with quivering fingers.

She wanted a drink more than she'd ever wanted anything in her life.

Her tongue darted across her lips. Her right hand moved on its own volition, closed around the neck of the glittering diamond-cut glass. Scarlett looked at her hand as if it belonged to a stranger, at the beautiful heavy crystal decanter and the promise of escape that lay within it. Slowly, watching her movements in the mirror, she lifted the decanter and backed away from her frightening reflection.

Then she drew in a long breath and swung her arm with all the strength she could find. The decanter sparkled blue and red and violet in the sunlight as it crashed into the huge mirror. For an instant Scarlett saw her face cracking into pieces, saw her twisted smile of victory. Then the silvered glass fragmented, and tiny shards spattered onto the sideboard. The top of the mirror seemed to lean forward from its frame, and huge jagged pieces fell crashing with a sound like cannon fire onto the sideboard, the floor, the pieces that had fallen first.

Scarlett was crying, and laughing, and shouting at the destruction of her own image. "Coward! Coward! Coward!"

She didn't feel the tiny cuts that flying bits of glass made on her arms and neck and face. Her tongue tasted salt; she touched the trickle of blood on her cheek and looked in surprise at her reddened fingers.

She stared at the place where her reflection had been, but it was gone. She laughed unevenly. Good riddance.

The servants had rushed to the door when they heard the noise. They stood very close to one another, afraid to enter the room, looking fearfully at Scarlett's rigid figure. She turned her head suddenly towards them, and Pansy let out a little cry of terror at the sight of her blood-smeared face.

"Go away," Scarlett said calmly. "I am perfectly all right. Go away. I want to be by myself." They obeyed without a word.

She was by herself whether she wanted to be or not, and no amount of brandy would make it any different. Rhett wasn't coming home, this house wasn't home to him any more. She'd known that for a long time but she'd refused to face it. She'd been a coward and a fool. No wonder she hadn't known that woman in the mirror. That cowardly fool wasn't Scarlett O'Hara. Scarlett O'Hara didn't—what did they call it?—drown her sorrows. Scarlett O'Hara didn't hide and hope. She faced the worst the world could hand her. And she went out into the danger to take what she wanted.

Scarlett shuddered. She had come so close to defeating herself.

No more. It was time—long past time—to take her life in her own hands. No more brandy. She had flung away that crutch.

Her whole body was crying out for a drink, but she refused to listen. She'd done harder things in her life, she could do this. She had to.

She shook her fist at the broken mirror. "Bring on your seven years bad luck, damn you." Her defiant laugh was ragged.

She leaned against the table for a moment while she gathered her strength. She had so much to do.

Then she walked over the destruction around her, her heels breaking the mirror into bits. "Pansy!" she called from the doorway. "I want you to wash my hair."

Scarlett was trembling from head to toe, but she made her legs carry her to the staircase and climb the long flight of stairs. "My skin must be like corduroy," she said aloud, concentrating her mind away from the cravings of her body. "I'll need to use quarts of rosewater and glycerine. And I have to get all new clothes. Mrs. Marie can hire extra sewing help."

It shouldn't take more than a few weeks to get over her weakness and get back to looking her best. She wouldn't let it.

She had to be strong and beautiful, and she had no time to waste. She'd lost too much of it already.

Rhett hadn't come back to her, so she'd have to go to him.

To Charleston.

High Stakes

10

Once her mind was made up, Scarlett's life changed radically. She had a goal, now, and all her energy poured into achieving it. She'd think later about exactly how she was going to get Rhett back, after she arrived in Charleston. For now, she had to get ready to go.

Mrs. Marie threw up her hands and declared it impossible to make a complete new wardrobe in only a few weeks; Uncle Henry Hamilton put his fingertips together and expressed his disapproval when Scarlett told him what she needed him to do. Their opposition made Scarlett's eyes gleam with the joy of battle, and in the end she won. By the beginning of November Uncle Henry had taken over the financial management of the store and saloon with a guarantee that the money would go to Joe Colleton. And Scarlett's bedroom was a chaos of color and laces—her new clothes laid out to be packed for the trip.

She was still thin, and there were faint bruise-like shadows under her eyes, because the nights had been torments of sleeplessness and fierce efforts of will to resist the rest promised by the decanter of brandy. But she had won that battle, too, and her normal appetite for food had returned. Her face was already filled out enough so that a dimple flickered when she smiled, and her bosom was enticingly plump. With a skillful application of rouge on her lips and cheeks, she looked almost like a girl again, she was sure.

It was time to go.

* * *

Goodbye, Atlanta, Scarlett said silently when the train pulled out of the station. You tried to beat me down, but I wouldn't let you. I don't care if you approve of me or not.

She told herself that the chill she felt must be from a draft. She wasn't afraid, not a bit. She was going to have a wonderful time in Charleston. Didn't people always say that it was the partyingest town in the whole South? And there was no question at all about being invited everywhere; Aunt Pauline and Aunt Eulalie knew everybody. They'd know all about Rhett, where he was living, what he was doing. All she'd have to do was ...

No sense thinking about that now. She'd decide when she got there. If she thought about it now, she might feel nervous about going, and she had made up her mind to go.

Gracious! It was silly even to imagine being nervous. It wasn't as if Charleston was the end of the world. Why, Tony Fontaine went off to Texas, a million miles away, just as easy as if it was no more than a ride over to Decatur. She'd been to Charleston before, too. She knew where she was going ...

It didn't mean a thing that she had hated it. After all, she'd been so young then, only seventeen, and a new widow with a baby, besides. Wade Hampton hadn't even cut his teeth yet. That was over twelve years ago. Everything would be completely different now. It was all going to work out just fine, just the way she wanted.

"Pansy, go tell the conductor to move our things, I want to sit closer to the stove. There's a draft from this window."

Scarlett sent a telegram to her aunts from the station in Augusta where she changed to the South Carolina railroad line:

> ARRIVING FOUR PM TRAIN FOR VISIT STOP ONLY ONE SERVANT
> STOP LOVE SCARLETT

She had thought it all out. Exactly ten words, and there was no risk that her aunts would wire back some excuse to keep her from coming, because she was already on her way. Not that they'd be likely to. Eulalie was forever begging her to come see them, and hospitality was still the unwritten law of the land in the South. But no sense gambling when you could have a sure thing, and she had to have her aunts' house and protection to begin with. Charleston was a mighty stuck-up, proud place, and Rhett was obviously trying to turn people against her.

No, she wouldn't think about that. She was going to love Charleston this time. She was determined. Everything was going to be different. Her whole life was going to be different. Don't look back, she'd always told herself. Now she truly meant it. Her whole life was behind her, further behind with each turn of the wheels. All the demands of her businesses were in Uncle Henry's hands, her responsibilities to Melanie were taken care of, her children were settled at Tara. For the first time in her adult life she was free to do anything she wanted to do, and she knew what that was. She'd prove to Rhett that he was wrong when he refused to believe that she loved him. She'd show him that she did. He'd see. And then he'd be sorry he'd left her. He'd put his arms around her and kiss her, and they'd be happy forever after ... Even in Charleston if he insisted on staying there.

Lost in her daydream, Scarlett didn't notice the man who got onto the train at Ridgeville until he lurched against the arm of her seat. Then she recoiled as if he had struck her. He was in the blue uniform of the Union Army.

A Yankee! What was he doing here? Those days were done, and she wanted to forget them forever, but the sight of the uniform brought them all back. The fear when Atlanta was under siege, the brutality of the soldiers when they stripped Tara of its pitiful store of food and set fire to the house, the explosion of blood when she shot the straggler before he could rape her ... Scarlett felt her heart pounding with terror all over again, and she almost cried out. Damn them, damn them all for destroying the South. Damn them most of all for making her feel helpless and afraid. She hated the feeling, and she hated them!

I won't let it upset me, I won't. I can't let anything bother me now, not when I need to be at my best, ready for Charleston and Rhett. I won't look at the Yankee, and I won't think about the past. Only the future counts now. Scarlett stared resolutely out the window at the hilly countryside, so similar to the land around Atlanta. Red clay roads through stands of dark pine woods and fields of frost-darkened crop stubble. She'd been travelling for more than a day, and she might as well have never left home. Hurry, she urged the engine, do hurry.

"What's Charleston like, Miss Scarlett?" Pansy asked for the hundredth time just as the light was beginning to fade outside the window.

"Very pretty, you'll like it fine," Scarlett answered for the hundredth time. "There!" She pointed at the landscape. "See that tree with the stuff hanging off it? That's the Spanish moss I told you about."

Pansy pressed her nose to the sooty pane. "Oooh," she whimpered. "It looks like ghosts moving. I'm scared of ghosts, Miss Scarlett."

"Don't be a ninny!" But Scarlett shivered. The long, swaying, gray wisps of moss were eerie in the gray light, and she didn't like the way it looked either. It meant that they were moving into the Lowcountry, though, close to the sea and to Charleston. Scarlett peered at her lapel watch. Five-thirty. The train was over two hours late. Her aunts would have waited, she was sure. But even so, she wished she wouldn't be arriving after dark. There was something so unfriendly about the dark.

The cavernous station in Charleston was poorly lit. Scarlett craned her neck, searching for her aunts or for a coachman who might be their servant, looking for her. What she saw instead were a half dozen more soldiers in blue uniform, carrying guns slung over their shoulders.

"Miss Scarlett—" Pansy tugged on her sleeve. "There's soldiers everywhere." The young maid's voice was quavering.

Her fear forced Scarlett to appear brave. "Just act like they're not here at all, Pansy. They can't hurt you, the War's been over for practically ten years. Come on." She gestured to the porter who was pushing the cart with her luggage. "Where would I find the carriage that's meeting me?" she asked haughtily.

He led the way outside, but the only vehicle there was a ramshackle buggy with a swaybacked horse and a dishevelled black driver. Scarlett's heart sank. Suppose her aunts were out of town? They went to Savannah to visit their father, she knew. Suppose her telegram was just sitting on the front stoop of a dark, empty house?

She drew in a long breath. She didn't care what the story was, she had to get away from the station and the Yankee soldiers. I'll break a window to get into the house if I have to. Why shouldn't I? I'll just pay to get it fixed the same way I paid to fix the roof for them and everything else. She'd been sending her aunts money to live on ever since they lost all of theirs during the War.

"Put my things in that hack," she ordered the porter, "and tell the driver to get down and help you. I'm going to the Battery."

The magic word "Battery" had exactly the effect she hoped for. Both driver and porter became respectful and eager to be of service. So it's still the most fashionable address in Charleston, Scarlett thought with relief. Thank goodness. It would be too awful if Rhett heard I was living in a slum.

* * *

Pauline and Eulalie threw open the door of their house the moment the buggy stopped. Golden light streamed out onto the path from the sidewalk, and Scarlett ran through it to the sanctuary it promised.

But they looked so old! she thought when she was close to her aunts. I don't remember Aunt Pauline being skinny as a stick and all wrinkled like that. And when did Aunt Eulalie get so fat? She looks like a balloon with gray hair on top.

"Look at you!" Eulalie exclaimed. "You've changed so, Scarlett, why I'd hardly know you."

Scarlett quailed. Surely she hadn't got old, too, had she? She accepted her aunts' embraces and forced a smile.

"Look at Scarlett, Sister," Eulalie burbled. "She's grown up to be the image of Ellen."

Pauline sniffed. "Ellen was never this thin, Sister, you know that." She took Scarlett's arm and pulled her away from Eulalie. "There is a clear resemblance, though, I will say that."

Scarlett smiled, this time happily. There was no greater compliment in the world that anyone could pay her.

The aunts fluttered and argued about the business of settling Pansy in the servants' quarters and getting the trunks and valises carried upstairs to Scarlett's bedroom. "Don't you lift a finger, honey," Eulalie said to Scarlett. "You must be worn out after that long trip." Scarlett settled herself gratefully on a settee in the drawing room, away from the fuss. Now that she was finally here, the feverish energy that had gotten her through the preparations seemed to have evaporated, and she realized that her aunt was right. She was worn out.

She all but dozed off during supper. Both her aunts had soft voices, with the characteristic Lowcountry accent that elongated vowels and blurred consonants. Even though their conversation consisted largely of politely expressed disagreement on everything, the sound of it was lulling. Also, they weren't saying anything that interested her at all. She'd learned what she wanted to know almost as soon as she stepped across the threshold. Rhett was living at his mother's house, but he was out of town.

"Gone North," Pauline said, with a sour expression.

"But for good reason, Sister," Eulalie reminded her. "He's in Philadelphia buying back some of the family silver that the Yankees stole."

Pauline relented. "It's a joy to see how devoted he is to his mother's happiness, finding all the things that she lost."

This time Eulalie was the critic. "He could have shown some of that devotion a lot sooner, if you ask me."

Scarlett didn't ask. She was busy with her own thoughts, which were concentrated on wondering how soon she could go up to bed. No sleeplessness would plague her tonight, she was sure of it.

And she was right. Now that she'd taken her life in her own hands and was on her way to getting what she wanted, she could sleep like a baby. She woke in the morning with a sense of well-being that she hadn't felt for years. She was welcome at her aunts', not shunned and lonely like in Atlanta, and she didn't even have to think yet about what she'd say to Rhett when she saw him. She could relax and be spoiled a little while she waited for him to get back from Philadelphia.

Her aunt Eulalie punctured Scarlett's bubble before she'd finished her first cup of breakfast coffee. "I know how anxious you must be to see Carreen, honey, but she only has visitors on Tuesdays and Saturdays, so we've planned something else for today."

Carreen! Scarlett's lips tightened. She didn't want to see her at all, the traitor. Giving her share of Tara away as if it meant nothing at all . . . But what was she going to say to the aunts? They'd never understand that a sister wouldn't be just dying to see another sister. Why, they even live together, they're so close. I'll have to pretend I want to see Carreen more than anything in the world and get a headache when it's time to go.

Suddenly she realized what Pauline was saying, and her head did begin to throb painfully at the temples.

". . . so we sent our maid Susie with a note to Eleanor Butler. We'll call on her this morning." She reached for the bowl of butter. "Would you please pass the syrup, Scarlett?"

Scarlett's hand reached out automatically, but she knocked over the pitcher, spilling the syrup. Rhett's mother. She wasn't ready to see Rhett's mother yet. She'd only met Eleanor Butler once, at Bonnie's funeral, and she had almost no memory of her, except that Mrs. Butler was very tall and dignified and imposingly silent. I know I'll have to see her, Scarlett thought, but not now, not yet. I'm not ready. Her heart pounded and she dabbed clumsily with her napkin at the spreading stickiness on the tablecloth.

"Scarlett, dear, don't rub the stain into the cloth like that." Pauline put her hand on Scarlett's wrist. Scarlett jerked her hand away. How could anyone worry about some silly old tablecloth at a time like this?

"I'm sorry, Auntie," she managed to say.

"That's all right, dear. It's just that you're practically putting a hole through it, and we have so few of our nice things left . . ." Eulalie's voice faded mournfully.

Scarlett clenched her teeth. She wanted to scream. What did a tablecloth matter when she had to face the mother Rhett practically worshipped?

Suppose he'd told her the truth about why he'd left Atlanta, that he had walked out on the marriage? "I'd better go look at my clothes," Scarlett said through the constriction in her throat. "Pansy'll have to press the wrinkles out of whatever I'm going to wear." She had to get away from Pauline and Eulalie, she had to pull herself together.

"I'll tell Susie to start heating the irons," Eulalie offered. She rang the silver bell near her plate.

"She'd better wash out this cloth before she starts on anything else," Pauline said. "Once a stain sets—"

"You might observe, Sister, that I have not yet finished my breakfast. Surely you don't expect me to let it get cold while Susie clears everything off the table."

Scarlett fled to her room.

"You won't need that heavy fur cape, Scarlett," said Pauline.

"Indeed not," said Eulalie. "We have a typical Charleston winter day today. Why, I wouldn't even wear this shawl if I didn't have a cold."

Scarlett unhooked the cape and handed it to Pansy. If Eulalie wanted everyone else to have a cold, too, she'd be glad to oblige her. Her aunts must take her for a fool. She knew why they didn't want her to wear her cape. They were just like the Old Guard in Atlanta. A person had to be shabby like them to be respectable. She noticed Eulalie eyeing the fashionable feather-trimmed hat she was wearing, and her jaw hardened belligerently. If she had to face Rhett's mother, at least she would do it in style.

"Let's be off, then," said Eulalie, capitulating. Susie pulled the big door open, and Scarlett followed her aunts out into the bright day. She gasped when she stepped down from the entrance. It was like May, not November. Sun reflected warmth from the white crushed shell of the path and settled on her shoulders like a weightless blanket. She tilted her chin up to feel it on her face and her eyes closed in sensuous pleasure. "Oh, Aunties, this feels wonderful," she said. "I hope your carriage has a fold-down top."

The aunts laughed. "Dear child," Eulalie said, "there's not a living soul in Charleston with a carriage any more, except for Sally Brewton. We'll walk. Everyone does."

"There are carriages, Sister," Pauline corrected. "The carpetbaggers have them."

"You could hardly call the carpetbaggers 'living souls,' Sister. Soulless is what they are, else they couldn't be carpetbaggers."

"Vultures," Pauline agreed with a sniff.

"Buzzards," said Eulalie. The sisters laughed again. Scarlett laughed with them. The beautiful day was making her feel almost giddy with delight. Nothing could possibly go wrong on a day like this. Suddenly she felt a great fondness for her aunts, even for their harmless quarreling. She followed them across the wide empty street in front of the house and up the short stairway on the other side of it. As she reached the top of it, a breeze fluttered the feathers on her hat and touched her lips with a taste of salt.

"Oh my goodness," she said. On the far side of the elevated promenade, the green-brown waters of Charleston's harbor stretched before her to the horizon. To her left, flags fluttered on the tall masts of ships along the wharves. To her right the trees of a long low island glowed a bright green. The sunlight glittered on the tips of tiny pointed wavelets, like diamonds scattered across the water. A trio of brilliantly white birds soared in the cloudless blue sky then swooped down to skim the tops of the waves. They looked as if they were playing a game, a weightless, carefree kind of follow-the-leader. The salt-sweet light breeze caressed her neck.

She'd been right to come, she was sure of it now. She turned to her aunts. "It's a wonderful day," Scarlett said.

The promenade was so wide, they walked three abreast along it. Twice they met other people, first an elderly gentleman in an old-fashioned frock coat and beaver hat, then a lady accompanied by a thin boy who blushed when he was spoken to. Each time, they stopped, and the aunts introduced Scarlett, ". . . our niece from Atlanta. Her mother was our sister Ellen, and she's married to Eleanor Butler's boy, Rhett." The old gentleman bowed and kissed Scarlett's hand, the lady introduced her grandson, who gazed at Scarlett as if he had been struck by lightning. For Scarlett the day was getting better with every passing minute. Then she saw that the next walkers approaching them were men in blue uniforms.

Her step faltered, she grabbed Pauline's arm.

"Auntie," she whispered, "there are Yankee soldiers coming at us."

"Keep walking," said Pauline clearly. "They'll have to get out of our way."

Scarlett looked at Pauline with shock. Who would have thought that her skinny old aunt could be so brave? Her own heart was thumping so loud that she was sure the Yankee soldiers would hear it, but she willed her feet to move.

When only three paces separated them, the soldiers drew aside, pressing their bodies against the railings of metal pipe that lined the edge of the walkway along the water. Pauline and Eulalie sailed past them as if they were not there. Scarlett lifted her chin to equal the tilt of her aunts' and kept pace.

Somewhere ahead of them a band began to play "Oh! Susanna." The rollicking, merry tune was as bright and sunny as the day. Eulalie and Pauline walked more quickly, keeping time with the music, but Scarlett's feet felt like lead. Coward! she berated herself. But inside she couldn't stop trembling.

"Why are there so many damned Yankees in Charleston?" she asked angrily. "I saw some at the depot, too."

"My goodness, Scarlett," said Eulalie, "didn't you know? Charleston is still under military occupation. They'll likely never leave us alone. They hate us because we threw them out of Fort Sumter and then held it against their whole fleet."

"And heaven only knows how many regiments," Pauline added. The sisters' faces were glowing with pride.

"Mother of God," Scarlett whispered. What had she done? Walked right into the arms of the enemy. She knew what military government meant: the helplessness and the rage, the constant fear that they'd confiscate your house or put you in jail or shoot you if you broke one of their laws. Military government was all-powerful. She had lived under its capricious rule for five harsh years. How could she have been such a fool as to stumble back into it again?

"They do have a pleasant band," said Pauline. "Come along, Scarlett, we cross here. The Butler house is the one with the fresh paint."

"Lucky Eleanor," said Eulalie, "to have such a devoted son. Rhett positively worships his mother."

Scarlett stared at the house. Not a house, a mansion. Shining white columns soared a hundred feet to support the roof overhang above the deep porches along the side of the tall, imposing brick house. Scarlett's knees felt weak. She couldn't go in, she couldn't. She'd never seen any place as grand, as impressive. How would she ever find anything to say to the woman who lived in such magnificence? Who could destroy all her hopes with one word to Rhett.

Pauline had her by the arm, hurrying her across the street. "'... with a banjo on my knee,'" she was singing in a low off-key murmur. Scarlett allowed herself to be led like a sleepwalker. In time, she found herself standing inside a door, looking at a tall elegant woman with shining white hair crowning a lined lovely face.

"Dear Eleanor," said Eulalie.

"You've brought Scarlett," said Mrs. Butler. "My dear child," she said to Scarlett, "you look so pale." She put her hands lightly on Scarlett's shoulders and bent to kiss her cheek.

Scarlett closed her eyes. The faint scent of lemon verbena surrounded her, floating gently from Eleanor Butler's silk gown and silken hair. It was the fragrance that had always been part of Ellen O'Hara, the scent for Scarlett of comfort, of safety, of love, of life before the War.

Scarlett felt her eyes spilling uncontrollable tears.

"There, there," Rhett's mother said. "It's all right, my dear. Whatever it is, it's all right now. You've come home at last. I've been longing for you to come." She put her arms around her daughter-in-law and held her close.

11

$\mathscr{E}$leanor Butler was a Southern lady.
Her slow, soft voice and indolent, graceful movements disguised a formidable energy and efficiency. Ladies were trained from birth to be decorative, to be sympathetic and fascinated listeners, to be appealingly helpless and empty-headed and admiring. They were also trained to manage the intricate and demanding responsibilities of huge houses and large, often warring, staffs of servants—while always making it seem that the house, the garden, the kitchen, the servants ran themselves flawlessly while the lady of the house concentrated on matching colors of silk for her delicate embroidery.

When the deprivations of war reduced the staffs of thirty or forty to one or two, the demands on women increased exponentially, but the expectations remained the same. The battered houses must continue to welcome guests, shelter families, sparkle with clean windows and shining brass, and have a well-groomed, imperturbable, accomplished mistress at leisure in the drawing room. Somehow the ladies of the South did it.

Eleanor soothed Scarlett with gentle words and fragrant tea, flattered Pauline by asking her opinion of the desk recently installed in the drawing room, diverted Eulalie with a plea to taste the pound cake and judge if the extract of vanilla bean was strong enough. She also murmured to Manigo, her manservant, that her maid Celie would help him and Scarlett's maid transfer Scarlett's things from her aunts' house to the big bedroom overlooking the garden where Mr. Rhett slept.

In under ten minutes, everything had been accomplished to move Scar-

lett without opposition, or injured feelings, or interruption to the
even rhythm of the tranquil life under Eleanor Butler's roof. Scarlett felt
like a girl again, safe from all harm, sheltered by a mother's all-powerful
love.

She gazed at Eleanor through misted, admiring eyes. This was what
she wanted to be, had always meant to be, a lady like her mother, like
Eleanor Butler. Ellen O'Hara had instructed her to be a lady, had planned
for it and wanted it. I can do it now, Scarlett told herself. I can make up
for all the mistakes I made. I can make Mother proud of me.

When she was a child, Mammy had described heaven to her as a land
of clouds like big feather mattresses where angels rested, amusing themselves by looking down at the goings-on below through cracks in the sky.
Ever since her mother died, Scarlett had had an uncomfortable childish
conviction that Ellen was watching her with unhappy concern.

I'll make it all better now, she promised her mother. Eleanor's affectionate welcome had, for the moment, erased all the fears and memories
that filled her heart and mind when she saw the Yankee soldiers. It had
even wiped out Scarlett's unacknowledged anxiety about her decision to
follow Rhett to Charleston. She felt safe and loved and invincible. She could
do anything, everything. And she would. She would win Rhett's love again.
She would be the lady Ellen always meant for her to be. She would be
admired and respected and adored by everyone. And she would never, ever,
be lonely again.

When Pauline closed the last tiny, ivory-inlaid drawer of the rosewood
desk and Eulalie hurriedly swallowed the last slice of cake, Eleanor Butler
stood, pulling Scarlett up with her. "I have to pick up my boots from the
cobbler this morning," she said, "so I'll take Scarlett along and introduce
her to King Street. No woman can possibly feel at home until she knows
where the shops are. Will youall join us?"

To Scarlett's immense relief, her aunts declined. She wanted Mrs. Butler all to herself.

The walk to Charleston's shops was pure pleasure in the warm bright
winter sunlight. King Street was a revelation and a delight. Stores lined
it for block after block; dry goods, hardware, boots, tobacco and cigars,
hats, jewelry, china, seeds, medicines, wines, books, gloves, candies—it
seemed that everything and anything could be bought on King Street.
There were crowds of shoppers, too, and dozens of smart buggies and
open carriages, with liveried drivers and fashionably dressed occupants.
Charleston was nowhere near as dreary as she had remembered it and
feared it to be. It was much bigger and busier than Atlanta. And no sign
of the Panic at all.

Unfortunately, Rhett's mother behaved as if none of the color and excitement and busyness existed. She walked past windows full of ostrich plumes and painted fans without looking at them, crossed the street without so much as a thank you to the women in the buggy that had stopped to avoid hitting her. Scarlett remembered what her aunts had told her: there wasn't a carriage to be had in Charleston except those owned by Yankees, carpetbaggers and scallywags. She felt a rush of white-hot rage at the vultures that were fattening on the defeated South. When she followed Mrs. Butler into one of the boot shops it did her heart good to see the proprietor turn over his richly dressed customer to a young assistant so that he could hurry forward to Rhett's mother. It was a pleasure to be with a member of the Old Guard in Charleston. She wished fervently that Mrs. Merriwether or Mrs. Elsing were there to see her.

"I left some boots to be resoled, Mr. Braxton," Eleanor said, "and I also want my daughter-in-law to know where to come for the finest footwear and the most agreeable service. Scarlett, dear, Mr. Braxton will take the same good care of you that he has of me for all these years."

"It will be my privilege, ma'am." Mr. Braxton bowed elegantly.

"How do you do, Mr. Braxton, and I thank you," Scarlett replied, with great refinement. "I believe I'll get a pair of boots today myself." She raised her skirt a few inches to display her fragile, thin leather shoes. "Something more suitable for city walking," she said proudly. No one was going to take her for a carriage-riding scallywag.

Mr. Braxton took an immaculate white handkerchief from his pocket and brushed off the spotless upholstery on two chairs. "If you ladies please . . ."

When he disappeared behind a curtain in the rear of the shop, Eleanor leaned close to Scarlett and whispered in her ear. "Look closely at his hair when he kneels to fit your boots. He colors it with boot polish."

It took all of Scarlett's self-control not to laugh when she saw that Mrs. Butler was right, especially when Eleanor was looking at her with such a conspiratorial twinkle in her dark eyes. When they left the shop, she began to giggle. "You shouldn't have told me that, Miss Eleanor. I nearly made a spectacle of myself in there."

Mrs. Butler smiled serenely. "You'll recognize him easily in the future," she said. "Now let's go to Onslow's for a dish of ice cream. One of the waiters there makes the best moonshine in all of South Carolina, and I want to order a few quarts for soaking the fruitcakes. The ice cream is excellent, too."

"Miss Eleanor!"

"My dear, brandy's not available for love nor money. We all have to make do the best we can, do we not? And there's something quite exciting about black-market dealings, don't you think?"

What Scarlett thought was that she didn't blame Rhett one bit for adoring his mother.

Eleanor Butler continued to initiate Scarlett into the inner life of Charleston by going to the fancy goods draper for a spool of white cotton (the woman behind the counter had killed her husband with a sharpened knitting needle through the heart, but the judge ruled that he had fallen on it when he was drunk, because everyone had seen the bruises on her arms and face for years) and to the pharmacist for some witch hazel (poor man, he was so nearsighted he once paid a small fortune for a peculiar tropical fish preserved in alcohol that he was convinced was a small mermaid—for real medicine, always go to the shop on Broad Street that I'll show you).

Scarlett was sorely disappointed when Eleanor said it was time to go home. She couldn't remember ever having had such fun, and she almost begged for visits to a few more shops. But, "I think perhaps we'll take the horsecar back downtown," Mrs. Butler said. "I'm feeling a little tired." And Scarlett immediately began to worry. Was Eleanor's pallor a sign of illness instead of the pale skin so prized by ladies? She held her mother-in-law's elbow when they stepped up into the brightly painted green and yellow tram and hovered over her until Eleanor settled into the wicker-covered seat. Rhett would never forgive her if she let something awful happen to his mother. She'd never forgive herself, either.

She looked from the corner of her eye at Mrs. Butler as the horsecar moved slowly along its tracks, but she couldn't see any outward sign of trouble. Eleanor was talking cheerfully about more shopping they would do together. "We'll go to the Market tomorrow, you'll meet everyone you should know there. It's the traditional place to learn all the news, too. The paper never prints the really interesting things."

The car jolted and turned to the left, then moved a block and stopped at an intersection. Scarlett gasped. Immediately outside the open window next to Eleanor she saw a soldier in blue, rifle on his shoulder, marching in the shadows of a tall colonnade. "Yankees," she whispered.

Mrs. Butler's gaze followed Scarlett's eyes. "That's right, Georgia's been rid of them for some time, hasn't it? We've been occupied so long that we hardly even notice them any more. Ten years next February. One gets accustomed to almost anything in ten years."

"I'll never get used to them," Scarlett whispered. "Never."

A sudden noise made her jump. Then she realized that it was the chime of a great clock somewhere above them. The horsecar moved into the intersection, turning to the right.

"One o'clock," said Mrs. Butler. "No wonder I'm tired; it was a long morning." Behind them the chimes ended their quartet of notes. A single bell rang once. "That's every Charlestonian's timekeeper," Eleanor Butler said, "the bells in Saint Michael's steeple. They record our births and our passings."

Scarlett was looking at the tall houses and walled gardens they were passing. Without exception they bore the scars of war. Pock-holes of shelling marred every surface, and poverty was visible on all sides: peeling paint, boards nailed over shattered windows that could not be replaced, gaps and rust disfiguring elaborate, lace-like wrought iron balconies and gates. The trees lining the street had thin trunks; they were youthful replacements for the giants broken by shelling. Damn the Yankees.

And yet the sun gleamed on brightly polished brass door knobs, and there was the scent of flowers blooming behind the garden walls. They've got gumption, these Charleston folks, she thought. They don't give in.

She helped Mrs. Butler down at the last stop, the end of Meeting Street. In front of them was a park, with neatly clipped grass and gleaming white paths that converged on and circled a freshly painted round bandstand with a shiny pagoda-like roof. Beyond it was the harbor. She could smell the water and the salt. A breeze rattled the sword-shaped fronds of palm trees in the park and swayed the long airy clumps of Spanish moss on the scarred limbs of liveoaks. Small children were running, rolling hoops, tossing balls on the grass under the watchful eyes of turbanned black nursemaids sitting on benches.

"Scarlett, I hope you'll forgive me; I know I shouldn't, but I have to ask." Mrs. Butler's cheeks had splotches of bright color.

"What is it, Miss Eleanor? Are you feeling bad? Do you want me to run get you something? Come sit down."

"No, no, I'm perfectly well. I just can't stand not knowing ... Have you and Rhett ever thought of another child? I understand that you'd be afraid to repeat the heartbreak you felt when Bonnie died ..."

"A baby ..." Scarlett's voice trailed off. Had Mrs. Butler read her mind? She was counting on getting pregnant as soon as possible. Rhett would never send her away then. He was crazy about children, and he'd love her forever if she gave him one. Her voice rang with sincerity when she spoke.

"Miss Eleanor, I want a baby more than anything else in the whole world."

"Thank God," said Mrs. Butler. "I do so long to be a grandmother again. When Rhett brought Bonnie to visit me, I could hardly keep from smothering her with hugging. You see, Margaret—that's my other son's wife, you'll meet her today—poor Margaret is barren. And Rosemary ...

Rhett's sister . . . I'm very much afraid that there'll never be anyone for Rosemary to marry."

Scarlett's mind worked furiously, fitting together the pieces of Rhett's family and what they meant to her. Rosemary could be a problem. Old maids were so nasty. But the brother—what was his name anyhow? Oh, yes, Ross, that was it. Ross was a man, and she'd never had any trouble charming men. Babyless Margaret wasn't worth bothering about. It wasn't likely she'd have any influence on Rhett. Fiddle-dee-dee, what did any of them matter? It was his mother that Rhett loved so much, and his mother wanted them together, with a baby, two babies, a dozen. Rhett had to take her back.

She kissed Mrs. Butler quickly on her cheek. "I'm just longing for a baby, Miss Eleanor. We'll convince Rhett, the two of us."

"You've made me very happy, Scarlett. Let's go home now, it's only around the corner there. Then I think I'll have a little rest before dinner. My committee is meeting at the house this afternoon, and I need to have my wits about me. I hope you'll join us, if only for tea. Margaret will be there. I don't want to pressure you to work, but of course if you were interested, I'd be pleased. We raise money with cake sales and bazaars of handcrafts and such for the Confederate Home for Widows and Orphans."

God's nightgown, were they all the same, these Southern ladies? It was just like Atlanta. Always Confederate this and Confederate that. Couldn't they admit the War was over and get on with their lives? She'd have a headache. Scarlett's step faltered, then resumed its steady pace, matching Mrs. Butler's. No, she'd go to the committee meeting, she'd even work on the committee if they asked her. She was never going to make the mistakes here she'd made in Atlanta. She was never going to be shut out and lonely again, not even if she had to wear the Stars and Bars embroidered on her corsets.

"That sounds mighty nice," she said. "I was always a little sad that I never had time for extra work in Atlanta. My former husband, Frank Kennedy, left a fine business as an inheritance for our little girl. I felt it was my duty to watch over it for her."

That should take care of that story Rhett was telling.

Eleanor Butler nodded comprehension. Scarlett lowered her lashes to hide the delight in her eyes.

While Mrs. Butler was resting, Scarlett wandered through the house. She hurried down the stairs to see what Rhett was so busy buying back from the Yankees for his mother.

The place looked mighty bare to her. Scarlett's eye wasn't educated to appreciate the perfection of what he had done. On the second floor, the magnificent double drawing rooms held exquisite sofas, tables, and chairs, placed so that each could be appreciated as well as used. Scarlett admired the obvious quality of the silk upholstery and the well-polished gleam of the wood, but the beauty of the space surrounding the furniture escaped her completely. She liked the small card room much better. The table and chairs filled it more, and besides, she loved to play cards.

The ground floor dining room was only a dining room to her; she'd never heard of Hepplewhite. And the library was just a place full of books, therefore boring. What pleased her most were the deep porches, because the day was so warm, and the view over the harbor included wheeling gulls and small sailboats that looked as if they might themselves soar into the air at any moment. Landlocked all her life, Scarlett found the broad expanse of water incredibly exotic. And the air smelled so good! It gave her an appetite, too. She'd be glad when Miss Eleanor finished her rest and they could eat dinner.

"Would you like to take coffee on the piazza, Scarlett?" asked Eleanor Butler when she and Scarlett were finishing their dessert. "It might be our last chance for a while. It looks as if weather is coming in."

"Oh, yes, I'd like that very much." The dinner had been very good, but she still felt restless, almost confined. Outside would be nice.

She followed Mrs. Butler to the second floor porch. My grief, it's turned chilly since I was here before dinner, was her first thought. Hot coffee's going to taste good.

She drank the first cup quickly and was about to ask for another when Eleanor Butler laughed and gestured toward the street. "Here comes my committee," she said. "I'd recognize that sound anywhere."

Scarlett heard it, too, a tinkling of tiny bells. She ran to the railing above the street to look.

A pair of horses was racing toward her, pulling a handsome dark green brougham with yellow-spoked wheels. The wheels gave off silver flashes of light and also the merry jingling sound. The carriage slowed, then stopped in front of the house. Scarlett could see the bells then, sleigh bells attached to a leather strap that was woven around and through the yellow spokes. She'd never seen such a thing. Nor had she ever seen anyone like the driver on the high seat on the front of the carriage. It was a woman, wearing a dark brown riding habit and yellow gloves. She was half standing, pulling on the traces with all her might, her ugly face screwed up with determination; she looked for all the world like a dressed-up monkey.

The brougham's door opened and a laughing young man stepped out onto the mounting block before the house. He held out his hand. A stout lady took it and stepped from the carriage. She, too, was laughing. The young man helped her down from the carriage block, then handed down a younger woman with a broad smile on her face. "Come inside, dear," Mrs. Butler said, "and help me with the tea things." Scarlett followed her eagerly, seething with curiosity. What a peculiar turnout of people. Miss Eleanor's committee sure is different from the bunches of old cats who run everything in Atlanta. Where did they find that monkey-woman driver? And who could the man be? Men didn't bake cakes for charity. He looked rather handsome, too. Scarlett paused to smooth her windblown hair at a mirror.

"You look a bit shaken, Emma," Mrs. Butler was saying. She and the stout woman touched cheeks, one side then the other. "Have a restful cup of tea, but first let me present Rhett's wife, Scarlett."

"It'll take more than a cup of tea to repair my nerves after that little ride, Eleanor," said the woman. She held out her hand. "How do you do, Scarlett? I'm Emma Anson, or rather what remains of Emma Anson."

Eleanor embraced the younger woman and led her to Scarlett. "This is Margaret, dear, Ross's wife. Margaret, meet Scarlett."

Margaret Butler was a pale, fair-haired young woman with beautiful sapphire-blue eyes that dominated her thin colorless face. When she smiled, a network of deep, premature lines bracketed them. "I'm delighted to know you at last," she said. She took Scarlett's hands in hers and kissed her cheek. "I always wanted a sister, and a sister-in-law is practically the same thing. I hope you and Rhett will come to us for supper sometime soon. Ross will be longing to meet you, too."

"I'd love to, Margaret, and I'm sure Rhett would, too," said Scarlett. She smiled, hoping she was telling the truth. Who could say whether Rhett would escort her to his brother's house or anyplace else? But it was going to be mighty hard for him to say no to his own family. Miss Eleanor and now Margaret were on her side. Scarlett returned Margaret's kiss.

"Scarlett," said Mrs. Butler, "do come meet Sally Brewton."

"And Edward Cooper," added a male voice. "Don't deprive me of the chance to kiss Mrs. Butler's hand, Eleanor. I'm already smitten."

"Wait your turn, Edward," Mrs. Butler said. "You young people have no manners at all."

Scarlett hardly looked at Edward Cooper, and his flattery escaped her altogether. She was trying not to stare, but staring nonetheless at Sally Brewton, the monkey-faced driver of the carriage.

Sally Brewton was a tiny woman in her forties. She was shaped like a thin, active young boy, and her face did, in fact, greatly resemble a monkey's. She wasn't in the least upset by Scarlett's rude stare. Sally was accustomed to the reaction; her remarkable ugliness—to which she had adapted long, long ago—and her unconventional behavior often astonished people who were strangers to her. She walked over to Scarlett now, her skirts trailing behind her like a brown river. "My dear Mrs. Butler, you must think us as mad as March hares. The truth is—boring though it may be—that there's a perfectly rational explanation for our—shall we say?—dramatic arrival. I am the only surviving carriage possessor in town and I find it impossible to keep a coachman. They object to ferrying my dispossessed friends, and I insist on it. So I've given up hiring men who are going to quit almost at once. And—if my husband is otherwise occupied—I do the driving myself." She put her small hand on Scarlett's arm and looked up into her face. "Now I ask you, doesn't that make perfectly good sense?"

Scarlett found her voice and said, "Yes."

"Sally, you mustn't trap poor Scarlett like that," said Eleanor Butler. "What else could she say? Tell her the rest."

Sally shrugged, then grinned. "I suppose your mother-in-law is referring to my bells. Cruel creature. The fact is that I am an appallingly bad driver. So whenever I take the carriage out, I'm required by my humanitarian husband to bedeck it in bells, as advance warning to people to get out of my way."

"Rather like a leper," offered Mrs. Anson.

"I shall ignore that," Sally said with an air of injured dignity. She smiled at Scarlett, a smile of such genuine good will that Scarlett felt warmed by it. "I do hope," she said, "that you'll call on me whenever you need the brougham, despite what you've seen."

"Thank you, Mrs. Brewton, you're very kind."

"Not at all. The fact is, I adore careening through the streets, scattering scallywags and carpetbaggers to the four winds. But I'm monopolizing you. Let me present Edward Cooper before he expires ..."

Scarlett responded automatically to the gallantries of Edward Cooper, smiling to create the beguiling dimple at the corner of her mouth and shamming embarrassment at his compliments while inviting more of them with her eyes. "Why, Mr. Cooper," she said, "how you do run on. I declare you're liable to turn my head. I'm just a country girl from Clayton County, Georgia, and I don't know what to make of a sophisticated Charleston gentleman like you."

"Miss Eleanor, please forgive me," she heard a new voice say. Scarlett turned and drew in a sharp breath. There was a girl in the doorway, a young girl with shining brown hair that grew in a widow's peak above her soft brown eyes. "I'm so sorry to be late," the girl continued. Her voice was soft, a little breathless. She was wearing a brown dress with white linen collar and cuffs and an old-fashioned bonnet covered in brown silk.

She looks for all the world like Melanie when I first knew her, Scarlett thought. Like a soft little brown bird. Could she be a cousin? I never heard the Hamiltons had any kin in Charleston.

"You're not late at all, Anne," said Eleanor Butler. "Come have some tea, you looked chilled to the bone."

Anne smiled gratefully. "The wind is picking up, and the clouds are coming in fast. I believe I beat the rain by only a few steps ... Good afternoon, Miss Emma, Miss Sally, Margaret, Mr. Cooper—" She stopped, her lips parted, her eyes on Scarlett. "Good afternoon. I don't think we've met. I'm Anne Hampton."

Eleanor Butler hurried to the girl's side. She was holding a steaming cup. "How barbaric of me," she exclaimed. "I was so busy with the tea that I forgot that of course you don't know Scarlett, my daughter-in-law. Here, Anne, drink this at once. You're white as a ghost ... Scarlett, Anne is our expert on the Confederate Home. She graduated from the school last year, and now she's teaching there. Anne Hampton—Scarlett Butler."

"How do you do, Mrs. Butler." Anne extended a cold little hand. Scarlett felt it quiver in her own warm one when she shook it.

"Please call me Scarlett," she said.

"Thank you ... Scarlett. I'm Anne."

"Tea, Scarlett?"

"Thank you, Miss Eleanor." She hurried to take the cup, glad to escape from the confusion she felt when she looked at Anne Hampton. She's Melly to the life. Just as frail, just as mousy, just as sweet—I can tell that already. She must be an orphan if she's at that Home place. Melanie was an orphan, too. Oh, Melly, how I miss you.

The sky was darkening outside the windows. Eleanor Butler asked Scarlett to draw the curtains when she finished her tea.

As she drew the curtains on the last window, she heard a rumbling of thunder in the distance and a spattering of rain on the glass.

"Let's come to order," said Miss Eleanor. "We've got a lot of business to do. Everyone take a seat. Margaret, will you keep passing the tea cakes and sandwiches? I don't want anyone distracted by an empty stomach. Emma, you'll continue to pour, won't you? I'll ring for more hot water."

"Let me go get it, Miss Eleanor," said Anne.

"No, dear, we need you here. Scarlett, just pull that bell rope, please, my dear. Now, ladies and gentleman, the first order of business is very exciting. I've received a large check from a lady in Boston. What shall we do with it?"

"Tear it up and send the pieces back to her."

"Emma! Is your brain asleep? We need all the money we can get. Besides, the donor is Patience Bedford. You remember her. We used to see her and her husband almost every year at Saratoga in the old days."

"Wasn't there a General Bedford in the Union Army?"

"There was not. There was a General Nathan Bedford Forrest in our army."

"The finest cavalryman we had," said Edward.

"I don't think Ross would agree with that, Edward." Margaret Butler put a plate of bread and butter down with a clatter. "After all, he was in the cavalry with General Lee."

Scarlett yanked the bell rope a second time. Great balls of fire! Did all Southerners have to refight the War every time they met? What difference did it make if the money came from Ulysses Grant himself? Money was money, and you took it anywhere you found it.

"Truce!" Sally Brewton waved a white napkin in the air. "If you would give Anne an opening, she's trying to say something."

Anne's eyes were glowing with emotion. "I've got nine little girls that I'm teaching to read, and only one book to teach from. If the ghost of Abe Lincoln came and offered to buy us some books, I'd—I'd kiss him!"

Good for you, cheered Scarlett silently. She looked at the astonishment on the faces of the other women. Edward Cooper's expression was something quite different. Why, he's in love with her, she thought. Just see the way he's looking at her. And she doesn't notice him at all, she doesn't even know he's yearning over her like a moon calf. Maybe I should tell her. He's really quite attractive if you like the type, sort of slender and dreamy-looking. Not all that different from Ashley, come to think of it.

Sally Brewton was watching Edward, too, Scarlett noticed. Sally's eyes met hers and they exchanged discreet smiles.

"We're agreed, then, are we?" said Eleanor. "Emma?"

"We're agreed. Books are more important than rancor. I'm being over-emotional. It must be dehydration. Is anyone ever going to bring that hot water?"

Scarlett rang again. Maybe the bell was broken; should she go down to the kitchen and tell the servants? She started from the corner, then saw the door opening.

"Did you ring for tea, Mrs. Butler?" Rhett pushed the door wider with his foot. His hands were holding a huge silver tray laden with gleaming tea pot, urn, bowl, sugar bowl, milk pitcher, strainer, and three tea caddies. "India, China, or chamomile?" He was smiling with delight at his surprise.

Rhett! Scarlett couldn't breathe. How handsome he was. He'd been in the sun somewhere, he was brown as an Indian. Oh, God, how she loved him, her heart was beating so hard that everyone must be able to hear it.

"Rhett! Oh, darling, I'm afraid I'm going to make a spectacle of myself." Mrs. Butler grabbed a napkin and wiped her eyes. "You said 'some silver' in Philadelphia. I had no idea it was the tea service. And intact. It's a miracle."

"It's also very heavy. Miss Emma, will you please push that makeshift china to one side? I heard you mention something about thirst, I believe. I'd be honored if you'd brew your heart's desire . . . Sally, my beloved, when are you going to agree to let me duel your husband to the death and abduct you?" Rhett placed the tray on the table, leaned across it, and kissed the three women sitting on the settee behind it. Then he looked around.

Look at me, Scarlett begged silently from the shadowy corner. Kiss me.

But he didn't see her. "Margaret, how lovely you look in that gown. Ross doesn't deserve you. Hello, Anne, it's a pleasure to see you. Edward, I can't say the same for you. I don't approve of your organizing yourself a harem in my house when I'm out in the rain in the sorriest hansom cab in North America, clutching the family silver to my bosom to protect it from the carpetbaggers." Rhett smiled at his mother. "Stop that crying, now, Mama dear," he said, "or I'll think you don't like your surprise."

Eleanor looked up at him, her face shining with love. "Bless you, my son. You make me very happy."

Scarlett couldn't stand another minute of it. She ran forward. "Rhett, darling—"

His head turned toward her, and she stopped. His face was rigid, blank, all emotion withheld by an iron control. But his eyes were bright; they faced one another for a breathless moment. Then his lips turned downward at one corner in the sardonic smile she knew so well and feared so much. "It's a fortunate man," he said slowly and clearly, "who receives a greater surprise than he gives." He held his hands out for hers. Scarlett put her trembling fingers into his palms, conscious of the distance his outstretched arms kept between them. His mustache brushed her right cheek, then her left.

He'd like to kill me, she thought, and the danger of it gave her a strange thrill. Rhett put his arm around her shoulders, his hand clamped like a vise around her upper arm.

"I'm sure you ladies—and Edward—will excuse us if we leave you," he said. There was an appealing mixture of boyishness and roguishness in his voice. "It's been much too long since I've had a chance to talk to my wife. We'll go upstairs and leave you to solve the problems of the Confederate Home."

He propelled Scarlett out the door without giving her an opportunity to make her goodbyes.

12

Rhett didn't speak while he rushed her up the stairs and into his bedroom. He closed the door and stood with his back against it. "What the hell are you doing here, Scarlett?"

She wanted to hold out her arms to him, but the hot rage in his eyes warned her not to. Scarlett made her eyes widen in innocent misunderstanding. Her voice was rushed and charmingly breathless when she spoke.

"Aunt Eulalie wrote and told me what you were saying, Rhett—about how you longed for me to be here with you, but I wouldn't leave the store. Oh, darling, why didn't you tell me? I don't care two pins for the store, not compared to you." She watched his eyes warily.

"It won't work, Scarlett."

"What do you mean?"

"None of it. Not the fervid explanation and not the innocent lack of understanding. You know you could never lie to me and get away with it."

It was true, and she did know it. She had to be honest.

"I came because I wanted to be with you." Her quiet statement had a simple dignity.

Rhett looked at her straight back and proudly lifted head, and his voice softened. "My dear Scarlett," he said, "we might have been friends in time, when the memories had softened to bittersweet nostalgia. Perhaps we might arrive at that yet, if we are both charitable and patient. But nothing more." He strode impatiently across the room. "What do I have to do to get through to you? I don't want to hurt you, but you force me. I don't want you here. Go back to Atlanta, Scarlett, leave me be. I no longer love you. I can speak no more clearly than that."

The blood had drained from Scarlett's face. Her green eyes glittered against her ghostly white skin. "I can speak clearly, too, Rhett. I am your wife and you are my husband."

"An unfortunate circumstance that I offered to correct." His words were like a whiplash. Scarlett forgot that she had to control herself.

"Divorce you? Never, never, never. And I'll never give you cause to divorce me. I'm your wife, and like a good dutiful wife should, I've come to your side, abandoning all I hold dear." A smile of triumph lifted the corners of her mouth and she played her trump card. "Your mother is overjoyed that I'm here. What are you going to tell her if you throw me out? Because I'll tell her the truth, and it'll break her heart."

Rhett paced heavily from end to end of the big room. Under his breath he muttered curses, profanity and vulgarity such as Scarlett had never heard. This was the Rhett that was only hearsay to her, the Rhett who had followed the gold rush to California and defended his claim with a knife and heavy boots. This was Rhett the rum-runner, habitué of the lowest taverns in Havana, Rhett the lawless adventurer, friend and companion of renegades like himself. She watched, shocked and fascinated and excited despite the menace in him. Suddenly his animal-like pacing stopped and he turned to face her. His black eyes glittered, but no longer with rage. They held humor, dark and bitter and wary. He was Rhett Butler, Charleston gentleman.

"Check," he said with a wry twisted smile. "I overlooked the unpredictable mobility of the queen. But not mate, Scarlett." He held out his opened palms in momentary surrender.

She didn't understand what he was saying, but the gesture and his tone of voice told her that she'd won . . . something.

"So I'll stay?"

"You'll stay until you want to go. I don't expect it to be very long."

"But you're wrong, Rhett! I love it here."

An old, familiar expression crossed his face. He was amused and skeptical and all-knowing. "How long have you been in Charleston, Scarlett?"

"Since last night."

"And you've learned to love it. Quick work, I congratulate you on your sensitivity. You were driven out of Atlanta—miraculously minus tar and feathers—and you've been treated decently by ladies who know no other way to treat people, and so you think you've found a refuge." He laughed at the look on her face. "Oh, yes, I still have associates in Atlanta. I know all about your ostracism there. Not even the scum you used to consort with will have anything to do with you any more."

"That's not true!" she cried. "I threw them out."

Rhett shrugged. "We needn't discuss that further. What matters is that now you are here, in my mother's house and under her wing. Because I care greatly for her happiness, I cannot for the moment do anything about it. However, I don't really have to. You'll do what's necessary without any action on my part. You'll reveal yourself for what you are; then everyone will feel pity for me and compassion for my mother. And I'll pack you up and ship you back to Atlanta to the genteelly silent cheers of the entire community. You think you can pass yourself off as a lady, don't you? You couldn't fool a blind deaf-mute."

"I am a lady, damn you. You just don't know what it's like to be a decent person. I'll thank you to remember that my mother was a Robillard from Savannah and that the O'Haras descend from the kings of Ireland!"

Rhett's grin in response was maddeningly tolerant. "Leave it alone, Scarlett. Show me the clothes you brought with you." He sat in the chair nearest him and stretched out his long legs.

Scarlett stared at him, too frustrated by his abrupt calm to speak without sputtering. Rhett took a cigar from his pocket and rolled it between his fingers. "You don't object if I smoke in my room, I hope," he said.

"Of course not."

"Thank you. Now show me your clothes. They're certain to be new; you'd never embark on an attempt to win back my favors without an arsenal of petticoats and silk frocks, all in the execrable taste that is your hallmark. I won't have you making my mother a laughingstock. So show them to me, Scarlett, and I'll see what can be salvaged." He took a cutter from his pocket.

Scarlett scowled, but nevertheless she stalked into the dressing room to collect her things. Maybe this was a good thing. Rhett had always supervised her wardrobe. He'd liked to see her in clothes that he had chosen, he'd been proud of how stylish and beautiful she looked. If he wanted to get involved with her appearance again, be proud of her again, she'd be willing to cooperate. She'd try them all on for him. That way he'd see her in her shimmy. Scarlett's fingers moved quickly to unhook the dress she was wearing and the cage with padding that supported the bustle. She stepped out of the pile of rich fabric, then gathered her new dresses in her arms and walked slowly into the bedroom, her arms bare, her bosom half-revealed, and her legs silk-stockinged.

"Dump them on the bed," said Rhett, "and put on a wrapper before you freeze. It's gotten colder with the rain, or haven't you noticed?" He blew a stream of smoke to his left, turning his head away from her. "Don't catch cold trying to be alluring, Scarlett. You're wasting your time." Scarlett's face became livid with anger, her eyes like green fire. But Rhett was not looking at her. He was examining the finery on the bed. "Rip off all this lace," he said about the first gown, "and keep only one of the avalanche of bows down the side. Then it won't be too bad ... Give this one to your maid, it's hopeless ... This will do if you take off the trim, replace the gold buttons with plain black ones, and shorten the train ..." It took only a few minutes for him to go through them all.

"You'll need some sturdy boots, plain black," he said when he finished with the clothes.

"I bought some this morning," Scarlett said, with ice in her voice. "When your mother and I went shopping," she added, emphasizing each word. "I don't see why you don't buy her a carriage since you love her so much. She got very tired with all the walking."

"You don't understand Charleston. That's why you'll be miserable here in no time at all. I could buy her this house, because ours was destroyed by the Yankees and everyone she knows still has a house just as grand. I can even furnish it more comfortably than her friends' are furnished because every piece in it is something that the Yankees looted or is a duplicate of what she once had, and her friends still have many of their things. But I cannot set her apart from her friends by buying her luxuries that they cannot afford."

"Sally Brewton has a carriage."

"Sally Brewton is unlike anyone else. She always has been. Sally is an original. Charleston has respect—even fondness—for eccentricity. But no tolerance for ostentation. And you, my dear Scarlett, have never been able to resist ostentation."

"I hope you're enjoying insulting me, Rhett Butler!"

Rhett laughed. "As a matter of fact, I am. Now you can start making one of those dresses decent to wear for this evening. I'm going to go drive the committee home. Sally shouldn't do it in this storm."

After he was gone, Scarlett put on Rhett's dressing gown. It was warmer than hers, and he was right—it had gotten much colder, and she was shivering. She pulled the collar of the robe up around her ears and went to sit in the chair where he had sat. His presence was still in the room for her, and she wrapped herself in it. Her fingers stroked the soft foulard that enveloped her—strange to think of Rhett choosing such a light, almost fragile-feeling wrapper when he was so solid and strong himself. But then, so many things about him mystified her. She didn't know him at all, never had. Scarlett felt a moment of dreadful hopelessness. She shook it off, stood up hurriedly. She had to get dressed before Rhett got back. Gracious heavens, how long had she been sitting in that chair daydreaming? It was already near dark. She rang sharply for Pansy. The bows and lace had to be picked off the pink gown so she could wear it tonight, and the curling tongs should be put to heat at once. She wanted to look especially pretty and feminine for Rhett ... Scarlett looked at the wide expanse of counterpane on the big bed, and her thoughts made her blush.

The lamplighter had not yet reached the upper part of the city where Emma Anson lived, and Rhett had to drive slowly, hunched forward to peer through the heavy rain at the dark street. Behind him only Mrs. Anson and Sally Brewton remained in the closed carriage. Margaret Butler had been taken home first to the tiny house on Water Street where she and Ross lived; then Rhett drove to Broad Street, where Edward Cooper had escorted Anne Hampton to the door of the Confederate Home under his large umbrella. "I'll walk the rest of the way," Edward called up to Rhett from the sidewalk, "no sense taking this dripping umbrella in with the ladies." He lived on Church Street, only a block away. Rhett touched the wide brim of his hat in salute and drove on.

"Do you think Rhett can hear us?" murmured Emma Anson.

"I can hardly hear you, Emma, and I'm only a foot from you," Sally answered tartly. "For goodness' sake, speak up. This downpour is deafening." She was irritated by the rain. It kept her from driving the brougham herself.

"What do you think of the wife?" Emma said. "She's not at all what I would have expected. Have you ever seen anything as grotesquely overdecorated as the walking-out costume she was wearing?"

"Oh, clothes are easily remedied, and lots of women have dreadful taste. No, what's interesting is that she's got possibilities," said Sally. "The only question is, will she grow into them? It can be a great handicap, being beautiful and having been a belle. Lots of women never recover from it."

"It was ridiculous, the way she flirted with Edward."

"Automatic, I think, not really ridiculous. There are plenty of men who expect just that kind of thing, too. Maybe they need it now more than ever before. They've lost everything else that once made them feel like men, all their wealth, their lands, and their power."

The two women were silent for a while, thinking of things better left unadmitted by a proud people under the heel of a military occupying force.

Sally cleared her throat, breaking the somber mood. "One good thing," she said in a positive way, "Rhett's wife is desperately in love with him. Her face lit up like a sunrise when he appeared in that doorway, did you see?"

"No, I didn't," said Emma. "I wish to God I had. What I saw was the same look—but it was on Anne's face."

13

Scarlett's eyes kept returning to the door. What was keeping Rhett so long? Eleanor Butler pretended not to notice, but a tiny smile nestled in the corners of her mouth. Her fingers moved a gleaming ivory shuttle rapidly back and forth, tatting an intricate web of loops. It should have been a cozy moment. The drawing room curtains were closed against the storm and the dark, lamps were lit on tables throughout the two beautiful adjoining rooms, and a golden, crackling fire banished chill and damp. But Scarlett's nerves were too drawn to be comforted by the domestic scene. Where was Rhett? Would he still be angry when he returned?

She tried to keep her mind on what Rhett's mother was saying, but she couldn't. She didn't care about the Confederate Home for Widows and Orphans. Her fingers touched the bodice of her dress, but there were no cascades of lace to fiddle with. Surely he wouldn't care about her clothes if he really didn't care about her, would he?

"... so the school just sort of grew by itself because there was no place else really for the orphans to go," Mrs. Butler was saying. "It's been more successful than we would have dared to hope. Last June, there were six graduated, all of them teachers now themselves. Two of the girls have gone to Walterboro to teach, and one actually had a choice of places, either Yemassee or Camden. Another one—such a sweet girl—wrote to us, I'll show you the letter . . ."

Oh, where is he? What could be taking him so long? If I have to sit still much longer, I'll scream.

The bronze clock on the mantel chimed and Scarlett jumped. Two . . . three . . . "I wonder what's keeping Rhett?" said his mother. Five . . . six. "He knows we have supper at seven, and he always enjoys a toddy first. He'll be soaked to the skin, too; he'll have to change his clothes." Mrs. Butler put her tatting down on the table at her side. "I'll just go see if the rain's stopped," she said.

Scarlett leapt to her feet. "I'll go." She walked quickly, released, and pulled back an edge of the heavy silk curtain. Outside a heavy mist was billowing over the sea-wall promenade. It swirled in the street and coiled upward like a live thing. The street lamp was a glowing, undefined brightness in the moving whiteness surrounding it. She drew back from the eerie formlessness and dropped the silk over the sight of it. "It's all foggy," she said, "but it's not raining. Do you think Rhett's all right?"

Eleanor Butler smiled. "He's been through worse than a little wet and fog, Scarlett, you know that. Of course he's all right. You'll hear him at the door any minute now."

As if the words had caused it, there came the sound of the great front door opening. Scarlett heard Rhett's laughter and the deep voice of Manigo, the butler.

"You best hand me them wet things, Mist' Rhett, boots, too. I got your house shoes right here," Manigo was saying.

"Thank you, Manigo. I'll go up and change. Tell Mrs. Butler I'll be with her in a minute. Is she in the drawing room?"

"Yessir, her and Missus Rhett."

Scarlett listened for Rhett's reaction, but she heard only his quick firm tread on the steps. It seemed a century before he came back down. The clock on the mantel had to be wrong. Each minute took an hour to pass.

"You look tired, dear," exclaimed Eleanor Butler when Rhett entered the drawing room.

Rhett lifted his mother's hand and kissed it. "Don't cluck over me, Mama, I'm more hungry than tired. Supper soon?"

Mrs. Butler started to rise. "I'll tell the kitchen to serve right now." Rhett gently touched her shoulder to halt her effort.

"I'll have a drink first, don't rush." He walked to the table holding the drinks tray. As he poured whiskey into a glass, he looked at Scarlett for the first time. "Will you join me, Scarlett?" His raised eyebrow taunted her. So did the smell of the whiskey. She turned away, as if insulted. So, Rhett was going to play cat and mouse, was he? Try to force her or trick her into doing something that would make his mother turn against her. Well, he'd have to be mighty smart to catch her out. Her mouth curved and her eyes began to sparkle. She'd have to be mighty smart herself to outwit him. A little pulse of excitement throbbed in her throat. Competition always thrilled her.

"Miss Eleanor, isn't Rhett shocking?" she laughed. "Was he a wicked little boy, too?" Behind her she sensed Rhett's abrupt movement. Ha! That had struck home. He'd felt guilty for years about the pain he'd caused his mother when his escapades made his father disown him.

"Supper's served, Miz Butler," said Manigo from the doorway.

Rhett offered his mother his arm, and Scarlett felt a stab of jealousy. Then she reminded herself that his devotion to his mother was the very thing that permitted her to stay, and she swallowed her anger. "I'm so hungry I could eat half a cow," she said, her voice bright, "and Rhett's just starving, aren't you, darling?" She had the upper hand now; he had admitted that much. If she lost it, she'd lose the whole game, she'd never get him back.

As it turned out, Scarlett needn't have worried. Rhett took command of the conversation the moment they were seated. He recounted his search for the tea service in Philadelphia, transforming it into an adventure, painting deft word portraits of the succession of people he talked to, mimicking their accents and idiosyncrasies with such skill that his mother and Scarlett found themselves laughing until their sides ached.

"And after following that long trail to get to him," Rhett concluded with a theatrical gesture of dismay, "just imagine my horror when the new owner seemed to be too honest to sell the tea service for the twenty times its value I offered. For a minute, I was afraid I'd have to steal it back, but fortunately he was receptive to the suggestion that we amuse ourselves with a friendly game of cards."

Eleanor Butler tried to look disapproving. "I do hope you didn't do anything dishonest, Rhett," she said. But there was laughter beneath the words.

"Mama! You shock me. I only deal from the bottom when I'm playing with professionals. This miserable ex-colonel in Sherman's army was such an amateur I had to cheat to let him win a few hundred dollars to ease his pain. He was like the reverse side of an Ellinton."

Mrs. Butler laughed. "Oh, the poor man. And his wife—my heart goes out to her." Rhett's mother leaned toward Scarlett. "Some of the skeletons in my side of the family," Eleanor Butler said in a mock whisper. She laughed again and began to reminisce.

The Ellintons, Scarlett learned, were famous all up and down the East Coast for the family weakness: they would gamble on anything. The first Ellinton to settle in Colonial America was part of the shipload only because he had won a land grant in a wager with the owner as to who could drink the most ale and remain standing. "By the time he won," Mrs. Butler said, in neat conclusion, "he was so drunk that he thought it made sense to go take a look at his prize. They say he didn't even know where he was going until he got there, because he won most of the sailors' rum ration playing dice."

"What did he do when he sobered up?" Scarlett wanted to know.

"Oh, my dear, he never did. He died only ten days after the ship made landfall. But in the meantime he had wagered some other gambler at dice and won a girl—one of the indentured servants from the ship—and, since later she turned out to be carrying his child, there was a sort of *ex post facto* wedding at his grave marker, and her son became one of my great-great-grandfathers."

"He was rather a gamester himself, wasn't he?" Rhett asked.

"Oh, of course. It truly ran in the family." And Mrs. Butler continued along the family tree.

Scarlett glanced at Rhett often. How many surprises were there in this man she hardly knew? She'd never seen him so relaxed and happy and totally at home. I never made a home for him, she realized. He never even liked the house. It was mine, done the way I wanted, a present from him, not his at all. Scarlett wanted to break in on Miss Eleanor's stories, to tell Rhett that she was sorry for the past, that she'd make up for all her mistakes. But she kept silent. He was content, enjoying himself and his mother's ramblings. She mustn't break this mood.

The candles in their tall silver holders were reflected in the polish of the mahogany table and in the pupils of Rhett's gleaming black eyes. They bathed the table and the three of them in a warm, still light, making an island of soft brilliance in the shadows of the long room. The world outside was closed off by the thick folds of curtains at the windows and by the intimacy of the small candlelit island. Eleanor Butler's voice was gentle, Rhett's laughter a quiet, encouraging chuckle. Love made an airy yet unbreakable web between mother and son. Scarlett had a sudden consuming yearning to be enclosed in that web.

Then Rhett said, "Tell Scarlett about Cousin Townsend, Mama," and she was safe in the warmth of the candlelight, included in the happiness that ringed the table. She wished that it could last forever, and she begged Miss Eleanor to tell about Cousin Townsend.

"Townsend's not really a cousin-cousin, you know, only a third cousin twice removed, but he is the direct descendent of Great-Great-Grandfather Ellinton, only son of an eldest son of an eldest son. So he inherited that original land grant, and the Ellinton gambler's fever, and the Ellinton luck. They were always lucky, the Ellintons. Except for one thing: there's another Ellinton family trait, the boys are always cross-eyed. Townsend married an extremely beautiful girl from a fine Philadelphia family—Philadelphia called it the wedding of beauty and the beast. But the girl's father was a lawyer and a very sensible man about property, and Townsend was fabulously rich. Townsend and his wife settled in Baltimore. Then, of course, the War came. Townsend's wife went running home to her family the minute Townsend went off to join General Lee's army. She was a Yankee, after all, and Townsend would more than likely get killed. He couldn't shoot a barn, much less a barn door, because of his cross eyes. However, he still had the Ellinton luck. He never got anything worse than chilblains although he served all the way through to Appomattox. Meanwhile, his wife's three brothers and her father were all killed, fighting in the Union Army. So she inherited everything piled up by her careful father and his careful ancestors. Townsend's living like a king in Philadelphia and doesn't care a fig that all his property in Savannah was confiscated by Sherman. Did you see him, Rhett? How is he?"

"More cross-eyed than ever, with two cross-eyed sons and a daughter that, thank God, takes after her mother."

Scarlett hardly heard Rhett's answer. "Did you say the Ellintons were from Savannah, Miss Eleanor? My mother was from Savannah," she said eagerly. The crisscross of relations that was so much a part of Southern life had long been a frustrating lack in her own. Everyone she knew had a network of cousins and uncles and aunts that covered generations and hundreds of miles. But she had none. Pauline and Eulalie had no children. Gerald O'Hara's brothers in Savannah were childless, too. There must be lots of O'Haras still in Ireland, but that did her no good, and all the Robillards except her grandfather were gone from Savannah.

Now here she was, again hearing about somebody else's family. Rhett had kin in Philadelphia. No doubt he was related to half of Charleston, too. It wasn't fair. But maybe these Ellinton people were tied to the Robillards somehow. Then she'd be part of the web that included Rhett. Perhaps she could find a connection to the world of the Butlers and Charleston, the world that Rhett had chosen and she was determined to enter.

"I remember Ellen Robillard very well," said Mrs. Butler. "And her mother. Your grandmother, Scarlett, was probably the most fascinating woman in all of Georgia, and South Carolina, too."

Scarlett leaned forward, enthralled. She'd heard only bits and pieces of stories about her grandmother. "Was she really scandalous, Miss Eleanor?"

"She was extraordinary. But when I knew her best, she wasn't scandalous at all. She was too busy having babies. First your Aunt Pauline, then Eulalie, then your mother. As a matter of fact, I was in Savannah when your mother was born. I remember the fireworks. Your grandfather hired some famous Italian to come down from New York and put on a magnificent fireworks display every time your grandmother gave him a baby. You wouldn't remember. Rhett, and I don't suppose you'll thank me for remembering, either, but you were scared witless. I took you outside especially to see them, and you cried so loud that I nearly died of shame. All the other children there were clapping their hands and shrieking with joy. Of course, they were older. You were still in dresses, barely over a year old."

Scarlett stared at Mrs. Butler, then at Rhett. It wasn't possible! Rhett couldn't be older than her mother. Why, her mother was—her mother. She'd always taken it for granted that her mother was old, past the age of strong emotions. How could Rhett be older? How could she love him so desperately if he was that old?

Then Rhett added shock upon shock. He dropped his napkin on the table, stood, stepped to Scarlett's side and kissed the top of her head, moved on to take his mother's hand in his and kiss it. "I'm off now, Mama," he said.

Oh, Rhett, no! Scarlett wanted to shout. But she was too stunned to say anything, even to ask where he was going.

"I wish you wouldn't go out in the rainy pitch dark, Rhett," his mother protested. "And Scarlett's here. You've barely had a chance to say hello to her."

"It's stopped raining, and the full moon's out," Rhett said. "I can't waste the chance to ride the tide upriver, and I've just enough time to catch it before it turns. Scarlett understands that you've got to check up on your workers if you go away and leave them—she's a businesswoman. Aren't you, my pet?" His eyes glittered from the candle flame reflected in them when he looked at her. Then he walked into the hall.

She pushed back from the table, almost upending her chair in her haste. Then, without a word to Mrs. Butler, she ran frantically after him.

He was in the vestibule, buttoning his coat, hat in his hand. "Rhett, Rhett, wait!" Scarlett cried. She ignored the warning in his look when he turned to face her. "Everything was so nice at supper," she said. "Why do you want to go?"

Rhett stepped past her and pushed the door from the vestibule to the hallway. It closed with a heavy dull click of the latch, shutting off the rest of the house. "Don't make a scene, Scarlett. They're wasted on me."

As if he could see inside her skull, he drawled his final words. "Don't count on sharing my bed, either, Scarlett."

He opened the door to the street. Before she could say a word, he was gone. The door swung slowly closed behind him.

Scarlett stamped her foot. It was an inadequate outlet for her anger and disappointment. Why did he have to be so mean? She grimaced—half anger, half unwilling laughter—in grudging acknowledgment of Rhett's cleverness. He'd known what she was planning easy enough. Well then, she'd have to be cleverer, that's all. She'd have to give up the idea of having a baby right away, think of something else. Her brow was furrowed when she went back to join Rhett's mother.

"There now, dear, don't be upset," Eleanor Butler said, "he'll be all right. Rhett knows the river like the back of his hand." She had been standing near the mantel, unwilling to go into the hall and risk intruding on Rhett's farewell to his wife. "Let's go into the library, it's cozy there, and let the servants clear the table."

Scarlett settled into a high-back chair, protected from drafts. No, she said, she didn't want a throw over her knees, she was just fine, thank you. "Let me tuck you in, Miss Eleanor," she insisted, taking the cashmere shawl from her. "You sit down now, and ease yourself." She bullied Mrs. Butler into comfort.

"What a dear girl you are, Scarlett, so like your darling mother. I remember how thoughtful she always was, such beautiful manners. All the Robillard girls were well behaved, of course, but Ellen was special . . ."

Scarlett closed her eyes and inhaled the faint whisper of lemon verbena. Everything was going to be all right. Miss Eleanor loved her, she'd make Rhett come home, and they'd all live happily together forever and ever.

Scarlett half-dozed in the deep-cushioned chair, lulled by the soft reminiscences of a gentler time. When the disturbance erupted in the hall beyond the door, she was jerked back to confused consciousness. For a moment she didn't know where she was or how she had gotten there, and she blinked, bleary-eyed, at the man in the doorway. Rhett? No, it couldn't be Rhett, not unless he'd shaved off his mustache.

The big man who wasn't Rhett stepped unevenly across the doorsill. "I came to meet my sister," he said. The words slurred together.

Margaret Butler ran towards Eleanor. "I tried to stop him," she cried, "but he was in one of those moods—I couldn't get him to listen, Miss Eleanor."

Mrs. Butler stood up. "Hush, Margaret," she said with quiet urgency. "Ross, I'm waiting for a proper greeting." Her voice was unusually loud, the words very distinct.

Scarlett's mind was clear now. So this was Rhett's brother. And drunk, too, by the look of him. Well, she'd seen drunk men before, they were no special novelty. She stood, smiled at Ross, her dimple flickering. "I declare, Miss Eleanor, how could one lady be so lucky as to have two sons, each one handsomer than the other? Rhett never told me he had such a good-looking brother!"

Ross staggered towards her. His eyes raked her body, then fastened on her tousled curls and rouged face. He leered rather than smiled. "So this is Scarlett," he said thickly. "I might have known Rhett would end up with a fancy piece like her. Come on, Scarlett, give your new brother a friendly kiss. You know how to please a man, I'm sure." His big hands ran up her arms like huge spiders and fastened themselves on her bare throat. Then his open mouth was over hers, his sour breath in her nose, his tongue forcing itself between her teeth. Scarlett tried to get her hands up to shove him away, but Ross was too strong, his body too closely pressed against hers.

She could hear Eleanor Butler's voice, and Margaret's, but she couldn't make out what they were saying. All her attention was focused on the need to break free of the repulsive embrace, and on the shame of Ross' insulting words. He had called her a whore! And he was treating her like one.

All of a sudden Ross thrust her away, tumbled her back into her chair. "I'll bet you're not so cold to my dear big brother," he growled.

Margaret Butler was sobbing against Eleanor's shoulder.

"Ross!" Mrs. Butler hurled the name like a knife. Ross turned with a clumsy lurch, sending a small table crashing to the floor.

"Ross!" his mother said again. "I have rung for Manigo. He will help you home and give Margaret decent escort. When you sober up, you will write letters of apology to Rhett's wife and to me. You have disgraced yourself, and Margaret, and me, and you will not be received in this house until I have recovered from the shame you've caused me."

"I'm so sorry, Miss Eleanor," Margaret wept.

Mrs. Butler put her hands on Margaret's shoulders. "I am sorry for you, Margaret," she said. Then she moved Margaret away from her. "Go home now. You will, of course, always be welcome here."

Manigo's wise old eyes took in the situation with one look, and he removed Ross, who surprisingly said not a word in protest. Margaret scuttled out behind them. "I'm so sorry," she repeated again and again, until the sound of her voice was cut off by the closing of the big front door.

"My darling child," Eleanor said to Scarlett, "there is no excuse I can make. Ross was drunk, he didn't know what he was saying. But that is no excuse."

Scarlett was shaking all over. From disgust, from humiliation, from anger. Why had she let it happen, let Rhett's brother revile her and put his hands and his mouth on her? I should have spit in his face, clawed him blind, hit his nasty, foul mouth with my fists. But I didn't, I just took it—as if I deserved it, as if it was true. Scarlett had never been so ashamed. Shamed by Ross' words, shamed by her own weakness. She felt defiled, dirty, and eternally humiliated. Better if Ross had hit her, or cut her with a knife. Her body would recover from a bruise or a wound. But her pride would never be healed from the sickness she felt.

Eleanor leaned over her, tried to put her arms around her, but Scarlett shrank from her touch. "Leave me alone!" she tried to shout, but it came out a moan.

"I won't," said Mrs. Butler, "not until you listen to me. You've got to understand, Scarlett, you have to hear me. There's so much you don't know. Are you listening?" She drew a chair close to Scarlett's, sat in it, only inches away.

"No! Go away." Scarlett put her hands over her ears.

"I won't leave you," said Eleanor. "And I'll tell you—again and again, a thousand times if need be—until you hear me . . ." Her voice went on and on, gentle but insistent, while her hand stroked Scarlett's bent head—comforting, caring, insinuating her kindness and her love through Scarlett's refusal to hear her. "What Ross did was unpardonable," she said, "I don't ask you to forgive him. But I must, Scarlett. He is my son, and I know the pain in him that made him do it. He wasn't trying to hurt you, my dear. It was Rhett he was attacking through you; he knows, you see, that Rhett is too strong for him, that he'll never be able to match Rhett in anything. Rhett reaches out and takes what he wants, he makes things happen, he gets things done. And poor Ross is a failure at everything.

"Margaret told me privately this afternoon that when Ross went to work this morning, they told him he was fired. Because of his drinking, you see. He always drank, men always do, but not the way he's been drinking since Rhett came back to Charleston a year ago. Ross was trying to make the plantation go, he's been slaving away at it ever since he came back from the War, but something always went wrong, and he never did get a decent rice crop. Everything was about to be sold up for taxes. So when Rhett offered to buy the plantation from him, Ross had to let it go. It would have been Rhett's anyhow, except that he and his father—but that's another story.

"Ross got a position as teller at a bank, but I'm afraid he thought that handling money was vulgar. Gentlemen always signed bills in the old days, or simply gave their word, and their factors took care of everything. At any rate, Ross made mistakes at his cage, his accounts never balanced, and one day he made a big mistake, and he lost his job. Worse, the bank said they were going to law to get the money from him that he'd paid out in error. Rhett made it good. It was like a dagger in Ross' heart. The heavy drinking started then, and now it's cost him another job. On top of that, some fool —or villain—let it slip that Rhett had arranged the job for him in the first place. He went right home and got so drunk he could hardly walk. Mean drunk.

"I love Rhett best, may God forgive me, I always have. He was my first-born, and I laid my heart in his tiny hands the moment he was put in my arms. I love Ross and Rosemary, but not the way I love Rhett, and I'm afraid they know it. Rosemary thinks it's because he was gone for so long, then came back like a genie from a bottle and bought me everything in this house, bought her the pretty frocks she'd been longing for. She doesn't remember what it was like before he went away. She was only a baby, she doesn't know that he always came first with me. Ross knows, he knew all the time, but he was first with his father, so he didn't care overmuch. Steven cast Rhett out, made Ross his heir. He loved Ross, he was proud of him. But now Steven is dead, seven years this month. And Rhett is home again, and the joy of it fills my life, and Ross cannot fail to see it."

Mrs. Butler's voice was hoarse, ragged from the effort of speaking the heavy secrets of her heart. It broke, and she wept bitterly. "My poor boy, my poor, hurting Ross."

I should say something, Scarlett thought, to make her feel better. But she couldn't. She was hurting too much herself.

"Miss Eleanor, don't cry," she said ineffectively. "Don't feel bad. Please, I need to ask you something."

Mrs. Butler breathed deeply; she wiped her eyes and composed her face. "What is it, my dear?"

"I have to know," Scarlett said urgently. "You've got to tell me. Truly, do I—what he said—do I look like that?" She needed reassurance, had to have the approval of this loving, lemon-scented lady.

"Precious child," said Eleanor, "it doesn't matter a tinker's dam what you look like. Rhett loves you, and therefore I love you, too."

Mother of God! She's saying that I look like a whore but it doesn't matter. Is she crazy? Of course it matters, it matters more than anything else in the world. I want to be a lady, like I was meant to be!

She grabbed Mrs. Butler's hands in a desperate grip, not knowing that she was causing her agonizing pain. "Oh, Miss Eleanor, help me! Please, I need you to help me."

"Of course, dear. Tell me what you want." There was only serenity and affection on Mrs. Butler's face. She had learned many years before how to hide any pain she felt.

"I need to know what I'm doing wrong, why I don't look like a lady.

I am a lady, Miss Eleanor, I am. You knew my mother, you must know it's so."

"Of course you are, Scarlett, and of course I know. Appearances are so deceiving, it's really not fair. We can take care of everything with practically no effort at all." Mrs. Butler gently disengaged her throbbing, swollen fingers from Scarlett's grasp. "You have so much vitality, dear child, all the vigor of the world you grew up in. It's misleading to people here in the old, tired Lowcountry. But you mustn't lose it, it's too valuable. We'll simply find ways to make you somewhat less visible, more like us. Then you'll be more comfortable."

And so will I, Eleanor Butler thought silently. She would defend to her dying breath the woman she believed Rhett loved, but it would be much easier if Scarlett stopped wearing paint on her face and expensive, ill-considered clothes. Eleanor welcomed the opportunity to remake Scarlett in the Charleston mold.

Scarlett gratefully swallowed Mrs. Butler's diplomatic assessment of her problem. She was too shrewd to believe it completely—she had seen Miss Eleanor manage Eulalie and Pauline. But Rhett's mother would help her, and that was what counted, at least for now.

14

The Charleston that had molded Eleanor Butler and drawn Rhett back after decades of adventuring was an old city, one of the oldest in America. It was crowded onto a narrow triangular peninsula between two wide tidal rivers that met in a broad harbor connected to the Atlantic. First settled in 1682, it had, from its earliest days, a romantic languor and sensuality foreign to the brisk pace and Puritan self-denial of the New England colonies. Salt breezes stirred palm trees and wisteria vines, and flowers bloomed year-round. The soil was black, rich, free of stones to blunt a man's plow; the waters teemed with fish, crab, shrimp, terrapin and oysters, the woods with game. It was a rich land, meant to be enjoyed.

Ships from all over the globe anchored in the harbor for cargoes of the rice grown on Charlestonians' vast plantations along the rivers; they delivered the world's luxuries for the pleasure and adornment of the small population. It was the wealthiest city in America.

Blessed by reaching its maturity in the Age of Reason, Charleston used its wealth in the pursuit of beauty and knowledge. Responsive to its climate and natural bounties, it used its riches also for the enjoyment of the senses. Each house had its chef and its ballroom, every lady her brocades from France and her pearls from India. There were learned societies and societies for music and dancing, schools of science and schools of fencing. It was civilized and hedonistic in a balance that created a culture of exquisitely refined grace in which incomparable luxury was tempered by a demanding discipline of intellect and education. Charlestonians painted their houses in all the colors of the rainbow and hung them with shaded porches through which sea breezes carried the scent of roses like a caress. Inside every house there was a room with globe, telescope, and walls of books in many languages. In the middle of the day they sat at dinner for six courses, each offering a choice of dishes in quietly gleaming, generations-old silver pieces. Conversation was the sauce of the meal, wit its preferred seasoning.

This was the world which Scarlett O'Hara, one-time belle of a rural county in the raw red frontier earth of north Georgia, now intended to conquer, armed only with energy, stubbornness, and a dreadful need. Her timing was terrible.

For more than a century, Charlestonians had been renowned for their hospitality. It wasn't unusual to entertain a hundred guests, fully half of whom were unknown to host and hostess except through letters of introduction. During Race Week—the climax of the city's social season—owners from England, France, Ireland, and Spain often brought their horses months in advance to accustom them to the climate and water. The owners stayed at the homes of their Charleston competitors; their horses were stabled, as guests, next to the horses the Charleston host would be running against them. It was an open-handed, open-hearted city.

Until the War came. Fittingly, the first shots of the Civil War were fired at Fort Sumter, in Charleston harbor. To most of the world Charleston was the symbol of the mysterious and magical, moss-hung, magnolia-scented South. To Charlestonians as well.

And to the North. "Proud and arrogant Charleston" was the refrain in New York and Boston newspapers. Union military officials were determined to destroy the flower-filled, pastel-painted old city. The harbor entrance was blockaded first; later, gun emplacements on nearby islands fired shells into narrow streets and houses in a siege that lasted for almost six hundred days; finally Sherman's Army came with its torches to burn the plantation houses on the rivers. When the Union troops marched in to occupy their prize, they faced a desolate ruin. Wild grasses grew in the streets and choked the gardens of windowless, shell-scarred, broken-roofed houses. They also faced a decimated population that had become as proud and arrogant as their Northern reputation.

Outsiders were no longer welcome in Charleston.

People repaired their roofs and windows as best they could and locked their doors. Among themselves, they restored the cherished habits of gaiety. They met for dancing in looted drawing rooms where they toasted the South in water from cracked and mended cups. "Starvation parties," they called their gatherings, and laughed. The days of French champagne in crystal flutes might be gone, but they were still Charlestonians. They had lost their possessions but they had almost two centuries of shared tradition and style. No one could take that from them. The War was over, but they weren't defeated. They would never be defeated, no matter what the damn Yankees did. Not so long as they stuck together. And kept everyone else out of their closed circle.

The military occupation and the outrages of Reconstruction tested their mettle, but they held fast. One by one the other states of the Confederacy were readmitted to the Union, their state governments restored to the state's population. But not South Carolina. And especially not Charleston. More than nine years after the end of the War, armed soldiers patrolled the old streets, enforcing curfew. Constantly changing regulations covered everything from the price of paper to the licensing of marriages and funerals. Charleston became more and more derelict outwardly, but ever stronger in its determination to preserve the old ways of life. The Bachelors' Cotillion was reborn, with a new generation to fill the gaps caused by the carnage of Bull Run, Antietam, and Chancellorsville. After their working hours as clerks or laborers, former plantation owners took the streetcars or walked to the outskirts of the city to rebuild the two-mile oval of the Charleston Race Course and to plant the blood-soaked churned mud of the land around it with grass seed bought with combined widow's mites.

Little by little, by symbols and by inches, Charlestonians were regaining the essence of their beloved lost world. But there was no room in it for anyone who didn't belong there.

15

*P*ansy couldn't hide her amazement at the orders Scarlett gave her when she was unlacing for bed the first night in the Butler house. "Take the green walking-out costume I wore this morning and give it a good brushing. Then take off every speck of trimming, including the gold buttons, and sew on some plain black buttons instead."

"Where I going to find any black buttons, Miss Scarlett?"

"Don't bother me with fool questions like that. Ask Mrs. Butler's maid—what's her name? Celie. And wake me up tomorrow at five o'clock."

"Five o'clock?"

"Are you deaf? You heard me. Now scoot. I want that green outfit ready to put on when I get up."

Scarlett sank gratefully into the feather mattress and down pillows on the big bed. It had been an over-full, over-emotional day. Meeting Miss Eleanor, then shopping, then that silly Confederate Home meeting, then Rhett appearing from nowhere with the silver tea service ... Her hand stretched over to the empty space beside her. She wanted him there, but perhaps it was better to wait a few days, until she was really accepted in Charleston. That miserable Ross! She wouldn't think about him or those horrible things he'd said and done. Miss Eleanor had denied him the house, and she wouldn't have to see him, she hoped not ever again. She'd think about something else. She'd think about Miss Eleanor, who loved her and who was going to help her get Rhett back, even if she didn't know that's what she was doing.

The Market, Miss Eleanor had said, was the place to meet everybody and hear all the news. So to the Market she would go—tomorrow. Scarlett would have been happier if it wasn't necessary to go so early, at six o'clock. But needs must. I have to say this for Charleston, she thought sleepily, it's plenty busy, and I like that. She was only halfway through a yawn when she fell asleep.

The Market was the perfect place for Scarlett to begin the life of a Charleston lady. The Market was an outward, visible distillation of Charleston's essence. From the city's earliest days it had been the place where Charlestonians bought their food. The lady of the house—or, in rare cases, the man—selected and paid for it, a maid or coachman received it and placed it in a basket hung over the arm. Before the War the food was sold by slaves who had transported it from their masters' plantations. Many of the vendors were in the places they had been before, only now they were free, and the baskets were carried by servants who were paid for their service; like the vendors, many of them were the same people, carrying the same baskets they had before. What was important to Charleston was that the old ways hadn't changed.

Tradition was the bedrock of society, the birthright of Charleston's people, the priceless inheritance that no carpetbagger or soldier could steal. It was made manifest in the Market. Outsiders could shop there; it was public property. But they found it frustrating. Somehow they could never quite catch the eye of the woman who was selling vegetables, the man selling crabs. Black citizens were as proudly Charlestonian as white ones. When the foreigner left, the whole Market rang with laughter. The Market was for Charleston's people only.

Scarlett hunched her shoulders to lift her collar higher on her neck. A cold finger of wind got inside it despite her efforts, and she shivered violently. Her eyes felt full of cinders, and she was sure her boots must be lined with lead. How many miles could there be in five city blocks? She couldn't see a thing. The street lamps were only a bright circle of mist within mist in the ghostly gray pre-dawn half-light.

How can Miss Eleanor be so cursed cheery? Chattering away as if it wasn't freezing cold and black as pitch. There was some light ahead—way ahead. Scarlett stumbled towards it. She wished the miserable wind would die down. What was that? In the wind. She sniffed the air. It was! It was coffee. Maybe she'd live after all. Her steps matched Mrs. Butler's in an eager, accelerated pace.

The Market was like a bazaar, an oasis of light and warmth, color and life in the formless gray mist. Torches blazed on brick pillars that supported tall wide arches open to the surrounding streets, illuminating the bright aprons and headscarves of smiling black women and highlighting their wares, displayed in baskets of every size and shape on long wooden tables painted green. It was crowded with people, most of them moving from table to table, talking—to other shoppers or to the vendors in a challenging, laughing ritual of haggling obviously enjoyed by all.

"Coffee first, Scarlett?"

"Oh, yes, please."

Eleanor Butler led the way to a nearby group of women. They held steaming tin mugs in their gloved hands, sipping from them while they talked and laughed with one another, oblivious to the din around them.

"Good morning, Eleanor ... Eleanor, how are you? ... Push over, Mildred, let Eleanor get through ... Oh, Eleanor, did you hear that Kerrison's has real wool stockings on sale? It won't be in the paper until tomorrow. Would you like to come with Alice and me? We're going after dinner today ... Oh, Eleanor, we were just talking about Lavinia's daughter. She lost the baby last night. Lavinia's prostrate with grief. Do you think your cook could make some of her wonderful wine jelly? Nobody does it the way she does. Mary has a bottle of claret, and I'll supply the sugar ..."

"Morning, Miz Butler, I saw you coming, your coffee's all ready."

"And another cup for my daughter-in-law, please, Sukie. Ladies, I want you to meet Rhett's wife, Scarlett."

All chattering stopped and all heads turned to look at Scarlett.

She smiled and inclined her head in a little bow. She looked apprehensively at the group of ladies, imagining that it must be all over town, what Ross said. *I shouldn't have come, I can't stand it.* Her jaw hardened, and an invisible chip settled on her shoulder. She expected the worst, and all her old hostility to Charleston's aristocratic pretensions returned in a flash.

But she smiled and bowed to each of the ladies as Eleanor introduced her ... *yes, I just love Charleston ... yes, ma'am, I am Pauline Smith's niece ... no, ma'am, I haven't seen the art gallery yet, I've only been here since night before last ... yes'm I do think the Market's real exciting ... Atlanta—more Clayton County actually, my folks had a cotton plantation there ... oh, yes, ma'am, the weather is a real treat, these warm winter days ... no, ma'am, I don't think I met your nephew when he was in Valdosta, that's quite a ways from Atlanta ... yes'm, I do enjoy a game of whist ... Oh, thank you so much, I've been positively aching for a taste of coffee ...*

She buried her face in the mug, her job done. *Miss Eleanor's got no* more sense than a pea hen, she thought mutinously. How could she just pitch me in to the middle like that? She must think I've got a memory like an elephant. So many names, and they all mix up together. They're all looking at me as if I was an elephant, too, or something else in a zoo. They know what Ross said, I know they do. Miss Eleanor might be fooled by their smiling, but I'm not. Bunch of old cats! Her teeth ground against the rim of the mug.

She wouldn't show her feelings, not if she went blind to keep from crying. But her cheeks were stained with high color.

When she finished her coffee, Mrs. Butler took her mug and handed it, with her own, to the busy coffee-seller. "I'll have to ask you for some change, Sukie," she said. She held out a five dollar bill. With no waste motion, Sukie dipped and swirled the mugs in a big pail of brownish water, set them on the table at her elbow, wiped her hands on her apron, took the bill and deposited it in a cracked leather pouch hanging from her belt, withdrawing a dollar bill without looking. "Here you is, Miz Butler, hope you enjoyed it."

Scarlett was aghast. Two dollars for a cup of coffee! Why, with two dollars you could buy the best pair of boots on King Street.

"I always enjoy it, Sukie, even though I have to do without food on the table to pay for it. Don't you ever feel ashamed of yourself for being such a robber?"

Sukie's white teeth flashed against her brown skin. "No ma'am, I surely don't!" she said, rumbling with amusement. "I can swear on the Good Book that ain't nothing disturbing my sleep."

The other coffee drinkers laughed. Each of them had had a similar exchange with Sukie many times.

Eleanor Butler looked around until she located Celie and her basket. "Come along, dear," she said to Scarlett, "we have a long list today. We'll have to get to it before everything's gone."

Scarlett followed Mrs. Butler to the end of the Market hall where the rows of tables were crowded with dented galvanized washtubs filled with seafood that emitted a strong acrid odor. Scarlett's nose wrinkled at the reek, and she looked at the tubs with disdain. She thought she knew fish well enough. Ugly, whiskered, bone-filled catfish were plentiful in the river that ran alongside Tara. They'd had to eat them when there was nothing else. Why anyone would actually buy one of the nasty little things was beyond her, but there were lots of ladies with one glove off poking into the tubs. Oh, bother! Miss Eleanor was going to introduce her to every single one of them. Scarlett readied her smile.

A tiny white-haired lady raised a big silvery beast of a fish from the tub in front of her. "I'd love to meet her, Eleanor. What do you think of this flounder? I was planning on sheepshead, but they're not in yet, and I can't wait. I don't know why the fishing boats can't be more punctual, and don't talk to me about no wind for the sails. My bonnet nearly blew right off my head this morning."

"I really prefer flounder myself, Minnie, it takes to a sauce so much better. Let me present Rhett's wife, Scarlett . . . This is Mrs. Wentworth, Scarlett."

"How do, Scarlett. Tell me, does this flounder look good to you?"

It looked disgusting to her, but Scarlett murmured, "I've always been partial to flounder myself." She hoped that all Miss Eleanor's friends wouldn't ask her opinion. She didn't even know what flounder was, for pity sakes, much less if it was any good or not.

In the next hour, Scarlett was introduced to more than twenty ladies, and a dozen varieties of fish. She was receiving a thorough education in seafood. Mrs. Butler bought crabs, going to five different sellers until she had accumulated eight. "I suppose I seem awfully picky to you," she said when she was satisfied, "but the soup's just not the same if it's made with he-crabs. The roe gives it a special flavor, you see. It's a lot harder to find she-crab this time of year, but it's worth the effort, I think."

Scarlett didn't care a bit what gender the crabs were. She was appalled that they were still alive, scuttling around in the tubs, reaching out their claws, making nervous rustling noises as they climbed on top of one another trying to reach up the sides to get out. And now she could hear them in Celie's basket, pushing at the paper sack that held them.

The shrimp were worse, even though they were dead. Their eyes were horrible black balls on stalks, and they had long trailing whiskers and feelers and spiky stomachs. She couldn't believe that she'd ever eaten anything that looked like that, much less enjoyed it.

The oysters didn't bother her; they just looked like dirty rocks. But when Mrs. Butler picked up a curved knife from a table and opened one, Scarlett felt her stomach heave. It looks like a hawk of spit floating in old dishwater, she thought.

After the seafood the meats had a reassuring familiarity even though the swarms of flies around the blood-soaked newspapers under them made her queasy. She managed to smile at a small black boy who was waving them off with a big heart-shaped fan made of some woven dried straw-like stuff. By the time they reached the rows of limp-necked birds, she was sufficiently herself again to think about trimming a hat with some of the feathers.

"Which feathers, dear?" asked Mrs. Butler. "The pheasant? Of course you may have some." She bargained briskly with the ink-black fat woman who was selling the birds, finally buying a large handful that she plucked herself for a penny.

"What in blue blazes is Eleanor doing?" said a voice at Scarlett's elbow. She looked around and saw Sally Brewton's monkey face.

"Good morning, Mrs. Brewton."

"Good morning, Scarlett. Why is Eleanor buying the inedible parts of that bird? Or has someone discovered a way to cook feathers? I have several mattresses that I'm not using right now."

Scarlett explained why she wanted them. She could feel herself getting red in the face. Maybe only "fancy pieces" wore trimmed hats in Charleston.

"What a good idea!" said Sally with genuine enthusiasm. "I have an old riding top hat that could be resurrected with a cockade of ribbon and some feathers trailing down from it. If I can find it, it's been so long since I used it last. Do you ride, Scarlett?"

"Not for years. Not since . . ." She tried to remember.

"Not since before the War. I know. Me, too. I miss it horribly."

"What do you miss, Sally?" Mrs. Butler joined them. She held out the feathers to Celie. "Tie a piece of string 'round these, at both ends, and be careful not to crush them." Then she gasped. "Excuse me," she said with a laugh, "I'll miss Brewton's sausage. Thank goodness I saw you, Sally, it had clean slipped my mind." She hurried away, with Celie in pursuit.

Sally smiled at Scarlett's puzzled expression. "Don't worry, she hasn't gone mad. The best sausage in the world is for sale on Saturdays only. It sells out early. The man who makes it was a footman of ours when he was a slave. Lucullus is his name. After he was freed, he added Brewton for a last name. Most of the slaves did that—you'll find all of Charleston's aristocracy here as far as names go. Of course there's a good number of Lincolns, too. Come walk with me, Scarlett. I've got to get my vegetables. Eleanor will find us."

Sally stopped before a table of onions. "Where the devil is Lila?—oh, there you are. Scarlett, this tiny young creature, if you can credit it, runs my entire household as if she were Ivan the Terrible. This is Mrs. Butler, Lila, Mister Rhett's wife."

The pretty young maid bobbed a curtsey. "We needs lots of onions, Miss Sally," she said, "for the artichoke pickles I'm putting up."

"Do you hear that, Scarlett? She thinks I'm senile. I know we need lots of onions," Sally grabbed one of the brown paper bags from the table and began to drop onions into it. Scarlett watched with dismay. Impulsively, she put her hand over the mouth of the bag.

"Excuse me, Mrs. Brewton, but those onions are no good."

"No good? How can onions be no good? They're not rotten or sprouting."

"These onions were dug up too soon," Scarlett explained. "They look fine enough, but they won't have any flavor. I know, because it's a mistake I made myself. When I had to run our place, I planted onions. Since I didn't know anything about growing things, I dug up a batch as soon as the tops started to brown, afraid they were dying and would rot. They were pretty as pictures, and I was proud as a peacock, because most of my planting came out mighty sorry. We ate them boiled and stewed and in fricassee to help the taste of the squirrels and raccoons. But they didn't have any bite to them at all. Later, when I dug up the row to plant something else, I came across one I'd missed. That one was what an onion's supposed to be. The fact is, they need time to flavor up. I'll show you what a good onion should be like." Scarlett sorted with expert eyes, hands, and nose through the baskets on the table. "These are the ones you want," she said at last. Her chin was belligerent. You can figure me for a country bumpkin if you want to, she was thinking, but I'm not ashamed that I got my hands dirty when I had to. You high-toned Charlestonians think you're the be-all and end-all, but you're not.

"Thank you," said Sally. Her eyes were thoughtful. "I'm grateful. I did you an injustice, Scarlett. I didn't think anyone as pretty as you could have any sense. What else did you plant? I wouldn't mind learning about celery."

Scarlett studied Sally's face. She saw the honest interest and responded to it. "Celery was too fancy for me. I had a dozen mouths to feed. I know about all there is to know about yams, though, and carrots and white potatoes and turnips. Cotton, too." She didn't care if she was bragging or not. She'd bet anything that no lady in Charleston had ever sweated in the sun picking cotton!

"You must have worked yourself to a shadow." Respect was written clear in Sally Brewton's eyes.

"We had to eat." She shrugged off the past. "Thank goodness that's way behind us." Then she smiled. Sally Brewton made her feel good. "It did make me mighty particular about root crops, though. Rhett said one time that he'd known plenty of people to send wine back but I was the only one who'd do it with carrots. We were at the fanciest restaurant in New Orleans, and did it ever cause a rumpus!"

Sally laughed explosively. "I think I know that restaurant. Do tell me. Did the waiter rearrange the napkin over his arm and look down his nose in disapproval?"

Scarlett giggled. "He dropped the napkin and it fell onto one of those frying pans they cook dessert in."

"And caught on fire?" Sally grinned wickedly.

Scarlett nodded.

"Oh, Lord!" Sally hooted. "I'd have given my eye teeth to have been there."

Eleanor Butler broke in. "What are you two talking about? I could use a good laugh. Brewton only had two pounds of sausage left, and he'd promised them to Minnie Wentworth."

"Get Scarlett to tell you," said Sally, still chuckling. "This girl of yours is a wonder, Eleanor, but I've got to go." She put her hand on the basket of onions that Scarlett had designated. "I'll take this," she said to the vendor. "Yes, Lena, the whole basket. Just pour them into a croaker sack and give them to Lila. How's your boy, is he still whooping?" Before she got involved in a discussion of cough remedies she turned to Scarlett and looked up into her face. "I hope you'll call me 'Sally' and come see me, Scarlett. I'm at home the first Wednesday of the month in the afternoon."

Scarlett didn't know it, but she had just advanced to the highest level of Charleston's tight-knit, stratified society. Doors that would have opened a polite crack for Eleanor Butler's daughter-in-law swung wide for a protégée of Sally Brewton's.

Eleanor Butler gladly accepted Scarlett's judgments on the potatoes and carrots she needed to buy. Then she made her purchases of cornmeal, hominy, flour, and rice. Finally, she bought butter, buttermilk, cream, milk, and eggs. Celie's basket was overflowing. "We'll have to take everything out and repack it," Mrs. Butler fretted.

"I'll carry something," Scarlett offered. She was impatient to be gone before she had to meet any more of Mrs. Butler's friends. They had stopped so often, the walk through the vegetable and dairy sections had taken them more than an hour. She didn't mind meeting the women who were selling the produce—she wanted to mark them down in her mind very clearly, because she was sure she'd be dealing with them in the future. Miss Eleanor was too soft. She was sure she could do better on the prices. It would be fun. As soon as she got the hang of things she'd offer to take over some of the shopping. Not the fishy things, though. They made her sick.

Not, she discovered, when she ate them. Dinner was a revelation. The she-crab soup was a velvety blend of tastes that made her open her eyes wide. She'd never tasted anything so subtly delicious, except in New Orleans. Of course! Now that she remembered it, Rhett had identified many of the dishes he ordered for them as one kind of seafood or another.

Scarlett had a second bowl of soup and relished every drop, then did full justice to the rest of the generous dinner, including dessert, a whipped-cream-topped, crusty nut and fruit confection that Mrs. Butler identified as Huguenot Torte.

That afternoon she had indigestion for the first time in her life. Not from overeating. Eulalie and Pauline upset her. "We're on our way to see Carreen," Pauline announced when they arrived, "and we figured Scarlett would want to go with us. Sorry to interrupt. I didn't know you'd just be finishing dinner." Her mouth was tight with disapproval of a meal that would last so long. Eulalie released a small sigh of envy.

Carreen! She didn't want to see Carreen at all. But she couldn't say that, her aunts would have a fit.

"I'd just love to go, Auntie," she cried, "but I'm really not feeling very well. I'm just going to put a cool cloth on my forehead and lie down." She dropped her eyes. "You know how it is." There! Let them think I'm having female troubles. They're much too prissy-nice to ask any questions.

She was right. Her aunts made the hastiest possible farewells. Scarlett saw them to the door, careful to walk as if she had cramping in her stomach. Eulalie patted her shoulder sympathetically when she kissed her goodbye. "You have yourself a good long rest, now," she said. Scarlett nodded meekly. "And come to our house in the morning at nine-thirty. It's a half-hour walk to Saint Mary's for Mass."

Scarlett stared, gape-mouthed with horror. Mass had never crossed her mind.

At that moment a genuine stab of pain made her almost double over.

All afternoon she cowered on the bed with her stays loosed and a hot water bottle on her stomach. The indigestion was uncomfortable and unfamiliar, therefore frightening. But far, far more frightening was her abject fear of God.

Ellen O'Hara had been a devout Catholic, and she had done her best to make religion part of the fabric of life at Tara. There were evening prayers, Litany and rosary, and constant gentle reminders to her daughters about their duties and obligations as Christians. The plantation's isolation was a sorrow to Ellen because she missed the consolations of the Church. In her quiet way, she tried to provide them to her family. By the time they were twelve years old, Scarlett and her sisters had the imperatives of the catechism firmly implanted by their mother's patient teaching.

Now Scarlett squirmed with guilt because she had neglected all religious observance for so many years. Her mother must be weeping in heaven. Oh, why did her mother's sisters have to live in Charleston? Nobody in Atlanta had ever expected her to go to Mass. Mrs. Butler wouldn't have fussed at her, or at worst, she might have expected her to go to the

Episcopal church with her. That wouldn't be so bad. Scarlett had some vague notion that God didn't pay attention to anything that happened in a Protestant church. But He would know the minute she stepped over the threshold of Saint Mary's that she was a fearful sinner who hadn't been to Confession since . . . since—she couldn't even remember the last time. She wouldn't be able to take Communion, and everyone would know that was why. She imagined the invisible guardian angels Ellen had told her about when she was a child. All of them were frowning; Scarlett pulled the covers up over her head.

She didn't know that her concept of religion was as superstitious and ill-formed as any Stone Age man's. She only knew that she was frightened and unhappy and angry that she was trapped in a dilemma. What was she going to do?

She remembered her mother's serene candlelit face telling her family and her servants that God loved the stray lamb most of all, but it wasn't much comfort. She couldn't think of any way to get out of going to Mass.

It wasn't fair! Just when things had started to go so well, too. Mrs. Butler had told her that Sally Brewton gave very exciting whist parties and she was sure to be invited.

16

*S*carlett did, of course, go to Mass. To her surprise the ancient ritual and the responses were strangely comforting, like old friends in the new life she was beginning. It was easy to remember her mother when her lips were murmuring the Our Father, and the smooth beads of the rosary were so familiar to her fingers. Ellen must be pleased to see her there on her knees, she was sure, and it made her feel good.

Because it was inescapable, she made a Confession and went to see Carreen, too. The convent and her sister turned out to be two more surprises. Scarlett had always imagined convents as fortress-like places with locked gates where nuns scrubbed stone floors from morning till night. In Charleston the Sisters of Mercy lived in a magnificent brick mansion and taught school in its beautiful ballroom.

Carreen was radiantly happy in her vocation, so changed from the quiet, withdrawn girl Scarlett remembered that she didn't seem like the same person at all. How could she be angry with a stranger? Especially a stranger who seemed somehow to be older than she, instead of her baby sister. Carreen—Sister Mary Joseph—was so extravagantly glad to see her, too. Scarlett felt warmed by the freely expressed love and admiration. If only Suellen was half as nice, she thought, she wouldn't feel so shut out at Tara. It was a positive pleasure to visit Carreen and take tea in the lovely formal garden at the convent, even if Carreen did talk so much about the little girls in her arithmetic class that it nearly put Scarlett to sleep.

In what seemed like almost no time at all, Sunday Mass, followed by breakfast at her aunt's house, and Tuesday afternoon tea with Carreen were welcome quiet moments in Scarlett's busy schedule.

For she was very busy.

A blizzard of calling cards had descended on Eleanor Butler's house in the week after Scarlett educated Sally Brewton about onions. Eleanor was grateful to Sally; at least she thought she was. Wise in the ways of Charleston, she was apprehensive for Scarlett. Even in the spartan conditions of post-War life, society was a quicksand of unstated rules of behavior, a Byzantine labyrinth of overelaborate refinements lying in wait to trap the unwary and uninitiated.

She tried to guide Scarlett. "You needn't call on all these people who left cards, dear," she said. "It's enough to leave your own cards with the corner turned down. That acknowledges the call made on you and your willingness to be acquainted and says that you aren't actually coming in the house to see the person."

"Is that why so many of the cards were all bent up? I thought they were just old and knocked around. Well, I'm going to go see every single one of them. I'm glad everybody wants to be friends; I do, too."

Eleanor held her tongue. It was a fact that most of the cards were "old and knocked around." No one could afford new ones—almost no one. And those who could wouldn't embarrass those who couldn't by having new ones made. It was accepted custom now to leave all cards received on a tray in the entrance hall for discreet retrieval by their owners. She decided that, for the moment, she wouldn't complicate Scarlett's education with that particular bit of information. The dear child had shown her a box of a hundred fresh white cards that she had brought from Atlanta. They were so new that they were still interleaved with tissue. They should last for a long time. She watched Scarlett set out with high-spirited determination, and she felt the way she had when Rhett, aged three, had called triumphantly to her from the topmost limb of a gigantic oak tree.

Eleanor Butler's apprehensions were unnecessary. Sally Brewton had been explicit. "The girl is almost totally lacking in education, and she has the taste of a Hottentot. But she has vigor and strength, and she's a survivor. We need her kind in the South, yes, even in Charleston. Perhaps especially in Charleston. I'm sponsoring her; I expect all my friends to make her feel welcome here."

Soon Scarlett's days were a whirlwind of activity. Beginning with an hour or more at the Market, then a big breakfast at the house—usually including Brewton's sausage—she was out and about by ten o'clock, freshly dressed, with Pansy trotting behind carrying her card case and personal supply of sugar, an expected accompaniment to all guests in rationing times.

There was enough time to pay as many as five calls before she returned for dinner. Afternoons were taken up by visits to ladies having their "at home" days or whist parties or excursions with new friends to King Street for shopping or receiving callers with Miss Eleanor.

Scarlett loved the constant activity. Even more, she loved the attention paid her. Most of all, she loved hearing Rhett's name on everyone's lips. A few old women were openly critical. They had disapproved of him when he was young, and they would never relent. But most of them forgave his earlier sins. He was older now, chastened. And he was devoted to his mother. Old ladies who had lost their own sons and grandsons in the War could well understand Eleanor Butler's glowing happiness.

The younger women regarded Scarlett with poorly concealed envy. They delighted in telling all the facts, and all the rumors, about what Rhett was doing when he left the city without explanation. Some said that their husbands knew for sure that Rhett was financing the political movement to throw out the carpetbagger government in the state capital. Others whispered that he was recapturing the Butler family portraits and furnishings at the point of a gun. All of them had stories about his exploits during the War, when his sleek dark ship raced through the Union blockade fleet like a death-dealing shadow. They had a special look on their faces when they talked about him, a mixture of curiosity and romantic imaginings. Rhett was more myth than man. And he was Scarlett's husband. How could they not envy her?

Scarlett was at her best when she was constantly busy, and these were good days for her. The social rounds were just what she needed after the terrifying loneliness of Atlanta, and she quickly forgot the desperation she had felt. Atlanta must have been wrong, that's all. She'd done nothing to deserve such cruelty or everybody in Charleston wouldn't like her so much. And they did, why else would they invite her?

The thought was immensely gratifying. She returned to it often. Whenever she was paying her calls, or receiving calls with Mrs. Butler, or visiting her specially chosen friend, Anne Hampton, at the Confederate Home, or gossiping over coffee at the Market, Scarlett always wished that Rhett could see her. Sometimes she even looked quickly around her, imagining that he was there, so intense was her desire. Oh, if only he'd come home!

He seemed closest to her in the quiet time after supper when she sat with his mother in the study and listened with fascination while Miss Eleanor talked. She was always willing to remember things Rhett had done or said when he was a little boy.

Scarlett enjoyed Miss Eleanor's other stories, too. Sometimes they were wickedly funny. Eleanor Butler, like most of her Charleston contemporaries, had been educated by governesses and travel. She was well-read but not intellectual, spoke the romance languages adequately, but with a terrible accent, was familiar with London, Paris, Rome, Florence, but only the famous historic attractions and luxury shops. She was true to her era and her class. She had never questioned the authority of her parents or her husband, and she did her duty in all respects, without complaining.

What set her apart from most women of her type was that she had an irrepressible, quiet sense of fun. She enjoyed whatever life brought her and found the human condition fundamentally entertaining, and she was a gifted teller of stories, with a repertoire that ranged from accounts of amusing incidents in her own life to the classic Southern storehouse of the skeletons in the closets of every family in the region.

Scarlett, if she had known the reference, could accurately have called Eleanor her personal Scheherazade. She never realized that Mrs. Butler was trying, indirectly, to stretch her mind and her heart. Eleanor could see the vulnerability and courage that had drawn her beloved son to Scarlett. She could also see that something had gone horribly wrong with the marriage, so wrong that Rhett wanted nothing more to do with it. She knew, without being told, that Scarlett was desperately determined to get him back, and for her own reasons she was even more eager for reconciliation than Scarlett was. She wasn't certain whether Scarlett could make Rhett happy, but she believed with all her heart that another child would make the marriage a success. Rhett had visited her with Bonnie; she would never forget the joy of it. She had loved the little girl and loved even more seeing her son so happy. She wanted that happiness again for him, and the joy again for herself. She was willing to do anything in her power to accomplish it.

Because she was so occupied, Scarlett had been in Charleston for more than a month before she noticed that she was bored. It happened at Sally Brewton's, the least boring place in town, when everyone was talking about fashion, a subject that had previously been of consuming interest to Scarlett. At first she was fascinated to hear Sally and her circle of friends mention Paris. Rhett had once brought her a bonnet from Paris, the most beautiful, most exciting gift she'd ever received. Green—to match her eyes, he'd said—with glorious wide silk ribbons to tie under her chin. She made herself listen to what Alicia Savage was saying—though what a skinny old lady like her could know about dressing was hard to figure. Or Sally, either. With her face and flat chest, nothing would make her look good.

"Do you remember Worth's fittings?" Mrs. Savage said. "I thought I'd collapse standing on the platform so long."

A half dozen voices spoke at once, sharing complaints about the brutality of Paris dressmakers. Others argued with them, saying that any in-convenience was a small price to pay for the quality that only Paris could supply. Several sighed over memories of gloves and boots and fans and perfume.

Scarlett turned automatically toward whatever voice was speaking, an interested expression on her face. When she heard laughter, she laughed. But she thought about other things—whether there was any of that good pie left from dinner to have for supper . . . her blue dress that could use a fresh collar . . . Rhett . . . She looked at the clock behind Sally's head. She couldn't leave for at least eight more minutes. And Sally had seen her looking. She'd have to pay attention.

The eight minutes seemed like eight more hours.

"All anybody talked about, Miss Eleanor, was clothes. I thought I'd go crazy I was so bored!" Scarlett collapsed into the chair opposite Mrs. Butler's. Clothes had lost their fascination for her when she was reduced to the four "serviceable" drab-colored frocks Rhett's mother helped her order from the dressmaker. Even the ballgowns that were being made held small interest. There were only two, for the upcoming six-week series of balls almost every night. They were dull, too—dull colors, one blue silk and one claret-colored velvet—and dull design, with hardly any trim. Still, even the dullest ball meant music—and dancing—and Scarlett dearly loved to dance. Rhett would be back from the plantation, too, Miss Eleanor had promised her. If only she didn't have to wait so long for the Season to start. Three weeks suddenly seemed unendurably boring to contemplate with nothing to do but sit around and talk to women.

Oh, how she wished something exciting would happen!

Scarlett's wish was granted very soon, but not in the way she wanted. Instead, the excitement was terrifying.

It started as malicious gossip that had people laughing all over town. Mary Elizabeth Pitt, a spinster in her forties, claimed that she had awakened in the middle of the night and seen a man in her room. "Just as plain as anything," she said, "with a kerchief over his face like Jesse James."

"If ever I heard wishful thinking," someone unkindly commented, "that's it. Mary Elizabeth must be twenty years older than Jesse James." The newspaper had been printing a series of articles romanticizing the daring exploits of the James brothers and their gang.

But the following day the story took an ugly turn. Alicia Savage was also in her forties, but she had been married twice, and everyone knew that she was a calm-natured, rational woman. She, too, had woken up and seen a man in her bedroom, standing beside her bed, looking at her in the moonlight. He was holding the curtain back to let the light in, and he was staring over a kerchief that hid the lower part of his face. The upper part was shadowed by the bill of his cap.

He was wearing the uniform of a Union soldier.

Mrs. Savage screamed and threw a book from her bedside table at him. He went through the curtains onto the piazza before her husband reached her room.

A Yankee! Suddenly everyone was afraid. Women alone were frightened for themselves; women with husbands were frightened for themselves and even more afraid for their husbands, because if a man injured a Union soldier, he'd go to prison or even be hanged.

The next night and the next, the soldier materialized in a woman's bedroom. On the third night, the report was the worst of all. It wasn't moonlight that woke Theodosia Harding, it was the movement of a warm hand on the coverlet over her breasts. Only darkness met her eyes when she opened them. But she could hear strangled breathing, feel a crouching presence. She cried out, then fainted from fear. No one knew what might have happened next. Theodosia had been sent to cousins in Summerville. Everyone said she was in a state of collapse. Near idiocy, added the ghoulish.

A delegation of Charleston men went to Army headquarters with the elderly lawyer Josiah Anson as their spokesman. They were going to begin their own night patrols in the old part of the city. If they surprised the intruder, they'd deal with him themselves.

The commandant agreed to the patrols. But he warned that if any Union soldier was hurt, the responsible man or men would be executed. There'd be no vigilante justice or random attacks on Northern troops under the guise of protecting Charleston's women.

Scarlett's fears—long years of them—crashed on her like a tidal wave. She had grown contemptuous of the occupation troops; like everyone else in Charleston she ignored them, acted as if they were not there, and they got out of her way as she walked briskly down the sidewalk on her way to pay a call or go shopping. Now she was afraid of every blue uniform she saw. Any one of them might be the midnight intruder. She could imagine him all too well, a figure springing out from the dark.

Her sleep was broken by hideous dreams—memories, really. Again and again she saw the Yankee straggler who'd come to Tara, smelled the rank smell of him, saw his filthy, hairy hands pawing through the trinkets in her mother's work box, his red-rimmed eyes hot with violent lust staring at her and his broken-toothed mouth wet and twisted in an anticipatory leer. She'd shot him. Obliterated the mouth and the eyes in an explosion of blood and bits of bone and viscous red-streaked gobbets of his brains.

She'd never been able to forget the echoing boom of the shot and the ghastly red spatterings and her fierce, rending triumph.

Oh, if only she had a pistol to protect herself and Miss Eleanor from the Yankee!

But there was no weapon in the house. She ransacked cupboards and trunks, wardrobes and dresser drawers, even the shelves behind the books in the library. She was defenseless, helpless. For the first time in her life she felt weak, unable to face and overcome any obstacle in her way. It all but crippled her. She begged Eleanor Butler to send a message to Rhett.

Eleanor temporized. Yes, yes, she'd send word. Yes, she'd tell him what Alicia had said about the hulking size of the man and the unearthly glint of moonlight in his inhumanly black eyes. Yes, she'd remind him that she and Scarlett were two women alone in the big house at night, that the servants all went to their own homes after supper except for Manigo, an old man, and Pansy, a small, weak girl.

Yes, she'd make the note urgent, and she'd dispatch it right away— on the very next trip of the boat that brought game from the plantation.

"But when will that be, Miss Eleanor? Rhett has to come now! That magnolia tree is practically a ladder from the ground to the piazza outside our rooms!" Scarlett clutched Mrs. Butler's arm, shook it for emphasis.

Eleanor patted her hand. "Soon, dear, it's bound to be soon. We haven't had any duck for a month, and roast duck is a particular favorite of mine. Rhett knows that. Besides, everything will be all right now. Ross and his friends are going to patrol every night."

Ross! Scarlett screamed inwardly. What could a drunk like Ross Butler do? Or any of the Charleston men? Most of them were old men or cripples or still boys. If they'd been any use, they wouldn't have lost the stupid War. Why should anyone trust them to fight the Yankees now?

She battered her need against Eleanor Butler's impenetrable optimism, and she lost.

For a while it seemed the patrols were effective. There were no reports of intruders, and everyone calmed down. Scarlett had her first "at home" day, which was so well attended that her Aunt Eulalie complained that there wasn't enough cake to go around. Eleanor Butler tore up the note she had written Rhett. People went to church, went shopping, played whist, took out their evening clothes to air them and make repairs before the Season began.

Scarlett came in from her round of morning calls with glowing cheeks from walking too quickly. "Where's Mrs. Butler?" she demanded of Manigo. When he replied that she was in the kitchen Scarlett ran to the back of the house.

Eleanor Butler looked up at Scarlett's rushed entry. "Good news, Scarlett! I had a letter from Rosemary this morning. She'll be home day after tomorrow."

"Better wire her to stay," Scarlett snapped. Her voice was harsh, emotionless. "The Yankee got to Harriet Madison last night. I just heard." She looked at the table near Mrs. Butler. "Ducks? Those are ducks you're plucking! The plantation boat came! I can go back to the plantation on it to get Rhett."

"You can't go alone in that boat with four men, Scarlett."

"I can take Pansy, whether she likes it or not. Here, give me a sack and some of those biscuits. I'm hungry. I'll eat them on the way."

"But Scarlett—"

"But me no buts, Miss Eleanor. Just hand me the biscuits. I'm going."

What am I doing? Scarlett thought, near panic. I should never have dashed off this way, Rhett's going to be furious with me. And I must look awful. It's bad enough just to show up where I don't belong; at least I could look pretty. I had it all planned so different.

She had thought about it a thousand times, what it would be like when next she saw Rhett. Sometimes she imagined that he'd come home to the house late; she'd be in her nightdress, the one with the drawstring neck—tied loose—and she'd be brushing her hair before bedtime. Rhett had always loved her hair, he said it was a live thing; sometimes—in the early days—he'd brush it for her, to see the blue cracklings of electricity.

Often she pictured herself at the tea table, dropping a piece of sugar into a cup with the silver tongs elegantly held in her fingers. She'd be chatting cozily with Sally Brewton, and he'd see how much at home she was, how welcomed by Charleston's most interesting people. He'd catch up her hand and kiss it, and the tongs would drop, but it wouldn't matter . . .

Or she was with Miss Eleanor after supper, the two of them in their chairs before the fire, so comfortable together, so close, but with a place waiting for him. Only once had she envisioned going to the plantation, because she didn't know what the place was like, except that Sherman's men had burned it. Her daydream began all right—she and Miss Eleanor arrived with hampers of cakes and champagne in a lovely green-painted boat, resting against piles of silk cushions, holding bright flowered parasols. "Picnic," they called out, and Rhett laughed and ran to them, his arms open. But then it fizzled out, in blankness. Rhett hated picnics, for one thing. He said you might as well live in a cave if you were going to eat sitting on the ground like an animal instead of in a chair at a table like a civilized human being.

Certainly she had never thought of the possibility that she'd show up like this, squashed amid boxes and barrels of God knows what on a scabby boat that smelled to high heaven.

Now that she was away from the city, she was more worried about Rhett's anger than about the prowling Yankee. Suppose he just tells the boatmen to turn right around and take me back?

The boatmen dipped their oars into the green-brown water only to steer; the tide's invisible, powerful, slow current carried them. Scarlett looked impatiently at the banks of the wide river. It didn't seem to her that they were moving at all. Everything was the same: wide stretches of tall brown grasses that swayed slowly—oh, so slowly—in the tidal current, and behind them thick woods draped with motionless gray curtains of Spanish moss, under them the tangled growth of overgrown evergreen shrubs. It was all so silent. Why weren't there any birds singing, for heaven's sake? And why was it getting so dark already?

It began to rain.

Long before the oars started a steady pull toward the left bank she was soaked to the skin and shivering, miserable in body and mind. The bump of the bow against a dock jarred her from her huddled desolation. She looked up through the blur of rain on her face and saw a figure in streaming black oilskins, illuminated by a blazing torch. The face was invisible under a deep hood.

"Throw me a line." Rhett leaned forward, one arm outstretched. "Good trip, boys?"

Scarlett pushed against the crates nearest her to stand. Her legs were too cramped to hold her, and she fell back, toppling the topmost crate with a crash.

"What the hell?" Rhett caught the noosed rope that snaked to him from the boatman and dropped the circle over a mooring post. "Toss up the stern line," he ordered. "What's making that racket? Are you men drunk?"

"No sir, Mister Rhett," the boatmen chorused. It was the first time they had spoken since they had left the dock in Charleston. One of them gestured toward the two women in the stern of the barge.

"My God!" said Rhett.

17

"Do you feel better now?" Rhett's voice was carefully controlled.

Scarlett nodded dumbly. She was wrapped in a blanket, wearing a coarse work shirt of Rhett's underneath, and sitting on a stool near an open fire with her bare feet in a tub of hot water.

"How are you doing, Pansy?" Scarlett's maid, on another stool in another blanket cocoon, grinned and allowed as how she was doing just fine excepting that she was powerful hungry.

Rhett chuckled. "And so am I. When you dry out, we'll eat."

Scarlett pulled the blanket more closely around her. *He's being too nice, I've seen him like this before, all smiles and warm as sunshine. Then it would turn out that he was really mad enough to spit nails all the time. It's because Pansy's here, that's why he's putting on this act. When she's gone, he'll turn on me. Maybe I can say I need her to stay with me—but for what? I'm already undressed, and I can't put my clothes on again until they dry, and Lord knows when that will be, with the rain outside and the inside so dank. How can Rhett bear to live in this place? It's awful!*

The room they were in was lit only by the fire. It was a large square, perhaps twenty feet to a side, with a packed-earth floor and stained walls that had lost most of their plaster. It smelled of cheap whiskey and tobacco juice, with an underlay of scorched wood and fabric. The only furniture was an assortment of crude stools and benches, plus a scattering of dented metal cuspidors. The mantelpiece over the wide fireplace and the frames around the doors and windows looked like some kind of mistake. They were made of pine, beautifully carved with a delicate fretwork design and oiled to a glowing golden brown. In one corner there was a rough staircase with splintered wooden treads and a sagging, unsafe railing. Scarlett's and Pansy's clothes were draped over the length of it. The white petticoats billowed from time to time when a draft caught them, like ghosts lurking in deep shadows.

"Why didn't you stay in Charleston, Scarlett?" Supper was over and Pansy had been sent to sleep with the old black woman who cooked for Rhett. Scarlett squared her shoulders.

"Your mother didn't want to disturb you in your paradise here." She looked around the room disdainfully. "But I believe you should know what's going on. There's a Yankee soldier creeping into bedrooms at night—ladies' bedrooms—and handling them. One girl went clean out of her mind and had to be sent off." She tried to read his face, but it was expressionless. He was looking at her, silent, as if he was waiting for something.

"Well? Don't you care that your mother and I could be murdered in our beds, or something worse?"

Rhett's mouth turned down in a derisive smile. "Am I hearing correctly? Maidenly timidity from the woman who drove a wagon through the entire Yankee army because it was in her way? Come, now, Scarlett. You've been known to tell the truth. Why did you come all this way in the rain? Were you hoping to catch me in the arms of a light o' love? Did Henry Hamilton recommend that as a way to get me to start paying your bills again?"

"What on earth are you talking about, Rhett Butler? What has Uncle Henry got to do with anything?"

"Such convincing ignorance! I compliment you. But you can't expect me to believe for an instant that your crafty old lawyer didn't notify you when I cut off the money I was sending to Atlanta. I'm too fond of Henry Hamilton to credit such negligence."

"Stopped sending the money? You can't do that!" Scarlett's knees turned to jelly. Rhett couldn't mean it. What would happen to her? The house on Peachtree Street—the tons of coal it took to heat it, the servants to clean and cook and wash and keep the garden and the horses and polish the carriages, the food for all of them—why, it cost a fortune. How could Uncle Henry pay the bills? He'd use her money! No, no that couldn't be. She'd scrabbled along with no food in her belly, broken shoes on her feet, her back breaking and her hands bleeding while she worked in the fields to keep from starving. She'd given up all her pride, turned her back on everything she'd been taught, done business with low-down people not fit to spit on, schemed and cheated, worked day and night for her money. She wouldn't let it go, she couldn't. It was hers. It was the only thing she had.

"You can't take my money!" she screamed at Rhett. But it came out a cracked whisper.

He laughed. "I haven't taken any away from you, my pet. I've only stopped adding to it. As long as you're living in the house I provide in Charleston, there's no reason for me to maintain an empty house in Atlanta. Of course, if you were to return to it, it would no longer be empty. Then I'd feel obliged to begin paying for it again." Rhett walked over to the fireplace where he could see her face in the light of the flames. His challenging smile disappeared and his forehead creased with concern.

"You really didn't know, did you? Hold on, Scarlett, I'll get you a brandy. You look like you're going to pass out."

He had to steady her hands with his to hold the glass to her lips. She was trembling uncontrollably. When the glass was empty, he dropped it on the floor and chafed her hands until they warmed and stopped shaking.

"Now tell me, in sober truth, is there really a soldier breaking into bedrooms?"

"Rhett, you didn't mean it, did you? You aren't going to stop sending the money to Atlanta?"

"To hell with the money, Scarlett, I asked you a question."

"To hell with you," she said, "I asked you one."

"I should have known you wouldn't be able to think of anything else once money was mentioned. All right, I'll send some to Henry. Now will you answer me?"

"You swear?"

"I swear."

"Tomorrow?"

"Yes! Yes, dammit, tomorrow. Now, once and for all, what's this story about a Yankee soldier?"

Scarlett's sigh of relief seemed to last forever. Then she drew breath into her lungs and told him everything she knew about the intruder.

"You say Alicia Savage saw his uniform?"

"Yes," Scarlett answered. Then she added spitefully, "He doesn't care how old they are. Maybe he's raping your mother right this minute."

Rhett's big hands clenched. "I should strangle you, Scarlett. The world would be a better place."

He questioned her for almost an hour, until she was drained of everything she'd heard.

"Very well," he said then, "we'll leave tomorrow as soon as the tide turns." He walked to a door and threw it open. "Good," he said, "the sky is clear. It'll be an easy run."

Past his silhouette Scarlett could see the night sky. There was a three-quarter moon. She stood wearily. Then she saw the mist from the river that covered the ground outside. The moonlight made it white, and for a confused moment she wondered if it had snowed. A billow of mist enveloped Rhett's feet and ankles, then dissipated into the room. He closed the door and turned. Without the moonlight, the room seemed very dark until a match flared, illuminating Rhett's chin and nose from below. He touched it to a lamp wick, and she could see his face. Scarlett ached with longing. He put the glass chimney on the lamp and held it high. "Come with me. There's a bedroom upstairs where you can sleep."

It was not nearly as primitive as the room downstairs. The tall four-post bed had a thick mattress and fat pillows and a bright woolen blanket over its crisp linen sheets. Scarlett didn't look at the other furnishings. She let the blanket fall from her shoulders and climbed the set of steps beside the bed to burrow under the covers.

He stood over her a moment before he left the room. She listened to his footsteps. No, he wasn't going downstairs, he'd be close by. Scarlett smiled, then slept.

The nightmare began as it had always begun—with the mist. It was years since Scarlett had dreamed it, but her unconscious mind remembered even as it created the dream, and she began to twist and thrash and whimper deep in the back of her throat, dreading what was to come. Then, again, she was running, with her straining heart pounding in her ears, running, stumbling and running, through a thick white fog that twined cold swirling tendrils around her throat and legs and arms. She was cold, as cold as death, and hungry, and terrified. It was the same, it had always been the same, and each time worse than the time before, as if the terror and hunger and cold accumulated, grew stronger.

And yet it was not the same. For in the past, she had been running and reaching for something unnamed and unknowable, and now ahead of her she could glimpse through streaks in the mist Rhett's broad back, always moving away. And she knew that he was what she was searching for, that when she reached him the dream would lose its power and fade away, never to return. She ran and ran, but he was always far ahead, always with his back turned on her. Then the fog thickened, and he began to disappear, and she cried out to him. "Rhett . . . Rhett . . . Rhett . . . Rhett . . . Rhett . . ."

"Hush, hush now. You're dreaming, it's not real."

"Rhett . . ."

"Yes, I'm here. Hush now. You're all right." Strong arms lifted her and held her, and she was warm and safe at last.

Scarlett half-woke with a start. There was no mist. Instead, a lamp on a table cast a glowing light and she could see Rhett's face bent close above hers. "Oh, Rhett," she cried. "It was so awful."

"The old dream?"

"Yes, yes—well, almost. There was something different, I can't remember . . . But I was cold and hungry and I couldn't see because of the fog, and I was so frightened, Rhett, it was terrible."

He held her close and his voice vibrated in his hard chest next to her ear. "Of course you were cold and hungry. That supper wasn't fit to eat, and you've kicked off your blankets. I'll pull them up, and you'll sleep just fine." He laid her down against the pillows.

"Don't leave me. It'll come back."

Rhett spread the blankets up over her. "There'll be biscuits for breakfast, and hominy, and butter enough to turn them yellow. Think about that—and country ham and fresh eggs—and you'll sleep like a baby. You've always been a good feeder, Scarlett." His voice was amused. And tired. She closed her heavy eyelids.

"Rhett?" It was a blurred, drowsy sound.

He paused in the doorway, his hand shading the lamplight. "Yes, Scarlett?"

"Thank you for coming to wake me. How did you know?"

"You were yelling loud enough to break the windows." The last sound she heard was his warm gentle laughter. It was like a lullaby.

True to Rhett's prediction, Scarlett ate an enormous breakfast before she went to look for him. He'd been up before dawn, the cook told her. He was always up before the sun. She looked at Scarlett with undisguised curiosity.

I should wear her out for her impudence, Scarlett thought, but she was so content she couldn't summon up any real anger. Rhett had held her, comforted her, even laughed at her. Just as he used to before things went wrong. She'd been so right to come to the plantation. She should have done it before, instead of frittering away her time at a million tea parties.

The sunlight made her narrow her eyes when she stepped outside the house. It was strong, already warm on her head although it was still very early. She shaded her eyes with her hand and looked around her.

A soft moan was her first reaction. The brick terrace under her feet continued to her left for a hundred yards. Broken, blackened and grassgrown, it was a frame for a monumental charred ruin. Jagged remnants of walls and chimneys were all that remained of what had been a magnificent mansion. Tumbled mounds of smoke- and fire-stained bricks within the fragments of walls were heart-stopping mementos of Sherman's Army.

Scarlett was heartsick. This had been Rhett's home, Rhett's life—lost forever before he could come back to reclaim it.

Nothing in her troubled life had ever been as bad as this. She'd never known the degree of pain he must have felt, must still feel a hundred times a day when he saw the ruins of his home. No wonder he was determined to rebuild, to find and regain everything he could of the old possessions.

She could help him! Hadn't she plowed and planted and harvested Tara's fields herself? Why, she'd wager Rhett didn't even know good seed corn from bad. She'd be proud to help, because she knew how much it meant, what a victory it was over the despoilers when the land was reborn with tender new growth. I understand, she thought triumphantly. I can feel what he's feeling. I can work with him. We can do this together. I don't mind a dirt floor. Not if it's with Rhett. Where is he? I've got to tell him!

Scarlett turned away from the shell of the house and found herself facing a vista unlike anything she'd ever seen in her life. The brick terrace on which she was standing led onto a grass-covered earth parterre, the highest of a series of grass terraces that unfolded in perfectly contoured sweeping movement down to a pair of sculpted lakes in the shape of gigantic butterfly wings. Between them a wide grassy path led to the river and the boat landing. The extravagant scale was so perfectly proportioned that the great distances appeared less, and the whole was like a carpeted outdoor room. The lush grass hid the scars of war, as though it had never been. It was a scene of sunlit tranquillity, of nature lovingly shaped into harmony with man. In the distance a bird sang an extended melody, as if in celebration. "Oh, how pretty!" she said aloud.

Movement to the left of the lowest terrace caught Scarlett's eye. It must be Rhett. She began to run. Down the terraces—the undulation increased her speed and she felt a giddy, intoxicating, joyful freedom; she laughed and threw her arms wide, a bird or a butterfly about to soar into the blue, blue skies.

She was breathless when she reached the place where Rhett was standing and watching her. Scarlett panted, her hand on her chest, until her breath returned. Then, "I've never had such fun!" she said, still half-gasping. "What a wonderful place this is, Rhett. No wonder you love it. Did you run down that lawn when you were a little boy? Did you feel like you could fly? Oh, my darling, how horrible to see the burning! I'm broken-hearted for you; I'd like to kill every Yankee in the world! Oh, Rhett, I've got so much to tell you. I've been thinking. It can all come back, darling, just like the grass. I understand, I really, truly do understand what you're doing."

Rhett looked at her strangely, cautiously. "What do you 'understand,' Scarlett?"

"Why you're here, instead of in town. Why you must bring the plantation back to life. Tell me what you've done, what you're going to do. It's so exciting!"

Rhett's face lit up, and he gestured toward the long rows of plants behind him. "They burned," he said, "but they didn't die. It looks as if perhaps they were even strengthened by the burning. The ashes may have given them something they needed. I've got to find out. I've got so much to learn."

Scarlett looked at the low stubby remains. She didn't know those dark green shiny leaves. "What kind of tree is it? Do you grow peaches here?"

"They're not trees. Scarlett, they're shrubs. Camellias. The first ones ever brought to America were planted here at Dunmore Landing. These are offshoots, over three hundred all told."

"Do you mean they're flowers?"

"Of course. The most nearly perfect flower in the world. The Chinese worship them."

"But you can't eat flowers. What crops are you planting?"

"I can't think about crops. I've got a hundred acres of garden to save."

"That's crazy, Rhett. What's a flower garden good for? You could grow something to sell. I know cotton doesn't grow 'round here, but there must be some good cash crop. Why, at Tara, we put every foot of land to use. You could plant right up to the walls of the house. Just look how green and thick that grass is. The land must be as rich as anything. All you'd have to do is plow it and drop in the seed, and it would probably sprout faster than you could get out of the way." She looked eagerly at him, ready to share her hard-earned knowledge.

"You're a barbarian, Scarlett," Rhett said heavily. "Go up to the house and tell Pansy to get ready. I'll meet you at the dock."

What had she done wrong? One minute he was full of life and excitement, then all of a sudden it was gone and he was cold, a stranger. She'd never understand him if she lived to be a hundred. She strode rapidly up the green terraces, blind now to their beauty, and into the house.

* * *

The boat moored to the landing was very different from the scabrous barge that had brought Scarlett and Pansy to the plantation. It was a sleek brown-painted sloop with bright brass fittings and gilt scroll trim. Beyond it in the river was another boat, one that she'd much prefer, Scarlett thought angrily. It was five times the size of the sloop and it had two decks with white and blue gingerbread scrollwork trim and a bright red rear paddle-wheel. Gaily colored bunting flags were strung from its smokestacks, and brightly dressed men and women crowded the rails on both decks. It looked festive and fun.

It's just like Rhett, Scarlett brooded, to go to the city in his dinky little boat instead of hailing the steamer to pick us up. She reached the landing just as Rhett took off his hat and made a sweeping, flamboyant bow to the people on the paddlewheeler.

"Do you know those folks?" she said. Maybe she was wrong, maybe he was signalling.

Rhett turned from the river, replacing his hat. "Indeed I do. Not individually, I hope, but in the whole. That's the weekly excursion boat from Charleston up the river and back. A highly profitable business for one of our carpetbagger citizens. Yankees buy tickets well in advance for the pleasure of seeing the skeletons of the burned-out plantation houses. I always greet them if it's convenient; it amuses me to see the confusion it engenders." Scarlett was too appalled to say a word. How could Rhett make a joke out of a bunch of Yankee buzzards laughing at what they'd done to his home?

She settled herself obediently on a cushioned bench in the small cabin, but as soon as Rhett stepped up on deck she jumped up to examine the intricate arrangement of cupboards, shelves, supplies and equipment, each thing in a place obviously designed for its storage. She was still busily satisfying her curiosity as the sloop moved slowly along the riverbank for a short distance and then tied up again. Rhett called out crisp orders. "Pass those bundles over and tie them down on the bow." Scarlett poked her head up from the hatch to see what was going on.

Gracious peace, what was all this? Dozens of black men were leaning on picks and shovels and watching as a series of bulky sacks were thrown to a crewman on the sloop. Where on earth could they be? This place looked like the back side of the moon. There was a huge clearing in the woods with a big pit dug in it and gigantic piles of what looked like pale chunks of rock on one side. Chalky dust filled the air and, soon, her nostrils, and she sneezed.

Pansy's echoing sneeze from the rear deck caught her attention. No fair, she thought. Pansy had a good view of everything. "I'm coming up," Scarlett shouted.

"Cast off," Rhett said at the same time.

The sloop moved quickly, caught by the fast river current, sending Scarlett tumbling down from the short ladder-stair into a graceless sprawl in the cabin. "Damn you, Rhett Butler, I could have broken my neck."

"You didn't. Stay put. I'll be down shortly."

Scarlett heard the creaking of ropes, and the sloop picked up speed. She scrambled to one of the benches and pulled herself up.

Almost immediately Rhett stepped easily down the ladder, his head bent to clear the hatch. He straightened up, and his head grazed the polished wood above it. Scarlett glared at him.

"You did that on purpose," she grumbled.

"Did what?" He opened one of the small portholes and closed the hatch. "Good," he said then, "we've got a following wind and a strong current. We'll be in the city in record time." He dropped onto the bench opposite Scarlett and lounged back, sleek and sinuous as a cat. "I assume you won't object if I smoke." His long fingers dipped into the interior pocket of his coat and extracted a cheroot.

"I object a lot. Why am I shut up down here in the dark? I want to go upstairs in the sun."

"Above," Rhett corrected automatically. "This is a rather small craft. The crew is black, Pansy is black, you are white and a woman. They get the cockpit, you get the cabin. Pansy can roll her eyes at the two men, laugh at their somewhat indelicate gallantries, and they'll all three have a pleasant time. Your presence would spoil it.

"So at the same time that the underclass is enjoying the journey, you and I, the privileged élite, will be thoroughly miserable cooped up in each other's company while you continue to pout and whine."

"I'm not pouting and whining! And I'll thank you not to talk to me as if I was a child!" Scarlett pulled in her lower lip. She hated it when Rhett made her feel foolish. "What was that quarry we stopped at?"

"That, my dear, was the salvation of Charleston and my passport back into the bosom of my people. It is a phosphate mine. There are dozens of them scattered along both rivers." He lit his cigar with prolonged appreciation and the smoke spiraled upward to the porthole. "I see your eyes gleaming, Scarlett. It's not the same as a gold mine. You can't make coins or jewelry out of phosphate. But, ground and washed and treated with certain chemicals, it makes the best quick-acting fertilizer in the world. There are customers waiting for as much of it as we can produce."

"So you're getting richer than ever."

"Yes, I am. But, more to the point, this is respectable, Charleston money. I can spend as much of my ill-gotten, speculator profit as I like now without disapproval. Everyone can tell themselves that it comes from phosphates, even though the mine is puny in size."

"Why don't you make it bigger?"

"I don't have to. It serves my purpose just as it is. I have a foreman who doesn't cheat me much, a couple of dozen laborers who work almost as much as they loaf, and respectability. I can spend my time and money and sweat on what I care about, and right now, that's restoring the gardens."

Scarlett was annoyed almost past bearing. Wasn't that just like Rhett to fall into a tub of butter? And to waste the chance? No matter how rich he was, he could stand to get richer. There was no such thing as too much money. Why, if he took over from the foreman and got a decent day's work out of those men, he could triple the yield. With another couple of dozen laborers, he could double that . . .

"Forgive me for interrupting your empire building, Scarlett, but I have a serious question to ask you. What would it take to convince you that you should leave me in peace and go back to Atlanta?"

Scarlett gaped at him. She was genuinely astonished. He couldn't possibly mean what he was saying, not after he had held her so tenderly last night. "You're joking," she accused.

"No, I am not. I've never been more serious in my life, and I want you to take me seriously. It has never been my habit to explain to anyone what I'm doing or what I'm thinking; nor do I have any real confidence that you will understand what I'm going to tell you. But I'm going to try.

"I am working harder than I've ever had to work in my life, Scarlett. I burned my bridges in Charleston so thoroughly and so publicly that the stench of the destruction is still in the nostrils of everyone in town. It's immeasurably stronger than the worst Sherman could do, because I was one of their own, and I defied everything they built their lives on. Winning my way back into Charleston's good graces is like climbing an ice-covered mountain in the dark. One slip, and I'm dead. So far I've been very cautious and very slow, and I've made some small headway. I can't take the risk of your destroying all I've done. I want you to leave, and I'm asking your price."

Scarlett laughed with relief. "Is that all? You can set your mind at rest if that's what's worrying you. Why, everybody in Charleston just loves me. I'm rushed off my feet with invitations to this and that, and not a day goes by that somebody doesn't come up to me in the Market and ask my advice about her shopping."

Rhett drew on his cigar. Then he watched the bright end of it cool and become ash. "I was afraid I'd be wasting my breath," he said at last. "I was right. I'll admit you've lasted longer and been more restrained than I expected—oh, yes, I hear some news from town when I'm on the plantation—but you're like a powder keg lashed to my back on that ice-mountain, Scarlett. You're dead weight—unlettered, uncivilized, Catholic, and an exile from everything decent in Atlanta. You could blow up in my face any minute. I want you gone. What will it take?"

Scarlett seized on the only accusation she could defend. "I'd be grateful if you'd tell me what's wrong with being a Catholic, Rhett Butler! We were God-fearing long before you Episcopalians were ever heard of."

Rhett's sudden laughter made no sense to her. "*Pax*, Henry Tudor," he said, which made no sense either. But his next words struck to the bone with their accuracy. "We won't waste time debating theology, Scarlett. The fact is—and you know it as well as I do—that, for no defensible reason, Roman Catholics are looked down on in Southern society. In Charleston today you can attend Saint Phillip's or Saint Michael's or the Huguenot church or First Scots Presbyterian. Even the other Episcopal and Presbyterian churches are slightly suspect, and any other Protestant denomination is considered rank individualistic display. Roman Catholicism is beyond the pale. It's not reasonable, and God knows it's not Christian, but it is a fact."

Scarlett was silent. She knew he was right. Rhett used her momentary defeat to repeat his original question. "What do you want, Scarlett? You can tell me. I've never been shocked at the darker corners of your nature."

He really means it, she thought with despair. All the tea parties I've sat through, and the dreary clothes I had to wear, and tramping through the cold dark every morning to the Market—it was all for nothing. She had come to Charleston to get Rhett back, and she had not won.

"I want you," Scarlett said with stark honesty.

This time it was Rhett who was silent. She could see only his outline and the pale smoke from his cigar. He was so near; if she moved her foot a few inches it would touch his. She wanted him so much that she felt physical pain. She wanted to double over to ease it, hold it inside her so it couldn't grow any worse. But she sat tall, waiting for him to speak.

18

*O*verhead Scarlett could hear a rumble of voices punctuated by Pansy's high-pitched giggle. It made the silence in the cabin seem even worse.

"A half million in gold," said Rhett.

"What did you say?" I must have heard wrong. I told him what was in my heart and he hasn't answered.

"I said I'll give you half a million dollars in gold if you will go away. Whatever pleasure you're finding in Charleston can hardly be worth that much to you. I'm offering you a handsome bribe, Scarlett. Your greedy little heart can't possibly prefer a futile attempt to save our marriage to a fortune bigger than you ever hoped for. As a bonus, if you agree I'll resume payments for expenses of that monstrosity on Peachtree Street."

"You promised last night that you'd send the money to Uncle Henry today," she said automatically. She wished he'd be quiet for a minute. She needed to think. Was it really "a futile attempt"? She refused to believe it.

"Promises are made to be broken," Rhett said calmly. "What about my offer, Scarlett?"

"I need to think."

"Think, then, while I finish my cigar. Then I want your answer. Think what it will be like if you have to pour your own money into that horror of a house you love so much on Peachtree Street; you have no conception of the cost. And then think about having a thousand times the money you've been hoarding all these years—a king's ransom, Scarlett, all at one time and all yours. More than even you could ever spend. Plus the house expenses paid by me. I'll even give you title to the property." The end of his cigar glowed bright.

Scarlett began to think with desperate concentration. She had to find a way to stay. She couldn't go away, not for all the money in the world.

Rhett rose to his feet and walked to the porthole. He threw the cigar out and looked through the opening at the riverbank for a moment until he saw a landmark. The sunlight was bright on his face. How much he's changed since he left Atlanta! thought Scarlett. Then he had been drinking as if he was trying to blot out the world. But now he was Rhett again, with his sun-darkened skin drawn tight over the fine sharp planes of his face and his clear eyes as dark as desire. Under his elegant tailored coat and linen, his muscles were hard, visibly swelling when he moved. He was everything a man should be. She wanted him back, and she was going to get him, no matter what. Scarlett took a deep breath. She was ready when he turned toward her and raised one eyebrow in interrogation. "What's it to be, Scarlett?"

"You want to make a deal you said, Rhett." Scarlett was businesslike. "But you're not bargaining, you're flinging threats at my head like rocks. Besides, I know you're just bluffing about cutting off the money you send to Atlanta. You're almighty concerned about being welcome in Charleston, and folks don't have a very high opinion of a man who doesn't take care of his wife. Your mother wouldn't be able to hold her head up if word got around.

"The second thing—the pile of money—you're right. I'd be glad to have it. But not if it means going back to Atlanta right now. I might as well show my cards 'cause you already know about it. I did some mighty foolish things, and there's no taking them back. Right this minute I haven't got a friend in the whole state of Georgia.

"I'm making friends in Charleston, though. You might not want to believe it, but it's true. And I'm learning a lot, too. As soon as people in Atlanta have enough time to forget a few things, I figure I can make up for my mistakes.

"So I've got a deal to offer you. You stop acting so hateful to me, you act nice and help me have a good time. We go through the Season like a devoted, happy husband and wife. Then, come spring, I'll go home and start over."

She held her breath. He had to say yes, he just had to. The Season lasted for almost eight weeks, and they'd be together every day. There wasn't a man on two feet that she couldn't have eating out of her hand if he was around her that much. Rhett was different from other men, but not that different. There'd never been a man she couldn't get.

"With the money, you mean."

"Well of course with the money. Do you take me for a fool?"

"That's not exactly my idea of a deal, Scarlett. There's nothing in it for me. You take the money I'm willing to pay you to leave, but you don't leave. How do I benefit?"

"I don't stay forever, and I don't tell your mother what a skunk you are." She was almost certain that she saw him smile.

"Do you know the name of the river we're on, Scarlett?"

What a silly question. And he hadn't yet agreed to the Season. What was going on?

"It's the Ashley River." Rhett pronounced the name with exaggerated distinctness. "It calls to mind that estimable gentleman, Mr. Wilkes, whose affections you once coveted. I was a witness to your capacity for dogged devotion, Scarlett, and your single-minded determination is a terrifying thing to behold. You have recently been so amiable as to mention that you have decided to put me in the elevated place once occupied by Ashley. The prospect fills me with alarm."

Scarlett interrupted, she had to. He was going to say no, she could tell. "Oh, fiddle-dee-dee, Rhett. I know there's no point in going after you. You're not nice enough to put up with it. Besides, you know me too well."

Rhett laughed, without humor. "If you recognize just how right you are, we might be able to do business," he said.

Scarlett was careful not to smile. "I'm willing to dicker," she said. "What did you have in mind?"

This time Rhett's abrupt laugh was genuine. "I do believe that the real Miss O'Hara has joined us," he said. "These are my terms: you will confide to my mother that I snore, and therefore we always sleep in separate rooms; after the Saint Cecilia Ball, which concludes the Season, you will express an urgent desire to rush back to Atlanta; and once there, you will immediately appoint a lawyer, Henry Hamilton or any other, to meet with my lawyers to negotiate a settlement and a binding separation agreement. Furthermore, you will never again set foot in Charleston. Nor will you write or otherwise send messages to me or to my mother."

Scarlett's mind was racing. She had almost won. Except for the "separate rooms." Maybe she should ask for more time. No, not ask. She was supposed to be bargaining.

"I might agree to your terms, Rhett, but not your timing. If I pack up the day after all the parties are done, everybody will notice. You'll be going back to the plantation after the Ball. It would make sense if I started thinking about Atlanta then. Why don't we say I'll go the middle of April?"

"I'm willing for you to tarry a while in town after I go to the country. But April first is more appropriate."

Better than she'd hoped for! The Season plus more than a month. And she hadn't said anything herself about staying in the city after he went to the plantation. She could follow him out there.

"I don't want to know which one of us is the April Fool you're talking about, Rhett Butler, but if you swear you'll be nice for the whole time before I leave, you've got a bargain. If you turn mean, then it's you that broke it, not me, and I won't leave."

"Mrs. Butler, your husband's devotion will make you the envy of every woman in Charleston."

He was mocking, but Scarlett didn't care. She'd won.

Rhett opened the hatch, admitting sharp salt air and sunlight and a surprisingly strong breeze. "Do you get seasick, Scarlett?"

"I don't know. I've never been in a boat till yesterday."

"You'll find out soon enough. The harbor's just ahead, and there's a sizable chop. Get a bucket out of the locker behind you just in case." He hurried onto the deck. "Let's get the jib up now and put her on a tack. We're losing way," he shouted into the wind.

A minute later the bench had tilted at an alarming angle, and Scarlett discovered that she was sliding helplessly from it. The slow upriver trip in the wide flat barge the day before hadn't prepared her for the action of a sailing vessel. Coming downriver in the current with a gentle wind half filling the mainsail had been faster, but just as placid as the barge. She scrambled to the short ladder and pulled herself up so that her head was above deck level. The wind took her breath away and lifted the feathered hat from her head. She looked up and saw it fluttering in the air while a sea gull squawked frantically and flapped its wings to soar away from the bird-like object. Scarlett laughed with delight. The boat heeled higher, and water washed over its low side, foaming. It was thrilling! Through the wind Scarlett heard Pansy scream in terror. What a goose that girl was!

Scarlett steadied herself and started up the ladder. The roar of Rhett's voice stopped her. He spun the wheel, and the sloop's deck returned to a bobbing level, its sails flapping. At his gesture, one of the crew took the wheel. The other one was holding Pansy steady while she vomited over the stern. In two steps, Rhett was at the top of the ladder, scowling at Scarlett. "You little idiot, you could have gotten your head knocked off by the boom. Get down below where you belong."

"Oh, Rhett, no! Let me come up where I can see what's happening. It's such fun. I want to feel the wind and taste the spray."

"You don't feel sick? Or frightened?"

The scornful look she gave him was her answer.

* * *

"Oh, Miss Eleanor, it was the most wonderful time I've ever had in my life! I don't know why every man in the world doesn't become a sailor."

"I'm glad you enjoyed yourself dear, but it was very wicked of Rhett to expose you to all that sun and wind. You're red as an Indian." Mrs. Butler ordered Scarlett to her room with glycerine and rosewater compresses on her face. Then she scolded her tall, laughing son until he hung his head in pretended shame.

"If I put up the Christmas greens I brought you, will you let me have dessert after dinner, or do I have to stand in the corner?" he asked in mock humility.

Eleanor Butler spread her hands in surrender. "I don't know what I'm going to do with you, Rhett," she said, but her effort not to smile was a total failure. She loved her son beyond all reason.

That afternoon, while Scarlett was submitting to a treatment of lotions for her sunburn, Rhett carried one of the holly wreaths he had brought from the plantation to Alicia Savage, as a gift from his mother.

"How kind of Eleanor, and of you, Rhett. Thank you. Would you like to have a pre-seasonal toddy?"

Rhett accepted the drink with pleasure, and they talked idly about the unusual weather, the winter thirty years earlier when it had actually snowed, the year it rained for thirty-eight days in a row. They had known each other as children. Their families had houses that shared a garden wall and a mulberry tree with sweet, finger-staining purple fruit on branches that reached low on both sides of the wall.

"Scarlett's scared half out of her wits about the Yankee bedroom prowler," said Rhett after he and Alicia finished reminiscing. "I hope you don't mind talking about it with an old friend who saw up your skirts when you were five."

Mrs. Savage laughed heartily. "I'll talk freely if you'll manage to forget my youthful antipathy to undergarments. I was the despair of the whole family for at least a year. It's funny now ... but this business with the Yankee isn't funny at all. Somebody's going to get trigger-happy and shoot a soldier, and then there'll be the devil to pay."

"Tell me what he looked like, Alicia. I have a theory about him."

"I only saw him for an instant, Rhett ..."

"That should be enough. Tall or short?"

"Tall, yes really very tall. His head was only a foot or so below the top of the curtains, and those windows are seven feet four inches."

Rhett grinned. "I knew I could count on you. You're the only person I've ever known who could identify the biggest scoop of ice cream at a birthday party from the other side of the room. 'Eagle eye' we called you behind your back."

"And to my face, I seem to remember, along with other unpleasant personal remarks. You were a horrid little boy."

"You were a loathsome little girl. I would have loved you even if you had worn underclothes."

"I would have loved you if you hadn't. I looked up your skirts plenty of times, but I couldn't see a thing."

"Be merciful, Alicia. At least call it a kilt."

They smiled companionably at one another. Then Rhett resumed the questioning. Alicia remembered a great many details once she began to think. The soldier was young—very young indeed—with the ungainly movements of a boy who had not gotten accustomed to the spurt of growth. He was very thin, too. The uniform hung loosely on his frame. His wrists showed clearly below the sleeve binding; the uniform might not have been his at all. His hair was dark—"not raven like yours, Rhett, and by the way the touch of gray is extremely becoming; no, his hair must have been brown and looked darker in the shadows." Yes, well cut and almost certainly undressed. She would have smelled Macassar oil. Bit by bit Alicia pieced together her memories. Then her words faltered.

"You know who it is, don't you, Alicia?"

"I must be wrong."

"You must be right. You have a son the right age—about fourteen or fifteen—and you're sure to know his friends. As soon as I heard about this I thought it had to be a Charleston boy. Do you really believe a Yankee soldier would break into a woman's bedroom just to look at the shape of her under a coverlet? This isn't a reign of terror, Alicia, it's a miserable boy who's confused about what his body is doing to him. He wants to know what a woman's body is like without corsets and bustles, wants to know so much that he's driven to stealing looks at sleeping women. Most likely he's ashamed of his thoughts when he sees one fully dressed and awake. Poor little devil. I suppose his father was killed in the War, and there's no man for him to talk to."

"He has an older brother—"

"Oh? Then maybe I'm wrong. Or you're thinking of the wrong boy."

"I'm afraid not. Tommy Cooper is the boy's name. He's the tallest of the lot of them, and the cleanest. Plus he all but choked to death when I said hello to him on the street two days after the incident in my bedroom. His father died at Bull Run. Tommy never knew him. His brother's ten or eleven years older."

"Do you mean Edward Cooper, the lawyer?"

Alicia nodded.

"It's no wonder, then. Cooper is on my mother's Confederate Home committee; I met him at the house. He's all but a eunuch. Tommy'll get no help from him."

"He's not a eunuch at all, he's just too much in love with Anne Hampton to see his brother's needs."

"As you like, Alicia. But I'm going to have a little conference with Tommy."

"Rhett, you can't. You'll scare the poor boy to death."

"The 'poor boy' is scaring the female population of Charleston to death. Thank God nothing has really happened yet. Next time he might lose control. Or he might get shot. Where does he live, Alicia?"

"Church Street, just around the corner from Broad. It's the middle one of the brick houses on the south side of Saint Michael's Alley. But Rhett, what are you going to say? You can't just walk in and haul Tommy out by the scruff of the neck."

"Trust me, Alicia."

Alicia put her hands on each side of Rhett's face and kissed him softly on the lips. "It's good to have you back home again, neighbor. Good luck with Tommy."

Rhett was sitting on the Coopers' piazza drinking tea with Tommy's mother when the boy came home. Mrs. Cooper introduced her son to Rhett, then sent him inside to leave his schoolbooks and wash his hands and face. "Mr. Butler is going to take you to his tailor, Tommy. He has a nephew in Aiken who's growing as fast as you are and he needs you to try on things so he can pick out a Christmas present that will fit."

Out of sight of the adults Tommy grimaced horribly. Then he remembered bits and pieces he'd heard about Rhett's flamboyant youth and he decided he'd be happy to go along and help out Mr. Butler. Maybe he'd even find the nerve to ask Mr. Butler a few questions about things that were bothering him.

Tommy didn't have to ask. As soon as they were well away from the house, Rhett put an arm around the boy's shoulders. "Tom," he said, "I have it in mind to teach you a few valuable lessons. The first is how to lie convincingly to a mother. While we're riding on the streetcar, you and I will talk in some detail about my tailor and his shop and his habits. You'll practice with my assistance until you've got your story straight. Because I don't have a nephew in Aiken, and we're not on our way to the tailor. We're going to ride to the end of the Rutledge Avenue line, then go for a healthy walk to the house where I want you to meet some friends of mine."

Tommy Cooper agreed without argument. He was accustomed to having his elders tell him what to do, and he liked the way Mr. Butler called him "Tom." Before the afternoon was over and Tom was delivered back to his mother, the boy was looking at Rhett with such hero-worship in his young eyes that Rhett knew he'd be saddled with Tom Cooper for years to come.

He was also confident that Tom would never forget the friends they'd gone to see. Among Charleston's many historic "firsts" was the first recorded whorehouse "for gentlemen only." It had moved its location many times in the nearly two centuries of its existence, but it had never missed a day's business, despite wars, epidemics, and hurricanes. One of the specialities of the house was the gentle, discreet introduction of young boys to the pleasures of manhood. It was one of Charleston's cherished traditions. Rhett speculated sometimes about how different his own life might have been if his father had been as diligent about that tradition as he had been about all the other things expected of a Charleston gentleman ... But the past was done. His lips curved in a rueful smile. He had been able, at least, to stand in for Tommy's dead father, who would have done the same for the boy. Traditions did have their uses. For one thing, there'd be no more Yankee midnight prowler. Rhett went home to have a self-congratulatory drink before it was time to pick up his sister at the train station.

19

"Suppose the train's early, Rhett?" Eleanor Butler looked at the clock for the tenth time in two minutes. "I hate to think of Rosemary being at the station with nobody there when it's getting dark. Her maid's only half-trained, you know. And half-witted, too, to my way of thinking. I don't know why Rosemary puts up with her."

"That train has never in its history been less than forty minutes late, Mama, and even if it were on time, that's a half hour from now."

"I asked you most particularly to allow plenty of time to get there. I should have gone myself, like I planned when I didn't know you'd be home."

"Try not to fret, Mama." Rhett explained again what he had already told his mother. "I hired a hackney to pick me up in ten minutes. Then it's a five-minute ride to the station. I'll be fifteen minutes early, the train will be an hour late or more, and Rosemary will arrive home on my arm just in time for supper."

"May I ride with you, Rhett? I'd love a breath of air." Scarlett pictured the hour enclosed in the small cab of the hackney. She'd ask Rhett all about his sister, he'd like that. He was crazy about Rosemary. And if he talked enough, then maybe Scarlett would know what to expect. She was terrified that Rosemary wouldn't like her, that she'd be another Ross. Her brother-in-law's florid letter of apology had done nothing to make her stop loathing him.

"No, my dear, you may not ride with me. I want you to stay just as you are on that couch with the compresses on your eyes. They're still swollen from sunburn."

"Do you want me to come, dear?" Mrs. Butler rolled up her tatting to put it away. "It is going to be a long wait, I'm afraid."

"I don't mind waiting at all, Mama. I've got some plans to work out in my head about spring planting at the plantation."

Scarlett settled back against the cushions, wishing that Rhett's sister wasn't coming home. She had no clear idea of what Rosemary would be like, and she'd rather not find out. She knew, from bits of gossip that she'd heard, that Rosemary's birth had caused a lot of hidden smiles. She was a "change" baby, born when Eleanor Butler was over forty years old. She was also an old maid, one of the domestic casualties of the War—too young to marry before it began, too plain and too poor to attract the attention of the few men available when it was over. Rhett's return to Charleston and his fabulous wealth had set tongues wagging. Rosemary would have a substantial dowry now. But she seemed to be always away, visiting a cousin or a friend in another town. Was she looking for a husband there? Weren't Charleston men good enough for her? Everyone had been waiting for the announcement of an engagement for more than a year, but there was not even a hint of an attachment, much less a betrothal. "Rich pickings for speculation" was the way Emma Anson described the situation.

Scarlett speculated on her own. She'd be delighted to have Rosemary marry, no matter what it cost Rhett. She didn't care to have her in the house. No matter if Rosemary was as plain as a mud fence, she was still younger than Scarlett and Rhett's sister to boot. She'd get too much of his attention. She tensed when she heard the outside door open, a few minutes before suppertime. Rosemary had arrived.

Rhett entered the library, and smiled at his mother.

"Your wandering girl is home at last," he said. "She's sound in mind and limb and as fierce as a lion from hunger. As soon as she gets her hands washed, she'll probably come in here and devour your flesh."

Scarlett looked at the door with apprehension. The young woman who came through it a moment later had a pleasant smile on her face. There was nothing jungle-like about her. But she was as shocking to Scarlett as if she had worn a mane and roared. She looks just like Rhett! No, it's not that. She's got the same black eyes and hair and white teeth, but that's not what's the same. It's more the way she is—she just kind of takes over, like he does. I don't like it, I don't like it at all.

Her green eyes narrowed and she studied Rosemary. She's not really as plain as people said, but she doesn't do anything with herself. Look at how she's got her hair all skinned back in that big knot on the nape. And she's not even wearing earbobs, though her ears are right pretty. Kind of sallow. I guess that's what Rhett's skin would be like if he wasn't always in the sun. But a bright-colored frock would take care of that. She picked the worst possible thing in that dull browny-green. Maybe I could help her out some.

"So this is Scarlett." Rosemary crossed the room in four strides. Oh, my, I'll have to teach her to walk, Scarlett thought. Men don't like women who gallop like that. Scarlett stood before Rosemary reached her, smiling a sisterly smile and tipped her face upward for a social kiss.

Instead of touching cheeks in the approved fashion, Rosemary stared frankly at Scarlett's face. "Rhett said you were feline," she said. "I see what he means, with those green eyes. I do hope you'll purr at me and not spit, Scarlett. I'd like for us to be friends."

Scarlett's mouth gaped soundlessly. She was too startled to speak.

"Mama, do say supper's ready," Rosemary said. She had already turned away. "I told Rhett he was a thoughtless brute not to bring a hamper to the station."

Scarlett's eyes found him, and her temper flared. Rhett was lounging against the frame of the door, his mouth twisted in sardonic amusement. Brute! she thought. You put her up to that. "Feline," am I? I wish I could show you feline. I'd like to scratch that laughter right out of your eyes. She looked quickly at Rosemary. Was she laughing, too? No, she was embracing Eleanor Butler.

"Supper," said Rhett. "I see Manigo coming to announce it."

Scarlett pushed her food around on her plate. Her sunburn was painful and Rosemary's bumptiousness was giving her a headache. For Rhett's sister was passionately and loudly opinionated and argumentative. The cousins she'd been visiting in Richmond were hopeless dolts, she declared, and she had hated every minute of the time there. She was absolutely certain that not one of them had ever read a book—at least, not one worth reading.

"Oh, dear," said Eleanor Butler softly. She looked at Rhett with mute entreaty.

"Cousins are always a trial, Rosemary," he said with a smile. "Let me tell you the latest on Cousin Townsend Ellinton. I saw him in Philadelphia recently, and the meeting left me with blurred vision for a week. I kept trying to look him in the eye and of course I get vertiginous."

"I'd rather be dizzy than bored to death!" his sister interrupted. "Can you picture having to sit around after supper and listen to Cousin Miranda read aloud from the Waverley novels? That sentimental claptrap!"

"I always rather enjoyed Scott, dear, and so did you, I thought," Eleanor said soothingly.

Rosemary was not soothed. "Mama, I didn't know any better, that was years ago."

Scarlett thought longingly of the quiet after supper hours she had been sharing with Miss Eleanor. Obviously there'd be no more of those with Rosemary in the house. How could Rhett possibly be so fond of her? Now she seemed bound and determined to pick a fight with him.

"If I were a man, you'd let me go," Rosemary was shouting at Rhett. "I've been reading the articles about Rome that Mr. Henry James is writing, and I feel like I'll perish of ignorance if I don't get to see it for myself."

"But you're not a man, my dear," Rhett said calmly. "Where on earth did you get copies of *The Nation?* You could be strung up for reading a liberal rag like that."

Scarlett's ears perked up and she broke into the conversation. "Why don't you let Rosemary go, Rhett? Rome's not so far. And I'm sure we must know somebody who has kin there. It can't be any farther than Athens, and the Tarletons have about a million cousins in Athens."

Rosemary gaped at her. "Who are these Tarletons and what does Athens have to do with Rome?" she said.

Rhett coughed to mask his laughter. Then he cleared his throat. "Athens and Rome are the names of country towns in Georgia, Rosemary," he drawled. "Would you like to pay them a visit?"

Rosemary put her hands to her head in a dramatic gesture of despair. "I cannot credit what I'm hearing. Who would want to go to Georgia, for pity's sake? I want to go to Rome, the real Rome, the Eternal City. In Italy!"

Scarlett felt the color rising in her cheeks. *I should have known she meant Italy.*

But before she could burst out as noisily as Rosemary, the door to the dining room crashed open with a bang that silenced all of them with shock, and Ross stumbled, panting for breath, into the candlelit room.

"Help me," he gasped, "the Guard is after me. I shot the Yankee who's been breaking into bedrooms."

In seconds Rhett was at his brother's side, holding his arm. "The sloop's at the dock, and there's no moon; the two of us can sail her," he said with calming authority. As he left the room, he turned his head to speak quietly over his shoulder. "Tell them I left as soon as I delivered

Rosemary so that I could catch the tide upriver, and you haven't seen Ross, don't know anything about anything. I'll send word."

Eleanor Butler rose from her chair without haste, as if this were a normal evening and she had finished eating supper. She walked to Scarlett, put an arm around her. Scarlett was shaking. The Yankees were coming. They'd hang Ross for shooting one of them, and they'd hang Rhett for trying to help Ross escape. Why couldn't he let Ross take care of himself? He had no right to leave his women unprotected and alone when the Yankees were coming.

Eleanor spoke, and there was steel in her voice even though it was as soft and slow as ever. "I'm going to take Rhett's dishes and silver into the kitchen. The servants must be told what to say and there must be no indication that he was here. Will you and Rosemary please rearrange the table for three settings?"

"What are we going to do, Miss Eleanor? The Yankees are coming." Scarlett knew she should stay calm; she despised herself for being so frightened. But she couldn't control her fear. She had come to think that the Yankees were toothless, only laughable and in the way. It was shattering to be reminded that the occupying Army could do anything it wanted, and call it law.

"We're going to finish our supper," said Mrs. Butler. Her eyes began to laugh. "Then I think I shall read aloud from *Ivanhoe*."

"Don't you have anything better to do with your time than bully a household of women?" Rosemary glared at the Union captain, her fisted hands on her hips.

"Sit down and be quiet, Rosemary," said Mrs. Butler. "I apologize for my daughter's rudeness, Captain."

The officer was not won over by Eleanor's conciliatory politeness. "Go ahead and search the house," he ordered his men.

Scarlett lay supine on the couch with chamomile compresses on her sunburned face and swollen eyes. She was grateful for their protection; she didn't have to look at the Yankees. What a cool head Miss Eleanor had, to think of arranging a sickroom scene in the library. Still, curiosity was nearly killing her. She couldn't tell what was going on with only sound to guide her. She could hear footsteps, and doors closing, and then silence. Was the captain gone? Were Miss Eleanor and Rosemary gone, too? She couldn't stand it. She moved one hand slowly up to her eyes and lifted a corner of the damp cloth that covered them.

Rosemary was sitting in the chair near the desk, calmly reading a book.

"Ssst," Scarlett whispered.

Rosemary quickly closed the book and covered the title with her hand. "What is it?" she said, also whispering. "Did you hear something?"

"No, I don't hear a thing. What are they doing? Where's Miss Eleanor? Did they arrest her?"

"For heaven's sake, Scarlett, what are you whispering for?" Rosemary's normal voice sounded terribly loud. "The soldiers are searching the house for weapons; they're confiscating all the guns in Charleston. Mama's following them around to make sure they don't confiscate anything else."

Was that all? Scarlett relaxed. There were no guns in the house; she knew because she'd looked for one herself. She closed her eyes and drifted near sleep. It had been a long day. She remembered the excitement of the water foaming alongside the swift-moving sloop, and for a moment she envied Rhett sailing under the stars. If only she could have been with him instead of Ross. She wasn't worried that the Yankees would catch him; she never worried about Rhett. He was invincible.

When Eleanor Butler returned to the library after seeing the Union soldiers out, she tucked her cashmere shawl around Scarlett, who had fallen into a deep sleep. "No need to disturb her," she said quietly, "she'll be comfortable here. Let's go to bed, Rosemary. You've had a long trip, and I'm tired, and tomorrow's bound to be very active." She smiled to herself when she saw the bookmark placed well along in the pages of *Ivanhoe*. Rosemary was a fast reader. And not nearly as modern as she liked to think she was.

The Market was abuzz with indignation and ill-conceived plans the next morning. Scarlett listened to the agitated conversations around her with scorn. What did they expect, the Charlestonians? That the Yankees would let people go around shooting them and do nothing? All they were going to do was make things worse if they tried to argue or protest. What difference did it make after all this time that General Lee had talked Grant into allowing Confederate officers to keep their sidearms after the surrender at Appomattox? It was still the end of the South, and what good did a revolver do you if you were too poor to buy bullets for it? As for duelling pistols! Who on earth would care about saving them? They weren't good for anything except men showing off how brave they were and getting their fool heads blown off.

She kept her mouth shut and concentrated on the shopping. Otherwise it would never get done. Even Miss Eleanor was running around like a chicken with its head cut off, talking to everybody in a barely audible, urgent tone.

"They say the men all want to finish what Ross started," she told Scarlett when they were walking home. "It's more than they can bear to have their homes ransacked by the troops. We women are going to have to manage things; the men are too hot under the collar."

Scarlett felt a chill of terror. She'd thought it was all talk. Surely no one was going to make things worse! "There's nothing to manage!" she exclaimed. "The only thing to do is lie low till it blows over. Rhett must have gotten Ross away safely or we'd have heard."

Mrs. Butler looked astonished. "We cannot allow the Union Army to get away with this, Scarlett, surely you see that. They've already searched our houses, and they've announced that curfew will be enforced, and they're arresting all the black-market dealers in rationed goods. If we let them keep on the way they're going, soon we'll be back where we were in 'sixty-four when they had their boots on our necks, governing every breath of our lives. It simply won't do."

Scarlett wondered if the whole world was going mad. What did a bunch of tea-drinking, lace-making Charleston ladies think they could do against an army?

She found out two nights later.

Lucinda Wragg's wedding had been scheduled for January twenty-third. The invitations were addressed, and waiting to be delivered on January second, but they were never used. "Terrible efficiency" was Rosemary Butler's tribute to the efforts of Lucinda's mother, her own mother, and all the other ladies of Charleston. Lucinda's wedding took place on December nineteenth, at Saint Michael's Church, at nine o'clock in the evening. The majestic chords of the wedding march sounded through the open doors and windows of the packed and beautifully decorated church precisely at the hour the curfew began. They could be heard clearly in the Guardhouse across the street from Saint Michael's. Some officer later told his wife in the hearing of their cook that he had never seen the men in his command so nervous, not even before they marched into the Wilderness. The whole city heard the story the following day. Everyone had a good laugh, but no one was surprised.

At nine-thirty the entire population of Old Charleston exited from Saint Michael's and went on foot along Meeting Street to the reception at the South Carolina Hall. Men and women and children, aged five to ninety-seven years old, strolled laughing in the warm night air, breaking the law with flagrant defiance. There was no way the Union command could claim to be unaware of the occurrence; it took place under their very noses. Nor was there any way they could arrest the miscreants. The Guardhouse had twenty-six jail cells. Even if the offices and corridors had been used, there was not enough room to hold all the people. Saint Michael's pews had had to be moved to its peaceful graveyard to create enough space for everyone to crowd inside, standing shoulder to shoulder.

During the reception people had to take turns to get out onto the columned porch outside the crowded ballroom for a breath of air and a view of the helpless patrol marching in futile discipline along the empty street.

Rhett had returned to the city that afternoon with the news that Ross was safely in Wilmington. Scarlett confessed to him out on the porch that she'd been afraid to go to the wedding, even with him as escort. "I couldn't believe that a bunch of tea-party ladies could lick the Yankee Army. I've got to say it, Rhett. These Charleston folks have got all the gumption in the world."

He smiled. "I love the arrogant fools, every one of them. Even poor old Ross. I do hope he never learns that he missed the Yankee by a mile, he'd be very embarrassed."

"He didn't even shoot him? I suppose he was drunk." Her voice was thick with contempt. Then it skidded high with fear. "Then the prowler's still around!"

Rhett patted her shoulder. "No. Rest assured, my dear, you'll hear no more of the prowler. My brother and little Lucinda's hasty wedding have put the fear of God into the Yankees." He chuckled with rich, private enjoyment.

"What's so funny?" demanded Scarlett suspiciously. She hated it when people laughed and she didn't know why.

"Nothing you would understand," said Rhett. "I was congratulating myself on single-handedly solving a problem and then my bungling brother went me one better: he inadvertently gave the whole city something to enjoy and feel proud about. Look at them, Scarlett."

The porch was more crowded than ever. Lucinda Wragg, now Lucinda Grimball, was throwing flowers from her bouquet down to the soldiers.

"Humph! I'd sooner throw brickbats myself!"

"I'm sure you would. You've always liked the obvious. Lucinda's way requires imagination." His amused, lazy drawl had become viciously cutting.

Scarlett tossed her head. "I'm going back inside. I'd a far sight rather be suffocated than insulted."

Unseen in the shadow of a nearby column, Rosemary cringed at the cruelty she heard in Rhett's voice and the angry hurt in Scarlett's. Later that night, after bedtime, she tapped on the door of the library where Rhett was reading, then entered and closed the door behind her.

Her face was blotched red from weeping. "I thought I knew you, Rhett," she blurted, "but I don't at all. I heard you talking to Scarlett tonight on the porch of the Hall. How could you be so mean to your own wife? Who are you going to turn on next?"

20

*R*hett rose quickly from his chair and started towards his sister with his arms outstretched. But Rosemary held her hands up in front of her, palms outward, and backed away. His face darkened with pain, and he stood very still, his arms at his sides. He wanted—above all things—to shield Rosemary from hurt, and now he was the source of her anguish.

His mind was filled with Rosemary's short sad story and his part in it. Rhett had never regretted or explained anything he had done in his tempestuous younger years. There was nothing he was ashamed of. Except the effects on his young sister.

Because of his rebellious defiance of family and society, his father had disowned him. Rhett's name was only an inked-over line in the Butler family Bible when Rosemary's birth was recorded. She was more than twenty years his junior. He did not even see her until she was thirteen, an awkward girl with long legs, large feet, and budding breasts. Their mother had disobeyed her husband for one of the few times in her life when Rhett began the dangerous life of blockade runner through the Union fleet and into Charleston Harbor. She came by night to the dock where his ship was moored, bringing Rosemary to meet him. The deep vein of loving tenderness in Rhett was inexpressively moved by the confusion and need that he sensed in his young sister, and he welcomed her to his heart with all the warmth that their father had never been able to give. In turn, Rosemary gave him the trust and loyalty that their father had never inspired. The bond between brother and sister had never been severed, despite the fact that they saw each other no more than a dozen times from first meeting until Rhett came home to Charleston eleven years later.

He had never forgiven himself for accepting their mother's reassurance that Rosemary was well and happy and sheltered by the money he lavished on them once his father was dead and could no longer intercept and return it. He should have been more alert, more attentive, he accused himself later. Then perhaps his sister would not have grown up distrusting men the way she did. Perhaps she would have loved and married and had children.

As it was, when he returned home he found a twenty-four-year-old woman with the same awkwardness of the thirteen-year-old he had first met. She was uncomfortable with all men except him; she used the distant lives in novels as a substitute for the uncertainty of life in the world; she rejected the conventions of society about how a woman should look and think and behave. Rosemary was a bluestocking, distressingly forthright, and totally lacking in feminine wiles and vanity.

Rhett loved her, and he respected her prickly independence. He couldn't make up for the years he'd missed, but he could give her the rarest gift of all—his inner self. He was completely honest with Rosemary, talked to her as an equal and, on occasion, even confided the secrets of his heart to her, as he had never done to any other person. She recognized the immensity of his gift, and she adored him. In the fourteen months that Rhett had been home, the over-tall, ill-at-ease, innocent spinster and the over-sophisticated, disillusioned adventurer had become the closest of friends.

Now Rosemary felt betrayed. She'd seen a side of Rhett that she hadn't known existed, a streak of cruelty in the brother she'd known as unfailingly kind and loving. She was confused and distrustful.

"You haven't answered my question, Rhett." Rosemary's reddened eyes were accusing.

"I'm sorry, Rosemary," he said cautiously. "I am deeply sorry you happened to hear me. It was something I had to do. I want her to go away and leave all of us alone."

"But she's your wife!"

"I left her, Rosemary. She wouldn't divorce me as I offered, but she knew the marriage was over."

"Then why is she here?"

Rhett shrugged. "Perhaps we should sit down. It's a long, tiring story."

* * *

Slowly, methodically, rigidly unemotional, Rhett told his sister about Scarlett's two earlier marriages, about his proposal and Scarlett's agreement to marry him for his money. He also told her about Scarlett's near-obsessive love for Ashley Wilkes throughout all the years he'd known her.

"But if you knew that, why on earth did you marry her?" Rosemary asked.

"Why?" Rhett's mouth twisted in a smile. "Because she was so full of fire and so recklessly, stubbornly brave. Because she was such a child beneath all her pretenses. Because she was unlike any woman I had ever known. She fascinated me, infuriated me, drove me mad. I loved her as consumingly as she loved him. From the day I first laid eyes on her. It was a kind of disease." There was a weight of sorrow in his voice.

He bowed his head into his two hands and laughed shakily. His voice was muffled and blurred by his fingers. "What a grotesque practical joke life is. Now Ashley Wilkes is a free man and would marry Scarlett on a moment's notice, and I want to be rid of her. Naturally that makes her determined to have me. She wants only what she cannot have."

Rhett raised his head. "I'm afraid," he said quietly, "afraid that it will all begin again. I know that she's heartless and completely selfish, that she's like a child who cries for a toy and then breaks it once she has it. But there are moments when she tilts her head at a certain angle, or she smiles that gleeful smile, or she suddenly looks lost—and I come close to forgetting what I know."

"My poor Rhett." Rosemary put her hand on his arm.

He covered it with his own. Then he smiled at her, and he was himself again. "You see before you, my dear, the man who was once the marvel of the Mississippi riverboats. I've gambled all my life, and I've never lost. I'll win this hand, too. Scarlett and I have made a deal. I couldn't risk having her here in this house too long. Either I would fall in love with her again or I would kill her. So I dangled gold in front of her, and her greed for money outbalanced the undying love she professes for me. She will be leaving for good when the Season is over. Until then all I have to do is keep her at a distance, outlast her, and outwit her. I'm almost looking forward to it. She hates to lose, and she lets it show. It's no fun beating someone who's a good loser." His eyes laughed at his sister. Then they sobered. "It would destroy Mama if she knew the truth about my miserable marriage, but she'd be ashamed if she knew that I'd walked out on it, no matter how unhappy it was. A terrible dilemma. This way, Scarlett will leave, I will be the injured but bravely stoic party, and there'll be no disgrace."

"And no regrets?"

"Only for having been a fool once—years ago. I'll have the very powerful solace of not being a fool the second time. It does a lot to erase the humiliation of the first time."

Rosemary stared, unabashedly curious. "What if Scarlett changed? She might grow up."

Rhett grinned. "To quote the lady herself—'when pigs fly.'"

21

*G*o away." Scarlett buried her face in a pillow.

"It's Sunday, Miss Scarlett, you can't sleep late. Miss Pauline and Miss Eulalie is expecting you."

Scarlett groaned. It was enough to make a person turn Episcopalian. At least they got to sleep later; the service at Saint Michael's wasn't until eleven o'clock. She sighed and got out of bed.

Her aunts wasted no time in beginning to lecture her about what would be expected of her in the upcoming Season. She listened impatiently while Eulalie and Pauline lectured her on the importance of decorum, inconspicuousness, deference to her elders, ladylike behavior. For heaven's sake! She'd cut her teeth on all those rules. Her mother and Mammy had drummed them into her from the time she could walk. Scarlett set her jaw mutinously and stared at her feet as they walked to Saint Mary's. She just wouldn't listen, that's all.

However, when they were back at the aunts' house having breakfast Pauline said something that forced her to pay attention.

"You needn't scowl at me, Scarlett. I'm only telling you for your own good what people are saying. There's a rumor that you have two brand new ball gowns. It's a scandal, when everyone else is happy to make do with what they've been wearing for years. You're new in town and you have to be careful of your reputation. Rhett's, too. People haven't made up their minds about him yet, you know."

Scarlett's heart gave a sickening lurch. Rhett would kill her if she ruined things for him. "What about Rhett? Please tell me, Aunt Pauline."

Pauline told. With relish. All the old stories—he was expelled from West Point, his own father had disowned him for his wild behavior, he was known to have made money in disreputable ways, as a professional gambler on Mississippi riverboats, in the brawling gold fields of California, and worst of all through consorting with scallywags and carpetbaggers. True, he'd been a brave soldier for the Confederacy, a blockade runner and a gunner in Lee's Army, and he'd given most of his dirty money to the Confederate cause—

Ha! Scarlett thought. Rhett sure is good at spreading stories.

—but nevertheless, his past was definitely unsavory. It was all well and good that he'd come home to take care of his mother and sister, but he'd taken his own sweet time getting around to it. If his father hadn't starved himself to death to pay for a big life insurance, his mother and sister would probably have died of neglect.

Scarlett ground her teeth to keep from shouting at Pauline. It wasn't true about the insurance! Rhett had never, never for a minute, stopped caring about his mother, but his father wouldn't let her accept anything from him! It was only when Mr. Butler died that Rhett was able to buy Miss Eleanor the house and give her money. And even Mrs. Butler had to put the story around about the insurance to account for her prosperity. Because Rhett's money was considered dirty. Money was money, couldn't these stiff-necked Charlestonians see that? What difference did it make where it came from if it kept a roof over their heads and food in their bellies?

Why didn't Pauline stop preaching at her? What on earth was she talking about now? The stupid fertilizer business. That was another joke. There wasn't enough fertilizer in the world to account for the money Rhett was throwing away on foolishness like chasing down his mother's old furniture and silver and pictures of great-grandparents, and paying perfectly healthy men to baby his precious camellias instead of growing good money crops.

". . . there are a number of Charlestonians doing very well from phosphates, but they don't make a show of it. You must guard against this tendency to extravagance and ostentation. He's your husband, it's your duty to warn him. Eleanor Butler thinks he can do no wrong, she's always spoiled him, but for her good as well as yours and Rhett's you've got to see to it that the Butlers don't make themselves conspicuous."

"I tried to speak to Eleanor," sniffed Eulalie, "but she didn't hear a word I said, I'm sure of it."

Scarlett's narrowed eyes glinted dangerously. "I'm more grateful than I can tell you," she said with exaggerated sweetness, "and I'll pay attention to every word. Now I really have to run. Thank you for the delicious breakfast." She stood, pecked a kiss on the cheek of each aunt, and hurried to the door. If she didn't get away this very minute, she'd scream. Still, she'd better talk to Rhett about what the aunts had said.

"You do see, don't you, Rhett, why I thought I'd better tell you about it? People are criticizing your mother. I know my aunts are tiresome old busybodies but it's tiresome old busybodies who always seem to cause all the trouble. You remember Mrs. Merriwether and Mrs. Meade and Mrs. Elsing."

Scarlett had hoped Rhett would thank her. She certainly wasn't prepared for his laughter. "Bless their interfering old hearts," he chuckled. "Come with me, Scarlett, you'll have to tell Mama."

"Oh, Rhett, I couldn't. She'll be so upset."

"You must. This is serious. Absurd, but the most serious matters always are. Come along. And take that look of daughterly concern off your face. You don't give a damn what happens to my mother as long as the party invitations keep arriving, and we both know it."

"That's not fair! I love your mother."

Rhett was halfway out the door, but he turned and strode back to face her. He took her shoulders in his hands and jolted her so that her face was turned up. His eyes were cold, examining her expression as if she were on trial. "Don't lie to me about my mother, Scarlett. I warn you, it's dangerous."

He was close to her, touching her. Scarlett's lips parted, she knew her eyes must be telling him how much she longed for him to kiss her. If he'd only lower his head a little, she'd meet his lips with hers. Her breath was caught in her throat.

Rhett's hands tightened, she felt them, he was going to pull her to him— A tiny sob of joy vibrated in her trapped breath.

"Damn you!" Rhett growled quietly. He pushed himself away from her. "Come downstairs. Mama's in the library."

Eleanor Butler dropped her tatting into her lap and laid her hands on it, left atop right. It was a signal that she was taking Scarlett's account seriously, giving her full concentration. At the end Scarlett waited nervously for Mrs. Butler's reaction. "Sit down, both of you," Eleanor said serenely. "Eulalie is quite wrong. I paid full attention when she spoke to me about spending so much money." Scarlett's eyes widened. "And I gave it considerable thought afterwards," Eleanor continued. "Particularly with regard to giving Rosemary the Grand Tour for her Christmas gift, Rhett. No one in Charleston has been able to do that for many years, practically since the time you would have gone, if you hadn't been such a handful that your father sent you to military school instead.

"However, I decided that there is no real risk of ostracism. Charlestonians are pragmatic; old civilizations always are. We recognize that wealth is desirable and poverty extremely disagreeable. And if one is poor oneself, it's helpful to have rich friends. People would consider it unforgivable—not merely deplorable—were I to serve scuppernong wine for champagne."

Scarlett's brow was knotted. She was having some trouble understanding. Not that it mattered—the even, peaceful tone of Mrs. Butler's voice told her that everything was all right. "Perhaps we have been a little too visible," Eleanor was saying, "but right now no one in Charleston can afford to disapprove of the Butlers because Rosemary might just decide to accept the courtship of a son or brother or cousin of the family, and her marriage settlement could solve any number of awkwardnesses."

"Mama, you're a shameless cynic." Rhett laughed.

Eleanor Butler simply smiled.

"What are you laughing at?" said Rosemary, as she opened the door. Her eyes moved quickly from Rhett to Scarlett and back again. "I could hear you guffawing halfway down the hall, Rhett. Tell me the joke."

"Mama was being worldly," he said. He and Rosemary had long since united in a pact to protect their mother from the realities of the world, and they smiled at one another like conspirators. Scarlett felt shut out, and she turned her back on them.

"May I sit with you a while, Miss Eleanor? I want to ask your advice about what to wear to the ball." See if I care, Rhett Butler, that you cater to your old maid sister like she was Queen of the May. And if you think you can upset me or make me jealous, you'll just have to think again!

Eleanor Butler watched, puzzled, as Scarlett's mouth fell half-open in surprise, and her eyes glittered with excitement. Eleanor looked behind her shoulder, wondering what Scarlett saw.

But although Scarlett's gaze was fixed, she wasn't looking at anything. She was blinded by the brightness of the thought that had come to her.

Jealous! What a fool I've been! Of course that's it. It explains everything. Why did it take me so long to see it? Rhett practically rubbed my nose in it when he made such a to-do about the name of the river. Ashley. He's still jealous of Ashley. He's always been crazy jealous of Ashley, that's why he wanted me so much. All I have to do is make him jealous again.

Not of Ashley—heavens no—if I so much as threw a smile in his direction
he'd be looking pitiful at me and begging me to marry him. No, I'll find
somebody else, somebody right here in Charleston. That won't be hard at
all. The Season starts in six days and there'll be parties and balls and dancing and sitting out to take a bite of cake and a cup of punch. This might
be fancy old snobby Charleston, but men don't change with geography. I'll
have a string of beaux hanging after me before the first party's half done. I
can hardly wait.

After Sunday dinner the whole family went to the Confederate Home
carrying baskets of greens from the plantation and two of Miss Eleanor's
whiskey-soaked fruitcakes. Scarlett almost danced along the sidewalk,
swinging her basket and singing a Christmas song. Her gaiety was infectious, and soon the four of them were carolling at houses on the way.
"Come in," cried the owners of each house they serenaded. "Come with
us," Mrs. Butler suggested instead, "we're going to decorate the Home."
There were more than a dozen willing helpers when they reached the lovely
shabby old house on Broad Street.

The orphans squealed with anticipation when the cakes were unpacked, but, "Grown-ups only," Eleanor said firmly. "However..." And
she took out the sugar cookies she had brought for them. Two of the
widows who lived at the Home hurriedly fetched cups of milk and settled
the children in chairs around a low table on the piazza. "Now we can hang
the greens in peace," said Mrs. Butler. "Rhett, you'll do the ladder-climbing
please."

Scarlett seated herself next to Anne Hampton. She liked being extra
nice to the shy young girl because Anne was so much like Melanie. It made
Scarlett feel that in some way she was making up for all the unkind
thoughts she had had about Melly all the years that Melly was so resolutely
loyal to her. Also, Anne was so openly admiring that her company was
always a pleasure. Her soft voice was almost animated when she complimented Scarlett on her hair. "It must be wonderful to have such dark, rich-
looking color," she said. "It's like the deepest black silk. Or like a painting
I saw once of a beautiful, sleek black panther." Anne's face shone with
innocent worship, then blushed for her impertinence in making such a personal remark.

Scarlett patted her hand kindly. Anne couldn't help it if she was like a
soft, timid, brown field mouse. Later, when the decorations were done and
the tall rooms smelled sweetly resinous from pine branches, Anne excused
herself to go usher in the children for carol singing. How Melly would have

loved this, thought Scarlett. There was a lump in her throat when she looked at Anne, her arms encircling two nervous little girls while they sang a duet. Melly was so crazy fond of children. For an instant Scarlett felt guilty that she hadn't sent more Christmas presents to Wade and Ella, but then the duet was over and it was time to join in the singing, and she had to concentrate on remembering all the verses of "The First Noël."

"What fun that was!" she exclaimed after they left the Home. "I do love Christmastime."

"I do, too," said Eleanor. "It's a good breathing spell before the Season. Though this year won't be as peaceful as usual. The poor Yankee soldiers will be down on our necks, more than likely. Their colonel can't just let it slide that we all broke curfew with such a bang." She giggled like a girl. "What fun that was!"

"Honestly, Mama!" said Rosemary. "How can you call those bluecoated wretches 'poor' Yankees?"

"Because they'd much rather be home with their own families for the holidays than here badgering us. I think they're embarrassed."

Rhett chuckled. "You and your cronies have something up your lace-edged sleeves, I'll bet."

"Only if we're driven to it." Mrs. Butler giggled again. "We figure today's calm was only because their colonel is such a Bible-thumper he won't order any action on the Sabbath. Tomorrow will tell the tale. In the old days they used to harass us by going through our baskets to search for contraband when we left the Market. If they try it again, they'll be dipping their hands into some interesting things underneath the turnip greens and rice."

"Innards?" guessed Rosemary.

"Broken eggs?" Scarlett offered.

"Itching powder," suggested Rhett.

Miss Eleanor giggled for the third time. "And a few more things, besides," she said complacently. "We developed a number of interesting tactics back then. This crop of soldiers wasn't around; it will all be new to them. I'll bet a lot of these men never even heard of poison sumac. I dislike being so uncharitable at Christmas, but they've got to learn that we quit being afraid of them a long time ago.

"I do wish Ross could be here," she added abruptly, all laughter gone. "When do you suppose it will be safe for your brother to come back home, Rhett?"

"It depends on how quickly you and your friends get the Yankees whipped into shape, Mama. Certainly in time for the Saint Cecilia."

"That's all right, then. It doesn't matter if he misses all the rest as long as he's home for the Ball." Scarlett could hear the capital B in Miss Eleanor's voice.

Scarlett was certain that the hours would drag by until the twenty-sixth and the beginning of the Season. But to her surprise the time passed so quickly that she could hardly keep up. The most entertaining part of it all was the battle with the Yankees. The colonel did, indeed, order retaliation for the curfew humiliation. And on Monday the Market rang with laughter as Charleston's ladies packed their baskets with the weapons of their choice.

The following day the soldiers were careful to keep their gloves on. Plunging a hand into some loathsome-feeling substance or suddenly being afflicted with fiery itching and swelling were not experiences they were willing to repeat.

"The fools should have known we'd expect them to do just what they did," Scarlett said to Sally Brewton at a whist party that afternoon. Sally agreed, with a happy reminiscent laugh.

"I had a loose-lidded box of lamp black in my shopping," she said. "What was yours?"

"Cayenne pepper. I was scared to death I'd start sneezing and give the whole trick away . . . speaking of tricks, I believe that's mine." New rationing regulations had been posted the day before, and the ladies of Charleston were now gambling for coffee, not money. With the black market effectively out of business for the time being, this was the highest-stakes card game Scarlett had ever been in. She loved it.

She loved tormenting the Yankees, too. There were still patrols on Charleston's streets but their noses had been tweaked and would be tweaked again and again until they admitted defeat. With her as one of the tweakers.

"Deal," she said, "I feel lucky." Only a few more days and she would be at a ball, dancing with Rhett. He was keeping away from her now, managing things so that they were never alone together, but on the dance floor they would be together—and touching—and alone, no matter how many other couples were on the floor.

Scarlett held the white camellias Rhett had sent her to the cluster of curls at the nape of her neck and twisted her head to see herself in the looking glass. "It looks like a glob of fat on a bunch of sausages," she said with disgust. "Pansy, you'll have to do my hair different. Pile it on top."

She could pin the flowers in between the waves, that wouldn't be too bad. Oh, why did Rhett have to be so mean, telling her that his precious old plantation flowers were the only jewels she could wear? It was bad enough that her ball gown was so dowdy. But with nothing to dress up the plainness except a bunch of flowers—she might as well wear a flour sack with a hole cut for her head. She'd counted on her pearls and her diamond earbobs.

"You don't have to brush a hole in my scalp," she grumbled at Pansy.

"Yes'm." Pansy continued to brush the long dark mass of hair with vigorous strokes, eradicating the curls that had taken so long to arrange.

Scarlett looked at her reflection with growing satisfaction. Yes, that was much better. Her neck was really too pretty to cover. It was much better to wear her hair up. And her earbobs would show up better. She was going to wear them, no matter what Rhett had told her. She had to be dazzling, she had to win the admiration of every man at the ball, and the hearts of at least a few. That would make Rhett sit up and take notice.

She fastened the diamonds into her earlobes. There! She tilted her head from side to side, pleased with the effect.

"Do you like this, Miss Scarlett?" Pansy gestured toward her handiwork.

"No. Do it fuller above the ears." Thank goodness Rosemary had turned down her offer to lend Pansy this evening. Though why Rosemary hadn't jumped at the chance was a mystery; she needed all the help she could get. She'd probably bundle her hair into the same lumpy old-maid bun she always wore. Scarlett smiled. Entering the ballroom with Rhett's sister would only call attention to how much prettier she was.

"That's fine, Pansy," she said, good humor restored. Her hair shone like a raven's wing. The white flowers would actually be very becoming. "Hand me some hairpins."

A half hour later, Scarlett was ready. She took one final look in the tall pier glass. The deep blue watered silk of her gown shimmered in the lamp light and made her powdered bare shoulders and bosom look as pale as alabaster. Her diamonds sparkled brilliantly, as did her green eyes. Black velvet ribbon in loops bordered the gown's train and a wide black velvet bow lined with paler blue silk sat atop the gown's bustle, emphasizing her tiny waist. Her slippers were made of blue velvet with black laces, and narrow black velvet ribbon was tied around her throat and each wrist. White camellias tied with black velvet bows were pinned to her shoulders and filled a silver-lace bouquet holder. She had never looked lovelier, and she recognized it. Excitement made her cheeks rosy with natural color.

* * *

Scarlett's first ball in Charleston was full of surprises. Almost nothing was the way she expected it to be. First she was told that she'd have to wear her boots, not her dancing slippers. They were going to walk to the Ball. She would have ordered a hackney if she'd known that, she couldn't believe that Rhett hadn't done it. It didn't help that Pansy was supposed to carry her slippers in a Charleston contraption called a "slipper bag" because she didn't have a slipper bag, and it took Miss Eleanor's maid fifteen minutes to find a basket to use instead. Why hadn't anyone told her she needed one of the miserable things? "We didn't think of it," Rosemary said. "Everybody has slipper bags."

Everybody in Charleston maybe, thought Scarlett, but not in Atlanta. People don't walk to balls there, they ride. Her happy anticipation of her first Charleston ball began to change to uneasy apprehension. What else was going to be different?

Everything, she discovered. Charleston had developed formalities and rituals in the long years of its history that were unknown in the vigorous semi-frontier world of North Georgia. When the fall of the Confederacy cut off the lavish wealth that had allowed the formality to develop, the rituals survived, the only thing that remained of the past, cherished and unchangeable for that reason.

There was a receiving line inside the door of the ballroom at the top of the Wentworth house. Everyone had to line up on the stairs, waiting to enter the room one by one and then shake hands and murmur something to Minnie Wentworth, then to her husband, their son, their son's wife, their daughter's husband, their married daughter, their unmarried daughter. While, all the time, the music was playing and earlier arrivals were dancing, and Scarlett's feet were itching to dance.

In Georgia, she thought impatiently, the people giving the party come forward to meet their guests. They don't keep them waiting in line like a chain gang. It's a sight more welcoming than this foolishness.

Just before she followed Mrs. Butler into the room, a dignified man-servant offered her a tray. A pile of folded papers was on it, little booklets held together by thin blue twine with a tiny pencil hanging from it. Dance cards? They must be dance cards. Scarlett had heard Mammy talk about balls in Savannah when Ellen O'Hara was a girl, but she'd never quite believed that parties were so peaceful that a girl looked in a book to see who she was supposed to dance with. Why, the Tarleton twins and the Fontaine boys would have split their britches laughing if anyone told them they had to write their names on a tiny piece of paper with a little pencil so dinky that it would break in a real man's fingers! She wasn't even sure she wanted to dance with the kind of pantywaist who'd be willing to do that.

Yes, she was! She was sure she'd dance with the devil himself, horns and tail and all, just to be able to dance. It seemed like ten years, not one, since the Masquerade Ball in Atlanta.

"I'm so happy to be here," said Scarlett to Minnie Wentworth, and her voice throbbed with sincerity. She smiled at all the other Wentworths, each in turn, and then she was through the line. She turned toward the dancing, her feet already moving in time to the music, and she drew in her breath. Oh, it was so beautiful—so strange and yet so familiar, like a dream she only half-remembered. The candlelit room was alive with music, with the colors and rustling of whirling skirts. Along the walls dowagers were sitting in fragile gold-painted chairs just as they always had, whispering behind their fans to one another about the things they had always whispered about: the young people who were dancing too close together, the latest horror story of someone's daughter's prolonged childbirth, the newest scandal about their dearest friends. Waiters in full-dress suits moved from group to group of men and women who weren't dancing with silver trays of filled glasses and frosted silver julep cups. There was a hum of blended voices, punctuated by laughter, high and deep, the age-old beloved noise of fortunate light hearted people enjoying themselves. It was as if the old world, the beautiful carefree world of her youth, still existed, as if nothing was changed, and there had never been a War.

Her sharp eyes could see the scabby paint on the walls and the spur-gouges in the floor under the layers of wax, but she refused to notice. Better to enter the illusion, to forget the War and the Yankee patrols on the street outside. There was music and there was dancing and Rhett had promised to be nice. Nothing more was needed.

Rhett was more than merely nice; he was charming. And no one on earth could be more charming than Rhett when he wanted to be. Unfortunately he was just as charming to everyone else as he was to her. She alternated wildly between pride that every other woman envied her and raging jealousy that Rhett was paying attention to so many others. He was attentive to her, she couldn't accuse him of neglect. But he was attentive to his mother, too, and to Rosemary, and to dozens of other women who were dreary old matrons in Scarlett's opinion.

She told herself that she mustn't care, and after a while she didn't. As each dance ended, she was immediately surrounded by men who insisted that her previous partner introduce them so that they could beg her for the dance to follow.

It was not simply that she was new in town, a fresh face in a crowd of people who all knew each other. She was compellingly alluring. Her decision to make Rhett jealous had added a reckless glitter to her fascinating, unusual green eyes, and a heated flush of excitement colored her cheeks like a red flag signalling danger.

Many of the men who vied for her dances were the husbands of friends she'd made, women she had called on, had partnered at the whist table, had gossiped with over coffee at the Market. She didn't care. Time enough to mend the damage after Rhett was hers again. In the meantime she was being admired and complimented and flirted with, and she was in her element. Nothing had really changed. Men still responded the same way to her fluttering eyelashes and flickering dimple and outrageous flattery. They'll believe any lie you tell them, long as it makes them feel like heroes, she thought, with a wicked smile of delight that made her partner miss a step. She jerked her toes out from under his foot. "Oh, do say you forgive me!" she begged. "I must have caught my heel in the hem of my dress. What a dreadful mistake to make, especially when I'm lucky enough to be waltzing with a wonderful dancer like you."

Her eyes were beguiling and the rueful pout that went with her apology made her lips look as if they were ready for a kiss. There were some things that a girl never forgot how to do.

"What a lovely party!" she said happily when they were walking back to the house.

"I'm pleased that you had a nice time," Eleanor Butler said. "And I'm very, very pleased for you, too, Rosemary. You seemed to be enjoying yourself."

"Hah! I hated it, Mama, you should know that. But I'm so happy that I'm going to Europe that it didn't bother me to go to the silly Ball."

Rhett laughed. He was walking behind Scarlett and Rosemary, his mother's hand in his left arm. His laughter was warm in the cold December night. Scarlett thought of the warmth of his body, imagined that she could sense it at her back. Why wasn't she on his arm, close to that warmth? She knew why: Mrs. Butler was old, it was appropriate that her son support her. But that didn't lessen Scarlett's longing.

"Laugh all you please, brother, dear," Rosemary said, "but I don't think it's funny." She was walking backwards now, half-trampling the train of her gown. "I didn't get to say two words to Miss Julia Ashley all night because I had to dance with all those ridiculous men."

"Who's Miss Julia Ashley?" Scarlett asked. The name commanded her interest.

"She's Rosemary's idol," said Rhett, "and the only person I've ever been afraid of in my adult life. You would have noticed Miss Ashley if you'd seen her, Scarlett. She always wears black, and she looks like she's been drinking vinegar."

"Oh, you—!" Rosemary sputtered. She ran to Rhett and hit him on the chest with her fists.

"*Pax!*" he cried. He put his right arm around her and pulled her close to his side.

Scarlett felt the wind cold off the river. She lifted her chin against it, turned forward and walked the remaining few steps to the house alone.

22

*A*nother Sunday meant another lecture from Eulalie and Pauline, Scarlett was sure of it. She was, in fact, more than a little frightened about her behavior at the Ball. Perhaps she'd been just a little bit too—lively, that was it. But she hadn't had fun like that in so long, and it wasn't her fault that she attracted so much more attention than the prissy Charleston ladies, was it? Besides, she was really only doing it for Rhett, so he would stop being so cold and distant to her. No one could blame a wife for trying to hold her marriage together.

She suffered in silence the heavy unexpressed disapproval of her equally silent aunts during the walk to and from Saint Mary's. Eulalie's mournful sniffling during Mass set her teeth on edge, but she managed to block it out by daydreaming about the moment when Rhett would abandon his stiff-necked pride and admit that he still loved her. For he did, didn't he? Whenever he held her in his arms to dance she felt like her knees had turned to water. Surely she couldn't feel the lightning in the air when they touched unless he felt it too. Could she?

She'd find out soon. He'd have to do more than just rest his gloved hand on her waist for dancing when New Year's Eve came. He'd have to kiss her at midnight. Only five more days to get through, and then their lips would meet and he'd have to believe how much she truly loved him. Her kiss would tell him more than words ever could . . .

The ancient beauty and mystery of the Mass unfolded before her unseeing eyes while Scarlett imagined her wishes coming true. Pauline's sharp elbow stabbed her whenever her responses were late.

The silence continued unbroken when they sat down for breakfast. Scarlett felt as if every nerve in her body were exposed to the air, to Pauline's icy stare, to the sound of Eulalie's sniffing. She couldn't stand it any longer, and she burst out in angry attack at them before they could attack her.

"You told me that everybody walked everywhere, and I've got broken blisters all over my feet from doing what you said. Last night the street in front of the Wentworths' ball was chock full of carriages!"

Pauline raised her eyebrows and tightened her lips. "Do you see what I mean, Sister?" she said to Eulalie. "Scarlett is determined to turn her back on everything that Charleston stands for."

"It's hard to see what importance the carriages have, Sister, compared with the things we agreed we should talk about to her."

"As an example," Pauline insisted. "It's an excellent example of the attitude behind all the other things."

Scarlett drained her cup of the pale, weak coffee Pauline had poured and set it down in the saucer with a crash. "I'll take it as a kindness if you'll stop talking about me as if I was deaf and dumb. You can preach at me till you're blue in the face if you want to, but first tell me who all those carriages belonged to!"

The aunts stared at her from wide eyes. "Why, the Yankees, of course," said Eulalie.

"Carpetbaggers," added Pauline with precision.

With corrections and amendments to every sentence spoken by the other, the sisters told Scarlett that the coachmen were still loyal to their pre-War owners, although they now worked for the new-rich, uptown people. During the Season they manipulated their employers in various clever ways so that they could drive "their white folks" to balls and receptions if the distance was too far or the weather too inclement for them to walk.

"On the night of the Saint Cecilia, they just flat out insist on having the evening off and the carriage for their own use," Eulalie added.

"They're all trained coachmen and very high-toned," Pauline said, "so the carpetbaggers are terrified of offending them." She was very close to laughter. "They know the coachmen despise them. House servants have always been the most snobbish creatures on earth."

"Certainly these house servants," said Eulalie gleefully. "After all, they're Charlestonians just as much as we are. That's why they care so much about the Season. The Yankees took whatever they could and tried to destroy everything else, but we still have our Season."

"And our pride!" Pauline announced.

With their pride and a penny, they could ride the streetcar anyplace it went, Scarlett thought sourly. But she was grateful that they'd gotten side-tracked onto the stories about faithful old family servants that occupied them for the rest of the meal. She was even careful to eat only half her breakfast so that Eulalie would be able to finish it as soon as she was gone. Aunt Pauline ran a mighty stingy household.

She was pleasantly surprised to find Anne Hampton at the Butler house when she got there. It would be nice to bask in Anne's admiration for a while after the hours of cold disapproval from her aunts.

But Anne and the widow from the Home who was with her were almost totally occupied with the bowls full of camellias that had been sent down from the plantation.

And so was Rhett. "Burnt to the ground," he was saying, "but stronger than ever once they're cleared of weeds."

"Oh, look!" Anne exclaimed. "There's the Reine des Fleurs."

"And a Rubra Plena!" The thin elderly widow cupped her pale hands to hold the vibrant red blossom. "I used to keep mine in a crystal vase on the pianoforte."

Anne's eyes blinked rapidly. "So did we, Miss Harriet, and the Alba Plenas on the tea table."

"My Alba Plena isn't as healthy as I'd hoped," Rhett said. "The buds are all kind of stunted."

The widow and Anne both laughed. "You won't see any flowers until January, Mr. Butler," Anne explained. "The Alba's a late bloomer."

Rhett's mouth twisted in a rueful smile. "So am I, it seems, where gardening is concerned."

My grief! thought Scarlett. Next thing I reckon they'll start chatting about is whether cow patties are better than horse droppings for fertilizer. What kind of sissyness is that for a man like Rhett to say! She turned her back on them and sat in a chair close to the settee where Eleanor Butler was doing her tatting.

"This piece is almost long enough to trim the neck of your claret gown when it needs freshening," she said to Scarlett with a smile. "Halfway through the Season it's always nice to have a change. I'll be finished with it by then."

"Oh, Miss Eleanor, you're always so sweet and thoughtful. I feel my bad mood going right away. Honestly, I marvel at you being such good friends with my Aunt Eulalie. She's not like you at all. She's forever sniffling and complaining and squabbling with Aunt Pauline."

Eleanor dropped her ivory tatting shuttle. "Scarlett, you astonish me.

Of course Eulalie's my friend; I think of her as practically a sister. Don't you know that she almost married my younger brother?"

Scarlett's jaw dropped. "I can't imagine anybody wanting to marry Aunt Eulalie," she said frankly.

"But, my dear, she was a lovely girl, simply lovely. She came to visit after Pauline married Carey Smith and settled in Charleston. The house they're in was the Smith town house; their plantation was over on the Wando River. My brother Kemper was smitten at once. Everyone expected them to marry. Then he was thrown from his horse and was killed. Eulalie's considered herself a widow ever since."

Aunt Eulalie in love! Scarlett couldn't believe it.

"I was sure you must know," said Mrs. Butler. "She's your family."

But I don't have any family, Scarlett thought, not the way Miss Eleanor means. Not close and caring and knowing all about everybody's heart secrets. All I have is nasty old Suellen, and Carreen with her nun's veil and her vows to the convent. Suddenly she felt very lonely despite the cheerful faces and conversation around her. I must be hungry, she decided, that's why I feel like bursting into tears. I should have eaten all my breakfast.

She was doing full justice to dinner when Manigo came in and spoke quietly to Rhett.

"Excuse me," Rhett said, "it seems we've got a Yankee officer at the door."

"What do you suppose they're up to now?" Scarlett wondered aloud.

Rhett was laughing when he returned a moment later. "Everything but a white flag of surrender," he said. "You've won, Mama. They're inviting all the men to come to the Guardhouse and take back the guns they confiscated."

Rosemary applauded loudly.

Miss Eleanor shushed her. "We can't take too much credit. They can't risk all these unprotected houses on Emancipation Day." She went on to answer Scarlett's questioning expression. "New Year's Day isn't what it used to be, a quiet time to nurse headaches from too much New Year's Eve. Mr. Lincoln issued the Emancipation Proclamation on a January first, so now it's the major day of celebration for all the former slaves. They take over the park down at the end of the Battery and shoot off firecrackers and pistols all day and all night while they get drunker and drunker. We lock up, of course, including all the shutters, just the way we do for a hurricane. But it helps to have an armed man in the house, too."

Scarlett frowned. "There aren't any guns in the house."

"There will be," said Rhett. "Plus two men. They're coming from the Landing just for the occasion."

"And when will you be going?" Eleanor asked Rhett.

"On the thirtieth. I have an appointment with Julia Ashley on the thirty-first. We need to plan our united-front strategy."

Rhett was leaving! Going to his wretched, smelly old plantation! He wouldn't be here to kiss her on New Year's Eve. Now Scarlett was sure she was going to cry.

"I'm going to the Landing with you," said Rosemary. "I haven't been there for months."

"You can't go to the Landing, Rosemary." Rhett was carefully patient.

"I'm afraid Rhett's right, dear," said Mrs. Butler. "He can't be with you all the time, he's got too much business to take care of. And you cannot be in the house or any place else with only that child you have for a maid. There's too much coming and going, too many rough people."

"I'll take your Celie, then. Scarlett will let you borrow Pansy to help you dress, won't you, Scarlett?"

Scarlett smiled. There was no need for tears. "I'll go with you, Rosemary," she said sweetly. "Pansy, too." New Year's Eve would come to the plantation, too. Without a ballroom full of people, just Rhett and her.

"How generous of you, Scarlett," Miss Eleanor said. "I know you'll miss going to the balls next week. You're luckier than you deserve, Rosemary, to have such a thoughtful sister-in-law."

"I don't think either of them should go, Mama, I won't allow it," said Rhett.

Rosemary opened her mouth to protest, but her mother's slightly raised hand stopped her. Mrs. Butler spoke quietly: "You're being rather inconsiderate, Rhett; Rosemary loves the Landing as much as you do, and she doesn't have the freedom to come and go the way you can. I believe you should take her, especially since you're also going to Julia Ashley's. She's very fond of your sister."

Scarlett's mind was racing. What did she care about missing some dances if she could be alone with Rhett? She'd get rid of Rosemary somehow—maybe this Miss Ashley would invite her to stay at her place. Then there would be only Rhett . . . and Scarlett.

She remembered him in her room when she was at the Landing before. He'd held her, comforted her, spoken with such tenderness . . .

"Just wait till you see Miss Julia's plantation, Scarlett," Rosemary said loudly. "It's what a plantation is supposed to be." Rhett was riding ahead of them, pushing aside or tearing the vines of honeysuckle that had grown across the trail through the pinewoods. Scarlett followed Rosemary, uninterested for the moment in what Rhett was doing, her mind busy with other things. Thank goodness this old horse is so fat and lazy. I haven't ridden horseback for so long that anything with spirit would throw me for sure. How I used to love to ride . . . back then . . . when the stables at Tara were full. Pa was so proud of his horses. And of me. Suellen had hands like anvils, she could ruin the mouth of an alligator. And Carreen was afraid, even of her pony. But I used to race with Pa, hell for leather on the roads, almost winning sometimes. "Katie Scarlett," he'd say, "you've got the hands of an angel and the nerve of the devil himself. It's the O'Hara in you, a horse will always recognize an Irishman and give his best for him." Darling Pa . . . Tara's woods smelled sharp, just like these, pine prickling in my nose. And the birds singing and the rustling leaves underfoot and the peace of it all. I wonder how many acres Rhett's got? I'll find out from Rosemary. She probably knows right down to the square inch. I hope this Miss Ashley isn't the dragon Rhett makes her out to be. What was it Rhett said? She looks like she drinks vinegar. He is funny when he's nasty—long as it's not about me.

"Scarlett! Catch up, we're almost there." Rosemary's call came from ahead. Scarlett flicked the neck of her horse with her crop and it walked marginally faster. Rhett and Rosemary were already out of the wood when she reached them. At first all she could see was Rhett, sharp-edged clear in the bright sunlight. How handsome he is, and how well he sits his horse, not a sluggish old thing like mine, but a real horse with plenty of fire to him. Look at the way the horse's muscles are twitching under his skin, yet he's still as a statue, just from the grip of Rhett's knees and his hands on the reins. His hands . . .

Rosemary gestured, catching Scarlett's eye, directing it to the scene ahead, and Scarlett caught her breath. She had never cared about architecture, never noticed it. Even the magnificent houses that made Charleston's Battery world-famous were to her just houses. However there was something about the severe beauty of Julia Ashley's house at Ashley Barony that she recognized as different from anything she'd ever known and grand in a way she couldn't define. It sat isolated in broad stretches of grass unadorned with garden, distant from the ancient huge live oak trees that were wide-spaced sentinels at the perimeter of the lawn. Square, made of brick with white-framed door and windows, the house was—"special," Scarlett whispered. No wonder that it alone of all the plantations on the river had been spared the torches of Sherman's Army. Even the Yankees wouldn't dare insult the mighty presence before her eyes.

There was a sound of laughter, followed by singing. Scarlett turned her head. The house awed and intimidated her. Far to her left she saw expanses of strong insistent green completely different from the familiar deep rich color of the grass. Dozens of black men and women were working and singing in the strange green. Why, they're field hands, tending the crop of whatever it is. So many of them, too. Her mind flew to the cotton fields at Tara that had once stretched as far as she could see, just as this strident green flowed without bounds along the river. Oh, yes, Rosemary's right. This is a real plantation, like a plantation's meant to be. Nothing was burned, nothing was changed, nothing would ever change. Time itself respected the majesty of Ashley Barony.

"It's good of you to meet with me, Miss Ashley," said Rhett. He bowed over the hand Julia Ashley held out to him; the back of his ungloved hand supported it respectfully, and his lips stopped the prescribed inch above it, for no gentleman would commit the impertinence of actually kissing the hand of a maiden lady, no matter how advanced her years.

"It's useful to us both, Mr. Butler," Julia said. "You're miserably ill-groomed as usual, Rosemary, but I'm glad to see you. Introduce your sister-in-law."

My grief, she really is a dragon, Scarlett thought nervously. I wonder if she expects me to curtsey?

"This is Scarlett, Miss Julia," Rosemary said, smiling. She didn't seem at all upset by the older woman's criticism.

"How do you do, Mrs. Butler."

Scarlett was sure that Julia Ashley didn't care to know how she did at all. "How do you do," she replied in kind. She inclined her head in a slight bow, the degree of inclination an exact replica of Miss Ashley's frigid politeness. Who did this old woman think she was anyhow?

"There is a tea tray in the drawing room," Julia said. "You may pour out for Mrs. Butler, Rosemary. Ring if you need more hot water. We'll do our business in my library, Mr. Butler, and take tea afterwards."

"Oh, Miss Julia, can't I listen while you and Rhett talk?" Rosemary begged.

"No, Rosemary, you may not."

And that's the end of that, I guess, Scarlett said to herself. Julia Ashley was walking away with Rhett obediently following behind.

"Come on, Scarlett, the drawing room's through here." Rosemary opened a tall door and gestured to Scarlett.

The room she entered was a surprise to Scarlett. There was none of the coldness of its owner about it and nothing intimidating. It was very large, bigger than Minnie Wentworth's ballroom. But the floor was covered with an old Persian rug with a background of faded red, and the draperies at the tall windows were a warm soft rose color. A bright fire crackled in the wide fireplace; sunlight poured through the sparkling window panes onto the brightly polished silver tea service, onto the gold and blue and rose velvet upholstery on broad, comfortable settees and winged chairs. And an enormous yellow tabby cat was sleeping on the hearth.

Scarlett shook her head slightly in wonder. It was difficult to believe that this cheerful, welcoming room had any connection with the stiff-backed woman in the black dress she had met outside its door. She sat next to Rosemary on a settee. "Tell me about Miss Ashley," she said, avid with curiosity.

"Miss Julia's wonderful!" Rosemary exclaimed. "She runs Ashley Barony herself; she says she's never had an overseer that didn't need overseeing. And she has practically as many rice fields as there were before the War. She could mine phosphate like Rhett, but she won't have anything to do with it. Plantations are for planting, she says, not for"—Rosemary's voice dropped to a shocked, pleased whisper—" 'raping the land to get what's underneath.' She keeps it all the way it was. There's sugar cane and a press to make her own molasses, and a blacksmith to shoe the mules and make wheels for the carts, and a cooper to make barrels for the rice and molasses, and a carpenter for fixing things, a tanner to make harness. She takes her rice into town for milling and she buys flour and coffee and tea, but everything else comes from the place. She's got cows and sheep and fowl and pigs and a dairy room and spring house and smoke house and storerooms full of canned vegetables and shelled corn and preserved fruit from the summer crops. She makes her own wine, too. Rhett claims she's even got a still out in the pine woods she gets her turpentine from."

"Does she still have slaves?" Scarlett's words were sharply sarcastic. The days of the great plantations were over and there was no bringing them back.

"Oh, Scarlett, you sound just like Rhett sometimes. I'd like to shake both of you. Miss Julia pays wages just like everybody else. But she makes the plantation earn enough to pay them. I'm going to do the same thing at the Landing if I ever get the chance. I think it's horrible that Rhett won't even try."

Rosemary began to clatter cups and saucers on the tea tray.

"I can't remember, do you take milk or lemon, Scarlett?"

"What? Oh—milk, please." Scarlett had no interest in tea. She was reliving the fantasy she'd had before, of Tara brought back to life, with its fields studded with white cotton for as far as the eye could see and its barns full and the house just the way it had been when her mother was alive.

Yes, there was some of the long-forgotten scent of lemon oil in this room and brass polish and floor wax. It was faint, but she was sure she could smell it, in spite of the sharp resinous tang of the pine logs in the fire.

Her hand automatically accepted the cup of tea that Rosemary offered and held it, letting it cool while she daydreamed. Why not make Tara what it had been? If that old lady can run this plantation, I can run Tara. Will doesn't know what Tara is, not the real Tara, the best plantation in Clayton County. "A two-mule farm," he calls it now. No, by all the saints, Tara's much much more than that! I could do it, too, I'll bet! Didn't Pa say a hundred times that I was a true O'Hara? Then I can do what he did, make Tara into what he made it. Maybe even better. I know how to keep books, how to squeeze out a profit where nobody else sees the possibilities. Why, practically all the places around Tara have gone back to scrub pine. I'll bet I could buy land for next to nothing!

Her mind leapt from one picture to another—rich fields, fat cattle; her old bedroom with crisp white curtains billowing into the room on a jasmine-scented spring breeze; riding through the woods—cleared of underbrush—miles of chestnut-rail fence outlining her land, stretching farther and farther into the red-earth countryside . . . She had to set the vision aside. Reluctantly she focused her attention on Rosemary's insistent loud voice.

Rice, rice, rice! Can't Rosemary Butler ever talk about anything but rice? What can Rhett possibly find to talk about with that old fright Miss Ashley for so long? Scarlett shifted position again on the settee. Rhett's sister had a habit of leaning toward her listener when she was excited about what she was saying. Rosemary had almost driven her into the corner of the long settee. She turned eagerly toward the door when it opened. Damn Rhett anyhow! What was he laughing about with Julia Ashley? He might think it was amusing to leave her to cool her heels for an age and a half, but she didn't.

"You always were a rogue, Rhett Butler," Julia was saying, "but I don't remember that you included impertinence in your list of sins."

"Miss Ashley, to the best of my knowledge, impertinence is a tag attached to the behavior of servants toward their masters and young people toward their elders. While I am, in all things, your obedient servant, you surely cannot be suggesting that you are my elder. Contemporary I'll grant with pleasure, but elder is out of the question."

Why, he's flirting with the old creature! I guess he must want something pretty bad if he's making a fool of himself like this.

Julia Ashley made a sound that could only be described as a dignified snort. "Very well, then," she said, "I'll agree, if only to put a halt to this absurdity. Now sit down and stop your foolishness."

Rhett moved a chair closer to the tea table and bowed ceremoniously when Julia seated herself in it. "Thank you, Miss Julia, for your condescension."

"Don't be such an ass, Rhett."

Scarlett frowned at both of them. Was that all? All that to-do about changing from "Miss Ashley" and "Mr. Butler" to "Rhett" and "Miss Julia"? Rhett was an ass, just like the old woman said. But "Miss Julia" was mighty close to acting like an ass herself. Why, she was practically simpering at Rhett. It was nothing short of disgusting the way he could wrap women around his little finger!

A maid hurried into the room and lifted the tray of tea things from the table in front of the settee. She was followed by a second maid, who quietly moved the tea table to a place in front of Julia Ashley, and a man-servant with a larger silver tray holding a different, larger silver service and stands of fresh sandwiches and cakes. Scarlett had to admit it: no matter how disagreeable Julia Ashley might be, the old woman did things with style!

"Rhett tells me you're to make the Tour, Rosemary," said Julia.

"Yes, ma'am! I'm so excited I could die."

"That would be inconvenient, I should imagine. Tell me, have you begun to map your itinerary?"

"Not really, Miss Julia. I've only known for a few days that I was going. The only thing I'm certain of is that I want to spend as long as possible in Rome."

"You must be sure to time it correctly. The summer heat is quite intolerable, even for a Charlestonian. And the Romans all abandon the city for the mountains or the sea. I still correspond with some delightful people whom you would enjoy. I'll give you letters of introduction, of course. If I might suggest—"

"Oh, please, Miss Julia. There's so much I want to know."

Scarlett breathed a small sigh of relief. She didn't put it past Rhett to tell Miss Ashley about the mistake she'd made, thinking that the only Rome was in Georgia, but he'd let the chance go by. Now he was putting his two cents in, talking a blue streak with the old woman about all the people with strange names. And Rosemary lapping it all up.

The conversation interested Scarlett not at all. But she wasn't bored. She watched, fascinated, every move that Julia Ashley made as she presided at the tea table. Without any break in the discussion of Roman antiquities

—except to ask Scarlett if she took milk or lemon and how many lumps of sugar—Julia filled cups and held each one up, to a level slightly below her right shoulder, for one of the maids to take it from her. She held it up, waited no longer than three seconds, then removed her hand.

She doesn't even look! Scarlett marvelled. If the maid wasn't there, or wasn't quick enough, the whole thing would just fall on the floor. But one of the maids was always there, and the cup was delivered silently to the correct person without a drop spilled.

Where did he come from? Scarlett was startled when the manservant appeared at her side, offering her a napkin with its folds shaken out and the three-tiered stand of sandwiches. She was just about to reach out and take one when the man produced a plate, which he held near her hand for her to take.

Oh, I see, there's a maid handing him things for him to hand to me! Mighty complicated for a fish-paste sandwich no bigger than a bite's worth.

But she was impressed by the elegance of it all, even more impressed when the man held an elaborate silver pincer in his white-gloved hand and lifted an assortment of sandwiches onto her plate. The final touch was the small table with a lace-edged cloth on it that the second maid placed beside her knees just when she was wondering how she was going to manage, with a cup and saucer in one hand and a plate in the other.

Despite her hunger and her curiosity about the sandwiches—what kind of fancy food called for such fancy serving?—Scarlett was more interested in the silent efficient routine of the servants as first Rosemary and then Rhett were provided with plate, sandwiches, table. It was almost a disappointment when Miss Ashley was given no special treatment, only a return of the stand to the table in front of her. Fiddle-dee-dee! She's even unfolding her napkin herself! It was a definite disappointment when she bit into the first sandwich and it was only bread and butter, even though the butter had something else in it—parsley, she thought; no, something stronger, maybe chives. She ate contentedly; all the sandwiches were good. And the cakes on the other stand looked even better.

My grief! They're still talking about Rome! Scarlett glanced toward the servants. They were standing still as posts, along the wall behind Miss Ashley. Obviously the cakes weren't going to be passed any time soon. For heaven's sake, Rosemary had only eaten one half of one sandwich.

"... but we're being inconsiderate," Julia Ashley said. "Mrs. Butler, what city would you like to visit? Or do you share Rosemary's conviction that all roads rightly lead to Rome?"

Scarlett put on her best smile. "I'm too enchanted by Charleston to even think about going any place else, Miss Ashley."

"A graceful response," said Julia, "although it does rather put a period to the conversation. May I offer you some tea?"

Before Scarlett could accept, Rhett spoke. "I'm afraid we have to go, Miss Julia. I haven't gotten the woods trails in condition yet for riding in the dark, and the days are so short."

"You could have avenues, not trails, if you'd put your men to work on the land instead of at that disgraceful phosphate mine."

"Now, Miss Julia, I thought we'd reached a truce."

"So we did. And I'll honor it. Furthermore, I'll admit that you should take care to be well home before dusk. I've been indulging myself with happy memories about Rome, and I haven't watched the time. Perhaps Rosemary might stay the night with me. I'd see her to the Landing tomorrow morning."

Oh, yes! thought Scarlett.

"Unfortunately, that won't do," Rhett said. "I might have to go out tonight, and I don't want Scarlett at the house with no one she knows except her Georgia maid."

"I don't mind, Rhett," Scarlett said loudly, "truly I don't. Do you think I'm some kind of sissy who's afraid of the dark?"

"You're quite right, Rhett," said Julia Ashley. "And you should cultivate some caution, Mrs. Butler. These are uncertain times."

Julia's tone was decisive. So was her abrupt movement. She stood and walked toward the door. "I'll see you out, then. Hector will have your horses brought around."

23

There were several large groups of angry-looking black men and one small group of black women in the horse-shoe-shaped grass area behind the house at the Landing. Rhett helped Scarlett and Rosemary step down from the mounting block near the makeshift stables and held on to their elbows while the stableboy gathered the reins and led the horses away. When the boy was out of earshot, Rhett spoke with hushed urgency. "I'm going to walk you around to the front of the house. Go inside and straight upstairs to one of the bedrooms. Close the door and stay in there until I come for you. I'll send Pansy up. Keep her with you."

"What's going on, Rhett?" Scarlett's voice had a quaver in it.

"I'll tell you later, there's no time now. Just do as I say." He kept hold of the two women, forcing them to match his purposeful but unhurried pace to the house and around its side. "Mist' Butler!" shouted one of the men. A half dozen others followed him as he started to walk towards Rhett. This isn't good, thought Scarlett, calling him Mr. Butler instead of Mr. Rhett. It's not friendly at all, and there must be close to fifty of them.

"Stay where you are," Rhett shouted back. "I'll be back to talk to you as soon as I get the ladies settled." Rosemary stumbled on a loose stone in the path and Rhett jerked her upright before she could fall. "I don't care if your leg's broken," he muttered, "keep walking."

"I'm all right," Rosemary said. She sounds cool as ice, thought Scarlett. She despised herself for feeling so nervous. Thank goodness they were almost at the house now. Only a few more steps and they'd be around it.

She was unaware that she was holding her breath until they neared the house front. When she saw the green terraces that stepped down to the butterfly lakes and the river, she let her breath out in a whoosh of release.

Then she drew it in sharply. As they turned the corner onto the brick terrace she saw ten white men sitting on it, leaning back against the house wall. They were all of them thin, lanky, their pale bare ankles showing between their clumsy heavy shoes and the bottoms of their faded overalls. Across their knees they held rifles or shotguns in a loose, accustomed grip. Battered wide-brimmed hats pulled low on their foreheads shadowed their eyes, but Scarlett knew they were looking at Rhett and his women. One of them expelled a stream of brown tobacco juice across the lawn in front of Rhett's fine riding boots.

"You can thank God you didn't spatter my sister, Clinch Dawkins," Rhett said, "or I'd have had to kill you. I'll talk to you boys in a few minutes, I've got other things to do right now." He spoke easily, casually. But Scarlett could feel the tension in his hand holding her arm. She lifted her chin and walked with firm strong steps to match Rhett's. No poor white trash was going to face Rhett down, or her either.

She blinked in the sudden darkness when she entered the house. What a stink! Her eyes adjusted rapidly and Scarlett saw the reason for the benches and spittoons in the main room downstairs. More weathered, hungry-looking poor whites were sprawled on the seats, filling every inch of space. They, too, were armed, and their hat brims made their eyes a secret. The floor was spotted with spit and pools of juice ringed the spittoons. Scarlett pulled her arm from Rhett's hold, gathered up her skirts to the top of her ankles and walked to the staircase. Two steps up, she dropped them again, letting the train of her riding habit drag through the dust. She'd be damned if she'd treat that rabble to a look at a lady's ankle. She mounted the rickety staircase as if she hadn't a care in the world.

"What's happening, Miss Scarlett? Ain't nobody will tell me nothing!" Pansy started wailing the moment the bedroom door closed behind her.

"Hush up!" Scarlett ordered. "Do you want everybody in South Carolina to hear you?"

"I don't want to have nothing to do with nobody in South Carolina, Miss Scarlett. I want to go back to Atlanta, to my own folks. I don't like this place."

"Nobody cares two pins what you like and don't like, so you just march yourself over to that corner and sit on that stool and keep quiet. If I hear one peep out of you, I'll . . . I'll do something terrible."

She looked at Rosemary. If Rhett's sister broke down, too, she didn't know what she'd do. Rosemary looked very pale, but she seemed composed enough. She was sitting on the edge of the bed, looking at the pattern of the coverlet as if she'd never seen one before.

Scarlett walked to the window that overlooked the back lawn. If she stayed to one side of it, no one below could see her looking out. She lifted the muslin curtain with cautious fingers and peered out. Was Rhett out there? Dear God, he was! She could just make out the top of his hat, a dark circle in the middle of a big crowd of dark heads and gesticulating dark hands. The separate groups of black men had come together in one threatening mass.

They could stomp him to death in half a minute flat, she thought, and there's nothing I can do to stop it. Her hand crumpled the thin curtain in anger at her helplessness.

"Better get away from that window, Scarlett," said Rosemary. "If Rhett starts worrying about you and me, he'll be distracted from whatever it is he has to do."

Scarlett whirled to the attack. "Don't you care what's happening?"

"I care plenty, but I don't know what's happening. And neither do you."

"I know that Rhett's about to be swamped by a bunch of raging darkies. Why don't those trashy tobacco spitters use the guns they're sitting around with?"

"Then we'd really be in a fix. I know some of the black men, they work at the phosphate mine. They don't want anything to happen to Rhett or they'd lose their jobs. Besides, plenty of them are Butler people. They belong here. It's the whites I'm scared of. I expect Rhett is, too."

"Rhett's not scared of anything!"

"Of course he is. He'd be a fool if he wasn't. I'm plenty scared and so are you."

"I am not!"

"Then you're a fool."

Scarlett's jaw dropped. The whiplash in Rosemary's voice shocked her more than the insult. Why, she sounds just like Julia Ashley. A half hour with that old she-dragon and Rosemary's turned into a monster.

She turned hurriedly to the window again. It was beginning to get dark. What was happening?

She couldn't see a thing. Only dark shapes on the dark ground. Was Rhett one of them? She couldn't tell. She put her ear against the windowpane and strained to hear. The only sound was a muffled whimpering from Pansy.

If I don't do something I'll go mad, she thought, and she began to pace back and forth across the small room. "Why does a big plantation like this have such cramped little bedrooms?" she complained. "You could fit two rooms like this into any one of the rooms at Tara."

"Do you really want to know? Then sit down. There's a rocker over by the other window. You can rock instead of walking. I'll light the lamp and I'll tell you all about Dunmore Landing if you'd like to hear."

"I can't bear to sit still! I'm going down there and find out what's going on." Scarlett groped in the darkness for the doorknob.

"If you do, he'll never forgive you," said Rosemary.

Scarlett's hand fell to her side.

The match striking was as loud as a pistol shot. Scarlett felt the nerves jump under her skin. Then she turned, surprised to see that Rosemary looked just the same as always. She was in the same place, too, sitting on the edge of the bed. The kerosene lamp made the random colors of the coverlet look very bright. Scarlett hesitated for a moment. Then she walked to the rocking chair and plopped down into it.

"All right. Tell me about Dunmore Landing." She began to rock with an angry push of her feet. The chair squeaked as Rosemary talked about the plantation that meant so much to her. Scarlett rocked with vicious pleasure.

The house they were in, Rosemary began, had small bedrooms because it was built as quarters for bachelor guests only. Above the floor they were on was another floor of small rooms for the guests' manservants. The rooms downstairs where Rhett's office and the dining room were now had been used as guest rooms also—a place for late-night toddies and card games and sociability. "All the chairs were red leather," Rosemary said softly. "I used to love to go in there and sniff the leather and whiskey and cigar smoke smell when all the men were out hunting.

"The Landing's named after the place the Butlers lived before our great-great-grandfather left England for Barbados. Our great-grandfather came to Charleston from there around a hundred and fifty years ago. He built the Landing and put in the gardens. His wife's name before she married great-grandfather was Sophia Rosemary Ross. That's where Ross and I get our names from."

"Where'd Rhett get his name?"

"He's named after our grandfather."

"Rhett told me your grandfather was a pirate."

"He did?" Rosemary laughed. "He would say that. Granddaddy ran the English blockade in the Revolution just like Rhett ran the Yankee blockade in our war. He was bound and determined to get his rice crop out, and he wouldn't let anything stop him. I imagine he did some pretty sharp trading on the side, but mainly he was a rice planter. Dunmore Landing has always been a rice plantation. That's why I get so mad at Rhett—"

Scarlett rocked faster. If she starts going on about rice again, I'll scream.

The loud double report of a shotgun crashed through the night and Scarlett did scream. She jumped up from the chair and ran toward the door. Rosemary leapt up and ran after her. She threw her strong arms around Scarlett's middle and held her back.

"Let me go, Rhett might be—" Scarlett croaked. Rosemary was squeezing the breath out of her.

Rosemary's arms tightened. Scarlett struggled to get free. She heard her own strangled breath loud in her ears and—strangely more distinct— the creak creak creak of the rocker, slowing even as her breath was slowing. The lighted room seemed to be turning dark.

Her flailing hands fluttered weakly and her straining throat made a faint rasping noise. Rosemary let her go. "I'm sorry," Scarlett thought she heard Rosemary say. It didn't matter. The only thing that mattered was to draw great gulps of air into her lungs. It even made no difference that she'd fallen onto her hands and knees. It was easier to breathe that way.

It was a long time before she could speak. She looked up then, saw Rosemary standing with her back against the door. "You almost killed me," Scarlett said.

"I'm sorry. I didn't mean to hurt you. I had to stop you."

"Why? I was going to Rhett. I've got to go to Rhett." He meant more to her than all the world. Couldn't this stupid girl understand that? No, she couldn't, she'd never loved anybody, never had anybody love her.

Scarlett tried to scrabble to her feet. Oh, sweet Mary, Mother of God, I'm so weak. Her hands found the bedpost. Slowly she pulled herself upright. She was as white as a ghost, her green eyes blazed like cold flames.

"I'm going to Rhett," she said.

Rosemary struck her then. Not with her hands or even her fists. Scarlett could have withstood that.

"He doesn't want you," Rosemary said quietly. "He told me so."

24

Rhett paused in midsentence. He looked at Scarlett and said, "What is this? No appetite? And they say that country air is supposed to make people hungry. You astonish me, my dear. I do believe this is the first time I've ever seen you peck at your food."

She looked up from her untouched plate to glare at him. How did he even dare to speak to her when he had been talking about her behind her back? Who else had he talked to besides Rosemary? Did everybody in Charleston know that he had walked out in Atlanta and that she'd made a fool of herself by coming after him?

She looked down and continued to push bits of food from place to place.

"So then what happened?" Rosemary demanded. "I still don't understand."

"It was just what Miss Julia and I expected. Her field hands and my phosphate diggers had cooked up a plot. You know that work contracts are signed on New Year's Day for the year to follow. Miss Julia's men were going to tell her that I paid my miners almost twice what she paid and that she'd have to jack up their salaries or they'd come to me. My men were going to play the same game, only the other way around. It never entered their heads that Miss Julia and I were on to them.

"The grapevine started humming the minute we rode over to Ashley Barony. All of them knew the game was up. You saw how industrious all the Barony workers were in the rice fields. They didn't want to risk losing their jobs, and they're all scared to death of Miss Julia.

"Things weren't quite that smooth here. Word had gotten out that the Landing blacks were scheming something, and the white sharecroppers across the Summerville road got edgy. They did what poor whites always do, grabbed their guns and got ready for a little shooting. They came to the house and broke in and stole my whiskey, then passed the bottle around to get up a good head of steam.

"After you were safely out of range I told them I'd take care of my business myself, and I high-tailed it out to the back of the house. The blacks were scared, as well they might be, but I persuaded them that I could calm the whites down and that they should go home.

"When I got back to the house, I told the sharecroppers that I'd settled everything with the workers and they should go on home, too. I probably gave it to them too fast. I was so relieved myself that there hadn't been any trouble that it made me careless. I'll be smarter next time. If, God forbid, there is a next time. Anyhow, Clinch Dawkins flew off the handle. He was looking for trouble. He called me a nigger lover and cocked that cannon of a shotgun he's got and turned it in my direction. I didn't wait to find out if he was drunk enough to shoot, I just stepped over and knocked it up. The sky got a couple of holes in it."

"Is that all?" Scarlett half-shouted. "You could have let us know."

"I was too busy, my pet. Clinch's pride was wounded, so he pulled a knife. I pulled mine and we had an active ten minutes or so before I cut off his nose."

Rosemary gasped.

Rhett patted her hand. "Only the end of it. It was too long anyhow. His looks are significantly improved."

"But Rhett, he'll come after you."

Rhett shook his head. "No, I can assure you he won't. It was a fair fight. And Clinch is one of my oldest companions. We were in the Confederate Army together. He was loader for the cannon I commanded. There's a bond between us that a small slice of nose can't damage."

"I wish he'd killed you," said Scarlett distinctly. "I'm tired and I'm going to bed." She pushed her chair back and walked with a dignified tread from the room.

Rhett's words, deliberately drawled, followed her. "No greater blessing can be granted a man than the devotion of a loving wife."

Scarlett's heart grew hot with anger. "I hope Clinch Dawkins is outside this house right this minute," she muttered, "just waiting for a clean shot."

For that matter, she wouldn't exactly cry her eyes out if the second barrel got Rosemary.

Rosemary lifted her wine glass to Rhett in a salute. "All right, now I know why you said supper was a celebration. I, for one, am celebrating this day being over."

"Is Scarlett sick?" Rhett asked his sister. "I was only half-joking about her appetite. It's not like her not to eat."

"She's upset."

"I've seen her upset more times than you can count, and she's eaten like a longshoreman every time."

"This isn't just her temper, Rhett. While you were chopping noses, Scarlett and I had a wrestling match ourselves." Rosemary described Scarlett's panic and her determination to go to him. "I didn't know how dangerous things might be downstairs, so I held her back. I hope I did right."

"You did absolutely right. Anything could have happened."

"I'm afraid I held a little too tight," Rosemary confessed. "She almost passed out, she couldn't breathe."

Rhett threw his head back and laughed. "By God, I wish I'd seen that. Scarlett O'Hara pinned to the mat by a girl. There must be a hundred women in Georgia who would have clapped the skin off their hands applauding you!"

Rosemary considered confessing the rest. She realized that what she'd said to Scarlett had hurt her more than the fight. She decided not to. Rhett was still chuckling; no sense in dimming his good mood.

Scarlett woke before dawn. She lay motionless in the dark room, afraid to move. Breathe like you're still asleep, she told herself, you wouldn't wake up in the middle of the night unless there'd been a noise or something. She listened for what seemed like an eternity, but the silence was heavy and unbroken.

When she realized that it was hunger that had wakened her, she almost cried with relief. Of course she was hungry! She'd had nothing to eat since breakfast the day before, except for a few tea sandwiches at Ashley Barony.

The night air was too cold for her to wear the elegant silk dressing gown she'd brought with her. She wrapped herself in the coverlet from the bed. It was heavy wool and still held in it the warmth of her body. It trailed awkwardly around her bare feet as she crept quietly through the dark hallway and down the stairs. Thank goodness, the banked fire in the great fireplace gave out some heat still, and enough light for her to see the door to the dining room and the kitchen beyond. She didn't care what she might find; even cold rice and stew would be all right. With one hand holding the dark coverlet around her, she groped for the doorknob. Was it to the left or the right? She hadn't noticed.

"Stop right there, or I'll blow a hole through your middle!" Rhett's harsh voice made her jump. The blanket fell away and cold air assaulted her.

"Great balls of fire!" Scarlett turned on him and bent to gather up the folds of wool. "Didn't I have enough to scare me witless yesterday? Do you have to start up again? You nearly made me jump out of my skin!"

"What are you doing wandering around at this hour, Scarlett? I could have shot you."

"What are you doing skulking around scaring people?" Scarlett draped the coverlet around her shoulders as if it were an imperial robe of ermine. "I'm going to the kitchen to get some breakfast," she said with all the dignity she could muster.

Rhett smiled at the absurdly haughty figure she cut. "I'll make up the fire in the stove," he said. "I was thinking of some coffee myself."

"It's your house. I reckon you can have coffee if you want some." Scarlett kicked the trailing coverlet behind her as if it were the train on a ball gown. "Well? Aren't you going to open the door for me?"

Rhett threw some logs into the fireplace. The hot coals touched off a flare of dried leaves on one branch of wood. He quickly sobered the expression on his face before Scarlett could see it. He opened the door to the dining room and stepped back. Scarlett swept past him, but had to stop almost at once. The room was completely dark.

"If you'll allow me—" Rhett struck a match. He touched it to the lamp above the table, then carefully adjusted the flame.

Scarlett could hear the laughter in his voice but somehow it didn't make her angry. "I'm so hungry I could eat a horse," she admitted.

"Not a horse, please," Rhett laughed. "I've only got three, and two of them are no damn good." He settled the glass chimney on the lamp and smiled down at her. "How about some eggs and a slice of ham?"

"Two slices," said Scarlett. She followed him into the kitchen and sat on a bench by the table with her feet tucked up under the blanket while he lit a fire in the big iron stove. When the pine kindling was crackling, she stretched her feet out to the warmth.

Rhett brought a half-eaten ham and bowls of butter and eggs from the pantry. "The coffee grinder's on the table behind you," he said. "The beans are in that can. If you'll grind some while I slice the ham, breakfast will be ready that much sooner."

"Why don't you grind them while I cook the eggs?"

"Because the stove's not hot yet, Miss Greedy. There's a pan of cold corn bread next to the grinder. That should tide you over. I'll do the cooking."

Scarlett swivelled around. The pan under the napkin had four squares of corn bread left in it. She dropped her wrap to reach for a piece. While she was chewing she put a handful of coffee beans into the grinder. Then she alternated taking bites of corn bread with turning the handle. When the corn bread was almost gone, she heard the sizzle as Rhett dropped ham slices into a skillet.

"That smells like heaven," she said happily. She finished grinding the coffee with a spurt of rapid cranks. "Where's the coffee pot?" She turned, saw Rhett, and began to laugh. He had a dishtowel tucked into the waistband of his trousers and a long fork in one hand. He waved the fork in the direction of a shelf by the door.

"What's so funny?"

"You. Dodging the fat spatters. Cover the stove hole or you'll set the whole pan on fire. I should have known you wouldn't know what to do."

"Nonsense, madam. I prefer the adventure of the open flame. It takes me back to the delightful days of frying fresh buffalo steaks at a campfire." But he slid the skillet to one side of the opening in the stove top.

"Did you really eat buffalo? In California?"

"Buffalo and goat and mule—and the meat off the dead body of the person who didn't make the coffee when I wanted it."

Scarlett giggled. She ran across the cold stone floor to get the pot.

They ate silently at the kitchen table, both concentrating hungrily on the food. It was warm and friendly in the dark room. An open door on the stove gave an uneven reddish light. The smell of coffee brewing on the stove was dark and sweet. Scarlett wanted the breakfast to last forever. *Rosemary must have lied. Rhett couldn't have told her he didn't want me.*

"Rhett?"

"Hmm?" He was pouring the coffee.

Scarlett wanted to ask him if the comfort and laughter could last, but she was afraid it would ruin everything. "Is there any cream?" she asked instead.

"In the pantry. I'll get it. Keep your feet warm by the stove."

He was gone only a few seconds.

While she stirred sugar and cream into her coffee, she stirred up her nerve. "Rhett?"

"Yes?"

Scarlett's words tumbled out in a burst, quickly so that he couldn't stop her. "Rhett, can't we have good times like this forever? This is a good time, you know it is. Why do you have to keep acting as though you hate me?"

Rhett sighed. "Scarlett," he said wearily, "any animal will attack if it's cornered. Instinct is stronger than reason, stronger than will. When you came to Charleston, you were backing me into a corner. Crowding me. You're doing it now. You can't leave well enough alone. I want to be decent. But you won't let me."

"I will, I will let you. I want you to be nice."

"You don't want kindness, Scarlett, you want love. Unquestioning, undemanding, unequivocal love. I gave you that once, when you didn't want it. I used it all up, Scarlett." Rhett's tone was growing colder, edged with harsh impatience. Scarlett shrank away from it, unconsciously touching the bench at her side, trying to find the warmth of the discarded coverlet.

"Let me put it in your terms, Scarlett. I had in my heart a thousand dollars' worth of love. It was in gold, not greenbacks. And I spent it on you, every penny of it. As far as love is concerned, I'm bankrupt. You've wrung me dry."

"I was wrong, Rhett, and I'm sorry. I'm trying to make up for it." Scarlett's mind was racing frantically. I can give him my heart's thousand dollars' worth of love, she thought. Two thousand, five, twenty, a thousand thousand. Then he'll be able to love me because he won't be bankrupt any more. He'll have it all back, and more. If he'll just take it. I have to make him take it . . .

"Scarlett," Rhett was saying, "there's no 'making up' for the past. Don't destroy the little that is left. Let me be kind, I'll feel better for it."

She seized on his words. "Oh, yes! Yes, Rhett, please. Be kind, the way you were before I ruined the happy time we were having. I won't crowd you. Let's just have fun, be friends, until I go back to Atlanta. I'll be content if we can just laugh together; I had such a good time at breakfast. My, you are a sight in that apron thing." She giggled. Thank God he couldn't see her any better than she could see him.

"That's all you want?" Relief took the edge from Rhett's voice. Scarlett took a big swallow of coffee while she planned what to say. Then she managed an airy laugh.

"Well, of course, silly. I know when I'm beat. I figured it was worth a try, that's all. I won't crowd you any more, but please make the Season good for me. You know how much I love parties." She laughed again. "And if you really want to be kind, Rhett Butler, you can pour me another cup of coffee. I don't have a hot-holder, and you do."

* * *

After breakfast Scarlett went upstairs to get dressed. It was still night, but she was much too excited to think about going back to sleep. She'd patched things up pretty well, she thought. His guard was down. He had enjoyed their breakfast, too, she was sure of it.

She put on the brown travelling costume she had worn on the boat to the Landing, then brushed her dark hair back from her temples and tucked combs in to hold it. Then she rubbed just a small amount of eau de cologne across her wrists and throat, just a whiff-reminder that she was feminine and soft and desirable.

Walking along the hall and down the stairs she was as quiet as she could be. The longer Rosemary stayed asleep, the better. The east-facing window on the stair landing was distinct in the darkness. It was nearly dawn. Scarlett blew out the flame in the lamp she was carrying. Oh, please let this be a good day, let me do everything right. Let it be like breakfast all day long. And all night after. It's New Year's Eve.

The house had the special quality of quiet that wraps the earth just before sunrise. Scarlett stepped carefully to make no noise until she reached the center room below. The fire was burning brightly; Rhett must have put more logs on while she was dressing. She could just make out the dark shape of his shoulders and head framed by the gray semi-light of a window beyond him. He was in his office with the door ajar, his back to her. She tiptoed across the room and tapped gently on the door frame with the tips of her fingers. "May I come in?" she whispered.

"I thought you'd gone back to bed," said Rhett. He sounded very tired. She remembered that he'd been up all night guarding the house. And her. She wished she could cradle his head against her heart and stroke his tiredness away.

"There wasn't much point to going to sleep, there'll be roosters crowing like crazy as soon as the sun's up." She put one foot tentatively across the doorsill. "Is it all right if I sit in here? There's not such a reek in your office."

"Come in," Rhett said without looking at her.

Scarlett moved quietly to a chair just inside the office. Over Rhett's shoulder she could see the window becoming more distinct. I wonder what he's looking for so hard. Are those Crackers outside again? Or Clinch Dawkins? A cock crowed, and her whole body jerked.

Then the first weak rays of red dawn light touched the scene outside the window. The jagged tumbled brick ruins of Dunmore Landing's house were dramatically lit, red against the dark sky behind them. Scarlett cried out. It looked as if they were still smoldering. Rhett was watching the death throes of his home.

"Don't look, Rhett," she begged, "don't look. It will only break your heart."

"I should have been here, I might have stopped them." Rhett's voice was slow, distant, as if he didn't know that he was speaking.

"You couldn't have. There must have been hundreds of them. They would have shot you and burned everything anyhow!"

"They didn't shoot Julia Ashley," said Rhett. But he sounded different now. There was a glimmer of wryness, almost humor, beneath his words. The red light outside was changing, becoming more golden, and the ruins were only blackened bricks and chimneys with the sun-touched sheen of dew on them.

Rhett's swivel chair swung around. He rubbed his hand over his chin, and Scarlett could almost hear the rasp of the unshaven whiskers. He had shadows under his eyes, visible even in the shadowy room, and his black hair was dishevelled, a cowlick standing up on the crown, an untidy lock falling on his forehead. He stood, yawned, and stretched. "I believe it's safe to sleep a little now. You and Rosemary stay in the house till I wake up." He lay down on a wooden bench and fell asleep at once.

Scarlett watched him as he slept.

I mustn't ever tell him again that I love him. That makes him feel pressured. And when he turns nasty, I feel small and cheap for having said it. No, I'll never say it again, not until he's told me first that he loves me.

25

$\mathcal{R}$hett was busy from the moment he woke after an hour's heavy sleep, and he told Rosemary and Scarlett bluntly to keep away from the butterfly lakes. He was building a platform there for the speeches and hiring ceremonies the next day "Working men don't take kindly to the presence of women." He smiled at his sister. "And I certainly don't want Mama asking me why I permitted you to learn such a colorful new vocabulary."

At Rhett's request, Rosemary led Scarlett on a tour of the overgrown gardens. The paths had been cleared but not gravelled, and Scarlett's hem was soon black from fine dust. How different everything was from Tara, even the soil. It seemed unnatural to her that the paths and the dust weren't red. The vegetation was so thick, too, and many of the plants were unfamiliar. It was too lush for her upland taste.

But Rhett's sister loved the Butler plantation with a passion that surprised her. Why, she feels about this place just the way I feel about Tara. Maybe I can get along with her after all.

Rosemary did not notice Scarlett's efforts to find a common ground. She was lost in a lost world: Dunmore Landing before the War. "This was called 'the hidden garden' because of the way the tall hedges along the paths kept you from seeing it until all of a sudden you were in it. When I was little I'd hide in here whenever bath time was coming. The servants were wonderful to me—they'd thrash around the hedges shouting back and forth about how they knew they'd never find me. I thought I'd been so clever. And when my Mammy stumbled through the gate, she'd always act surprised to see me . . . I loved her so much."

"I had a Mammy, too. She—"

Rosemary was already moving on. "Down this way is the reflecting pool. There were black swans and white ones. Rhett says maybe they'll come back once the reeds are cut out and all that filthy algae cleaned up. See that clump of bushes? It's really an island, purpose built for the swans to nest on. It was all grass, of course, clipped when it wasn't nesting season. And there was a miniature Greek temple of white marble. Maybe the pieces are somewhere in the tangle. A lot of people are afraid of swans. They can do terrible injury with their beaks and wings. But ours let me swim with them once the cygnets were out of the nest. Mama used to read me *The Ugly Duckling* sitting on a bench by the pool. When I learned my letters, I read it to the swans . . .

"This path goes to the rose garden. In May you could smell them for miles on the river before you ever got to the Landing. Inside the house, on rainy days with the windows closed, the sweetness from all the big arrangements of roses made me feel sick as a dog . . .

"Down there by the river was the big oak with the treehouse in it. Rhett built it when he was a boy, then Ross had it. I'd climb up with a book and some jam biscuits and stay for hours and hours. It was much better than the playhouse Papa had the carpenters make for me. That was much too fancy, with rugs on the floors and furniture in my size and tea sets and dolls . . .

"Come this way. The cypress swamp is over there. Maybe there'll be some alligators to watch. The weather's been so warm they're not likely to be in their winter dens."

"No, thank you," said Scarlett. "My legs are getting tired. I believe I'll sit on that big stone for a while."

The big stone turned out to be the base of a fallen, broken statue of a classically draped maiden. Scarlett could see the stained face in a thicket of brambles. She wasn't really tired of walking, she was tired of Rosemary. And she certainly had no desire to see any alligators. She sat with the sun warm on her back and thought about what she'd seen. Dunmore Landing was beginning to come to life in her mind. It hadn't been at all like Tara, she realized. Life here had been lived on a scale and in a style she knew nothing about. No wonder Charleston people had a reputation for thinking they were the be-all and end-all. They had lived like kings.

Despite the warmth of the sun she felt chilled. If Rhett worked day and night for the rest of his life, he'd never make this place what it once was, and that was exactly what he was determined to do. There wasn't going to be much time in his life for her. And knowing about onions and yams wouldn't be much help to her in sharing his life, either.

Rosemary returned, disappointed. She hadn't seen a single 'gator. She talked nonstop while they were walking back to the house, giving their old names to gardens that were now only areas of rank weeds, boring Scarlett with complex descriptions of the varieties of rice once grown in fields that were now gone to marsh grass, reminiscing about her childhood. "I hated it when summer came!" she complained.

"Why?" asked Scarlett. She had always loved summer when there were parties every week and lots of visitors and noisy, shouting racing on back roads between the fields of ripening cotton.

Rosemary's answer wiped away the apprehensions that were preying on her mind. In the Lowcountry, Scarlett learned, summertime was city-time. There was a fever that rose from the swamps to lay whites low. Malaria. Because of it everyone left their plantations from the middle of May until after the first frost in late October.

So Rhett would have time for her, after all. There was the Season, too, for nearly two more months. He had to be there to escort his mother and sister—and her. She'd be glad to let him fiddle with his flowers for five months a year if she could have the other seven. She'd even learn the names of his camellias.

What was that? Scarlett stared at the tremendous white stone object. It looked like an angel was standing on a big box.

"Oh, that's our tomb," said Rosemary. "A century and a half of Butlers, all in neat rows. When I go toes up, that's where I'll be put, too. The Yankees shot off big chunks of the angel's wings, but they had the decency to leave the dead alone. I heard that some places they dug up graves to look for jewelry."

Child of an Irish immigrant father, Scarlett was overwhelmed by the permanence of the tomb. All those generations, and all the generations to come, forever and ever, amen. "I'm going back to a place with roots that go deep," Rhett had said. Now she understood what he had meant. She felt sorrow for what he had lost, and envy that she had never had it.

"Come on, Scarlett. You're standing there as if you were planted. We're almost back to the house. You can't be too tired to walk that little bit."

Scarlett remembered why she had agreed in the first place to go on the walk with Rosemary. "I'm not the least bit tired!" she insisted. "I think we should gather some pine branches and things to decorate the house a little. These are the holidays, after all."

"Good idea. They'll cut the stink. There's plenty of pine, and holly, too, in the wood next to where the stables used to be."

And mistletoe, Scarlett added silently. She wasn't taking any chances with the New Year's Eve midnight ritual.

"Very nice," said Rhett when he came up to the house after the platform was built and draped with red, white, and blue bunting. "It looks festive, just right for the party."

"What party?" asked Scarlett.

"I invited the sharecropper families. It makes them feel important, and God willing the men will be too hungover from rotgut whiskey to make trouble tomorrow when the blacks are here. You and Rosemary and Pansy will go upstairs before they come. It's likely to get rough."

Scarlett watched the Roman candles arc through the sky from her bedroom window. The fireworks to celebrate the New Year lasted from midnight until nearly one o'clock. She wished with all her heart that she had stayed in the city. Tomorrow she'd be cooped up all day while the blacks celebrated, and by the time they got back to town on Saturday it would probably be too late to wash and dry her hair for the Ball.

And Rhett had never kissed her.

During the days that followed, Scarlett recaptured all the giddy excitement of what she remembered as the best time of her life. She was a belle, with men clustered around her at receptions, with her dance card filled as soon as she entered the ballroom, with all her old games of flirtation producing the same admiration that they had before. It was like being sixteen again, with nothing to think about other than the last party and the compliments she'd been paid, and the next party and how she would wear her hair.

But it was not long before the thrills became flat. She was not sixteen, and she didn't really want a string of beaux. She wanted Rhett, and she was no closer to winning him back than she had been. He kept up his end of their bargain: he was attentive to her at parties, pleasant to her whenever they were together in the house—with other people. Yet she was sure that he was looking at the calendar, counting the days until he'd be rid of her. She began to feel moments of panic. What if she lost?

The panic always bred anger. She focused it on young Tommy Cooper. The boy was always hanging around Rhett with hero-worship clear on his face. And Rhett responded, too. It enraged her. Tommy had been given a small sailboat for Christmas, and Rhett was teaching him to sail. There was a handsome brass telescope in the card room on the second floor, and Scarlett ran to it whenever she could on the afternoons that Rhett was out with Tommy Cooper. Her jealousy was like probing an aching tooth with her tongue, but she couldn't resist the compulsion to cause herself pain. *It's not fair! They're laughing and having fun and skimming the water as free as a bird. Why not take me sailing? I loved it so that time we came back from the Landing, I'd love it even more in that tiny boat the Cooper boy has. Why, it's alive, it moves so quickly, so lightly, so . . . so happily!*

Fortunately, there were few afternoons that she was at home and near the spy glass. Although the evening receptions and balls were the main events of the Season, there were also other things to be done. The dedicated whist players continued to gamble, Miss Eleanor's Confederate Home committee had meetings about fund raising to buy books for the school and to repair a leak that suddenly appeared in the roof, there were still calls to pay and to receive. Scarlett became hollow-eyed and pale from fatigue.

It would all have been worth it if Rhett was the one feeling jealous and not her. But he seemed to be unaware of the admiration she was provoking. Or worse, uninterested.

She had to make him notice, make him care! She decided to choose one man from her dozens of admirers. Someone handsome . . . rich . . . younger than Rhett. Someone he'd have to feel jealous of.

Heavens, she looked like a ghost! She put on rouge, and heavy perfume, and her most innocent expression for the hunt.

Middleton Courtney was tall and fair, with sleepy-lidded pale eyes and extremely white teeth that he flashed in a wicked-looking smile. He was the epitome of what Scarlett considered a sophisticated man about town. Best of all, he, too, had a phosphate mine and it was twenty times the size of Rhett's.

When he bowed over her hand in greeting, Scarlett closed her fingers over his. He looked up from his bow and smiled. "Dare I hope that you'll honor me with the next dance, Mrs. Butler?"

"If you hadn't asked me, Mr. Courtney, it would have broken my poor heart."

When the polka ended Scarlett opened her fan in the slow unfurling known as "languishing fall." She fluttered it near her face to lift the appealing tendrils of hair above her green eyes. "My goodness," she said breathlessly, "I'm afraid that if I don't get a little air I'm liable to keel right over into your arms, Mr. Courtney. Will you be so kind?" She took his proffered arm and leaned on it while he escorted her to a bench beneath a window.

"Oh, please, Mr. Courtney, do sit here beside me. I'll get a terrible crick in my neck if I have to look up at you."

Courtney seated himself. Rather close. "I'd hate to be the cause of any injury to such a beautiful neck," he said. His eyes moved slowly down her throat to her white bosom. He was as skillful as Scarlett was at the game they were playing.

She kept her eyes modestly lowered, as if she didn't know what Courtney was doing. Then she glanced up through her eyelashes and quickly down again.

"I hope my silly weak spell isn't keeping you from dancing with the lady closest to your heart, Mr. Courtney."

"But the lady you speak of is the lady closest to my heart right now, Mrs. Butler."

Scarlett looked him directly in the eyes and smiled enchantingly. "You be careful, Mr. Courtney. You're liable to turn my head," she promised.

"I certainly intend to try," he murmured close to her ear. His breath was warm on her neck.

Very soon the public romance between them was the most talked-about topic of the Season. The number of times they danced together at each ball ... the time Courtney took Scarlett's punch cup from her hand and put his lips where hers had been on the edge ... overheard snippets of their innuendo-laden raillery ...

Middleton's wife, Edith, looked increasingly drawn and pale. And no one could understand Rhett's imperturbability.

Why didn't he do something? the little world of Charleston society wondered.

26

The yearly races were second only to the Saint Cecilia Ball as the crowning event of Charleston's social season. Indeed there were many people—largely bachelors—who considered them the only event. "You can't gamble on a bunch of waltzes," they grumbled mutinously.

Before the War, the Season had included a full week of racing, and the Saint Cecilia Society hosted three balls. Then came the years of siege; an artillery shell ignited a path of fire through the city that consumed the building where the balls had always been held; and the long, landscaped oval track, its clubhouse, and its stables were used as a Confederate Army encampment and hospitals for the wounded.

In 1865 the city surrendered. In 1866 an enterprising and ambitious Wall Street banker named August Belmont bought the monumental carved stone entrance pillars of the old Race Course and had them transported north to become the entrance to his Belmont Park racetrack.

The Saint Cecilia Ball found a borrowed home only two years after the end of the War and Charlestonians rejoiced that the Season could begin again. It took longer to regain and restore the fouled and rutted land of the Race Course. Nothing was quite the same— there was one ball, not three; Race Week was Race Day; the entrance pillars could not be recovered, and the Clubhouse had been replaced by half-roofed tiers of wooden benches. But on the bright afternoon in late January 1875, the entire remaining population of old Charleston was *en fête* for the second year of racing. The streetcars of all four City Railway lines were diverted to the Rutledge Avenue route that ended near the Race Course, the cars were hung with green and white bunting, the Club colors, and the horses pulling them had green and white ribbons braided in their tails and manes.

Rhett presented his three ladies with green and white striped parasols when they were ready to leave the house and inserted a white camellia into his buttonhole. His white smile was brilliant in his tanned face. "The Yankees are taking the bait," he said. "The esteemed Mr. Belmont himself has sent down two horses, and Guggenheim has one. They don't know about the brood mares Miles Brewton hid in the swamp. Their get grew into a mettlesome family—a bit shaggy from swamp living and unbeautiful from cross-breeding with strays from the cavalry—but Miles has a wonder of a three-year-old that's going to make every big-money pocket a lot lighter than it expected to be."

"You mean there's betting?" Scarlett asked. Her eyes glittered.

"Why else would anyone race?" Rhett laughed. He tucked folded banknotes into his mother's reticule, Rosemary's pocket, and Scarlett's glove. "Put it all on Sweet Sally and buy yourselves a trinket with your winnings."

What a good mood he's in, Scarlett thought. He put the banknote inside my glove. He could have just handed it to me, he didn't have to touch my hand that way—no, not my hand, my bare wrist. Why, it was practically a caress! He's noticing me now that he thinks I'm interested in somebody else. Really noticing me, not just paying polite attention. It's going to work!

She'd been worried that maybe letting Middleton have every third dance was going too far. People had been talking, she knew. Well, let them talk if a little gossip would bring Rhett back to her.

When they entered the grounds of the Race Course, Scarlett gasped. She'd had no idea it was so big! Or that there'd be a band! And so many people. She looked around with delight. Then she caught hold of Rhett's sleeve. "Rhett ... Rhett ... there are Yankee soldiers all over the place. What does it mean? Are they going to stop the races?"

Rhett smiled. "Don't you think Yankees gamble, too? Or that we should mind relieving them of some of their money? God knows, they didn't object to taking all of ours. I'm glad to see the gallant colonel and his officers sharing in the simple pleasures of the vanquished. They've got a lot more money to lose than our kind do."

"How can you be so sure they'll lose it?" Her eyes were narrowed, calculating. "The Yankee horses are thoroughbreds, and Sweet Sally is nothing but a swamp pony."

Rhett's mouth twisted. "Pride and loyalty don't weigh much for you when there's money involved, do they, Scarlett? Well, go ahead, my pet, lay your bet on Belmont's filly to win. I gave you the money, you can do what you like with it." He walked away from her, took his mother's arm and gestured up at the stand. "I think you'll have a good view from higher up, Mama. Come along, Rosemary."

Scarlett started to run after him. "I didn't mean—" she said, but his wide back was like a wall. She shrugged angrily, then looked from right to left. Where did she go to place a bet, anyhow?

"Can I help you, ma'am?" said a man nearby.

"Why, yes, maybe you can." He looked like a gentleman, and his accent sounded like Georgia. She smiled gratefully. "I'm not used to such complicated racing. Back home somebody would just yell, 'I bet you five dollars I can beat you to the crossroads,' and then everybody would holler back and start riding lickety-split."

The man took off his hat and held it against his chest with both hands. He sure is looking at me peculiar, Scarlett thought uneasily. Maybe I shouldn't have spoken.

"Excuse me, ma'am," he said earnestly, "I'm not surprised you don't remember me, but I believe I know you. You're Mrs. Hamilton, aren't you? From Atlanta. You nursed me in the hospital there when I was wounded. My name's Sam Forrest, from Moultrie, Georgia."

The hospital! Scarlett's nostrils flared, an involuntary reaction to the memory of the stench of blood and gangrene and filthy, lice-ridden bodies.

Forrest's face was a picture of embarrassed discomfort. "I—I beg your pardon, Mrs. Hamilton," he stammered. "I shouldn't have made any claim to knowing you. I didn't mean to offend."

Scarlett returned the hospital to the corner of her mind reserved for the past and closed the door on it. She put her hand on Sam Forrest's arm and smiled at him. "Land, Mr. Forrest, you didn't offend me at all. I was just thrown off by being called Mrs. Hamilton. I married again, you see, and I've been Mrs. Butler for years and years. My husband's a Charlestonian, that's why I'm here. And I must say hearing your good Georgia talk makes me mighty homesick. What brings you here?"

Horses, Forrest explained. After four years in the cavalry, there was nothing about horses that he didn't know. When the War was over he'd saved the money he made as a laborer and started buying horses. "Now I've got a fine breeding and boarding business. I've brought the prize of the stable to race for the prize money. I tell you, Mrs. Hamil—sorry—Mrs. Butler, it was a happy day when the news got to me that the Charleston Race Course was open again. There's nothing else like it any place in the South."

Scarlett had to pretend to listen to more horse talk while he accompanied her to the booth set up for taking bets, then escorted her back to the stands. Scarlett said goodbye to him with a feeling of escape.

The stands were very nearly full, but she had no trouble finding her place. The green and white striped parasols were a beacon. Scarlett waved hers at Rhett, then began to climb the risers. Eleanor Butler returned her salute. Rosemary looked away.

Rhett seated Scarlett between Rosemary and his mother. She was barely settled when she felt Eleanor Butler stiffen. Middleton Courtney and his wife, Edith, were taking seats in the same row not far away. The Courtneys nodded and smiled a friendly greeting. The Butlers returned it. Then Middleton began to point out the starting gate and finish line to his wife. At the same time Scarlett said, "You'll never guess who I met, Miss Eleanor, a soldier that was in Atlanta when I first went to live there!" She could feel Mrs. Butler relax.

An excited stir ran through the crowd. The horses were coming onto the track. Scarlett stared open-mouthed, eyes shining. Nothing had prepared her for the smooth grass oval and the bright checkerboards and stripes and harlequin diamonds of the racing silks. Gaudy and shining and festive, the riders paraded past the grandstand while the band played a rollicking oom-pah tune. Scarlett laughed aloud without knowing it. It was a child's laughter, free and unconsidered, expressing pure joyful surprise. "Oh, look!" she said. "Oh, look!" She was so enraptured that she was unaware of Rhett's eyes watching her, instead of the horses.

There was an interval for refreshments after the third race. A tent hung with green and white streamers sheltered long tables of food, and waiters circulated throughout the crowd bearing trays of champagne-filled glasses. Scarlett took one of Emma Anson's glasses from one of Sally Brewton's crested trays, pretending that she didn't recognize Minnie Wentworth's butler, who was serving. She'd learned Charleston's ways of dealing with shortages and loss. Everyone shared their treasures and their servants, acting as if they belonged to the host or hostess of the event. "That's just about the silliest thing I ever heard," she'd said when Mrs. Butler first explained the charade. Lending and borrowing she could understand. But pretending that Emma Anson's initials belonged on Minnie Wentworth's napkins made no sense at all. Still, she went along with the deception, if that was the term for it. It was just one more of the peculiarities of Charleston.

"Scarlett." She turned quickly to the speaker. It was Rosemary.

"They'll be sounding the bell any minute. Let's go back before the rush starts."

People were starting to return to the stands. Scarlett looked at them through the opera glasses she'd borrowed from Miss Eleanor. There were her aunts; thank heaven she hadn't run into them in the refreshment tent. And Sally Brewton with her husband Miles. He looked almost as excited as she did. Good grief! Miss Julia Ashley was with them. Fancy *her* betting on the horses.

She moved the glasses from side to side. It was fun to be able to watch people when they didn't know you were looking. Hah! There was old Josiah Anson dozing off. While Emma was talking to him, too. He'd get an earful if she found out he was asleep! Ugh! Ross! Too bad he had come back, but Miss Eleanor was pleased. Margaret looked nervous, but she always did. Oh, there's Anne. My grief, she looks like the old woman in the shoe with all those children she's got with her. They must be the orphans. Does she see me? She's turning this way. No, she's not looking high enough.

My stars, she's positively glowing. Has Edward Cooper proposed at last? Must be; she's looking up at him as if he could walk on water. She's practically melting

Scarlett moved the glasses upward to see if Edward was being as obvious as Anne . . . a pair of shoes, trousers, jacket—

Her heart leapt into her throat. It was Rhett. He must be talking to Edward. Her gaze lingered for a moment. Rhett looked so elegant. She shifted the glasses, and Eleanor Butler came into view. Scarlett froze, not even breathing. It couldn't be. She scanned the area near Rhett and his mother. Nobody was there yet. Slowly she moved the glasses back to look at Anne again, then again at Rhett, then back to Anne. There was no doubt about it. Scarlett felt sick. Then searingly angry.

That miserable little sneak! She's been praising me to the skies all this time to my face, and she's wildly in love with my husband behind my back. I could strangle her to death with my bare hands!

Her hands were sweating, she almost lost hold of the glasses when she swung them back to Rhett. Was he looking at Anne? . . . No, he was laughing with Miss Eleanor . . . they were chatting with the Wentworths . . . greeting the Hugers . . . the Halseys . . . the Savages . . . old Mr. Pinckney . . . Scarlett kept Rhett in view until her eyes blurred.

He hadn't looked in Anne's direction even once. She was staring at him like she could eat him with a spoon, and he didn't even notice it.

There's nothing to fret about. It's just a silly girl with a crush on a grown-up man.

Why shouldn't Anne have a crush on him? Why shouldn't every woman in Charleston? He's so handsome and so strong and so . . .

She looked at him with yearning naked on her face, the glasses in her lap. Rhett was bent down to adjust Miss Eleanor's shawl across her shoulders. The sun was low in the sky and a cold fitful wind had begun to blow. He placed his hand under her elbow and they began to climb the steps to their seats, the very picture of a dutiful son with his mother. Scarlett waited eagerly for them to arrive.

The partial roof over the grandstand cast an angled shadow over the seats. Rhett changed places with his mother so that she could be warmed by what sunlight there was, and Scarlett had him beside her at last. She forgot Anne at once.

When the horses came out on the track for the fourth race, the spectators stood up, first two, then several groups of people, then everyone, in a tidal wave of anticipation. Scarlett was almost dancing with excitement.

"Having a good time?" Rhett was smiling.

"Wonderful! Which horse is Miles Brewton's, Rhett?"

"I suspect Miles rubbed his down with shoe-polish. It's number five, the very glossy black. The dark horse, you might say. Number six is Guggenheim's; Belmont managed post position; his pace-setter is number four."

Scarlett wanted to ask what "pace-setter" and "post position" meant, but there was no time, they were about to start.

Number five's rider anticipated the starter's pistol shot, and there were loud groans from the stands. "What happened?" Scarlett asked.

"False start, they'll have to line up again," Rhett explained. He tilted his head in gesture. "Look at Sally."

Scarlett looked. Sally Brewton's face was more monkey-like than ever, contorted with rage, and she was shaking her fist in the air. Rhett laughed affectionately. "I might just jump the fence and keep going if I were the jockey," he said. "Sally's ready to use his skin for a hearth rug."

"I don't blame her one bit," Scarlett declared, "and I don't think it's one bit funny either, Rhett Butler."

He laughed again. "May I dare assume that you put your money on Sweet Sally after all?"

"Of course I did. Sally Brewton's a dear friend of mine—and besides, if I lost, it was your money, not mine."

Rhett looked at Scarlett in surprise. She was smiling impishly at him.

"Well done, madam," he murmured.

The pistol shot sounded, and the race had begun. Scarlett didn't know that she was shouting, jumping up and down, pounding on Rhett's arm. She was even deaf to the shouts of the people all around them. When Sweet Sally won by a half-length she let out a yell of victory. "We won! We won! Isn't it marvelous? We won!"

Rhett rubbed his biceps. "I think I'm crippled for life, but I agree. It's marvelous, truly a marvel. The swamp rat over the best bloodstock in America."

Scarlett frowned at him. "Rhett! Do you mean to tell me you're surprised? After what you said this afternoon? You sounded so confident."

He smiled. "I despise pessimism. And I wanted everyone to have a good time."

"But didn't you bet on Sweet Sally, too? Don't tell me you bet on the Yankees!"

"I didn't bet at all." His jaw was hard with resolve. "When the gardens at the Landing are cleared and planted, I'm going to begin bringing the stables back to life. I've already retrieved some of the cups that Butler horses won when our colors were known all over the world. I'll place my first bet when I have a horse of my own to bet on." He turned to his mother. "What will you buy with your winnings, Mama?"

"That's for me to know and you not to find out," she replied, with a jaunty toss of her head.

Scarlett, Rhett, and Rosemary laughed together.

27

$\mathcal{S}$carlett received small spiritual benefit from Mass the next day. Her whole focus was on her own spirits, and they were very low. She'd hardly laid eyes on Rhett at the big party given by the Jockey Club after the races.

Walking back after Mass, she tried to make an excuse that would get her out of eating with her aunts, but Pauline wouldn't hear of it. "We have something very important to discuss with you," she'd said. Her tone was portentous. Scarlett braced herself for a lecture about dancing too much with Middleton Courtney.

As it turned out, his name wasn't mentioned at all. Eulalie was mournful and Pauline censorious about something else altogether.

"We've learned that you haven't written to your grandfather Robillard for years, Scarlett."

"Why should I write to him? He's nothing but a crabby old man who's never lifted a finger for me in my whole life."

Eulalie and Pauline were shocked speechless. Good! thought Scarlett. Her eyes gleamed triumphantly at them above the rim of her cup while she drank her coffee. You don't have an answer to that, do you? He's never done anything for me, and he's never done a thing for you, either. Who gave you the money to keep body and soul together when this house was about to go for taxes? Not your precious father, that's for sure. It was me. It was me who paid for Uncle Carey to get a decent burial when he died, too, and it's my money that puts clothes on your backs and food on your table—if Pauline can bear to open the pantry door on the stuff she hoards in there. So you can gape at me like a pair of goggle-eyed frogs, but there's not one single thing you can say!

But Pauline, echoed by Eulalie, found plenty to say. About respect for one's elders, loyalty to one's family, duty and manners and good breeding.

Scarlett set her cup on its saucer with a crash. "Don't you dare preach over me, Aunt Pauline. I'm sick to death of it! I don't care a fig for Grandfather Robillard. He was horrid to Mother and he's been horrid to me, and I hate him. And I don't care if I burn in Hell for it!"

It felt good to lose her temper. She'd been holding it in too long. There'd been too many tea parties, too many receiving lines, too many calls, and too many callers. Too many times when she'd had to curb her tongue—she who'd always said what she thought and devil take the hindmost. Most of all, too many hours of listening politely to Charlestonians brag about the glories of their fathers and grandfathers and great-grandfathers, on and on, all the way back to the Middle Ages. The very last thing Pauline should have mentioned was respect due to her family.

The aunts cowered before Scarlett's outburst, and their frightened faces gave her an intoxicating joyful feeling of power. She'd always been contemptuous of weakness, and in the months she'd spent in Charleston she had had no power, she'd been the weak one, and she'd begun to feel contempt for herself. Now she unleashed on her aunts all the disgust she had felt at her own craven desire to please.

"There's no need to sit there staring at me as if I had horns on my head and a pitchfork in my hand, either! You know I'm right, but you're just too lily-livered to say it for yourself. Grandfather treats everybody like dirt. I'll bet you a hundred dollars that he never answers all the mealymouth letters you write him. He likely doesn't even read them. I know I never once read one all the way through. I didn't have to, they were all always the same thing—whining for more money!"

Scarlett covered her mouth with her hand. She'd gone too far. She'd broken three of the unwritten, inviolate rules of the Southern code of behavior: she'd said the word "money," she'd reminded her dependents of the charity she'd given, and she'd kicked a downed foe. Her eyes when she looked at her weeping aunts were stricken with shame.

The mended china and darned linen on the table reproached her. I haven't even been very generous, she thought. I could have sent them much more and never missed it.

"I'm sorry," she whispered, and she began to cry.

A moment passed before Eulalie wiped her eyes and blew her nose.

"I heard that Rosemary has a new suitor," she said in a watery voice. "Have you met him, Scarlett? Is he an interesting person?"

"Is he from a good family?" Pauline added.

Scarlett winced, but only slightly. "Miss Eleanor knows his people," she said, "and says they're very nice. Rosemary won't have anything to do with him. You know how she is." She looked at her aunts' worn faces with real affection and respect. They had kept the code. She knew they would keep it until the day they died and never refer to the way she had broken it. No Southerner would ever deliberately shame another.

She straightened her shoulders and lifted her chin. "His name is Elliott Marshall," she said, "and he's the funniest-looking thing you'd ever want to see—skinny as a stick and solemn as an owl!" She forced a lilt into her voice. "He must be mighty brave, though. Rosemary could pick him up and break him in pieces if she got irritated enough." She leaned forward and widened her eyes. "Did you hear that he's a Yankee?"

Pauline and Eulalie gasped.

Scarlett nodded rapidly, emphasizing the impact of the revelation. "From Boston," she said slowly, giving each word full weight. "And I figure you can't get much more Yankeefied than that. Some big fertilizer outfit opened an office down here, and he's the manager . . ."

She settled back more comfortably in her chair, ready for a long stay.

When the morning was spent she marvelled at the time and rushed to the hall to get her wrap. "I shouldn't have stayed so long, I promised Miss Eleanor I'd be home for dinner." She rolled her eyes upward. "I do hope Mr. Marshall won't be calling. Yankees don't have sense enough to know when they're not welcome."

Scarlett kissed Pauline and Eulalie goodbye at the front door. "Thank you," she said simply.

"You come right back and have dinner with us if that Yankee's there," Eulalie giggled.

"Yes, you do that," said Pauline. "And do try if you can to come with us to Savannah for Father's birthday party. We're taking the train on the fifteenth, after Mass."

"Thank you, Aunt Pauline, but I couldn't possibly manage it. We've already accepted invitations for every single day and night of the Season."

"But my dear, the Season will be over by then. The Saint Cecilia's on Friday the thirteenth. I think that's unlucky myself, but nobody else seems to care."

Pauline's words were blurred in Scarlett's ears. How could the Season be so short? She'd thought there was lots of time left to get Rhett back.

"We'll see," she said hurriedly, "I've got to go now."

* * *

Scarlett was surprised to find Rhett's mother at home alone. "Julia Ashley invited Rosemary to dinner at her house," Eleanor told her. "And Rhett took pity on the Cooper boy. He's out sailing."

"Today? It's so cold."

"It is. Just when I'd begun to think we were going to escape winter altogether this year, too. I felt it yesterday at the races. The wind had a real bite to it. I took a bit of a chill, I believe." Mrs. Butler suddenly smiled in a conspiratorial manner. "What do you say to a quiet dinner on the card table before the fire in the library? It will offend Manigo's dignity, but I can bear it if you can. It'll be so cozy, just the two of us."

"I'd like that very much, Miss Eleanor, I really would." Suddenly it was what she wanted above all things. It was so nice when we used to have our quiet suppers that way, she thought. Before the Season. Before Rosemary came home. A voice in her mind added: before Rhett came back from the Landing. It was true, though she hated to admit it. Life was so much easier when she wasn't constantly listening for his step, watching for his reactions, trying to guess what he was thinking.

The warmth of the fire was so relaxing that Scarlett caught herself yawning. "Excuse me, Miss Eleanor," she said hastily, "it's not the company."

"I feel exactly the same way," said Mrs. Butler. "Isn't it pleasant?" She yawned, too, and the contagion caught both of them, until helpless laughter took the place of their yawns. Scarlett had forgotten how much fun Rhett's mother could be.

"I love you, Miss Eleanor," she said without thinking.

Eleanor Butler took her hand. "I'm so glad, dear Scarlett. I love you, too." She sighed softly. "So much so that I'm not going to ask any questions or make any unwelcome comments. I just hope you know what you're doing."

Scarlett squirmed inwardly. Then she bridled at the implied criticism. "I'm not 'doing' anything!" She pulled her hand away.

Eleanor ignored Scarlett's anger. "How are Eulalie and Pauline?" she asked easily. "I haven't seen either of them to talk to for ages. The Season wears me out."

"They're fine. Bossy as ever. They're trying to make me go to Savannah with them for Grandfather's birthday."

"Good heavens!" Mrs. Butler's tone was incredulous. "You mean he's not dead yet?"

Scarlett began to laugh again. "That was the first thing I thought, too, but Aunt Pauline would have skinned me alive if I'd said so. He must be about a hundred."

Eleanor's brow creased in thought and she mumbled under her breath as she worked out the arithmetic. "Over ninety for sure," she said at last. "I know he was in his late thirties when he married your grandmother in 1820. I had an aunt—she's dead long since—who never got over it. She was mad about him, and he'd been quite attentive to her. But then Solange—your grandmother—decided to notice him and poor Aunt Alice didn't stand a chance. I was only ten at the time, but that was old enough to know what was going on. Alice tried to kill herself, and everything was in an uproar."

Scarlett felt wide awake now. "What did she do?"

"Drank a bottle of paregoric. It was touch and go whether she'd live or not."

"Over *Grandfather?*"

"He was an incredibly dashing man. So handsome, with that wonderful straight bearing that soldiers have. And a French accent, of course. When he said 'good morning' he sounded like a hero from an opera. Dozens of women were in love with him. I heard my father say one time that Pierre Robillard was solely responsible for the roof on the Huguenot church. He'd come up from Savannah once in a while for the services because they're in French. The church walls would practically bulge with a congregation full of women, and the collection plate was filled to overflowing." Eleanor smiled reminiscently. "Come to think of it, my Aunt Alice eventually married a professor of French Literature at Harvard. So all the language practicing she must have done came in handy after all."

Scarlett refused to let Mrs. Butler be sidetracked. "Never mind that, tell me more about Grandfather. And Grandmother. I asked you about her once, but you just brushed it off."

Eleanor shook her head. "I don't know how to describe your grandmother. She wasn't like anybody else in the world."

"Was she very beautiful?"

"Yes—and no. That's the problem with talking about her, she was always changing. She was so—so French. They have a saying, the French, that no woman can be truly beautiful who is not also sometimes truly ugly. They're such a subtle people, and so wise, and so impossible for an Anglo-Saxon to understand."

Scarlett couldn't understand what Miss Eleanor was trying to say. "There's a portrait of her at Tara and she looks beautiful," she said stubbornly.

"Yes, she would, for her portrait. She could be beautiful or not, as she chose. She chose to be anything she liked. She had a quality of absolute stillness sometimes, and you'd almost forget she was there. Then she'd turn her slanted dark eyes on you, and suddenly you'd find yourself irresistibly drawn to her. Children swarmed to her. Animals, too. Even women felt it. It drove men out of their minds.

"Your grandfather was every inch the military man, accustomed to command. But your grandmother had only to smile, and he became her slave. She was considerably older than he was, and it made no difference. She was a Catholic, and it made no difference; she insisted on a Catholic household and Catholicism for their children, and he agreed to everything, although he was rigidly Protestant. He would have agreed to let them be Druids, if that was her desire. She was all the world to him.

"I remember when she decided that she must be surrounded by pink light because she was getting older. He said that no soldier would live in a room with so much as a pink shade on a lamp. It was too effeminate. She said it would make her happy, lots of pink. It ended up that not only the walls of the rooms inside were painted, but even the house itself. He would do anything to make her happy." Eleanor sighed. "It was all wonderfully mad and romantic. Poor Pierre. When she died, he died too, in a way. He kept everything in the house exactly the way she had left it. It was hard on your mother and her sisters, I fear."

In the portrait Solange Robillard was wearing a dress that clung to her body so tightly that it suggested that she was wearing nothing under it. That must be what drove men out of their minds, including her husband, Scarlett thought.

"Often you remind me of her," Eleanor said, and Scarlett was suddenly interested again.

"How so, Miss Eleanor?"

"Your eyes are shaped the same, that little upward tilt at the corner of them. And you have the same intensity, you fairly vibrate with it. Both of you strike me as in some way more fully alive than most people."

Scarlett smiled. She felt very satisfied.

Eleanor Butler looked at her fondly. "Now I believe I'll have my nap," she said. She thought she'd handled that conversation very well. She'd said nothing untrue, but she'd managed to avoid saying too much. She certainly didn't want her son's wife to know that her grandmother had had many lovers and that dozens of duels had been fought over her. No telling what kind of ideas that might put in Scarlett's head.

Eleanor was profoundly disturbed by the obvious trouble between her son and his wife. It was not something she could ask Rhett about. If he wanted her to know, he would have told her. And Scarlett's reaction to her hint about the unpleasant situation with the Courtney man made it clear that she didn't want to confide her feelings either.

Mrs. Butler closed her eyes and tried to rest. When all was said and done, there was nothing she could do except hope for the best. Rhett was a grown man and Scarlett a grown woman. Even though, in her opinion, they were behaving like undisciplined children.

Scarlett was trying to rest, too. She was in the card room, telescope at hand. There had been no sight of Tommy Cooper's sailboat when she looked. Rhett must have taken him up the river instead of into the harbor.

Maybe she shouldn't even look for them. When she'd looked through the opera glasses at the races, she'd lost faith in Anne, she was still hurting from it. For the first time in her life she felt old. And very tired. What difference did it make, any of it? Anne Hampton was hopelessly in love with another woman's husband. Hadn't she done the same thing when she was Anne's age? Fallen in love with Ashley and ruined her life with Rhett by clinging to that hopeless love long after she could see—but wouldn't—that the Ashley she loved was only a dream. Would Anne waste her youth the same way, dreaming of Rhett? What was the use of love if all it did was ruin things?

Scarlett rubbed the back of her hand across her lips. What's wrong with me? I'm brooding like an old hen. I've got to do something—go for a walk—anything—to shake off this awful feeling.

Manigo knocked gently on the door. "You got a caller if you is home, Missus Rhett."

Scarlett was so happy to see Sally Brewton that she nearly kissed her. "Take this chair, Sally, it's the closest to the fire. Isn't it a shock to have winter settle in at last? I told Manigo to bring the tea tray. Honestly, I think seeing Sweet Sally win that race was about the most exciting thing I ever saw in my life." She was babbling from relief.

Sally amused her with a highly colored account of Miles kissing their horse, and the jockey too. It lasted until Manigo had set the tea tray on the table in front of Scarlett and left.

"Miss Eleanor's having a rest, or I'd let her know you were here," said Scarlett. "When she wakes up—"

"I'll be gone," Sally interrupted. "I know Eleanor naps in the afternoon, and Rhett is out sailing, and Rosemary is at Julia's. That's why I picked this time to come. I want to talk to you alone."

Scarlett spooned tea leaves into the pot. She was mystified. Sally

Brewton, of all people, sounded uneasy, and nothing ever fazed Sally. She poured hot water onto the leaves and put the lid on the pot.

"Scarlett, I'm going to do the unforgivable," said Sally briskly. "I'm going to meddle in your life. What's much worse, I'm going to give you some unsolicited advice.

"Go ahead and have an affair with Middleton Courtney if you want to, but for God's sake be discreet. What you're doing is in appallingly poor taste."

Scarlett's eyes widened in shock. Have an affair? Only loose women did things like that. How dare Sally Brewton insult her this way? She drew herself up to her tallest. "I'll have you know, Mrs. Brewton, that I'm just as much a lady as you are," she said stiffly.

"Then act like it. Meet Middleton somewhere in the afternoons and pleasure yourself all you like, but don't make your husband and his wife and everyone in town watch you two panting at each other in a ballroom like a dog after a bitch in heat."

Scarlett thought that nothing could be as horrifying as Sally's words. The next ones proved her wrong.

"I should warn you, though, that he's not very good in bed. He's Don Juan in the ballroom but a village idiot once he takes off his dancing pumps and tailcoat."

Sally reached over to the tray and shook the teapot. "If you let this steep much longer, we'll be able to tan hides with it. Do you want me to pour?" She peered closely at Scarlett's face.

"My God," she said slowly, "you're as ignorant as a newborn babe, aren't you? I am sorry, Scarlett, I didn't realize. Here—let me give you a cup of tea with lots of sugar."

Scarlett drew back into her chair. She wanted to cry, to cover her ears. She'd admired Sally, been proud to be a friend of hers, and Sally had turned out to be no better than trash!

"My poor child," said Sally, "if I had known, I would have been a lot easier on you. As it is, consider this an accelerated education. You're in Charleston and married to a Charlestonian, Scarlett. You can't afford to wrap your backwoods innocence around you as a shield. This is an old city with an old civilization. An essential part of being civilized is consideration for the sensibilities of others. You can do anything you like, provided you do it discreetly. The unpardonable sin is to force your peccadilloes down the throats of your friends. You must make it possible for others to pretend they don't know what you're doing."

Scarlett couldn't believe what she was hearing. This was not at all like pretending that initialed napkins belonged to someone else. This was—

disgusting. Although she had married three times while she was in love with someone else, she had never thought of physically betraying any one of her husbands. She could yearn for Ashley, imagine Ashley's embraces, but she would never have sneaked off to meet him for an hour in bed.

I don't want to be civilized, she thought with despair. She'd never be able to look at any woman in Charleston again without wondering if she and Rhett were lovers or had ever been lovers.

Why had she come to this place? She didn't belong here. She didn't want to belong in the kind of place Sally Brewton was talking about.

"I think you'd better go home," she said. "I don't feel very well."

Sally nodded ruefully. "I do apologize for upsetting you, Scarlett. It may make you feel better to know that there are lots of other innocents in Charleston, my dear; you're not the only one. Unmarried girls and maiden ladies of all ages are never told about things they'd rather not know. There are many faithful wives, too. I'm lucky enough to be one of them. I'm sure Miles has strayed a time or two, but I've never been tempted. Perhaps you're the same way; I rather hope so, for your sake. I apologize again for my clumsiness, Scarlett.

"I'll go now. Pull yourself together and drink your tea . . . And behave better with Middleton."

Sally pulled on her gloves with quick, practiced motions and started for the door.

"Wait!" said Scarlett. "Please wait, Sally. I've got to know. Who? Rhett and who?"

Sally's monkey face crumpled in sympathy. "Nobody we know," she said gently. "I swear to you. He was only nineteen when he left Charleston, and at that age boys go to a bordello or to a willing poor white girl. Since he returned he's demonstrated great delicacy in refusing all offers without hurting any feelings.

"Charleston isn't a sink of iniquity, dear. People don't feel any social pressure to be constantly rutting. I'm sure that Rhett is faithful to you.

"I'll see myself out."

As soon as Sally was gone Scarlett ran upstairs to her bedroom and locked herself in. She threw herself across the bed and wept uncontrollably.

Grotesque visions assaulted her mind of Rhett with one woman . . . another . . . still another, and another and another of the ladies she saw at parties every day.

What a fool she'd been to believe that he would be jealous of her.

When she could no longer bear her thoughts, she rang for Pansy, then washed and powdered her face. She couldn't sit and smile and talk with Miss Eleanor when she woke up. She had to get away, at least for a while.

"We're going out," she told Pansy. "Hand me my pelisse."

Scarlett walked for miles—quickly and silently, uncaring whether Pansy was keeping up. As she passed Charleston's tall, beautiful old houses, she didn't see their crumbling pastel stucco walls as proud evidence of survival, she saw only that they cared not how they looked to passers-by and turned their shoulders to the street to face inward toward their private walled gardens.

Secrets. They keep their secrets, she thought. Except from each other. Everyone pretends about everything.

28

It was nearly dark when Scarlett got back, and the house looked silent and forbidding. No light showed through the curtains, drawn each day at sundown. She opened the door carefully, making no sound. "Tell Manigo that I have a headache and I don't want any supper," she said to Pansy while they were still in the vestibule. "Then come undo my laces. I'm going straight to bed."

Manigo would have to notify the kitchen and the family. She couldn't face conversation with anyone. She crept quietly up the stairs past the open doors of the warmly lit drawing room. Rosemary's loud voice was proclaiming Miss Julia Ashley's opinion about something or other. Scarlett hastened her footsteps.

She extinguished the lamp and curled up tightly under the covers after Pansy undressed her, trying to hide from her own desperate unhappiness. If only she could sleep, forget Sally Brewton, forget everything, escape. Darkness was all around her, mocking her dry sleepless eyes. She couldn't even cry; all her tears had been spent in the emotional storm after Sally's hellish revelations.

The latch grated, and light poured into the room as the door swung open. Scarlett turned her head towards it, startled by the sudden brightness.

Rhett was standing in the doorway, a lamp in his raised hand. It cast harsh shadows on the strong planes of his wind-burned face and salt-stiff black hair. He was still wearing the clothes he'd worn sailing; they clung, wet, to his hard chest and muscled arms and legs. His expression was dark with barely controlled emotion, and he loomed huge and dangerous.

Scarlett's heart leapt with primitive fear, yet her breath quickened from excitement. This was what she had dreamed of—Rhett coming into her bedroom with passion overriding his cool self-control.

He strode to the bed, closing the door with a kick. "You can't hide from me, Scarlett," he said. "Get up." In one motion his arm swept the unlit lamp off the table onto the floor with a splintering crash, and his big hand set the lighted one down with such force that it rocked perilously. He threw back the quilts, grabbed her arms, and dragged her from the bed onto her feet.

Her dark tumbled hair fell across her neck and shoulders and over his hands. The lace that edged the open neck of her nightdress quivered from the pounding of her heart. Hot blood stained her cheeks red and deepened the green color of her eyes, fixed on his. Rhett threw her painfully against the bed's thick carved post and backed away.

"Damn you for an interfering fool," he said hoarsely. "I should have killed you the minute you set foot in Charleston."

Scarlett held on to the bedpost to keep from falling. She felt the surging thrill of danger in her veins. What had happened to put him in such a state?

"Don't play the frightened maiden with me, Scarlett. I know you better than that. I'm not going to kill you, I'm not even going to beat you, although God knows you deserve it."

Rhett's mouth twisted. "How fetching you look, my dear. Bosom heaving and eyes wide with innocence. The pity of it is that you probably are innocent by your warped definition. Never mind the pain you've caused a harmless woman by casting your net over her witless husband."

Scarlett's lips curved in an uncontrollable smile of victory. He was furious about her conquest of Middleton Courtney! She had done it—made him admit that he was jealous. Now he'd have to admit that he loved her, she'd make him say it—

"I don't give a damn that you made a spectacle of yourself," Rhett said instead. "In fact it was rather diverting to watch a middle-aged woman convince herself that she was still an irresistible nubile girl. You can't grow past sixteen, can you, Scarlett? The height of your ambition is to remain eternally the belle of Clayton County.

"Today the joke ceased to be funny," he shouted. Scarlett recoiled from the sudden noise. He clenched his fists, visibly took command of his fury. "As I left church this morning," he said quietly, "an old friend, who is also a close cousin, drew me to one side and volunteered to serve as my second when I challenge Middleton Courtney to a duel. He never doubted that that must be my intention. Regardless of the truth of the matter, your good name had to be defended. For the sake of the family."

Scarlett's small white teeth bit into her lower lip. "What did you say to him?"

"Exactly what I am about to say to you. 'A duel will not be necessary. My wife is unaccustomed to society and acted in a way subject to misinterpretation because she didn't know any better. I'll instruct her in what is expected of her.'"

His arm moved as rapidly as a striking snake, and his hand closed cruelly around her wrist. "Lesson one," he said. He pulled her to him with a sudden jerk. Scarlett was pinned against his chest with her arm twisted and held high on her back. Rhett's face was close above her, his eyes boring into hers. "I do not mind if the entire world thinks I'm a cuckold, my dear, devoted little wife, but I will not be forced to fight Middleton Courtney." Rhett's breath was warm and salty in her nose and on her lips. "Lesson two," he said.

"If I kill the jackass, I will have to leave town or be hung by the military, and that would be inconvenient for me. And I certainly have no intention of making myself an easy target for him. He might accidentally shoot straight and wound me, which would be another kind of inconvenience."

Scarlett struck at him with her free hand, but he trapped it easily in his and twisted it up next to the other. His arms were a cage holding her against him. She could feel the moisture in his shirt seeping through her nightdress to her skin. "Lesson three," said Rhett. "It would be the irony of the age for me—or even an imbecile like Courtney—to risk death in order to save your dishonest little soul from dishonor. Therefore—lesson four: you will follow my instructions for your behavior at all public appearances until the Season is ended. No head-hanging chagrin, my pet. It's not your style and it would only add fuel to the fire of gossip. You will hold your curled head high and continue your relentless pursuit of lost youth. But you will distribute your attentions more evenly among the beguiled male population. I will be happy to advise you which gentlemen to favor. In fact I will insist on giving you advice." His hands released her wrists and closed over her shoulders, thrusting her away.

"Lesson five: you will do exactly what I tell you to do." Away from the heat of Rhett's body, the wet silk nightdress felt like ice on Scarlett's breasts and stomach. She crossed her arms over herself for warmth, but it was useless. Her mind was as icy as her body, and the things he had said rang clearly through it. He didn't care . . . he had been laughing at her . . . he was concerned only with his "convenience."

How dare he? How dare he laugh at her in public and revile her to his kin and throw her around in her own room like a sack of meal? A

"Charleston gentleman" was as much a lie as a "Charleston lady." Two-faced, lying, double-dealing—

Scarlett lifted her fists to hit him, but he was still gripping her shoulders, and her balled hands fell ineffectually on his chest.

She twisted and broke free. Rhett raised his palms to ward off her blows, and laughter rumbled low in his brown throat.

Scarlett lifted her hands—only to push her wild hair back from her face. "You can save your breath, Rhett Butler. I'll need no advice from you because I won't be here to ignore it. I hate your precious Charleston, and I despise everybody in it, especially you. I'm leaving tomorrow." She faced him head-on, her hands on her hips, her head high, her chin out. Her body was visibly trembling in the clinging silk.

Rhett looked away. "No, Scarlett," he said. His tone was leaden. "You will not leave. Flight would only serve to confirm guilt, and I'd still have to kill Courtney. You blackmailed me into allowing you to stay for the Season, Scarlett, and stay you will.

"And you will do what I tell you to do, and you will appear to like it. Or I swear before God that I will break every bone in your body, one after another."

He walked to the door. With his hand on the latch, he looked back at her and smiled mockingly. "And don't try to do anything clever, my pet. I will be watching every move you make."

"I hate you!" Scarlett shouted at the closing door. When she heard a key turning in the lock, she threw the mantel clock, then the fireplace poker, at it.

Too late she thought of the piazza and the other bedrooms. When she ran to their doors they, too, were locked on the outside. She returned to her own room and paced its length and width until she was exhausted.

At last she slumped into a chair and pounded weakly on its armrests until her hands were sore. "I am going to leave," she announced aloud, "and there's no way he can stop me." The tall, thick, locked door silently gave her the lie.

There was no point in fighting Rhett, she'd have to outwit him somehow. There had to be a way, and she'd find it. No need to burden herself with luggage, she could go with only the clothes on her back. That's what she'd do. She'd go to a tea or a whist party or something and just walk away in the middle, straight to the horsecar and on to the depot. She had plenty of money for a ticket to—where?

As always when Scarlett was heartsore, she thought of Tara. There was peace there, and new strength . . .

. . . and Suellen. If only Tara was hers, all hers. She saw again the daydreams she'd invented when she visited Julia Ashley's plantation. How could Carreen have thrown away her share the way she had?

Scarlett's head snapped up like a woods animal scenting water. What good was a share in Tara to the convent in Charleston? They couldn't sell it, even if there was a buyer, because Will would never agree, nor would she. Maybe they got a third share of any profit from the cotton crop, but how much could that possibly be? At best thirty or forty dollars a year. Why, they would jump at a chance to sell to her.

Rhett wanted her to stay, did he? Fine! She'd stay, but only if he helped her get Carreen's third of Tara. Then, with two-thirds in her hand, she'd offer to buy out Will and Suellen. If Will refused to sell, she'd throw them out.

A stab of conscience halted her thoughts, but Scarlett pushed it away. What did it matter how much Will loved Tara? She loved it more. And she needed it. It was the only place she cared about, the only place where anyone had ever cared about her. Will would understand; he'd see that Tara was her only hope.

She ran to the bellpull and yanked on it. Pansy came to the door, tried it, turned the key and opened it.

"Tell Mr. Butler I want to see him, here in my room," Scarlett said. "And bring up a supper tray. I'm hungry after all."

She changed into a dry nightdress and a warm velvet dressing gown, then brushed her hair smooth and tied it back with a velvet ribbon. Her bleak eyes met themselves in the reflection of the looking glass.

She had lost. She wasn't going to get Rhett back.

It wasn't supposed to be like this.

Too much—too fast—her whole world had turned upside down in only a few hours. She was still reeling from the shock of what Sally Brewton told her. She couldn't stand staying in Charleston after what she'd learned. It would be like trying to build a house on shifting sands.

Scarlett pressed her hands to her forehead as if to contain the maelstrom of confused thoughts. She couldn't make sense of so many things spinning through her brain at one time. There had to be one thing she could concentrate on. All her life she'd been successful if she put all her attention on one goal.

Tara . . .

Tara it would be. When she finished gaining control of Tara, then she would think about all the rest . . .

"Here's your supper, Miss Scarlett."

"Put the tray on that table, Pansy, and leave me alone. I'll ring when I'm done with it."

"Yes'm. Mr. Rhett he say he'll be along after he eats."

"Leave me alone."

Rhett's expression was unreadable except for the wariness in his eyes. "You wanted to see me, Scarlett?"

"Yes, I do. Don't worry, I'm not looking for a fight. I want to offer you a trade."

His expression did not change. He said nothing.

Scarlett kept her voice cool and businesslike when she continued. "You and I both know that you can force me to stay in Charleston and go to the balls and receptions. And we both know that once you get me to one, there's not a single thing you can do about what I might say or do. I'm offering to stay and to act however you want me to act, if you'll help me get something I want that has nothing to do with you or Charleston."

Rhett sat down, took out a thin cheroot, clipped and lit it. "I'm listening," he said.

She explained her plan, growing more intense with each word she spoke. She waited eagerly for Rhett's opinion when she finished.

"I have to admire your nerve, Scarlett," said Rhett. "I never questioned whether you could hold your own against General Sherman and his army, but trying to outwit the Roman Catholic Church might be biting off more than you can chew."

He was laughing at her, but it was a friendly laugh, even admiring. As if he, too, were back in the early days when they were friends.

"I'm not trying to outwit anybody, Rhett, just make an honest deal, that's all."

Rhett grinned. "You? Make an honest deal? You disappoint me, Scarlett. Are you losing your touch?"

"Honestly! I don't know why you have to talk so ugly. You know very well I wouldn't take advantage of the Church." Scarlett's prim outrage made Rhett laugh even more.

"I don't know anything of the kind," he said. "Tell me the truth, is this why you've been trotting off to Mass every Sunday rattling your beads? Have you been planning this all along?"

"No I haven't. I can't imagine why it took me so long to think of it." Scarlett covered her mouth with her hand. How did Rhett do it? He always could surprise her into telling more than she meant to. She lowered her hand and scowled at him. "Well? Are you going to help me or not?"

"I'm willing to help, but I don't see how I can. What if the Mother Superior turns you down? Will you still stay through the Season?"

"I said I would, didn't I? Besides, there's no reason for her to turn me down. I'm going to offer much more than Will can possibly send her. You can use your influence. You know everybody in the world, you can always get things done."

Rhett smiled. "What touching faith you have in me, Scarlett. I know every rascal and crooked politician and dishonest businessman within a thousand miles, but I have no influence at all with the good people in this world. The best I can do for you is give you a little advice. Don't try to pull the wool over the lady's eyes. Tell her the truth if you can, and agree to anything she asks. Don't bargain."

"What a ninny you are, Rhett Butler! Nobody pays asking price except a fool. The convent doesn't really need money anyhow. They've got that big house and all the sisters work for no wages and there are gold candlesticks and a big gold cross on the altar in the chapel."

" 'Though I speak with the tongues of men and of angels . . .' " Rhett murmured with a chuckle.

"What on earth are you talking about?"

"Just quoting."

He forced his face into a serious expression, but his dark eyes were gleeful. "I wish you all the luck in the world, Scarlett," he said. "Consider it my benediction." He left her room with his composure intact, then he laughed with genuine delight. Scarlett would keep her promise, she always did. With her help, he'd smooth over the scandal; then, in only two weeks the Season would end and Scarlett would be gone. He'd be free of the tension she had brought to the life he was trying to build in Charleston, and he'd be free to get back to the Landing. There was so much that he wanted to do on the plantation. Scarlett's bullheaded assault on the Mother Superior of Carreen's convent should be a good entertainment to divert him until his life was his own again.

I'd bet on the Roman Catholic Church, Rhett said to himself. It thinks of time in aeons, not in weeks. But I wouldn't want to bet much. When Scarlett takes the bit between her teeth she's a formidable force to reckon with. He laughed quietly for a long time.

As Rhett had expected, Scarlett's relations with the Mother Superior were far from simple. "She won't say yes and she won't say no and she doesn't even listen when I try to explain the good sense of selling!" Scarlett complained after her first visit to the convent. And her second visit, third, fifth. She was baffled and frustrated. Rhett listened with kind, patient attention while she raged, keeping his laughter inside. He knew that he was the only person she had to talk to.

In addition, Scarlett's efforts provided him with fresh delights almost daily as she escalated her assault on the Holy Mother Church. She began going to Mass every morning, confident that word of her devotion would get back to the convent. Then she started visiting Carreen so often that she learned the names of all the other nuns and almost half of the students. After a week of gentle, noncommittal responses from the Mother Superior, Scarlett was so desperate that she even began to accompany her aunts when they paid calls on friends of theirs who were also elderly Catholic ladies in straitened circumstances.

"I believe I'm wearing my rosary beads down to half their size, Rhett," she exclaimed angrily. "How can that awful old woman be so mean?"

"Maybe she thinks this will save your soul," Rhett suggested.

"Fiddle-dee-dee! My soul is just fine, thank you very much. It's making me gag at the smell of incense, that's what it's doing, all this church stuff. And I look like a hag because I never get enough sleep. I do wish there wasn't a big party every single night."

"Nonsense. Those shadows under your eyes make you look spiritual. They must impress the Mother Superior enormously."

"Oh! Rhett, what a horrid thing to say. I'll have to go powder right this minute."

In fact the lack of sleep was beginning to show on Scarlett's face. And frustration was etching small vertical lines between her eyebrows. Everyone in old Charleston was talking about what they assumed to be some kind of religious fervor. Scarlett was a different person. At receptions and balls she was polite but abstracted. The belle-temptress had retired. She no longer accepted invitations to play whist, and she'd stopped calling on the ladies at whose at-home days she had become a fixture. "I'm all in favor of honoring God," Sally Brewton said one day. "I even give up something I really love for Lent. But I think Scarlett's going too far. It's extravagant."

Emma Anson disagreed. "It makes me think much better of her than I did before. You know I thought you were foolish to sponsor her the way you did, Sally. She was obviously an ignorant, vain little climber. Now I'm willing to eat my words. There's something admirable about anyone with serious religious feelings. Even Popish ones."

Wednesday morning in the second week of Scarlett's siege was dark and cold and rainy. "I just can't walk all the way to the convent through this downpour," she moaned, "I'll ruin my only pair of boots." She thought with longing of the Butlers' former coachman, Ezekiel. He had showed up, like a magical genie from a bottle, on the two rainy nights they were going out. All this Charleston pretense is crazy and disgusting, but I'd be glad to put up with it today if I could just ride in a nice warm dry carriage. But I can't. And I have to go, so I will.

"Mother Superior left this morning early to go to Georgia for a meeting at the Order's school there," said the nun who opened the convent's door. No one knew exactly how long the meeting would last. Perhaps one day, or several, or maybe a week or more.

I don't have a week or more, Scarlett shouted inwardly, I can't even afford to waste a day.

She plodded back to the house through the rain. "Throw away these damned boots," she ordered Pansy. "And get me out some dry clothes."

Pansy was even more soaked than she was. With an ostentatious fit of pitiful coughing, she limped off to do Scarlett's bidding. I should take a strap to that girl, Scarlett said to herself, but she was more heartsick than angry.

The rain stopped in the afternoon. Miss Eleanor and Rosemary decided to go up to King Street shopping. Scarlett didn't even want to do that. She sat in her room brooding until the walls seemed to be closing in on her, then she went downstairs to the library. Maybe Rhett would be there to provide some sympathy. She couldn't talk to anyone else about her frustration because she hadn't told anyone else what she was doing.

"How goes the reformation of the Catholic Church?" he asked, raising one eyebrow.

She burst into an angry account of the Mother Superior's flight. He made sympathetic noises while he cut and lit a thin cigar. "I'm going out onto the piazza to smoke," he said when it was glowing to his satisfaction. "Come out and get some air. The rainstorm brought summer back again; it's very warm now that it's blown out to sea."

The sunlight was dazzling after the dim interior of the dining room. Scarlett shaded her eyes, breathing in the damp green smell of the garden and the salt tang of the harbor and the pungent masculinity of cigar smoke. Suddenly she was acutely aware of Rhett's presence. She was so disturbed that she walked away several paces, and his voice when he spoke seemed to come from a great distance.

"I believe that the school the Sisters have in Georgia is in Savannah. You might go down after the Saint Cecilia for your grandfather's birthday. Your aunts have been nagging you enough. If it's an important Church meeting the Bishop will be there; perhaps you'll have better luck with him."

Scarlett tried to think about Rhett's suggestion, but she couldn't concentrate. Not with him so near. Strange to feel so shy when lately they'd been so comfortable together. He was leaning against one of the columns, placidly enjoying his smoke.

"I'll see," she said, and she left in a rush, before she began to cry.

What on earth is wrong with me? she thought as tears streamed from her eyes. I'm turning into a spineless cry-baby, just the kind of creature I despise. So what if it takes a little longer to get what I want? I will have Tara . . . and Rhett, too, if it takes a hundred years.

29

"I have never been so annoyed in all my long years," said Eleanor Butler. Her hands were shaking when she poured the tea. A crushed thin paper sheet was on the floor near her feet. The telegram had arrived while she and Rosemary were out shopping: Cousin Townsend Ellinton and his wife were coming down from Philadelphia to visit.

"Two days' notice!" Eleanor exclaimed. "Can you credit it? You'd think they'd never heard of the War."

"They'll be staying in a suite at the Charleston Hotel, Mama," Rhett said soothingly, "and we'll take them to the Ball. It won't be too bad."

"It will be awful," said Rosemary. "I don't see any reason we have to put ourselves out to be nice to Yankees."

"Because they're our kin," said her mother severely. "And you will be extremely nice. Besides, your Cousin Townsend isn't a Yankee at all. He fought with General Lee."

Rosemary frowned and was silent.

Miss Eleanor began to laugh. "I must stop complaining," she said. "It'll be worth it in the long run to see Townsend and Henry Wragg meet each other. Townsend's cross-eyed, and Henry's wall-eyed. Do you suppose they'll be able to manage to shake hands?"

The Ellintons weren't so bad, Scarlett thought, even though you didn't know where to look when you talked to Cousin Townsend. His wife Hannah wasn't as beautiful as Miss Eleanor had predicted, which was agreeable. However, her pearl-sewn ruby brocade ball gown and diamond dog-collar made Scarlett feel miserably frumpy in her tired claret velvet and camellias. Thank Heaven this was the last ball, and the end of the Season.

I would have called anybody a liar if they'd said I could ever get tired of dancing, but I've had more than my fill. Oh, if only everything was settled about Tara! She had followed Rhett's advice, she'd thougnt about going to Savannah. But the prospect of day after day with her aunts was more than she could bear, and she had decided to wait for the Mother Superior's return to Charleston. Rosemary was going to visit Miss Julia Ashley, so that thorn would be out of her flesh. And Miss Eleanor was always good company.

Rhett was going to the Landing. She wouldn't think about that now. If she did, she'd never be able to get through the evening.

"Do tell, Cousin Townsend," Scarlett said brightly, "all about General Lee. Is he really as handsome as everybody says?"

Ezekiel had polished the carriage and groomed the horses until they looked fit to carry royalty. He stood by the carriage block, holding the door open, ready to assist if needed when Rhett helped his ladies to step up into the carriage.

"I still say that the Ellintons should be riding with us," Eleanor stewed.

"We'd be squashed to death," Rosemary grumbled. Rhett told her to be quiet.

"There's nothing to fret about, Mama," he said. "They're directly in front of us in the finest rig Hannah's money can rent. When we get to Meeting Street we'll pass them so we can be there first to escort them in. There's nothing whatsoever to worry about."

"There's plenty, and you know it, Rhett. Yes, they're nice people and Townsend's kin, but that doesn't alter the fact that Hannah's a dyed-in-the-wool Yankee. I'm afraid she'll be polited to death."

"Be what?" asked Scarlett.

Rhett explained. Charlestonians had a particularly vicious and cunning game, developed after the War. They treated outsiders with so much graciousness and consideration that their politeness became a weapon. "Visitors end up feeling as if they're wearing shoes for the first time in their lives. It's said that only the strongest ever recover from the experience. I hope we won't be treated to a display of it tonight. The Chinese never developed a torture to match it, although they're a very subtle people."

"Rhett! Please stop," begged his mother.

Scarlett said nothing. That's what they've been doing to me, she thought grimly. Well, let them. I don't have to put up with Charleston much longer.

After the turn onto Meeting Street the carriage moved into place at the end of a long line of carriages. One by one they stopped to release passengers, then slowly moved on. It'll be over before we get there at this rate, Scarlett thought. She looked out the window at people walking, the ladies followed by their maids carrying their slipper bags. I wish we'd walked, too. It would be lovely to be out in the warm air instead of cooped up in this stuffy little space. She was startled by the sharp clanging of a streetcar bell to their left.

How can there be a streetcar running? she wondered. They always stopped at nine o'clock. She heard the bells from St. Michael's steeple ring two full rounds. It was half past.

"Isn't it nice to see the streetcar with nobody on it but people dressed for a ball?" said Eleanor Butler. "Did you know, Scarlett, that they always stop running the cars early on the night of the Saint Cecilia so they can scrub them out before they make the special runs to take people to the ball?"

"I didn't know that, Miss Eleanor. How do people get home?"

"Oh, they run another special at two when the ball's over."

"What if somebody wants to ride who isn't going to the ball?"

"They can't, of course. Nobody would even think of it. Everybody knows the cars don't run after nine o'clock."

Rhett laughed. "Mama, you sound like the duchess in *Alice in Wonderland*."

Eleanor Butler began to laugh, too. "I suppose I do," she sputtered cheerfully, then laughed even harder.

She was still laughing when the carriage moved forward and stopped and the door was pulled open. Scarlett looked out onto a scene that made her catch her breath. This was the way a ball should be! Tall black iron poles held a pair of enormous lanterns brightly lit with a half dozen gas jets. They illuminated the deep portico and towering white columns of a temple-like building set back from the street behind a tall iron fence. A gleaming white canvas walkway led from the scoured white marble carriage block to the portico's steps. Over walkway and block a white canvas awning had been erected.

"Just think," she said, marvelling, "you could go from your carriage to the Ball in the pouring rain and not a drop of water would touch you."

"That's the idea," Rhett agreed, "but it's never been tested. It never rains on the night of the Saint Cecilia. God wouldn't dare."

"Rhett!" Eleanor Butler was genuinely shocked.

Scarlett smiled at Rhett, pleased that he could make fun of something that he took as seriously as this ball. He'd told her all about it, how many years and years it had been going on—everything in Charleston seemed to have been around for at least a hundred years—how it was completely run by men. Only men could be members of the Society.

"Step down, Scarlett," said Rhett, "you should feel right at home here. This building is the Hibernian Hall. Inside you'll see a plaque with the harp of Ireland in best gold paint."

"Don't be rude," scolded his mother.

Scarlett stepped out with her pugnacious chin—so like her Irish father's—held high.

What were those Yankee soldiers doing? Scarlett's throat contracted with momentary fear. Were they planning to cause trouble because they'd been beaten by the ladies before? Then she saw the crowds behind them, eager faces bobbing from side to side in an effort to see the figures emerging from the carriages. Why, the Yankees are holding people back to make a path for us! Just like servants, like the torch boys or the footmen. Serves them right. Why don't they just give up and go away? Nobody pays them any mind anyhow.

She looked over the heads of the soldiers and smiled brilliantly at the staring crowds before she stepped down from the carriage block. If only she could have had a new gown instead of this tired old thing. She'd just have to make the best of it. She took three steps forward, then expertly cast the gown's train from across her arm to fall behind her. It spread out on the white walkway, untouched by dust, to sweep regally behind her as she promenaded into The Ball of the Season.

She paused in the entrance hall, waiting for the others. Her eyes were drawn upward, following the graceful arc of the staircase to the second floor's wide landing and the glittering candlelit crystal chandelier suspended over the soaring open space. It was like the biggest, brightest jewel in the world.

"Here are the Ellintons," said Mrs. Butler. "Come this way, Hannah, we'll leave our wraps in the ladies' cloakroom."

But Hannah Ellinton stopped short in the doorway and backed away involuntarily. Rosemary and Scarlett had to move aside quickly to avoid running into the ruby brocade figure in front of them.

What could be wrong? Scarlett craned her neck to see. The scene had become so familiar to her during the Season that she couldn't imagine why Hannah was so shocked. Several girls and women were seated on a low bench near the wall. Their skirts were pulled up above their knees, their feet in basins of soapy water. While they gossiped and laughed with one another, their maids washed and dried and powdered their feet, then unrolled their mended stockings up their legs and put their dancing slippers on. It was the regular routine for all the women who walked through the city's dusty streets to the Season's balls. What did the Yankee woman expect? That people would dance in their boots? She nudged Mrs. Ellinton. "You're blocking the door," she said.

Hannah apologized and moved on inside. Eleanor Butler turned from the mirror where she was rearranging her hairpins. "Good," she said, "I was afraid for a minute that I'd lost you." She hadn't seen Hannah's reaction. "I want you to meet Sheba. She'll take care of anything you need tonight." Mrs. Ellinton was led unprotestingly to the corner of the room where the fattest woman she had ever seen was sitting in a wide, worn, faded brocade wing chair, her golden-brown skin only a tone darker than the gold brocade. Sheba pushed herself up from her throne to be presented to Mrs. Butler's guest.

And to Mrs. Butler's daughter-in-law. Scarlett hurried over, eager to see the woman she'd heard so much about. Sheba was famous. Everyone knew that she was the best seamstress in all Charleston, trained when she was the Rutledges' slave by the modiste Mrs. Rutledge imported from Paris to make her daughter's trousseau. She still sewed for Mrs. Rutledge and her daughter and a few select ladies of her choosing. Sheba could remake rags and flour sacks into creations as elegant as anything in *Godey's Lady's Book*. Baptized Queen of Sheba by her lay-preacher father, she was indeed a queen in her own world. She ruled the ladies' cloakroom at the Saint Cecilia every year, supervising her two neatly uniformed maids, and any maids accompanying the ladies, in rapid, effective action to meet any and all feminine emergencies. Torn hems, spots and stains, lost buttons, drooping curls, faintness, overeating, bruised insteps, broken hearts—Sheba and her minions dealt with them all. Every ball had a room set aside for ladies' needs and maids to staff it, but only the Saint Cecilia had Queen of Sheba. She politely refused to work her magic at any ball other than the finest.

She could afford to be particular. Rhett had told Scarlett what most people knew but no one said aloud. Sheba owned the most lavish and profitable whorehouse on notorious "Mulatto Alley," the stretch of Chalmers Street, only two blocks from the Saint Cecilia, where officers and soldiers of the occupying military forces spent the better part of their pay packets on cheap whiskey, crooked gambling wheels, and women of every age, every shade of skin, and every price.

Scarlett looked at Hannah Ellinton's bewildered expression. I'll bet she's one of those abolitionists who's never seen a black person close up in her life, she thought. I wonder what she'd do if somebody told her about Sheba's other business. Rhett said Sheba's got more than a million dollars in gold in a vault in a bank in England. I doubt the Ellintons can match that.

30

*W*hen Scarlett reached the entrance to the ballroom, it was her turn to stop short, unaware that there were others following her. She was overwhelmed by a beauty that was magical, too lovely to be real.

The huge ballroom was lit brilliantly, yet softly, by candlelight. From four cascades of crystal that seemed to float high above. From paired gilt-and-crystal sconces on the long side walls. From tall gilt-framed mirrors that reflected the flames again and again in opposing images. From night-black tall windows that acted as mirrors. From tall multi-armed silver candelabra on long tables at each side of the door, holding monumental silver punch bowls that held curving light reflections golden in their rounded sides.

Scarlett laughed with delight and stepped across the sill.

"Are you having a good time?" Rhett asked her much later.

"My, yes! It really is the best ball of the Season." She meant it, the evening had been everything a ball should be, filled with music and laughter and happiness on all sides. She'd been less than pleased when she was given her dance card, even though it was presented with a bouquet of gardenias framed in silver-lace paper. The Governors of the Society, it seemed, filled in the names on all the ladies' cards in advance. But then she saw that the regimentation was masterfully orchestrated. She was partnered by men she knew, men she had never met before, old men, young men, long-time Charlestonians, visiting guests, Charlestonians who lived in many other places but always came home for the Saint Cecilia. So that every dance held the tantalizing potential of surprise and the assurance of change. And no embarrassment. Middleton Courtney's name wasn't on her card. She had nothing to think about except the pleasure of being in the exquisite room dancing to the beautiful music.

It was the same for everyone. Scarlett giggled when she saw her aunts dancing every dance; even Eulalie's usually sorrowful face was alight with pleasure. There were no wallflowers here. And no awkwardnesses. The terribly young debutantes in their fresh white gowns were paired with men skillful at both dancing and conversation. She saw Rhett with at least three of them, but never with Anne Hampton. Scarlett wondered briefly how much the wise old Governors knew. She didn't care. It made her happy. And it made her laugh to see the Ellintons.

Hannah was obviously feeling like the belle of the Ball. She must be dancing with the biggest flatterers in Charleston, Scarlett thought maliciously. No, she decided, Townsend looked like he was having an even better time than his wife. Somebody sure must be sweet talking him. They'd certainly never forget this night. For that matter, neither would she. The sixteenth dance was coming up soon. It was reserved, Josiah Anson told her when they were waltzing, for sweethearts and married couples. At the Saint Cecilia, husbands and wives were always newly in love, he said with mock solemnity. He was President of the Society, so he knew. It was one of the Saint Cecilia's rules. She would be dancing it with Rhett.

So when he took her in his arms and asked her if she was enjoying herself, she said yes with all her heart.

At one o'clock the orchestra played the last phrase of the "Blue Danube Waltz," and the Ball was over. "But I don't want it to be over," Scarlett said, "not ever."

"Good," replied Miles Brewton, one of the Governors, "that's exactly how we hope everyone will feel. Now everyone goes downstairs for supper. The Society prides itself on its oyster stew almost as much as on its punch. I hope you've had a cup of our famous mixture?"

"Indeed I have. I thought the top of my head was going to lift right off." The Saint Cecilia punch was composed largely of excellent champagne mixed with superlative brandy.

"We old fellows find it helpful for a night of dancing. It goes to our feet, not our heads."

"Fiddle-dee-dee, Miles! Sally always said that you were the best dancer in Charleston, and I thought she was just bragging. But now I know she was only telling the simple truth." Scarlett's dimpling, smiling, extravagant raillery was so automatic that she didn't even have to think what she was saying. What was taking Rhett so long? Why was he talking to Edward Cooper instead of escorting her to supper? Sally Brewton would never forgive her for tying Miles up this way.

Oh, thank goodness, Rhett was coming.

"I'd never let you claim your enchanting wife if you weren't so much bigger than I, Rhett." Miles bowed over Scarlett's hand. "A great privilege, ma'am."

"A great pleasure, sir," she replied, with a curtsey.

"My God," Rhett drawled, "I might as well go beg Sally to run away with me. She's turned me down the last fifty times, but my luck might have changed."

The three of them went, laughing, in search of Sally. She was sitting on a windowsill holding her slippers in her hand. "Who ever said that the proof of the perfect ball is that you dance through the soles of your slippers?" she asked plaintively. "I did and now I've got blisters on both feet."

Miles picked her up. "I'll carry you down, you troublesome woman, but then you cover your feet like a respectable person and hobble to supper."

"Brute!" said Sally. Scarlett saw the look they exchanged and her heart cramped with envy.

"What fascinating thing were you talking about with Edward Cooper for so long? I'm starving." She looked at Rhett, and the pain grew worse. I won't think about it. I won't ruin this perfect night.

"He was informing me that, due to my bad influence, Tommy's grades in school are falling. As a punishment he's selling the little boat the boy loves so much."

"That's cruel!" Scarlett exclaimed.

"The boy will get it back. I bought it. Now let's get to supper before all the oysters are gone. For once in your life, Scarlett, you're going to have more food than you can possibly eat. Even ladies gorge themselves. It's traditional. The Season is over, and it's almost Lent."

It was shortly after two when the doors to the Hibernian Hall opened. The young black torch boys were yawning when they took their positions to light the revellers out. As their torches were lit, the dark waiting streetcar on Meeting Street came to life on its tracks. The driver turned up the blueglobed lamp on its roof and the tall-chimneyed lanterns by the doors. The horses stamped their feet and bobbed their heads. A white-aproned man swept the canvas walkway free of the scattering of leaves that had accumulated then slid back the long iron bolt and swung wide the gates. He disappeared into the shadows just as the sound of voices poured from the building. For three blocks along the street carriages waited to move in turn to collect their passengers. "Wake up, they're coming," Ezekiel growled to the sleeping boys in the footman livery. They jerked at his prodding finger, then grinned and scrambled down from their resting place at his feet.

People came pouring through the open doors, talking, laughing, pausing on the porch, reluctant to see the end of the evening. As they did every year, they said that this had been the best Saint Cecilia ever, the best orchestra, the best food, the best punch, the best time they had ever had.

The streetcar driver spoke to his horses. "I'll get you to your stable, boys, don't you fret." He pulled the handle near his head and the brightly polished bell beside the blue light clanged its summons.

"Good night, good night," cried obedient riders to the people on the porch and first one couple, then three, then a laughing avalanche of young people ran along the white canvas path. Their elders smiled and made comments about the tirelessness of youth. They moved at a slower, more dignified pace. In some cases their dignity failed to hide a certain unsteadiness of the legs.

Scarlett plucked Rhett's sleeve. "Oh, do let's ride the car, Rhett. The air feels so good and the carriage will be stuffy."

"There's a long walk after we get off."

"I don't care. I'd love to walk some."

He took a deep breath of the fresh night air. "I would, too," he said. "I'll tell Mama. Go on to the car and save us a place."

They hadn't far to ride. The streetcar turned east on Broad Street, only a block away, then moved grandly through the silent city to the end of Broad in front of the Post Office building. It was a merry, noisy continuation of the party. Almost everyone on the crowded car joined in the song started by three laughing men when the car teetered around the corner. *"Oh, the Rock Island Line, it is a mighty fine line! The Rock Island Line, it is the road to ride . . ."*

Musically the performance left much to be desired but the singers neither knew nor cared. Scarlett and Rhett sang as loudly as the rest. When they stepped down from the car she continued to join in every time the chorus was repeated. *"Get your ticket at the station for the Rock Island Line."*

Rhett and three other volunteers helped the driver unharness the horses, lead them to the opposite end of the car, and rehitch them for the journey back along Broad then up Meeting to the terminal. They returned waves and cries of "good night" as the car moved away, taking the singers with it.

"Do you suppose they know any other song?" Scarlett asked.

Rhett laughed. "They don't even know that one, and to tell the truth neither do I. It didn't seem to make much difference."

Scarlett giggled. Then she put her hand over her mouth. Her giggle had sounded very loud now that "The Rock Island Line" was faint in the distance. She watched the lighted car become smaller, then stop, then start, then disappear as it turned the corner. It was very quiet, and very dark outside the pool of light thrown by the street lamp in front of the Post Office. A breath of wind played with the fringe on her shawl. The air was balmy and soft. "It's real warm," she whispered to Rhett.

He murmured a wordless affirmative and took out his pocket watch, held it in the lamplight. "Listen," he said quietly.

Scarlett listened. Everything was still. She held her breath to listen harder.

"Now!" said Rhett. Saint Michael's bells chimed once, twice. The notes hung in the warm night for a long time. "Half past," Rhett said with approval. He replaced the watch in its pocket.

Both of them had taken quite a bit of punch. They were in the condition known as "high flown," where everything was somewhat magnified in effect. The darkness was blacker, the air warmer, the silence deeper, the memory of the pleasant evening even more enjoyable than the ball itself. Each felt a quietly glowing inner well-being. Scarlett yawned happily and tucked a hand into Rhett's elbow. Without a word they began to walk into the darkness toward home. Their footsteps were loud on the brick sidewalk, bounced back from the buildings. Scarlett looked uneasily from side to side, and over her shoulder at the looming Post Office. She couldn't recognize anything. It's so quiet, she thought, like we were the only people on the face of the earth.

Rhett's tall form was a part of the darkness, his white shirt front covered by his black evening cape. Scarlett tightened her hold on his arm, above the crook of the elbow. It was firm and strong, the powerful arm of a powerful man. She moved a little closer to his side. She could feel the warmth of his body, sense the bulk and strength of it.

"Wasn't that a wonderful party?" she said too loudly. Her voice echoed, sounding strange to her ears. "I thought I'd laugh out loud at old look-down-your-nose Hannah. My grief, when she got a taste of how

Southerners treat folks, her head was so turned I expected her to start walking backwards to see where she was going."

Rhett chuckled. "Poor Hannah," he said, "she may never again in her life feel so delightfully attractive and witty. Townsend's no fool. He told me he wants to move back to the South. This visit will probably make Hannah agree. There's a foot of snow on the ground in Philadelphia." Scarlett laughed softly into the balmy darkness, then smiled with warm contentment. When she and Rhett walked through the light of the next streetlamp, she saw that he was smiling, too. There was no further need to talk. It was enough that they were both feeling good, both smiling, walking together, in no hurry to be any place else.

Their route took them past the docks. The sidewalk abutted a long row of ships chandlers, narrow buildings with tightly shuttered shops on street level and the darkened windows of living quarters above. Many of the windows were open to the almost-summery warmth of the night. A dog barked half-heartedly at the sound of their steps. Rhett commanded it to be quiet, his own voice muted. The dog whimpered once, then was still.

They walked forward, past widely spaced street lamps. Rhett adjusted his long stride automatically to match Scarlett's shorter one, and the sound of heels on brick became a single clack clack clack clack—testimony of the comfortable unity of the moment.

One street lamp had gone out. In the patch of greater darkness Scarlett noticed for the first time that the sky seemed very near, its spangling of stars brighter than she could remember them ever before. One star looked almost close enough to touch. "Rhett, look at the sky," she said softly. "The stars look so close." He stopped walking, put his hand over hers to signal her to stop, too. "It's because of the sea," he said, the sound of his voice low and warm. "We're past the warehouses now, and there's only water. Listen and you can hear it breathing." They stood very still.

Scarlett strained to hear. The rhythmic slap slap of the moving water against the invisible pilings of the seawall became audible. Gradually it seemed to get louder, until she was amazed she hadn't been hearing it all the time. Then another sound merged with the cadence of the tidal river. It was music, a thin high slow procession of notes. The purity of them made her eyes fill with unexpected tears.

"Do you hear it?" she asked fearfully. Was she imagining things?

"Yes. It's a homesick sailor on the ship anchored out there. The tune is 'Across the Wide Missouri.' They make those flute-like whistles themselves. Some of them have a real gift for playing. He must have the watch. See, there's a lantern in the rigging, that's where the ship is. The lantern's supposed to warn any other ship traffic that she's anchored there, but you always have a man on watch, too, to look for anything approaching. Maybe two in busy lanes like this river. There are always small boats, people who know the river moving at night when no one can see them."

"Why would they do that?"

"A thousand reasons, all of them either dishonest or noble, depending on who's telling the story." Rhett sounded as if he were talking to himself more than to Scarlett.

She looked at him but it was too dark to see his face. She looked back at the ship's lantern that she had mistaken for a star and listened to the tide and the music of the yearning, anonymous sailor. Saint Michael's bells rang the three-quarter hour.

Scarlett tasted salt on her lips. "Do you miss the blockade running, Rhett?"

He laughed once. "Let's just say I'd like to be ten years younger." He laughed again, lightly mocking, amused at himself. "I play with sailboats under the guise of being kind to confused young men. It gives me the pleasure of being on the water and feeling the wind blowing free. There's nothing like it for making a man feel like a god." He moved forward, pulling Scarlett into motion. Their pace was slightly faster, but still in step.

Scarlett tasted the air and thought of the wing-like sails of the small boats that skimmed the harbor, almost flying. "I want to do that," she said, "I want to go sailing more than anything in the whole world. Oh, Rhett, will you take me? It's as warm as summer, you don't absolutely have to go back to the Landing tomorrow. Say you will, please, Rhett."

He thought for a moment. Very soon she'd be out of his life forever.

"Why not? It's a shame to waste the weather," he said.

Scarlett pulled at his arm. "Come on, let's hurry. It's late, and I want to get an early start."

Rhett held back. "I won't be able to take you sailing if you've got a broken neck, Scarlett. Watch your step. We've only got a few more blocks to go."

She fell into step with him again, smiling to herself. It was wonderful to have something to look forward to.

Just before they reached the house Rhett stopped, stopping her. "Wait a second." His head was lifted up, listening.

Scarlett wondered what he was hearing. Oh, for heaven's sake, it was just Saint Michael's clock again. The chimes ended and the deep reverberating single bell tolled three times. Distant but distinct in the warm darkness the voice of the watchman in the steeple called to the sleeping old city.

"Three . . . o'clock . . . and all's well!"

31

$\mathcal{R}$hett looked at the costume Scar-
lett had assembled with such care, and one eyebrow skidded upward while
his mouth twitched downward at the corner.

"Well, I didn't want to get sunburned again," she said defensively.
She was wearing a wide-brimmed straw hat that Mrs. Butler kept near
the garden door for protection from the sun when she went out to cut
flowers. She had wrapped yards of bright blue tulle around the crown
of the hat and tied the ends under her chin in a bow that she thought
very becoming. She had her favorite parasol with her, a saucy pale blue
flowered silk pagoda-shape with a dark blue tasselled fringe. It kept her
dull, proper brown twill walking-out costume from being so boring, she
thought.

What made Rhett think he could criticize anybody else, anyhow? He
looked like a field hand, she thought, in those beat-up old breeches and
that plain shirt without so much as a collar, never mind a proper cravat and
coat. Scarlett set her jaw. "You said nine o'clock, Rhett, and that's what it
is. Shall we go?"

Rhett made a sweeping bow, then picked up a battered canvas bag
and slung it over his shoulders. "We shall go," he said. There was something suspicious about his voice. He's up to something, Scarlett thought,
but I'm not about to let him get away with it.

* * *

She'd had no idea that the boat was so small. Or that it would be at the bottom of a long ladder that looked so slimy wet. She looked accusingly at Rhett.

"Nearly low tide," he said. "That's why we had to get here by nine-thirty. After the tide turns at ten, we would have a hard time getting into the harbor. Of course it will be a help bringing us back up the river to dock. . . . If you're quite certain that you want to go."

"Quite, thank you." Scarlett put her white-gloved hand on one projecting rail of the ladder and started to turn around.

"Wait!" said Rhett. She looked up at him with a stonily determined face. "I'm not willing to let you break your neck to spare me the trouble of taking you out for an hour. That ladder's very slippery. I'll go down one rung before you to make sure you don't lose your footing in those foolish city boots. Stand by while I get ready." He opened the drawstring of the canvas bag and took out a pair of canvas shoes with rubber soles. Scarlett watched in silent stubbornness. Rhett took his time, removing his boots, putting on the shoes, placing the boots in the bag, tightening the drawstring, making an intricate-looking knot in it.

He looked at her with a sudden smile that took her breath away. "Stay right there, Scarlett, a wise man knows when he's beaten. I'll stow this gear and come back for you." In a flash he hoisted the bag on his shoulder and was halfway down the ladder before Scarlett understood what he was talking about.

"You skinnied down and up that thing like greased lightning," she said with honest admiration when Rhett was beside her again.

"Or a monkey," he corrected. "Come on, my dear, time and tide wait for no man, not even a woman."

Scarlett was no stranger to ladders, and she had a good head for heights. As a child she had climbed trees to their topmost swaying branches and scampered up into the hayloft of the barn as if its narrow ladder were a broad flight of stairs. But she was grateful for Rhett's steadying arm around her waist on the algae-coated rungs, and very glad to reach the relative stability of the small boat.

She sat quietly on the board seat in the stern while Rhett efficiently attached the sails to the mast and tested the lines. The white canvas lay in heaps, on the covered bow and inside the open cockpit. "Ready?" he said.

"Oh, yes!"

"Then let's cast off." He freed the lines that hugged the tiny sloop to the dock and pushed away from the barnacle-crusted pier support with a paddle. The fast-running ebb tide grabbed the little boat at once and pulled it into the river. "Sit where you are and keep your head down on your knees," Rhett ordered. He hoisted the jib, cleated halyard and sheet, and the narrow sail filled with wind, luffing gently.

"Now." Rhett sat on the seat beside Scarlett and hooked his elbow over the tiller between them. With his two hands he began to haul up the mainsail. There was a great noise of creaking and rattling. Scarlett stole a sideways look without lifting her head. Rhett's eyes were squinting against the sun and he was frowning in concentration. But he looked happy, as happy as she had ever seen him.

The mainsail bellied out with a booming snap and Rhett laughed. "Good girl!" he said. Scarlett knew that he wasn't talking to her.

"Are you ready to go in?"

"Oh, no, Rhett! Not ever." Scarlett was in a transport of delight with the wind and the sea, unconscious of the spray spotting her clothes, the water running across her boots, the total ruin of her gloves and Miss Eleanor's hat, the loss of her parasol. She had no thoughts, only sensation. The sloop was a mere sixteen feet long, its hull sometimes barely inches above the sea. It rode waves and current like an eager young animal, climbing to the crests, then swooping into the troughs with a dashing plunge that left Scarlett's stomach somewhere high up near her throat and threw a fan of salty droplets into her face and open, exultant mouth. She was part of it— she was the wind and the water and the salt and the sun.

Rhett looked at her rapt expression, smiled at the sodden foolish tulle bow under her chin. "Duck," he ordered, and put the tiller over for a short tack into the wind. They'd stay out a bit longer. "Would you like to take the tiller?" he offered. "I'll teach you to sail her."

Scarlett shook her head. She had no desire to control, she was happy simply to be.

Rhett knew how remarkable it was for Scarlett to turn down an opportunity to rule, understood the depth of her response to the joyous freedom of sail on sea. He had felt the same rapture often in his youth. Even now he had brief moments of it from time to time, moments that sent him back onto the water again and again in search of more.

"Duck," he said again. And put the little sloop into a long reach. The suddenly increased speed brought water foaming onto the deep-slanted edge of the hull. Scarlett let out a cry of delight. Overhead the cry was repeated by a soaring sea gull, bright white against the high wide cloudless blue sky. Rhett looked up and grinned. The sun was warm on his back, the wind sharp and salty on his face. It was a good day to be alive. He lashed the tiller and moved forward in a stoop to get the canvas bag. The sweaters he pulled out of it were stretched and misshapen with age, stiff with dried brine. They were made of thick wool in a blue so dark that it looked almost black. Rhett crab-walked back to the stern and sat down on the raked outer edge of the cockpit. The cant of the hull dropped with his weight, and the lively little boat hissed through the water on an almost even keel.

"Put this on, Scarlett." He held one of the sweaters out to her.

"I don't need it. It's like summertime today."

"The air's warm enough, but not the water. It's February whether it seems like summer or not. The spray will chill you without your knowing it. Put on the sweater."

Scarlett made a face, but she took the sweater from him. "You'll have to hold my hat."

"I'll hold your hat." Rhett pulled the second, grimier sweater over his head. Then he helped Scarlett. Her head emerged, and the wind assaulted her dishevelled hair, pulling it free from dislodged combs and hairpins and tossing it in long, dark leaping streamers. She shrieked and grabbed wildly at it.

"Now look what you've done!" she shouted. The wind whipped a thick strand of hair into her open mouth, making her sputter and blow. When she pulled the hair free it tore out of her grasp and flew into snarled witches' locks with the rest. "Give me my hat quick before I'm bald-headed," she said. "My grief, I'm a mess."

She had never in her life looked so beautiful. Her face was alight with joy, rosy from windburn, glowing amid the wild dark cloud of hair. She tied the ridiculous hat firmly on her head, tucked her subdued tangled hair into the back of the sweater. "I don't suppose you have anything to eat in that bag of yours, do you?" she asked hopefully.

"Only sailors' rations," said Rhett, "hardtack and rum."

"That sounds delicious. I've never tasted either one."

"It's not much past eleven, Scarlett. We'll be home for dinner. Restrain yourself."

"Can't we stay out all day? I'm having such a good time."

"Another hour; I have a meeting with my lawyers this afternoon."

"Bother your lawyers," said Scarlett, but under her breath. She refused to get angry and spoil her pleasure. She looked at the sun-spangled water and the white curls of foam on each side of the bow, then flung out her arms and arched her back in a luxurious cat-like stretch. The sleeves of the sweater were so long that they extended past her hands, flapping in the wind.

"Careful, my pet," Rhett laughed, "you might blow away." He freed the tiller, preparing to come about, looking automatically for any other vessels that might be in his proposed path.

"Look, Scarlett," he said urgently, "quick. Out there to starboard—to your right. I'll bet you've never seen that before."

Scarlett's eyes scanned the marshy shore in the near distance. Then—halfway between boat and shore—a gleaming gray shape curved above the water for a moment before disappearing beneath it.

"A shark!" she exclaimed. "No, two—three sharks. They're coming right at us, Rhett. Do they want to eat us?"

"My dear imbecilic child, those are dolphins, not sharks. They must be heading for the ocean. Hold tight and duck. I'm going to bring her around tight. Maybe we can travel with them. It's the most charming thing in the world to be in the middle of a school of them. They love to play."

"Play? Fish? You must think I'm mighty gullible, Rhett." She bent under the swinging boom.

"They aren't fish. Just watch. You'll see."

There were seven dolphins in the pod. By the time Rhett maneuvered the sloop onto the course the sleek mammals were following, the dolphins were far ahead. Rhett stood and shaded his eyes against the sun. "Damn!" he said. Then, immediately in front of the sloop, a dolphin leapt from the water, bowed its back, and dived with a splash back into the water.

Scarlett pounded on Rhett's thigh with a sweater-mittened fist. "Did you see that?"

Rhett dropped onto the seat. "I saw it. He came to tell us to get a move on. The others are probably waiting for us. Look!" Two dolphins had broken water ahead. Their graceful leaps made Scarlett clap her hands. She pushed the sweater sleeves up her arms and clapped again, this time successfully. Two yards to her right the first dolphin surfaced, cleared his blow hole with a spurt of spume, then lazily rocked back down into the water.

"Oh, Rhett, I never saw anything so darling. It was smiling at us!"

Rhett was smiling, too. "I always think they're smiling, and I always smile back. I love dolphins, always have."

The dolphins treated Rhett and Scarlett to what could only be called a game. They swam alongside, under, across the bow, sometimes singly, sometimes in twos or threes. Diving and surfacing, blowing, rolling, leaping, looking from eyes that seemed human, seemed to be laughing above the engaging smile-like mouth at the clumsy, boat-bound man and woman.

"There!" Rhett pointed when one burst from the surface in a leap, and "There!" Scarlett yelled when another leapt in the opposite direction. "There!" and "There!" and "There!" whenever the dolphins broke water. It was a surprise each time, always in a spot that was different from the places where Scarlett and Rhett were looking.

"They're dancing," Scarlett insisted.

"Frolicking," Rhett suggested.

"Showing off," they agreed. The show was enchanting.

Because of it Rhett was careless. He didn't see the dark patch of cloud that was spreading across the horizon behind them. His first warning was when the steady fresh wind suddenly dropped. The taut billowing sails went limp, and the dolphins nosed abruptly down into the water and disappeared. He looked then—too late—over his shoulder and saw the squall racing over the water and the sky.

"Get down into the belly of the boat, Scarlett," he said quietly, "and hold on. We're about to have a storm. Don't be frightened, I've sailed through much worse."

She looked behind and her eyes widened. How could it be so sunny and blue in front of them and so black back there? Without a word she slid down and found a handhold beneath the seat where she and Rhett had been sitting.

He was making rapid adjustments to the rigging. "We'll have to run before it," he said, then he grinned. "You'll get wet, but it will be a hell of a ride." At that moment the squall hit. Day turned to liquid near-night as the clouds blackened the sky and loosed sheets of rain on them. Scarlett opened her mouth to cry out, and it was immediately filled with water.

My God, I'm drowning, she thought. She bent over and spat and coughed until her mouth and throat were clear. She tried to lift her head, to see what was happening, to ask Rhett what was that terrible noise. But her giddy battered hat was collapsed onto her face, and she couldn't see anything. I've got to get rid of it or I'll suffocate. She tore at the tulle bow under her chin with her free hand. Her other hand was desperately gripping the metal handle she had found. The boat was pitching and yawing, creaking as if it was coming apart. She could feel the sloop racing down, down —it must be almost standing on its nose, it's going to go straight through the water, right to the bottom of the sea. Oh, sweet Mother of God, I don't want to die!

With a shudder the sloop stopped its plunge. Scarlett pulled the wet tulle roughly over her chin, over her face, and she was free of the smothering folds of wet straw. She could see!

She looked at the water, then up, at water, then up ... up ... up. There was a wall of water higher than the tip of the mast, ready to fall and smash the frail wooden shell to bits. Scarlett tried to scream, but her throat was paralyzed by fear. The sloop was shaking and groaning; it rode with a sickening slide up the side of the wall, then hung on the top, shuddering, for an endless terrifying moment.

Scarlett's eyes were narrowed against the rain pouring down on her head with terrible pounding blows, streaming down over her face. On all sides there were angry, surging, foam-streaked mountainous waves with curling breaking white tops streaming fans of spume into the furious wind and rain. "Rhett," she tried to shout. Oh God, where was Rhett? She turned her head from side to side, trying to see through the rain. Then, just as the sloop dove furiously down the other side of the wave, she found him.

God damn his soul! He was kneeling, his back and shoulders straight, his head and chin high, and he was laughing into the wind and the rain and the waves. His left hand gripped the tiller with corded strength, and his right hand was outstretched, holding on to the line that was wrapped around his elbow and forearm and wrist, the sheet that led to the fearful pull of the huge wind-filled mainsail. He's loving this! The fight with the wind, the death danger. He loves it.

I hate him!

Scarlett looked up at the towering threat of the next wave and for a wild, despairing instant she waited for it to topple, to trap, to destroy her. Then she told herself that she had nothing to fear. Rhett could manage anything, even the ocean itself. She lifted her head, as his was lifted, and gave herself over to the wild perilous excitement.

Scarlett did not know about the chaotic power of the wind. As the little sloop rode up the side of the thirty-foot wave, the wind stopped. It was only for a few seconds, a freak of the center of the squall, but the mainsail flattened, and the boat slewed to broadside, carried erratically by water current only in a perilous climb. Scarlett was aware that Rhett was rapidly freeing his arm from the encircling slack line, that he was doing something different with the swinging tiller, but she had no hint that anything was wrong until the crest of the wave was nearly under the keel and Rhett shouted, "Jibe! Jibe," and threw his body painfully over hers.

She heard a rattling, creaking noise close to her head and sensed the slow then faster then rushing swing of the heavy boom above. Everything happened very fast, yet it seemed to be terribly, unnaturally slow, as though the whole world were stopping. She looked without understanding at Rhett's face so near to hers, and then it was gone and he was on his knees again doing something, she didn't know what, except that heavy loops of thick rope were falling on her.

She didn't see the crosswind ruffle, then suddenly fill, the wet canvas of the mainsail and propel it to the opposite side of the wayless sloop with an ever-mounting force so mightly that there was a *crack* like the sound of lightning striking and the thick mast broke and was carried into the sea by the momentum and weight of the sail. The hull of the boat bucked, then lifted to starboard and rolled slowly, following the pull of the fouled rigging, until it was upside down. Capsized in the cold storm-torn sea.

She'd never known such cold could exist. Cold rain pelting her, colder waters surrounding her, pulling at her. Her whole body must be frozen. Her teeth were chattering uncontrollably, making such a noise in her head that she couldn't think, couldn't understand what was happening, except that she must be paralyzed, because she couldn't move. And yet she was moving, in sickening swings and surging lifts and terrible, terrible falling, falling.

I'm dying. Oh God, don't let me die! I want to live.

"Scarlett!" The sound of her name was louder than the clacking of her teeth and it penetrated to her consciousness.

"Scarlett!" She knew that voice, it was Rhett's voice. And that was Rhett's arm around her, holding her. But where was he? She couldn't see anything through the water that kept hitting her face, glazing and stinging her eyes.

She opened her mouth to answer and at once it was filled with water. Scarlett craned her head up as hard as she could and blew the water from her mouth. If only her teeth would be still!

"Rhett," she tried to say.

"Thank God." His voice was very close. Behind her. She was beginning to make some kind of sense of things.

"Rhett," she said again.

"Now listen carefully, my darling, listen harder than you've ever listened in your life. We've got one chance, and we're going to take it. The sloop is right here; I'm holding on to the rudder. We've got to get under it and use it for protection. That means we've got to go under the water and come up under the hull of the boat. Do you understand?"

Everything in her cried out, No! If she went under the water she'd drown. It was pulling her already, dragging at her. If she went under, she'd never come up! Panic seized her. She couldn't breathe. She wanted to hold on to Rhett, and she wanted to scream and scream and scream—

Stop it. The words were clear. And the voice was her own. You've got to live through this, and you'll never do it if you act like a gibbering idiot.

"Wh-wh-what sh-should I d-d-d-do?" Damn this chattering.

"I'm going to count. At 'three' take a deep breath and close your eyes. I've got you. I'll get us there. You'll be all right. Are you ready?" He didn't wait for her to answer, but began at once to shout "One ... two ..."

Scarlett inhaled in jerky spurts. Then she was pulled down, down, and water filled her nose and ears and eyes and consciousness. In seconds, it was over. She gulped air gratefully.

"I've been holding your arms, Scarlett, so you wouldn't grab me and drown us both." Rhett moved his grip to her waist. The freedom felt wonderful. If only her hands weren't so cold. She began to rub them together.

"That's the way," said Rhett. "Keep your circulation going. But not quite yet. Take hold of this cleat. I must leave you for a few minutes. Don't panic. It won't be long. I'm going to duck back up and cut away the fouled lines and the mast before they pull the boat under. I'm going to cut the laces on your boots, too, Scarlett. Don't kick when you feel something grab your foot. It'll be me. Those heavy skirts and petticoats will have to go, too. Just hold on tight. I won't be long."

It seemed like forever.

Scarlett used the time to assess her surroundings. Things weren't too bad—if she could ignore the cold. The overturned sloop made a roof over her head, so that the rain was not hitting her. For some reason the water was calmer, too. She couldn't see it; the inside of the hull was totally dark; but she knew it was so. Although the boat was rising and falling with the surge of the waves in the same dizzying rhythm, the surface of the sheltered water was almost flat, no choppy little waves to break against her face.

She felt Rhett's touch on her left foot. Good! I'm not really paralyzed. Scarlett took a deep breath for the first time since the storm hit. How strange her feet felt. She'd had no idea how heavy and constricting boots were. Oh! The hand at her waist was strange-feeling. She could sense the sawing motion of the knife. Then suddenly a tremendous weight slid down her legs and her shoulders bobbed up out of the water. She cried out in surprise. The sound of her cry reverberated in the hollow space beneath the wooden hull. It was so loud that she almost lost her handhold from the shock of it.

Then Rhett burst through the water. He was very close to her. "How do you feel?" he asked. It sounded as if he was shouting.

"Shhh," said Scarlett. "Not so loud."

"How do you feel?" he asked quietly.

"Frozen nearly to death, if you really want to know."

"The water's cold, but not that cold. If we were in the North Atlantic—"

"Rhett Butler, if you tell me one of your blockade-running adventure stories, I'll--I'll drown you!"

His laughter filled the air around them and it seemed somehow to make it warmer. But Scarlett was still furious. "How you can laugh at a time like this is beyond me. It's not funny to be dangling in freezing water in the middle of a terrible storm."

"When things are at their worst, Scarlett, the only thing to do is find something to laugh about. It keeps you sane ... and it stops your teeth chattering from fear."

She was too exasperated to speak. The worst of it was that he was right. The chattering had stopped when she stopped thinking that she was going to die.

"Now I'm going to cut the laces on your corset, Scarlett. You can't breathe easily in that cage. Just hold still so I don't cut your skin." There was an embarrassing intimacy in the movement of his hands under the sweater, tearing open her basque and her shirtwaist. It had been years since he had last put his hands on her body.

"Now, breathe deep," said Rhett when he pulled the cut corset and camisole away. "Women today never learn how to breathe. Fill your lungs all the way. I'm rigging a support for us with some line I cut. You'll be able to turn loose that cleat when I'm done and massage your hands and arms. Keep breathing. It'll warm up your blood."

Scarlett tried to do what Rhett said, but her arms felt terribly heavy when she lifted them. It was much easier just to let her body rest in the harness-like rope support under her arms and rise and fall, limp, with the rise and fall of the waves. She was feeling very sleepy ... Why did Rhett have to keep talking so much? Why did he insist on fussing at her about rubbing her arms?

"Scarlett!" The sound was very loud. "Scarlett! You cannot go to sleep. You've got to keep moving. Kick your feet. Kick me if you want to, but move your legs." Rhett began to rub her shoulders vigorously, then her upper arms; his touch was rough.

"Stop it. That hurts." Her words were weak, like the mewing of a kitten. Scarlett closed her eyes, and the darkness became darker. She didn't feel so cold any more, only very tired, and sleepy.

With no warning Rhett slapped her face so hard that her head jerked backwards and hit the wooden hull with a crash that echoed in the enclosed space. Scarlett came full awake, shocked and angry.

"How dare you! I'll pay you back for that when we get out of here, Rhett Butler, just see if I don't!"

"That's better," said Rhett. He continued to rub her arms roughly, though Scarlett was trying to push his hands away. "Keep talking, I'll do the massage. Give me your hands so I can rub them."

"I certainly will not! I'll keep my hands to myself and I'll thank you to do the same. You're rubbing my flesh right off my bones."

"Better my rubbing than crabs eating it," said Rhett harshly. "Listen to me. If you let yourself give in to the cold, Scarlett, you'll die. I know you want to sleep but that's the sleep of death. And, by God, if I have to beat you black and blue, I will not allow you to die. You stay awake, and breathe, and keep moving. Talk; keep talking; I don't give a damn what you say, just let me hear your cantankerous fishwife tones so I'll know you're alive."

Scarlett was aware of the paralyzing cold again as Rhett rubbed life back into her flesh. "Are we going to get out of this?" she asked without emotion. She tried to move her legs.

"Of course we are."

"How?"

"The current is carrying us ashore; it's an incoming tide. It'll take us back where we came from."

Scarlett nodded in the darkness. She remembered all the fuss about leaving before the tide turned. Nothing in Rhett's voice revealed his knowledge that the power of gale-force winds would make all normal tidal activity meaningless. The storm might be carrying them through the mouth of the harbor into the vast reaches of the Atlantic Ocean.

"How long before we get there?" Scarlett's tone was querulous. Her legs felt like huge tree trunks. And Rhett was rubbing her shoulders raw.

"I don't know," he answered. "You'll need all your courage, Scarlett."

He sounds as solemn as a sermon! Rhett, who always makes fun of everything. Oh, my God! Scarlett willed her lifeless legs to move and forced terror away with iron determination. "I don't need courage half as much as something to eat," she said. "Why the devil didn't you grab that dirty old bag of yours when we turned over?"

"It's stowed under the bow. By God, Scarlett, your gluttony may be the saving of us. I'd forgotten all about it. Pray it's still there."

The rum spread life-restoring tentacles of warmth through her thighs, her legs, her feet, and Scarlett began to push them back and forth. The pain of returning circulation was intense, but she welcomed it. It meant she was alive, all of her. Why, rum just might be better than brandy, she thought after a second drink. It sure did warm a person up.

Too bad that Rhett insisted on rationing it, but she knew he was right. It would be too awful to run out of the warmth in the bottle before they were safe on land. In the meantime she was even able to join in Rhett's tribute to their prize. " '*Yo, ho, ho, and a bottle of rum!*' " she sang with him when he finished each verse of the sea chanty.

And afterwards Scarlett thought of "*Little brown jug, how I love thee.*"

Their voices echoed so loudly inside the hull that it was possible to pretend that they weren't growing weaker as the cold gripped their bodies. Rhett put his arms around Scarlett and held her close to his body to share its warmth. And they sang all the favorites they could remember, while the sips of rum came closer together with less and less effect.

"How about 'The Yellow Rose of Texas'?" Rhett suggested.

"We sang that twice already. Sing that song Pa loved so much, Rhett. I remember the two of you staggering down the street together in Atlanta bellowing like stuck pigs."

"Sure and we sounded like a choir of angels," Rhett said, mimicking Gerald O'Hara's brogue. " '*When first I saw sweet Peggy, 'twas on a market day* . . .' " He sang the first verse of "Peg in a Low Back'd Car," then admitted he didn't know the rest. "You must know every word of it, Scarlett. Sing it for me."

She tried, but couldn't find the strength. "I've forgotten," she said, to cover her weakness. She was so tired. If only she could rest her head against Rhett's warmth and sleep. His arms felt so wonderful holding her. Her head dropped. It was too heavy to hold up any longer.

Rhett shook her. "Scarlett, do you hear me? Scarlett! I feel a change in the current, I swear it, we're very near shore. You can't give up now. Come on, my darling, let me see some more of that gumption of yours. Hold up your head, my pet, it's almost over."

". . . so cold . . ."

"Damn you for a quitter, Scarlett O'Hara! I should have let Sherman get you in Atlanta. You weren't worth saving."

The words registered slowly in her fading consciousness, and produced only a feeble stirring of anger. But it was enough. Her eyes opened and her head lifted to meet the dimly sensed challenge.

"Take a deep breath," Rhett commanded. "We're going in." He put his big hand over her nose and mouth and dove under the water with her feebly struggling body held close. They surfaced outside the hull, near a line of tall, cresting combers. "Almost there, my love," Rhett gasped. He bent one arm around Scarlett's neck and held her heavy head in his hand while he swam expertly through a breaking wave and used its power to carry them into the shallows.

A thin rain was falling, blown almost horizontal by the gusting wind. Rhett cradled Scarlett's limp form to his chest and huddled over it, kneeling in the white frothing edge of the water. A comber rose far behind him and raced toward the beach. It began to curl over on itself, then the foam-streaked gray water crashed, surged toward land, and the rolling, roiling forces in it struck Rhett's back and roared across his sheltering body.

When the wave had passed over and spent itself, he rose unsteadily to his feet and stumbled forward onto the beach, clasping Scarlett to him. His bare feet and legs were cut in a hundred places by the fragments of shell that the breaker had thrown against him, but he was uncaring. He ran clumsily through the deep clinging sand to an opening in the line of immense sand dunes and climbed a short way into a bowl-like area sheltered from the winds. There he gently placed Scarlett's body on the soft sand.

His voice broke as he called Scarlett's name over and over again while he tried to bring life into her chilled whiteness by rubbing every part of her with his two hands. Her snarled, glistening black hair was spilled around her head and shoulders and her black eyebrows and lashes were shocking streaks across her colorless wet face. Rhett slapped her cheeks softly and urgently with the backs of his fingers.

When her eyes opened their color looked as strong as emeralds. Rhett shouted in primitive triumph.

Scarlett's fingers half closed around the shifting solidity of the rain-hardened sand. "Land," she said. And she began to cry in gasping sobs.

Rhett put one arm under her shoulders and lifted her into the protection of his bent crouching body. With his free hand he touched her hair, her cheeks, mouth, chin. "My darling, my life. I thought I'd lost you. I thought I'd killed you. I thought— Oh, Scarlett, you're alive. Don't cry, my dearest, it's all over. You're safe. It's all right. Everything—" He kissed her forehead, her throat, her cheeks. Scarlett's pale skin warmed with color, and she turned her head to meet his kissed with her own.

And there was no cold, no rain, no weakness—only the burning of Rhett's lips on her lips, on her body, the heat of his hands. And the power she felt under her fingers when she gripped his shoulders. And the pounding of her heart in her throat against his lips, the strong beat of his heart beneath her palms when she tangled her fingers in the thick curling hair on his chest.

Yes! I did remember it, it wasn't a dream. Yes, this is the dark swirling that draws me in and closes out the world and makes me alive, so alive, and free and spinning up to the heart of the sun. "Yes!" she shouted again and again, meeting Rhett's passion with her own, her demands the same as his. Until in the swirling, spiraling rapture there were no longer words or thoughts, only a union beyond mind, beyond time, beyond the world.

32

*H*e loves me! What a fool I was to doubt what I knew. Scarlett's swollen lips curved in a lazy surfeited smile, and she slowly opened her eyes.

Rhett was sitting beside her. His arms were wrapped across his knees, his face hidden in the hollow they made.

Scarlett stretched luxuriantly. For the first time she felt the rasping sand against her skin, noticed her surroundings. Why, it's pouring down rain. We'll catch our death. We'll have to find some shelter before we make love again. Her dimples flickered, and she stifled a giggle. Maybe not, we sure didn't pay any attention to the weather just now.

She reached out her hand and traced Rhett's spine with her fingernails.

He jerked away as if she'd burned him, turning in a rush to face her, then springing to his feet. She couldn't read his expression.

"I didn't want to wake you," he said. "Try to get some more rest if you can. I'm going to look for some place to dry out and build a fire. There are shacks on all these islands."

"I'll go with you." Scarlett struggled to get up. Rhett's sweater was across her legs, and she was still wearing hers. She felt burdened by their water-laden weight.

"No. You stay here." He was walking away, up the steep dunes. Scarlett gaped foolishly, not believing her eyes.

"Rhett! You can't leave me. I won't let you."

But he kept climbing. She could see only his broad back with his wet shirt clinging to it.

At the top of the dune he halted. His head turned slowly from side to side. Then his hunched shoulders squared. He turned and slid recklessly down the steep slope.

"There's a cottage. I know where we are. Get up." Rhett held his hand out to help Scarlett rise. She clasped it eagerly.

The cottages that some Charlestonians had built on the nearby islands were designed to capture the cooler sea breezes in the hot humid days of the long Southern summer. They were retreats from the city and the city's formality, little more than unornamented shacks with deep shaded porches and weathered clapboard siding perched on creosoted timbers to raise them above the blistering summer sands. In the cold driving rain the shelter Rhett had found looked derelict and inadequate to stand against the buffeting wind. But he knew these island houses had stood for generations, and had kitchen fireplaces where meals were prepared. Exactly the shelter needed for shipwreck survivors.

He broke open the door to the cottage with a single kick. Scarlett followed him inside. Why was he so silent? He'd hardly said a word to her, not even when he was carrying her in his arms through the thicket of low shrubs at the base of the sand dunes. I want him to talk, Scarlett thought, I want to hear his voice saying how much he loves me. Lord knows he made me wait long enough.

He found a worn patchwork quilt in a cupboard. "Take off those wet things and wrap up in this," he said. He tossed the quilt onto her lap. "I'll have a fire started in a minute."

Scarlett dropped her torn pantalets on top of the soaked sweater and dried herself on the quilt. It was soft, and it felt good. She wrapped it shawl-fashion then sat down again on the hard kitchen chair. The quilt made an envelope for her feet on the floor. She was dry for the first time in hours, but she began to shiver.

Rhett brought dry wood in from a box on the porch outside the kitchen. In a few minutes there was a small fire in the big fireplace. Almost at once it bit into the teepee of logs and a tall orange burst of flame leapt into crackling life. It lit his brooding face.

Scarlett hobbled across the room to warm herself at the fire. "Why don't you get out of your wet things, too, Rhett? I'll let you have the quilt to dry off on; it feels wonderful." She dropped her eyes as if she were embarrased by her boldness. Her thick lashes fluttered on her cheeks. Rhett did not respond.

"I'll just get soaked again when I go back out," he said. "We're only a couple of miles from Fort Moultrie. I'll go get help." Rhett walked into the small pantry adjoining the kitchen.

"Bother Fort Moultrie!" Scarlett wished he'd stop rooting around in the pantry like that. How could she talk to him when he was in another room?

Rhett emerged with a bottle of whiskey in one hand. "The shelves are pretty bare," he said with a brief smile, "but the necessities are there." He opened a cupboard and took down two cups. "Clean enough," he said. "I'll pour us a drink." He set cups and bottle down on the table.

"I don't want a drink. I want—"

He interrupted before she could tell him what she wanted. "I need a drink," he said. He poured the cup half full, drank it in one long swallow, then shook his head. "No wonder they left it here; it's real rotgut. Still . . ." He poured again.

Scarlett watched him with a look of amused indulgence. Poor darling, how nervous he is. When she spoke her voice was heavy with loving patience. "You don't have to be so skittery, Rhett. It's not like you compromised me or anything. We're two married people who love each other, that's all."

Rhett stared at her over the rim of the cup, then put it carefully down on the table. "Scarlett, what happened out there had nothing to do with love. It was a celebration of survival, that's all. You see it after every battle in wartime. The men who don't get killed fall on the first woman they see and prove they're still alive by using her body. In this case you used mine, too, because you'd narrowly escaped dying. It had nothing to do with love."

The harshness of his words took Scarlett's breath away.

But then she remembered his hoarse voice in her ear, the words "my darling," "my life," "I love you," repeated a hundred times. No matter what Rhett might say, he loved her. She knew it in the innermost center of her soul, the place where there were no lies. He's still afraid that I don't really love him! That's why he won't admit how much he loves me.

She began to move toward him. "You can say anything you like, Rhett, but it won't change the truth. I love you and you love me and we made love to prove it to each other."

Rhett drank the whiskey. Then he laughed harshly. "I never thought you were a silly little romantic, Scarlett. You disappoint me. You used to have some sense in your hard little head. A primitive, hasty coupling should never be confused with love. Though God knows it happens often enough to fill churches with wedding ceremonies."

Scarlett continued to walk. "You can talk till you're blue, but that won't change anything." She put a hand to her face and wiped away the tears that were pouring from her eyes. She was very close to him now. She could smell the salt on his skin, the whiskey on his breath. "You do love me," she sobbed, "you do, you do." The quilt fell to the floor when she let go of it to reach out to Rhett. "Take me in your arms and tell me you don't love me and then I'll believe it."

Rhett's hands abruptly caught her head and he kissed her with bruising possessive strength. Scarlett's arms closed behind his neck as his hands moved down her throat and her shoulders, and she gave herself up to abandonment.

But Rhett's fingers suddenly closed around her wrists and he pried her arms apart, away from his neck, away from him, and his mouth was no longer seeking hers, his body was drawing away.

"Why?" she cried. "You want me."

He cast her away, releasing her wrists, stumbling backwards in the first uncontrolled action she had ever seen him take. "Yes, by Christ! I do want you, and sicken for you. You're a poison in my blood, Scarlett, a sickness of my soul. I've known men with a hunger for opium that was like my hunger for you. I know what happens to an addict. He becomes enslaved, then destroyed. It almost happened to me, but I escaped. I won't risk it again. I won't destroy myself for you." He crashed through the door and out into the storm.

The wind howled through the open door, icy against Scarlett's bare skin. She grabbed up the quilt from the floor and wrapped it around her. She pushed against the wind to the yawning doorway but could see nothing through the rain. It took all her strength to pull the door closed. She had very little strength left.

Her lips still felt warm from Rhett's kiss. But the rest of her was shivering. She curled up in front of the fire with the quilt wrapped securely around her. She was tired, so very tired. She'd have a little nap until Rhett came back.

She slid into a sleep so profound that it was more nearly coma.

"Exhaustion," said the army doctor Rhett brought back from Fort Moultrie, "and exposure. It's a miracle your wife isn't dead, Mr. Butler. Let's hope she doesn't lose the use of her legs; the circulation's all but shut down. Wrap her in those blankets and let's get her back to the fort." Rhett swaddled Scarlett's limp body quickly and lifted her in his arms.

"Here, now, give her to the sergeant. You're not in such good condition yourself."

Scarlett's eyes opened. Her clouded mind registered the blue uniforms around her, then her eyes rolled back in her head. The doctor closed the eyelids with fingers practiced in battlefield medicine. "Better hurry," he said, "she's slipping away."

"Drink this, honey." It was a woman's voice, soft yet authoritative, a voice she almost recognized. Scarlett opened her lips obediently. "That's a good girl, take another little sip. No, I don't want to see no ugly screwed-up face like that. Don't you know if you make that kind of face it's liable to stick? Then what'll you do? A pretty little girl turned ugly. That's better. Now open up. Wider. You going to drink this good hot milk and medicine if it takes all week. Come on, now, lamb. I'll stir some more sugar in it."

No, it wasn't Mammy's voice. So close, so nearly the same, but not the same. Weak tears seeped from the corners of Scarlett's closed eyes. For a minute she'd thought she was home, at Tara, with Mammy tending her. She forced her eyes to open, to focus. The black woman bending over her smiled. Her smile was beautiful. Compassionate. Wise. Loving. Patient. Unyieldingly bossy. Scarlett smiled back.

"There, now, ain't that just what I told them? What this little girl need, I say, is a hot brick in her bed and a mustard plaster on her chest and old Rebekah rubbing out the chill from her bones, with a milk toddy and a talk with Jesus to finish the cure. I done talk with Jesus while I rub, and He bring you back like I knowed He would. Lord, I tell Him, this ain't no real work like Lazarus, this here is just a little girl feeling poorly. It won't hardly take a minute of Your everlasting time to cast Your eye this way and bring her back.

"He done so, and I'm going to thank Him. Soon's you finish drinking your milk. Come on, honey, there's two fresh spoons of sugar in it. Drink it down. You don't want to keep Jesus waiting for Rebekah to say thank You, do you? That don't set too well in Heaven."

Scarlett swallowed. Then she gulped. The sweetened milk tasted better than anything she'd tasted in weeks. When it was all gone she rubbed her mouth with the back of her hand to erase the milk mustache. "I'm mighty hungry, Rebekah, could I have something to eat?"

The big black woman nodded. "Just a second," she said. Then she closed her eyes and put her palms together in prayer. Her lips moved silently and she rocked back and forth, giving thanks in an intimate talk with her Lord.

When she finished, she pulled the coverlet up over Scarlett's shoulders and tucked it around them. Scarlett was asleep. The medicine in the milk was laudanum.

Scarlett tossed fitfully while she slept. When she thrashed off the coverlet, Rebekah tucked her in again and stroked her forehead until the lines of distress were soothed away. But Rebekah could do nothing about the dreams.

They were disjointed, chaotic, fragments of Scarlett's memories and fears. There was hunger, the never-ending desperate hunger of the bad days at Tara. And Yankee soldiers, coming closer and closer to Atlanta, looming in the shadows of the piazza outside her window, handling her and whispering that her legs would have to come off, sprawling in a pool of blood on the floor at Tara, the blood spurting, spreading, becoming a torrent of red that rose into a mountainous wave higher and still higher over a screaming small Scarlett. And there was cold, with ice covering trees and shrivelling flowers and forming a shell around her so that she couldn't move and couldn't be heard although she was calling "Rhett, Rhett, Rhett come back" inside the icicles that were falling from her lips. Her mother passed through her dream, and Scarlett smelled lemon verbena, but Ellen never spoke. Gerald O'Hara jumped a fence, then another, then fence after fence into infinity, sitting backwards on a shining white stallion that was singing with Gerald in a human voice about Scarlett in a Low Back'd Car. The voices changed, became women's voices, became hushed. She couldn't hear what they were saying.

Scarlett licked her dry lips and opened her eyes. Why, it's Melly. Oh, she looks so worried, poor thing. "Don't be frightened," Scarlett said hoarsely. "It's all right. He's dead. I shot him."

"She been having a nightmare," said Rebekah.

"The bad dreams are all over now, Scarlett. The doctor said you're going to be well in no time at all." Anne Hampton's dark eyes were shining with earnestness.

Eleanor Butler's face appeared over her shoulder. "We've come to take you home, my dear," she said.

"This is ridiculous," Scarlett complained. "I can perfectly well walk." Rebekah clamped a hand on her shoulder and continued to push the wheelchair slowly along the crushed oyster-shell road. "I feel like a fool," grumbled Scarlett, but she slumped back in the chair. Her head was throbbing with sharp dagger-like pains. The rainstorm had brought back weather suitable for February. The air was crisp, with a bite in the wind that was still blowing. At least Miss Eleanor brought my fur cape, she thought. I must have had a mighty close call if I'm allowed to wear the furs she thought were so showy.

"Where is Rhett? Why isn't he taking me home?"

"I wouldn't let him go out again," said Mrs. Butler firmly. "I sent for our doctor and told Manigo to put Rhett straight to bed. He was blue with cold."

Anne spoke quietly, bending near Scarlett's ear. "Miss Eleanor was alarmed when the storm came up so suddenly. We rushed from the Home to the mooring basin and when they said the boat hadn't come back she got frantic. I doubt that she sat down once all afternoon, she was just pacing back and forth on the piazza looking out into the rain."

Under a nice roof, thought Scarlett impatiently. It's all well and good for Anne to sound so concerned for Miss Eleanor, but she wasn't the one freezing to death!

"My son told me you worked a miracle tending his wife," Miss Eleanor said to Rebekah. "I don't know how we'll ever thank you."

"Wasn't me, Missus, it was the good Lord. I talked to Jesus for her, poor little shivering thing. I said this ain't Lazarus, Lord . . ."

While Rebekah repeated her story to Mrs. Butler, Anne answered Scarlett's question about Rhett. He had waited until the doctor said that Scarlett was out of danger, then he'd taken the ferry to Charleston to set his mother's mind at rest, knowing how worried she must be. "It gave us all a shock when we saw a Yankee soldier coming through the gate," Anne laughed. "He'd borrowed dry clothes from the sergeant."

Scarlett refused to leave the ferry in the wheelchair. She insisted that she was perfectly capable of walking to the house and she did walk, stepping out as if nothing had happened.

But she was tired when they arrived, so tired that she accepted Anne's help to climb the stairs. And after a tray with a hot bean soup and corn muffins, she fell again into a deep sleep.

There were no nightmares this time. She was in the familiar soft luxury of linen sheets and feather mattress, and she knew that Rhett was only a few steps away. She slept for fourteen strength-restoring hours.

She saw the flowers the minute she woke up. Hothouse roses. There was an envelope propped against the vase. Scarlett reached greedily for it.

His bold slashing handwriting was starkly black on the cream-colored paper. Scarlett touched it lovingly before she began to read.

There is nothing that I can say about what happened yesterday except that I am profoundly ashamed and sorry to have been the cause of such great pain and danger for you.

Scarlett wriggled with pleasure.

Your courage and valiant spirits were truly heroic, and I shall always regard you with admiration and respect.

I regret bitterly all that occurred after we escaped from the long ordeal. I said things to you that no man should say to a woman, and my actions were reprehensible.

I cannot, however, deny the truth of anything I said. I must not and will not ever see you again.

According to our agreement, you have the right to remain in Charleston at my mother's house until April. I am frankly hoping that you will not choose to do so, because I will visit neither the city house nor Dunmore Landing until I receive information that you have returned to Atlanta. You cannot find me, Scarlett. Don't try.

The cash settlement I promised will be transferred to you immediately in care of your Uncle Henry Hamilton.

I ask you to accept my sincere apologies for everything about our lives together. It was not meant to be. I wish you a happier future.

Rhett

Scarlett stared at the letter, at first too shocked to hurt. Then too angry. Finally she held it in her two hands and tore the heavy paper slowly into shreds, talking as she destroyed the thick dark words. "Not this time you don't, Rhett Butler. You ran away from me that time before, in Atlanta, after you made love to me. And I drooped around, lovesick, waiting for you to come back. Well, now I know a lot more than I did then. I know you can't get me out of your head, no matter how hard you try. You can't live without me. No man could make love to a woman the way you made love to me and then never see her again. You'll come back, just like you came back before. But you won't find me waiting. You'll have to come find me. Wherever I am."

She heard Saint Michael's tolling the hour . . . six . . . seven . . . eight . . . nine . . . ten. Every other Sunday, she had gone to Mass at ten o'clock. Not today. She had more important things to do.

She slid out of bed and ran to the bellpull. Pansy'd better come quick. I want to be packed and at the station in time for the train to Augusta. I'll go home, and I'll make sure Uncle Henry's got my money, and then I'll start right in on the work at Tara.

. . . But I haven't got it yet.

"Morning, Miss Scarlett. It's mighty fine to see you looking so fit after what happen—"

"Stop that babbling and get out my valises." Scarlett paused. "I'm going to Savannah. It's my grandfather's birthday."

She'd meet her aunts at the train depot. The train left for Savannah at ten of twelve. And tomorrow she'd find the Mother Superior and make her talk to the Bishop. No point in going home to Atlanta without the deed to Tara in her hand.

"I don't want that nasty old dress," she said to Pansy. "Get out the ones I brought when I came here. I'll wear what I like. I'm over being so eager to please."

"I wondered what all the fuss was about," said Rosemary. She eyed Scarlett's fashionable clothes with curiosity. "Are you going someplace, too? Mama said you probably would sleep all day."

"Where is Miss Eleanor? I want to tell her goodbye."

"She's already left for church. Why don't you write her a note? Or I can give her a message."

Scarlett looked at the clock. She hadn't much time. The hackney was waiting outside. She dashed into the library and grabbed paper and pen. What should she say?

"Your carriage is waiting, Missus Rhett," said Manigo.

Scarlett scrawled a few sentences, saying that she was going to her grandfather's birthday and was sorry to miss seeing Eleanor before she left. *Rhett will explain everything*, she added. *I love you.*

"Miss Scarlett—" called Pansy nervously. Scarlett folded the note and sealed it.

"Please give this to your mother," she said to Rosemary. "I must hurry. Goodbye."

"Goodbye, Scarlett," said Rhett's sister. She stood in the doorway to watch Scarlett and her maid and her luggage move off down the street. Rhett hadn't been so well organized when he departed late the night before.

She had begged him not to go because he'd looked so unwell. But he had kissed her goodbye and set off into the darkness on foot. It wasn't hard to figure out that somehow Scarlett was driving him away.

With slow deliberate movements Rosemary struck a match and burned Scarlett's note. "Good riddance," she said aloud.

New Life

33

Scarlett clapped her hands with delight when the hackney pulled up in front of Grandfather Robillard's house. It was pink, just like Miss Eleanor had said. To think that I didn't even notice when I visited before! Well, no matter, it was so long ago; what counts is now.

She hurried up one curving arm of the double iron-railed steps and through the opened door. Her aunts and Pansy could see to the luggage, she was dying with curiosity about the inside of the house.

Yes, it was pink everywhere—pink and white and gold. The walls were pink, and the covers on the chairs, and the draperies. With shiny white woodwork and columns, all trimmed with glimmering gilt. Everything looked perfect, too, not peeling and shabby like the paint and fabrics in most of the houses in Charleston and Atlanta. What a perfect place to be when Rhett came after her. He'd see that her family was every bit as important and impressive as his.

Rich, too. Her eyes moved rapidly, assessing the value of the meticulously maintained furnishings she could see through the open door to the drawing room. Why, she could paint every wall of Tara, inside and out, for what it must cost to gold leaf the plastered ceiling corners.

The old skinflint! Grandfather never sent a penny to help me after the War, and he doesn't do a thing for the aunts, either.

Scarlett prepared for battle. Her aunts were terrified of their father, but she wasn't. The fearful loneliness she'd known in Atlanta had made her timid, apprehensive, eager to please in Charleston. Now she had taken her life back into her own hands, and she felt vibrant with strength. Not man nor beast could bother her now. Rhett loved her, and she was queen of the world.

She coolly removed her hat and her fur cape and dropped them on a marble-topped console in the hall. Then she began to take off her apple green kid gloves. She could feel her aunts staring. They'd done plenty of that already. But Scarlett was very pleased to be wearing her green and brown plaid travelling costume instead of the drab outfits she'd worn in Charleston. She fluffed up the dark green taffeta bow that made her eyes sparkle so. When her gloves had joined hat and cape, she pointed to them. "Pansy, take these things upstairs and put them away in the prettiest bedroom you can find. Stop cringing in the corner like that, nobody's going to bite you."

"Scarlett, you can't . . ."

"You must wait . . ." The aunts were wringing their hands.

"If Grandfather's too mean to come out and meet us, we'll just have to shift for ourselves. God's nightgown, Aunt Eulalie! You grew up here, you and Aunt Pauline, can't you just make yourselves at home?"

Scarlett's words and manner were bold enough, but when a basso voice bellowed "Jerome!" from the rear of the house, she felt her palms grow damp. Her grandfather, she suddenly remembered, had eyes that cut right through you and made you wish you were anywhere except under his gaze.

The imposing black manservant who had admitted her now gestured Scarlett and her aunts toward the open door at the end of the hall. Scarlett let Eulalie and Pauline go first. The bedroom was a tremendous high-ceilinged space that had formerly been a spacious parlor. It was crowded with furniture, all the sofas and chairs and tables that had been in the parlor, plus a massive four-posted bed with gilt eagles crouching on top of the posts. In one corner of the room was a flag of France and a headless tailor's dummy wearing the gold-epauletted medal-hung uniform that Pierre Robillard had worn when he was a young man and an officer in Napoleon's army. The old man Pierre Robillard was in the bed, sitting erect against a mass of huge pillows, glaring at his visitors.

Why, he's shrunk up to almost nothing. He was such a big old man, but he's practically lost in that big bed, nothing but skin and bones. "Hello, Grandfather," Scarlett said, "I've come to see you for your birthday. It's Scarlett, Ellen's daughter."

"I haven't lost my memory," said the old man. His strong voice belied his fragile body. "But apparently your memory fails you. In this house, young people do not speak unless they are spoken to."

Scarlett bit her tongue to keep silent. I'm not a child to be talked to that way, and you should be grateful anybody comes to see you at all. No wonder Mother was so happy to have Pa take her away from home!

"*Et vous, mes filles. Qu'est-ce-que vous voulez cette fois?*" Pierre Robillard growled at his daughters.

Eulalie and Pauline rushed to the bedside, both speaking at once.

My grief! They're talking French! What on earth am I doing here? Scarlett sank down onto a gold brocade sofa, wishing she was some place —any place—else. Rhett better come after me soon or I'll go crazy in this house.

It was getting dark outside, and the shadowed corners of the room were mysterious. The headless soldier seemed about to move. Scarlett felt cold fingers on her spine and told herself not to be silly. But she was glad when Jerome and a sturdy-looking black woman came in carrying a lamp. While the maid pulled the curtains Jerome lit the gas lamps on each wall. He asked Scarlett politely if she would move so that he could get behind the sofa. When she stood, she saw her grandfather's eyes on her, and she turned away from them. She found herself facing a big painting in an ornate gilt frame. Jerome lit one lamp, then a second, and the painting came to life.

It was a portrait of her grandmother. Scarlett recognized her at once from the painting at Tara. But this one was very different. Solange Robillard's dark hair was not piled high on her head as in Tara's portrait. It fell, instead, like a warm cloud over her shoulders and down her bare arms to the elbow, bound only by a fillet of gleaming pearls. Her arrogant thin nose was the same, but her lips held a beginning smile instead of a sneer, and her tip-tilted dark eyes looked from their corners at Scarlett with the laughing, magnetic intimacy that had challenged and lured everyone who'd ever known her. She was younger in this painting, but nevertheless a woman, not a girl. The provocative round breasts half-exposed at Tara were covered by the thin white silk gown she wore. Covered yet visible through the gauzy silk, a glimmer of white flesh and rosy nipples. Scarlett felt herself blushing. Why, Grandma Robillard doesn't look like a lady at all, she thought, automatically disapproving as she'd been taught she should. Involuntarily she remembered herself in Rhett's arms and the wild hunger for his hands on her. Her grandmother must have felt the same hunger, the same ecstasy, it was in her eyes and her smile. So it can't be wrong, what I felt. Or was it? Was it some taint of shamelessness in her blood, handed down from the woman who smiled at her from the painting? Scarlett stared at the woman above her on the wall, fascinated.

"Scarlett." Pauline whispered in her ear. "Père wants us to leave now. Say goodnight quietly, and come with me."

* * *

Supper was a skimpy meal. Hardly enough, in Scarlett's opinion, for one of the bright-plumaged fantasy birds painted on the plates that held it. "That's because the cook's preparing Père's birthday feast," Eulalie explained in a whisper.

"Four days ahead of time?" Scarlett said loudly. "What's she doing, watching the chicken grow up?" Good heavens, she grumbled to herself, she'd be as skinny as Grandfather Robillard by Thursday if it was going to be like this. After the house was asleep she made her way silently down to the basement kitchen and ate her fill of the cornbread and buttermilk in the larder. Let the servants go hungry for a change, she thought, pleased that her suspicions had proven accurate. Pierre Robillard might keep the loyalty of his daughters when their stomachs were only half-filled, but his servants wouldn't stay unless they had plenty to eat.

The next morning she ordered Jerome to bring her eggs and bacon and biscuits. "I saw plenty in the kitchen," she added. And she got what she wanted. It made her feel much better about her meekness the night before. It's not like me to knuckle under that way, she thought. Just because Aunt Pauline and Aunt Eulalie were shaking like leaves, that's no reason for me to let the old man scare me. I won't let it happen again.

Still, she was just as glad that she had the servants to deal with and not her grandfather. She could see that Jerome was offended, and it rather pleased her. She hadn't had a show-down with anyone in a long time, and she did love to win. "The other ladies will have bacon and eggs, too," she told Jerome. "And this isn't enough butter for my biscuits."

Jerome stalked off to report to the other servants. Scarlett's demands were an affront to them all. Not because they meant more work; in fact she was only asking for what the servants always had for breakfast themselves. No, what bothered Jerome and the others was her youth and energy. She was a loud disruption of the house's shrine-like, muted atmosphere. The servants could only hope that she would leave soon, and without wreaking too much havoc.

After breakfast, Eulalie and Pauline took her into each of the rooms on the first floor, talking eagerly about the parties and receptions they had seen in their youth, correcting each other constantly and arguing about decades-old details. Scarlett paused for a long time in front of the portrait of three young girls, trying to see her mother's composed adult features in the chubby-cheeked five-year-old of the painting. Scarlett had felt isolated in Charleston's web of intermarried generations. It was good to be in the house where her mother had been born and reared, in a city where she was part of the web.

"You must have about a million cousins in Savannah," she said to the aunts. "Tell me about them. Can I meet them? They're my cousins, too."

Pauline and Eulalie looked confused. Cousins? There were the Prudhommes, their mother's family. But only one very old gentleman was in Savannah, the widower of their mother's sister. The rest of the family had moved to New Orleans many years ago. "Everyone in New Orleans speaks French," Pauline explained. And as for the Robillards, they were the only ones. "Père had lots of cousins in France, brothers, too—two of them. But he was the only one to come to America."

Eulalie broke in. "But we have many, many friends in Savannah, Scarlett. You can certainly meet them. Sister and I will be paying calls and leaving cards today, if Père doesn't need us to stay home with him."

"I'll have to be back by three," Scarlett said quickly. She didn't want to be out when Rhett arrived, nor did she want to be other than at her best. She'd need plenty of time to bathe and dress before the train from Charleston got in.

But Rhett didn't come, and when Scarlett left the carefully chosen bench in the immaculately maintained formal garden behind the house she felt chilled to the bone. She had refused her aunts' invitation to accompany them that evening to the musicale they'd been invited to. If it was going to be anything like the tedious reminiscences of the old ladies they'd called on that morning, she'd be bored to death. But her grandfather's malevolent eyes when he received his family for ten minutes before supper made her change her mind. Anything would be better than being alone in the house with Grandfather Robillard.

The Telfair sisters, Mary and Margaret, were the recognized cultural guardians of Savannah, and their musicale was nothing like the ones Scarlett had known before. Usually they were just ladies singing, showing off their "accomplishments," accompanied by other ladies on the pianoforte. It was obligatory that ladies sing a little, play the piano a little, draw or paint watercolors a little and do fancy needlework a little. At the Telfairs' house on Saint James' Square, the standards were much more demanding. The handsome double drawing rooms had rows of gilt chairs across their centers, and at the curved end of one of the rooms a piano and a harp and six chairs with music stands in front of them promised some real performances. Scarlett made mental notes of all the arrangements. The double drawing rooms at the Butler house could easily be fixed the same way, and it would be a different kind of party from what everyone else did. She'd have a reputation as an elegant hostess in no time at all. She wouldn't be old and frumpy looking like the Telfair sisters, either. Or as dowdy as the younger women who were here. Why was it that everywhere in the South people thought they had to look poor and patched to prove they were respectable?

The string quartet bored her, and she thought the harpist would never finish. She did enjoy the singers, even though she had never heard of opera; at least there was a man singing with the woman instead of two girls together. And after the songs in foreign languages, they did a group of songs she knew. The man's voice was wonderfully romantic in "Beautiful Dreamer" and it throbbed with emotion when he sang "Come Back to Erin, Mavourneen, Mavourneen." She had to admit he sounded a lot better than Gerald O'Hara in his cups.

I wonder what Pa would make of all this? Scarlett almost giggled aloud. He'd probably sing along and add something from a flask to the punch, too. Then he'd ask for "Peg in a Low Back'd Car." Just as she had asked Rhett to sing it . . .

The room and the people in it and the music disappeared for her, and she heard Rhett's voice booming inside the overturned sloop, felt his arms holding her to his warmth. He can't do without me. He'll come to me this time. It's my turn.

Scarlett didn't realize that she was smiling during a touching rendition of "Silver Threads Among the Gold."

The next day she sent a telegram to her Uncle Henry, giving her address in Savannah. She hesitated, then added a question. Had Rhett transferred any money to her?

What if Rhett tried to play some kind of game again and stopped sending the money to keep up the house on Peachtree Street? No, surely he wouldn't do that. Just the opposite. His letter said he was sending the half million.

It couldn't be true. He was only bluffing when he wrote all those hurtful things. Like opium, he'd said. He couldn't do without her. He'd come after her. It would be harder for him to swallow his pride than it would for any other man, but he'd come. He had to. He couldn't do without her. Especially not after what happened on the beach . . .

Scarlett felt a warm weakness travelling through her body, and she forced herself to remember where she was. She paid for the telegram and listened attentively when the telegraph operator gave her directions to the Convent of the Sisters of Mercy. Then she set off at such a rapid pace that Pansy almost had to run to keep up. While she was waiting for Rhett to come, she should have just enough time to track down Carreen's Mother Superior and get her to talk to the Bishop, as Rhett had suggested.

Savannah's Convent of the Sisters of Mercy was a big white building with a cross over its tall closed doors, surrounded by a tall iron fence with closed gates surmounted by iron crosses. Scarlett's rapid pace slowed, then she stopped. It was very different from the handsome brick house in Charleston.

"Is you going in there, Miss Scarlett?" Pansy's voice had a quaver in it. "I better wait outside. I'm a Baptist."

"Don't be such a goose!" Pansy's fearfulness gave Scarlett courage. "It's not a church, just a home for nice ladies like Miss Carreen." The gate opened at her touch.

Yes, said the elderly nun who opened the door when Scarlett rang the bell, yes, Charleston's Mother Superior was there. No, she couldn't ask her to see Mrs. Butler right now. There was a meeting in progress. No, she didn't know how long it would last, nor whether the Mother Superior would be able to see Mrs. Butler when it was over. Perhaps Mrs. Butler would like to see the schoolrooms; the convent was very proud of its school. Or it was possible that a tour of the new Cathedral building could be arranged. After that, perhaps the Mother Superior could be sent a message, if the meeting had ended.

Scarlett forced herself to smile. The last thing on earth I want to do is admire a bunch of children, she thought angrily. Or look at some church, either. She was about to say that she'd simply come back later, then the nun's words gave her an idea. They were building a new Cathedral, were they? That cost money. Maybe her offer to buy back Carreen's share of Tara would be looked on more favorably here than it had been in Charleston, just like Rhett said. After all, Tara was Georgia property, probably controlled by the Bishop of Georgia. Suppose she offered to buy a stained glass window in the new Cathedral as Carreen's dowry? The cost would be much higher than Carreen's share of Tara was worth, and she'd make it clear that the window was in exchange, not in addition. The Bishop would listen to reason, and then he'd tell the Mother Superior what to do.

Scarlett's smile became warmer, wider. "I'd be honored to see the Cathedral, Sister, if you're sure it's not too much trouble."

* * *

Pansy's mouth gaped open when she looked up at the soaring twin spires of the handsome Gothic-design Cathedral. The workmen on the scaffolding that surrounded the nearly completed towers looked small and nimble, like brightly garbed squirrels high in paired trees. But Scarlett had no eyes for the drama overhead. Her pulse was quickened by the organized hubbub on the ground, the sounds of hammering, sawing, and especially by the familiar resiny smell of fresh-cut lumber. Oh, how she missed the lumber mills and lumberyards. Her palms itched with the yearning to run her hands over the clean wood, to be busy, to be doing something, making a difference, running things—instead of taking tea from dainty cups with washed-out, dainty old ladies.

Scarlett heard barely a word of the descriptive wonders outlined by the young priest who was her escort. She did not even notice the surreptitious admiring looks of the burly laborers who stood back from their work to allow the priest and his companion free passage. She was too preoccupied to listen or notice. What fine straight trees had given up these timbers? It was the best heart pine she'd ever seen. She wondered where the mill was, what kind of saws it had, what kind of power. Oh, if only she was a man! Then she could ask, could go see the mill instead of this church. Scarlett scuffled her feet through a mound of fresh wood shavings and inhaled the tonic of the sharp scent of them.

"I must get back to the school for dinner," said the priest apologetically.

"Of course, Father, I'm ready to go." She wasn't but what else could she say? Scarlett followed him out of the Cathedral and onto the sidewalk.

"Begging your pardon, Father." The speaker was a huge, red-faced man wearing a red shirt that was heavily whitened by mortar dust. The priest looked diminutive and pale beside him.

"If you could be saying a small blessing on the work, Father? The lintel to the Chapel of the Sacred Heart was set not an hour ago."

Why, he sounds just like Pa at his most Irish. Scarlett bowed her head for the priest's blessing, as did the groups of workmen. Her eyes smarted from the tang of the cut pine and the quick tears for her father that she blinked away.

I'll go see Pa's brothers, she decided. No matter that they must be about a hundred years old, Pa would want me to go and say hello at least.

She walked with the priest back to the convent, and another placid refusal by the elderly nun when she asked to see the Mother Superior.

Scarlett kept her temper, but her eyes were dangerously bright. "Tell her I'll be back this afternoon," she said.

As the tall iron gate swung closed behind her Scarlett heard the sound of church bells from a few blocks away. "Bother!" she said. She was going to be late for dinner.

$\mathcal{S}$carlett smelled fried chicken as soon as she opened the door of the big pink house. "Take these things," she said to Pansy, and she got out of her cape and hat and gloves with record speed. She was very hungry.

Eulalie looked at her with huge mournful eyes when she entered the dining room. "Père wants to see you, Scarlett."

"Can't it wait until after dinner? I'm starving."

"He said 'the minute she comes in.' "

Scarlett picked up a steaming hot roll from the bread basket and took an angry bite as she swung on her heel. She finished it while she marched to her grandfather's room.

The old man frowned at her over the tray that rested on his lap in the big bed. His plate, Scarlett saw, held only mashed potatoes and a mound of soggy-looking bits of carrot.

My grief! No wonder he looks so fierce. There's not even any butter on the potatoes. Even if he doesn't have a tooth in his head, they could feed him better than that.

"I do not tolerate a disregard for the schedule of my house," said the old man.

"I'm sorry, Grandfather."

"Discipline is what made the Emperor's armies great; without discipline there is only chaos."

His voice was deep, strong, fearsome. But Scarlett saw the sharp old bones jutting under his heavy linen nightshirt, and she felt no fear.

"I said I was sorry. May I go now? I'm hungry."

"Don't be impertinent, young lady."

"There's nothing impertinent about being hungry, Grandfather. Just because you don't want to eat your dinner, it doesn't mean nobody else should have any."

Pierre Robillard pushed angrily at his tray. "Pap!" he growled. "Not fit for pigs."

Scarlett edged toward the door.

"I have not dismissed you, Miss."

She felt her stomach growl. The rolls would be cold by now, the chicken might even be gone, with Aunt Eulalie's appetite being what it was.

"God's nightgown, Grandfather, I'm not one of your soldiers! And I'm not scared of you like my aunts, either. What are you going to do to me, do you think? Shoot me for desertion? If you want to starve yourself to death, that's up to you. I'm hungry, and I'm going to go have whatever dinner is left." She was halfway out the door when a strange choking sound made her turn back. Dear God, have I given him apoplexy? Don't let him die on me.

Pierre Robillard was laughing.

Scarlett put her hands on her hips and glared at him. He'd scared her half to death.

He waved her away with a long-fingered bony hand. "Eat," he said, "eat." Then he began laughing again.

"What happened?" asked Pauline.

"I didn't hear shouting, did I, Scarlett?" said Eulalie.

They were sitting at table waiting for dessert. The dinner was gone. "Nothing happened," Scarlett said through her teeth. She picked up the small silver bell on the table and shook it furiously. When the stout black maid appeared carrying two small dishes of pudding, Scarlett stalked over to her. She put her hands on the woman's shoulders and turned her around. "Now you march, and I mean march, not amble along. You go down to the kitchen and bring me my dinner. Hot and plenty of it and in a hurry. I don't care which one of you was planning to eat it, but you'll have to make do with the back and the wings. I want a thigh and a breast and plenty of gravy on my potatoes and a bowl of butter, with the rolls nice and hot. Go on!"

She sat down with a flounce, ready to do battle with her aunts if they said so much as one word. Silence filled the room until her dinner was served.

Pauline contained herself until Scarlett's food was half-eaten. Then, "What did Père say to you?" she asked politely.

Scarlett wiped her mouth with her napkin. "He just tried to bully me the way he does you and Aunt 'Lalie, so I gave him a piece of my mind. It made him laugh."

The two sisters exchanged shocked looks. Scarlett smiled and ladled more gravy onto the potatoes left on her plate. What geese her aunts were. Didn't they know that you had to stand up to bullies like their father or else they'd trample right over you?

It never occurred to Scarlett that she was able to resist being bullied because she was a bully herself, or that her grandfather's laughter was caused by his recognition of her resemblance to him.

When dessert was served, the bowls of tapioca had somehow become larger. Eulalie smiled gratefully at her niece. "Sister and I were just saying how much we enjoyed having you with us in our old home, Scarlett. Don't you find Savannah a lovely little city? Did you see the fountain in Chippewa Square? And the theater? It's nearly as old as Charleston's. I remember how Sister and I used to look out of the windows of our schoolroom at the thespians coming and going. Don't you remember, Sister?"

Pauline remembered. She also remembered that Scarlett had not told them she was going out that morning, nor where she had been. When Scarlett reported that she'd been to the Cathedral, Pauline put her finger to her lips. Père, she said, was unfortunately extremely opposed to Roman Catholicism. It had something to do with French history, she wasn't sure what, but he got very angry about the Church. That was the reason she and Eulalie always left Charleston after Mass to come to Savannah and left Savannah on Saturday to return to Charleston. This year there was a particular difficulty; because Easter was so early, they would be in Savannah for Ash Wednesday. Naturally they had to attend Mass, and they could leave the house early and unobserved. But how could they keep their father from seeing the smudges of ash on their foreheads when they returned to the house?

"Wash your face," said Scarlett impatiently, thereby revealing her ignorance and the recent date of her return to religion. She dropped her napkin on the table. "I've got to be off," she said briskly. "I . . . I'm going to visit my O'Hara uncles and aunts." She didn't want anyone to know that she was trying to buy the convent's share of Tara. Especially not her aunts, they gossiped too much. Why, they might even write to Suellen. She smiled sweetly. "What time do we leave in the morning for Mass?" She'd be sure to mention it to the Mother Superior. No need to let on that she'd forgotten all about Ash Wednesday.

What a bother it was that she'd left her rosary in Charleston. Oh, well, she could buy a new one at her O'Hara uncles' store. If she remembered correctly, they had everything in there from bonnets to plows.

"Miss Scarlett, when are we going home to Atlanta? I don't feel comfortable with the folks in your Grandpa's kitchen. They is all so old. And my shoes is just about wore out from all this walking. When are we going home where you got all the fine carriages?"

"Stop that everlasting complaining, Pansy. We'll go when I say go and where I say go." Scarlett's response had no real heat in it; she was trying to remember where her uncles' store was, and having no luck. I must be catching old folks' forgetfulness. Pansy's right about that part. Everybody I know in Savannah is old. Grandfather, Aunt Eulalie, Aunt Pauline, all their friends. And Pa's brothers are the oldest of all. I'll just say hello and let them give me a nasty dry old man's kiss on the cheek and buy my rosary and leave. There's no real call to see their wives. If they cared about seeing me, they would have done something about keeping up all these years. Why, for all they know I could be dead and buried and not so much as a condolence note to my husband and children. A mighty tacky way to treat a blood relative, I call it. Maybe I'll just forget about going to see any of them at all. They don't deserve any visits from me after the way they neglected me, she thought, ignoring the letters from Savannah that she'd never answered, until finally they stopped coming.

She was ready to consign her father's brothers and their wives permanently to oblivion in the recesses of her mind now. She was fixed on two things, getting control of Tara and getting the upper hand with Rhett. Never mind that the two were contradictory goals, she'd find a way to have both. And they demanded all the thinking she had time for. I'm not going to go trailing around looking for that musty old store, Scarlett decided. I've got to track down the Mother Superior and the Bishop. Oh, I do wish I hadn't left those beads in Charleston. She looked quickly along the storefronts on the other side of Broughton Street, Savannah's place to shop. Surely there must be a jeweler somewhere close by.

The bold gilt letters that spelled out O'HARA stretched across the wall above five gleaming windows almost directly opposite. My, they've come up in the world since I was here last, Scarlett thought. That doesn't look musty at all. "Come on," she said to Pansy, and she plunged into the tangled traffic of wagons, buggies, and pushcarts that filled the busy street.

The O'Hara store smelled of fresh paint, not long-settled dust. A green tarlatan banner draped across the front of the counter in the rear gave the reason in gold letters: GRAND OPENING. Scarlett looked around enviously. The store was more than twice the size of her store in Atlanta, and she could see that the stock was fresher and more varied. Neatly labelled boxes and bolts of bright fabrics filled shelves to the ceiling; barrels of meals and flours were lined up along the floor, not far from the big potbellied stove in the center; and huge glass jars of candy stood temptingly on the tall counter. Her uncles were moving up in the world for sure. The store she'd visited in 1861 wasn't in the central, fashionable part of Broughton Street, and it was dark, cluttered, even more so than hers in Atlanta. It would be interesting to find out what this handsome expansion had cost her uncles. She might just consider a few of their ideas for her own business.

She walked quickly to the counter. "I'd like to see Mr. O'Hara, if you please," she said to the tall, aproned man who was measuring out some lamp oil into a customer's glass jug.

"In a moment, if you'll be so kind as to wait, ma'am," the man said without looking up. His voice had just a hint of brogue in it.

That makes sense, thought Scarlett. Hire Irish for a shop run by Irishmen. She looked at the labels on the shelved boxes in front of her while the man wrapped the oil in brown paper and made change. Hmmm, she should be keeping gloves that way, too, by size not by color. You could see the colors quick enough when you opened the box, but it was a real bother to search for the right size in a box of gloves that were all of them black. Why hadn't she thought of it before?

The man behind the counter had to speak again before Scarlett heard him. "I'm Mr. O'Hara," he repeated. "How might I be of service to you?"

Oh, no, this wasn't the uncles' store after all! They must still be where they'd always been. Scarlett explained hurriedly that she'd made a mistake. She was looking for an elderly Mr. O'Hara, Mr. Andrew or Mr. James. "Can you direct me to their store?"

"But this is their store. I'm their nephew."

"Oh . . . oh, my goodness. Then you must be my cousin. I'm Katie Scarlett, Gerald's daughter. From Atlanta." Scarlett held out both her hands. A cousin! A big, strong, not-an-old-man cousin of her own. She felt as if she'd just been given a surprise present.

"Jamie, that's me," said her cousin with a laugh, taking her hands in his. "Jamie O'Hara at your service, Scarlett O'Hara. And what a gift you are to a weary businessman, to be sure. Pretty as a sunrise, and dropping from out of the blue like a falling star. Tell me now, how do you come to be here for the grand opening of the new store? Come—let me get you a chair."

Scarlett forgot all about the rosary she'd meant to buy. She forgot about the Mother Superior, too. And about Pansy, who settled herself on a low stool in a corner and went to sleep at once with her head resting on a neat pile of horse blankets.

Jamie O'Hara mumbled something under his breath when he returned from the back room with a chair for Scarlett. There were four customers waiting to be served. In the next half hour more and more came in, so that there was no chance for him to say a word to Scarlett. He looked at her from time to time with apology in his eyes, but she smiled and shook her head. There was no need to apologize. She was pleased just to be there, in a warm, well-run store that was doing a good business, with a new-found cousin whose competence and skillful treatment of his customers was a delight to observe.

At last there was a brief moment when the only customers were a mother and her three daughters who were looking through four boxes of laces. "I'll talk like a rushing river, then, while I can," said Jamie. "Uncle James will be longing to see you, Katie Scarlett. He's an old gentleman, but still active enough. He's here every day until dinnertime. You may not know it, but his wife died, God rest her soul, and Uncle Andrew's wife as well. It took the heart out of Uncle Andrew, and he followed her within a month. May they all be resting in the arms of the angels. Uncle James lives in the house with me and my wife and children. It's not far from here. Will you come to tea this afternoon and see them all? My boy Daniel will be back soon from making deliveries, and I'll walk you to the house. We're celebrating my daughter Patricia's birthday today. All the family will be there."

Scarlett said she'd love to go to tea. Then she took off her hat and cape and walked over to the ladies at the laces. There was more than one O'Hara who knew how to run a store. Besides, she was too excited to sit still. A birthday for her cousin's daughter! Let's see, she'll be my first cousin once removed. Although Scarlett had grown up without the usual many-generation family network of the South, she was still a Southerner, and could name the exact relationship of cousins to the tenth remove. She had revelled in watching Jamie while he worked, because he was the living confirmation of everything Gerald O'Hara had told her. He had the dark curly hair and blue eyes of the O'Haras. And the wide mouth and short nose in the round, florid face. Most of all, he was a big man, tall and broad through the chest with strong thick legs like the trunks of trees that could withstand any storm. He was an impressive figure. "Your Pa is the runt of

the litter," Gerald had said without shame for himself but with enormous
pride in his brothers. "Eight children my mother had, and all boys, and me
the last and the only one not as big as a house." Scarlett wondered which
of the brothers was Jamie's father. No matter, she'd find out at the tea. No,
not tea, the birthday party! For her first cousin once removed.

35

_S_carlett looked up at her cousin Jamie with carefully concealed curiosity. In the daylight of the open street the lines and pouches beneath his eyes weren't blended away by shadows, the way they were inside the store. He was a middle-aged man, running to weight and softness. She'd assumed somehow that because he was her cousin he must be her age. When his son came in, she was shocked to be introduced to a grown man, not a boy who delivered packages. And a grown man with flaming red hair, to boot. It took some getting used to.

So did the sight of Jamie in daylight. He ... he wasn't a gentleman. Scarlett couldn't specify how she knew that, but it was as clear as glass. There was something wrong with his clothes; his suit was dark blue, but not dark enough, and it fit him too closely through the chest and shoulders and too loosely everywhere else. Rhett's clothing was, she knew, the result of superlative tailoring and, on his part, demanding perfectionism. She wouldn't expect Jamie to dress like Rhett—she'd never known any man who dressed like Rhett. But, still, he could do something—whatever it was that men did—so that he wouldn't look so ... so common. Gerald O'Hara had always looked like a gentleman, no matter how worn or rumpled his coat might be. It didn't occur to Scarlett that her mother's quiet authority and influence might have been at work on her father's transformation to gentleman landowner. Scarlett only knew that she'd lost most of her joy in discovering the existence of her cousin. Well, I only have to have a cup of tea and a piece of cake, and then I can leave. She smiled brilliantly at Jamie.

"I'm so thrilled to be meeting your family that I've taken leave of my senses, Jamie. I should have bought a present for your daughter's birthday."

"Aren't I bringing her the best gift of all when I walk in with you on my arm, Katie Scarlett?"

He does have a twinkle in his eye, just like Pa, Scarlett told herself. And Pa's teasing brogue. If only he wasn't wearing a Derby hat! Nobody wears Derby hats.

"We'll be walking past your grandfather's house," Jamie said, striking horror to Scarlett's heart. What if her aunts saw them—suppose she had to introduce them? They always thought Mother married beneath her; Jamie would be all the proof they could ever want. What was he saying? She had to pay attention.

". . . leave off your servant-girl there. She'd feel out-of-place with us. We don't have any servants."

No servants? Good Lord! Everybody has servants, everybody! What kind of place do they live in, a tenement? Scarlett squared her jaw. This is Pa's own brother's son, and Uncle James is Pa's own brother. I won't disgrace his memory by being too cowardly to take a cup of tea with them, even if there are rats running across the floor. "Pansy," she said, "when we get to the house, you go on in. I'll be back directly, you tell them . . . You will walk me home, won't you, Jamie?" She was brave enough to face a rat running across her foot, but she wasn't willing to ruin her reputation for all time by walking alone on the street. Ladies just didn't do that.

To Scarlett's relief they walked along the street behind her grandfather's house, not by the square in front of it where her aunts liked to promenade under the trees for their "constitutionals." Pansy went willingly through the gate into the garden, already yawning in anticipation of going back to sleep. Scarlett tried not to look anxious. She'd heard Jerome complaining to her aunts about the deterioration of the neighborhood. Only a few blocks to the east the fine old homes had degenerated into ramshackle boardinghouses for the sailors who manned the ships in and out of Savannah's busy port. And for the waves of immigrants who arrived on some of the ships. Most of them, according to the snobbish, elegant old black man, were unwashed Irish.

James escorted her straight ahead, and she sighed silently with relief. Then, very soon, he turned onto the handsome, well-kept avenue called South Broad and announced, "Here we are," in front of a tall, substantial brick house.

"How nice!" Scarlett said, with all her heart.

It was almost the last thing she got to say for some time. Instead of climbing the stairs to the big door on the high stoop, Jamie opened a smaller door at street level and ushered her into the kitchen and an overwhelming onslaught of people, all of them redheaded and all of them noisily welcoming when he shouted out above the hubbub of greetings, "This is Scarlett, my uncle Gerald O'Hara's beautiful daughter come all the way from Atlanta to see Uncle James."

There are so many of them, Scarlett thought when they rushed toward her. Jamie's laughter when the youngest girl and a little boy grabbed him around the knees made it impossible to understand what he was saying.

Then a large stout woman, with hair redder than any of them, held out a roughened hand to Scarlett. "Welcome to the house," she said placidly. "I'm Jamie's wife, Maureen. Pay no attention to these savages; come sit by the fire and have a cup of tea." She took Scarlett's arm in a firm grip and drew her into the room. "Quiet, you heathens, let your Pa catch his breath, can't you? Then wash your faces and come meet Scarlett one by one." She plucked Scarlett's fur cape from her shoulders. "Put this in a safe place, Mary Kate, else the baby will think it's a kitten to pull the tail on, so soft is it." The larger of the girls bobbed a curtsey in Scarlett's direction and held out eager hands for the fur. Her blue eyes were huge with admiration. Scarlett smiled at her. And at Maureen, even though Jamie's wife was pushing her down onto a Windsor chair as if she thought Scarlett was one of her children to be ordered around.

In an instant Scarlett found herself holding the biggest cup she had ever seen in one hand while, with the other, she was shaking hands with a startlingly beautiful young girl who whispered, "She looks like a princess," to her mother, and, "I'm Helen," to Scarlett.

"You should touch the furs, Helen," said Mary Kate importantly.

"Is Helen the guest here, then, that you're addressing yourself to her?" Maureen said. "What a disgrace for a mother to have such an eejit child." Her voice was warm with affection and suppressed laughter.

Mary Kate's cheeks stained with embarrassment. She curtseyed again and held out her hand. "Cousin Scarlett, I ask your pardon. I forgot myself in looking at your elegances. I'm Mary Kate, and it's proud I am to be cousin to such a grand lady."

Scarlett wanted to say no pardon was needed, but she had no chance. Jamie had taken off his hat and his suit coat and unbuttoned his vest. Under his right arm he was holding a child, a kicking, squealing, chubby, redheaded bundle of delighted struggle. "And this little devil is Sean, named John like a good American boy because he was born right here in Savannah.

We call him Jacky. Say hello to your cousin, Jacky, if you've got a tongue in your head."

"Hello!" shouted the little boy, then shrieked with excitement when his father turned him upside down.

"What's all this now?" The noise, except for Jacky's giggles, died down at once when the thin querulous tones cut through the racket. Scarlett looked across the kitchen and saw a tall old man who must be her Uncle James. There was a pretty girl with dark curly hair at his side. She looked alarmed and timid.

"Jacky woke Uncle James from his rest," she said. "Is he hurt, then, to be howling so and to bring Jamie home early?"

"Not a bit of it," said Maureen. She raised her voice. "You have a visitor, Uncle James. Come special to see you. Jamie left the store with Daniel so he could bring her to you. Come by the fire, tea's ready. And see Scarlett."

Scarlett stood up and smiled. "Hello, Uncle James, do you remember me?"

The old man stared at her. "Last time I saw you, you were mourning your husband. Have you found another one yet?"

Scarlett's mind raced backwards. Good heavens, Uncle James was right. She'd come to Savannah after Wade was born, when she was wearing black for Charles Hamilton. "Yes, I have," she said. And what would you say if I told you I found two husbands since then, nosy old man?

"Good," pronounced her uncle. "There are too many unmarried women in this house already."

The girl beside him let out a tiny cry, then turned and ran out of the room.

"Uncle James, you shouldn't be tormenting her so," said Jamie severely.

The old man walked to the fire and rubbed his hands before its warmth. "She shouldn't be such a weeper," he said. "The O'Haras don't weep over their troubles. Maureen, I'll have my tea now while I talk to Gerald's girl." He sat in the chair next to Scarlett's. "Tell me about the funeral. Did you bury your father in fine style? My brother Andrew had the finest burial this city has seen in many a year."

In her mind's eye Scarlett saw the pitiful band of mourners around Gerald's grave at Tara. So few of them. So many who should have been there were dead before her father, dead before their time.

Scarlett fixed her green eyes on the old man's faded blue ones. "He had a glass-sided hearse with four black horses and black plumes on their heads, a blanket of flowers on his coffin and more on the roof, and two hundred mourners following the hearse in their rigs. He's in a marble tomb, not a grave, and the tomb has a carved angel on top, seven feet high." Her voice was cold and harsh. Take that, old man, she thought, and leave Pa alone.

James rubbed his dry hands together. "God rest his soul," he said happily. "I always said Gerald had the most style of any of us; didn't I tell you that, Jamie? The runt of the litter, and the quickest to fly off at an insult. He was a fine small man, was Gerald. Do you know how he came by that plantation of his? Playing poker with my money, that's how. And not a penny of the profit did he offer to me." James' laughter was full and strong, the laughter of a young man. It was warm with life and rich amusement.

"Tell about how he came to leave Ireland, Uncle James," said Maureen, refilling the old man's cup. "Perhaps Scarlett never heard the tale."

Great balls of fire! Are we going to have a wake? Scarlett stirred angrily in her chair. "I heard it a hundred times," she said. Gerald O'Hara loved to boast about fleeing Ireland with a price on his head after he killed an English landlord's rent agent with one blow of his fist. Everyone in Clayton County had heard it a hundred times, and no one believed it. Gerald was noisy in his rages, but the whole world could see the gentleness underneath.

Maureen smiled. "A mighty man, for all his small size, so I've always been told. A father to make a woman proud."

Scarlett felt her throat clog with tears.

"He was that," said James. "When do we have the birthday cake, Maureen? And where is Patricia?"

Scarlett looked around the circle of crimson-topped faces. No, she was sure she hadn't heard the name Patricia. Maybe it was the dark-haired girl who had run away.

"She's fixing her own feast, Uncle James," said Maureen. "You know how particular she is. We're to go next door as soon as Stephen comes to tell us she's ready."

Stephen? Patricia? Next door?

Maureen saw the questions on Scarlett's face. "Did Jamie not tell you, Scarlett? There are three households of O'Haras here now. You've only just begun to meet your people."

I'll never get them all straight, thought Scarlett desperately. If only they'd stay in one place!

But there was no hope of that. Patricia was holding her birthday party in the double parlors of her house, with the sliding doors between them open as wide as they would go. The children—and there were many of them—were playing games that required a great deal of running and hiding and popping out from behind chairs and draperies. The adults darted from time to time after a child who was getting too boisterous, or swooped to pick up one of the small ones who had fallen and needed comforting. It didn't seem to matter whose child it was. All the adults played parent to all the children.

Scarlett was grateful for Maureen's red hair. All her children—the ones Scarlett had met next door, plus Patricia, plus Daniel, the son at the store, plus another grown boy whose name she couldn't remember—were at least recognizable. The others were a hopeless muddle.

So were their parents. Scarlett knew that one of the men was named Gerald, but which one? They were all big men, with curly dark hair and blue eyes and winning smiles.

"Isn't it confusing?" said a voice beside her. It was Maureen. "Don't let it bother you, Scarlett, you'll puzzle them out in time."

Scarlett smiled and nodded politely. But she had no intention of "puzzling them out." She was going to ask Jamie to walk her home just as soon as she could. It was too noisy here with all those brats running around. The silent pink house on the square seemed like a refuge. At least there she had her aunts to talk to. Here she couldn't say a word to a soul. They were all too busy chasing children or hugging and kissing Patricia. Asking her about her baby, for heaven's sake! As if they didn't know that the only decent thing to do was pretend that you didn't notice when a woman was pregnant. She felt like a stranger. Left out. Unimportant. Just like Atlanta. Just like Charleston. And these were her own kin! It made things a hundred times worse.

"We'll be cutting the cake now," Maureen said. She slipped her arm through Scarlett's. "Then we'll have a bit of music."

Scarlett clenched her teeth. My grief, I've sat through one musicale already in Savannah. Can't these people do anything else? She walked with Maureen to a settee covered in red plush and settled herself stiffly on the edge of the seat.

A knife clattering against a glass demanded everyone's attention. Something that was almost silence came into the crowd. "I thank you for as long as it lasts," Jamie said. He waved his knife menacingly at the laughter. "We've come to celebrate Patricia's birthday, even though it will not arrive until next week. Today is Shrove Tuesday, a better time for feasting than the middle of Lent." He threatened the laughter again. "And we have a further cause for celebration. A beautiful long lost O'Hara has been found again. I lift this glass for all the O'Haras in a toast to Cousin Scarlett and bid her welcome to our hearts and our homes." Jamie threw back his head and poured the dark contents of his glass down his throat. "Bring on the feast!" He commanded with a sweeping gesture. "And the fiddle!"

There was an outburst of giggles from the doorway and the sound of hissing calls for silence. Patricia came over and seated herself next to Scarlett. Then, from a corner, a fiddle began to play. Jamie's beautiful daughter Helen walked in carrying a platter of steaming small meat pies. She bent over to show them to Patricia and Scarlett, then carefully carried them to the heavy round parlor table in the center of the room and set the platter on the velvet cloth that covered it. Helen was followed by Mary Kate, then the pretty girl who had been with Uncle James, then the youngest of the O'Hara wives. All of them presented the platters they were carrying to Scarlett and Patricia before adding them to the food on the table. A roast of beef, a clove-studded ham, a bulging turkey. Then Helen appeared again with a huge bowl of steaming potatoes, followed more quickly now by the others with creamed carrots, roast onions, whipped sweet potatoes. Again and again the procession came until the table was covered with food and relishes of every kind. The fiddle—Scarlett saw that Daniel from the store was playing—played a flourishing arpeggio, and Maureen entered carrying a tower of a cake liberally trimmed with huge, vividly pink icing roses.

"Bakery cake!" screamed Timothy.

Jamie was immediately behind his wife. He held his two arms over his head. He was carrying three bottles of whiskey in each hand. The fiddle began to play an exuberant rapid tune, and everyone laughed and clapped. Even Scarlett. The drama of the procession was irresistible.

"Now Brian," said Jamie. "You and Billy. The queens on their throne to the hearth." Before Scarlett knew what was happening the settee was lifted and she was holding on to Patricia while they were swung back and forth and moved to a place near the glowing coals in the fireplace.

"Uncle James," Jamie ordered, and the old man was carried, laughing, in his high-backed chair to the other side of the mantel.

The girl who had been with James began to shoo the children, as if they were chickens, into the other parlor, where Mary Kate laid a tablecloth on the floor for them to sit on in front of the second fireplace.

In a surprisingly short time there was calm where there had been chaos. And while they ate and talked, Scarlett tried to "puzzle out" the adults.

Jamie's two sons were so much alike that she could hardly believe that Daniel, at twenty-one, was almost three years older than Brian. When she smiled at Brian and said as much, he blushed as only a redhead can. The only other young man began to tease him unmercifully, but he stopped when the pink-cheeked girl next to him put her hand on his and said, "Stop it, Gerald."

So that was Gerald. Pa would be so pleased to know that big hand-some fellow was named after him. He called the girl Polly, and they're so shiny with love they must be fresh-married. And Patricia's being mighty bossy to the one Jamie called Billy, so they must be husband and wife, too.

But Scarlett had little time to listen for the names of the others. Every-one, it seemed, wanted to talk to her. And everything she said was cause for exclamation, repetition, admiration. She found herself telling Daniel and Jamie all about her store, Polly and Patricia about her dressmaker, Uncle James about the Yankees setting Tara on fire. She talked mostly about her lumber business and how she'd built it from one small mill into two mills, lumberyards, and now a whole village of new houses on the edge of At-lanta. Everyone was loudly approving. At last Scarlett had found people who didn't think that talking about money was taboo. They were like she was, willing to work hard and determined to make money from it. She had already made hers, and they told her she was wonderful. She couldn't imag-ine why she had ever wanted to leave this marvelous party and go back to the deadly quiet at her grandfather's house.

"Will you give us some music, then, Daniel, if you've finished eating most of your sister's cake?" said Maureen when Jamie uncorked a bottle of whiskey, and suddenly everyone except Uncle James was up and moving around in what seemed to be a practiced routine. Daniel began playing a rapid, squeaking tune on the fiddle and the others shouted criticism while the women quickly cleared the table and the men moved the furniture back against the walls, leaving Scarlett and her uncle sitting as if on an island. Jamie presented James with a glass of whiskey and waited, half bent, for the old man's opinion.

"It'll do," was the judgment.

Jamie laughed. "Indeed I hope so, old man, for we have no other kind."

Scarlett tried to catch Jamie's eye, failed, finally called out to get his attention. She had to go now. Everyone was pulling chairs into a circle around the fire, and the smaller children were taking places on the floor at the adults' feet. Obviously they were getting ready for the musicale, and once it started, it would be terribly rude to get up and go.

Jamie stepped over a small boy to get to Scarlett. "Here you are, then," he said. To her horror he handed her a glass with several fingers of whiskey in it. What kind of person did he think she was? A lady didn't drink whis-key. She didn't drink anything stronger than tea, except champagne or a party punch or perhaps a very small glass of sherry. He couldn't possibly know about the brandy she used to drink. Why, he was insulting her! No, he wouldn't do that, it must be a joke. She forced a brittle laugh. "It's time for me to go, Jamie. I've had a delightful time, but it's getting late . . ."

"You'll not be leaving just when the party begins, Scarlett?" Jamie turned toward his son. "Daniel, you're driving your new-found cousin away with that screeching. Play a song for us, boy, not a cat fight."

Scarlett tried to speak, but her words were drowned out by the cries of "play decent, Daniel," and "give us a ballad," and "a reel, boy, let's have a reel."

Jamie grinned. "I can't hear you," he shouted over the din. "I'm deaf as a stone to anyone asking to go."

Scarlett felt her temper rising. When Jamie offered her the whiskey again, she stood up in a rage. Then, before she could knock the glass from his hand, she realized what Daniel had begun to play. It was "Peg in a Low Back'd Car."

Pa's favorite. She looked at Jamie's ruddy Irish face and saw her father's image. Oh, if only he could be here, he'd love this so. Scarlett sat down. She shook her head at the proffered drink, smiled weakly at Jamie. She was close to tears.

The music wouldn't allow sadness. The rhythm was too infectious, too merry, and everyone was singing now, and clapping their hands. Scarlett's foot began involuntarily to tap the beat under cover of her skirts.

"Come on, Billy," said Daniel, singing it, really, to the tune. "Play with me."

Billy opened the lid of a window seat and took out a concertina. The pleated leather bellows opened with a wheeze. Then he walked up behind Scarlett, reached over her head, and picked up something shiny from the mantel. "Let's have some real music. Stephen—" He tossed a thin glinting tube to the dark silent man. "You, too, Brian." There was another arc of silver through the air. "And, for you, dear mother-in-law—" His hand dropped something in Maureen's lap.

A young boy clapped wildly. "The bones! Cousin Maureen's going to play the bones."

Scarlett stared. Daniel had stopped playing, and with the music gone she felt sad again. But she no longer wanted to leave. This party had nothing to do with the Telfairs' musicale. There was easiness here, warmth, laughter. The parlors that had been so neatly arranged before were all hodge-podge now, furniture moved, chairs from both rooms crowded in a straggling half circle around the fire. Maureen lifted her hand with a clacking noise, and Scarlett saw that the "bones" were really thick pieces of smooth wood.

Jamie was still pouring and passing whiskey. Why, the women are drinking, too! Not in secret, not ashamed. They're having as much fun as the men. I'll have a drink, too. I'll celebrate the O'Haras. She almost called out to Jamie, then she remembered. I'll be going to grandfather's. I can't drink. Somebody would smell it on my breath. No matter. I feel as warm inside as if I had just had a drink. I don't need it.

Daniel pulled the bow over the strings. "The Maid Behind the Bar," he said. Everyone laughed. Including Scarlett, though she didn't know why. In an instant the big room rang with the music of an Irish reel. Billy's concertina whined vigorously, Brian piped the tune on his tin whistle, Stephen played his tin whistle in rippling counterpoint that wove in and out of Brian's melody. Jamie beat time with his foot, the children clapped, Scarlett clapped, everyone clapped. Except Maureen. She threw up the hand holding the bones and the sharp staccato clacking made an insistent rhythm that held everything together. Faster, the bones demanded, and the others obeyed. The whistles soared higher, the fiddle scraped louder, the concertina puffed to keep up. A half dozen children got up and began to leap and hop across the bare floor in the center of the room. Scarlett's hands grew hot from clapping, and her feet were moving as if she wanted to leap about with the children. When the reel came to an end, she fell back against the settee, exhausted.

"Come along, Matt, show the babies how to dance," cried Maureen with a tempting rattle of the bones. The older man near Scarlett stood up.

"God save us, wait a bit," Billy begged. "I need a bit of a rest. Give us a song, instead, Katie." He squeezed a few notes out of the concertina.

Scarlett started to protest. She couldn't sing, not here. She didn't know any Irish songs except "Peg" and her father's other favorite, "The Wearing o' the Green."

But, she saw, Billy didn't mean her. A plain dark woman with big teeth was handing her glass to Jamie and standing. "*There was a wild Colonial boy,*" she sang in a pure sweet high voice. Before the line was finished, Daniel and Brian and Billy were accompanying her. "*Jack Duggan was his name,*" sang Katie. "*He was born and raised in Ireland.*" and Stephen's whistle entered, an octave higher, with a strange heartbreaking silvery plaintiveness.

"*. . . in a house called Castlemaine . . .*" Everyone began to sing, except Scarlett. But she didn't mind not knowing the words. She was still part of the music. It was all around her. And when the sad, brave song was over, she saw that everyone else had glistening eyes just like hers.

There was a happy song next, started by Jamie, then one that made Scarlett laugh and blush at the same time when she understood the double meaning of the words.

"Now me," Gerald said. "I'll sing my sweet Polly the 'Londonderry Air.'"

"Oh, Gerald!" Polly hid her blushing face in her hands. Brian played the first few notes. Then Gerald began to sing and Scarlett caught her breath. She'd heard talk of the Irish tenor, but she wasn't prepared for the reality. And that voice like an angel's was coming from her Pa's namesake. Gerald's loving young heart was exposed for all to see on his face and for all to hear in the high pure notes from his vibrating strong throat. Scarlett's own throat felt choked by the beauty of it and the sharp painful longing to know love like that, so fresh and open. Rhett! her heart cried, even as her mind mocked the notion of simple directness from his dark complex nature.

At the end of the song Polly threw her arms around Gerald's neck and hid her face in his shoulder. Maureen lifted the bones above her shoulder. "We'll have a reel now," she announced firmly. "My toes are fairly twitching." Daniel laughed and began to play.

Scarlett had danced the Virginia reel a hundred times or more, but she'd never seen dancing like what happened next at Patricia's birthday party. Matt O'Hara began it. With his shoulders straight and his arms stiff at his side he looked like a soldier when he stepped away from the circle of chairs. Then his feet began to pound and flash and twist and move so quickly that they blurred in Scarlett's vision. The floor became a resounding drum under his heels, became like polished ice under his intricate impossible steps forward and back. He must be the best dancer in the whole world, Scarlett thought. And then Katie danced out to face him, her skirts held up in her two hands so that her feet were free to match his steps. Mary Kate was next, then Jamie joined his daughter. And beautiful Helen with a cousin, a little boy who couldn't be older than eight. I don't believe it, Scarlett thought. They're magic, all of them. The music's magic, too. Her feet moved, faster than they'd ever moved before, trying to mimic what she was seeing, trying to express the excitement of the music. I've got to learn to dance like that, I've just got to. It's like . . . like you spin right up to the sun.

A sleeping child under the settee woke at the sounds of the dancing feet and began to cry. Like a contagion, crying spread to the other smallest children. The dancing and the music stopped.

"Make some mattresses from folded blankets in the other parlor," Maureen said placidly, "and give them dry bottoms. Then we'll close the doors most shut and they'll sleep right along. Jamie, the bone-woman has a terrible thirst. Mary Kate, hand your Pa my glass."

Patricia asked Billy to carry their three-year-old son. "I'll get Betty," she said, reaching beneath the settee. "Hush, hush." She cradled the crying child to her. "Helen, close the curtains in the back, darling. There'll be a strong moon tonight."

Scarlett was still half in a trance from the spell of the music. She looked vaguely at the windows and was jolted back to reality. It was getting dark. The cup of tea she'd come for had stretched into hours. "Oh, Maureen, I'm going to be late for supper," she gasped. "I've got to go home. My grandfather will be furious."

"Let him be, the old loo-la. Stay for the party. It's only beginning."

"I wish I could," said Scarlett fervently. "It's the best party I've ever been to in my life. But I promised I'd be back."

"Ah, well, then. A promise is a promise. You'll come again?"

"I'd love to. Will you invite me?"

Maureen laughed comfortably. "Will you listen to the girl?" she said to the room at large. "There's no inviting done here. We're all a family, and you're a part of it. Come anytime you like. My kitchen door has no lock, and there's always a fire on the hearth. Jamie's a fine hand with the fiddle himself, too ... Jamie! Scarlett's got to go. Put your coat on, man, and give her your arm."

Just before they turned the corner Scarlett heard the music begin again. It was faint because of the thick brick walls of the house and the windows closed against the winter night. But she recognized what the O'Haras were singing. It was "The Wearing o' the Green."

I know all the words to that one; oh, I wish I hadn't had to leave.

Her feet made little dance steps. Jamie laughed and matched her. "I'll teach you the reel next time," he promised.

36

*S*carlett bore her aunts' tightlipped disapproval with easy disregard. Even being called on the carpet by her grandfather failed to upset her. She remembered Maureen O'Hara's offhanded dismissal of him. Old loo-la, she thought, and giggled internally. It made her brave and impertinent enough to sashay over to his bed and kiss his cheek after he dismissed her. "Good night, Grandfather," she said cheerfully.

"Old loo-la," she whispered when she was safely in the hall. She was laughing when she joined her aunts at table. Her supper was brought promptly. The plate was covered with a brightly shining silver dish cover to keep the food hot. Scarlett was sure it was newly polished. This house could run really properly, she thought, if it just had someone to keep the servants in line. Grandfather lets them get away with murder. Old loo-la.

"What do you find so amusing, Scarlett?" Pauline's tone was icy.

"Nothing, Aunt Pauline." Scarlett looked down at the mountain of food revealed when Jerome ceremoniously lifted the silver cover. She laughed aloud. For once in her life she wasn't hungry, not after the feast at the O'Haras'. And there was enough food in front of her to feed a half dozen people. She must have put the fear of God into the kitchen.

The following morning at Ash Wednesday Mass Scarlett took her place beside Eulalie in the pew favored by the aunts. It was genteelly unobtrusive, entered from a side aisle and located well towards the back. Her knees had just begun to hurt from kneeling on the cold floor when she saw her cousins enter the church. They walked—of course, thought Scarlett— straight up the center aisle to almost the front, where they took up two full pews. What very large people they are, and so full of life. And color. Jamie's sons' heads look like warm fires in the light from the red stained glass, and not even their hats can hide the bright hair on Maureen and the girls. Scarlett was so engrossed in admiration and memories of the birthday party that she almost missed the arrival of the nuns from the convent. After she'd hurried her aunts to get to church early, too. She wanted to make sure that the Mother Superior from Charleston was still at hand in Savannah.

Yes, there she was. Scarlett ignored Eulalie's frantic whispers ordering her to turn back around and face the altar. She studied the nun's serene expression as she walked past. Today the Mother Superior would see her. Scarlett was determined. She spent her time during Mass daydreaming about the party she'd give after she restored Tara to all its former beauty. There'd be music and dancing, just like last night, and it would go on and on for days and days.

"Scarlett!" Eulalie hissed. "Stop humming like that."

Scarlett smiled into her missal. She hadn't realized she was humming. She had to admit that "Peg in a Low Back'd Car" wasn't exactly church music.

"I don't believe it!" Scarlett said. Her pale eyes were bewildered and hurt beneath her smudged forehead, and her fingers were closed like claws on the rosary she'd borrowed from Eulalie.

The elderly nun repeated her message with emotion-free patience. "The Mother Superior will be in retreat all day, in prayer and fasting." She took pity on Scarlett and added an explanation. "This is Ash Wednesday."

"I know it's Ash Wednesday," Scarlett almost shouted. Then she curbed her tongue. "Please say that I am very disappointed," she said softly, "and I'll come back tomorrow."

As soon as she reached the Robillard house she washed her face.

Eulalie and Pauline were visibly shocked when she came downstairs and joined them in the drawing room, but neither of them said anything. Silence was the only weapon they felt it safe to use when Scarlett was in a temper. But when she announced that she was going to order breakfast, Pauline spoke up. "You'll regret that before the day is out, Scarlett."

"I can't imagine why," Scarlett answered. Her jaw was set.

It sagged when Pauline explained. Scarlett's reintroduction to religion was so recent that she thought fasting meant simply having fish on Fridays instead of meat. She liked fish and had never objected to the rule. But what Pauline told her was objectionable in the extreme.

Only one meal a day during the forty days of Lent, and no meat at that meal. Sundays were the exception. Still no meat, but three meals were allowed.

"I don't believe it!" Scarlett exclaimed for the second time within an hour. "We never did that at home."

"You were children," said Pauline, "but I'm sure your mother fasted as she should. I cannot understand why she didn't introduce you to Lenten observance when you passed childhood, but then she was isolated out in the country without a priest's guidance, and there was Mr. O'Hara's influence to offset . . ." Her voice trailed off.

Scarlett's eyes lit for battle. "And just what do you mean by 'Mr. O'Hara's influence,' I'd like to know?"

Pauline dropped her gaze. "Everyone knows that the Irish take certain freedoms with the laws of the Church. You can't really blame them, poor illiterate nation that they are." She crossed herself piously.

Scarlett stamped her foot. "I'm not going to stand here and listen to such high and mighty French snobbery. My Pa was never anything but a good man, and his 'influence' was kindness and generosity, something you don't know anything about. Furthermore, I'll have you know, I spent all afternoon yesterday with his kin, and they're fine people, every one of them. I'd a sight rather be influenced by them than by your whey-faced religious prissiness."

Eulalie burst into tears. Scarlett scowled at her. Now she'll sniff that sniff of hers for hours, I reckon. I can't bear it.

Pauline sobbed loudly. Scarlett turned, staring. Pauline never wept.

Scarlett looked helplessly at the two bent gray heads and hunched shoulders, Pauline's so thin and fragile looking.

My grief! She walked over to Pauline and touched her aunt's knobby back. "I'm sorry, Auntie. I didn't mean what I said."

When peace had been restored, Eulalie suggested that Scarlett join her and Pauline for their walk around the square. "Sister and I always find that a constitutional is a great restorative," she said brightly. Then her mouth quivered pathetically. "It keeps one's mind off food, too."

Scarlett agreed at once. She had to get out of the house. She was convinced she could smell bacon frying in the kitchen. She walked with her aunts around the square of green in front of the house, then the short distance to the next square, around it, then to the next square, and the next and the next. By the time they returned to the house she was dragging her feet almost as much as Eulalie was, and she was positive that she'd walked through or around every single one of the twenty-some squares that dotted Savannah and gave it its claim to unique charm. She was also positive that she was half-starved to death and bored to screaming-point. But at least it was time for dinner ... She couldn't remember ever tasting fish that was quite so delicious.

What a relief! Scarlett thought when Eulalie and Pauline went upstairs for their after-dinner naps. A little of their reminiscences of Savannah goes a long way. A lot of it could drive a person to murder. She wandered restlessly through the big house picking up bits of china and silver from tables and putting them back without really seeing them.

Why was the Mother Superior being so difficult? Why wouldn't she talk to her at least? Why on earth would a woman like that have to spend a whole day in retreat, even a holy day like Ash Wednesday? Surely a Mother Superior was already as good as a person could be. Why did she need to spend a day in prayer and fasting?

Fasting! Scarlett ran back to the drawing room to look at the tall clock. It couldn't be only four o'clock. Not even. It was seven minutes to four. And there'd be nothing at all to eat until dinnertime tomorrow. No, it wasn't possible. It didn't make sense.

Scarlett walked to the bell pull and jerked it four times. "Go put your coat on," she told Pansy when the girl came running. "We're going out."

"Miss Scarlett, how come we going to the bakery? Cook, she say bakery stuff ain't fit to eat. She does all the baking her own self."

"I don't care what Cook says. And if you tell one single soul we've been here, I'll skin you alive."

Scarlett ate two cookies and a dinner roll in the store. She carried two sacks of baked goods home and up to her room, hiding them under her cape.

A telegram had been placed neatly in the center of her bureau. Scarlett dropped the sacks of breads and cookies on the floor and ran to get it.

"Henry Hamilton," it said as signature. Damn! She'd thought it was from Rhett, begging her to come home or telling her that he was on his way to fetch her. She crumpled the flimsy paper angrily in her fist.

Then she smoothed it out. Better see what Uncle Henry had to say. As she read the message, Scarlett began to smile.

YOUR TELEGRAM RECEIVED STOP ALSO LARGE BANK DRAFT FROM YOUR
HUSBAND STOP WHAT FOOLISHNESS IS THIS QUESTION MARK RHETT ASKED
ME TO NOTIFY HIM YOUR WHEREABOUTS STOP LETTER FOLLOWS STOP
HENRY HAMILTON

So Rhett was looking for her. Just what she'd expected. Hah! She'd
been so right to come to Savannah. She hoped Uncle Henry had had the
sense to tell Rhett right away and by telegram, not letter. Why, he might
be reading his right this minute, just like she was reading hers.

Scarlett hummed a waltz tune and danced around the room holding
the telegram against her heart. He might even be on his way now. The
train from Charleston arrived just about this time of day. She ran to the
mirror to smooth her hair and pinch color into her cheeks. Should she
change her dress? No, Rhett would notice, and it would make him think
she wasn't doing anything except wait for him. She rubbed toilet water on
her throat and temples. There. She was ready. Her eyes, she saw, were
glowing green like a prowling cat's. She'd have to remember to drop her
lashes over them. She took a stool to the window, seated herself where
she'd be hidden by the curtain but still able to see out.

An hour later, Rhett hadn't come. Scarlett's small white teeth tore at a
roll from the bakery bag. What a bother this Lent business was! Imagine
having to hide in her room and eat rolls without even any butter to put on
them. She was in a very bad mood when she went downstairs.

And there was Jerome with her grandfather's supper tray! It was almost enough to make her turn Huguenot or Presbyterian like the old man.

Scarlett stopped him in the hall. "This food looks terrible," she said.
"Take it back and put big lumps of butter on the mashed potatoes. Put a
thick slice of ham on the plate, too; I know you've got a ham down there,
I saw it hanging in the larder. And add a pitcher of cream to pour on that
pudding. A little bowl of strawberry jam, too."

"Mr. Robillard, he can't chew no ham. And his doctor say he's not
supposed to eat sweets, nor cream and butter neither."

"The doctor doesn't want him to starve to death, either. Now do what
I say."

Scarlett looked angrily at Jerome's stiff back until he disappeared down
the stairs. "Nobody should have to go hungry," she said. "Not ever." Her
mood changed abruptly and she giggled. "Not even an old loo-la."

37

ortified by her rolls, Scarlett was cheerfully singing under her breath when she went downstairs Thursday. She found her aunts in a nervous frenzy of preparation for her grandfather's birthday dinner. While Eulalie wrestled with branches of dark green magnolia leaves for arrangements on the sideboard and mantel, Pauline was going through stacks of heavy linen tablecloths and napkins, trying to find the ones she remembered as her father's favorite.

"What difference does it make?" Scarlett asked impatiently. Talk about a tempest in a teapot! Grandfather wouldn't even see the dining room table from his room. "Just pick the one that shows the darning least."

Eulalie dropped an armload of rattling leaves. "I didn't hear you come in, Scarlett. Good morning."

Pauline nodded coldly. She had forgiven Scarlett for her insults, as a good Christian woman should, but in all likelihood she'd never forget them. "There are no darns in Mère's linens, Scarlett," she said. "They're all in perfect condition."

Scarlett looked at the stacks that covered the long table and remembered the worn, mended cloths that her aunts had in Charleston. If it was up to her, she'd pack up all this stuff and take it back to Charleston when they left on Saturday. Grandfather wouldn't miss it, and the aunts could use it. I'll never in my life be as afraid of anybody as they are of that old tyrant. But if I said what I think, Aunt Eulalie would start to sniffle, and Aunt Pauline would lecture me for an hour about duty to my elders. "I have to go buy a present for him," she said aloud. "Is there any shopping you want me to do for you?"

And don't dare, she said silently, offer to come with me. I've got to go to the convent to see the Mother Superior. She can't still be in retreat. If I have to, I'll stand by the gate and grab her when she comes out. I'm almighty tired of being turned away.

They were much too busy, her aunts said, to go shopping, and they were astonished that Scarlett had not yet selected and wrapped a gift for her grandfather. Scarlett left before they could describe the extent of their busyness and depth of their astonishment. "Old loo-las," she said under her breath. She wasn't at all sure what the Irish phrase meant, but the sound of it was enough to make her smile.

The trees in the square looked somehow thicker, the grass greener than the day before. The sun was warmer, too. Scarlett felt the quickened optimism that always accompanied the first hint of spring. Today would be a good day, she was sure of it—in spite of her grandfather's birthday party. "Walk up, Pansy," she said automatically, "don't drag along like a turtle," and she set off at a brisk pace along the packed sand-and-shell sidewalk.

The sound of hammering and men's voices shouting at the Cathedral building carried clearly through the still, sunlit air. Scarlett wished for a moment that the priest would take her on another tour of the site. But that wasn't what she was here for. She turned into the gate of the convent.

The same elderly nun answered the doorbell. Scarlett readied herself for combat.

But, "The Mother Superior is expecting you," said the nun. "If you'll follow me . . ."

Scarlett was almost dazed when she left the convent ten minutes later. It had been so easy! The Mother Superior agreed at once to talk to the Bishop. She'd send word, she said, very soon. No, she couldn't say just when that would be, but certainly within a short time. She herself would be returning to Charleston the following week.

Scarlett was euphoric. Her smile and her eyes were so bright that the grocer in the small shop on Abercorn Street nearly forgot to charge her for the bow-bedecked box of chocolate candies she selected for her grandfather's birthday present.

Her high spirits carried her through the final preparations for the birthday dinner that engulfed her when she got back to the Robillard house. They began to dim slightly when she learned that her grandfather would actually come to table for the six courses of his particularly favorite foods. Her spirits plummeted when the aunts informed her that she wasn't allowed to eat many of the delicacies that would be served.

"Flesh is forbidden during Lent," said Pauline sternly. "Be certain that no gravy touches the rice or vegetables you eat."

"But be careful, Scarlett. Don't let Père notice," added Eulalie in a whisper. "He doesn't approve of fasting." Her eyes were rheumy with sorrow.

Brooding about missing out on the food, thought Scarlett unkindly. Then—I don't blame her. The aromas from the kitchen were making her mouth water.

"There'll be soup for us. And fish," Eulalie said with sudden cheerfulness. "Cake, too, a beautiful, beautiful cake. A true feast, Scarlett."

"Remember, Sister," warned Pauline, "gluttony is a sin."

Scarlett left them; she could feel herself losing control of her temper. It's only a dinner, she reminded herself, just calm down. Even with Grandfather at table with us, it can't be all that bad. After all, what could one old man do?

He could, Scarlett learned at once, refuse to allow anything other than French to be spoken. Her "Happy Birthday, Grandfather," was ignored as if she hadn't said it. Her aunts' greetings were acknowledged by a cold nod, and he sat down in the huge throne-like chair at the head of the table.

Pierre Auguste Robillard was no longer a night-shirted, frail elderly man. Impeccably clothed in an old-fashioned frock coat and starched linen, his thin body looked larger, and his erect military bearing was impressive even when he was seated. His white hair was like an old lion's ruff, his eyes were hawk-like under his thick white brows, and his big bony nose looked like a predator's beak. The certainty that it was a good day began to ooze out of Scarlett. She unfolded the huge starched linen napkin over her lap and knees and braced herself for she knew not what.

Jerome entered, bearing a big silver tureen on a silver tray the size of a small tabletop. Scarlett's eyes widened. She'd never seen silver like that in her life. It was encrusted with ornamentation. An entire forest of trees circled the base of the tureen, their branches and leaves curving upward to surround the rim. Within the forest there were birds and animals—bears, deer, wild boar, hares, pheasant, even owls and squirrels on the limbs of the trees. The lid of the tureen was shaped like a tree stump covered with thick vines, each vine bearing clusters of miniature, perfect ripe grapes. Jerome placed the tureen in front of his master and lifted the lid with a white-gloved hand. Steam poured out, clouding the silver and spreading the delicious aroma of shrimp bisque throughout the room.

Pauline and Eulalie leaned forward, smiling anxiously.

Jerome took a soup plate from the sideboard and held it next to the tureen. Pierre Robillard lifted a silver ladle and silently filled the bowl. Then he watched with half-hooded eyes while Jerome carried the bowl and deposited it in front of Pauline.

The ceremony was repeated for Eulalie, then for Scarlett. Her fingers itched to grab her spoon. But she kept her hands in her lap while her grandfather served himself and tasted the soup. He shrugged eloquent dissatisfaction and dropped his spoon into his bowl.

Eulalie let out a strangled sob.

You old monster! Scarlett thought. She began to eat her soup. It was a velvety richness of flavor. She tried to catch Eulalie's eyes so that she could show her aunt that she was enjoying the soup, but Eulalie was downcast. Pauline's spoon was in the bowl, like her father's. Scarlett lost all sympathy for her aunts. If they were going to be terrorized this easily, they deserved to go hungry. She wasn't going to let the old man keep her from her dinner!

Pauline asked her father something, but because she was speaking French, Scarlett had no idea what her aunt had said. Her grandfather's reply was so brief, and Pauline's face so white, that he must have said something very insulting. Scarlett began to get angry. He's going to ruin everything, and on purpose, too. Oh, I wish I could speak French. I wouldn't just sit and take his nastiness.

She kept silent while Jerome removed the soup plates and the silver place plates and set down dinner plates and fish knives and forks. It seemed to take forever.

But the planked shad, when it came, was worth the wait. Scarlett looked at her grandfather. He wouldn't dare pretend that he didn't like this. He ate two small bites. The sound of knives and forks was terribly loud when they touched the plates. Pauline first, then Eulalie, gave up with most of their fish still on their plates. Scarlett looked defiantly at her grandfather over each forkful that she carried to her mouth. But even she was beginning to lose her appetite. The old man's displeasure was souring.

The next dish revived her appetite. The potted doves looked as tender as dumplings, and their gravy was a rich brown river over puréed potatoes and turnips molded into light-as-air nests for the meat of the tiny birds. Pierre Robillard dipped the tines of his fork into the gravy, then touched them to his tongue. That was all.

Scarlett thought she would explode. Only the desperate entreaty in her aunts' eyes kept her silent. How could anyone be as hateful as her grandfather? It was just plain impossible that he didn't like the food. It wasn't too hard for him to eat, even if he did have bad teeth. Or none at all, for that matter. She knew he liked tasty food, too. After she'd buttered and gravied the pap he was usually served, his plate had gone back to the kitchen as clean as if a dog had licked it. No, there must be some other reason he wasn't eating. And she could see it in his eyes. They gleamed when he looked at her aunts' pitiful disappointment. He'd rather make them suffer than enjoy eating his dinner. His birthday dinner, too.

What a difference between this birthday feast and the one for her cousin Patricia!

Scarlett looked at her grandfather's skeletal ramrod body and his self-satisfied impassive face, and she despised him for the way he was torment-ing her aunts. But even more she despised them for tolerating his tortures. They don't have a shred of gumption. How can they just sit there like that and take it? Sitting silently at her grandfather's table, in the gracious pink room in the handsome pink house, she seethed with loathing for everything and everyone. Even herself. I'm as bad as they are. Why on earth can't I just speak up and tell him how nasty he's acting? I don't have to talk French to do it, he understands English as well as I do. I'm a grown woman, not a child who mustn't speak until spoken to. What's wrong with me? This is downright silly.

But she continued to sit quietly, her back not touching the chair, her left hand in her lap at all times. Just as if she were a child on her best company behavior. Her mother's presence was unseen, not even imagined, but Ellen Robillard O'Hara was there, in the house where she'd grown up, at the table where she had so often sat as Scarlett was sitting, with her left hand resting on the starched linen napkin across her lap. And, for love of her, for need of her approval, Scarlett was incapable of defying the tyranny of Pierre Robillard.

She sat for what seemed an eternity, watching Jerome's stately slow service. Plates were replaced again and again by new plates, knives and forks by fresh knives and forks; it seemed to Scarlett that the feast would never end. Pierre Robillard consistently tasted and rejected each carefully selected and prepared dish that was offered him. By the time Jerome brought in the birthday cake, the tension and misery of Scarlett's aunts was palpable, and Scarlett herself was barely able to sit still in her chair, so urgent was her longing to escape.

The cake was coated in glossy swirled meringue that had been sprin-kled liberally with silver dragées. A silver filigreed bud vase on top held curling fronds of Angel Hair ferns and miniature silk flags of France, the Emperor Napoleon's army, and the regiment in which Pierre Robillard had served. The old man grunted, perhaps with pleasure, when it was placed before him. He turned his hooded eyes on Scarlett. "Cut it," he said in English.

He hopes I'll knock over the flags, she thought, but I'm not going to give him that pleasure. As she accepted the cake knife from Jerome with her right hand, with her left she quickly lifted the shining bud vase from the cake and put it on the table. She looked directly into her grandfather's eyes and smiled her sweetest smile.

His lips twitched.

"And did he eat it?" Scarlett asked dramatically. "He did not! The old horror managed to get no more than two crumbs on the tip of his fork— after he scraped off that beautiful meringue as if it was mold or something else horrible—and put them in his mouth like he was doing the biggest favor in the world. Then he said he was too tired to open his presents, and he went back to his room. I wanted to wring his scrawny neck!"

Maureen O'Hara rocked back and forth, laughing with delight.

"I don't see what's so funny," Scarlett said. "He was mean and rude." She was disappointed in Jamie's wife. She'd expected sympathy, not amusement.

"But of course you see, Scarlett. It's the roguishness of it all. Your poor old aunts plotting their hearts out to please him, and himself sitting in his nightshirt like a wee toothless babe, plotting against them. The old villain. I've always had a weak spot in my heart for the deviltry of a rascal. I can see him now, sniffing the dinner to come and making his plans.

"And don't you know he's got that man of his sneaking in all those wonderful dishes for him to eat his fill behind his closed door? The old rascal. It does make me laugh, the clever wickedness of him." Maureen's laughter was so contagious that Scarlett finally joined in. She'd done the right thing, coming to Maureen's never-locked kitchen door after the disastrous birthday dinner.

"Let's have our own piece of cake, then," said Maureen comfortably. "You're in practice, Scarlett, cut it for us; it's under that towel there on the dresser. Cut some extra slices, too, the young ones will be home from school before long. I'll be brewing some fresh tea."

Scarlett had just seated herself near the fire with cup and plate when the door flew open with a bang and five young O'Haras invaded the quiet kitchen. She recognized Maureen's redhaired daughters Mary Kate and Helen. The little boy, she soon learned, was Michael O'Hara; the two younger girls were his sisters Clare and Peg. All of them had dark curly hair that needed combing, dark-lashed blue eyes, and grubby little hands that Maureen told them to wash at once.

"But we don't need clean hands," Michael argued, "we're going to the cowshed to play with the pigs."

"Pigs live in the pigpen," said tiny Peg with a self-important air. "Don't they, Maureen?"

Scarlett was shocked. In her world, children never called adults by their first name. But Maureen seemed to find it nothing out of the ordinary. "They live in the pigpen if no one lets them out," she said with a wink. "You weren't thinking of taking the piglets out of the pen to play with, now, were you?"

Michael and his sisters laughed as if Maureen's joke was the funniest thing they'd ever heard. Then they ran through the kitchen to the back door that led into a large yard shared by all the houses.

Scarlett's eyes took in the glowing coals on the hearth, the shiny copper of the tea kettle on the crane, and the pans hanging above the mantel. Funny, she'd thought she would never set foot in a kitchen again once the bad days at Tara were over. But this was different. It was a place to live, a happy place to be, not just the room where food was prepared and dishes washed. She wished she could stay. The static beauty of her grandfather's drawing room made her shiver inside when she thought of it.

But she belonged in a drawing room, not a kitchen. She was a lady, accustomed to servants and luxury. She drained her cup hurriedly and put it down in its saucer. "You've saved my life, Maureen, I thought I'd go crazy if I had to stay with my aunts. But I've really got to go back now."

"What a pity. You haven't even had your cake. I'm told my cakes are worth eating."

Helen and Mary Kate edged up to their mother's chair, empty plates in hand. "Take a piece, then, but not all of it. The little ones will be in soon."

Scarlett began to pull on her gloves. "I've got to go," she repeated.

"If you must, then you must. I'll hope you'll stay longer for the dancing on Saturday, Scarlett? Jamie told me he's going to teach you the reel. Maybe Colum will be back by then, too."

"Oh, Maureen! Are you having another party on Saturday?"

"Not to say a party. But there's always the music and the dancing when the week's work is done and the men bring home their pay packets. You'll be here?"

Scarlett shook her head. "I can't. I'd love to, but I won't still be in Savannah." Her aunts expected her to go back to Charleston with them on Saturday morning's train. She didn't think she would, she'd never thought so. Surely Rhett would come for her long before then. Maybe he was at her grandfather's right now. She shouldn't have left the house.

She jumped to her feet. "I've got to run. Thank you, Maureen. I'll stop by again before I leave."

Maybe she'd bring Rhett to meet the O'Haras. He'd fit right in, another big dark-haired man with all the big dark-haired O'Haras. But he might slouch against the wall in that infuriating elegant way he had and laugh at all of them. He'd always laughed at her half-Irishness, mocked her when she repeated what Pa told her a hundred times. The O'Haras were great and powerful landowners for centuries. Until the Battle of the Boyne.

I don't know why he found that so funny. Just about everybody we know lost their land to the Yankees, it makes sense that Pa's folks lost theirs the same way to whoever, the English, I think. I'll ask Jamie or Maureen about it, if I get a chance. If Rhett doesn't take me away first.

38

$\mathcal{H}$enry Hamilton's promised letter was delivered to the Robillard house just as dark was setting in. Scarlett grabbed it like a line thrown to the drowning. She'd been listening to her aunts quarrelling for more than an hour about who was to blame for their father's reaction to his birthday.

"This is about my Atlanta property," Scarlett said. "Please excuse me, I'll take it up to my room." She didn't wait for them to agree.

She locked the door to her room. She wanted to savor every word in private.

"*What mess have you made this time?*" the letter began, without salutation. The old lawyer's handwriting was so agitated that it was difficult to read. Scarlett made a face and held it closer to the lamp.

What mess have you made this time? On Monday I was visited by a pompous old fool I generally go out of my way to avoid. He presented me with an astonishing draft drawn on his bank and payable to you. The amount was one-half million dollars, and it was paid by Rhett.

On Tuesday I was badgered by another old fool, this one a lawyer, asking me where you were. His client—your husband—wanted to know. I did not tell him you were in Savannah

* * *

Scarlett groaned. Who was Uncle Henry calling an old fool when he was such an old fool himself? No wonder Rhett hadn't come for her. She peered again at Henry's spidery script.

because your telegram arrived after he left, and at the time he called on me I didn't know where you were. I have not told him yet, because I do not know what you're up to, and I have a pretty good idea that I want no part of it.

This courthouse lawyer had two questions from Rhett. The first was your whereabouts. The second was—do you want a divorce?

Now, Scarlett, I don't know what you're holding over Rhett's head to get that kind of money from him and I don't want to know. Whatever he might have done to give you grounds to divorce him is none of my business either. I've never dirtied my hands with a divorce action, and I'm not going to start now. You would be wasting your time and money, besides. There is no divorce in South Carolina, and that is Rhett's legal residence now.

If you persist in this tomfoolery, I will give you the name of a lawyer in Atlanta who is almost respectable, even though he has done two divorces that I've heard of. But I warn you that you'll have to give him or someone else all your legal business. I won't handle anything for you any more. If you're thinking of divorcing Rhett so you'll be free to marry Ashley Wilkes, let me say that you'd do well to think again. Ashley is doing much better than anyone expected he would. Miss India and my silly sister keep a comfortable house for him and his boy. If you push yourself into his life, you'll ruin everything. Leave the poor man alone, Scarlett.

Leave Ashley alone, indeed! I'd like to know how comfortable and prosperous he'd be if I had left him alone. Uncle Henry, of all people, should have better sense than to fuss at me like a prissy old maid and jump to all kinds of nasty conclusions. He knows all about building the houses on the edge of town. Scarlett's feelings were deeply wounded. Uncle Henry Hamilton was the closest thing she had to a father—or a friend in Atlanta —and his accusations cut deep. She scanned the few remaining lines quickly then scrawled a response for Pansy to take to the telegraph office.

SAVANNAH ADDRESS NO SECRET STOP
DIVORCE NOT WANTED
STOP MONEY IN GOLD QUESTION MARK

If Uncle Henry hadn't sounded so much like an old clucking hen, she would have trusted him to have bought gold and put it in her safe box. But anyone who didn't have sense enough to give Rhett her address might not have sense about other things, too. Scarlett chewed on the knuckle of her left thumb, worried about her money. Maybe she should go to Atlanta and talk to Henry and her bankers and Joe Colleton. Maybe she should buy some more land out there on the edge of town, put up some more houses. Things would never be cheaper than they were now, with the aftereffects of the Panic still depressing business.

No! She had to put first things first. Rhett was trying to find her. She smiled to herself, and the fingers of her right hand smoothed the reddened skin over her thumb knuckle. He doesn't fool me with that divorce talk. Or by transferring the money as if our deal was being carried out. What counts—the only thing that counts—is that he wants to know where I am. He won't stay away long once Uncle Henry tells him.

"Don't be ridiculous, Scarlett," said Pauline in a cold tone, "of course you'll be going home tomorrow. We always go back to Charleston on Saturday."

"That doesn't mean I have to. I told you, I've decided to stay in Savannah for a while." Scarlett wouldn't let Pauline bother her, nothing could bother her now that she knew Rhett was looking for her. She'd receive him right here, in this elegant pink and gold room, and she'd make him beg her to come back. After he'd been adequately humbled, she'd agree, and then he'd take her in his arms and kiss her . . .

"Scarlett! Will you have the kindness to answer me when I address a question to you?"

"What is it, Aunt Pauline?"

"What do you propose to do with yourself? Where are you going to stay?"

"Why, here, of course." It had not entered Scarlett's head that she might not be welcome to stay as long as she liked at her grandfather's house. The tradition of hospitality was still fiercely cherished in the South, and it was unheard of for a guest to be asked to leave until he or she decided it was time.

"Père doesn't like surprises," Eulalie offered sadly.

"I believe that I can instruct Scarlett in the habits of this household without your help, Sister."

"Of course you can, Sister, I'm sure I never suggested otherwise."

"I'll just go ask Grandfather," Scarlett said, standing up. "Do you want to come along?"

Twittering, she thought, that's what they're doing. Terrified that visiting him without an express invitation might make Grandfather mad. Great balls of fire! What meanness can he do them that he hasn't already done? She strode along the hallway, followed by her whispering, anxious aunts, and knocked on the old man's door.

"*Entrez*, Jerome."

"It's not Jerome, Grandfather, it's me, Scarlett. May I come in?"

There was a moment's silence. Then Pierre Robillard's deep strong voice called "Come in." Scarlett tossed her head and smiled triumphantly at her aunts before she opened the door.

Her boldness flagged a bit when she looked at the stern hawk-like face of the old man. But she couldn't stop now. She advanced halfway across the thick carpet with a confident air. "I just wanted to tell you, Grandfather, that I'm going to stay for a while after Aunt Eulalie and Aunt Pauline leave."

"Why?"

Scarlett was nonplussed. She wasn't about to explain her reasons. She didn't see why she should have to. "Because I want to," she said.

"Why?" the old man asked again.

Scarlett's determined green eyes met his suspicious faded blue ones. "I have my reasons," she said. "Do you object?"

"What if I do?"

This was intolerable. She could not, would not go back to Charleston. It would be equivalent to surrender. She had to stay in Savannah.

"If you don't want me here, I'll go to my cousins. The O'Haras have already invited me."

Pierre Robillard's mouth jerked, a travesty of a smile. "You don't mind sleeping in the parlor with the pig, I take it."

Scarlett's cheeks reddened. She'd always known her grandfather disapproved of her mother's marriage. He'd never accepted Gerald O'Hara in his house. She wanted to defend her father, and her cousins, from his prejudice against the Irish. If only she didn't have this terrible suspicion that the children brought the baby pigs into the house to play with.

"Never mind," said her grandfather. "Stay if you like. It's a matter of supreme indifference to me." He closed his eyes, dismissing her from his sight and his attention.

Scarlett refrained with difficulty from slamming the door when she left the room. What a horrid old man! Still, she had gotten what she wanted. She smiled at her aunts. "Everything's all right," she said.

For the remainder of the morning, and all afternoon Scarlett cheerfully went along with her aunts to leave their cards at the houses of all their friends and acquaintances in Savannah. "P.P.C." they hand-lettered in the lower left corner. "*Pour prendre congé*—to take leave." The custom had never been observed in Atlanta, but in the older cities of coastal Georgia and South Carolina, it was a required ritual. Scarlett thought it a great waste of time to inform people you were leaving. Especially when, only a handful of days earlier, her aunts had worn themselves out leaving cards at the same houses to inform the same people that they had arrived. She was sure that most of those people hadn't bothered to leave cards at the Robillard house. Certainly there had been no callers.

On Saturday she insisted on going to the train depot with them, and she saw to it that Pansy put their valises exactly where they wanted them, in full view so that no one could steal them. She kissed their papery wrinkled cheeks, returned to the busy platform, and waved goodbye while the train chugged out of the station.

"We'll stop at the bakery on Broughton Street before we go back to the house," she told the driver of the rented carriage. It was still a long time until dinner.

She sent Pansy to the kitchen to order a pot of coffee and then took off her hat and gloves. How lovely and quiet the house was with the aunts gone. But that was definitely a film of dust on the hall table. She'd have to have a few words with Jerome. The other servants, too, if necessary. She wasn't going to have things looking shabby when Rhett arrived.

As if he'd read her mind, Jerome appeared behind her. Scarlett jumped. Why on earth couldn't the man make a decent amount of noise when he walked?

"This message come for you, Miss Scarlett." He held out a silver tray with a telegram on it.

Rhett! Scarlett grabbed the thin paper with too-eager, clumsy fingers. "Thank you, Jerome. See to my coffee, please." The butler was too curious by half, in her opinion. She didn't want him reading over her shoulder.

As soon as he was gone, she ripped open the message. "Damn!" she said. It was from Uncle Henry.

The normally thrifty old lawyer must have been deeply agitated because the telegram was wastefully wordy.

I HAVE NOT AND WILL NOT HAVE ANYTHING WHATSOEVER TO DO WITH INVESTING OR OTHERWISE INVOLVING MYSELF WITH THE MONEY THAT WAS TRANSFERRED BY YOUR HUSBAND STOP IT IS IN YOUR ACCOUNT AT YOUR BANK STOP I HAVE EXPRESSED MY REPUGNANCE FOR THE CIRCUM-STANCES SURROUNDING THIS TRANSACTION STOP DO NOT EXPECT ANY HELP FROM ME STOP

Scarlett sank onto a chair when she read it. Her knees were like water, and her heart was racing. The old fool! A half million dollars—that was probably more money than the bank had seen since before the War. What was to stop the officers from just pocketing it and closing the bank? Banks were still closing all over the country, it was in the paper all the time. She'd have to go to Atlanta at once, change the money to gold, add it to her safe box. But that would take days. Even if there was a train today, she wouldn't get to the bank before Monday. Plenty of time for her money to disappear.

A half million dollars. More money than she'd have if she sold everything she owned twice over. More money than her store and her saloon and her new houses would make in thirty years. She had to protect it, but how? Oh, she could kill Uncle Henry!

When Pansy came upstairs proudly carrying the heavy silver tray with the gleaming coffee service on it, she was met by a pale, wild-eyed Scarlett. "Put that thing down and get your coat on," said Scarlett. "We're going out."

She had herself under control; there was even a little color in her cheeks from the walk when she hurried into the O'Hara store. Cousin or not, she didn't want Jamie to know too much about her business. So her voice was charmingly girlish when she asked him to recommend a banker. "I've been so giddy that I just haven't paid any attention to my spending money, and now that I've decided to stay a while longer, I need to have a few dollars transferred from my bank at home, but I don't know a soul here in Savannah. I figured you'd be able to put in a good word for me, being a prosperous businessman and all."

Jamie grinned. "I'll be proud to escort you to the president of the bank, and I'll vouch for him because Uncle James has done business with him for fifty years and more. But you'll do better, Scarlett, to tell him you're old Robillard's granddaughter than that you're O'Hara's cousin. The word is, he's a very warm old gentleman. Wasn't he the smart one who sent his brass to France when Georgia decided to follow South Carolina out of the Union?"

But that meant her grandfather was a traitor to the South! No wonder he still had all that heavy silver and that undamaged house. Why hadn't he been lynched? And how could Jamie laugh about it? Scarlett remembered Maureen laughing about her grandfather, too, when she should by rights have been shocked. It was all very complicated. She didn't know what to think. In any case, she didn't have time to think about it now, she had to get to the bank and arrange about her money.

"You'll watch the store, then, Daniel, while I walk out with Cousin Scarlett?" Jamie was beside her, offering his arm. Scarlett put her hand in the bend of his elbow and waved goodbye to Daniel. She hoped it wasn't far to the bank. It was nearly noon.

"Maureen will be delighted that you'll be with us for a bit," said Jamie as they walked along Broughton Street with Pansy trailing behind. "Will you be coming over this evening, then, Scarlett? I could call for you on my way home to walk you there."

"I'd like that very much, Jamie," she said. She'd go crazy in that big house with no one to talk to but her grandfather, and him only for ten minutes. If Rhett came, she could always send Pansy to the store with a note saying she'd changed her mind.

As it turned out, she was waiting impatiently in the front hall for Jamie when he arrived. Her grandfather had been exceptionally nasty when she told him she was going out for the evening. "This is not a hotel where you can come and go as you please, miss. You'll match your schedule to the routine of my house, and that means in your bed by nine o'clock."

"Of course, Grandfather," she had said meekly. She was sure she'd be home long before then. And besides, she was regarding him with increased respect ever since her visit to the bank president. Her grandfather must be much, much richer than she'd imagined. When Jamie introduced her as Pierre Robillard's granddaughter, the man nearly split his britches bowing and scraping. Scarlett smiled, remembering. Then, after Jamie left, when I told him I wanted to rent a safe box and transfer a half million to it, I thought he'd swoon at my feet. I don't care what anybody says, having lots of money is the best thing in the world.

"I can't stay late," she told Jamie when he arrived. "I hope that's all right. You won't mind walking me back by eight-thirty?"

"I'll be honored to walk you anywhere at any time at all," Jamie vowed.

Scarlett truly had no idea that she wouldn't be back until almost dawn.

39

The evening started quietly enough. So quietly, in fact, that Scarlett was disappointed. She'd been expecting music and dancing and some kind of celebration, but Jamie escorted her to the now familiar kitchen of his house. Maureen greeted her with a kiss on each cheek and a cup of tea in her hand, then returned to the preparation of supper. Scarlett sat down next to Uncle James, who was dozing. Jamie took off his coat, unbuttoned his vest, and lit a pipe, then settled down in a rocking chair for a quiet smoke. Mary Kate and Helen were setting the table in the adjoining dining room, chattering to one another over the rattle of knives and forks. It was a comfortable family scene, but not very exciting. Still, thought Scarlett, at least there's going to be supper. I knew Aunt Pauline and Aunt Eulalie must be wrong about the whole fasting nonsense. Nobody would live on only one meal a day for weeks and weeks on purpose.

After a few minutes the shy girl with the cloud of beautiful dark hair came in from the hall with little Jacky by the hand. "Oh, there you are, Kathleen," said Jamie. Scarlett made a mental note of the name. It suited the girl, so soft and youthful. "Bring the little man to his old Pa." Jacky pulled his hand away and ran to his father, and the brief tranquillity was over. Scarlett winced at the little boy's shouts of joy. Uncle James snorted in sudden waking. The street door opened and Daniel came in with his younger brother Brian. "Look what I found sniffing at the door, Ma," said Daniel.

"Oh, so you've decided to grace us with your presence, then, Brian," Maureen said. "I'll have to tell the newspaper so they can put it on the front page."

Brian grabbed his mother around the waist in a bear hug. "You wouldn't turn a man out to starve, now, would you?"

Maureen made a pretense of anger, but she was smiling. Brian kissed the coiled masses of red hair on top of her head and released her.

"Now look what you've done to my hair, you wild Indian," Maureen complained. "And shaming me in the bargain by not greeting your cousin Scarlett. You, too, Daniel."

Brian leaned down from his great height and grinned at Scarlett. "Will you forgive me?" he said. "You were so small and elegantly silent there that I missed you altogether, Cousin Scarlett." His thick red hair was bright in the glow from the fire, and his blue eyes were infectiously merry. "Will you plead for me with my cruel mother that I can have a few scraps from her table?"

"Go on with you, savage, and wash the dust off your hands," Maureen ordered.

Daniel took his brother's place when Brian headed for the sink. "We're all glad you're here with us, Cousin Scarlett."

Scarlett smiled. Even with the racket from Jacky bouncing on Jamie's knee, she was glad to be there, too. There was so much life in these big redheaded cousins of hers. It made the cold perfection of her grandfather's house seem like a tomb.

While they ate at the big table in the dining room Scarlett learned the story behind Maureen's mock anger at her son. Brian had moved a few weeks earlier from the room he had shared with Daniel, and Maureen was only semi-reconciled to his burst of independence. Granted he was only a few steps away, at his sister Patricia's house; still, he was gone. It gave Maureen immense satisfaction that Brian still preferred her cooking to Patricia's fancier menus. "Ah, well, what can you expect," she said complacently, "when Patricia won't allow the smell of fish to get into her fine lace curtains?" And she piled four glistening butter-coated fried fish on her son's plate. "It's a hardship to be such a lady during Lent, I'm sure."

"Bite your tongue, woman," said Jamie, "that's your own daughter you're maligning."

"And who has a better right than her own mother?"

Old James spoke up then. "Maureen has a point. I well remember my own mother's sharp tongue ..." He rambled fondly through a series of memories of his youth. Scarlett listened intently for mention of her father. "Now, Gerald," said Old James, and she leaned toward him, "Gerald was always the apple of her eye, being the baby and all. He always got off with no more than a small scolding." Scarlett smiled. It was just like Pa to be his mother's favorite. Who could resist the soft heart he tried to hide under all his blustering? Oh, how she wished he could be here now with all his family.

"Are we going to Matthew's after supper?" Old James asked. "Or is everyone coming here?"

"We're going to Matt's," Jamie replied. Matt was the one who'd started the dancing at Patricia's birthday, Scarlett remembered. Her feet began to tap.

Maureen smiled at her. "I believe there's a readiness for a reel," she said. She picked up the spoon by her plate, reached across Daniel and took his; then, placing their bowls back to back, she held the tips of the handles loosely together and tapped the spoons against her palm, against her wrist, her forearm, Daniel's forehead. The rhythm of the beating was like playing the bones, but lighter, and the sheer silliness of making music with a pair of mismatched tablespoons was cause for delighted, spontaneous laughter from Scarlett. Without thinking about it, she began to pound on the table with her open hands, matching the beat of the spoons.

"It's time we were going," Jamie laughed. "I'll get my fiddle."

"We'll bring the chairs," said Mary Kate.

"Matt and Katie only have two," Daniel explained to Scarlett. "They're the newest O'Haras to come to Savannah."

It didn't matter at all that Matt and Katie O'Hara's double parlors held almost no furniture. They had fireplaces for warmth, gaslit ceiling globes for light, and a broad, polished wood floor for dancing. The hours Scarlett passed in those bare rooms that Saturday were among the happiest she'd ever known.

Within the family the O'Haras shared love and happiness as freely and unconsciously as they shared the air they breathed. Scarlett felt within her the growth of something she had lost too long ago to remember. She became, like them, unaffected and spontaneous and open to carefree joy. She could shed the artifice and calculation that she'd learned to use in the battles for conquest and dominance that were part of being a belle in Southern society.

She had no need to charm or conquer; she was welcome as she was, one of the family. For the first time in her life she was willing to relinquish the spotlight to let someone else be the center of attention. The others were fascinating to her, primarily because they were her new-found family, but also because she'd never known anyone like them in her life.

Or almost never. Scarlett looked at Maureen, with Brian and Daniel making music behind her, Helen and Mary Kate clapping in time with the rhythm she was setting with the bones, and for a moment it was as if the vivid redheads were the youthful Tarletons come back to life. The twins, tall and handsome, the girls squirming with juvenile impatience to move on to the next adventure life held for them. Scarlett had always envied the Tarleton girls their free-and-easy ways with their mother. Now she saw the same easiness between Maureen and her children. And she knew that she, too, was welcome to laugh with Maureen, to tease and be teased, to share in the bounteous affection that Jamie's wife showered on everyone around her.

At that moment Scarlett's near-worship of her serene, self-contained mother shivered and suffered a tiny crack, and she began to free herself of the guilt she'd always felt because she couldn't live up to her mother's teachings. Perhaps it was all right if she wasn't a perfect lady. The idea was too rich, too complicated. She'd think about it later. She didn't want to think about anything now. Not yesterday, not tomorrow. The only thing that mattered was this moment and the happiness it held, the music and singing and clapping and dancing.

After the formal rituals of Charleston's balls, the spontaneous home-made pleasures were intoxicating. Scarlett breathed deep of the joy and laughter around her, and it giddied her.

Matt's daughter Peggy showed her the simplest steps of the reel, and there was, in some strange way, a rightness to learning from a seven-year-old child. And a rightness to the outspoken encouragement and even the teasing of the others, adults and children alike, because it was the same for Peggy as it was for her. She danced until her knees were wobbly, then she collapsed, laughing, in a heap on the floor at Old James' feet, and he patted her head as if she were a puppy, and that made her laugh all the more, until she was gasping for breath when she cried out, "I'm having so much fun!"

There had been very little fun in Scarlett's life, and she wanted it to last forever, this clean, uncomplicated joyfulness. She looked at her big, happy cousins, and she was proud of their strength and vigor and talent for music and for life. "We're a fine lot, we O'Haras. There's none can touch us." Scarlett heard her father's voice, boasting, saying the words he had so often said to her, and she knew for the first time what he had meant.

"Ah, Jamie, what a wonderful night this was," she said when he was walking her home. Scarlett was so tired she was practically stumbling, but she was chattering like a magpie, too exhilarated to accept the peaceful silence of the sleeping city. "We're a fine lot, we O'Haras."

Jamie laughed. His strong hands caught her around the waist and he lifted her up and swung her in a giddy circle. "There's none can touch us," he said when he set her down.

"Miss Scarlett . . . Miss Scarlett!" Pansy woke her at seven with a message from her grandfather. "He wants you right this minute."

The old soldier was formally dressed and fresh-shaven. He looked disapprovingly at Scarlett's hastily combed hair and dressing gown from his imperial position in the great armchair at the head of the dining room table.

"My breakfast is unsatisfactory," he announced.

Scarlett stared at him, slack-jawed. What did his breakfast have to do with her? Did he think she'd cooked it? Maybe he had lost his mind. Like Pa. No, not like Pa. Pa had had more than he could bear, that's all, and so he retreated to a time and a world where the terrible things hadn't happened. He was like a confused child. But there's nothing confused or childlike about Grandfather. He knows exactly where and who he is and what he's doing. What does he mean by waking me up after only a couple of hours' sleep and complaining to me about his breakfast?

Her voice was carefully calm when she spoke. "What's wrong with your breakfast, Grandfather?"

"It's tasteless and it's cold."

"Why don't you send it back to the kitchen, then? Tell them to bring what you want and make sure it's hot."

"You do it. Kitchens are women's business."

Scarlett put her hands on her hips. She looked at her grandfather with eyes as steely as his. "Do you mean to tell me that you got me out of bed to send a message to your cook? What do you take me for, some kind of servant? Order your own breakfast or starve, it's all the same to me. I'm going back to bed." Scarlett turned with a flounce.

"That bed belongs to me, young woman, and you occupy it by my grace and favor. I expect you to obey my orders as long as you're under my roof."

She was in a fine rage now, all hope of sleep gone. I'll pack my things this minute, she thought. I don't have to put up with this.

The seductive aroma of fresh coffee stopped her before she spoke. She'd have coffee first, then tell the old man off . . . And she'd better think a minute. She wasn't ready to leave Savannah yet. Rhett must know, by now, that she was here. And she should get a message about Tara from the Mother Superior any minute.

Scarlett walked to the bell pull by the door. Then she took a chair at her grandfather's right. When Jerome came in, she glared at him. "Give me a cup for my coffee. Then take this plate away. What is it, Grandfather, cornmeal mush? Whatever it is, Jerome, tell the cook to eat it herself. After she fixes some scrambled eggs and ham and bacon and grits and biscuits. With plenty of butter. And I'll have a pitcher of thick cream for my coffee right this minute."

Jerome looked at the erect old man, silently urging him to put Scarlett in her place. Pierre Robillard looked straight ahead, not meeting his butler's eyes.

"Don't stand there like a statue," Scarlett snapped. "Do as you're told." She was hungry.

So was her grandfather. Although the meal was as silent as his birthday dinner had been, this time he ate everything that was brought to him. Scarlett watched him suspiciously from the corner of her eye. What was he up to, the old fox? She couldn't believe that there wasn't something behind this charade. In her experience, getting what you wanted from servants was the easiest thing in the world. All you had to do was shout at them. And Lord knows Grandfather's good at terrifying people. Look at Aunt Pauline and Aunt Eulalie.

Look at me, for that matter. I hopped out of bed quick enough when he sent for me. I'll not do that again.

The old man dropped his napkin by his empty plate. "I'll expect you to be suitably dressed for future meals," he said to Scarlett. "We shall leave the house in precisely one hour and seven minutes to go to church. That should provide adequate time for your grooming."

Scarlett hadn't intended to go to church at all, now that her aunts weren't there to expect it and she'd gotten what she wanted from the Mother Superior. But her grandfather's high-handedness had to be stopped. He was violently anti-Catholic, according to her aunts.

"I didn't know you attended Mass, Grandfather," she said. Sweetness dripped from the words.

Pierre Robillard's thick white brows met in a beetling frown. "You do not subscribe to that papist idiocy like your aunts, I hope."

"I'm a good Catholic, if that's what you mean. And I'm going to Mass with my cousins, the O'Haras. Who—by the way—have invited me to come stay with them any time I want, for as long as I like." Scarlett stood and marched in triumph from the room. She was halfway up the stairs before she remembered that she shouldn't have eaten anything before Mass. No matter. She didn't have to take Communion if she didn't want to. And she'd certainly showed Grandfather. When she reached her room, she did a few steps of the reel that she'd learned the night before.

She didn't for a minute believe that the old man would call her bluff about staying with her cousins. Much as she loved going to the O'Haras' for music and dancing, there were far too many children there to make a visit possible. Besides, they didn't have any servants. She couldn't get dressed without Pansy to lace her stays and fix her hair.

I wonder what he's really up to, she thought again. Then she shrugged. She'd probably find out soon enough. It wasn't really important. Before he came out with it, Rhett would probably have come for her anyhow.

40

One hour and four minutes after Scarlett went up to her room, Pierre Auguste Robillard, soldier of Napoleon, left his beautiful shrine of a house to go to church. He wore a heavy overcoat and a wool scarf, and his thin white hair was covered with a tall hat made of sable that had once belonged to a Russian officer who died at Borodino. Despite the bright sun and the promise of spring in the air, the old man's thin body was cold. Still, he walked stiffly erect, seldom using the malacca cane he carried. He nodded in a correct abbreviated bow to the people who greeted him on the street. He was very well known in Savannah.

At the Independent Presbyterian Church on Chippewa Square he took his place in the fifth pew from the front, the place that had been his ever since the gala dedication of the church nearly sixty years earlier. James Monroe, then president of the United States, had been at the dedication and had asked to be introduced to the man who had been with Napoleon from Austerlitz to Waterloo. Pierre Robillard had been gracious to the older man, even though a President was nothing impressive to a man who had fought alongside an Emperor.

When the service ended, he had a few words with several men who responded to his gesture and hurried to join him on the steps of the church. He asked a few questions, listened to a great many answers. Then he went home, his stern face almost smiling, to nap until dinner was served to him on a tray. The weekly outing to church grew more tiring all the time.

He slept lightly, as the very old do, and woke before Jerome brought his tray. While he waited for it, he thought about Scarlett.

He had no curiosity about her life or her nature. He hadn't given her a thought for many years, and when she appeared in his room with his daughters he was neither pleased nor displeased to see her. She caught his attention only when Jerome complained to him about her. She was causing disruption in the kitchen with her demands, Jerome said. And she would cause Monsieur Robillard's death if she continued to insist on adding butter and gravy and sweets to his meals.

She was the answer to the old man's prayer. He had nothing to look forward to in his life except more months or years of the unchanging routine of sleep and meals and the weekly excursion to church. It did not disturb him that his life was so featureless; he had his beloved wife's likeness before his eyes and the certainty that, in due time, he would be reunited with her after death. He spent the days and nights dreaming of her when he slept and turning memories of her in his mind when he was awake. It was enough for him. Almost. He did miss having good food to eat, and in recent years it had been tasteless, cold when it wasn't burnt, and of a deadly monotony. He wanted Scarlett to change that.

Her suspicions of the old man's motives were unfounded. Pierre Robillard had recognized the bully in her at once. He wanted it to function in his behalf now that he no longer had the strength to get what he wanted for himself. The servants knew that he was too old and tired to dominate them. But Scarlett was young and strong. He didn't seek her companionship or her love. He wanted her to run his house the way he had once run it himself—which meant in accordance with his standards and subject to his dominance. He needed to find a way to accomplish that, and so he thought about her.

"Tell my granddaughter to come here," he said when Jerome came in.

"She ain't home yet," said the old butler with a smile. He anticipated the old man's anger with delight. Jerome hated Scarlett.

Scarlett was at the big City Market with the O'Haras. After the confrontation with her grandfather she had dressed, dismissed Pansy, and escaped through the garden to hurry, unaccompanied, the two short blocks to Jamie's house. "I've come to have company going to Mass," she told Maureen, but her real reason was to be someplace where people were nice to one another.

After Mass the men went in one direction, the women and children in another. "They'll have a haircut and a gossip in the barber shop at the

Pulaski House Hotel," Maureen told Scarlett. "And most likely a pint or two in the saloon. It's better than a newspaper for hearing what's going on. We'll get our own news at the Market while I buy some oysters for a nice pie."

Savannah's City Market had the same purpose and the same excitement as the Market in Charleston. Until she was back in the familiar hubbub of bargaining and buying and friends greeting friends, Scarlett hadn't realized how much she'd missed it when the Season took precedence for women's time.

She wished now that she'd taken Pansy with her after all; she could have filled a basket with the exotic fruits that came in through Savannah's busy seaport if only she'd had her maid to carry it. Mary Kate and Helen were doing that chore for the O'Hara women. Scarlett let them carry some oranges for her. And she insisted on paying for the coffee and caramel rolls they all had at one of the stands.

Still, she refused when Maureen invited her to come home for dinner with them. She hadn't told her grandfather's cook that she wouldn't be at the house. And she wanted to catch up on the sleep she'd missed. It wouldn't do to look like death warmed over if Rhett came in on the afternoon train.

She kissed Maureen goodbye at the Robillard doorstep, called goodbye to the others. They were almost a block behind, slowed down by the unsteady steps of the little children and Patricia's burdened by pregnancy pace. Helen ran up with a bulging paper sack. "Don't forget your oranges, Cousin Scarlett."

"I'll take that, Miss Scarlett." It was Jerome.

"Oh. All right. Here. You shouldn't be so quiet, Jerome, you gave me a shock. I didn't hear the door open."

"I've been looking out for you. Mr. Robillard, he wants you." Jerome looked at the straggle of O'Haras with unconcealed disdain.

Scarlett's chin stiffened. Something was going to have to be done about the butler's impertinence. She sailed into her grandfather's room with an angry complaint on her lips.

Pierre Robillard gave her no time to speak. "You are dishevelled," he said coldly, "and you have ruptured the schedule of my house. While you were consorting with those Irish peasants, the dinner hour has passed."

Scarlett leapt hotly to the bait. "I'll thank you to keep a civil tongue when you refer to my cousins."

The old man's eyelids half hid the gleam in his eyes. "What do you call a man who's in trade?" he said quietly.

"If you're talking about Jamie O'Hara, I call him a successful, hardworking businessman, and I respect him for what he's accomplished."

Her grandfather set the hook. "And no doubt you admire his garish wife, too."

"Indeed I do! She's a kind and generous woman."

"I believe that's the impression her trade tries to make. You are aware, are you not, that she was a barmaid in an Irish saloon."

Scarlett gasped like a landed fish. It couldn't be true! Unwelcome pictures filled her mind. Maureen holding up her glass for another whiskey ... playing the bones and singing lustily all the verses of bawdy songs ... brushing her tousled bright hair off her red face without trying to pin it back up ... lifting her skirts to her knees to dance the reel ...

Common. Maureen was common.

They were all kind of common.

Scarlett felt like crying. She'd been so happy with the O'Haras, she didn't want to lose them. But ... here in this house where her mother had grown up, the gulf between Robillard and O'Hara was too broad to ignore. No wonder Grandfather's ashamed of me. Mother would be heartbroken if she could see me walking on the street with a bunch like I just came home with. A woman in public without so much as a shawl over her pregnant belly, and a million children running all over the place like wild Indians, and not even a maid to carry the shopping. I must have looked as trashy as the rest of them. And Mother tried so hard to teach me to be a lady. She'd be happy she was dead if she knew that her daughter was friends with a woman who worked in a saloon.

Scarlett looked anxiously at the old man. Could he possibly know about the building she owned in Atlanta and rented to a saloonkeeper?

Pierre Robillard's eyes were closed. He seemed to have slipped into the sudden sleep of old age. Scarlett tiptoed out of the room. When she closed the door behind her, the old soldier smiled, then went to sleep.

Jerome brought her the mail on a silver tray. He was wearing white gloves. Scarlett took the envelopes from the tray, a short nod her only thank you. It wouldn't do to show her gratification, not if she was going to keep Jerome in his place. The previous evening, after waiting for an eternity in the drawing room for Rhett, who never showed up, she had given the servants a tongue-lashing they'd never forget. Jerome in particular. It was a godsend that the butler was so nearly impertinent; she needed someone to unload her anger and disappointment on.

Uncle Henry Hamilton was furious that she'd transferred the money to the Savannah bank. Too bad. Scarlett crumpled up his brief letter and dropped it on the floor.

The fat envelope was from Aunt Pauline. Her meandering complaints could wait, and they were sure to be complaints. Scarlett opened the stiff square envelope next. She didn't recognize the handwriting on the front.

It was an invitation. The name was unfamiliar, and she had to think hard before she remembered. Of course. Hodgson was the married name of one of those old ladies, the Telfair sisters. The invitation was for a ceremony of dedication for Hodgson Hall, with a reception to follow. "New home of the Georgia Historical Society." It sounded even deadlier than that awful musicale. Scarlett made a face and put the invitation aside. She'd have to find some letter paper and send her regrets. The aunts liked to be bored to death, but not she.

The aunts. Might as well get it over with. She tore open Pauline's letter.

> . . . *profoundly ashamed of your outrageous behavior. If we had known that you were coming with us to Savannah without so much as a word of explanation to Eleanor Butler, we would have insisted that you leave the train and go back.*

What the devil was Aunt Pauline saying? Was it possible that Miss Eleanor didn't mention the note I left for her? Or that she didn't get it? No, it wasn't possible. Aunt Pauline was just making trouble.

Scarlet's eyes moved quickly over Pauline's complaints about the folly of Scarlett's travelling after her ordeal when the boat capsized and about Scarlett's "unnatural reticence" in not telling her aunts that she'd been in the accident.

Why couldn't Pauline tell her what she wanted to know? There wasn't a word about Rhett. She went through page after page of Pauline's spiky handwriting, looking for his name. God's nightgown! Her aunt could lecture longer than a hellfire preacher. There. At last.

> . . . *dear Eleanor is understandably concerned that Rhett felt it necessary to travel all the way to Boston for the meeting about his fertilizer shipments. He should not have gone to the chill of the Northern climate immediately after the ordeal of his long immersion in cold water following the capsizing of his boat . . .*

Scarlett let the pages fall into her lap. Of course! Oh, thank God. That's why Rhett hadn't come after her yet. Why didn't Uncle Henry tell me Rhett's telegram came from Boston? Then I wouldn't have driven myself crazy expecting him to show up on the doorstep any minute. Does Aunt Pauline say when he's coming back?

Scarlett pawed through the jumble of letter sheets. Where had she stopped? She found her place and read eagerly to the end. But there was no mention of what she wanted to know. Now what am I going to do? Rhett might be gone for weeks. Or he might be on his way back right this very minute.

Scarlett picked up the invitation from Mrs. Hodgson again. At least it would be someplace to go. She'd have a screaming fit if she had to stay in this house day after day.

If only she could run over to Jamie's every now and then, just for a cup of tea. But no, that was unthinkable.

And yet, she couldn't not think of the O'Haras. The next morning she went with the sullen cook to the City Market to supervise what she bought and how much she paid for it. With nothing else to occupy her, Scarlett was determined to see her grandfather's house in order. While she was having coffee, she heard a soft hesitant voice speak her name. It was lovely, shy young Kathleen. "I'm not familiar with all the American fishes," she said. "Will you help me choose the best prawns?" Scarlett was bewildered until the girl gestured toward the shrimp.

"The angels must have sent you, Scarlett," Kathleen said when her purchase was made. "I'd be lost for sure without you. Maureen wants only the best. We're expecting Colum, you see."

Colum—am I supposed to know him? Maureen or somebody mentioned that name once, too. "Why's Colum so important?"

Kathleen's blue eyes widened in amazement that the question could be asked. "Why? Well ... because Colum's Colum, that's all. He's ..." She couldn't find the words she was looking for. "He's just Colum, that's all. He brought me here, don't you know? He's my brother, like Stephen."

Stephen. The quiet dark one. Scarlett hadn't realized he was Kathleen's brother. Maybe that's why he's so quiet. Maybe they're all shy as mice in that family. "Which one of Uncle James' brothers is your father?" she asked Kathleen.

"Ah, but my father's dead, God rest his soul."

Was the girl simple? "What was his name, Kathleen?"

"Oh, it's his name you're wanting to know! Patrick, that was his name, Patrick O'Hara. Patricia's called after him, being Jamie's firstborn and Patrick his own father's name."

Scarlett's forehead creased in concentration. So Jamie was Kathleen's brother, too. So much for thinking the whole family was shy. "Do you have any other brothers?" she asked.

"Oh, yes," Kathleen said with a happy smile, "brothers, and sisters, too. Fourteen of us all told. Still living, I mean." And she crossed herself.

Scarlett drew away from the girl. Oh, Lord, more than likely the cook's been listening, and it'll get back to grandfather. I can hear him now. Talking about Catholics breeding like rabbits.

But in fact Pierre Robillard made no mention at all of Scarlett's cousins. He summoned her for a presupper visit, announced that his meals were proving satisfactory, then dismissed her.

She stopped Jerome to check over the supper tray, examined the silver to see that it was gleaming and free of fingerprints. When she put the coffee spoon down it tapped against the soup spoon. I wonder if Maureen would teach me to play the spoons? The thought caught her off guard.

That night she dreamed about her father. She woke in the morning with a smile still on her lips, but her cheeks stiff with the dried streaks of tears.

At the City Market she heard Maureen O'Hara's distinctive gusty laughter just in time to dart behind one of the thick brick piers and miss being seen. But she could see Maureen, and Patricia, looking as big as a house, and a straggle of children behind them. "Your father's the only one of us not in a fever for your uncle to arrive," she heard Maureen say. "He's enjoying the special treats I fix for supper every night in hopes of Colum."

I'd like a special treat myself, Scarlett thought rebelliously. I'm getting mighty tired of food soft enough for Grandfather. She turned on the cook. "Get some chicken, too," she ordered, "and fry up a couple of pieces for my dinner."

Her bad mood cleared up long before dinner, however. When she got back to the house, there was a note from the Mother Superior. The Bishop was going to consider Scarlett's request to allow her to buy back Carreen's dowry.

Tara. I'm going to get Tara! So busy was her mind with planning Tara's rebirth that she didn't notice the time passing at all, nor was she conscious of what was on her plate at mealtime.

She could see it so clearly in her mind. The house, gleaming fresh white on top of the hill; the clipped lawn green, so green, and thick with clover; the pasture, shimmering green with its deep satiny grass bending before the breeze, unrolling like a carpet down the hill and into the mysterious shadowy dark green of the pines that bordered the river and hid it from view. Spring with clouds of tender dogwood blossoms and the heady scent of wisteria; then summer, the crisp starched white curtains billowing from the open windows, the thick sweetness of honeysuckle flowing through them into all the rooms, all restored to their dreaming, polished quiet perfection. Yes, summer was the best. The long, lazy Georgia summer when twilight lasted for hours and lightning bugs signalled in the slow thickening darkness. Then the stars, fat and close in the velvet sky, or a moon round and white, as white as the sleeping house it lit on the dark, gently rising hill.

Summer ... Scarlett's eyes widened. That was it! Why hadn't she realized it before? Of course. Summer—when she loved Tara most—summer was when Rhett couldn't go to Dunmore Landing because of the fever. It was perfect. They'd spend October to June in Charleston, with the Season to break the monotony of all those stuffy boring tea parties, and the promise of summer at Tara to break the monotony of the Season. She could bear it, she knew she could. As long as there was the long summer at Tara.

Oh, if only the Bishop would hurry!

41

ierre Robillard escorted Scarlett to the dedication ceremonies at Hodgson Hall. He was an imposing figure in his old-fashioned dress suit, with its satin knee breeches and velvet tailcoat, the tiny red rosette of the Legion of Honor in his buttonhole and a broad diagonal red sash across his chest. Scarlett had never seen anyone look quite so distinguished and aristocratic as her grandfather.

He could be proud of her, too, she thought. Her pearls and diamonds were of the first water, and her gown was magnificent, a shining column of gold brocaded silk trimmed with gold lace and a gold brocaded train that was a full four feet long. She'd never had a chance to wear it, because she'd had to dress so dowdy in Charleston. How lucky, after all, that she'd had all those clothes made before she went to Charleston. Why, there were a half dozen dresses that had hardly been on her back. Even without the trim that Rhett had taunted her into removing, they were much prettier than anything she'd seen on anybody in Savannah. Scarlett was preening as Jerome handed her up into the hired carriage to sit across from her grandfather.

The ride to the south end of town was silent. Pierre Robillard's white-crowned head nodded, half-sleeping. It jerked upright when Scarlett exclaimed, "Oh, look!" There were crowds of people on the street outside the iron-fenced classical building, there to watch the arrival of Savannah's elite society. Just like the Saint Cecilia. Scarlett held her head arrogantly high as a liveried attendant helped her from the carriage to the sidewalk.

She could hear murmurs of admiration from the crowds. While her grandfather slowly stepped down to join her, she bobbed her head to set her earbobs flashing in the lamplight and cast her train from over her arm to spread out behind her for her entrance up the tall, red-carpeted steps to the Hall's door.

"Ooooh," she heard from the crowd and, "aaah," "beautiful," "who is she?" As she extended her white-gloved hand to rest on her grandfather's velvet sleeve a familiar voice called out clearly, "Katie Scarlett, darling, you're as dazzling as the Queen of Sheba!" She looked quickly, in a panic, to her left, then, even more quickly, turned away from Jamie and his brood as if she didn't know them, and proceeded at Pierre Robillard's slow, stately pace to mount the stairs. But the picture was seared into her mind. Jamie had his left arm around the shoulders of his laughing, bright-haired untidy wife, his Derby hat tipped carelessly on the back of his curly head. Another man stood at his right side, illuminated by the street lamp. He was only as tall as Jamie's shoulder, and his overcoated figure was thick, stocky, a dark block. His florid round face was bright, his eyes flashing blue, and his uncovered head a halo of silver curls. He was the very image of Gerald O'Hara, Scarlett's Pa.

Hodgson Hall had a handsome, serious interior, appropriate to its scholarly purpose. Rich, polished wood panelling covered the walls and framed the Historical Society's collection of old maps and sketches. Huge brass chandeliers fitted with white glass-globed gaslights hung from the tall ceiling. They cast an unkind, bright, bleaching light on the pale, lined aristocratic faces below them. Scarlett sought instinctively for some shadow. Old. They all look so old.

She felt panicky, as if somehow she was aging rapidly, as if old age were a contagion. Her thirtieth birthday had come and gone unnoticed while she was in Charleston, but now she was acutely aware of it. Everyone knew that once a woman was thirty, she just as well be dead. Thirty was so old that she'd never believed it could happen to her. It couldn't be true.

"Scarlett," said her grandfather. He held her arm above the elbow and propelled her toward the receiving line. His fingers were cold as death; she could feel the cold through the thin leather of the glove that covered her arm almost to her shoulder.

Ahead of her the elderly officers of the Historical Society were welcoming elderly guests, one by one. I can't! Scarlett thought frantically. I can't shake all those dead cold hands and smile and say I'm happy to be here. I've got to get away.

She sagged against her grandfather's stiff shoulder. "I'm not well," she said. "Grandfather, I feel ill all of a sudden."

"You are not permitted to feel ill," he said. "Stand straight, and do what's expected of you. You may leave after the ceremony of dedication, not before."

Scarlett stiffened her spine and stepped forward. What a monster her grandfather was! No wonder that she'd never heard her mother say much about him; there was nothing nice to say. "Good evening, Mrs. Hodgson," she said. "I'm so happy to be here."

Pierre Robillard's progress along the lengthy receiving line was much slower than Scarlett's. He was still bowing stiffly over the hand of a lady halfway along when Scarlett was finished. She pushed her way through a group of people and hurried to the door.

Outside, she gulped the crisp air with desperation. Then she ran. Her train glittered in the lamplight on the stairs, on the gala red carpet, stretching up behind her as if it were floating free in the air. "The Robillard carriage. Quickly!" she begged the attendant. Responding to her urgency, he ran to the corner. Scarlett ran after him, heedless of her train on the rough bricks of the sidewalk. She had to get away before anyone could stop her.

When she was safely inside the carriage, she breathed in short gasps. "Take me to South Broad," she told the driver when she could speak. "I'll show you which house." Mother left these people, she thought, she married Pa. She can't blame me if I run away, too.

She could hear the music and laughter through the door to Maureen's kitchen. Her two fists beat on it until Jamie opened it.

"It's Scarlett!" he said with pleased surprise. "Come in, Scarlett darling, and meet Colum. He's here at last, the best of all the O'Haras, saving only yourself."

Now that he was close to her, Scarlett could see that Colum was years younger than Jamie and not really all that much like her father, except for his round face and short stature among his taller cousins and nephews. Colum's blue eyes were darker, more serious, and his round chin had a firmness that Scarlett had seen on her father's face only when he was on horseback, commanding his mount to take a jump higher than sanity allowed.

Colum smiled when Jamie introduced them, and his eyes were almost lost in a network of creases. Yet the warmth gleaming from them made Scarlett feel that meeting her was the happiest experience of his entire life. "And are we not the luckiest family on the face of the earth, to have such a creature one of us?" he said. "It only wants a tiara to complete your gold splendor, Scarlett darling. If the Queen of the Fairies could see you, wouldn't she tear her spangled wings to ribbons in envy? Let the little girls have a look, Maureen, it will give them something to aspire to, to grow up as breathtaking as their cousin."

Scarlett dimpled with pleasure. "I believe I'm hearing the famous Irish blarney," she said.

"Not a bit of it. I wish only that I had the gift of poetry to say all I'm thinking."

Jamie hit his brother on the shoulder. "You're not doing too badly, for all that, you rogue. Step aside and give Scarlett a seat. I'll fetch her a glass ... Colum found us a keg of real Irish ale on his travels, Scarlett darling. You must have a taste." Jamie spoke name and endearment the way Colum did, as if they made one word: Scarlettdarling.

"Oh, no, thank you," she said automatically. Then, "Why not? I've never tasted ale." She would have had champagne without thinking anything of it. The dark foamy brew was bitter, and she made a face.

Colum took the mug from her. "She adds to her perfection with every second that passes," he said, "even to leaving all the drink for those with the bigger thirst." His eyes smiled at her over the rim when he drank.

Scarlett returned the smile. It was impossible not to. As the evening wore on, she noticed that everyone smiled at Colum a lot, as if reflecting his pleasure. He was clearly enjoying himself so much. He was leaning back in a straight chair, tipped to rest against the wall near the fire, waving his hand to direct and encourage Jamie's fiddling and Maureen's rat-tat-tat with the bones. His boots were off, and his stockinged feet fairly danced on the rungs of the chair. He was the picture of a man at his ease; even his collar was off, and the neck of his shirt was open so that his laughter could vibrate in his throat.

"Tell us, Colum, about your travels," someone would urge from time to time, but Colum always put them off. He needed music, he said, and a glass, to refresh his heart and his dusty throat. Tomorrow was time enough for talking.

Scarlett's heart, too, was refreshed by the music. But she couldn't stay very long. She had to be home and in bed before her grandfather returned. *I hope the driver keeps his promise and doesn't tell him he brought me here. Grandfather wouldn't care two pins how much I needed to get away from that mausoleum and have a little fun.*

She barely made it. Jamie was hardly out of sight when the carriage rolled up to the door. She ran up the stairs with her slippers in her hand and her train bunched up under her arm. She pressed her lips together to keep from giggling. Playing truant was fun when you got away with it.

But she didn't get away with it. Her grandfather never learned what she had done, but Scarlett knew, and the knowledge stirred the emotions that had warred within her all her life. Scarlett's essential self was as much her heritage from her father as was her name. She was impetuous, strong-willed, and had the same coarse, forthright vitality and courage that had carried him across the dangerous waters of the Atlantic and to the pinnacle of his dreams—master of a great plantation and husband to a great lady.

Her mother's blood gave her the fine bones and creamy skin that spoke of centuries of breeding. Ellen Robillard also instilled in her daughter the rules and tenets of aristocracy.

Now her instincts and her training were at war. The O'Haras drew her like a lodestone. Their earthy vigor and lusty happiness spoke to the deepest and best part of her nature. But she wasn't free to respond. Everything she'd been taught by the mother she revered forbid her that freedom.

She was torn by the dilemma, and she couldn't understand what was making her so miserable. She roamed restlessly through the silent rooms of her grandfather's house, blind to their austere beauty, imagining the music and dancing at the O'Haras', wishing with all her heart that she was with them, thinking as she'd been taught that such boisterous merriment was vulgar and lower class.

Scarlett didn't care really that her grandfather looked down on her cousins. He was a selfish old man, she thought accurately, who looked down on everyone, including his own daughters. But her mother's gentle inculcation had marked her for life. Ellen would have been proud of her in Charleston. In spite of Rhett's jeering prediction, she had been recognized and accepted as a lady there. And she had liked it. Hadn't she? Of course she had. It was also what she wanted, what she was meant to be. Why, then, was it so hard to stop herself from envying her Irish kin?

I won't think about that now, she decided. I'll think about it later. I'll think about Tara instead. And she retreated into the idyll of her Tara, as it had been and as she'd make it again.

Then a note came from the Bishop's secretary, and her idyll exploded in her face. He wouldn't grant her request. Scarlett didn't think at all. She clutched the note to her breast and ran, heedless and hatless and alone, to the unlocked door into Jamie O'Hara's house. They'd understand how she felt, the O'Haras would. Pa told me so, again and again. "To anyone with a drop of Irish blood in them the land they live on is like their mother. It's the only thing that lasts, that's worth working for, worth fighting for ..."

She burst through the door with Gerald O'Hara's voice in her ear, and ahead of her she saw the compact stock body and silver head of Colum O'Hara, so like her father's. It seemed right that he should be the one, certain that he'd feel what she felt.

Colum was standing in the doorway, looking into the dining room.

When the outside door crashed open and Scarlett stumbled into the kitchen, he turned.

He was dressed in a dark suit. Scarlett looked at him through the daze of her pain. She stared at the unexpected white line across his throat that was his Roman collar. A priest! No one had told her Colum was a priest. Thank God. You could tell a priest anything, even the deepest secrets of your heart.

"Help me, Father," she cried. "I need someone to help me."

42

So there you have it," Colum concluded. "Now, what can be done to remedy it? That's what we must find." He sat at the head of the long table in Jamie's dining room. All the adults from the three O'Hara houses were in chairs around the table. Mary Kate and Helen's voices could be heard through the closed door to the kitchen, where they were feeding the children. Scarlett was seated at Colum's side, her face swollen and blotched from earlier storms of weeping.

"You mean to say, Colum, that the farm doesn't go intact to the eldest child in America?" Matt asked.

"So it would seem, Matthew."

"Well, then, Uncle Gerald was foolish not to leave a will and testament."

Scarlett roused herself to glare at him. Before she could speak, Colum intervened. "The poor man wasn't granted his old age, he had no time to think about his death and after, God rest his soul."

"God rest his soul," echoed the others, making the sign of the cross. Scarlett looked without hope at their solemn faces. What can they do? They're just Irish immigrants.

But she soon learned that she was wrong. As the talking went on, Scarlett felt more and more hopeful. For there was quite a lot these Irish immigrants could do.

Patricia's husband, Billy Carmody, was foreman of all the bricklayers working on the Cathedral. He had come to know the Bishop very well.

"To my sorrow," he complained. "The man interrupts the work three times a day to tell me it's not being done fast enough." There was a real urgency, Billy explained, because a Cardinal from Rome itself would be touring America in the autumn, and he might come to Savannah for the dedication.

If it was done to suit his schedule.

Jamie nodded. "An ambitious man, our Bishop Gross, would you say? Not unwilling to be noticed by the Curia."

He looked at Gerald. So did Billy, Matt, Brian, Daniel, and Old James. And the women—Maureen, Patricia, and Katie. Scarlett did, too, although she didn't know why they were all looking.

Gerald took his young bride's hand in his. "Don't be shy, sweet Polly," he said, "you're an O'Hara now, same as the rest of us. Tell us which of us you would choose to talk to your Pa."

"Tom MacMahon's contractor for the whole job," Maureen murmured to Scarlett. "A mention from Tom that the work might be slowed would make Bishop Gross promise anything. Doubtless he's scared to trembling of MacMahon. Everyone else in the world is."

Scarlett spoke up. "Let Colum do it." She had no doubt that he was the best to do anything that needed doing. For all his small size and disarming smile, there was strength and power in Colum O'Hara.

A chorus of agreement sounded from all the O'Haras. Colum was the one to do what needed doing.

He smiled around the table, then at Scarlett alone. "We'll help you, then. Isn't it a grand thing to have a family, Scarlett O'Hara? Especially one with in-laws that can help, too? You'll have your Tara, wait and see."

"Tara? What's this about Tara?" Old James demanded.

"'Tis the name Gerald gave his plantation, Uncle James."

The old man laughed until it made him cough. "That Gerald," he said when he could speak again, "for a small bit of a man, he always did have a high opinion of himself!"

Scarlett stiffened. No one was going to make fun of her Pa, not even his brother.

Colum spoke very softly to her. "Whist, now, he means no insult. I'll explain it all later."

And so he did, when he was escorting her to her grandfather's house.

"Tara is a magical word to all us Irish, Scarlett, and a magical place. It was the center of all Ireland, the home of the High Kings. Before there was a Rome, or an Athens, far, far back when the world was young and hopeful, there ruled in Ireland great Kings who were as fair and beauteous as the sun. They passed laws of great wisdom and gave shelter and riches to poets. And they were brave giants of men who punished wrong with fearful wrath and fought the enemies of truth and beauty and Ireland with blood-gouted swords and stainless hearts. For hundreds and thousands of years they ruled their sweet green island, and there was music throughout the land. Five roads led to the hill of Tara from every corner of the country, and every third year did all the people come to feast in the banquet hall and hear the poets sing. This is not a story only, but a great truth, for all the histories of other lands record it, and the sad words of the end are written in the great books of the monasteries. 'In the Year of Our Lord five hundred fifty and four was held the last feast of Tara.' "

Colum's voice faded slowly on the last word, and Scarlett felt her eyes sting. She was spellbound by his story and his voice.

They walked on in silence for a while. Then Colum said, "It was a noble dream your father had to build a new Tara in this new world of America. He must have been a fine man indeed."

"Oh, he was, Colum. I loved him very much."

"When next I go to Tara, I'll think of him and of his daughter."

"When next you go? Do you mean it's still there? It's a real place?"

"As real as the road beneath our feet. It's a gentle green hill with magic in it and sheep grazing on it, and from the top you can see for great distances all around the same beautiful world the High Kings saw. It's not far from the village where I live, where your father and mine were born, in County Meath."

Scarlett was thunderstruck. Pa must have gone there, too, must have stood where the High Kings stood! She could picture him sticking out his chest and strutting the way he did when he was pleased with himself. It made her laugh softly.

When they reached the Robillard house she stopped reluctantly. She would have liked to walk for hours listening to Colum's lilting voice. "I don't know how to thank you for everything," she told him. "I feel a million times better now. I'm so sure you'll make the Bishop change his mind."

Colum smiled. "One thing at a time, Cousin. First the fierce Mac-Mahon. But what name shall I tell him, Scarlett? I see the band on your finger. You're not O'Hara to the Bishop."

"No, of course not. My married name is Butler."

Colum's smile collapsed, then returned. "It's a powerful name."

"In South Carolina it is, but I don't see that it's done me much good here. My husband's from Charleston, his name is Rhett Butler."

"I'm surprised he's not helping you with your troubles."

Scarlett smiled brightly. "He would if he could, but he had to go up North on business. He's a very successful businessman."

"I understand. Well, I'm happy to stand in as your helper, as best I can."

She felt like hugging him, the way she used to hug her father when he gave her what she wanted. But she had an idea you shouldn't go around hugging priests, even if they were your cousin. So she simply said good night and went into the house.

Colum walked away whistling "Wearing o' the Green."

"Where have you been?" Pierre Robillard demanded. "My supper was quite unsatisfactory."

"I've been at my cousin Jamie's house. I'll order you another tray."

"You've been seeing those people?" The old man quivered with outrage.

Scarlett's anger swelled to meet his. "Yes, I have, and I intend to see them again. I like them very much." She stalked out of the room. But she did see to a fresh supper tray for her grandfather before she went up to her room.

"What about your supper, Miss Scarlett?" Pansy asked. "You wants I should fetch you a tray upstairs?"

"No, just come up now and get me out of these clothes. I don't want any supper."

Funny, I don't feel hungry at all, and I only had a cup of tea. All I want now is some sleep. All that crying wore me out. I could hardly get out the words to tell Colum about the Bishop, I was crying so hard. I believe I could sleep for a week, I've never felt so washed out in my life.

Her head felt light, her whole body heavy and relaxed. She sank into the soft bed and plunged at once into a deep refreshing sleep.

In all Scarlett's life, she had faced her crises alone. Sometimes she had refused to admit she needed help, more often there had been nowhere she could turn. It was different now, and her body recognized the difference before her mind did. There were people to help her. Her family had willingly lifted her burden from her shoulders. She wasn't alone any more. She could allow herself to let go.

Pierre Robillard slept little that night. He was disturbed by Scarlett's defiance. Just so had her mother defied him, so many years before, and he had lost her forever. His heart had broken then; Ellen was his favorite child, the daughter most like her mother. He didn't love Scarlett. All the love he had was in the grave with his wife. But he wouldn't let Scarlett go without a fight. He wanted his last days to be comfortable, and she could see to it. He sat erect in bed, his lamp finally fading when the oil was gone, and he planned his strategy as if he were a general facing superior numbers.

After a fitful hour of rest shortly before dawn, he woke with his decision made. When Jerome brought his breakfast, the old man was signing a letter he had written. He folded and sealed it before he made room across his knees for the tray.

"Deliver this," he said, handing the letter to his butler. "And wait for a reply."

Scarlett opened the door a crack and stuck her head through. "You sent for me, Grandfather?"

"Come in, Scarlett."

She was surprised to see that there was someone in the room. Her grandfather never had guests. The man bowed, and she inclined her head.

"This is my lawyer, Mr. Jones. Ring for Jerome, Scarlett. He'll show you to the drawing room, Jones. Wait there until I send for you."

Scarlett had hardly touched the bellpull before Jerome opened the door.

"Pull that chair up closer, Scarlett. I have a great deal to say to you, and I don't want to strain my voice."

Scarlett was mystified. The old man had all but said "please." He sounded kind of feeble, too. *Lord, I hope he's not getting ready to die on me. I don't want to have to deal with Eulalie and Pauline at his funeral.* She moved a chair to a spot near the head of the bed. Pierre Robillard studied her from under lowered eyelids.

"Scarlett," he said quietly when she was seated, "I am almost ninety-four years old. I am in good health, considering my age, but it is not likely in simple mathematics that I will live much longer. I am asking you, my grandchild, to stay with me for the time I have left."

Scarlett started to speak, but the old man raised one thin hand to stop her. "I haven't finished," he said. "I do not appeal to your sense of family duty, even though I know that you have acted responsibly toward the needs of your aunts for many years.

"I am prepared to make you a fair offer, even a generous one. If you will remain in this house as its chatelaine and see to my comforts and conform with my wishes, you will inherit my entire estate when I die. It is not inconsiderable."

Scarlett was dumbfounded. He was offering her a fortune! She thought about the obsequiousness of the bank manager, wondered just how much her grandfather was worth.

Pierre Robillard misunderstood Scarlett's hesitation while her mind worked. He thought she was overcome with gratitude. His information did not include a report from the same bank manager, and he was unaware of her gold in the vaults. Satisfaction glimmered in his faded eyes. "I do not know," he said, "nor do I wish to know what circumstances have led you to consider dissolving your marriage." His posture and voice were stronger now that he believed he had the winning position. "But you will abandon any idea of divorce—"

"You've been reading my mail!"

"Anything that comes under this roof is rightfully my business."

Scarlett was so enraged she couldn't find words to express it. Her grandfather continued to speak. Precisely. Coldly. His words like icy needles.

"I despise rashness and stupidity, and you have been stupidly rash, leaving your husband without thought for your position. If you had had the intelligence to consult a lawyer, as I have done, you would have learned that South Carolina law does not encompass divorce for any reason. It is unique among the United States in this respect. You have fled to Georgia, it is true, but your husband is legally resident in South Carolina. There can be no divorce."

Scarlett was still concentrating on the indignity of strangers pawing over her private letters. It must have been that sneak Jerome. He put his hands on my things, went through my bureau. And my own blood kin, my grandfather, put him up to it. She stood up and leaned forward, her fists pressed on the bed beside Pierre Robillard's skeletal hand.

"How dare you send that man into my room?" she shouted at him, and she pounded on the thick layers of quilts.

Her grandfather's hand darted upward as quickly as a snake's striking. He caught her two wrists in the bony grip of his long fingers. "You will not raise your voice in this house, young woman. I detest noise. And you will conduct yourself with suitable decorum, as my granddaughter should. I am not one of your shanty Irish relations."

Scarlett was shocked at his strength, and a little frightened. What had become of the feeble old man she'd almost felt sorry for? His fingers were like iron bands.

She burst out of his grip, then backed away until the chair stopped her. "No wonder my mother left this house and never came back," she said. She hated her voice for its fearful quaver.

"Stop being melodramatic, girl. It tires me. Your mother left this house because she was headstrong and too young to listen to reason. She'd been disappointed in love and she took the first man who asked her. She lived to regret it, but what was done was done. You're not a girl, as she was;

you're old enough to use your head. The contract is drawn up. Bring Jones in here; we will sign it and proceed as though your unseemly outburst had never occurred."

Scarlett turned her back on him. I don't believe him. I won't listen to that kind of talk. She lifted the chair and carried it back to its usual place. With great care she set it down so that the feet fit the indentations they had made in the carpet over the years. She no longer felt afraid of him or sorry for him or even angry with him. When she turned to face him again, it was as if she'd never seen him before. He was a stranger. A tyrannical, sneaky, boring old man whom she didn't know and didn't care to know.

"There's not enough money ever been minted to keep me here," she said, and she was talking to herself more than to him. "Money can't make living in a tomb bearable." She looked at Pierre Robillard with blazing green eyes in a deathly pale face. "You belong here—you're dead already except you won't admit it. I'll leave first thing in the morning." She walked quickly to the door and pulled it open.

"I figured you'd be there listening, Jerome. Go on in."

43

$\mathcal{D}$on't be a cry-baby, Pansy, nothing's going to happen to you. The train goes straight through to Atlanta, then it stops. Just don't get off it before it gets there. I've pinned some money in a handkerchief and pinned the handkerchief in your coat pocket. The conductor already has your ticket, and he's promised to look out for you. Great balls of fire! You've been snivelling about how much you wanted to go home, and now you're going, so stop carrying on like that."

"But Miss Scarlett, I never been on a train by myself."

"Fiddle-dee-dee! You're not by yourself at all. There are plenty of folks on the train. You just look out the window and eat that basket full of food Mrs. O'Hara fixed you and you'll be home before you know it. I've sent a telegram to tell them to come meet you at the depot."

"But Miss Scarlett, what am I to do without you to do for? I'm a lady's maid. When are you going to be home?"

"When I get there. It all depends. Now climb up in that car, the train's ready to leave."

It all depends on Rhett, Scarlett thought, and Rhett better come pretty soon. I don't know if I'm going to manage with my cousins or not. She turned and smiled at Jamie's wife. "I don't know how I'm ever going to thank you for taking me in, Maureen. I'm thrilled to death at the idea, but it's caused you so much trouble." It was her bright, girlish, social voice.

Maureen took Scarlett's arm and walked her away from the train and Pansy's forlorn face in the dust-streaked window of the coach. "Everything is grand, Scarlett," she said. "Daniel is delighted to give you his room because he gets to move to Patricia's with Brian. He's been wanting to do it, but he didn't dare say so. And Kathleen is near floating with joy that she'll be your lady's maid. It's what she wants to train for anyhow, and she worships the ground under your feet. It's the first time the silly girl's been happy since she came here. You belong with us, not at the beck and call of that old loo-la. The brass of him, expecting that you'd stay there to housekeep for him. We want you for the love of you."

Scarlett felt better. It was impossible to resist Maureen's warmth. Still, she hoped it wouldn't be long. All those children!

Just like a colt about to shy, Maureen thought. Under the light pressure of her hand she could feel the tension in Scarlett's arm. What she needs, Maureen decided, is to open her heart and likely have a good old-fashioned bawling. It's not natural for a woman to never tell nothing about herself, and this one hasn't mentioned her husband at all. It makes a person wonder ... But Maureen didn't waste any time wondering. She'd observed when she was a girl washing glasses in her father's bar that given enough time everyone came around to airing his troubles sooner or later. She couldn't imagine that Scarlett would be any different.

The O'Hara houses were three tall brick houses in a row, with windows front and rear and shared interior walls. Inside, the layouts were identical. Each floor had two rooms: kitchen and dining room on the street level, double parlors on the first floor, and two bedrooms on each of the top two floors. A narrow hall with a handsome staircase ran the length of each house, and behind each one was an ample yard and a carriage house.

Scarlett's bedroom was on the third floor of Jamie's house. It had two single beds in it—Daniel and Brian had shared it until Brian moved to Patricia's—and it was very plain, as befitted two young men, with only a wardrobe and a writing table and chair for furniture in addition to the beds. But there were brightly colored patchwork quilts on the beds and a big red and white rag rug on the polished floor. Maureen had hung a mirror over the writing table and covered it with a lace cloth, so Scarlett had a dressing table. Kathleen was surprisingly good with her hair, and she was eager to learn how to please, and she was right at hand. She slept with Mary Kate and Helen in the other third-floor bedroom.

The only little child in Jamie's house was four-year-old Jacky, and he was usually over at one of the other houses, playing with cousins near his age.

During the day, with the men at work and the older children in school, the row of houses was a world of women. Scarlett expected to hate it. But nothing in Scarlett's life had prepared her for the O'Hara women.

There were no secrets among them, and no reticences. They said whatever they thought, confided intimacies that made her blush, quarrelled when they disagreed, and hugged one another, weeping, when they made up. They treated all the houses as one, were in and out of the others' kitchens at any hour for a cup of tea, shared the duties of shopping and baking and tending the animals in the yard and the carriage houses that had been converted into sheds.

Most of all they enjoyed themselves, with laughter and gossip and confidences and harmless intricate conspiracies against their men. They included Scarlett from the moment she arrived, assuming that she was one of them. Within days she felt she was. She went to the City Market with Maureen or Katie every day to search for the best foods at the best prices, and she giggled with young Polly and Kathleen about tricks with curling iron and ribbons, and she looked through swatches of upholstery fabric with house-proud Patricia long after Maureen and Katie threw up their hands at her finickiness. She drank innumerable cups of tea and listened to accounts of triumphs and worries; and, although she shared none of her own secrets, no one pressured her or held back the frank confession of their own. "I never knew that so many interesting things happened to people," Scarlett told Maureen with genuine surprise.

The evenings had a different pattern. The men worked hard and were tired when they got home. They wanted a good meal and a pipe and a drink. And they always got it. After that the evening evolved by itself. Often the whole family ended up at Matt's house, because he had five young children asleep upstairs. Maureen and Jamie could leave Jacky and Helen in Mary Kate's care, and Patricia could bring her sleeping two-year-old and three-year-old without waking them. Before too long the music would begin. Later, when Colum came in, he would be the leader.

The first time Scarlett saw the *bodhran*, she thought it was an outsize tambourine. The metal-framed circle of stretched leather was more than two feet across, but it was shallow, like a tambourine, and Gerald was holding it in his hand, like a tambourine. Then he sat down, braced it on his knee and tapped on it with a wooden stick that he held in the middle, rocking it to strike one end, then the other, against the skin, and she saw that it was really a drum.

Not much of a drum, she thought. Until Colum picked it up. His left hand spread against the underside of the taut leather as if caressing it, and his right wrist was suddenly as fluid as water. His arm moved from top to bottom to top to center of the drum while his right hand made a curious, careless-looking motion that pounded the stick with a steady, blood-stirring rhythm. The tone and volume differed, but the hypnotic, demanding beat never varied, as fiddle, then whistle, then concertina joined in. Maureen held the bones lifeless in her hand, too caught up in the music to remember them.

Scarlett gave herself over to the drumbeat. It made her laugh, it made her cry, it made her dance as she'd never dreamed she could dance. It was only when Colum laid the *bodhran* down on the floor beside him and demanded a drink, saying "I've drummed myself dry," that she saw that everyone else was as transported as she was.

She looked at the short, smiling pug-nosed figure with a shiver of awestruck wonder. This man was not like other men.

"Scarlett darling, you understand oysters better than I do," said Maureen when they entered the City Market. "Will you find us the best of them? I want to make a grand oyster stew for Colum's tea today."

"For tea? Oyster stew's rich enough for a meal."

"And isn't that the reason for it? He's speaking at a meeting tonight, and he'll need the strength of it."

"What kind of meeting, Maureen? Will we all go?"

"It's at the Jasper Greens, the American Irish volunteer soldiering group, so there'll be no women. We wouldn't be welcome."

"What does Colum do?"

"Ah, well, first he reminds them they're Irish, no matter how long they've been Americans, then he brings them to tears with longing and love for the Old Country, then he gets them to empty their pockets for the aid of the poor in Ireland. He's a mighty speechmaker, says Jamie."

"I can imagine. There's something magic about Colum."

"So you'll find us some magical oysters, then."

Scarlett laughed. "They'll not have pearls," she said, mimicking Maureen's brogue, "but they'll make a glory of a broth."

Colum looked down at the steaming, brimming bowl, and his eyebrows rose. "Maureen, this is a hearty tea you serve."

"The oysters looked particularly fat today at Market," she said with a grin.

"Do they not print calendars in the United States of America?"

"Whist, Colum, eat your stew before it's cold."

"It's Lent, Maureen, you know the rules for fasting. One meal a day, and that one we took at midday."

So her aunts had been right! Scarlett slowly put her spoon down on the table. She looked at Maureen with sympathy. This good meal wasted. She'd have to do a terrible penance and she must feel miserably guilty. Why did Colum have to be a priest?

She was astonished to see Maureen smiling and dipping in her spoon to capture an oyster. "I'm not worried about Hell, Colum," she said. "I have the O'Hara dispensation. You're an O'Hara, too, so eat your oysters and enjoy them."

Scarlett was bewildered. "What's the O'Hara dispensation?" she asked Maureen.

Colum answered her, but without Maureen's good humor. "Thirty years or so gone by," he said, "Ireland was struck with famine. One year and again the next people starved. There was no food, so they ate grass, and then there was not even grass. It was a terrible thing, terrible. So many died, and there was no way to help them. Those that lived through it were granted dispensation from future hungers by priests in some parishes. The O'Haras lived in such a parish. They need not fast, save for forsaking meat." He was staring down into the thick butter-flecked liquid in his bowl.

Maureen caught Scarlett's eye. She put her finger to her lips for silence, then gestured with her spoon, urging Scarlett to eat.

After a long while Colum picked up his spoon. He did not look up while he ate the succulent oysters, and his thanks were perfunctory. Then he left to go to Patricia's, where he shared a room with Stephen.

Scarlett looked at Maureen with curiosity. "Were you there in the Famine?" she asked cautiously.

Maureen nodded. "I was there. My father owned a bar, so we didn't fare as bad as some. People will always find money for drink, and we could buy bread and milk. It was the poor farmers got the worst of it. Ah, it was terrible." She put her arms across her breasts and shuddered. Her eyes were full of tears, and her voice broke when she tried to talk. "They only had potatoes, you see how it was. The corn they grew and the cows they raised and the milk and butter they got from them were always sold so they could pay the rent for their farms. For themselves they had a bit of butter and the skimmed milk and maybe a few chickens so that there was sometimes an egg for Sunday. But mostly they had potatoes to eat, only potatoes, and they made that enough. Then the potatoes turned to rot under the earth, and they had nothing." She was silent, rocking back and forth holding herself. Her mouth was trembling. It became a shaking circle, and she gave a harsh, tormented cry, remembering.

Scarlett jumped up and put her arms around Maureen's heaving shoulders.

Maureen wept against Scarlett's breast. "You cannot imagine what it is to have no food."

Scarlett looked at the smouldering coals on the hearth. "I know what it's like," she said. She held Maureen close, and she told about going home to Tara from burning Atlanta. There were no tears in Scarlett's eyes or in her voice when she talked about the desolation and the long months of relentless gnawing hunger and near starvation. But when she spoke about finding her mother dead when she reached Tara, and her father's pitiful broken mind, Scarlett broke down.

Then Maureen held her while she wept.

44

It seemed that the dogwood trees came into bloom overnight. Suddenly one morning, when Scarlett and Maureen were walking to the Market, there were clouds of blossoms above the grassy median in the avenue outside the house.

"Ah, isn't it a lovely sight?" Maureen sighed gustily. "The morning light shining through the tender petals making them almost pink. By noon they'll be white as a swan's breast. It's a grand thing, this city that plants flowering beauty for all to see!" She drew in a deep breath. "We'll have a picnic in the park, Scarlett. To taste the spring green in the air. Come quickly, there's a grand shopping to do. I'll bake this afternoon, and after Mass tomorrow we'll spend the day at the park."

Was it Saturday already? Scarlett's mind raced, calculating and remembering. Why, she'd been in Savannah almost a full month! A vise squeezed her heart. Why hadn't Rhett come? Where was he? His business in Boston couldn't have taken this long.

". . . Boston," said Maureen, and Scarlett stopped short. She grabbed Maureen's arm and glared at her suspiciously. How could Maureen have known Rhett was in Boston? How could she know anything about him? I haven't said a word to her.

"What's the matter, Scarlett, darling? Have you turned your ankle?"

"What were you saying about Boston?"

"I said 'tis a shame Stephen won't be with us for the picnic. He's leaving today for Boston. There'll be no trees flowering there, I'm bound.

Still, he'll have a chance to see Thomas and his family and bring back news of them. That'll please Old James. To think of all the brothers scattering through America, it's a wonderful thing . . ."

Scarlett walked quietly at Maureen's side. She was ashamed of herself. How could I have been so horrid? Maureen's my friend, the closest friend I ever had. She wouldn't spy on me, pry into my private life. It's just that it's been so long, and I hadn't even noticed. That's why I'm so jumpy, probably, why I barked at Maureen like that. Because it's been so long, and Rhett hasn't come.

She murmured unthinking agreement to Maureen's suggestions about food for the picnic while questions battered against the walls of her mind like birds trapped in a cage. Had she made a mistake not going back to Charleston with her aunts? Had she been wrong to leave in the first place?

This is driving me crazy. I can't think about it or I'll scream!

But her mind would not stop questioning.

Maybe she should talk to Maureen about it. Maureen was so comforting, and she was smart, really, about so many things. She'd understand. Maybe she could help.

No, I'll talk to Colum! Tomorrow, at the picnic, there'll be lots of time. I'll tell him I want to talk, ask him to go for a walk. Colum will know what to do. In his own way, Colum was like Rhett. He was complete in himself, like Rhett, and everyone else looked unimportant next to him, just the way men seem somehow to become only boys, and Rhett the only man in the room. Colum got things done, too, just like Rhett, and laughed about the doing, just like Rhett.

Scarlett laughed to herself at the memory of Colum talking about Polly's father. "Aye, he's a grand, bold man, the mighty builder MacMahon. Arms like sledgehammers he has, fairly popping the seams of his costly coat, doubtless chosen by Mrs. MacMahon to match her parlor suite, else why would it be such a plushy object? A Godly man, too, with proper reverence for the shine it gives his soul to build God's own house here in Savannah, America. I blessed him for it, in my own humble way. 'Faith!' I said. 'It's my belief you're such a religious that you're not taking a penny more than forty percent profit from the parish.' Then didn't his eyes flash and his muscles swell like a bull's and his plushy sleeves make pretty little popping sounds along their silk-sewn seams? 'Sure it is, Master Builder,' says I, 'that any other man would have made it fifty, seeing that the Bishop's not an Irishman?'

"And then the good man showed his merit. 'Gross!' he roared, till I feared the windows would fly out into the street. 'What manner of name is that for a Catholic?' Then he told me stories about the iniquities of the Bishop that my collar forbids me to credit. I shared his sorrows and a glass or two with him, then I told him about the suffering of my poor little cousin. Righteous wrath he showed, the good man. It was all I could do to stop him tearing down the steeple with his own strong hands. It's my belief he won't call all the men out on strike, but I cannot be altogether certain. He will, he tells me, express to the Bishop his concern for Scarlett's easiness of mind in terms the nervous little man cannot fail to understand, and as often as may be necessary to convince him of the gravity of the problem."

Maureen said, "And why are you smiling at the cabbages, I'd like to know?"

Scarlett turned the smile onto her friend. "Because I'm happy that it's spring and we're going to have a picnic," she said. And because she was going to have Tara, she was sure.

Scarlett had never seen Forsyth Park. Hodgson Hall was just across the street from it, but it had been dark when she went to the dedication ceremony. It caught her unaware, and it took her breath away. A pair of stone sphinxes flanked the entrance. The children looked longingly at the beasts they were forbidden to climb, then ran at full speed along the central path. They had to run around Scarlett. She was stopped in the middle of the path, staring ahead.

The fountain was two blocks from the entrance, but it was so enormous that it looked very close. Arcs and jets of water lifted and fell like showering diamonds from every direction. Scarlett was spellbound; she'd never seen anything so spectacular.

"Come along now," said Jamie, "it gets better as you get closer."

And it did. There was a bright sun that made rainbows in the dancing waters; they flashed, vanished, reappeared with every step Scarlett took. The whitewashed trunks of the trees that lined the path glimmered in the dappled shade from their leaves, leading to the sparkling dazzle of the fountain. When she reached the iron fence that circled the fountain's basin, she had to tilt her head back to near dizziness to look at the nymph atop its third tier, a statue bigger than she was, the arm held high, grasping a staff that threw a plume of water high, high toward the brilliant blue sky.

"I like the serpent-men myself," Maureen commented. "They always look to me like they're enjoying themselves." Scarlett looked where Maureen was pointing. The bronze mermen knelt in the huge basin on their elegantly coiled scaly tails with one hand on hip, the other holding a horn to the lips.

The men spread rugs under the oak tree Maureen selected, and the women put down their baskets. Mary Kate and Kathleen deposited Patricia's little girl and Katie's smallest boy on the grass to crawl. The older children were running and jumping in some game of their own design.

"I'll rest my feet," Patricia said. Billy helped her to sit with her back against the tree trunk. "Go on," she said crossly, "no need for you to spend all day at my elbow." He kissed her cheek, slid the straps of the concertina off his shoulder, and put it down beside her.

"I'll play you a fine tune later," he promised. Then he strolled toward a group of men in the distance who were playing baseball.

"Go get in trouble with him, Matt," Katie suggested to her husband.

"Yes, go on, the lot of you," Maureen said. She made shooing motions with her hands. Jamie and his tall sons set off at a run. Colum and Gerald walked behind them with Matt and Billy.

"They'll be starving when they get back," Maureen said. Her voice was rich with pleasure. "It's a good thing we packed food for an army."

What a mountain of food, Scarlett thought at first. Then she realized that it would probably all be gone inside an hour. Big families were like that. She looked with real affection at the women of her family, would feel equally fond of the men when they came back carrying their coats and hats, their collars open and their sleeves rolled up. She had put aside her class pretensions without noticing their departure. She no longer remembered her uneasiness when she learned that her cousins had been servants on the great estate near where they lived in Ireland. Matt was a carpenter there, Gerald a worker under him doing repairs on the dozens of buildings and miles of fence. Katie was a milkmaid, Patricia a parlormaid. And it made no difference. Scarlett was happy to be one of the O'Haras.

She knelt beside Maureen and began to help her. "I hope the men don't dawdle," she said. "This fresh air is making me right peckish."

When there were only two pieces of cake and an apple left, Maureen began to boil water for tea over a spirit lamp. Billy Carmody picked up his concertina and winked at Patricia. "What'll it be, Patsy? I promised you a tune."

"Shhh, not yet, Billy," said Katie. "The little ones are almost asleep." Five small bodies were on one of the rugs in the densest shade of the tree. Billy began to whistle softly, then took up the tune with the concertina, almost muted. Patricia smiled at him. She smoothed the hair from Timothy's forehead then started to sing the lullaby Billy was playing.

> On wings of a wind o'er the dark rolling sea
> Angels are coming to watch o'er thy sleep;
> Angels are coming to watch over thee,
> So list to the wind coming over the sea.

Hear the wind blow love, hear the wind blow,
Hang your head over, hear the wind blow.
The currachs are sailing way out on the blue,
Chasing the herring of silvery hue.
Silver the herring and silver the sea
Soon they'll be silver for my love and me.
Hear the wind blow love, hear the wind blow,
Hang your head over, hear the wind blow.

There was a moment of silence, then Timothy opened his eyes. "Again, please," he said drowsily.

"Oh, yes, please, miss, sing it again."

Everyone looked up, startled, at the strange young man who was standing nearby. He was holding a ragged cap in rough, dirty hands in front of his patched jacket. He looked about twelve years old, except that he had a stubble of dark whiskers on his chin.

"Begging your pardon, ladies and gentlemen," he said earnestly. "I know I'm being too bold, crashing in on your party and all that. But my mam used to sing that song to me and me sisters, and when I heard it, it called my heart over."

"Sit down, lad," said Maureen. "There's cake here with no one to eat it, and some grand cheese and bread in the basket. What's your name, and where are you from?"

The boy knelt by her. "Danny Murray, milady." He pulled on the stringy black hair over his forehead, then wiped his hand on his sleeve and held it out for the bread Maureen had taken out of the basket. "Connemara's me home, when I'm there." He bit hugely into the bread. Billy began to play.

"*On wings of a wind . . .*" sang Katie. The hungry boy swallowed and sang with her.

"*. . . hear the wind blow,*" they finished after three full repetitions. Danny Murray's dark eyes were shining like black jewels.

"Eat, then, Danny Murray," Maureen said. Her voice was rough with sentiment. "You'll need your strength later. I'm going to brew up a pot of tea, then we'll want to hear more of your singing. Your angel's voice is like a gift from heaven." It was true. The boy's Irish tenor was as pure as Gerald's.

The O'Haras busied themselves arranging teacups so the boy could eat unobserved.

"I learned a new song I think you might like," he said while Maureen was pouring the tea. "I'm on a ship that stopped in Philadelphia before it come here. Shall I sing it for you?"

"What's it called, Danny? I might know it," Billy said.

" 'I'll Take You Home' ?"

Billy shook his head. "I'll be glad to learn it from you."

Danny Murray grinned. "I'll be glad to show you." He tossed the hair off his face and took a breath. Then he opened his lips, and music poured out of him like shining silver thread.

I'll take you home again, Kathleen
Across the ocean wild and wide
To where your heart has ever been
Since first you were my bonny bride.
The roses all have left your cheek.
I've watched them fade away and die.
Your voice is sad when e'er you speak
And tears be-dim your loving eyes.
And I will take you back, Kathleen.
To where your heart will feel no pain.
And when the hills are fresh and green
I will take you to your home, Kathleen.

Scarlett joined in the applause. It was a lovely song.

"That was so grand I forgot to learn," Billy said ruefully. "Sing it again, Danny, for me to get the tune."

"No!" Kathleen O'Hara jumped to her feet. Her face was streaked with tears. "I can't listen again, I can't!" She wiped her eyes with her palms. "Forgive me," she sobbed. "I have to go." She stepped carefully over the sleeping children and ran away.

"I'm sorry," said the boy.

"Whist, it's not your fault, lad," said Colum. "It's real pleasure you've given. The poor girl's pining for Ireland is the truth of it, and by chance her name is Kathleen. Tell me, do you know 'The Curragh of Kildare'? It's a specialty of Billy's, him with the music box. It would be a rare favor were you to sing with him playing and make him sound like a musician."

The music went on until the sun dropped behind the trees and the breeze became chill. Then they went home. Danny Murray couldn't accept Jamie's invitation to supper. He had to be back at his ship by dark.

* * *

"Jamie, I'm thinking I should take Kathleen with me when I go," said Colum. "She's been here long enough to get over being homesick, but her heart's still aching."

Scarlett nearly poured boiling water on her hand instead of in the teapot. "Where are you going, Colum?"

"Back to Ireland, darling. I'm only visiting."

"But the Bishop hasn't changed his mind about Tara, yet. And there's something else I want to talk to you about."

"Well, I'm not leaving this minute, Scarlett darling. There's time for everything. What do you think, with your woman's heart? Should Kathleen go back?"

"I don't know. Ask Maureen. She's been up there with her ever since we got back." What difference did it make what Kathleen did? It was Colum that mattered. How could he just pick up and leave when she needed him? Oh, why did I just sit there singing with that filthy dirty boy? I should have gotten Colum to go for a walk the way I planned.

Scarlett only picked at the cheese toast and potato soup they had for supper. She felt like crying.

"Oof," Maureen groaned when the kitchen was tidy again. "I'm going to take my old bones to bed early tonight. Sitting on the ground all those hours has me stiff as a plow handle. You, too, Mary Kate and Helen. Tomorrow's a school day."

Scarlett felt stiff, too. She stretched in front of the fire. "Good night," she said.

"Stay a bit," Colum said, "while I finish my pipe. Jamie's yawning so, I can tell he's about to abandon me."

Scarlett took a chair across from Colum's, and Jamie patted her head on his way to the stairs.

Colum drew on his pipe. The smell of the tobacco was sweetly acrid. "A glowing hearth is good for talking by," he said after a while. "What's on your mind and your heart, Scarlett?"

She sighed deeply. "I don't know what to do about Rhett, Colum. I'm afraid I might have ruined everything." The kitchen was warm and dimly lit, the perfect setting for opening her heart. In addition, Scarlett had a muddled notion that, because Colum was a priest, everything she told him would be kept secret from the rest of the family, as if she were confessing in the cramped little closed booth in the church.

She started from the beginning, with the truth about her marriage. "I didn't love him, at least I didn't know it if I did. I was in love with someone else. And then, when I knew it was Rhett I loved, he didn't love me any more. That's what he said, anyhow. But I don't believe that's true, Colum; it just can't be."

"Did he leave you?"

"Yes. But then I left him. That's what I wonder, if it was a mistake."

"Let me get this straight . . ." With infinite patience Colum unravelled the tangle of Scarlett's story. It was well after midnight when he knocked the dottle out of his long-cold pipe and put it in his pocket.

"You did just what you should have, my dear," he said. "Because we wear our collars backwards some people think that priests are not men. They're wrong. I can understand your husband. I can even feel great compassion for his problem. It's deeper and more hurtful than yours, Scarlett. He's fighting himself, and for a strong man that's a mighty battle. He'll come after you, and you must be generous to him when he does, for he will be battlesore."

"But when, Colum?"

"That I cannot tell you. I know this, though. It's he that must do the seeking, you can't do it for him. He has to fight himself alone, until he faces his need for you and admits it is good."

"You're sure he'll come?"

"That I'm sure of. And now I'm to bed. You do the same."

Scarlett nestled into her pillow and tried to fight the heaviness of her eyelids. She wanted to stretch this moment, to enjoy the satisfaction that Colum's certainty had given her. Rhett would be here—maybe not as soon as she wanted, but she could wait.

45

Scarlett was none too pleased when Kathleen woke her up the next morning. After sitting up so late talking to Colum, she'd much rather have slept longer.

"I've brought your tea," said Kathleen softly. "And Maureen asks will you be wanting to go to the Market with her this morning?"

Scarlett turned her head away and closed her eyes again. "No, I think I'll go back to sleep." She could feel Kathleen hovering. Why didn't the silly girl just go away and let her sleep? "What do you want, Kathleen?"

"Begging your pardon, Scarlett, I wondered if you'd be getting dressed? Maureen wants me to go in your place if you're not going, and I don't know when we'll be back."

"Mary Kate can help me." Scarlett mumbled into her pillow.

"Oh, no. She's been off to school for ages. It's all but nine already."

Scarlett forced her eyes open. She felt as if she could sleep forever— if people would let her. "All right," she sighed, "get my things out. I'll wear the red and blue plaid."

"Oh, you do look so lovely in that one," Kathleen said happily. She said the same whatever Scarlett chose. Kathleen considered Scarlett quite the most elegant and beautiful woman in the world.

Scarlett drank her tea while Kathleen arranged her hair in a thick fig-ure-eight across the nape of the neck. I look like the wrath of God, she thought. There were faint shadows under her eyes. Maybe I should wear the pink dress, it's better with my skin, but then Kathleen would have to do the laces again, the pink has a smaller waist, and her fussing is driving me crazy. "That's fine," she said when the last hairpin was in, "now go on."

"Would you care for another cup of tea?"

"No. Go on." I'd really like coffee, Scarlett thought. Maybe I should go to the Market after all . . . No, I'm too tired to walk up and down, up and down, looking at every single thing. She powdered under her eyes and made a face at herself in the looking glass before she went downstairs to rummage up some breakfast.

"My grief!" she said when she saw Colum reading the newspaper in the kitchen. She'd thought there was no one in the house.

"I came to ask you a favor," he said. He wanted some feminine advice in selecting things for people back in Ireland. "I can manage the lads myself, and their fathers, but the lasses are a mystery. Scarlett will know, I told myself, what's the latest thing in America."

She laughed at his perplexed expression. "I'd love to help, Colum, but you have to pay me—with a cup of coffee and a sweet roll at the bakery on Broughton Street." She no longer felt tired at all.

"I don't know why you asked me to come with you, Colum! You don't like a single thing I've suggested." Scarlett looked with exasperation at the piles of kid gloves, lace handkerchiefs, clocked silk stockings, beaded bags, painted fans, and lengths of silks, velvets, and satins. The drapers' assistants had pulled out all the choicest wares of the most fashionable shop in Savannah, and Colum had shaken his head no to everything.

"I apologize for all the trouble I've given," he said to the stiffly smiling clerks. He offered Scarlett his arm. "I beg your pardon, too, Scarlett. I fear I didn't make it clear enough what I was wanting. Come along, and I'll pay the debt I owe you; then we'll try once more. A cup of coffee would be welcome."

It was going to take more than a cup of coffee to make her forgive him for this wild goose chase! Scarlett ostentatiously ignored the proffered arm and sailed out of the shop.

Her temper improved when Colum suggested they go to the Pulaski House for coffee. The huge hotel was very fashionable, and Scarlett had never been there. When they were seated on a tufted velvet settee in one of the ornate, marble-columned reception rooms, she looked around her with satisfaction. "This is nice," she said happily when a white-gloved waiter brought a laden silver tray to the marble-topped table in front of them.

"You look right at home in your elegant finery amidst all the grand marble and potted palms," he said, smiling. "That's why we crossed paths instead of travelling together." People in Ireland, he explained, led lives more simple than Scarlett knew. More simple, perhaps, than she could even imagine. They lived on their farms, in the countryside, with no city nearby at all, only a village with a church and a blacksmith and a public house where the mail-coach stopped. The only store at all was a room in the corner of the public house where you could mail a letter and buy tobacco and a few foodstuffs. Travelling wagons came by with ribbons and trinkets and papers of pins. People found their entertainment by going to other people's houses.

"But that's just like plantation life," Scarlett exclaimed. "Why, Tara's five miles from Jonesboro, and when you get there there's nothing much but a train depot and a puny little feed store."

"Ah, no, Scarlett. Plantations have mansion houses, not simple white-washed farmers' homes."

"You don't know what you're talking about, Colum O'Hara! The Wilkes' Twelve Oaks was the only mansion house in all Clayton County. Most folks have houses that started out with a couple of rooms and a kitchen, then added on what they needed."

Colum smiled and admitted defeat. Nevertheless, he said, the gifts for the family couldn't be city things. The girls would do better with a length of cotton than one of satin, and they wouldn't know what to do with a painted fan.

Scarlett put her cup in its saucer with a decisive clink. "Calico!" she said. "I'll bet you they'd love calico. It comes in all kinds of bright patterns and makes up into pretty frocks. We all had calico for everyday stay-at-home dresses."

"And boots," Colum said. He took a thick packet of paper from his pocket and unfolded it. "I have the names and sizes here."

Scarlett laughed at the length of the paper. "They sure saw you coming, Colum."

"What?"

"Never mind. It's an American saying." Every man, woman, and child in County Meath must have put their name on Colum's list, she thought. It was just like Aunt Eulalie's "As long as you're going shopping, would you just pick up something for me?" Somehow she never remembered to pay for whatever it was, and Scarlett would bet Colum's Irish friends would turn out just as forgetful.

"Tell me more about Ireland," she said. There was plenty of coffee left in the pot.

"Ah, it's a rare beautiful island," said Colum softly. He talked with love in his lilting voice about green hills crowned with castles, of rushing streams rimmed with flowers and leaping with fish, of walking between fragrant hedgerows in misty rain, of music everywhere, of a sky wider and higher than any other sky with a sun as gentle and warming as a mother's kiss . . .

"You sound almost as homesick as Kathleen."

Colum laughed at himself. "I won't weep when the ship sails, it's true. There's none who admire America more than I do, and I look forward to visiting, but I will not shed a tear when the ship sails for home."

"Maybe I will. I don't know what I'll do without Kathleen."

"Don't do without her, then. Come with us and see the home of your people."

"I couldn't do that."

"It would be a grand adventure. Ireland's beautiful any time, but in the spring the tenderness of it would break your heart."

"I don't need a broken heart, thank you, Colum. What I need is a maid."

"I'll send you Brigid, she's longing to come. I suppose she should have been the one all along, not Kathleen, only we wanted Kathleen away."

Scarlett scented gossip. "Why would you want to send that sweet girl away?"

Colum smiled. "Women and their questions," he said. "You're all alike both sides of the ocean. We didn't approve of the man who wanted to court her. He was a soldier, and a heathen besides."

"You mean a Protestant. Did she love him?"

"Her head was turned by his uniform, that was the all of it."

"Poor girl. I hope he's waiting for her when she gets home."

"Thanks be to God, his regiment's gone back to England. He'll bother her no more."

Colum's face was hard as granite. Scarlett held her tongue.

"What about that list?" she asked after she gave up expecting Colum to speak. "We'd better get back to our shopping. You know, Colum, Jamie has everything you want at his store. Why don't we just go there?"

"I couldn't put him in a fix. He'd feel bound to make me a price that would hurt him."

"Honestly, Colum, you don't have the brains of a flea about business! Even if Jamie sells to you at cost, it will make him look better to his suppliers, and he'll get a bigger discount next order." She laughed at Colum's bewilderment. "I have a store myself, I know what I'm saying. Let me explain . . ."

She talked a blue streak while they walked to Jamie's. Colum was fascinated and obviously impressed, asking question after question.

"Colum!" Jamie boomed when they entered the store. "We were just wishing for you. Uncle James, Colum's here." The old man came out from the storeroom with his arms full of bunting fabric.

"You're the answer to a prayer, man," he said. "Which is the color that we want?" He spilled the fabric onto a counter. It was all green, but four closely related shades.

"That one's the prettiest," Scarlett said.

Jamie and her uncle asked Colum to make a choice.

Scarlett was miffed. She'd already told them which was the best. What would a man know, even Colum?

"Where will you have it?" he asked.

"Over the window outside and in," Jamie replied.

"Then we'll look at it there, for the light on it," said Colum. He looked as serious as if he was picking out the color to print money, Scarlett thought crossly. What was all the fuss about?

Jamie noticed her pout. "It's to decorate for Saint Paddy's Day, Scarlett darling. Colum's the one to say what's closest to the true green of a shamrock. It's been too long since we've seen them, Uncle James and me."

The O'Haras had been talking about Saint Patrick's Day ever since the first time she met them. "When is it?" Scarlett asked, more polite than interested.

The three men gaped at her.

"You don't know?" Old James said incredulously.

"I wouldn't ask if I knew, would I?"

"It's tomorrow," Jamie said, "tomorrow. And, Scarlett darling, you're going to have the finest time of your life!"

Savannah's Irish—like the Irish everywhere—had always celebrated on March 17. It was the feast day of the patron saint of Ireland, and feast day was the secular meaning, as well as the canonical. Although it came during Lent, there was no fasting on Saint Patrick's Day. There was, instead, food and drink and music and dancing. Catholic schools were closed, and Catholic businesses, except for saloons, which expected and achieved one of their biggest days of the year.

There had been Irish in Savannah from its earliest days—the Jasper Greens first fought in the American Revolution—and Saint Patrick's Day had always been a major holiday for them. But during the bleak depressed decade since the defeat of the South, the entire city had begun to join in.

March 17 was Savannah's Spring Festival, and for one day everyone was Irish.

There were gaily decorated booths in every square selling food and lemonade, wine, coffee, and beer. Jugglers and men with trick dogs gathered crowds on street corners. Fiddlers played from the steps of City Hall and proud, peeling houses throughout the city. Green ribbons fluttered from flowering tree branches, shamrocks made of paper or of silk were for sale from boxes carried by enterprising men, women, and children from square to square. Broughton Street was bedecked with green bunting in shop windows, and ropes of fresh green vines strung between lampposts to canopy the parade route.

"Parade?!" Scarlett exclaimed when she was told. She touched the green silk ribbon rosettes Kathleen had pinned in her hair. "Are we finished? Do I look all right? Is it time to go?"

It was time. First early Mass, and then a celebration all day and into the night. "Jamie tells me there'll be fireworks starring the sky over the park until you're fair giddy from the splendor of it all," Kathleen said. Her face and eyes were shining with excitement.

Scarlett's green eyes were suddenly calculating. "I'll bet you don't have parades and fireworks in your village, Kathleen. You'll be sorry if you don't stay in Savannah."

The girl smiled radiantly. "I'll remember it forever and tell the tale by all the hearths of all the houses. Once home, it will be a grand thing to have seen America. Once home."

Scarlett gave up. There was no budging the silly girl.

Broughton Street was lined with people, all of them sporting green. Scarlett laughed aloud when she saw one family. With all those scrubbed-up children wearing green bows or scarves or feathers in their hats, they were just like the O'Haras. Except that they were all black. "Didn't I tell you everyone is Irish today?" Jamie said with a grin.

Maureen elbowed her. "Even the loo-las are wearing the green," she said, jerking her head toward a pair nearby. Scarlett craned her neck to see. Good grief! It was her grandfather's stuffy lawyer and a boy who must be his son. Both of them were wearing green cravats. She looked curiously up and down the street at the smiling people, searching for other familiar faces. There was Mary Telfair with a group of ladies, all of them with green ribbons on their hats. And Jerome! Where had he found a green coat, for pity's sake? Surely her grandfather wasn't here; please, God, don't let him be. He'd manage to make the sun stop shining. No, Jerome was with a black woman wearing a green sash. Fancy that, old prune-face Jerome with a girlfriend! At least twenty years younger, too.

A street vendor was handing out lemonade and coconut candy cakes to each O'Hara in turn, starting with the eager children. When he got to her, Scarlett accepted with a smile and bit into the candy. She was eating on the street! No lady would do that, even if she were dying of starvation. Take that, Grandfather! she thought, delighted by her own wickedness. The coconut was fresh, moist, sweet. Scarlett enjoyed it very much, even though it lost its thrilling defiance when she saw that Miss Telfair was nibbling on something that she was holding between her kid-gloved thumb and forefinger.

"I still say the cowboy in the green hat was the best," Mary Kate insisted. "He did all those fancy things with the rope, and he was so hand-some."

"You just say that because he smiled at us," Helen said scornfully. Ten years old was too young to be sympathetic with the romantic dreams of fifteen. "The best was the float with the leprechauns dancing on it."

"Those weren't leprechauns, silly. There aren't any leprechauns in America."

"They were dancing around a big bag of gold. Nobody would have a bag of gold except leprechauns."

"You're such a child, Helen. They were boys in costumes is all. Couldn't you see that the ears were false? One of them had fallen off."

Maureen intervened before the argument could get out of hand. "It was a grand parade, every bit of it. Come along, girls, and hold on to Jacky's hand."

Strangers the day before, strangers again the day after, on Saint Patrick's Day people joined hands and danced, joined voices and sang. They shared the sun and the air and the music and the streets.

"It's wonderful," Scarlett said when she tasted a chicken drumstick from one of the food stalls. And, "It's wonderful," she said when she saw the green chalk shamrocks on the brick paths of Chatham Square. "It's wonderful," about the mighty granite eagle with a green ribbon around its neck on the Pulaski Monument.

"What a wonderful, wonderful, wonderful day," she cried, and she spun around and around before she sank exhausted onto a newly vacated bench next to Colum. "Look, Colum, I've got a hole in the bottom of my boot. Where I come from everybody says you can tell the best parties because they're the ones where you dance your slippers right through. And these aren't even slippers, they're boots. This must be the best party ever!"

"It's a grand day, to be sure, and there's the evening still to come, with the Roman candles and all. You'll be worn through just like your boot, Scarlett darling, if you don't take a little rest. It's near four o'clock. Let's go to the house now for a bit."

"I don't want to. I want to dance some more and eat some more pork barbecue and have one of those green ices and taste that awful green beer Matt and Jamie were drinking."

"And so you shall tonight. You observe, do you not, that Matt and Jamie gave up an hour ago or more?"

"Sissies!" Scarlett proclaimed. "But you're not. You're the best of the O'Haras, Colum. Jamie said so, and he was right."

Colum smiled at her flushed cheeks and sparkling eyes. "Saving only yourself," he said. "Scarlett, I'm going to take off your boot now, hold it up, the one with the hole in it." He unlaced the neat black kid lady's boot, removed it and upended it to empty the sand and crushed shell fragments. Then he picked up a discarded ice cream cornet and folded the thick paper to fit inside the boot. "This should get you home. I'm supposing you've got more boots there."

"Of course I do. Oh, that does feel much better. Thank you, Colum. You always know what to do."

"What I know right now is we'll go home and have a cup of tea and a rest."

Scarlett hated to admit it, even to herself, but she was tired. She walked slowly beside Colum along Drayton Street, smiling at the smiling people thronging the street. "Why is Saint Patrick the patron saint of Ireland?" she asked. "Is he the saint of any place else?"

Colum blinked once, astonished by her ignorance. "All saints are saints for every person and every place in the world. Saint Patrick is special to the Irish because he brought us Christianity when we were still being lied to by the Druids, and he drove out all the snakes from Ireland to make it like the Garden of Eden without the serpent."

Scarlett laughed. "You're making that up."

"Indeed I am not. There's not a single snake the length and breadth of Ireland."

"That's wonderful. I do purely hate snakes."

"You really should come with me when I go home, Scarlett. You'd love the Old Country. The ship takes only two weeks and a day to Galway."

"That's very fast."

"It is that. The winds blow towards Ireland and carry the homesick travellers home as fast as a cloud flying across the sky. It's a grand sight to see all the sails set, and the big ship fairly dancing over the sea. The white gulls fly out with her until the land is almost lost from view, then they turn back, crying because they cannot come all the way. The dolphins take over the escort then, and sometimes a great whale, spouting like a fountain with astonishment to have the beautiful sail-topped companion. It's a lovely thing, sailing. You feel so free you think you could fly."

"I know," said Scarlett. "That's just what it's like. You feel so free."

$\mathcal{S}$carlett thrilled Kathleen by wearing her green watered silk gown to the festivities at Forsyth Park that night, but she horrified the girl by insisting on wearing her thin green morocco leather slippers instead of boots. "But the sand and the bricks are that rough, Scarlett, they'll take out the soles of your elegant slippers!"

"I want them to. I want, one time in my life, to dance through two pairs of shoes at one party. Just brush my hair, please, Kathleen, and put the green velvet ribbon on to hold it. I want to feel it loose and flying when I dance." She had slept for twenty minutes and felt that she could dance until dawn.

The dancing was on the broad plaza of granite blocks that surrounded the fountain, the water glittering like jewels and whispering beneath the merry, driving rhythms of the reel and the lilting beauty of the ballads. She danced one reel with Daniel, her small feet in their dainty slippers flashing like little green flames in the intricate patterns of the dance. "You're a marvel, Scarlett darling," he shouted. He put his hands around her waist and lifted her above his head, then turned, turned, turned while his feet pounded to the insistent beat of the *bodhran*. Scarlett stretched her arms wide and lifted her face to the moon, turning, turning in the fountain's silver mist.

"That's how I feel tonight," she told her cousins when the first Roman candle flew up into the sky and burst into showering brightness that made the moon look wan.

* * *

Scarlett hobbled Wednesday morning. Her feet were swollen and bruised. "Don't be silly," she said when Kathleen exclaimed about the condition of her feet, "I had a wonderful time." She sent Kathleen downstairs as soon as her corset was laced. She didn't want to talk yet about all the pleasures of Saint Patrick's Day; she wanted to turn over the memories slowly, by herself. It didn't really make any difference if she was a little late for breakfast; she wouldn't be walking to the Market today anyhow. She'd just leave off stockings and wear her felt house slippers and stay in.

There certainly were a lot of steps from the third floor down to the kitchen. Scarlett had never noticed how many when she was running down them. Now each one meant a stab of pain if she didn't carefully ease her weight down. No matter. It was worth staying in for a day—or even two —to have had the joyful dancing. Maybe she could ask Katie to shut the cow in her shed. Scarlett was afraid of cows, she always had been, all her life. If Katie shut it up, though, she could sit outside in the yard. The spring air smelled so fresh and sweet through the open windows that she longed to be out in it.

There . . . almost to the parlor floor. I'm over halfway. I wish I could go faster. I'm hungry.

As Scarlett gingerly lowered her right foot to the first step on the final flight of stairs to the kitchen, the smell of frying fish rose up to meet her. Damn, she thought, it's no-meat time again. What I'd really like is some nice thick bacon.

Suddenly, without warning, her stomach contracted and her throat filled. Scarlett turned in panic and lurched to the window. She held on to the open curtains with frantic grasping hands while she leaned out of the window and vomited into the thick green leaves of the young magnolia tree in the yard. She was sick again and again until she was weak, and her face was wet with tears and clammy sweat. Then she slid helplessly down into a huddled miserable heap on the hall floor.

She wiped her mouth with the back of her hand, but the feeble gesture did nothing to erase the sour, bitter taste inside. If only I could have a drink of water, she thought. Her stomach contracted in response, and she gagged.

Scarlett put her hands over her middle and wept. I must have eaten something gone to poison in the heat yesterday. I'm going to die right here, like a dog. She took short panting breaths. If only she could loosen her stays; they were cramping her aching stomach, cutting off the air she needed. The rigid whalebones felt like a cruel iron cage.

She had never in all her life felt so sick.

* * *

She could hear the family's voices from below, Maureen asking where she was, Kathleen saying she'd be down any minute. Then a door banged, and she heard Colum. He was asking for her, too. Scarlett clenched her teeth. She had to get up. She had to go downstairs. She would not be discovered like this, bawling like a baby because she had partied too much. She wiped the tears from her face with the hem of her skirt, and pulled herself upright.

"There she is," Colum said when Scarlett appeared in the doorway. Then he hurried to her. "Poor little Scarlett darling, you look like you're walking on broken glass. Here, let me put you at ease." He picked her up before she could say a word and carried her to the chair that Maureen quickly pulled up close to the hearth.

Everyone bustled about, their breakfast forgotten, and in only seconds Scarlett found herself with her feet on a cushion and a cup of tea in her hands. She blinked back the tears in her eyes, tears of weakness and happiness. It was so nice to be taken care of, to be loved. She felt a thousand times better now. She took a cautious small sip of tea, and it was good.

She had a second cup, then a third and a piece of toast. But she averted her eyes from the fried fish and potatoes. No one seemed to notice. There was too much hubbub getting the children's books and lunchbags sorted out and shooing them off to school.

When the door closed behind them, Jamie kissed Maureen on the lips, Scarlett on the top of her head, Kathleen on her cheek. "I'll be off to the store now," he said. "The bunting must come down and the headache remedy must be put on the counter where all the sufferers can get to it easy. Celebrating is a fine thing, but the day after can be a fearsome burden."

Scarlett bent her head to hide her blushing face.

"Now you just stay as you are, Scarlett," Maureen ordered. "Kathleen and I will have the kitchen cleared in no time, then we'll go to the Market while you have a little rest. Colum O'Hara, you stay where you are, too; I don't want your big boots getting in my way. I want you under my eye, too; it's little enough I get to see of you. If it wasn't for Old Katie Scarlett's birthday, I'd beg you not to leave so soon for Ireland."

"Katie Scarlett?" said Scarlett.

Maureen dropped the sudsy cloth she was holding. "And did no one think to tell you?" she said. "Your grandmother that you were named for is going to be a century old next month."

"And still as sharp-tongued as when she was a girl," Colum chuckled. "It's something for all the O'Haras to pride themselves on."

"I'll be home for the feast," Kathleen said. She glowed with happiness.

"Oh, I wish I could go," Scarlett said. "Pa used to tell so many stories about her."

"But you can, Scarlett darling. And think what a joy for the old woman."

Kathleen and Maureen rushed to Scarlett's side, urging, encouraging, persuading, until Scarlett was giddy. Why not? she asked herself.

When Rhett came for her, she would have to go back to Charleston. Why not put it off a little longer? She hated Charleston. The drab dresses, the interminable calls and committees, the walls of politeness that shut her out, the walls of decaying houses and broken gardens that shut her in. She hated the way Charlestonians talked—the flat, drawn-out vowels, the private language of cousins and ancestors; the words and phrases in French and Latin and God only knew what other languages, the way they all knew places she'd never been and people she'd never heard of and books she'd never read. She hated their society—the dance cards and receiving lines and the unspoken rules that she was supposed to know and didn't, the immorality that they accepted, and the hypocrisy that condemned her for sins she never committed.

I don't want to wear colorless dresses and say "yes ma'am" to old biddies whose grandfather on their mother's side was some famous Charleston hero or something. I don't want to spend every single Sunday morning listening to my aunts picking at each other. I don't want to have to think the Saint Cecilia Ball is the be-all and end-all of life. I like Saint Patrick's Day better.

Scarlett laughed aloud. "I'm going to go!" she said. Suddenly she felt wonderful, even in her stomach. She stood up to hug Maureen and she barely noticed the pain in her feet.

Charleston could wait until she got back. Rhett could wait, too. Lord knows she'd waited for him often enough. Why shouldn't she visit the rest of her O'Hara kin? It was only two weeks and a day on a great sailing ship to that other Tara. And she'd be Irish and happy for a while yet before she settled down to Charleston's rules.

Her tender, wounded feet tapped out the rhythm of a reel.

Only two days later, she was able to dance for hours at the party to celebrate Stephen's return from Boston. And not long after that, she found herself in an open carriage with Colum and Kathleen, on her way to the docks along Savannah's riverfront.

It had been no trouble at all to get ready. Americans did not need passports for entrance to the British Isles. They didn't even need letters of credit, but Colum insisted that she get one from her banker. "Just in case," Colum said. He didn't say in case of what. Scarlett didn't care. She was intoxicated with the adventure of it all.

"You're sure we'll not miss our boat, Colum?" Kathleen fretted. "You were late coming for us. Jamie and them left an hour ago to walk over."

"I'm sure, I'm sure," Colum soothed. He winked at Scarlett. "And if I was tardy a bit, it was no fault of mine, seeing that Big Tom MacMahon wanted to pledge his promise about the Bishop in a glass or two, and I couldn't insult the man."

"If we miss our boat, I'll die," Kathleen moaned.

"Whist, stop your worrying, Kathleen mavourneen. The captain won't sail without us; Seamus O'Brien's a friend of many years' standing. But he'll be no friend of yours if you call the *Brian Boru* a boat. A ship she is, and a fine shining vessel she is, too. You'll see for yourself soon enough."

At that moment the carriage turned beneath an arch, and they plunged, skidding and jolting, down a dark, slippery, cobblestoned ramp. Kathleen screamed. Colum laughed. Scarlett was breathless from the thrill of it.

Then they were at the river. The tumult and color and chaos were even more exciting than the precipitous ride down to it. Ships of every size and kind were tied up to jutting wooden piers, more ships than she'd ever seen in Charleston. Loaded wagons pulled by heavy dray horses rattled wooden or iron wheels over the wide cobbled street in a constant din. Men shouted. Barrels rolled down wooden chutes onto wooden decks with a deafening clatter. A steamship blew its piercing whistle; another rang its clangorous bell. A row of barefooted loaders moved across a gangplank, carrying bales of cotton and singing. Flags in bright colors and gaudy decorated pennants snapped in the wind. Gulls swooped and squawked.

Their driver stood up and cracked his whip. The buggy jerked forward, scattering a crowd of gaping pedestrians. Scarlett laughed into the gusty wind. They careened around a phalanx of barrels awaiting loading, clattered past a slow-moving dray, and pulled to a jouncing halt.

"I hope you're not expecting to be paid extra for the white hairs you've put on my head," Colum said to the driver. He jumped down and held up his hand to Kathleen to help her down.

"You've not forgotten my box, Colum?" she said.

"All the traps are here betimes, darling. Go on over, now, and give your cousins a kiss to say goodbye." He pointed towards Maureen. "You can't miss that red hair shining like a beacon."

When Kathleen ran off, he spoke quietly to Scarlett. "You'll not forget what I told you about the name, now, Scarlett darling?"

"I won't forget." She smiled, enjoying the harmless conspiracy.

"You'll be Scarlett O'Hara and no other on this voyage and in Ireland," he had told her with a wink. "It's nothing to do with you or yours, Scarlett darling, but Butler is a powerful famous name in Ireland, and all of its fame is heinous."

Scarlett didn't mind at all. She was going to enjoy being an O'Hara for as long as she could.

The *Brian Boru* was, as Colum had promised, a fine, shining ship. Her hull was gleaming white with gilt scroll trim. Gilt trimmed the emerald-colored cover of the gigantic paddle wheels as well, and her name in gilt letters two feet high was painted on them in a frame of gilt arrows. The Union Jack flew from her flagstaff, but a green silk banner decorated with a golden harp waved boldly from her forward mast. She was a luxury passenger ship, catering to the expensive tastes of rich Americans who travelled to Ireland for sentiment—to see the villages where emigrant grandfathers were born—or for show—to visit, in all their finery, the villages where they had been born. The public rooms and staterooms were oversized and overdecorated. The crew was trained to satisfy every whim. There was a disproportionately large hold, compared to the usual passenger ship, because Irish-Americans carried with them gifts for all their relatives and returned with multiple souvenirs of their visits. The baggage handlers treated every trunk and every crate as if it were full of glass. Often it was. It was not unknown for prosperous third-generation American Irish wives to light every room in their new houses with Waterford crystal chandeliers.

A broad platform with sturdy railings was built across the top of the paddle wheel on which Scarlett stood with Colum and a handful of adventurous passengers to wave a final goodbye to her cousins. There'd been time only for hasty farewells on the dock because the *Brian Boru* had to catch the outgoing tide. She blew excited kisses to the massed O'Haras. There'd been no school this morning for the children, and Jamie had even closed the store for an hour so that he and Daniel could come down and see them off.

Slightly behind and to one side of the others stood quiet Stephen. He raised his hand once in a signal to Colum.

It signified that Scarlett's trunks had been opened and repacked en route to the ship. Among the layers of tissue paper and petticoats and frocks and gowns were the tightly wrapped, oiled rifles and the boxes of ammunition he had purchased in Boston.

Like their fathers and grandfathers and generations before them, Stephen, Jamie, Matt, Colum, and even Uncle James were all militantly opposed to English rule over Ireland. For more than two hundred years the O'Haras had risked their lives to fight, sometimes even kill, their foes, in abortive, ill-fated small actions. Only in the past ten years had an organization begun to grow. Disciplined and dangerous, financed from America, the Fenians were becoming known throughout Ireland. They were heroes to the Irish peasant, anathema to English landowners, and to English military forces revolutionaries fit only for death.

Colum O'Hara was the most successful fund-raiser and one of the foremost clandestine leaders of the Fenian Brotherhood.

The Tower

47

The *Brian Boru* moved ponderously between the banks of the Savannah River, pulled by steam-driven tugboats. When at last it reached the Atlantic, its deep whistle saluted the departing tugs and its great sails were loosed. The passengers cheered as the ship's prow dipped into the gray-green waves at the river's mouth and the tremendous paddle wheels began to churn.

Scarlett and Kathleen stood side by side watching the flat shoreline recede quickly into a soft blur of green, then disappear.

What have I done? Scarlett thought, and she grabbed the deck rail in momentary panic. Then she looked ahead at the limitless expanse of sun-flecked ocean, and her heart beat faster with the thrill of adventure.

"Oh!" Kathleen cried out. Then, "Oooh," she moaned.

"What's wrong, Kathleen?"

"Oooh. I'd forgot the seasickness," the girl gasped.

Scarlett held back her laughter. She put her arm around Kathleen's waist and led her to their cabin. That evening, Kathleen's chair at the captain's table was empty. Scarlett and Colum did full justice to the gargantuan meal that was served. Afterwards, Scarlett took a bowl of broth to her unfortunate cousin and spoon-fed her.

"I'll be all right in a day or two," Kathleen promised in a weak voice. "You won't need to be tending me forever."

"Hush up and take another sip," said Scarlett. Thank heavens I haven't got a puny stomach, she thought. Even the food poisoning from Saint Patrick's Day is over now, or I couldn't have enjoyed my dinner so much.

* * *

She woke abruptly when the first red streaks of dawn were on the horizon and ran with frantic clumsiness into the small convenience room that adjoined the cabin. There she fell to her knees and vomited into the flower-decorated china receptacle of the mahogany chaise privée.

She couldn't be seasick, not her. Not when she loved sailing so much. Why, in Charleston, when the tiny sailboat was climbing the waves in the storm, she hadn't even felt queasy, nor when it slid down into the trough of the wave. The *Brian Boru* was steady as a rock compared to that. She couldn't imagine what was wrong with her . . .

. . . Slowly, slowly Scarlett's bent head rose from its drooping weakness. Her mouth and eyes opened wide with discovery. Excitement raced through her, hot and strengthening, and she laughed deep in her throat.

I'm pregnant. I'm pregnant! I remember; this is how it feels.

Scarlett leaned back against the wall and threw her arms wide in a luxurious stretch. Oh, I feel wonderful. I don't care how awful my stomach feels, I feel wonderful. I've got Rhett now. He is mine. I can't wait to tell him.

Sudden tears of happiness poured down her cheeks, and her hands flew down to cover her middle in a protective cradling of the new life growing within. Oh, how she wanted this baby. Rhett's baby. Their baby. It would be strong, she knew it, she could feel its tiny strength already. A bold, fearless little thing, like Bonnie.

Scarlett's mind flooded with memories. Bonnie's little head had fit into her palm, hardly bigger than a kitten's. She'd fit into Rhett's big hands like a doll. How he had loved her. His wide back bent over the cradle, his deep voice making silly baby-talk sounds—never in all the world was there a man so besotted with a baby. He was going to be so happy when she told him. She could see his dark eyes flashing with the joy of it, his white smile gleaming in his pirate's face.

Scarlett smiled, too, thinking of it. I'm happy, too, she thought. This is the way it's supposed to be when you have a baby, Melly always said so.

"Oh, my God," she whispered aloud. Melly died trying to have one, and my insides are all messed up, Dr. Meade said, after I had the miscarriage. That's why I didn't know I was pregnant, I didn't even notice I missed my time of month, because it's been so undependable for so long. Suppose having this baby kills me? Oh, God, please, please, God, don't let me die just when I finally get what I need to be happy. She crossed herself again and again in confused entreaty, propitiation, superstition.

Then she shook her head angrily. What was she doing? Just being silly. She was strong and healthy. Not like Melly at all. Why, Mammy always said it was downright shameful the way she dropped a baby with hardly more fuss than an alley cat. She was going to do just fine, and her baby would be fine, too. And her life would be fine, with Rhett loving her, loving their baby. They'd be the happiest, lovingest family in the whole world. Gracious, she hadn't even thought of Miss Eleanor. Talk about baby-loving! Miss Eleanor was going to pop her buttons with pride. I can see her now, at the Market, telling everybody, even the bent-up old man who sweeps out the trash. This baby's going to be the talk of Charleston before it even draws its first breath.

... Charleston ... That's where I should be going. Not to Ireland. I want to see Rhett, to tell him.

Maybe the *Brian Boru* could put in there. The captain's a friend of Colum's; Colum could persuade him to do it. Scarlett's eyes sparkled. She got to her feet and washed her face, then rinsed the sour taste out of her mouth. It was too early to talk to Colum, so she went back to bed and sat up against the pillows making plans.

When Kathleen got up, Scarlett was sleeping, a contented smile on her lips. There was no need to hurry, she had decided. No need to talk to the captain. She could meet her grandmother and her Irish kin. She could have her adventure of crossing the ocean. Rhett had kept her waiting for him in Savannah. Well, he could wait awhile to learn about the baby. There were months and months to go before it was born. She was entitled to have some fun before she went back to Charleston. Sure as fate, she wouldn't be allowed to do so much as stick her nose out of the door there. Ladies in a delicate condition weren't supposed to stir a stump.

No, she'd have Ireland first. She'd never have another chance.

She'd enjoy the *Brian Boru* too. Her morning sickness had never lasted much more than a week with the other babies. It must be almost over now. Like Kathleen, in a day or two she'd be just fine.

Crossing the Atlantic on the *Brian Boru* was like a continuous Saturday night at the O'Haras' in Savannah—only more so. At first Scarlett loved it.

The ship soon had a full complement of passengers who boarded at Boston and New York, but they didn't seem like Yankees at all, Scarlett thought. They were Irish and proud of it. They had the vitality that was so appealing in the O'Haras, and they took advantage of everything the ship had to offer. All day there was something to do: checkers tournaments, heated competitions at quoits on deck, excited participation in games of chance, such as wagering on the number of miles the ship would cover the following day. In the evening they sang along with the professional musicians and danced energetically to all the Irish reels and Viennese waltzes.

Even when the dancing was done, the amusement continued. There was always a game of whist in the Ladies' Card Saloon, and Scarlett was always in demand as a partner. Except for Charleston's rationed coffee, the stakes were higher than any she'd known, and every turn of a card was exciting. So were her winnings. The *Brian Boru*'s passengers were living proof that America was the Land of Opportunity, and they didn't mind spending their lately gained wealth.

Colum, too, benefitted from their opened pockets. While the women played cards, the men generally retired to the ship's bar for whiskey and cigars. There, Colum brought tears of pity and pride to eyes that were normally shrewd and dry. He talked about Ireland's oppression under English rule, called the roll of martyrs to the cause of Irish freedom, and accepted lavish donations for the Fenian Brotherhood.

A crossing on the *Brian Boru* was always a profitable enterprise, and Colum made the trip at least twice a year, even though the excessive luxury of the staterooms and the gargantuan meals secretly sickened him when he thought of the poverty and need of the Irish in Ireland.

By the end of the first week, Scarlett, too, was looking at their fellow passengers with a disapproving eye. Both men and women changed clothes four times a day, the better to show off the extent of their costly wardrobes. Scarlett had never seen so many jewels in her life. She told herself she was glad that she'd left hers in the vault of the Savannah bank; they'd pale next to the array in the dining saloon every night. But in truth she wasn't glad at all. She had grown accustomed to having more of everything than anyone she knew—a bigger house, more servants, more luxury, more things, more money. It put her nose decidedly out of joint to see display more conspicuous than hers had ever been. In Savannah, Kathleen, Mary Kate, and Helen had been ingenuously blatant in their envy, and all the O'Haras had fed her need for admiration. These people on the ship didn't envy her, or even admire her all that much. Scarlett wasn't at all pleased with them. She couldn't bear a whole country full of Irish if this was what they were like. If she heard "Wearing o' the Green" one more time she'd scream.

"You're just not taken with the American New-Rich, Scarlett darling," Colum soothed. "You're a grand lady, that's why." It was exactly the right thing for him to say.

A grand lady was what she had to be after this vacation was over. She'd have this final fling of freedom and then she'd go to Charleston, put on her drab clothes and company manners, and be a lady for the rest of her life.

At least now when Miss Eleanor and everybody else in Charleston talked about their trips to Europe before the War, she'd not feel so left out. She wouldn't say she'd disliked it, either. Ladies didn't say things like that. Unconsciously, Scarlett sighed.

"Ach, Scarlett darling, it can't be as bad as all that," Colum said. "Look at the bright side. You're cleaning out their deep pockets at the card table."

She laughed. It was true. She was winning a fortune—some evenings as much as thirty dollars. Wait till she told Rhett! How he'd laugh. He'd been a gambler on Mississippi riverboats for a while, after all. Come to think of it, it was a good thing, really, that there was still a week at sea. She wouldn't have to touch a penny of Rhett's money.

Scarlett's attitude toward money was a complex mixture of miserliness and generosity. It had been her measure of safety for so many years that she guarded every penny of her hard-earned fortune with angry suspicion of anyone who made any real or imagined demands for a dollar of it. And yet she accepted the responsibility to support her aunts and Melanie's family without question. She had taken care of them even when she didn't know where she'd find the means to take care of herself. If some unforeseen calamity befell, she would continue to take care of them, even if it meant that she had to go hungry. She didn't think about it; it was simply the way things were.

Her feelings about Rhett's money were equally inconsistent. As his wife she spent profligately on the Peachtree Street house, with its prodigious expenses, and on her wardrobe and luxuries. But the half million he had given her was different. Inviolable. She intended to give it back to him intact when they were once again truly man and wife. He had offered it as payment for separation, and she could not accept it because she would not accept separation.

It bothered her that she'd had to take some of it out of the bank vaults to bring on the trip. Everything had happened so fast, there'd been no time to get any of her own money from Atlanta. But she'd put an IOU in the box with the remaining gold in Savannah, and she was determined to spend as little as possible of the gold coins that were now keeping her back straight and her waist small, filling the channels in her corset where steel strips had once been. It was much better to win at whist and have her own money to spend. Why, in another week, with any luck, she'd add at least another $150 to her purse.

But still, she'd be glad when the voyage was over. Even with all the sails bellied taut with wind, the *Brian Boru* was too big for her to feel the thrill she remembered from racing ahead of the storm in Charleston Harbor. And she hadn't seen even one dolphin, despite Colum's poetic promises.

"There they are, Scarlett darling!" Colum's usually calm, melodious voice rose in excitement; he took Scarlett's arm and drew her to the ship's rail. "Our escorts are here. We'll be seeing land soon."

Overhead the first gulls circled the *Brian Boru*. Scarlett hugged Colum impulsively. Then again when he pointed to the sleek silvery forms on the nearby sea. There were dolphins after all.

Much later, she stood between Colum and Kathleen trying to hold her hat on her head against the attack of the strong wind. They were entering harbor under steam. Scarlett stared in astonishment at the island of rock to starboard. It seemed impossible that anything, even the towering wall of craggy stone, could withstand the crashing waves that beat against it and threw white foam high against its face. She was accustomed to the low rolling hills of Clayton County. This soaring stark cliff was the most exotic sight she'd ever seen.

"Nobody tries to live there, do they?" she asked Colum.

"No bit of earth is wasted in Ireland," he replied. "But it takes a hardy breed to call Inishmore home."

"Inishmore." Scarlett repeated the beautiful strange name. It sounded like music. And like no name she'd ever heard before.

Then she was silent; so were Colum and Kathleen; each of them looked at the broad blue sparkling waters of Galway Bay with private thoughts.

Colum saw Ireland ahead and his heart swelled with love for her and pain for her sufferings. As he did many times every day, he renewed his vow to destroy the oppressors of his country and to restore her to her own people. He felt no anxiety about the weapons concealed in Scarlett's trunks. Customs officials in Galway concentrated mainly on ships' cargoes, making sure that duty owed to the British government was paid. They'd look at the *Brian Boru* with sneers. They always did. Successful Irish-Americans gratified their sense of superiority over both—the Irish and the Americans. Even so, it was very good fortune, Colum thought, that he'd managed to convince Scarlett to come. Her petticoats were much better for hiding guns than the dozens of American boots and calicoes he'd bought. And she might even loosen her purse strings a bit when she saw the poverty of her own people. He didn't have high hopes; Colum was a realist, and he'd gotten Scarlett's measure from the first. He did not like her less because she was so unthinkingly self-centered. He was a priest, and human frailty was forgivable—so long as the humans were not English. In fact, even when he was manipulating Scarlett, he was fond of her, just as he was fond of all the O'Hara children.

Kathleen held tight to the ship's rail. I'd jump over and swim did I not anchor myself, she thought, I'm that happy to be nearing Ireland, I know I'd be faster than the ship. Home. Home. Home . . .

Scarlett drew in her breath with a tiny squeaking noise. There was a castle on that little low island. A castle! It couldn't be anything else, it had tooth-like things on top. What matter that it was half-fallen-down. It was really, truly a castle, just like pictures in a child's book. She could hardly wait to discover what this Ireland was like.

When Colum escorted her down the gangplank she realized that she had entered a completely different world. The docks were busy, like the docks in Savannah, noisy, crowded, perilous with hurrying wagons and laden men loading or unloading barrels and crates and bales. But the men were all white, and they shouted to one another in a tongue that had no meaning for her.

"It's the Gaelic, the old Irish language," Colum explained, "but you needn't fret, Scarlett darling. The Gaelic's hardly known anyplace in Ireland any more save here in the west. Everyone speaks English; you'll have no trouble."

As if to prove him wrong, a man spoke to him with an accent so pronounced that Scarlett didn't realize at first that he was speaking English.

Colum laughed when she told him. "It's a queer sound, and that's the truth of it," he agreed, "but it's English for sure. English the way the English speak it, all up in their noses like they're strangling from it. That was a sergeant of Her Majesty's Army."

Scarlett giggled. "I thought he was a button salesman." The sergeant's elaborately decorated short, tight uniform jacket was fronted with more than a dozen bars of thick gold braid between pairs of brightly polished brass buttons. It looked like fancy dress to her.

She tucked her hand in Colum's elbow. "I'm awfully glad I came," she said. And she was. Everything was so different, so new. No wonder people liked to travel so much.

"Our baggages will be brought to the hotel," Colum said when he returned to the bench where he'd left Scarlett and Kathleen. "It's all arranged. Then tomorrow we'll be on our way to Mullingar and home."

"I wish we could go right now," Scarlett said hopefully. "It's early yet, barely noon."

"But the train left at eight, Scarlett darling. The hotel's a fine one, with a good kitchen, too."

"I remember," Kathleen said. "This time I'll do all those fancy sweets justice." She was radiant with happiness, hardly recognizable as the girl Scarlett had known in Savannah. "Coming the other way I was too sorrowful to put food in my mouth. Oh, Scarlett, you can't know what it is to me to have the Irish ground under my feet. I feel like getting on my knees to kiss it."

"Come along, the two of you," Colum said. "We'll have competition getting a hackney, today being Saturday and Market Day."

" 'Market Day?' " Scarlett echoed.

Kathleen clapped her hands. "Market Day in a big city like Galway! Oh, Colum, it should be something grand."

It was beyond imagination, "grand" and exciting and foreign to Scarlett. The entire grass-covered square in front of the Railway Hotel was teeming with life, alive with color. When the hackney set them down on the hotel steps, she begged Colum to join in at once, never mind seeing their rooms or eating dinner. Kathleen echoed her. "There's food aplenty at the stalls, Colum, and I want to take some stockings home to gift the girls. There's none like them in America, or I would have them bought already. Brigid's fair pining away for want of some, I know it."

Colum grinned. "And Kathleen O'Hara's pining a bit herself, I wouldn't be amazed. All right, then. I'll see to the rooms. You see to Cousin Scarlett so she doesn't get lost. Have you any money?"

"A fistful, Colum. Jamie gave it me."

"That's American money, Kathleen. You can't spend it here."

Scarlett grabbed Colum's arm in panic. What did he mean? Wasn't her money any good over here?

"It's not the same kind, is all, Scarlett darling. You'll find English money much more diverting. I'll do the exchanging for all of us. What would you like?"

"I have all my winnings from whist. In greenbacks." She said the word with contempt and anger. Everybody knew that greenbacks weren't worth the numbers written on them. She should have made the losers pay her in silver or gold. She opened her purse and took out the folded wad of five and ten and one dollar bills. "Change these if you can," she said, handing the money to Colum. His eyebrows rose.

"So much? I'm glad you never asked me to play cards with you, Scarlett darling. You must have almost two hundred dollars here."

"Two forty-seven."

"Look at this, Kathleen mavourneen. You'll never see such a fortune in one place again. Would you like to hold it?"

"Oh, no, I wouldn't dare." She backed away, her hands behind her back, her wide eyes fixed on Scarlett.

You'd think I was green instead of the money, Scarlett thought uncomfortably. Two hundred wasn't all that much. She'd paid practically that for her furs. Surely Jamie must clear at least two hundred a month in the store. There was no need for Kathleen to carry on so.

"Here." Colum was holding out his hand. "Here's a few shillings for each of you. You can shop a bit while I do the banking, then meet me at that pie stall for a bite." He pointed toward a fluttering yellow flag in the center of the busy square.

Scarlett's eyes followed the direction of his finger and her heart sank. The street between the hotel steps and the square was filling with slowly moving cattle. She couldn't get across it!

"I'll manage for the both of us," Kathleen said. "Here's my dollars, Colum. Come on, Scarlett, take my hand."

The shy girl Scarlett had known in Savannah was gone. Kathleen was home. Her cheeks were glowing, and her eyes. And her smile was as bright as the sun overhead.

Scarlett tried to make an excuse, to protest, but Kathleen was having none of it. She pushed through the herd of cows pulling Scarlett behind her. In seconds they were on the grass of the square. Scarlett had no time to scream with fear in the midst of the cows or to scream out her anger at Kathleen. And once in the square, she was too fascinated to remember either fear or anger. She'd loved the markets in Charleston and Savannah for their busyness and color and array of produce. But they were nothing in comparison with Market Day in Galway.

There was something going on everywhere she looked. Men and women were bargaining, buying, selling, arguing, laughing, praising, criticizing, conferring—over sheep, chickens, roosters, eggs, cows, pigs, butter, cream, goats, donkeys. "How darling," Scarlett said when she saw the baskets of squealing pink piglets ... the tiny furry donkeys with their long, pink-lined ears ... and—over and over again—the colorful clothes worn by the dozens of young women and girls. When she saw the first one, she thought the girl must be in costume; then she saw another, and another, and yet another, until she realized they were almost all dressed the same. No wonder Kathleen had been talking about stockings! Everywhere Scarlett looked she saw ankles and legs in bright stripes of blue and yellow, red and white, yellow and red, white and blue. The Galway girls wore low-cut, low-heeled black leather shoes, not boots, and their skirts were four to six inches above their ankles. What skirts, too! Full, swinging, bright as the stockings in solid reds or blues or greens or yellows. Their shirtwaists were darker shades, but still colorful, with long buttoned sleeves and crisp white linen fichus folded and pinned over the front.

"I want some stockings, too, Kathleen! And one of the skirts. And a shirtwaist and kerchief. I've got to have them. They're lovely!"

Kathleen smiled with pleasure. "You like Irish clothes, then, Scarlett? I'm so glad. Your things are so elegant I thought you'd laugh at ours."

"I wish I could dress like that every day. Is that what you wear when you're home? You lucky girl, no wonder you wanted to come back."

"These are best dressing, for Market Day and to catch the eyes of the lads. I'll show you everyday things, too. Come." Kathleen caught Scarlett by the wrist again and led her through the masses of people just as she'd led her through the cows. Near the square's center there were tables—boards across trestles—piled with finery for women. Scarlett goggled. She wanted to buy everything she saw. Look at all the stockings . . . and wonderful shawls, so soft to the touch . . . goodness gracious, what lace! Why, my dressmaker in Atlanta would practically sell her soul to get her hands on rich heavy lace like that. There they were, the skirts! Oh, the darlings, how wonderful she'd look in that shade of red—and the blue, too. But wait—there was another blue on that next table, a darker one. Which was best? Oh, and lighter reds over there—

She felt giddy from the lavishness of choice. She had to touch them all—the wool was so soft, thick, alive with warmth and color under her gloved hand. Quickly, carelessly, she stripped off a glove so she could feel the woven wools. It was like no fabric she'd ever touched.

"I've been waiting by the pies, with water filling my mouth from hunger," said Colum. He put his hand on her arm. "Don't fret, now, you can come back, Scarlett darling." He lifted his hat and nodded to the black-clad women behind the tables. "May the sun shine forever on your fine work," he said. "I ask your pardon for my American cousin here. She lost her tongue in admiration. I'm going to feed her now and, please Saint Brigid, she'll be able to talk to you when she returns." The women grinned at Colum, stole another sideways glance at Scarlett, said "Thank you, Father," as Colum hauled her away.

"Kathleen told me you'd gone completely daft," he said with a chuckle. "She plucked at your sleeve a dozen times, poor girl, but devil a look you'd give her."

"I forgot all about her," Scarlett admitted. "I've never seen so many wonderful things all at once. I figured I'd buy a costume for a party. But I don't know if I can wait to wear it. Tell me the truth, Colum, do you think it would be all right if I dressed like the Irish girls while I'm here?"

"I don't believe you should do other, Scarlett darling."

"What fun! What a lovely vacation, Colum. I'm so glad I came."
"So are we all, Cousin Scarlett."

She didn't understand the English money at all. The pound was paper and weighed less than an ounce. The penny was huge, big as a silver dollar, and the thing called a tuppence, which meant two pennies, was smaller than the one penny. Then there were coins called half pennies and others called shillings . . . It was all too confusing. Besides, it didn't really matter, it was all free, from whist winnings. The only thing that counted was that the skirts cost two of the shilling things, the shoes were one. The stockings were only pennies. Scarlett gave the drawstring bag of coins to Kathleen. "Make me stop before I run out," she said, and she began to shop.

All three of them were loaded down when they went to the hotel. Scarlett had bought skirts in every color and every weight—the thinner ones were also worn for petticoats, Kathleen told her—and dozens of stockings—for herself, for Kathleen, for Brigid, for all the other cousins she was going to meet. She had shirts, too, and yards and yards of lace, wide and narrow and made into collars and fichus and cunning little caps. There was a long blue cape with a hood, plus a red one because she couldn't make up her mind, plus a black one because Kathleen said most people wore black for every day, and a black skirt for the same reason, which could have colored petticoats underneath. Linen fichus and linen shirt-waists and linen petticoats—all like no linen she'd ever seen—and six dozen linen handkerchiefs. Stacks of shawls; she'd lost count.

"I'm worn out," Scarlett groaned happily when she dropped down onto the plush settee in the living room of their suite. Kathleen dropped the money bag into her lap. It was still more than half full. "My grief," said Scarlett, "I'm really going to love Ireland!"

48

$\mathcal{S}$carlett was entranced with her bright "costumes." She tried to wheedle Kathleen into "dressing up" with her and returning to the square, but the girl was politely adamant in her refusal. "We'll be eating dinner late, Scarlett, according to the English custom of the hotel, and we've an early start to make tomorrow. There are lots of market days; we have one every week in the town near our village."

"But not like Galway's, judging from what you said," Scarlett noted suspiciously. Kathleen admitted that the town of Trim was much, much smaller. Nonetheless, she didn't want to go back to the square. Scarlett grudgingly stopped nagging.

The dining room of the Railway Hotel was known for its fine food and service. Two liveried waiters seated Kathleen and Scarlett at a large table beside a tall, much-curtained window, then stood behind their chairs to serve them. Colum had to make do with the tail-coated waiter in charge of the table. The O'Haras ordered a dinner of six courses, and Scarlett was thoroughly enjoying a delicately sauced cutlet of Galway's famous salmon when she heard music from the square. She pulled back the heavily fringed draperies, the silk curtain beneath them, and the thick lace panel beneath that. "I knew it!" she announced. "I knew we should have gone back. They're dancing in the square. Let's go right this minute."

"Scarlett, darling, we've only begun to have dinner," Colum argued.

"Fiddle-dee-dee! We all ate ourselves practically sick on the ship; the last thing we need is another endless dinner. I want to put on my costume and dance."

Nothing would dissuade her.

"I'm not understanding you at all, Colum," Kathleen said. The two of them were on one of the square's benches near the dancing, in case Scarlett got into any trouble. Wearing a blue skirt over red and yellow petticoats, she was dancing the reel as if she'd been born to it.

"What is it you don't understand, then?"

"Why are we staying at this fine English hotel, like kings and queens, at all? And if we're doing it, why could we not eat our fancy dinner? It's the last we'll have, I know that. Couldn't you say to Scarlett, 'No, we'll not go,' as I did?"

Colum took her hand in his. "The way of it is this, my little sister, Scarlett is not yet ready for the truth of Ireland, or the O'Haras in it. I hope to make it easier for her. Better she should see wearing Irish garb as a merry adventure than weeping when she learns that her fancy silk trains will get covered with muck. She's meeting Irish people out there in the reel and finding them pleasing, for all their rough garments and dirty hands. It's a grand event, though I'd rather be sleeping."

"But we go home tomorrow, do we not?" Kathleen's longing throbbed in the question.

Colum squeezed her hand. "We go home tomorrow, that I promise you. We'll be in a first class carriage on the train, though, and you mustn't remark it. Also, I'm putting Scarlett to stay with Molly and Robert, and you're not to say a word."

Kathleen spit on the ground. "That for Molly and her Robert. But so long as it's Scarlett with them and not me, I'm willing to keep my tongue."

Colum frowned, but not at his sister. Scarlett's current dancing partner was trying to embrace her. Colum had no way of knowing that Scarlett had been an expert since she was fifteen at inciting men's attentions and escaping them. He stood up quickly and moved toward the dancing. Before he got there, Scarlett had slipped away from her admirer. She ran to Colum. "Have you come to dance with me at last?"

He took her outstretched hands. "I've come to take you away. It's past time to be sleeping."

Scarlett sighed. Her flushed face looked bright red under the pink paper lantern hanging over her head. Throughout the square brightly colored lights swung from the branches of tall, wide-crowned trees. With the fiddles playing and the thick crowd laughing and calling as they danced, she hadn't heard exactly what Colum said, but his meaning was clear.

She knew he was right, too, but she hated to stop dancing. She had never known such intoxicating freedom before, not even on Saint Patrick's Day. Her Irish costume was not made to wear with stays, and Kathleen had laced her only enough to keep her corset from falling down to her knees. She could dance forever and never get short of breath. It felt like she wasn't held in at all, not in any way.

Colum looked tired, in spite of the pink glow of the lamp. Scarlett smiled and nodded. There would be plenty more dancing. She'd be in Ireland for two weeks, until after her grandmother celebrated her hundredth birthday. The original Katie Scarlett. I wouldn't miss that party for all the world!

This makes much more sense than our trains at home, Scarlett thought when she saw all the open doors to the individual compartments. How nice to have your own little room instead of sitting in a car with a bunch of strangers. No walking forever in the aisle, either, getting on and off, or people half-falling in your lap when they walked past your seat. She smiled happily at Colum and Kathleen. "I love your Irish trains. I love everything about Ireland." She settled comfortably in the deep seat, eager to pull out of the station so she could look at the countryside. It was bound to be different from America.

Ireland didn't disappoint her. "My stars, Colum," she said after they'd been travelling for an hour, "this country's positively peppered with castles! There's one on practically every hill, and more in the flat country, too. Why are they all falling down? Why don't people live in them?"

"They're very old, for the most part, Scarlett darling, four hundred years or more. People found more comfortable ways to live."

She nodded. That made sense. There must have been a lot of running up and down stairs in the towers. Still, they were awfully romantic. She pressed her nose to the window again. "Oh," she said, "what a shame. My castle watching's over. It's starting to rain."

"It will stop," Colum promised.

As it did, before they reached the next station.

"Ballinasloe," Scarlett read the name aloud. "What beautiful names your towns have. What's the name of the place the O'Haras live?"

"Adamstown," Colum replied. He laughed at the expression on Scarlett's face. "No, it's not very Irish. I'd change it for you if I could, I'd change it for all of us if I could. But the owner's English, and he'd not like it."

"Somebody owns the whole town?"

"It's not a town, that's just the English bragging. It's hardly even a village. It was named for the son of the Englishman who first built it, a small gift for Adam, the estate was. It's been inherited since then by his son and grandson and so on. The one that has it now never sees it. He lives mostly in London. It's his agent who manages things."

There was a bite of bitterness in Colum's words. Scarlett decided she'd better not ask questions. She contented herself with looking for castles.

Just as the train began to slow for the next station she saw an enormous one that hadn't crumbled at all. Surely somebody lived there! A knight? A prince? Far from it, said Colum; it was a military barracks for a regiment of the British Army.

Oh, I've put my foot in it this time for sure, thought Scarlett. Kathleen's cheeks were flaming. "I'll get us some tea," Colum said when the train stopped. He pulled the window down from the top and leaned out. Kathleen stared at the floor. Scarlett stood next to Colum. It felt good to straighten her knees. "Sit down, Scarlett," he said firmly. She sat. But she could still see the groups of smartly uniformed men on the platform, and the shake of Colum's head when he was asked if any seats were vacant in the compartment. What a cool customer he was. No one could see past him because his shoulders filled the window, and there were three large empty seats going begging. She'd have to remember that next time she rode an Irish train, just in case Colum wasn't with her.

He handed in mugs of tea and a lumpy folded cloth just as the train began to move. "Try an Irish specialty," he said, smiling now, "it's called barm brack." The rough linen cloth held great slabs of delicious, fruit-filled light bread. Scarlett ate Kathleen's, too, and asked Colum if he could get some more for her when they stopped at the next station.

"Can you stay hungry another half hour or so? We'll be getting off the train then and we can have a proper meal." Scarlett was delighted to agree. The novelty of the train and the castle-peppered views had begun to wear off. She was ready to get wherever it was they were going.

But the station sign said "Mullingar," not "Adamstown." Poor lamb, Colum said, hadn't he told her? They could only go part way on the train. After they ate their dinner, they'd make the rest of the journey by road. It was only twenty miles or so; they'd be home before dark.

Twenty miles! Why, that was as far as from Atlanta to Jonesboro. It would take ages, and they'd already been on the train for practically six hours. It took all her will to smile pleasantly when Colum introduced his friend Jim Daly. Daly wasn't even good-looking. His wagon was, however. It had tall wheels painted bright red and glossy blue sides with J. DALY on them in bold gilt. Whatever business he's in, thought Scarlett, he's doing well at it.

Jim Daly's business was a bar and brewery. Even though she was landlord to a saloon, Scarlett had never been in it; it made her feel pleasantly wicked to be entering the malty-smelling large room. She looked curiously at the long, polished oak bar, but she had no time to take in the details before Daly opened another door and ushered her through it into a hallway. The O'Haras were having dinner with him and his family in their private quarters above the public house.

It was a good dinner, but she might just as well have been in Savannah. There was nothing strange or foreign about leg of lamb with mint sauce and mashed potatoes. And all the talk was about the Savannah O'Haras, their health and their doings. Jim Daly's mother, it turned out, was another O'Hara cousin. Scarlett couldn't tell that she was in Ireland at all, much less right upstairs over a saloon. No one of the Dalys seemed very interested in her opinion about anything, either. They were all too busy talking among themselves.

Things improved after dinner. Jim Daly insisted on taking her on his arm for a walk to see the sights of Mullingar. Colum and Kathleen followed them. Not that there's all that much to see, Scarlett thought. It's a pokey little town, just one street and five times as many bars as shops, but it does feel good to stretch my legs. The town square wasn't half the size of Galway's, and nothing was happening in it at all. A young woman with a black shawl over her head and breast came up to them with one cupped hand held forward. "God bless you, sir and lady," she whined. Jim dropped a few coins into her hand, and she repeated the blessing while she curtseyed. Scarlett was appalled. Why, that girl was begging, bold as brass! She certainly wouldn't have given her anything; there wasn't any reason the girl couldn't go out and work for a living, she looked healthy enough.

There was an outburst of laughter, and Scarlett turned to see what caused it. A group of soldiers had entered the square from a side street. One of them was teasing the begging woman by holding a coin out to her, higher than she could reach. Brute! But what can she expect, if she's going to make a spectacle of herself, begging on a public street. And from soldiers, too. Anybody would know that they'd be coarse and rude ... Although, she had to admit, you could hardly credit that bunch as soldiers. They looked more like big toys for a little boy in those silly fancy uniforms. Obviously they did no more soldiering than marching in parades on holidays. Thank heavens there weren't any real soldiers in Ireland, like the Yankees. No snakes and no Yankees.

The soldier threw the coin into a filthy, scum-coated puddle and laughed again with his friends. Scarlett saw Kathleen's two hands grab Colum's arm. He pulled away and walked over to the soldiers and the beggar. Oh, Lord, what if he started lecturing them about being good Christians? Colum pushed up his sleeve, and she caught her breath. He looks so much like Pa! Is he going to wade in fighting?

Colum knelt on the cobbled square and fished the coin out of the noisome puddle. Scarlett let her breath out in a slow, relieved hiss. She wouldn't for a minute worry about Colum holding his own against one of those sissy-britches soldiers, but five might just be too much even for an O'Hara. What did he have to make such a fuss over a beggarwoman's problems for, anyhow?

Colum stood, his back turned to the soldiers. They were visibly uncomfortable at the turn their joke had taken. When Colum took the woman's arm and led her away, they turned in the opposite direction and walked quickly to the next corner.

Well, that's that and no harm done, thought Scarlett. Except to the knees of Colum's breeches. I suppose they get plenty of wear and tear anyhow, him being a priest and all. Funny, I forget that most of the time. If Kathleen hadn't dragged me out of bed at dawn I wouldn't have remembered we had to go to Mass before we took the train.

The balance of the town tour was very brief. There were no boats to be seen on the Royal Canal, and Scarlett wasn't interested in the slightest by Jim Daly's enthusiasm for travelling to Dublin that way instead of by train. Why should she care about getting to Dublin? She wanted to be on the way to Adamstown.

Before long she got her wish. There was a small, shabby carriage outside Jim Daly's bar when they got back. An aproned man in shirtsleeves was loading their trunks on the top of it; the valises were already strapped on the back. If Scarlett's trunk weighed much less now than it had at the depot when Jim Daly and Colum put it in Daly's wagon, no one mentioned it. When the trunks were secure, the shirtsleeved man disappeared into the bar. He returned wearing a coachman's caped coat and top hat. "Name's Jim, too," he said briefly. "Let's be going." Scarlett stepped up and took a seat on the far side. Kathleen sat beside her, Colum opposite. "May God travel your road with you," called the Dalys. Scarlett and Kathleen waved their handkerchiefs out the window. Colum unbuttoned his coat and took off his hat.

"I cannot speak for anyone else here, but I'm going to try to sleep a bit," he said. "I hope you ladies will excuse my feet." He removed his boots and stretched out, his stockinged feet on the seat between Scarlett and Kathleen.

They looked at each other, then bent to unlace their boots. Within minutes they, too, were settled with their hatless heads resting against the corners of the carriage and their feet flanking Colum. Oh, if only I had on my Galway costume, I'd be as snug as a bug, Scarlett thought. One gold-filled corset stay was stabbing her in the ribs no matter how she arranged herself. Nevertheless she drifted quickly and easily into sleep.

She woke once when rain began to spatter on the window, but soon the soft sound of it lulled her back to sleep. The next time she woke the sun was shining. "Are we there?" she asked sleepily.

"No, we've a way to go yet," Colum replied. Scarlett looked out and clapped her hands at what she saw. "Oh, look at all the flowers! I could reach out and pick one. Colum, open the window, do. I'll get a bouquet."

"We'll open it when we stop. The wheels stir up too much dust."

"But I want some of those flowers."

"'Tis only a hedgerow, Scarlett darling. You'll have the same all the way home."

"This side, too, you see," Kathleen said. It was true, Scarlett saw. The unknown vine and its bright pink flowers were barely an arm's length away from Kathleen, too. What a wonderful way to travel with walls of flowers on both sides of you. When Colum's eyes closed, she slowly let the window down.

49

*W*e'll be reaching Ratharney soon," Colum said, "then a few more miles and we're in County Meath."

Kathleen sighed happily. Scarlett's eyes sparkled. County Meath. Pa talked like it was paradise, and I guess I can see why. She sniffed the sweet afternoon through the open window, a blend of faint perfume from the pink flowers, a rich country smell of sun-warmed grass from the invisible fields beyond the thick hedgerows, and a pungent herbal tang from within the hedgerows themselves. If only he could be here with me, it would be perfect. I'll just have to enjoy it twice as much, for him as well as me. She inhaled deeply and caught a hint of the freshness of water in the air. "I think it's going to rain again," she said.

"It won't last," Colum promised, "and everything will smell the sweeter when it's past."

Ratharney came and went so quickly that Scarlett hardly saw anything. One minute there was the hedgerow, then it was gone and solid wall was in its place and she was looking through the carriage window and another open window the same size with a face in it looking out at her. She was still trying to get over the shock of the stranger's eyes appearing from nowhere when the carriage rattled past the last of the row of buildings and the hedgerow was back again. They had not even slowed their pace.

It slowed very soon. The road had begun to wind in sharp short bends. Scarlett had her head halfway through the window, trying to look at the road ahead. "Are we in County Meath yet, Colum?"

"Very soon."

They passed a tiny cottage, moving at hardly more than a walk, so Scarlett had a good look. She smiled and waved at the red-haired little girl who was standing inside the door. The child smiled in return. Her front milk teeth were gone, and the gap gave her smile a special charm. Everything about the cottage charmed Scarlett. It was made of stone and the walls were bright white with small square windows, their frames painted red. The door was red also and divided in half, with the top half open into the house. The child's head reached barely above the half door; beyond it Scarlett could see a brightly burning fire in a shadowy room. Best of all the cottage was topped by a straw roof, and the roof made scallops where it met the house. It was like a picture from a fairy tale. She turned to smile at Colum. "If that little girl had blond hair, I'd expect to see the three bears any minute."

She could tell from Colum's expression that he didn't know what she was talking about. "Goldilocks, silly!" He shook his head. "My grief, Colum, it's a fairy tale. Don't you have fairy tales in Ireland?"

Kathleen began to laugh.

Colum grinned. "Scarlett darling," he said, "I don't know about your fairy tales or your bears, but if it's fairies you're wanting, sure you've come to the right place. Ireland is teeming with fairies."

"Colum, be serious."

"But I am serious. And you'll have to learn about the fairies or you might get in fearful trouble. Most of them, mind you, are no more than a small nuisance, and there are those, like the shoemaker leprechaun that every man would like to have a meeting with—"

The carriage had stopped suddenly. Colum put his head out the window. When he was back inside, he was no longer smiling. He reached across Scarlett and seized the leather strap that moved the window. With a rapid pull, he raised the glass. "Sit very still and don't speak to anyone," he said in a harsh undertone. "Keep her still, Kathleen." He thrust his feet into his boots and his fingers were quick with the lacing.

"What is it?" Scarlett asked.

"Hush," said Kathleen.

Colum opened the door, grabbed his hat, stepped down into the road and closed the door. His face was like gray stone as he walked away.

"Kathleen?"

"Hush. It's important, Scarlett. Be quiet."

There was a dull reverberating thudding sound, and the leather walls of the carriage vibrated. Even through the closed windows Scarlett and Kathleen could hear the loud clipped words shouted by a man somewhere in front of them. "You! Driver! Move along. This is no entertainment for you to gawp at. And you! Priest! Get back in your box and out of here." Kathleen's hand closed around Scarlett's.

The carriage rocked on its springs and moved slowly toward the right side of the narrow road. The stiff branches and thorns of the hedgerow tore at the thick leather. Kathleen moved away from the rasp on the window and closer to Scarlett. There was another thud, and both of them jerked. Scarlett's hand tightened on Kathleen's. What was going on?

As the carriage edged along, they came upon another cottage, identical to the one Scarlett had thought idyllic for Goldilocks. Standing in the fully open door was a black-uniformed, gold-braid-trimmed soldier who was placing two small, three-legged stools atop a table outside the door. To the left of the door there was a uniformed officer on a skittish bay horse, and to the right of it was Colum. He was talking quietly to a small weeping woman. Her black shawl had slipped from her head, and her red hair was straggling over her shoulders and cheeks. She held a baby in her arms; Scarlett could see its blue eyes and the russet down on its round head. A little girl who might have been the twin of the smiling child at the half-door was sobbing into the mother's apron. Both mother and child were bare-footed. A straggle of soldiers stood in the center of the road near a huge tripod of tree trunks. A fourth trunk hung, swaying, from ropes attached to the tripod's apex.

"Move on, Paddy," the officer shouted. The carriage creaked and tore along the hedgerow. Scarlett could feel Kathleen trembling. Something terrible was happening here. *That poor woman, she looks like she's about to faint . . . or go stark crazy. I hope Colum can help her.*

The woman dropped to her knees. *My Lord, she's fainting, she'll drop the baby!* Scarlett reached for the door-latch, and Kathleen grabbed her arm. "Kathleen, let me—"

"Quiet. For the love of God, quiet." The desperate urgency in Kathleen's whisper made Scarlett stop.

What on earth? Scarlett watched, disbelieving her own eyes. The weeping mother was clutching Colum's hand, kissing it. Above her head he made the sign of the cross. Then he raised her to her feet. He touched the head of the baby, and of the little girl, and with his two hands on her shoulders he turned the mother to face away from her cottage.

The carriage moved on, slowly, and the dull, heavy thudding began again, behind them. They began to move away from the hedgerow, into the road, then into the center of it. "Driver, stop!" Scarlett shouted before Kathleen could stop her. They were leaving Colum behind, and she couldn't allow that to happen.

"Don't, Scarlett, don't," Kathleen begged, but Scarlett had the door open even before the carriage ceased moving. She scrambled down to the road and ran back toward the noise, oblivious of her fashionable trailing skirts dragging through the thin mud.

The sight and sound that met her eyes and ears halted her, and she cried out in shocked protest. The swinging tree trunk battered the cottage walls again, and its front collapsed inward, shattering windows, showering bright bits of clean, polished glass. Red window frames fell into the dust raised by the tumbling white stones, and the two-part red door folded upon itself. The noise was horrendous—grinding ... crashing ... shrieking like a live thing.

For a moment, then, silence followed, and then another sound—a crackling that became a roar—and the thick, smothering smell of smoke. Scarlett saw the torches in the hands of three soldiers, the flames that were eating hungrily into the straw thatch of the roof. She thought of Sherman's Army, of the scorched walls and chimneys of Twelve Oaks, of Dunmore Landing, and she moaned with grief and with terror. Where was Colum? Oh, dear heaven, what had happened to him?

His dark-suited form stepped hurriedly from the dark smoke that was billowing across the road. "Move on," he shouted to Scarlett. "Back to the carriage."

Before she could break the trance of horror that held her fixed in place, Colum was beside her, his hand clasping her arm. "Come along, Scarlett darling, don't tarry," he said with controlled urgency. "We must be going home now."

The carriage lurched off with all the speed the horses could manage on the winding road. Scarlett was tossed from side to side between the closed window and Kathleen, but she barely noticed. She was still shaking from the strange and terrible experience. It was only when the carriage slowed to a quietly creaking movement that her heart stopped pounding and she could catch her breath.

"What was going on back there?" she asked. Her voice sounded odd to her.

"The poor woman was being evicted," said Kathleen sharply, "and Colum was comforting her. You shouldn't have interfered like that, Scarlett. You might have caused trouble for us all."

"Softly, now, Kathleen, you mustn't be scolding so," Colum said. "There was no way for Scarlett to know, being from America."

Scarlett wanted to protest that she knew worse, much worse, but she stopped herself. She wanted more urgently to understand. "Why was she being evicted?" she asked instead.

"They didn't have the rent money," Colum explained. "And the worst of it is, her husband tried to stop the process when the militia came the first time. He hit a soldier, and they took him off to jail, leaving her with the little ones and afraid for him besides."

"That's sad. She looked so pitiful. What will she do, Colum?"

"She's a sister in a cottage along the road, not too far. I sent her there."

Scarlett relaxed somewhat. It was pitiful. The poor woman was so distraught. Still, she'd be all right. Her sister must be in the Goldilocks cottage, and that wasn't far. And, after all, people really did have an obligation to pay their rent. She'd find a new saloonkeeper in nothing flat if her tenant tried to hold out on her. As for the husband hitting the soldier, that was just unforgivable. He must have known he'd go to jail for it. He should have given some mind to his wife before he did such a stupid thing.

"But why did they destroy the house?"

"To keep the tenants from going back to live in it."

Scarlett said the first thing that came into her head. "How silly! The owner could have rented it to somebody else."

Colum looked tired. "He doesn't want to rent it at all. There's a little piece of land goes with it, and he's doing the thing they call 'organizing' his property. He'll put it all in grazing and send the fattened cattle to market. That's why he raised all the rents past paying. He's no longer interested in farming the land. The husband knew it was coming; they all know once it starts. They've got months of waiting before they've got nothing left to sell to raise the rent money. It's those months that build up the anger in a man and make him try to win with his fists . . . For the women, it's despair that tears at them, seeing their man's defeat. That poor creature with her babe on her breast was trying to put her little body and bones between the ram and her man's cottage. It was all he had to make him feel like a man."

Scarlett couldn't think of anything to say. She'd had no idea things like that could happen. It was so mean. The Yankees were worse, but that had been war. Not destruction so that a bunch of cows could have more grass. The poor woman. Why, that could have been Maureen holding Jacky when he was a baby. "Are you sure she'll go to her sister's?"

"She agreed to it, and she's not the kind to lie to a priest."

"She'll be all right, then, won't she?"

Colum smiled. "Don't worry, Scarlett darling. She'll be all right."

"Until the sister's farm is organized." Kathleen's voice was hoarse. Rain spattered, then poured down the windows. Water sheeted the inside of the carriage near Kathleen's head, gushing through a rip torn by the hedgerow. "Will you give me your big handkerchief, then, Colum, to stuff this peephole with?" Kathleen said with a laugh. "And will you say a priestly prayer for the sun to return?"

How could she be so cheerful after all that and with that huge leak on top of everything else? And, for goodness sake, Colum was actually laughing with her.

The carriage was going faster, much faster. The driver must be crazy. Nobody could possibly see through a downpour like this, and the road was so narrow, too, and full of curves. They'd tear ten thousand leaks open.

"Do you not feel the eagerness coming over Jim Daly's grand horses, Scarlett darling? They think they're on a race course. But I know a racing stretch like this could only be found in County Meath. We're nearing home for sure. I'd better tell you about the little people before you meet a leprechaun and don't know who you're talking to."

Suddenly there was sunlight slanting low through the rain-wet windows, turning drops of water into shards of rainbow. There's something unnatural about rain one minute and sun the next and then rain again, Scarlett thought. She looked away from the rainbows, toward Colum.

"You saw the mockery of them in Savannah's parade," Colum began, "and I tell you it's a good thing for all who saw it that there are no leprechauns in America, because their wrath would have been terrible and would have called in all their fairy kinfolk for taking the revenge. In Ireland, however, where they're given proper respect, they bother no one if no one bothers them. They find a pleasant spot and settle themselves there to ply their trade of cobbler. Not as a group, mind you, for the leprechaun is a solitary, but one in one place, another in another, and so on until—if you listen to enough tales—you could come to count on finding one by every stream and stone in the country. You know he's there by the tap-tap-tap of his hammer tacking on the sole and heel of the shoe. Then, if you creep as quiet as a caterpillar, you may catch him unaware. Some say you must hold him in your grip by an arm or an ankle, but for the most part there's general agreement that fixing your gaze on him is sufficient for the capture.

"He'll beg you to let him go, but you must refuse. He'll promise you your heart's desire, but he's notorious for lying, and you must not believe him. He'll threaten some great woe, but he cannot harm you, so you disdain his blustering. And in the end he'll be forced to buy his freedom with the treasure he has concealed in a safe hidden spot nearby.

"Such a treasure it is, too. A crock of gold, not looking like much, perhaps, to the uneducated eye, but the crock is made with great and deceptive leprechaun cunning, and there's no bottom to it, so you may take out and take out gold to the end of your days, and there'll always be more.

"All this he'll give, just to be set free; he likes not company so much. Solitary is his nature, at any cost. But fearful cunning is his nature, too, so much so that he outwits almost all who capture him by distracting the attention. And if your grip eases, or your eye looks away, he's gone in an instant, and you're none the richer save for a story to tell of your adventure."

"It doesn't sound hard to me for a person to hold on or keep staring if it means getting the treasure," Scarlett said. "That story doesn't make sense."

Colum laughed. "Practical and businesslike Scarlett darling, you're just the sort the little people delight in tricking. They can count on doing what they like because you'd never credit them as the cause. If you were strolling through a lane and heard a tapping, you'd never bother to stop and look."

"I would so, if I believed that kind of nonsense."

"There you are, then. You don't believe and you wouldn't stop."

"Fiddle-dee-dee, Colum! I see what you're doing. You're putting the fault on me for not catching something that's not there in the first place." She was beginning to get angry. Word games and mind games were too slippery, and they served no purpose.

She didn't notice that Colum had turned her attention away from the eviction.

"Have you told Scarlett about Molly, yet, Colum?" Kathleen asked. "She has a right to a warning, I would say."

Scarlett forgot all about leprechauns. She understood gossip, and relished it. "Who's Molly?"

"She's the first of the Adamstown O'Haras you'll meet," said Colum, "and a sister to Kathleen and me."

"Half sister," Kathleen corrected, "and that's a half too much, by my thinking."

"Tell," Scarlett encouraged.

The telling took so long that the trip was almost over when it was done, but Scarlett wasn't conscious of the time or the miles going by. She was hearing about her own family.

Colum and Kathleen were also half brother and sister, she learned. Their father, Patrick—who was one of Gerald O'Hara's older brothers— had married three times. The children by his first wife included Jamie, who'd gone to Savannah, and Molly, who was, said Colum, a great beauty.

When she was young, maybe, according to Kathleen.

After his first wife died, Patrick married his second wife, Colum's mother; and, after her death, he married Kathleen's mother, who was also the mother of Stephen.

The silent one, Scarlett commented silently.

There were ten O'Hara cousins for her to meet in Adamstown, some with children and even grandchildren of their own. Patrick, God rest his soul, was dead these fifteen years, come November 11.

In addition there was her uncle Daniel, who was still living, and his children and grandchildren. Of them, Matt and Gerald were in Savannah, but six had stayed in Ireland.

"I'll never get them all straight," Scarlett said with apprehension. She still got some of the O'Hara children in Savannah confused.

"Colum's starting you out easy," Kathleen said. "Molly's house has no O'Haras in it at all, save her, and she'd just as soon deny her own name."

Colum, with Kathleen's acid commentary, explained about Molly. She was married to a man named Robert Donahue, a "warm" man in material terms, with a prosperous big farm of a hundred and some acres. He was what the Irish called a "strong farmer." Molly had first worked in the Donahue kitchen as a cook. When Donahue's wife died, Molly became, after a suitable time of mourning, his second wife, and stepmother to his four children. There were five children of this second marriage—the eldest of them very big and healthy for all that he was nearly three months early—but they were all grown now and gone to homes of their own.

Molly was not devoted to her O'Hara kinfolk, Colum said neutrally, and Kathleen snorted, but that was perhaps because her husband was their landlord. Robert Donahue rented acreage in addition to his own farm; he sublet a smaller farm to the O'Haras.

Colum began to enumerate and name Robert's children and grandchildren, but by this time Scarlett had already started dismissing the overwhelming onslaught of names and ages as "the begats." She paid no close attention until he spoke about her own grandmother.

"Old Katie Scarlett still lives in the cottage her husband built for her when they married in 1789. Nothing will persuade her to move. My father, and Kathleen's, married first in 1815 and took his bride to live in the crowded cottage. When the children started coming, he built nearby a grand big place with room to grow in, and with a warm bed by the fire especially for his mother in her old age. But the Old One will have none of it. So Sean, he lives in the cottage with our grandmother, and the girls—like Kathleen here—do for them."

"When there's no escaping it," Kathleen added. "Grandmother needs no doing for really, except a pass with the broom and the dust cloth, but Sean goes out of his way to find mud to track in on a clean floor. And the mending that man creates! He can go through a new shirt before the buttons are hardly sewed on. Sean's the brother to Molly and only a half to us. He's a poor model of a man, nearly as nothing as Timothy, though he's a full twenty years older and more."

Scarlett's brain was reeling. She didn't dare ask who Timothy was, for fear of having another dozen names thrown at her.

In any case, there wasn't time. Colum opened the window and shouted up to the driver. "Haul up, Jim, if you please, and I'll get out and join you on the box. We'll be turning into a lane just ahead; I'll need to show you the way."

Kathleen caught his sleeve. "Oh, Colum darling, say I can get down with you and make my own way home. I can't wait longer. Scarlett won't mind riding along to Molly's, will you, Scarlett?" She smiled at Scarlett with such shining hope that Scarlett would have agreed even if she hadn't wanted a few minutes by herself.

She wasn't about to go to the house of the O'Hara family beauty—no matter how faded—without spitting on a handkerchief and wiping the dust off her face and her boots. Then some toilet water from the silver vial in her purse and some powder and maybe just a very, very small touch of rouge.

50

The lane to Molly's house ran through the center of a small apple orchard; twilight tinted the airy blossoms mauve against the dark blue low sky. Strict ribbon beds of primroses edged the angularity of the square house. Everything was very tidy.

Inside, as well. The rigid horsehair suite of furniture in the parlor wore antimacassars, each table was covered with a starched white lace-edged cloth, the coal fire was ashless in the brightly polished brass grate.

Molly herself was impeccable in dress and in manner. Her burgundy gown was trimmed with dozens of silver buttons, all gleaming; her dark hair was shining and neatly coiled beneath a delicate white cap of drawn work with lace lappets. She offered her right cheek and then her left for Colum's kiss and expressed "a thousand welcomes" to another O'Hara when Scarlett was presented.

And she didn't even know I was coming. Scarlett was favorably impressed, in spite of Molly's undeniable beauty. She had the most velvety clear skin Scarlett had ever seen, and her bright blue eyes were free of shadows or pouches. Hardly any crows' feet, either, and not a line worth mentioning except from her nose to her mouth, and even girls can have those, Scarlett summed up in her rapid appraisal. Colum must have been mistaken, Molly couldn't possibly be in her fifties. "I'm so happy to meet you, Molly, and just too grateful for words that you're going to put me up in your lovely house," Scarlett gushed. Not that the house was all that much. Clean as fresh paint, granted, but the parlor wasn't any bigger than the smallest bedroom in her Peachtree Street house.

* * *

"My grief, Colum! How could you have gone off and left me there all by myself?" she complained the next day. "That awful Robert is the most boring man in the world, talking about his cows—for pity's sake!—and how much milk every one of them gives. I felt like I was going to start mooing before we finished eating. Dinner, as they told me about fifty-eight times, not supper. What on earth difference does it make?"

"In Ireland the English have dinner in the evening, the Irish have supper."

"But they're not English."

"They have aspirations. Robert had a glass of whiskey once in the Big House with the Earl's agent when he was paying the rents."

"Colum! You're joking."

"I'm laughing, Scarlett darling, but I'm not joking. Don't worry yourself about it; what matters is, was your bed comfortable?"

"I suppose so. I could have slept on corncobs I was so tired. It feels good to be walking, I must say. That was a long ride yesterday. Is it far to Grandmother's place?"

"A quarter mile, no more, by this boreen."

" 'Boreen.' What pretty words you've got for things. We'd say 'track' for a skinny little path like this. It wouldn't have these hedgerows either. I think I'll try them at Tara instead of some of the fences. How long does it take to get them this thick?"

"It depends on what kind of planting you use for the foundation. What kind of shrubs grow in Clayton County? Or do you have a tree you can prune low?"

Colum was surprisingly well informed about growing things, for a priest, Scarlett thought as he explained and demonstrated the art of creating a hedgerow. But he had a lot to learn about measurements. The narrow twisting path was much longer than a quarter mile.

They emerged suddenly into a clearing. Ahead of them was a thatched cottage, its white walls and small blue-framed windows fresh and bright. A thick stream of smoke painted a pale line across the sunny blue sky from the low chimney in the roof, and a calico cat was sleeping on the blue sill of one of the open windows. "It's adorable, Colum! How do people keep their cottages so white? Is it all the rain?" It had showered three times during the night, Scarlett knew, and that was only in the hours before she went to sleep. The muddiness of the boreen made her think there might have been more.

"The wet helps a bit," Colum said with a smile. He was pleased with her for not complaining about what the walk was doing to her hems and her boots. "But really it's that you're visiting at a good time. We do our buildings twice a year without fail, for Christmas and for Easter, inside and out, whitewash and paint. Will we go see if Grandmother's not dozing?"

"I'm nervous," Scarlett confessed. She didn't say why. In fact she was afraid of what a person looked like who was almost a hundred years old. Suppose it turned her stomach to look at her own grandmother? What would she do?

"We'll not stay long," said Colum, as if he read her mind, "Kathleen's expecting us for a cup of tea." Scarlett followed him around the cottage to the front. The top half of the blue door was open, but she couldn't see anything inside except shadows. And there was a strange smell, earthy and sort of sour. It made her nose wrinkle. Was that what very old age smelled like?

"Are you sniffing the peat fire, then, Scarlett darling? You're smelling the true warm heart of Ireland. Molly's coal fire is naught but more Englishness. It's the turf burning that means home. Maureen told me she dreams of it some nights and wakes with a heart full of longing. I mean to take her a few bricks when we go back to Savannah."

Scarlett inhaled curiously. It was a funny smell, like smoke, but not really. She followed Colum through the low doorway into the cottage, blinking to adjust her eyes to the dark interior.

"And is that you at last, Colum O'Hara? Why, I want to know, have you brought Molly to see me when Bridie promised me the gift of my own Gerald's girl?" Her voice was thin and cantankerous, but not cracked or weak. Relief and a kind of wonder filled Scarlett's being. This was Pa's mother that he told about so many times.

She pushed past Colum and went to kneel beside the old woman, who was sitting in a wooden armchair next to the chimney. "I am Gerald's girl, Grandmother. He named me after you, Katie Scarlett."

The original Katie Scarlett was small and brown, her skin darkened by nearly a century of open air and sun and rain. Her face was round, like an apple, and withered, like an apple kept too long. But the faded blue eyes were unclouded and penetrating. A thick wool shawl of bright blue lay across her shoulders, across her breast, the fringed ends in her lap. Her thin white hair was covered by a knitted red cap. "Let me look at you, girl," she said. Her leathery fingers lifted Scarlett's chin.

"By all the saints, he told the truth! You've got eyes green as a cat's." She crossed herself rapidly. "Where did they come from, I'd like to know. I thought Gerald must be drink-taken when he wrote me such a tale. Tell me, Young Katie Scarlett, was your dear mother a witch?"

Scarlett laughed. "She was more like a saint, Grandmother."

"Is that so? And married to my Gerald? The wonder of it all. Or maybe it's that being married to him made a saint of her with all the tribulation of it. Tell me, did he stay quarrelsome to the end of his days, God rest his soul?"

"I'm afraid so, Grandmother." The fingers pushed her away.

" 'Afraid,' is it? It's grateful I am. I prayed America wouldn't ruin him. Colum, you'll light a candle of thanksgiving for me in the church."

"That I will."

The old eyes scrutinized Scarlett again. "You meant no ill, Katie Scarlett. I'll forgive you." She smiled suddenly, eyes first. The small pursed lips spread into a smile of heartbreaking tenderness. There was not a tooth in the rose-petal-pink gums. "I'll order another candle for the blessing granted me of seeing you with me own eyes before I go to my grave."

Scarlett's eyes filled with tears. "Thank you, Grandmother."

"Not at all, not at all," said Old Katie Scarlett. "Take her away, Colum, I'm ready for my rest now." She closed her eyes and her chin dropped onto her warm, shawled chest.

Colum touched Scarlett's shoulder. "We'll go."

Kathleen ran out through the open red door of the cottage nearby, sending the hens in the yards scattering and complaining. "Welcome to the house, Scarlett," she cried joyfully. "Tea's in the pot stewing, and there's a fresh loaf of barm brack for your pleasure."

Scarlett was amazed again at the change in Kathleen. She looked so happy. And so strong. She was wearing what Scarlett still thought of as a costume, an ankle-high brown skirt over blue and yellow petticoats. Her skirt was pulled up on one side and tucked into the top of the homespun apron that was tied around her waist, showing the bright petticoats. Scarlett owned no gown as becoming. But why, she wondered, was Kathleen bare-legged and barefooted when striped stockings would have finished off the outfit?

She had thought about asking Kathleen to come over to Molly's to stay. Even if Kathleen made no bones about her dislike for her half sister, she should be able to put up with her for ten days, and Scarlett really needed her. Molly had a parlor maid, who acted as lady's maid as well, but the girl was hopeless at arranging hair. But this Kathleen, happy at home and sure of herself, was not someone who'd jump to do her bidding, Scarlett could tell. There was no point in even hinting at the move, she'd just have to make do with a clumsy chignon, or wear a snood. She swallowed a sigh and went into the house.

It was so small. Bigger than Grandmother's cottage, but still too small for a family. Where did they all sleep? The outside door led directly to the kitchen, a room twice the size of the kitchen in the small cottage but only half the size of Scarlett's bedroom in Atlanta. The most noticeable thing in the room was the big stone fireplace in the center of the right-hand wall. Perilously steep stairs rose up to an opening high in the wall to the left of the chimney; a door to its right led to another room.

"Take a chair by the fire," Kathleen urged. There was a low turf fire directly on the stone floor inside the chimney. The same worked stone extended outward, flooring the kitchen. It gleamed pale from scrubbing, and the smell of soap mingled with the sharp aroma of the burning peat.

My soul, Scarlett thought, my family's really very poor. Why on earth did Kathleen cry her eyes out to come back to this? She forced a smile and sat down in the Windsor chair Kathleen had pushed forward to the hearth.

In the hours that followed Scarlett saw for herself why Kathleen had found the space and relative luxury of life in Savannah an inadequate replacement for life in the small whitewashed thatched cottage in County Meath. The O'Haras in Savannah had created a sort of island of happiness, populated by themselves, reproducing the life they'd known in Ireland. Here was the original.

A steady succession of heads and voices appeared in the open top half of the door, calling out, "God bless all here," followed by the invitation to "come in and sit by the fire," and then by the entrance of the owners of the voices. Women, girls, children, boys, men, babies came and went in overlapping ones, twos, threes. The musical Irish voices greeted Scarlett and welcomed her, greeted Kathleen and welcomed her home again, all with a warmth so heartfelt that Scarlett could all but hold it in her hand. It was as different from the formal world of paying and receiving calls as day differs from night. People told her they were related, and how. Men and women told her stories about her father—reminiscences from older ones, events told them by their parents or grandparents repeated by younger ones. She could see Gerald O'Hara's face in so many of the faces around the hearth, hear his voice in their voices. It's like Pa was here himself, she thought; I can see how he must have been when he was young, when he was here.

There was the gossip of the village and town to catch Kathleen up on, told and retold as people came and went so that before long Scarlett felt that she knew the blacksmith and the priest and the man who kept the bar and the woman whose hen was laying a double-yolk egg almost every day. When Father Danaher's bald head appeared in the doorway, it seemed the most natural thing in the world, and when he came in she looked automatically, with everyone else, to see if his cassock had been mended yet where the rough corner on the gate to the churchyard had torn it.

It's like the County used to be, she thought; everybody knows everybody, and knows everybody's business. But smaller, closer, more comfortable somehow. What she was hearing and sensing, without recognizing it, was that the tiny world she was seeing was kinder than any she had ever known. She knew only that she was enjoying being in it very much.

This is the best vacation a person could possibly have. I'll have so much to tell Rhett. Maybe we'll come back together sometime; he's always thought nothing of going off to Paris or London at the drop of a hat. Of course we couldn't live like this, it's too ... too ... peasanty. But it's so quaint and charming and fun. Tomorrow I'm going to wear my Galway clothes when I come over to see everybody, and no corset at all. Shall I put on the yellow petticoat with the blue skirt, or would the red ...?

In the distance a bell tolled, and the young girl in the red skirt who was showing her baby's first teeth to Kathleen jumped up from her seat on a low three-legged stool. "The Angelus! Who'd have believed I could let my Kevin come home and no dinner on the fire?"

"Take some of the stew, then, Mary Helen, we've got too much. Didn't Thomas greet me when I came home with four fat rabbits he'd snared?" In less than a minute, Mary Helen was on her way with her baby on her hip and a napkin-covered bowl in her arm.

"You'll help me pull out the table, Colum? The men will be coming to dinner. I don't know where Bridie's got to."

One by one, close on the heels of the one before, the men of the cottage came in from their work in the fields. Scarlett met her father's brother Daniel, a tall, vigorous, spare angular man of eighty, and his sons. There were four of them, aged twenty to forty-four, plus, she remembered, Matt and Gerald in Savannah. The house must have been like this when Pa was young, him and his big brothers. Colum looked so astonishingly short, even seated at table, in the midst of the big O'Hara men.

The missing Bridie ran through the door just as Kathleen was ladling stew into blue and white bowls. Bridie was wet. Her shirt clung to her arms, and her hair dripped down her back. Scarlett looked through the door, but the sun was shining.

"Did you tumble into a well, then, Bridie?" asked the youngest brother, the one named Timothy. He was glad to deflect attention away from himself. His brothers had been teasing him about his weakness for an unnamed girl they referred to only as "Golden Hair."

"I was washing myself in the river," Bridie said. Then she began to eat, ignoring the uproar caused by her statement. Even Colum, who rarely criticized, raised his voice and banged the table.

"Look at me and not the rabbit, Brigid O'Hara. Do you not know the Boyne claims a life for every mile of its length every year?"

The Boyne. "Is that the same Boyne as the Battle of the Boyne, Colum?" Scarlett asked. The whole table fell silent. "Pa must have told me about that a hundred times. He said the O'Haras lost all their lands because of it." Bowls and spoons resumed their clatter.

"It is, and we did," Colum said, "but the river continued in its course. It marks the boundary of this land. I'll show it to you if you want to see, but not if you're thinking of using it like a washtub. Brigid, you've got better sense. What possessed you?"

"Kathleen told me Cousin Scarlett was coming, and Eileen told me a lady's maid must be washed every day before she touches the lady's clothes or her hair. So I went to wash." She looked full at Scarlett for the first time. "It's my intention to please, so you'll take me back to America with you." Her blue eyes were solemn, her soft rounded chin thrust out with determination. Scarlett liked the look of her. There'd be no homesick tears from Bridie, she was sure. But, she could only use her until the trip was over. No Southerner ever had a white maid. She looked for the right words to tell the girl.

Colum did it for her. "It was already decided you'd go to Savannah with us, Bridie, so you could have avoided risking your life . . ."

"Hoo-rah!" Bridie shouted. Then she blushed crimson. "I'll not be so rowdy when I'm in service," she said earnestly to Scarlett. And, to Colum, "I was only at the ford, Colum, where the water's barely to the knee. I'm not such a fool as all that."

"We'll find out just what manner of fool you are, then," Colum said. He was smiling again. "Scarlett will have the task of telling you what a lady's needs might be, but you'll not be after her for schooling before it's the hour to depart. There's two weeks and a day you'll be sharing quarters on the ship, time enough to learn all you're able to learn. Bide your time till then, with Kathleen and the house your better and your duty."

Bridie sighed heavily. "It's a mountain of burden, being the youngest."

Everyone hooted her loudly. Except Daniel, who spoke not at all throughout the meal. When it was over, he pushed back his chair and stood. "The ditching's best done in this dry spell," he said. "Finish your meal and get back to your labors." He bowed ceremoniously to Scarlett. "Young Katie Scarlett O'Hara, you honor my house and I bid you welcome. Your father was greatly loved and his absence has been a stone in my breast for all these fifty years and more."

She was too surprised to say a word. By the time she thought of something, Daniel was out of sight behind the barn, on his way to his fields.

Colum pushed back his chair, then moved it near the hearth. "There's no way for you to know it, Scarlett darling, but you've made your mark on this house. That's the first time I've heard Daniel O'Hara use words on anything that hadn't to do with the farm. You'd better watch your step or the widows and spinsters of the region will buy a spell to lay on you. Daniel's a widower, you know, and could use a new wife."

"Colum! He's an old man!"

"And isn't his mother still thriving at a hundred? He's got plenty of good years left. You'd better remind him you've got a husband back home."

"Maybe I'll remind my husband that he's not the only man in the world. I'll tell him he's got a rival in Ireland." The thought made her smile, Rhett jealous of an Irish farmer. But why not, really? One of these days she might just mention it, not saying that it was her uncle, or that he was old as the hills. Oh, she was going to have a fine time when she had Rhett where she wanted him! An unexpected pang of longing struck her like physical pain. She wouldn't tease him about Daniel O'Hara or anything else. All she wanted was to be with him, to love him, to have this baby for them both to love.

"Colum's right about one thing," said Kathleen. "Daniel's given you the blessing of the head of the house. When you can't bear another minute of Molly, you'll have a place here if you want it."

Scarlett saw her chance. She'd been consumed with curiosity. "Where do you put everybody?" she asked bluntly.

"There's the loft, divided in two. The boys have their side, Bridie and me the other. And Uncle Daniel took the bed by the fire when Grandmother didn't want it. I'll show you." Kathleen pulled on the back edge of a wooden settle along the wall beyond the stairs, and it folded open and down to reveal a thick mattress covered by a woolen blanket. "He said that's why he was taking it, to show her she'd missed a good thing, but I've always thought he felt too lonely above the room after Aunt Theresa died."

" 'Above the room'?"

"Through there." Kathleen gestured toward the door. "We fitted it as a parlor, no sense wasting it. The bed's still there for you any time you've the mind."

Scarlett couldn't imagine that she ever would. Seven people in one small house were at least four or five too many in her opinion. Particularly such big people. No wonder Pa was called the runt of the litter, she thought, and no wonder he always carried on like he thought he was ten feet tall.

She and Colum visited her grandmother again before going back to Molly's, but Old Katie Scarlett was asleep by the fire. "Do you think she's all right?" Scarlett whispered.

Colum just nodded. He waited until they were outside before he spoke. "I saw the stewpot on the table, and it was almost empty. She'll have fixed Sean's dinner and shared it since we were there. She always has a small nap after meals."

The tall hedgerows that bordered the boreen were sweet with blossoms of hawthorn, and the singing of birds poured down from the branches at the top, two feet above Scarlett's head. It was wonderful to walk along, in spite of the wet ground. "Is there a boreen to the Boyne, Colum? You said you'd take me."

"And so I did. In the morning, if it please you. I promised Molly I'd have you home in good time today. She's having a tea party in your honor."

A party! For her! What a good idea it was, coming to meet her kinfolks before she settled in Charleston.

51

The food was good, but that's the only good thing I can find to say, Scarlett thought. She smiled brilliantly and shook hands with each of Molly's departing guests. God's nightgown! What limp droopy fingers these women have, and they all talk like they've got something stuck in their throat. I've never seen such a tacky bunch of people in all my born days.

The competitive overrefinement of provincial, would-be gentry was something Scarlett had never run into. There was an earthy forthrightness to Clayton County landowners and a true aristocracy that scorned pretension in Charleston and in the circle she'd thought of as "Melly's friends" in Atlanta. The elevated little finger of the hand lifting the teacup and the dainty, mouse-sized bites of scones and sandwiches that characterized Molly and her acquaintances seemed as ridiculous to her as in fact they were. She had eaten the excellent food with excellent appetite and ignored the hinted invitations to deplore the vulgarity of people who dirtied their hands with farm work. "What does Robert do, Molly—wear kid gloves all the time?" she'd asked, delighted to see that lines did show up in Molly's perfect skin when she frowned.

I reckon she'll have a few words to say to Colum about bringing me here, but I don't care. It served her right for talking about me like I wasn't an O'Hara at all, or her either. And where did she come up with that idea that a plantation is the same thing as—what did she call it?—an English manor. I might have to have a few words with Colum myself. Their faces were a treat, though, when I told them all our servants and field hands were always black. I don't think they've ever heard of dark skin, much less seen any. This is a strange place, all around.

"What a lovely party, Molly," said Scarlett. "I declare I ate till I could fairly pop. I think I might just take a little rest up in my room for a while."

"You must, naturally, do whatever you like, Scarlett. I had the boy bring around the trap so we could have a drive, but if you'd prefer to sleep . . ."

"Oh, no, I'd love to go out. Can we go to the river, do you think?" She'd planned to get away from Molly, but it was too good a chance to miss. The truth was she'd rather ride to see the Boyne than walk there. She didn't trust Colum one bit when he said it wasn't far.

Rightly so, as it turned out. Wearing yellow gloves to match the yellow spokes of the trap's tall wheels, Molly drove all the way back to the main road, then through the village. Scarlett looked at the row of dispirited-looking buildings with interest.

The trap rolled through the biggest gates Scarlett had ever seen, tremendous creations of wrought iron topped with gold spear points, each side centered by a gold-surrounded brightly colored plaque of intricate design. "The Earl's coat of arms," said Molly lovingly. "We'll drive to the Big House and see the river from the garden. It's all right, he's not there, and Robert got permission from Mr. Alderson."

"Who's that?"

"The Earl's land agent. He manages the entire manor. Robert knows him."

Scarlett tried to look impressed. Clearly, she was supposed to be bowled over, though she couldn't think why. What could be so important about an overseer? They were only hired help.

Her question was answered after a long drive on a perfectly straight, wide, gravelled road through spreading expanses of clipped lawn that reminded her for a moment of the great sweeping terraces of Dunmore Landing. The thought was pushed aside by her first sight of the Big House.

It was immense, not one building, it seemed, but a cluster of crenellated roofs and towers and walls. It was more like a small city than like any house Scarlett had ever seen or even heard of. She understood why Molly was so respectful of the agent. Managing a place like this would take more people and more work than the biggest plantation that had ever been. She craned her neck to look up at the stone walls and marble-framed tracery windows. The mansion Rhett had built for her was the largest and—to Scarlett's mind—most impressive residence in Atlanta, yet it could be put down in one corner of this place and hardly take up enough room to be noticed. I'd love to see the inside . . .

Molly was horrified that Scarlett would even ask. "We have permission to walk in the garden. I'll tie the pony to that hitching post, and we'll go through the gate there." She pointed to a steeply pointed arched entry. The iron gate was ajar. Scarlett jumped down from the trap.

The archway led through to a gravelled terrace. It was the first time Scarlett had ever seen gravel raked into a pattern. She was almost timid about walking on it. Her footprints would ruin the perfection of the S-curves formed by the raking. She looked apprehensively at the garden beyond the terrace. Yes, the paths were gravel. And raked. Not in curves, thank heaven, but still there wasn't a footprint to be seen. *I wonder how they do that? The man with the rake has to have feet.* She took a deep breath and crunched boldly onto the terrace and across it to the marble steps into the garden. The sound of her boots on the gravel was as loud as gunfire to her ears. She was sorry she'd come.

Where was Molly anyway? Scarlett turned around as quietly as she could. Molly was walking carefully, fitting her steps into the prints Scarlett had left. It made her feel much better that her cousin—for all her airs—was even more intimidated than she was. She looked up at the house, waiting for Molly to catch up. It seemed much more human from this side. There were French windows from the terrace to the rooms. Closed and curtained, but not too big to walk in and out of, not overwhelming like the doors on the front of the house. It was possible to believe that people might live here, not giants.

"Which way is the river?" Scarlett called to her cousin. She wasn't going to let an empty house make her whisper.

But she didn't care to linger, either. She refused Molly's suggestion that they walk through all the paths and all the gardens. "I just want to see the river. I'm bored sick of gardens; my husband makes too much fuss about them." She fended off Molly's transparent curiosity about her marriage while they followed the center path toward the trees that marked the end of the garden.

And then suddenly it was there, through an artfully natural-looking gap between two clumps of trees. Brown and gold, like no water Scarlett had ever seen. The sunlight lay on top of the river like molten gold swirling in slow eddies of water as dark as brandy. "It's beautiful," she said aloud, her voice soft. She hadn't expected beauty.

To hear Pa talk it should be red from all the blood that was spilled, and rushing and wild. But it hardly looks like it's moving at all. So this is the Boyne. She'd heard about it all her life and now she was close enough to reach down and touch it. Scarlett felt an emotion unknown to her, something she couldn't name. She searched for some definition, some understanding; it was important, if she could just find it . . .

"That's the view," Molly said in her cramped, most refined diction. "All the best houses have a view from their gardens."

Scarlett wanted to hit her. She'd never find it now, whatever she'd been looking for. She looked where Molly indicated and saw a tower on the other side of the river. It was like the ones she'd seen from the train, made of stone and part crumbled away. Moss stained the base of it and vines clung to its sides. It was much bigger than she'd thought they would be when she saw them at a distance; it looked like it might be as much as thirty feet across and twice that high. She had to agree with Molly that it was a romantic view.

"Let's go," she said after one more look at the river. All of a sudden she felt very tired.

"Colum, I think I'm going to kill dear cousin Molly. If you could have heard that horrible Robert last night at dinner telling us how privileged we were to walk on the Earl's dumb garden paths. He must have said it about seven hundred times, and every single time Molly chirped away for ten minutes about what a thrill it was.

"And then, this morning, she practically swooned when she saw me in these Galway clothes. No chirpy little lady voice then, let me tell you. She lectured me about ruining her position and being an embarrassment to Robert. To Robert! He should be embarrassed every time he sees his dumb fat face in a looking glass. How dare Molly lecture me about disgracing him?"

Colum patted Scarlett's hand. "She's not the best companion I'd wish for you, Scarlett darling, but Molly has her virtues. She did lend us the trap for the day, and we'll have a grand outing with no thought of her to cloud it. Look at the blackthorn flowers in the hedges, and the wild cherries blooming their hearts out in that farmyard. It's too fine a day to waste on rancor. And you look like a lovely Irish lass in your striped stockings and red petticoat."

Scarlett stretched out her feet and laughed. Colum was right. Why should she let Molly ruin her day?

They went to Trim, an ancient town with a rich history that Colum knew would interest Scarlett not at all. So he told her instead about Market Day every Saturday, just like Galway, only, he had to acknowledge, considerably smaller. But with a fortune-teller most Saturdays, something you seldom found in Galway, and a glorious fortune promised if you paid tuppence, reasonable happiness for a penny, and tribulation foretold only if your pocket could produce merely a ha'penny.

Scarlett laughed—Colum could always make her laugh—and touched the drawstring bag hanging between her breasts. It was hidden by her shirt and her Galway blue cloak. No one would ever know she was wearing two hundred dollars in gold instead of a corset. The freedom was almost indecent. She had not been out of the house without stays since she was eleven years old.

He showed her Trim's famous castle, and Scarlett pretended interest in the ruins. Then he showed her the store where Jamie had worked from the time he was sixteen until he went to Savannah at the age of forty-two, and Scarlett's interest was real. They talked with the shopkeeper, and of course nothing would do but to close the shop and accompany the owner upstairs to meet his wife, who would surely die from the sorrow of it if she couldn't hear the news from Savannah straight from Colum's own lips and meet the visiting O'Hara who was already the talk of the countryside for her beauty and her American charm.

Then neighbors had to be told what a special day it was and who was there, and they hurried to the rooms above the shop until Scarlett was sure the walls must be bulging.

Then, "The Mahoneys will be wounded by the slight if we come to Trim without seeing them," Colum said when at last they left Jamie's former employer. Who? They're Maureen's family, to be sure, with the grandest bar in all Trim and had Scarlett ever tried a bit of porter? The number of people was even larger this time, with more arriving every minute, and soon there were fiddlers and food. The hours sped by, and the long twilight was setting in when they started the short journey to Adamstown. The first shower of the day—a phenomenon to have so much sun, said Colum—intensified the scent of the blossoms in the hedgerows. Scarlett pulled up the hood of her cloak, and they sang all the way to the village.

"I'll stop in here in the bar and learn if there's a letter for me," Colum said. He looped the pony's reins around the village pump. In an instant heads thrust through the open half doors of all the buildings.

"Scarlett," cried Mary Helen, "the baby's got another tooth, come have a cup of tea and admire it."

"No, Mary Helen, you come along here with babe and tooth and husband and all," said Clare O'Gorman, née O'Hara. "Isn't she my own first cousin and my Jim dying to meet her?"

"And my cousin, too, Clare," shouted Peggy Monaghan. "And me with a barm brack on my hearth because I learned her partiality for it."

Scarlett didn't know what to do. "Colum!" she called.

It was easy enough, he said. They'd just go to each house in turn, starting with the closest, gathering friends as they went. When the entire village was in one of the houses, that's where they'd stay for a while.

"Not too long, mind you, because you'll have to get into your finery for Molly's dinner table. She has her imperfections, as do we all, but you cannot thumb your nose at her under her own roof. She's tried too hard to shed those kinds of petticoats to be able to support seeing them in her dining room."

Scarlett put her hand on Colum's arm. "Do you think I can stay at Daniel's?" she asked. "I truly hate being at Molly's . . . What are you laughing about, Colum?"

"I've been wondering how I could persuade Molly to let us have the trap one more day. Now I think she can be convinced to make it available for the rest of your visit. You take yourself in there to see the new tooth, and I'll go have a small talk with Molly. Don't take this wrong, Scarlett darling, but she'll likely promise anything if I promise to take you elsewhere. She'll never live down what you said about Robert's elegant kid gloves for cow tending. It's the most cherished story in every kitchen from here to Mullingar."

Scarlett was installed in the room "above" the kitchen by suppertime. Uncle Daniel even smiled when Colum told the tale of Robert's gloves. This remarkable occurrence was added to the tale, making it an even better story for the next telling.

Scarlett adjusted with astonishing ease to the simplicity of Daniel's two-room cottage. With a room of her own, a comfortable bed, and Kathleen's tireless unobtrusive cleaning and cooking, Scarlett had only to enjoy herself on her holiday. And she did—enormously.

52

$\mathscr{D}$uring the following week Scarlett was busier and, in some ways, happier than she had ever been. She felt stronger physically than she could remember ever feeling. Freed from the constriction of fashionable tight lacing and the metal cage of corset stays, she could move more quickly and breathe deeply for the first time in many years. In addition, she was one of those women whose vitality increased in pregnancy as if in response to the needs of the life growing within her. She slept deeply and woke at cockcrow with a raging appetite for breakfast and for the day ahead.

Which always produced both the comfortable delight of familiar pleasures and the stimulation of new experience. Colum was eager to take her out "adventuring," as he called it, in Molly's pony trap. But first he had to tear her away from her new friends. They poked their heads in at Daniel's door immediately after breakfast. For a visit, to invite her to visit them, with a story she might not have heard yet, or a letter from America that could use some explanation of the meaning of some words or phrases. She was the expert on America and was begged to tell what it was like, over and over again. She was also Irish, though she'd suffered, poor dear, from the lack of knowing it, and there were dozens of things to tell her and teach her and show her.

There was an artlessness about the Irish women that disarmed her; it was as if they were from another world, as foreign as the world they all believed in where fairies of all kinds did magical and enchanting things.

She laughed openly when Kathleen put a saucer of milk and a plate of crumbled bread on the doorstep every evening in case any "little people" passing by were hungry. And when both saucer and plate were empty and clean in the morning Scarlett said sensibly that one of the barn cats must have been at them. Her skepticism bothered Kathleen not at all, and Kathleen's fairy supper became, for Scarlett, one of the most charming things about living with the O'Haras.

Another was the time she spent with her grandmother. She's tough as shoe leather, Scarlett thought with pride, and she fancied that her grandmother's blood in her veins was what had gotten her through the desperate times in her life. She ran over to the little cottage often, and if Old Katie Scarlett was awake and willing to talk, she'd sit on a stool and ask for stories about her Pa growing up.

Eventually she'd give in to Colum's urgings and climb up into the trap for the day's adventure. Warm in her wool skirts, protected by cloak and hood, she learned within a few days to pay no attention to the gusting wind from the west or the brief light rains that so often rode on it.

Just such a rain was falling when Colum took her to "the real Tara." Scarlett's cloak billowed around her when she reached the top of the uneven stone steps up the side of the low hill where Ireland's High Kings had ruled and made music, and loved and hated, and feasted and battled and, in the end, been defeated.

There's not even a castle. Scarlett looked around her and saw nothing except a scattering of grazing sheep. Their fleece looked gray under the gray sky in the gray light. She shivered, surprising herself. A goose walked over my grave. The childhood explanation flickered in her mind, making her smile.

"It pleases you?" asked Colum.

"Um, yes, it's very pretty."

"Don't lie, Scarlett darling, and don't search for prettiness at Tara. Come with me." He held out his hand and Scarlett put hers in it.

Together they walked slowly across the rich grass to an uneven area of what looked to her like grassy lumps in the earth. Colum walked over some of them and stopped. "Saint Patrick himself stood where we are standing now. He was a man then, a simple missionary, no bigger, likely, than I am. Sainthood came later and he grew in people's minds to a giant of a man, invincible, armed with God's Holy Word. It's better, I believe, to remember that he was a man first. He must have been frightened—alone, in his sandals and frieze cloak, facing the power of the High King and his magicians. Patrick had only his faith and his mission of truth and the need to tell it. The wind must have been cold. His need must have been like a consuming flame. He had already broken the High King's law, lighting a great bonfire on a night when it was the law that all fires should be put out. He could have been killed for the trespass, he knew that. He had purposed the great risk to draw the eye of the King and prove to him the magnitude of the message he, Patrick, bore. He did not fear death; he feared only that he would fail God. That he did not do. King Laoghaire, from his ancient jewelled throne, gave the bold missionary the right to preach without hindrance. And Ireland became Christian."

There was, in Colum's quiet voice, something that compelled Scarlett to listen and to try to understand what he was saying and something more besides. She'd never thought about saints as people, as able to be afraid. She'd never really thought about saints at all; they were just names of holy days. Now, looking at Colum's short stocky figure and ordinary face and graying hair tousled by the wind, she could imagine the face and figure of another ordinary-looking man, in the same stance of readiness. He wasn't afraid to die. How could anyone not be afraid to die? What must it be like? She felt a human wrench of envy of Saint Patrick, of all the saints, even, somehow, of Colum. I don't understand, and I never will, she thought. The realization came slowly, a heavy weight. She had learned a great and painful and stirring truth. There are things too deep, too complex, too conflicted for explanation or everyday understanding. Scarlett felt alone and exposed to the western wind.

Colum walked on, leading her. It was only a few dozen paces to the place where he stopped. "There," he said, "that row of low mounds, do you see it?" Scarlett nodded.

"You should have music and a glass of whiskey to stave off the wind and open your eyes, but I have none to give you, so perhaps you should close them to see. That is all we have left of the banqueting hall of the thousand candles. The O'Haras were there, Scarlett darling, and the Scarletts, and everyone you know—Monaghan, Mahoney, MacMahon, O'Gorman, O'Brien, Danaher, Donahue, Carmody—others you've yet to meet, as well. All the heroes were there. The food, it was grand and plentiful, and the drink. And music to lift the heart right out of your body. A thousand guests it held, lit by the thousand candles. Can you see it, Scarlett? The flames glowing twice, thrice, ten times over, reflected as they were in the gold bracelets on their arms and in the gold cups that travelled to their mouths, and in the deep reds and greens and blues of the great gold-clasped jewels that held their carmine cloaks across their shoulders. What mighty appetites they had—for the venison and boar and roast goose gleaming in its fat—for the mead and the poteen—for the music that brought their fists to pounding on the tables with gold plates jouncing and rattling one upon the next. Can you see your Pa? And Jamie? And that rascal young Brian with his side-looking gaze at the women? Ach, what revelry! Can you see it, Scarlett?"

She laughed with Colum. Yes, Pa would have been bellowing out "Peg in a Low Back'd Car" and calling for his cup to be filled just one more time because singing put such a terrible thirst on a man. How he would have loved it. "There'd be horses," she said confidently. "Pa always had to have a horse."

"Horses as strong and beautiful as great waves rushing at the shore."

"And somebody patient to put him to bed after."

Colum laughed. He put his arms around her and hugged her, then let her go. "I knew you'd feel the glorious fact of it," he said. There was pride in his words, pride in her. Scarlett smiled at him, her eyes like living emeralds.

The wind blew her hood onto her shoulders, and warmth touched her bare head. The shower was past. She looked up at the clean-washed blue sky; clouds, dazzling white, moved like dancers before the gusting winds. So close they seemed, so warm and sheltering the Irish sky.

Then her gaze fell and she saw Ireland before her, green upon green of fresh-growth fields and tender new leaves and hedgerows thick with life. She could see so far, to the mist-edged curve of the earth. Something ancient and pagan stirred deep within her, and the barely tamed wildness that was her hidden being surged hotly through her blood. This was what it was to be a king, this height above the world, this nearness to the sun and the sky. She threw her arms wide to embrace being alive, on this hill, with the world at her feet.

"Tara," said Colum.

"I felt so strange, Colum, not like me at all." Scarlett stepped on one of the wheel's yellow spokes and then up onto the seat of the trap.

"It's the centuries, Scarlett darling. All the life lived there, all the joy and all the sorrow, all the feasts and battles, they're in the air around and the land beneath you. It's time, years beyond our counting, weighing without weight on the earth. You cannot see it or smell it or hear it or touch it, but you feel it brushing your skin and speaking without sound. Time. And mystery."

Scarlett pulled her cloak close around her in the warm sun. "It was like at the river, it made me feel peculiar, too, somehow. I almost could put a word to it, but then I lost it." She told him about the Earl's garden and the river and the view of the tower.

" 'The best gardens have views,' do they?" Colum's voice was terrible with anger. "Is that what Molly said?"

Scarlett drew her body deeper into the cloak. What had she said that was so wrong? She'd never seen Colum like this, he was a stranger, not Colum at all.

He turned to her and smiled, and she saw that she'd been mistaken. "How would you like to encourage me in my weakness, Scarlett darling? They'll be introducing the horses to the race course in Trim today. I'd like to look them over and choose one to carry a small wager for me in Sunday's race."

She'd like that very much.

It was almost ten miles to Trim—not far, Scarlett thought. But the road twisted and turned and veered off from time to time, in directions away from the one they wanted, only to twist and turn some more until finally they were going again where they wanted to go. Scarlett agreed enthusiastically when Colum suggested they stop in a village for a cup of tea and a bite. Back in the trap they went a short way to a crossroads, then turned onto a wider, straighter road. He whipped up the pony to a smart pace. A few minutes later he whipped it again, harder, and they raced through a large village so quickly that the trap teetered on its high wheels.

"That place looked deserted," she said when they slowed again. "Why is that, Colum?"

"No one will live in Ballyhara; it has a bad history."

"What a waste. It looked right handsome."

"Have you ever been horse racing, Scarlett?"

"Only once to a real one, in Charleston, but at home we had pick-up races all the time. Pa was the worst. He couldn't bear just to ride along and talk to the rider next to him. He made a race out of every mile of road."

"And why not?"

Scarlett laughed. Colum was so like Pa sometimes. "They must have closed Trim down," Scarlett commented when she saw the crowds at the race course. "Everybody's here." She saw a lot of familiar faces. "They've closed Adamstown, too, I reckon." The O'Hara boys waved and smiled. She didn't envy them if Old Daniel happened to see them. The ditching wasn't done yet.

The packed-earth oval was three miles long. Workmen were just completing installation of the final jump. The race would be a steeplechase.

Colum hitched the pony to a tree some distance from the track, and they worked their way into the crowd.

Everyone was in high spirits, and everyone knew Colum; they all wanted to meet Scarlett, "the little lady that inquired about Robert Donahue's habit of wearing gloves for farming."

"I feel like the belle of the ball," she whispered to Colum.

"And who better for the position?" He led the way, with many stops, to the area where the horses were being led in circles by riders or trainers.

"But Colum, they're magnificent. What are horses like that doing in a pokey little town's race?"

He explained that the race was neither little nor "pokey." It had a purse of fifty pounds for the winner, more than many a shopowner or farmer earned in a year. Also, the jumps were a real test. A winner at Trim could hold his own against the field in the more famous races at Punchestown or Galway, or even Dublin. "Or win by ten lengths any race at all in America," he added with a grin. "Irish horses are the best in the world, it's accepted knowledge everywhere."

"Just like Irish whiskey, I suppose," said Gerald O'Hara's daughter. She'd heard both claims all her life. The hurdles looked impossibly high to her; maybe Colum was right. It should be an exciting race meet. And even before the races, there'd be Trim Market Day. Truly, no one could wish for a better vacation.

A sort of undercurrent rumble ran through the talking, laughing, shouting crowd. "Fight! Fight!" Colum climbed up on the rail to see. A big grin spread across his face, and his fisted right hand smacked into his cupped left palm.

"Will you be wanting to place a small wager, then, Colum?" invited the man next to him on the rail.

"That I will. Five shillings on the O'Haras."

Scarlett nearly toppled Colum when she grabbed his ankle. "What's happening?"

The crowd was flowing away from the oval toward the disturbance. Colum jumped down, took Scarlett by the wrist, and ran.

Three or four dozen men, young and old, were grunting and yelling in a melee of fists and boots and elbows. The crowd made a broad uneven circle around them, shouting encouragement. Two piles of coats to one side were testimony to the sudden eruption of the fight; many of the coats had been stripped off so quickly that their sleeves were inside out. Within the ring shirts were getting red with spilled blood, from the shirt's owner or the man he was hitting. There was no pattern, no order. Each man hit whoever was closest to him, then looked around for his next target. Anyone knocked down was pulled up roughly by the person nearest him and shoved back into the fray.

Scarlett had never seen men fighting with their fists. The sounds of blows landing and the spurting blood from mouths and noses horrified her. All four of Daniel's sons were there, and she begged Colum to make them stop.

"And lose my five shillings? Don't be daft, woman."

"You're awful, Colum O'Hara, just awful."

She repeated the words later, to Colum and to Daniel's sons and to Michael and Joseph, two of Colum's brothers she hadn't met before. They were all in the kitchen at Daniel's house. Kathleen and Brigid were calmly washing the wounds, ignoring the yelps of pain and accusations of rough handling. Colum was passing around glasses of whiskey.

I don't think it's funny at all, no matter what they claim, Scarlett said to herself. She couldn't believe that faction fights were part of the fun of fairs and public events for the O'Haras and their friends. "Just high spirits," indeed! And the girls were worse, if anything, the way they were tormenting Timothy because he had nothing worse than a black eye.

53

*T*he next day Colum surprised her by showing up before breakfast riding a horse and leading a second. "You said you liked to ride," he reminded her. "I borrowed us some mounts. But they're to go back by noon Angelus, so grab us what's left of last night's bread and come along before the house fills with visitors."

"There's no saddle, Colum."

"Whist, are you a rider or not? Get the bread, Scarlett darling, and Bridie'll make a hand for you to step on."

She hadn't ridden bareback and astride since she was a child. She'd forgotten the feeling of being one creature with the horse. It all came back, as if she'd never stopped riding this way, and soon she barely needed the reins at all; the pressure of her knees told the horse what they were going to do.

"Where are we going?" They were in a boreen she'd never walked.

"To the Boyne. I've something to show you."

The river. Scarlett's pulse quickened. There was something there that drew her and repelled her at the same time.

It began to rain, and she was glad Bridie had made her bring a shawl. She covered her head, then rode silently behind Colum, hearing the rain on the leaves of the hedge and the slow, walking clopping of the horses' hooves. So peaceful. She felt no surprise when the rain stopped. Now the birds in the hedges could come out again.

The boreen ended, and the river was there. The banks were so low that the water all but lapped over them. "This is the ford where Bridie does her washing," said Colum. "Would you fancy a bath?"

Scarlett shivered dramatically. "I'm not that brave. The water must be freezing."

"You'll find out, but only a bit of splashing. We're going across. Get your reins steady." His horse stepped cautiously into the water. Scarlett gathered up her skirts and tucked them under her thighs, then followed.

On the opposite bank, Colum dismounted. "Come down and have breakfast," he said. "I'll tie the horses to a tree." Trees grew close to the river here; Colum's face was dappled by their shade. Scarlett slid to the ground and handed him her reins. She found a sunny patch to sit in, her back sloped against a tree trunk. Small yellow flowers with heart-shaped leaves carpeted the bank. She closed her eyes and listened to the quiet voice of the river, the sibilant rustle of the leaves above her head, the songs of birds. Colum sat beside her, and she opened her eyes slowly. He broke the half loaf of soda bread in two pieces, gave her the larger.

"I've a story to tell you while we eat," he said. "This land we're on is called Ballyhara. Two hundred years ago, less a few, it was home to your people, our people. This is O'Hara land."

Scarlett sat up, suddenly wide awake. This? This was O'Hara land? And "Ballyhara"—wasn't that the name of the deserted village they had driven through so fast? She turned eagerly towards Colum.

"Quiet, now, and eat your good bread, Katie Scarlett. It's a longish story," he said. Colum's smile silenced the questions on her lips. "Two thousand years ago, plus a few, the first O'Haras settled here and made the land their own. One thousand years ago—you see how close we're coming—the Vikings, Norsemen we'd call them now, discovered the green richness of Ireland and tried to take it for their own. Irish—like the O'Haras—watched the rivers where the dragon-headed longboats might invade and built strong protections against the enemy." Colum tore a corner of bread and put it in his mouth. Scarlett waited impatiently as he chewed. So many years . . . her mind couldn't grasp so many years. What came after a thousand years ago?

"The Vikings were driven away," said Colum, "and the O'Haras tilled their land and fattened their cattle for two hundred years and more. They built a strong castle with room for themselves and their servants, because the Irish have long memories and just as the Vikings had come before, invasion could come again. And so it did. Not Vikings but English who had once been French. More than half of Ireland was lost to them, but the O'Haras prevailed behind their strong walls, and tended their land for another five hundred years.

"Until the Battle of the Boyne, which piteous story you know. After two thousand years of O'Hara care, the land became English. The O'Haras were driven across the ford, those that were left, the widows and babes. One of those children grew up a tenant farmer for the English across the river. His grandson, farmer of the same fields, married our grandmother, Katie Scarlett. At his father's side he looked across the brown waters of the Boyne and saw the castle of the O'Haras torn down, saw an English house rise in its place. But the name remained. Ballyhara."

And Pa saw the house, knew this land was O'Hara land. Scarlett wept for her father, understood the rage and sorrow she'd seen in his face and heard in his voice when he roared about the Battle of the Boyne. Colum went to the river and drank from his hands. He washed them, then cupped them again and brought water to Scarlett. After she drank, he wiped the tears from her cheeks with his gentle wet fingers.

"I wanted not to tell you this, Katie Scarlett—"

Scarlett interrupted angrily. "I have a right to know."

"And so I believe also."

"Tell me the rest. I know there's more. I can tell by your face."

Colum was pale, as a man in pain beyond bearing. "Yes, there's more. The English Ballyhara was built for a young lord. He was as fair and handsome as Apollo, they say, and he thought himself a god, as well. He determined to make Ballyhara the finest estate in all Ireland. His village— for he possessed Ballyhara to the last stone and leaf—must be more grand than any other, more grand than Dublin herself. And so it was, though not so grand as Dublin, save for the single street of it, which was wider than the capital's widest street. His stables were like a cathedral, his windows as clear as diamonds, his gardens a soft carpet to the Boyne. Peacocks spread their jewelled fans on his lawns and beauteous ladies decked in jewels graced his entertainments. He was lord of Ballyhara.

"His only sorrow was that he had but one son, and he the only child. But he lived to see his grandson born, before he went to Hell. And that grandson, too, had neither brother nor sister. But he was handsome and fair, and he became lord of Ballyhara and its cathedral stable and grand village. As did his son after him.

"I remember him, the young lord of Ballyhara. I was but a child and I thought him all things wondrous and fine. He rode a tall roan horse, and when the gentry trampled our corn under the hooves of their horses as they hunted the fox, he always threw coins to us children. He sat so tall and slim in his pink coat and white breeches and high, shining boots. I couldn't understand why my father took the coins away from us and broke them and cursed the lord for the giving of them."

Colum stood and began to pace the riverbank. When he continued his story, his voice was thin from the strain of controlling it. "The Famine came, and with it the starvation and death. 'I cannot stand to see my tenants under such suffering,' said the lord of Ballyhara. 'I will buy two strong ships and give them free and safe passage to America, where there is food in abundance. I care not that my cows lament because there is no one to milk them and my fields fill with nettles because there is no one to cultivate them. I care more for the people of Ballyhara than for the cattle or the corn.'

"The farmers and villagers kissed his hand for his goodness, and many of them prepared for their voyage. But not all could bear the pain of leaving Ireland. 'We will stay, though we starve,' they told the young lord. He sent word, then, through the countryside that any man or woman had but to ask, and the untaken berth would be given free, with gladness.

"My father cursed him again. He raged at his two brothers, Matthew and Brian, for accepting the Englishman's gift. But they were firm to go . . . They drowned, with all the rest, when the rotten ships sank in the first heavy sea. They gained the bitter name 'coffin ships.'

"A man of Ballyhara lay in wait in the stables, not caring that they were as beautiful as a cathedral. And when the young lord came to mount his tall roan horse, he seized him and he hanged the golden-haired lord of Ballyhara in the tower by the Boyne where once O'Haras watched for dragon ships."

Scarlett's hand flew to her mouth. Colum was so pale, pacing and talking in that voice that wasn't his voice. The tower! It must be the same. Her hand closed tight across her lips. She mustn't speak.

"No one knows," Colum was saying, "the name of the man in the stable. Some say one name, some say another. When the English soldiers came, the men left at Ballyhara would not point to him. The English hanged them all, in payment for the death of the young lord." Colum's face was white in the sun-spattered shade of the trees. A cry burst from his throat. Wordless and inhuman.

He turned to Scarlett, and she shrank away from his wild eyes and tormented face. "A VIEW?" he shouted; it was like a cannon firing. He sank to his knees on the yellow bank of flowers and bent forward to hide his face. His body shuddered.

Scarlett's hands reached toward him, then fell limply in her lap. She didn't know what to do.

"Forgive me, Scarlett darling," said the Colum she knew, and he raised his head. "Me sister Molly is the eejit of the Western world for saying such a thing. She always did have a talent for enraging me." He smiled, and the smile was almost convincing. "We have time to ride across Ballyhara if you want to see it. It's been deserted for near thirty years, but there's been no vandalism. No one will go near it."

He held out his hand, and the smile in his ashen face was real. "Come. The horses are just here."

Colum's horse broke a path through the brambles and tangled growth, and soon Scarlett could see the mammoth stone walls of the tower ahead of them. He held up his hand to alert her, then he reined in. He cupped his hands in a funnel around his mouth. "*Seachain*," he shouted, "*seachain*." The strange syllables echoed from the stones.

He turned his head, and his eyes were merry. There was color in his cheeks. "That's Gaelic, Scarlett darling, the Old Irish. There's a *cailleach*, a wise woman, lives in a hut somewhere nearby. She's a witch as old as Tara, some say, and the wife that ran off from Paddy O'Brien of Trim twenty years back, if you listen to others. I called out to warn her we're passing. She might not like being surprised. I don't say I believe in witches, mind, but it never does any harm to be respectful."

They rode on to the clearing around the tower. Up close Scarlett could see that the stones had no mortar between them and yet they had not shifted even an inch from their places. How old did Colum say it was? A thousand years? Two thousand? No matter. She wasn't afraid of it, the way she'd been when Colum was talking in that unnatural way. The tower was only a building, the finest work she'd ever seen. It's not scary at all. In fact, it kind of invites me over. She rode closer, ran her fingers over the joins.

"You're very brave, Scarlett darling. I warned you, there are those who say the tower's haunted by a hanging man."

"Fiddle-dee-dee! There's no such thing as ghosts. Besides, the horse wouldn't come close if it was here. Everybody knows that animals can sense those things."

Colum chuckled.

Scarlett laid her hand against the stone. It was smooth from aeons of weathering. She could feel the warmth of the sun in it and the cold of the rain and the wind. An unaccustomed peacefulness entered her heart. "You can tell it's old," she said, knowing that her words were inadequate, knowing that it didn't matter.

"It survived," Colum said. "Like a mighty tree with roots that go deep to the center of the earth."

"Roots that go deep." Where had she heard that before? Of course. Rhett said that about Charleston. Scarlett smiled, stroking the ancient stones. She could tell him a thing or two about roots going deep. Just wait till the next time he started bragging about how old Charleston was.

The house at Ballyhara was built of stone as well, but its stone was dressed granite, each block a perfect rectangle. It looked strong, enduring; the broken windowpanes and paint-lost windowframes were a jarring incongruity in the untouched permanence of the stone. It was a big house, with flanking wings that were themselves bigger than almost any house Scarlett knew. Built to last, she said to herself. It was really a shame nobody lived in it, a waste. "Didn't the Ballyhara lord have any children?" she asked Colum.

"No." He sounded satisfied. "There was a wife, I believe, who went back to her own people. Or to an asylum. Some say she went mad."

Scarlett sensed she'd better not admire the house to Colum. "Let's look at the village," she said. It was a town, too large to be a village, and there was not a whole window anywhere, or an unbroken door. It was derelict and despised, and it made Scarlett's flesh crawl. Hatred had done this. "What's the best way home?" she asked Colum.

54

"The Old One's birthday is tomor-
row," Colum said when he left Scarlett at Daniel's house. "A man with any
judgment would be called away until then, and I like to pretend I am one
of those men. Tell the family I'll be back on the morning."

Why was he so skittish? Scarlett wondered. There couldn't be all that
much to do for one old woman's birthday. A cake, of course, but what else
was there? She'd already decided to give her grandmother the lovely lace
collar she'd bought in Galway. There'd be plenty of time to buy another
on the way home. Good heavens, that's the end of this week!

Scarlett discovered as soon as she was through the door that what she
was going to have was a lot of hard manual labor. Everything in Old Katie
Scarlett's house had to be scrubbed and polished, even if it was already
clean, and in Daniel's house as well. Then the farmyard outside the old
cottage had to be weeded and swept clean, ready for the benches and chairs
and stools to hold everyone who couldn't squeeze into the cottage itself.
And the barn cleaned and scrubbed and fresh straw put down for all who
would sleep the night. It was going to be a very big party; not many made
it to a hundred years.

"Eat and be gone," Kathleen told the men when they came in for
dinner. She put a pitcher of buttermilk and four loaves of soda bread and a
bowl of butter on the table. They were as meek as lambs, ate more quickly
than Scarlett had known a person could eat, and left, bending to go through
the low door, without a word.

"Now we start," Kathleen announced when they were gone. "Scarlett, I'll need lots of water from the well. The buckets are there by the door." Scarlett, like the O'Hara men, never thought of arguing.

After dinner all the village women came to the house, with their children, to help with the work. Everything was noisy, the work was sweaty, Scarlett got blisters on the ridge of soft flesh at the base of her fingers. And she enjoyed herself more than she could credit. Barefoot like the others, with her skirts tucked up, a big apron around her waist, her sleeves rolled to the elbow, she felt as if she were a child again, playing in the kitchen yard, infuriating Mammy because she was dirtying her pinafore and had taken off her shoes and stockings. Only now she had playmates who were fun, instead of whiny Suellen and baby Carreen who was too young to enter in.

How long ago that was . . . not when you think about something as old as the tower, I guess. Roots that go deep . . . Colum was frightening this morning . . . that awful story about the ships . . . Those were my uncles, Pa's own brothers drowning. Damn that English lord. I'm glad they hung him.

There had never been a party the likes of Old Katie Scarlett's birthday celebration. O'Haras from all over County Meath and beyond came in donkey carts and wagons, on horseback, on foot. Half the population of Trim was there, and every soul that lived in Adamstown. They brought gifts and stories and food made especially for the feast, although Scarlett had thought that there was already food enough for an army. Mahoney's wagon from Trim rolled up with kegs of ale, and so did Jim Daly's from Mullingar. Seamus, Daniel's eldest son, rode the plow horse into Trim and returned with a box of clay pipes strapped on his back like a huge angular hump, tobacco in two sacks hung like saddlebags. For every man—and many women, too—must be given a new pipe on such a momentous occasion.

Scarlett's grandmother received the stream of guests and gifts like a queen, sitting in her high-backed chair, wearing her new lace collar on her good black silk, dozing when it pleased her and drinking whiskey in her tea.

When the evening Angelus bell rang, there were over three hundred people standing in and outside the tiny cottage, come to do honor to Katie Scarlett O'Hara on her one hundredth birthday.

She'd asked for "the old ways," and there was an elderly man in the place of honor by the fire opposite hers. With loving gnarled fingers he turned back linen wrappings to reveal a harp; three hundred and more voices sighed with joy. This was MacCormac, the only true inheritor of the music of the bards now that the great O'Carolan was dead. He spoke, and his voice was like music already. "I tell you the words of the master Turlough O'Carolan: 'I spend my time in Ireland happy and contented, drinking with every strong man who is a real lover of music.' And I add these words of my own making: I drink with every strong man and every strong woman such as Katie Scarlett O'Hara." He bowed to her. "That is to say, when drink is offered." Two dozen hands filled glasses. He carefully chose the largest, which he raised to Old Katie Scarlett, then drained. "Now I will sing you the tale of the coming of Finn MacCool," he said. His worn bent fingers touched the strings of the harp and magic filled the air.

And forever after there was music. Two pipers had come with their *pibs willeann*, there were fiddlers beyond counting, and pennywhistles by the dozens, and concertinas, and hands leaping with clacking bones, and the stirring, inciting beat of *bodhrans* following the strong lead of Colum O'Hara.

Women filled plates with food, Daniel O'Hara presided over the small barrels of poteen, dancing filled the center of the farmyard, and no one slept at all, save Old Katie Scarlett whenever she had a mind to.

"I didn't know there could ever be such a party," Scarlett said. She was breathing in short gasps, catching up before rejoining the pink-washed dancing in the sunrise.

"You mean you've never celebrated May Day?" exclaimed shocked cousins from she knew not where.

"You'll have to stay for May Day, Young Katie Scarlett," Timothy O'Hara said. A chorus of urging echoed him.

"I can't. We've got to catch the ship."

"There'll be other ships, surely?"

Scarlett jumped up from the bench. She'd had enough rest, and the fiddlers were starting a new reel. While she danced herself breathless again, the question sang in her head with the rollicking tune. There must be other ships. Why not stay and have fun dancing the reel in her striped stockings a little longer? Charleston would still be there when she arrived—with the same tea parties in the same crumbling houses behind the same high, unfriendly walls.

Rhett would still be there, too. Let him wait. She'd waited for him long enough in Atlanta, but things were different now. The baby in her womb made Rhett hers any time she wanted to claim him.

Yes, she decided, she might just stay for May Day. She was having such a good time.

The next day she asked Colum if he knew about another sailing, after May Day.

There was indeed another sailing. A fine ship, that stopped first at Boston, where he had to go while he was in America. She and Bridie would do very well on their own for the balance of the journey to Savannah. "She sails the evening of the ninth. You'll only have a half day to do your shopping in Galway."

She didn't need even that long; she'd already thought about it. No one in Charleston would ever wear Galway stockings or Galway petticoats. They were too bright and vulgar. She was only going to keep a few of those she'd bought for herself. They'd be wonderful souvenirs. She'd give the others to Kathleen and her new friends in the village.

"May ninth. That's a lot later than we planned, Colum."

"It's but a week and a day after May Day, Katie Scarlett. No time at all, once you're dead."

It was true! She'd never have this chance again. Besides, it would be a nice thing to do for Colum. The trip from Savannah to Boston and back would be a real hardship for him. After he'd been so nice to her, it was the least she should do for him . . .

On April 26 the *Brian Boru* sailed from Galway with two staterooms unoccupied. She had arrived on the twenty-fourth, a Friday, with passengers and mail. The mail was sorted in Galway on Saturday; Sunday being Sunday, the small bag for Mullingar left on Monday. On Tuesday the coach from Mullingar to Drogheda left a smaller bag at Navan, and on Wednesday a post rider set out with a packet of letters for the postmistress at Trim. There was a big thick envelope for Colum O'Hara from Savannah, Georgia. He got a lot of mail, did Colum O'Hara, a grand devoted family the O'Haras, and the Old One's birthday a night he wouldn't soon forget. The post rider dropped it off at the bar in Adamstown. "No reason to wait a further twenty-four hours I was thinking," he said to Matt O'Toole, who operated the bar and the tiny shop and post station in the corner of it. "At Trim they'll only put it in a slot marked 'Adamstown' until tomorrow, when another man will bring it." He accepted with alacrity the glass of porter Matt O'Toole offered him on Colum's behalf. Small and needing paint O'Toole's bar might be, but it served a fine dark glass.

Matt O'Toole called his wife in from the yard where she was spreading the wash to dry. "Mind the place, Kate, I'm walking up the boreen to Uncle Daniel's." Matt's father was the brother of Daniel O'Hara's dead wife, Theresa, God rest her soul.

* * *

"Colum! That's wonderful!" Included in Colum's envelope from Jamie was a letter from Tom MacMahon, the contractor for the Cathedral. The Bishop—with a little persuading—had agreed to allow Scarlett to redeem her sister's dowry. Tara. My Tara. I'll do such marvelous things.

Great balls of fire! "Colum, did you see this? That skinflint Bishop is asking five thousand dollars for Carreen's third of Tara! God's nightgown! You could buy the whole of Clayton County for five thousand dollars. He'll have to come down in his price."

Bishops of the Church did not haggle, Colum told her. If she wanted the dowry, and she had the money, she should pay it. She'd also be financing the work of the Church, if that made the transaction more palatable to her.

"You know it doesn't, Colum. I hate to be taken for a ride by anybody, even the Church. I'm sorry if that offends you. Still, I must have Tara, my heart's set on it. Oh, what a fool I was to let you talk me into staying over. We could be halfway to Savannah by now!"

Colum didn't bother to correct her. He left her looking for a piece of paper and a pen. "I've got to write to Uncle Henry Hamilton right this minute! He can handle everything; it'll all be done when I get there."

On Thursday Scarlett went to Trim by herself. It was annoying that Kathleen and Bridie were busy at the farm, and infuriating that Colum had just disappeared without telling a soul where he was going or when he'd be back. Still, it couldn't be helped once he was gone. And she had so much to do. She wanted some of those lovely pottery bowls that Kathleen used in the kitchen, and lots of the baskets—every shape, and there were so many of them—and piles and piles of the thick linen cloths and napkins; there was no linen like that in the stores at home. She was going to make the kitchen at Tara warm and friendly, like the Irish ones. After all, wasn't the name Tara just about as Irish as you could get?

As for Will and Suellen, she'd do something very generous for them, for Will anyhow, he deserved it. There was lots of good land just going begging in the County. Wade and Ella would come live with her and Rhett in Charleston. Rhett really was fond of them. She'd find a good school, one with a short vacation time. Rhett would probably frown the way he always did about the way she treated the children, but when the baby was born and he saw how much she loved it, he'd stop criticizing her all the time. And in the summer, they'd be at Tara, a Tara reborn and beautiful and home.

Scarlett knew she was building castles in the air. Maybe Rhett would never leave Charleston, and she'd have to be satisfied with occasional visits to Tara. But why not daydream all she wanted on a beautiful spring day like this, driving a smart pony cart and wearing stockings striped in red and blue? Why not?

She giggled, touched the whip to the pony's neck. Listen to me—I sound downright Irish.

May Day was everything that had been promised. There was food and dancing on every street in Trim, plus four tremendous Maypoles on the green within the walls of the ruined castle. Scarlett's ribbon was red, and she had a wreath of flowers for her hair, and an English officer asked her to walk down to the river, and she told him off in no uncertain terms.

They went home after the sun came up; Scarlett walked the four miles with the rest of the family because she didn't want the night to end, even though it was now day. And because she was already starting to miss her cousins, all the people she'd met. She was longing to get home, to settle the details about Tara, to begin the work on it, but she was still glad that she'd stayed for May Day. There was only a week left now. It seemed a very short time.

On Wednesday, Frank Kelly, the post rider from Trim, stopped at Matt O'Toole's for a pipe and a pint. "There's a bulging letter for Colum O'Hara," he said. "What do you fancy it could be about?" They speculated pleasantly, and wildly. In America, anything might be true. And they might just as well speculate. Father O'Hara was a friendly man, as everyone agreed, and a grand talker. But when all was said and over, he never told much.

Matt O'Toole didn't take Colum's letter to him. There was no need. He knew that Clare O'Gorman was going to visit her old grandmother that afternoon. She'd take the letter, if Colum didn't stop in before. Matt hefted the envelope in his hand. It must be exceptionally fine news to warrant spending that much money to send such a weight. Or else a truly major disaster.

"There's post for you, Scarlett. Colum put it on the table. And a cup of tea when you want it. Did you have a pleasant visit with Molly?" Kathleen's voice was rich with anticipation.

Scarlett didn't disappoint her. With a giggle in her voice, she described

the visit. "Molly had the doctor's wife with her, and her teacup rattled fit
to break when I walked in. She didn't know whether she could get away
with saying I was the new hired girl or not, I reckon. So then the doctor's
wife said in a little fluty voice, 'Oh, the rich American cousin. What an
honor.' And she didn't bat an eye at my clothes. Molly jumped up like a
scalded cat and rushed over to give me one of her double kisses on the
cheek when she heard that. I promise you, Kathleen, she got tears in her
eyes when I said I'd only come to fetch a travelling costume out of my
trunk. She was just dying for me to stay, no matter what I looked like. I
gave her the kiss-kiss when I got ready to leave. And the doctor's wife,
too, for good measure. Might as well go the whole hog."

Kathleen was bent over with laughter, her sewing dropped in a heap
on the floor. Scarlett dropped her travelling suit beside it. She was sure it
was going to need easing through the waist. If the baby wasn't making her
thicker through the middle, then wearing easy clothes and eating so much
was to blame. Whichever it was, she had no intention of taking the long
trip laced so tight she couldn't breathe.

She picked up the envelope and held it in the doorway so the light
could fall on it. It was covered with writing and rubber-stamped dates.
Honestly! Her grandfather was the nastiest man in the world. Or else that
horrible Jerome was responsible, more likely him. The envelope had gone
to her care of her grandfather and he hadn't sent it to Maureen's for weeks.
She tore it open impatiently. It was from some government bureau in Atlanta, mailed originally to the Peachtree Street house. She hoped she hadn't
missed paying some tax or something. Between the money to the Bishop
for Tara and the cost of the houses she was building, her reserves were
getting too low to throw money away on late payment penalties. And she
was going to need a lot for the work on Tara. Not to mention buying a
place for Will. Her fingers touched the pouch beneath her shirt. No, Rhett's
money was Rhett's money.

The document was dated March 26, 1875. The day she'd sailed from
Savannah on the *Brian Boru*. Scarlett's eyes skimmed over the first few lines,
then stopped. It made no sense. She went back to the beginning and read
more slowly. All the color drained from her face. "Kathleen, where's
Colum, do you know?" Why, I sound perfectly ordinary. That's funny.

"He's with the Old One, I think. Clare came to get him. Can't it wait
a bit? I'm nearly finished with fixing this dress of mine for Bridie to wear
on the voyage, and I know she wants to try it on for you to comment."

"I can't wait." She had to see Colum. Something had gone terribly
wrong. They had to leave today, this minute. She had to get home.

Colum was in the yard in front of the cottage. "There's never been a spring so sunny," he said. "The cat and I are basking a bit."

Scarlett's unnatural calm vanished when she saw him, and she was screaming when she reached his side. "Take me home, Colum. Damn you and all the O'Haras and Ireland. I should never have left home."

Her hand was clutched painfully, nails biting into flesh. Crumbled in it was a statement from the sovereign state of Georgia that it had entered into its permanent records the absolute decree of divorce granted to one Rhett Kinnicutt Butler on the grounds of desertion by his wife, one Scarlett O'Hara Butler, by the Military District of South Carolina administered by the Federal Government of the United States of America.

"There is no divorce in South Carolina," said Scarlett. "Two lawyers told me so." She said it again and again, always the same words, until her throat was raw and she could no longer force sound through it. Then her chapped lips formed the words silently while her mind said them. Again and again.

Colum led her to a quiet corner of the vegetable garden. He sat beside her and talked, but he couldn't make her listen, so he took her clenched hands in his for comfort and stayed quiet beside her. Through the light shower that came with twilight. Through the brilliant sunset. Into the darkness. Bridie came looking for them when supper was ready, and Colum sent her away.

"Scarlett's off her head, Bridie. Tell them in the house not to worry, she only needs a bit of time to get over the shock. The news came from America: her husband's grievously sick. She's afraid he'll die without her by his side."

Bridie ran back to report. Scarlett was praying, she said. The family prayed too; their supper was cold when they finally began to eat. "Take a lantern out, Timothy," said Daniel.

The light reflected from Scarlett's glazed eyes. "Kathleen sent a shawl, too," Timothy whispered. Colum nodded, placed it over Scarlett's shoulders, waved Timothy away.

Another hour went by. Stars glowed in the nearly moonless sky; they were brighter than the light from the lantern. There was a brief small cry from a nearby wheat field, then a nearly soundless flutter of wings. An owl had made a kill.

"What am I to do?" Scarlett's rasping voice was loud in the darkness. Colum sighed quietly and thanked God. The worst of the shock was over.

"We'll go home as we planned, Scarlett darling. There's nothing happened that can't be remedied." His voice was calm, certain, soothing.

"Divorced!" There was an alarming rise of hysteria in the cracked sound. Colum chafed her hands briskly.

"What's done can be undone, Scarlett."

"I should have stayed. I'll never forgive myself."

"Whist, now. Should-haves solve nothing. It's the next thing to happen that needs thinking about."

"He'll never take me back. Not if his heart's so hard that he'd divorce me. I kept waiting for him to come after me, Colum, I was so sure he would. How could I have been such a fool? You don't know the all of it. I'm pregnant, Colum. How can I have a baby when I don't have a husband?"

"There, there," said Colum quietly. "Doesn't that take care of it? You've only got to tell him."

Scarlett's hands flew to her belly. Of course! How could she have been such a fool? Jagged laughter tore at her throat. There was no piece of paper ever written that would make Rhett Butler give up his baby. He could have the divorce cancelled, erased from all the records. Rhett could do anything. He'd just proved it again. There was no divorce in South Carolina. Unless Rhett Butler made up his mind to get one.

"I want to go right now, Colum. There must be a ship sailing earlier. I'll go crazy waiting."

"We're leaving early Friday, Scarlett darling, and the ship sails Saturday. If we go tomorrow there'll still be a day to fill before the sailing. Wouldn't you rather spend it here?"

"Oh, no, I've got to know I'm going. Even if it's only partway, I'll be heading home to Rhett. Everything's going to work out, I'll make it work out. It's going to be all right . . . isn't it, Colum? Say that it's going to be all right."

"That it is, Scarlett darling. You should eat now, at least a cup of milk. With a drop in it, perhaps. You need sleep, too. You have to keep up your strength, for the good of the baby."

"Oh, yes! I will. I'll take wonderful care of myself. But first I've got to see about my frock, and my trunk needs repacking. And, Colum, how will we find a carriage to get to the train?" Her voice was rising again. Colum got up and pulled her to her feet.

"I'll take care of it, with the help of the girls for the trunk. But only if you'll eat something while you see to your frock."

"Yes! Yes, that's what we'll do." She was a little calmer, but still perilously edgy. He'd have to see to it that she drank the milk and whiskey as soon as they reached the house. Poor creature. If only he knew more about women and babies he would feel a lot easier in his mind. She'd been going sleepless and dancing like a dervish of late. Could that bring on a baby too soon? If she lost it, he feared for her reason.

55

$\mathcal{L}$ike so many people before him, Colum underestimated the strength of Scarlett O'Hara. She insisted that her baggage be brought from Molly's that night, and she gave orders to Brigid to pack her things while Kathleen fitted her frock on her. "Watch the lacing, Bridie," she said sharply when she put her corset on. "You're going to have to do this on the ship, and I won't be able to see behind me to tell you what to do." Her feverish manner and ragged voice had already put Bridie in a terror. Scarlett's sharp cry of pain when Kathleen yanked on the laces made Bridie cry out, too.

It doesn't matter that it hurts, Scarlett reminded herself, it always hurts, always has. I'd just forgotten how much. I'll get used to it again after a while. I'm not hurting the baby. I always wore stays as long as I could when I was pregnant, and it was always a lot later than this. I'm not even ten weeks gone yet. I've got to get into my clothes, I've just got to. I'll be on that train tomorrow if it kills me.

"Pull, Kathleen," she gasped. "Pull harder."

Colum walked to Trim and arranged to get the carriage a day earlier. Then he made the rounds, spreading the word about Scarlett's terrible worry. When he was finished it was late and he was tired. But now there'd be no one wondering why the American O'Hara had gone off like a thief in the night without saying goodbye.

She did very well with her goodbyes to the family. The previous day's shock had armored her in a shell of numbness. She broke down only once, when she said goodbye to her grandmother. Or, rather, when Old Katie Scarlett said goodbye to her. "God go with you," the old woman said, "and the saints guide your footsteps. It's happy I am you were here for my birthday, Gerald's girl. The only pity is you'll not be at my wake . . . What are you weeping for, girl? Do you not know there's no party for the living half as grand as a wake? It's a shame to miss it."

Scarlett sat silent in the carriage to Mullingar and in the train to Galway. Bridie was too nervous to speak, but her excited happiness showed in her bright cheeks and large fascinated eyes. She'd never been more than ten miles from her home in all her fifteen years.

When they reached the hotel Bridie stared openmouthed at its grandeur. "I'll see you ladies to your room," said Colum, "and be back in time to escort you to the dining room. I'm just going to go down to the harbor and arrange about loading the trunks. I'd like to see which staterooms they've given us, too. Now's the time to change if they're not the best."

"I'll go with you," said Scarlett. It was the first time she'd spoken.

"There's no need, Scarlett darling."

"There is for me. I want to see the ship or I won't feel certain it's really there."

Colum humored her. And Bridie asked if she might come, too. The hotel was too overwhelming for her. She didn't want to stay there alone.

The early evening breeze off the water was sweet with salt. Scarlett breathed deeply of it, remembering that Charleston always had salted air. She was unaware of the slow tears rolling down her cheeks. If only they could sail now, at once. Would the captain consider? She touched the pouch of gold between her breasts.

"I'm looking for the *Evening Star*," Colum said to one of the longshoremen.

"She's down there," the man gestured with his thumb. "Been in just under an hour."

Colum concealed his surprise. The ship had been due to land thirty hours earlier. No reason to let Scarlett know that the delay might mean trouble.

Gangs were moving methodically to and from the *Evening Star*. She carried cargo as well as passengers. "This is no place for a woman right now, Scarlett darling. Let's go back to the hotel, and I'll come back later."

Scarlett's jaw set. "No. I want to talk to the Captain."

"He'll be too busy to see anyone, even someone as lovely as yourself."

She was in no mood for compliments. "You know him, don't you, Colum? You know everybody. Fix it so I can see him now."

"The man's a stranger to me; I've never laid eyes on him, Scarlett. How should I be knowing him? This is Galway, not County Meath."

A uniformed man came off the *Star*'s gangplank. The two big canvas sacks on his shoulders seemed to burden him not at all; his gait was light and quick, unusual for a man of his size and girth.

"And isn't that Father Colum O'Hara himself?" he bellowed when he came near them. "What finds you so far from Matt O'Toole's bar, Colum?" He heaved one of the sacks to the ground and took off his hat to Scarlett and Bridie. "Didn't I always say that the O'Haras have the devil's own luck with the ladies?" he roared, laughing at his own humor. "Did you tell them you were a priest, Colum?"

Scarlett's smile was perfunctory when she was introduced to Frank Mahoney, and she paid no attention at all to the chain of cousinships that connected him to Maureen's family. She wanted to talk to the Captain!

"I'm just taking the post from America over to the station for sorting tomorrow," said Mahoney. "Will you want a look, Colum, or will you wait till you're back home again to read your perfumed love letters?" He laughed uproariously at his wit.

"That's kind of you, Frank. I'll take a look if you'll let me." Colum untied the sack near his feet, pulled it nearer the tall gas lamp that lighted the pier. He found the envelope from Savannah with ease. "Luck's in my pocket today," he said. "I knew from his last letter that another'd be coming soon from my brother, but I'd given up hope of it. I thank you, Frank. Would you allow me to buy you a pint?" His hand reached into his pocket.

"There's no need. I did it for the pleasure of breaking the English rules." Frank hoisted the sack again. "The God-rotting supervisor will be looking at his gold watch, I can't tarry. Good evening to you, ladies."

There were a half dozen smaller letters in the envelope. Colum flicked through them, searching for Stephen's distinctive handwriting. "Here's one for you, Scarlett," he said. He put the blue envelope in her hand, found Stephen's letter, tore it open. He had just begun to read it when he heard a high, prolonged cry, and felt a weight sliding against him. Before he could throw out his arms, Scarlett was lying at his feet. The blue envelope and thin pages fluttered in her limp hand, then the breeze scattered them across the cobbles. While Colum lifted Scarlett's shoulders and held his fingers to the pulse in her throat, Bridie ran after the pages.

The hackney cab jounced and swayed from the speed of their race back to the hotel. Scarlett's head rolled grotesquely from side to side, even though Colum tried to hold her firmly in his arms. He carried her quickly through the hotel lobby. "Call a doctor," he shouted to the liveried attendants, "and get out of my way." Once in Scarlett's room, he laid her on the bed.

"Come on, Bridie, help me get her clothes off," he said. "We've got to get some breath into her." He took a knife from a leather sheath inside his coat. Bridie's fingers moved nimbly along the buttons on the back of Scarlett's dress.

Colum cut the corset laces. "Now," he said, "help me lift her head up on the pillows, and cover her with something warm." He rubbed Scarlett's arms roughly, slapped her cheeks gently. "Have you got smelling salts?"

"I don't, Colum, nor do she, far's I know."

"The doctor will. I hope it's only a faint."

"She fainted, that's all, Father," said the doctor when he left Scarlett's bedroom, "but it's a deep one. I've left some tonic with the girl for when she comes out of it. These ladies! They will cut off all their circulation for the sake of fashion. Nothing to worry about, though. She'll be fine."

Colum thanked him, paid him, saw him out. Then he sat heavily on a chair by the lamplit table, put his head in his hands. There was a great deal to worry about, and he questioned whether Scarlett O'Hara would ever be "fine" again. The crumpled, water-spotted pages of the letter were strewn on the table beside him. In their midst was a neatly trimmed clipping from a newspaper. "Yesterday evening," it read, "in a private ceremony at the Confederate Home for Widows and Orphans, Miss Anne Hampton was joined in matrimony to Mr. Rhett Butler."

56

$\mathcal{S}$carlett's mind spiralled up, up, spinning, swirling, up, up out of the black toward consciousness, but some instinct forced it downward again, sliding, slipping back into darkness, away from the unbearable truth lying in wait for her. Again and again it happened, the struggle tiring her so much that she lay exhausted, motionless and pale in the big bed, as if dead.

She dreamed, a dream full of movement and urgency. She was at Twelve Oaks, and it was whole again and beautiful, as it had been before Sherman's torches. The gracious curving staircase turned through space as if magically suspended, and her feet were lightly nimble on its treads. Ashley was ahead of her, climbing, unaware of her cries to stop. "Ashley," she called, "Ashley, wait for me," and she ran after him.

How long the staircase was. She didn't remember it being so tall; it seemed to be growing ever higher as she ran, and Ashley was so far above her. She had to reach him. She didn't know why, but she knew she must, and she ran faster, always faster, until her heart was pounding in her breast. "Ashley!" she cried. "Ashley!" He paused, and she found strength she didn't know she possessed; she climbed, running even faster.

Relief flooded her body and her soul when her hand touched his sleeve. Then he turned toward her, and she screamed without sound. He had no face, only a pale featureless blur.

Then she was falling, tumbling through space, her eyes fixed in terror on the figure above her, her throat straining to scream. But the only sound was laughter, from below, rising like a cloud to surround her and mock her muteness.

I'm going to die, she thought. Terrible pain will crush me and I'll die.

But suddenly, strong arms closed around her and drew her gently from the falling. She knew them, she knew the shoulder that pillowed her head. It was Rhett. Rhett had saved her. She was safe in his embrace. She turned her head, lifted it to look into his eyes. Icy terror paralyzed her whole body. His face was formless, like mist or smoke, like Ashley's. Then the laughter began again, from the blankness that should be Rhett's face.

Scarlett's mind jolted into consciousness, fleeing from horror, and she opened her eyes. Darkness surrounded her, and the unknown. The lamp had burned out, and Bridie was asleep in her chair, unseen in a corner of the huge room. Scarlett stretched out her arms over the expanse of the big, unfamiliar bed. Her fingers touched soft linen, nothing else. The sides of the mattress were too distant to reach. She seemed to be marooned on a strange vastness of softness, without definition. Perhaps it went on forever into the silent darkness— Her throat constricted with fear. She was alone and lost in the dark.

Stop it! Her mind forced panic away, demanded that she take hold of herself. Scarlett carefully pulled her legs up, turned over into a kneeling crouch. Her movements were slow, so as to make no sound. Anything might be out there in the darkness, listening. She crawled with agonized caution until her hands felt the edge of the bed, then down to the hard solidity of the wooden frame.

What a ninnyhammer you are, Scarlett O'Hara, she told herself when tears of relief ran over her cheeks. Of course the bed is strange, and the room. You fainted, like some silly weak vaporish girl, and Colum and Bridie brought you to the hotel. Stop this scaredy-cat nonsense.

Then, like a physical blow, memory attacked her. Rhett was lost to her ... divorced from her ... married to Anne Hampton. She couldn't believe it, but she had to, it was true.

Why? Why had he done such a thing? She'd been so sure he loved her. He couldn't have done it, he couldn't.

But he had.

I never knew him. Scarlett heard the words as if she'd spoken them aloud. I never knew him at all. Who was it that I loved? Whose child am I carrying?

What's going to become of me?

That night, in the frightening darkness of an unseen hotel room in a country thousands of miles from her homeland, Scarlett O'Hara did the most courageous thing she had ever been called on to do. She faced up to failure.

It's all my fault. I should have gone back to Charleston as soon as I knew I was pregnant. I chose to have fun, and those weeks of fun have cost me the only happiness I really care about. I just didn't think about what Rhett might believe when I ran away, I didn't think past the next day, the next reel. I didn't think at all.

I never have.

All the impetuous, unconsidered errors of her life crowded around Scarlett in the black silence of the night, and she forced herself to look at them. Charles Hamilton—she had married him to spite Ashley, she hadn't cared for him at all. Frank Kennedy—she'd been horrid to him, lied to him about Suellen so that Frank would marry her and give her money to save Tara. Rhett—oh, she'd made too many mistakes to count. She'd married him when she didn't love him, and she'd made no effort to make him happy, she'd never even cared that he wasn't happy—not until it was too late.

Oh, God, forgive me, I never thought once about what I was doing to them, about what they were feeling. I hurt and hurt and hurt all of them, because I didn't stop to think.

Melanie, too, especially Melly. I can't bear to remember how nasty I was to her. I never once felt grateful for the way she loved me and stood up for me. I never even told her I loved her, too, because I didn't think of it until the end, when there was no chance.

Have I ever in my life paid attention to what I was doing? Have I—even once—ever thought about the consequences?

Despair and shame gripped Scarlett's heart. How could she have been such a fool? She despised fools.

Then her hands clenched and her jaw hardened and she stiffened her spine. She would not wallow in picking at the past and feeling sorry for herself. She would not whine—not to anyone else, and not to herself.

She stared at the darkness above her through dry eyes. She wouldn't cry, not now. She'd have the rest of her life to cry. Now she had to think, and think carefully, before she decided what to do.

She had to think about the baby.

For a moment she hated it, hated her thickening waist and the clumsy, heavy body that lay ahead. It was supposed to have given Rhett back to her, and it hadn't. There were things a woman could do—she'd heard of women who had rid themselves of unwanted babies . . .

. . . Rhett would never forgive her if she did that. And what difference did that make? Rhett was gone, forever.

A forbidden sob broke from Scarlett's lips despite all her willpower.

Lost. I lost him. I'm beaten. Rhett won.

Then sudden anger coursed through her, cauterizing her pain, energizing her exhausted body and spirit.

I'm beaten, but I'll get even with you, Rhett Butler, she thought with bitter triumph. I'll hit you harder than you've hit me.

Scarlett laid her hands gently on her belly. Oh, no, she wasn't going to get rid of this baby. She'd take care of it better than any baby in the history of the whole world.

Her mind filled with images of Rhett and Bonnie. He always loved Bonnie more than he loved me. He'd give anything—he'd give his life to have her back. I'll have a new Bonnie, all my own. And when she's old enough—when she loves me, and only me, more than anything or anyone on earth, then I'll let Rhett see her, see what he's missed . . .

What am I thinking? I must be crazy. Only a minute ago I realized how much I hurt him, and I hated myself. Now I'm hating him and planning to hurt him worse. I won't be like that, I won't let myself imagine such things, I won't.

Rhett's gone; I've admitted it. I can't give in to regrets or revenge, that's a waste when what I have to do is make a new life from scratch. I've got to find something fresh, something important, something to live for. I can do it if I put my mind to it.

Throughout the remainder of the night, Scarlett's mind moved methodically along the avenues of possibility. She found dead ends, she found and overcame obstacles, she found surprising corners of memory and of imagination and of maturity.

She remembered her youth and the County and the days before the War. The memories were somehow painless, distant, and she understood that she was no longer that Scarlett, that she could let go of her, permit the old days and their dead to rest.

She concentrated on the future, on realities, on consequences. Her temples began to throb, then to pound, then her whole head ached abominably, but she continued to think.

Just when the first sounds began in the street outside, all the pieces fell into place inside her mind, and Scarlett knew what she was going to do. As soon as enough light filtered through the drawn curtains into the room, Scarlett called out, "Bridie?"

The girl jumped up from the chair, blinking sleep from her eyes. "Thanks be to God you're restored!" she exclaimed. "The doctor left this tonic. I'll just find the spoon, it's on this table somewhere."

Scarlett opened her mouth meekly for the bitter medicine. "There," she said firmly, "I'll have no more of being sick. Open the curtains, it must be day by now. I need some breakfast, my head is aching, and I've got to get my strength back."

It was raining. A real rain, not the misty showers that were customary. Scarlett felt a dark satisfaction.

"Colum will want to know you're better, he's been that worried. Can I tell him to come in?"

"Not now. Tell him I'll want to see him later, I want to talk to him. But not yet. Go on. Tell him. And ask him to show you how to order up my breakfast."

57

$\mathcal{S}$carlett forced herself to swallow bite after bite of food, even though she wasn't even aware of what she was eating. As she'd said to Bridie, she needed her strength.

After breakfast she sent Bridie away, with instructions to return after two hours. Then she sat down at the writing table near the window and, with a small frown of concentration, rapidly filled sheet after sheet of thick, creamy, unmarked letter paper.

After she had written, folded, and sealed two letters, she stared at the blank paper in front of her for a long time. She had planned it all out in the dark hours of the night, she knew what she was going to write, but she couldn't bring herself to pick up the pen and begin. Her very marrow shrank from what she had to do.

Scarlett shivered and looked away from the page. Her eyes fell on a pretty little porcelain clock on a nearby table, and she drew in her breath, shocked. So late! Bridie would be back in only forty-five minutes.

I can't put it off any longer, it won't change things no matter how long I do. There's no other way. I've got to write to Uncle Henry, eat humble pie, and ask him sweetly to help me. He's the only one I can trust. Scarlett gritted her teeth and reached for the pen. Her usually neat handwriting was cramped and uneven from strained determination when she put the words on paper that would turn over control of her Atlanta businesses and her precious hoard of gold in the Atlanta bank to Henry Hamilton.

It was like cutting the ground out from under her feet. She felt physically ill, almost dizzy. There was no fear that the old lawyer would cheat her, but there was no chance that he would watch every penny the way she always had. It was one thing to have him collect and bank the receipts from the store and the rent from the saloon. It was another thing altogether to give him control of store inventory and prices, and the amount of rent to charge the saloonkeeper.

Control. She was giving up control of her money, her safety, her success. Just when control was most needed. Buying Carreen's share of Tara was going to dig a deep hole in her accumulated gold, but it was too late now to stop the deal with the Bishop, and Scarlett wouldn't stop it even if she could. Her dream of spending summers at Tara with Rhett was dead now, but Tara was still Tara, and she was determined to make it hers.

Building the houses on the edge of town was another drain on her resources, but it had to be done. If only she wasn't certain that Uncle Henry would agree with everything Sam Colleton suggested, without asking the cost.

Worst of all, she wouldn't know what was going on, for good or for ill. Anything might happen.

"I can't do it!" Scarlett groaned aloud. But she continued to write. She had to do it. She was going to take a long vacation, she wrote, do some travelling. She would be out of touch, with no address where mail could reach her. She looked at the words. They blurred, and she blinked the tears away. None of that, she told herself. It was absolutely essential to cut all ties, or Rhett would be able to track her down. And he must not know about the baby until she chose to tell him.

But how could she bear not knowing what Uncle Henry was doing with her money? Or if the Panic was getting worse, threatening her savings? Or if her house burned down? Or, worse, her store?

She had to bear it, so she would. The pen scratched hurriedly across the pages, detailing instructions and advice that Henry Hamilton would probably disregard.

When Bridie returned, all the letters were on the blotter, folded and sealed. Scarlett was sitting in an armchair, her ruined corset in her lap.

"Oh, I forgot," Bridie moaned. "We had to cut you out, to let the breath into you. What will you have me do? There might be a shop nearby I could go to—"

"Never mind, it's not important," Scarlett said. "You can baste me into a frock, and I'll wear a cloak to hide the stitches in the back. Come on, now, it's getting late, and I've got a lot to do."

Bridie looked at the window. Late, was it? Her country-accustomed eyes could tell it wasn't yet nine in the morning. She went obediently to unpack the sewing kit Kathleen had helped her put together for her new role as lady's maid.

Thirty minutes later, Scarlett knocked on the door of Colum's room. She was hollow-eyed from lack of sleep, but immaculately groomed and perfectly composed. She didn't feel at all tired. The worst was over; now she had things to do. It restored her strength.

She smiled at her cousin when he opened his door. "Will your collar protect your reputation if I come in?" she asked. "I have things to talk about that are private."

Colum bowed and swung the door wide. "A thousand welcomes," he said. "It's good to see you smiling, Scarlett darling."

"It won't be long before I'll be able to laugh, I hope ... Did the letter from America get lost?"

"No. I have it. Private. I understand what happened."

"Do you?" Scarlett smiled again. "Then you're wiser than I am. I know, but I'll likely never understand. Still, that's neither here nor there." She put the three letters she'd written on a table. "I'll tell you about these in a minute. First I have to tell you that I'm not going with you and Bridie. I'm going to stay in Ireland." She held up her hand. "No, don't say anything. I've thought it all through. There's nothing for me in America any more."

"Ah, no, Scarlett darling, you're being too hasty. Didn't I tell you there's nothing done that can't be undone? Your husband got a divorce once, he'll do it again when you go back and tell him about the baby."

"You're wrong, Colum. Rhett will never divorce Anne. She's his kind, from his people, from Charleston. And besides she's like Melanie. That doesn't mean anything to you, you never knew Melly. But Rhett did. He knew how rare she was long before I did. He respected Melly. She was the only woman he ever did respect, except maybe his mother, and he admired her the way she deserved. This girl he's married is worth ten of me, the same as Melly was, and Rhett knows it. She's worth ten of Rhett, too, but she loves him. Let him carry that cross." There was a savage bitterness in the words.

Ach, the suffering, he thought. There must be a way to help her. "You've got your Tara now, Katie Scarlett, and you've such dreams for it. Won't that comfort you till your heart's healed? You can build the world you want for the child you're carrying, a grand plantation made by his grandfather and his mother. If it's a boy, he can be called Gerald."

"You're not thinking anything I haven't already thought. Thank you, but you can't find an answer if I couldn't, Colum, believe me. One thing, I already have a son, a child you don't know about, if there's inheritance to consider. But the main thing is this baby. I can't go back to Tara to have his baby, I can't take this baby to Tara after it's born. People would never believe it was made in wedlock. They've always thought—in the County and in Atlanta—that I was no better than I should be. And I left Charleston the day after—after the baby was started." Scarlett's face blanched with painful longing. "No one would ever believe it was Rhett's baby. We slept in separate rooms for years. They'd call me a whore and my baby a bastard, and they'd smack their lips with pleasure in the calling."

The ugly words were marked on her twisted mouth.

"Not so, Scarlett, not so. Your husband knows the truth. He'll acknowledge the baby."

Scarlett's eyes flamed. "Oh, he'd acknowledge it all right, and he'd take it from me. Colum, you can't imagine how Rhett is about babies, his babies. He's like a madman with love. And he's got to own the child, be the best loved, be the all. He'd take this baby soon as it had the first breath in its little body. Don't think he couldn't do it, either. He got the divorce when it couldn't be gotten. He'd change any law or make a new one. There's nothing he can't do." She was whispering hoarsely, as if afraid. Her face was contorted with hatred and a wild, unreasoned terror.

Then suddenly, like a veil falling, it changed. It became smooth, and tranquil, except for her blazing green eyes. A smile appeared on her lips; it made Colum O'Hara's spine chill. "This is my baby," said Scarlett. Her quiet low-pitched voice was like a giant cat's purr. "Mine alone. He'll never know about it till I want him to, when it's too late for him. I'm going to pray for a girl. A beautiful blue-eyed girl."

Colum crossed himself.

Scarlett laughed harshly. "Poor Colum. You must have heard about the woman scorned, don't be so shocked. Don't fret, I won't frighten you any more." She smiled, and he could almost believe he'd imagined what he'd seen in her face a moment earlier. Scarlett's smile was open and affectionate.

"I know you're trying to help me, and I'm grateful, Colum, I really am. You've been so good to me, such a good friend, probably the best friend I ever had except Melly. You're like a brother. I always wished I had a brother. I hope you'll always be my friend."

Colum assured her that he would. He thought to himself that he'd never seen a soul so in need of help.

"I want you to take these letters to America for me, please, Colum. This one's to my Aunt Pauline. I want her to know I got her letter so she'll get all the pleasure possible out of her love for telling people 'I told you so.' And this one's to my Atlanta lawyer, there's business I have to settle.

Both should be posted in Boston, I don't want anyone to know where I really am. This one I want you to hand-deliver. It'll mean more travel for you, but it's terribly important. It's to the bank in Savannah. I have a pile of gold and my jewelry in their vault, and I'm counting on you to bring it back safe for me. Did Bridie give you the bag I had 'round my neck? Good. That'll do me to get started with. Now I need you to find me a lawyer I can trust, if there is such a thing. I'm going to use Rhett Butler's money. I'm going to buy Ballyhara, where the O'Haras began. This child's going to have a heritage he could never provide. I'll show him a thing or two about roots that go deep."

"Scarlett darling, I beseech you. Wait a bit. We can stay in Galway awhile, with Bridie and me to take care of you. You're not over the shocks. One right on top the other the way they came, it's been too much for you to be making such big decisions."

"You think I've gone crazy, I suppose. Maybe I have. But this is my way, Colum, and I mean to take it. With your help or without it. No reason for you and Bridie to stay, either. I plan to go back to Daniel's tomorrow and ask them to take me in again until Ballyhara's mine. If you're afraid I need looking after, you can surely trust Kathleen and them.

"Come on, Colum," Scarlett said, "admit it. I've got you beat."

He spread his hands and admitted it.

Later he escorted her to the office of an English lawyer with a reputation for successful completion of whatever he put his hand to, and the search for the owner of Ballyhara was set into motion.

The following day Colum went to the Market as soon as the first tables were set up. He took the purchases Scarlett wanted back to the hotel. "Here you are then, Mrs. O'Hara," he said. "Black skirts and shirts and shawl and cloak and stockings for the poor new widow, and I've told Bridie that's what the news was that gave you the collapse. Your husband was taken by sickness before there was time for you to reach his side. And here you are as well—a wee gift from me. I'm thinking that when widow's weeds pull your spirits down, you'll feel better for knowing you've got them on." Colum deposited a heap of bright colored petticoats in Scarlett's lap.

Scarlett smiled. Her eyes brimmed with emotion. "How did you know I was kicking myself for giving all my Irish clothes to the cousins in Adamstown?" She waved at her trunk and valises. "I won't need these things any more. Take them with you and give them to Maureen to dole out."

"That's foolish extravagance and impetuosity, Scarlett."

"Fiddle-dee-dee! I took out my boots and my shimmies. The frocks are no use to me. I'm never going to be squeezed into a corset again, never.

I'm Scarlett O'Hara, an Irish lass with a free-swinging skirt and a secret red petticoat. Free, Colum! I'm going to make a world for myself by my rules, not anybody else's. Don't worry about me. I'm going to learn to be happy." Colum averted his eyes from the grimly determined expression on Scarlett's face.

58

The ship's sailing was delayed two days, so Colum and Bridie were able to escort Scarlett to the train station on Sunday morning. First they all went to Mass.

"You must have a word with her, now, Colum," Bridie whispered in his ear when they met in the hallway. She rolled her eyes toward Scarlett.

Colum hid his smile with a cough. Scarlett was dressed like a widowed peasant, even to wearing a shawl instead of a cloak.

"We'll go along with her, Brigid," he said firmly. "She has a right to mourn any way she sees fit."

"But, Colum—this grand English hotel, all the people will be staring, and talking."

"And don't they have their rights, too? Let them stare and say what they will. We'll give no notice." He took Bridie's arm in a firm grasp, offered his other hand to Scarlett. She rested hers elegantly on top of it, as if he were leading her into a ballroom.

When she was seated in her first-class compartment on the train, Colum watched with relish, Bridie with horror, as one group of English travellers after another opened the door to the compartment, then backed away.

"The authorities shouldn't allow those people to buy first-class tickets," one woman said loudly to her husband.

Scarlett's hand shot out to hold the door before the Anglo could close it. She called out to Colum, who was on the platform nearby. "Faith! I forgot my basket of boiled taties, Father. Will you say a prayer to the Blessed Virgin that there'll be a peddler selling some food on this train?" Her brogue was so exaggerated that Colum could barely understand the words. He was still laughing when a station attendant closed the door, and the train began to move. The English couple, he was pleased to see, abandoned all dignity in their scramble into another compartment.

Scarlett waved goodbye, smiling, as her window moved out of his sight.

Then she sat back in her seat and allowed her face to relax, permitted a single tear to escape. She was bone tired and dreading the return to Adamstown. Daniel's two-room cottage had seemed quaint and delightfully different from all she was accustomed to, as long as she was on a vacation visit. Now it was a cramped, crowded house with no luxuries, and it was the only place she could call home—for who knew how long. The lawyer might not be able to find the owner of Ballyhara. The owner might not be willing to sell. The price might be more, even, than all the money Rhett had given her.

Her carefully thought-out plan was riddled with holes, and she had no certainty about anything.

I won't think about it now, there's nothing I can do about any of those things. At least nobody'll be crowding in here wanting to chatter at me. Scarlett folded up the arms separating the three deeply cushioned seats, stretched out with a sigh, and fell asleep, her ticket on the floor where the conductor could see it. She had made a plan, and she was going to see it through as far as she could. It would be a lot easier if she wasn't tired half to death.

The first step proceeded without a hitch. She bought a pony and trap in Mullingar and drove it home to Adamstown. It wasn't as stylish a rig as Molly's; the trap was distinctly shabby looking. But the pony was younger and larger and stronger. And she'd made a start.

The family were shocked when she returned, and sympathetic for her loss in the best possible way. Once expressed, they never again spoke of their feelings; instead they asked was there anything they could do for her.

"You can teach me," said Scarlett. "I want to learn about an Irish farm." She followed Daniel and his sons through their work routines. She even set her jaw and forced herself to learn how to handle cattle, including milking the cow. After she'd learned all she could about Daniel's farm, Scarlett put herself out to charm Molly, then Molly's loathsome husband, Robert. His farm was five times the size of Daniel's. After Robert it was the turn of his boss, Mr. Alderson, manager of the Earl's entire estate. Not even in the days when she was captivating every man in Clayton County had Scarlett been so charming. Or worked so hard. Or succeeded so well. She had no time to notice the austerity of the cottage. All that mattered was the soft mattress at the end of the long, long summer day of work.

After a month, she knew almost as much about Adamstown as Alderson, and she'd identified at least six ways it could be improved. It was just about that time that she received the letter from her Galway lawyer.

The widow of Ballyhara's deceased owner had remarried only a year after his death and had herself died five years ago. Her heir and eldest son, now twenty-seven, lived in England where he was also heir to the estate of his father, who was still living. He had said he would give consideration to any offer in excess of fifteen thousand pounds. Scarlett studied the copy of the survey map of Ballyhara that was attached to the letter. It was much bigger than she'd thought.

Why, it's both sides of the road to Trim. And there's another river. The boundary's the Boyne on this side and—she squinted at the tiny lettering—the Knightsbrook on the other. What an elegant name. Knightsbrook. Two rivers. I've got to have it. But—fifteen thousand pounds!

She already knew from Alderson that ten pounds was a price paid only for prime growing land, and a high price at that. Eight was more like it, seven and a half for a shrewd bargainer. Ballyhara had a sizable area of bog, too. Useful for fuel, there was enough peat to last a few centuries. But nothing grew on bog, and the fields around it were too acid for wheat. Plus the land had gone to ruin in thirty years. It all needed clearing of scrub growth and tap-rooted weeds. She shouldn't pay more than four, four and a half. For 1,240 acres, that came to £4,960 or £5,580 at the most. There was the house, of course; it was huge. Not that she cared. The buildings in the town were more important. Forty-six of them all told, plus two churches. Five of the houses were quite grand, two dozen were only cottages.

But all were deserted. Likely to stay that way, too, with no one tending to the estate. Taken all in all, ten thousand pounds would be more than fair. He'd be lucky to get it. Ten thousand pounds—that was fifty thousand dollars! Scarlett was horrified.

I've got to start thinking in real money, I get too careless otherwise. Ten thousand doesn't sound like all that much of anything, but fifty thousand dollars is different. I know that's a fortune. With all that scrimping and saving and sharp dealing at the lumber mills and the store . . . and selling the mills outright . . . and the rent for the saloon . . . and never spending a penny I didn't absolutely have to, year in and year out, in ten years I only managed to put together a little over thirty thousand dollars. And I wouldn't have half that if Rhett hadn't paid for everything for almost the last seven years. Uncle Henry says I'm a rich woman with my thirty thousand, and I reckon he's right. Those houses I'm building don't cost more than a hundred to put up. What on earth kind of people have fifty thousand dollars to pay for a ramshackle ghost town and unworked land?

People like Rhett Butler, that's who. And I've got five hundred thousand of his dollars. To buy back the land stolen from my people. Ballyhara wasn't just land, it was O'Hara land. How could she even think about what she should or shouldn't pay? Scarlett made a firm offer of fifteen thousand pounds—take it or leave it.

After her letter was in the post, she shook all over, from head to toe. Suppose Colum didn't come back with her gold in time? There was no way of knowing how long the lawyer would take or when Colum would return. She barely said goodbye to Matt O'Toole after she gave him the letter. She was in a hurry.

She walked as quickly as the uneven ground would allow, wishing for rain. The tall thick hedges held the June heat in the narrow path between them. She had no hat to keep her head cool and to protect her skin from the sun. She almost never wore one; the frequent showers and the clouds that preceded and followed them made hats unnecessary. As for parasols, they were only ornaments in Ireland.

When she reached the ford over the Boyne she tucked up her skirts and stood in the water until her body was cooled. Then she went to the tower.

During the month she'd been back at Daniel's, the tower had become very important to her. She always went there when she was worried about anything or bothered or sad. Its great stones held heat and cool both; she could lay her hands on them or her cheek against them and find the solace and comfort she needed in its enduring ancient solidity. Sometimes she talked to it as if it were her father. More rarely she stretched her arms over its stones and wept upon it. She never heard a sound other than her own voice and the song of birds and the whisper of the river. She never sensed the presence of the eyes that were watching her.

Colum returned to Ireland on June 18. He sent a telegram from Galway: WILL ARRIVE TWO FIVE JUNE WITH SAVANNAH GOODS. The village was in an uproar. There had never been a telegram in Adamstown. There had never been a rider from Trim who was so uninterested in Matt O'Toole's porter, or a horse so swift carrying a rider.

When, two hours later, a second rider galloped into the village on an even more noteworthy horse, people's excitement knew no bounds. Another telegram for Scarlett from Galway. OFFER ACCEPTED STOP LETTER AND CONTRACT FOLLOW.

It took little discussion before the villagers agreed to do the only sensible thing. O'Toole's and the smithy would close. The doctor would close his door. Father Danaher would be spokesman, and they would all walk up to Daniel O'Hara's to find out what was going on.

Scarlett had driven out in her pony trap, they learned, and no more, because Kathleen knew no more than they did. But everyone got to hold and read the telegrams. Scarlett had left them on the table for all the world to see.

Scarlett drove the tortuous roads to Tara with a jubilant heart. Now she could really begin. Her plan was clear in her head, each step following logically upon the previous one. This trip to Tara was not one of the steps; it had come into her mind when the second telegram arrived, more as a compulsion than as an impulse. It was compellingly necessary on this glorious sunlit day to see from Tara's hill the sweet green land that was now her chosen home.

There were many more sheep grazing today than when she'd been here before. She looked over their wide backs and thought about wool. No one grazed sheep in Adamstown; she'd have to learn about the problems and profits of raising sheep from a fresh source.

Scarlett stopped in her tracks. There were people on the mounds that had once been the great banqueting hall of Tara. She'd expected to be alone. They're English too, damn them for the interlopers they are. Resentment of the English was part of every Irishman's life, and Scarlett had absorbed it with the bread she ate and the music she danced to. These picnickers had no right to spread rugs and a tablecloth where the High Kings of Ireland had once dined, or to talk in their honking voices where harps had played.

Particularly when that spot was where Scarlett O'Hara intended to stand, solitary, to look at her country. She glowered with frustration at the dandified men in their straw hats and the women with their flowered silk parasols.

I won't let them spoil my day, I'll go where they're out of my sight. She walked to the twice-ringed mound that had been the wall-encircled house of King Cormac, builder of the banquet hall. The Lia Fail was here, the stone of destiny. Scarlett leaned against it. Colum had been shocked when she did that the day he first brought her to Tara. The Lia Fail was the coronation test of the ancient kings, he told her. If it cried aloud, the man being tested was acceptable as Ireland's High King.

She'd been so strangely elated that day that nothing would have surprised her, not even if the weathered granite pillar had called her by name. As, of course, it had not. It was almost as tall as she was; the top made a good resting place for the hollow at the base of her skull. She looked dreamily at the racing clouds above her in the blue sky and felt the wind lifting the loose locks of hair from her forehead and temples. The English voices were now only muted background to the gentle tinkling bells on the necks of some of the sheep. So peaceful. Maybe that's why I needed to come to Tara. I've been so busy I'd forgotten to be happy, and that was the most important part of my plan. Can I be happy in Ireland? Can I make it my real home?

There is happiness here in the free life I live. And how much more there'll be when my plan is complete. The hard part is done, the part that other people controlled. Now it's all up to me, the way I want it. And there's so much to do! She smiled at the breeze.

The sun slipped in and out of the clouds, and the lush long grass smelled richly alive. Scarlett's back slid down the stone and she sat on the green. Maybe she'd find a shamrock; Colum said they grew more thickly here than any place in Ireland. She'd tried lots of grassy patches, but never yet seen the unmistakable Irish clover. On an impulse Scarlett rolled down her black stockings and took them off. How white her feet looked. Ugh! She pulled her skirts up above her knees to let the sun warm her legs and feet. The yellow and red petticoats under her black skirt made her smile again. Colum had been right about that.

Scarlett wiggled her toes in the breeze.

What was that? Her head snapped erect.

And the tiny stir of life moved again in her body. "Oh," she whispered, and again, "Oh." She placed her hands gently over the small swelling under her skirts. The only thing she could feel was the bulky folded wool. It was no surprise that the quickening wasn't touchable; Scarlett knew it would be many weeks before her hands could feel the kicking.

She stood, facing the wind, and thrust out her cradled belly. Green and gold fields and summer-thick green trees filled the world as far as her eyes could see. "All this is yours, little Irish baby," she said. "Your mother will give it to you. By herself!" Scarlett could feel the cool windblown grass beneath her feet, and the warm earth beneath the grass.

She knelt then and ripped up a tuft of grass. Her face was unearthly when she dug into the ground beneath it with her nails, when she rubbed the moist fragrant earth in circles over her belly, when she said, "Yours, your green high Tara."

They were talking about Scarlett in Daniel's house. That was nothing new; Scarlett had been the villagers' chief topic of conversation ever since she first arrived from America. Kathleen took no offense, why should she? Scarlett fascinated and mystified her too. She had no trouble understanding Scarlett's decision to stay in Ireland. "Wasn't I that heartsore my own self," she said to one and all, "missing the mists and the soft earth and all in that hot, closed-in city? When she saw what was better, she knew not to give it up."

"Is it true, then, Kathleen that her husband beat her something wonderful, and she ran from him to save her baby?"

"Not at all, Clare O'Gorman, and who'd be spreading such terrible lies as that?" Peggy Monaghan was indignant. "It's a well-known fact that the sickness that took him in the end was already upon him, and he sent her away lest it reach into her womb."

"It's a terrible thing to be a widow and all alone with a baby on the way," sighed Kate O'Toole.

"Not so terrible as it might be," said Kathleen, the knowledgeable one, "not when you're richer than the Queen of England."

Everyone settled more comfortably in their seats around the fire. Now they were coming to it. Of all the intriguing speculation about Scarlett, the most enjoyable was to talk about her money.

And wasn't it a grand thing to see a fortune in Irish hands for once instead of the English?

None of them knew that the richest days of gossip were just about to begin.

Scarlett flapped the reins of the pony's back. "Get a move on," she said, "this baby's in a hurry for a home." She was on her way to Ballyhara at last. Until everything was certain about buying it she hadn't allowed herself to go any farther than the tower. Now she could look closely, see what she had.

"My houses in my town . . . my churches and my bars and my post office . . . my bog and my fields and my two rivers . . . What a wonderful lot there is to do!"

She was determined that the baby would be born in the place that would be its home. The Big House at Ballyhara. But everything else had to be done, too. Fields were most important. And a smithy in town to repair hinges and fashion plows. And leaks mended, windows reglazed, doors replaced on their hinges. The deterioration would have to be stopped immediately, now that the property was hers.

And the baby's, of course. Scarlett concentrated on the life within her, but there was no movement. "Smart child," she said aloud. "Sleep while you can. We're going to be busy all the time from now on." She only had twenty weeks to work in before the birth. It wasn't hard to calculate the date. Nine months from February 14, Saint Valentine's Day. Scarlett's mouth twisted. What a joke that was . . . She wouldn't think about that now—or ever. She had to keep her mind on November 14 and the work to be done before then. She smiled and started to sing.

> *When first I saw sweet Peggy, 'twas on a market day.*
> *A low backed car she drove and sat upon a truss of hay.*
> *But when that hay was blooming grass and deck'd with flow'rs of spring,*
> *No flow'r was there that could compare to the blooming girl I sing.*
> *As she sat in her low backed car*
> *The man at the turnpike bar*
> *Never asked for the toll*
> *But just rubbed his ould poll*
> *And look'd after the low backed car . . .*

What a good thing it was to be happy! This excited anticipation and these unexpected good spirits definitely added up to happiness. She'd said, back in Galway, that she was going to be happy, and she was.

"To be sure," Scarlett added aloud, and she laughed at herself.

59

*C*olum was surprised when Scarlett met his train in Mullingar. Scarlett was surprised when he stepped out of the baggage car and not the coach. And when his companion stepped out after him. "This is Liam Ryan, Scarlett darling, Jim Ryan's brother." Liam was a big man, as big as the O'Hara men—Colum excepted—and he was dressed in the green uniform of the Royal Irish Constabulary. How on earth could Colum befriend one of them? she thought. The Constabulary were even more despised than the English militia, because they policed and arrested and punished their own people, under orders from the English.

Did Colum have the gold, Scarlett wanted to know. He did, and Liam Ryan with his rifle to guard it. "I've escorted many a package in my day," Colum said, "but never a time have I been nervous until now."

"I've got men from the bank to take it," said Scarlett. "I'm using Mullingar for safety, it's got the biggest garrison of military." She'd learned to loathe the soldiers, but where the safety of her gold was involved she was glad to use them. She could use the bank in Trim for convenience—for small sums.

As soon as she saw the gold stored in the security of the vault and signed the papers for the purchase of Ballyhara, Scarlett took Colum's arm and hurried him out onto the street.

"I've a pony trap, we can get going right away. There's so much to do, Colum. I've got to find a blacksmith right away and get the smithy going. O'Gorman's no good, he's too lazy. Will you help me find one? He'll be well paid to move to Ballyhara and well paid after he gets there, for there'll be all the work he can handle. I've bought scythes and axes and shovels, but they'll need sharpening. Oh! I need workmen too, to clear the fields, and carpenters to mend the houses, and glaziers and roofers and painters—everything imaginable!" Her cheeks were pink with excitement, her eyes shining. She was incredibly beautiful in her peasant black clothing.

Colum extricated himself from her grasp, then took her arm in his firm hand. "All will be done, Scarlett darling, and almost as quickly as you'd like. But not on an empty stomach. We'll be going now to Jim Ryan's. It's seldom he gets to see his Galway brother, and it's rare to find as grand a cook as Mrs. Ryan."

Scarlett made an impatient gesture. Then she forced herself to calm down. Colum's authority was quietly impressive. Also, she did try to remember to eat properly and drink quantities of milk for the baby's sake. The subtle movements could be felt many times every day now.

But after dinner she couldn't contain her anger when Colum said he wouldn't come with her at once. She had so much to show him, to talk about, to plan, and she wanted it all now!

"I've things to do in Mullingar," he said with placid, unshakable firmness. "I'll be home in three days, you've my word on it. I'll even set the time. Two in the afternoon we'll meet at Daniel's."

"We'll meet at Ballyhara," said Scarlett. "I've already moved in. It's the yellow house halfway down the street." She turned her back on him then and strode angrily away to get her trap.

Late that evening, after Jim Ryan's bar was closed for the night, its door was left on the latch for the men who quietly slipped in one by one to meet in a room upstairs. Colum laid out in detail the things they had to do. "It's a God-sent opportunity," he said with incandescent fervor, "an entire town of our own. All Fenian men, all their skills concentrated in one place, where the English would never think to look. The whole world already thinks my cousin's daft for paying such a price for property she might have bought for nothing just to spare the owner paying the taxes on it. She's American, too, a race known to be peculiar. The English are too busy laughing at her to be suspicious of what goes on in her property. We've long needed a secure headquarters. Scarlett's begging us to take it, though she doesn't know it."

*   *   *

Colum rode into Ballyhara's weed-grown street at 2:43. Scarlett was standing in front of her house, arms akimbo. "You're late," she accused.

"Ah, but sure and you'll forgive me, Scarlett darling, when I tell you that following me on the road comes your smith and his wagon with forge and bellows and all that."

Scarlett's house was a perfect portrait of her, work first and comfort later, if at all. Colum observed everything with deceptively lazy eyes. The parlor's broken windows were neatly covered with squares of oiled paper glued over the panes. Farm implements of new shiny steel were stacked in the corners of the room. The floors were swept clean but not polished. The kitchen had a plain narrow wooden bedstead with a thick straw mattress covered by linen sheets and a woolen blanket. There was a small turf fire in the big stone fireplace. The only cooking implements were an iron kettle and small pot. Above, on the mantelshelf, were tins of tea and oatmeal, two cups, saucers, spoons, and a box of matches. The only chair in the room was placed by a big table under the window. The table held a large account book, open, with entries in Scarlett's neat hand. Two large oil lamps, a pot of ink, a box of pens and pen wipes, and a stack of paper were at the back of the table. A larger stack of paper was near the front. The sheets were covered with notes and calculations, held down with a large washed stone. The surveyor's map of Ballyhara was nailed to the wall nearby. So was a mirror, above a shelf that held Scarlett's silver-backed comb and brushes, and silver-topped jars of hairpins, powder, rouge, and rosewater-glycerine cream. Colum restrained a smile when he saw them. But when he saw the pistol next to them, he turned angrily. "You could get jailed for owning that weapon," he said, too loudly.

"Fiddle-dee-dee," she said, "the Captain of the militia gave it to me. A woman living alone who's known to have a lot of gold should have some protection, he said. He'd have posted one of his sissy-britches soldiers at the door if I'd let him."

Colum's laughter made her eyebrows rise. She didn't think what she'd said was all that amusing.

The larder shelves held butter, milk, sugar, a rack with two plates in it, a bowl of eggs, a ham hanging from the ceiling, and a loaf of stale bread. Buckets of water stood in a corner with a tin of lamp oil and a washstand outfitted with bowl, pitcher, soap dish and soap, and a towel rack with one towel on it. Scarlett's clothes hung from nails on the wall.

"You're not using the upstairs, then," Colum commented.

"Why should I? I have all I need here."

"You've done wonders, Colum, I'm really impressed." Scarlett stood in the center of Ballyhara's famously wide street and looked at the activity everywhere along the length of it. Hammering could be heard from every direction; there was the smell of fresh paint; new windows sparkled in a dozen buildings; and in front of her, a man on a ladder was putting up a gold-lettered sign above the door of the building that Colum had first earmarked for work.

"Did we really need to finish the bar first?" Scarlett asked. She'd been asking the same thing ever since Colum made the announcement.

"You'll find more willing workers if there's a place for them to have a pint when their work's done," he said for the thousandth time.

"So you've said, every time you opened your mouth, but I still can't see why it won't just make them worse. Why, if I didn't keep after them, nothing would ever get done on time. They'd be just like them!" Scarlett jerked her thumb at the groups of interested observers along the street. "They should be back wherever they come from, doing their own work, not watching while other people work."

"Scarlett darling, it's the national character to take the pleasures life has to offer first and worry about duties later. It's what gives the Irish their charm and their happiness."

"Well, I don't think it's charming, and it doesn't make me one bit happy. It's practically August already and not one single field's been cleared yet. How can I possibly plant in the spring if the fields aren't cleared and manured in the fall?"

"You've got months yet, Scarlett darling. Just look what you've already done in only weeks."

Scarlett looked. The frown disappeared from her forehead and she smiled. "That's true," she said.

Colum smiled with her. He said nothing about the soothing and pressuring he had had to do to prevent the men putting down their tools and walking away. They didn't take well to being bossed by a woman, especially one as demanding as Scarlett. If the underground links of the Fenian Brotherhood hadn't committed them to the resurrection of Ballyhara, he didn't know how many would be left, even with Scarlett paying above-average wages.

He, too, looked along the busy street. It would be a good life for these men, and others too, he thought, when Ballyhara was restored. Already he had two more barkeepers asking to come in, and a man who owned a profitable dry-goods store in Bective wanted to relocate. The houses, even the smallest ones, were better than the hovels occupied now by most of the farm laborers he'd chosen. They were as eager as Scarlett for the roofs and windows to be repaired so that they could leave their landlords and get started on the fields of Ballyhara.

Scarlett darted into her house and out again, gloves and covered milk jug in her hand. "I hope you'll keep everybody working and not have a big celebration to open the bar while I'm gone," she said. "I'll ride over to Daniel's for some bread and milk." Colum promised to keep the work going. He said nothing about the folly of her jouncing along on a saddleless pony in her condition. She'd already bitten his head off for suggesting that it was unwise.

"For pity's sake, Colum, I'm barely past five months. That's hardly pregnant at all!"

She was more worried than she'd ever let him know. None of her earlier babies had given her so much trouble. She had an ache in her lower back that never went away, and occasionally there were spots of blood on her underclothes or her sheets that made her heart turn over. She washed them out with the strongest soap she had, the one meant for floors and walls, as if she could wash out the unknown cause together with the spots. Dr. Meade had warned her after her miscarriage that the fall had injured her severely, and she had taken an unconscionably long time to recover, but she refused to admit there might be anything really wrong. The baby wouldn't be kicking so strong if it wasn't healthy. And she had no time to be vaporish.

Frequent trips had created a well-defined track through Ballyhara's overgrown fields to the ford. The pony followed it almost by itself now, and Scarlett had time to think. She'd better get a horse pretty soon, she was getting too heavy for the pony. That was different, too. She'd never gotten so big before when she was carrying a baby. Suppose she had twins! Wouldn't that just be something? That would really pay Rhett back. She already had two rivers on her place to his one at Dunmore Landing. Nothing would please her more than to have two babies, just in case Anne had one. The thought of Rhett giving Anne a baby was too painful to bear. Scarlett turned her eyes and her mind onto the fields of Ballyhara. She just had to get started on them, she just had to, no matter what Colum said.

As always she paused by the tower before she rode to the ford. What good builders those long-ago O'Haras were, and how smart. Old Daniel had actually talked for almost a full minute when she mentioned how sorry she was that the stairs were gone. There were never any stairs outside, he said, only inside. A ladder gave people access to the door, set twelve feet up from the ground. When danger came people could run to the tower, pull the ladder up behind them, and fire arrows or throw stones or pour hot oil down on the attackers from the narrow slit windows, safe from assault by enemies below them.

One of these days I'll haul a ladder back here and have a look inside. I hope there aren't any bats. I do hate bats. Why didn't Saint Patrick get rid of them too when he was cleaning out the snakes?

Scarlett looked in on her grandmother, found her asleep, then stuck her head in Daniel's door. "Scarlett! What a happy thing it is to see you. Come in, do, and tell us the latest wonders you've done at Ballyhara." Kathleen reached for the teapot. "I was hoping you'd come. There's warm barm brack." Three of the village women were there. Scarlett pulled up a stool and joined them.

"How's the baby?" asked Mary Helen.

"Perfect," said Scarlett. She looked around the familiar kitchen. It was friendly and comfortable but she could hardly wait for Kathleen to have her new kitchen, the one in the largest house in Ballyhara town.

Scarlett had already mentally designated the houses she was going to give the family. They'd all have grand, spacious homes. Colum's was the smallest, only one of the gate houses where the estate adjoined the town, but he had chosen it for himself, so she wouldn't argue. And he'd never have a family anyhow, being a priest. But there were much bigger houses in the town. She'd chosen the best for Daniel because Kathleen was with him and they'd probably want Grandmother with them too, plus there had to be room for Kathleen's family when she married, which she'd easily do with the dowry Scarlett would give her, including the house. Then a house for each of Daniel's and Patrick's sons too, even spooky Sean who lived with Grandmother. Plus farmland, as much as they wanted, so that they'd be able to marry, too. She thought it was terrible the way that young men and women couldn't get married because they had no land and no money to get any. The English landlords were truly heartless, the way they kept the Irish ground down under their heels. The Irish did all the labor to grow the wheat or oats, fatten the cattle and sheep, and then they had to sell to the English, at the prices the English set, for the English to export the grain and stock to England, where they'd make more money for more Englishmen. No farmer ever had much left when his rent was paid, and that could be raised at the whim of the English. It was worse than sharecropping, it was like being under the Yankees after the War, when they took anything they wanted, then boosted the taxes on Tara sky high. No wonder the Irish hated the English so. She'd hate the Yankees till her dying day.

But soon the O'Haras would be free of all that. They'd be so surprised when she told them! It wouldn't be much longer, either. When the houses were finished and the fields ready—she wasn't about to give them halfway-done presents, she wanted everything to be perfect. They'd been so good to her. And they were her family.

The gifts were her cherished secret; she hadn't even told Colum yet. She'd been hugging it to herself ever since the night in Galway when the plan came to her. It added to her pleasure every time she looked at Bally-hara's street that she knew just which houses would be O'Hara houses. She'd have lots of places to go then, lots of fires to pull up a stool to, lots of homes with cousins in them for her baby to play with and go to school with and have huge holiday celebrations with at the Big House.

Because naturally that's where she and the baby would be. In the huge, enormous, fantastically elegant Big House. Bigger than the house on East Battery, bigger than the house at Dunmore Landing, even before the Yankees burned nine-tenths of it. And with land that had been O'Hara land before anybody ever heard of Dunmore Landing or Charleston, South Carolina, or Rhett Butler. How his eyes would bug out, how his heart would break when he saw his beautiful daughter—oh, please let it be a girl—in her beautiful home, and she was an O'Hara and her mother's child alone.

Scarlett cherished the daydream of sweet revenge. But that was years away, and the O'Hara houses were soon. As soon as she could make them ready.

60

*C*olum appeared at Scarlett's door late in August when the sky was still rosy with dawn. Ten burly men stood silently behind him in the mist-heavy half light. "Here are the men to clear your fields," he said. "Are you happy at last?"

She screeched with delight. "Let me get my shawl against the damp," she said, "and I'll be right out. Take them down to the first field beyond the gate." She hadn't finished dressing yet, her hair was all tumbled and her feet were bare. She tried to hurry but excitement made her clumsy. She'd been waiting so long! And it was getting more difficult every day to get her boots on. *My grief, I'm as big as a house already. I must be going to have triplets.*

The devil take it! Scarlett piled her unbrushed hair into a wad and stabbed hairpins in it to hold it, then she grabbed her shawl and ran along the street with her feet bare.

The men were grouped glumly around Colum on the weed-choked drive inside the open gate. "Never seen such a sight . . . those be more like trees than weeds . . . looks like all nettles to me . . . a man could spend a lifetime an acre . . ."

"A fine lot you are," Scarlett said clearly. "Are you afraid to get your hands dirty?"

They looked at her with disdain. They'd all heard about the little woman with the driving ways, nothing womanly about her.

"We were discussing the best way to get started," Colum said soothingly.

Scarlett was in no mood to be placated. "You don't get started at all if you discuss long enough. I'll show you how you get started." She put her left hand on the lower curve of her distended belly to support it, then she leaned over, and her right hand grasped a big handful of nettles at the base. With a grunt and a heave she ripped them from the earth. "There," she said contemptuously, "now you're started." She threw the spiny plants at the men's feet. Blood was oozing from wounds all over her hand. Scarlett spit in her palm then wiped her hand on her black widow's skirt and walked heavily away on her pale, fragile-looking feet.

The men stared at her back. First one, then another, then all of them took their hats off.

They were not the only ones who had learned to respect Scarlett O'Hara. Painters had discovered that she would climb the tallest ladder they had, moving like a crab to accommodate her shape, in order to point out overlooked spots or uneven brush strokes. Carpenters who attempted to use inadequate numbers of nails would find her hammering when they came to work. She slammed newly made or newly hung doors with a bang "that would wake the dead" to test hinges, and stood up inside chimneys with a flaming bundle of rushes in her hand to look for soot and test how well they drew. The roofers reported with awe that "only Father O'Hara's strong arm kept her from walking the roof tree and counting the slates." She drove everyone hard and herself harder.

And when it grew too dark to work, there were three free pints at the bar for every man who had stayed on the job that late, and even when their drinking and bragging and complaining was done, they could see her through her kitchen window bending over her papers and writing by lamplight.

"Did you wash your hands?" Colum asked when he entered the kitchen.

"Yes, and put some salve on too. It was a mess. I just get so mad sometimes I don't think what I'm doing. I'm fixing breakfast. Want some?"

Colum sniffed the air. "Porridge without salt? I'd rather have some boiled nettles."

Scarlett grinned. "Then pick your own. I'm leaving out salt for a while, it'll keep my ankles from swelling the way they've taken to doing lately . . . not that it's going to make much difference soon. I can't see my boots to lace them now, I won't be able to reach them in a week or two. I've figured it out, Colum. I'm having a litter, not a baby."

"I've 'figured it out,' as you say, myself. You need a woman to help you." He expected Scarlett to protest; she automatically denied every suggestion that she couldn't do everything herself. But she agreed. Colum smiled; he had just the woman for the job, he said, someone who could help with everything, even the bookkeeping if necessary. An older woman, but not too old to accept Scarlett's rule, and not so spineless that she wouldn't stand up to her when necessary. She was experienced at managing work and people and money, too. In fact, she was housekeeper at a Big House of an estate near Laracor, on the other side of Trim. She had knowledge of childbirth, though she was no midwife. She'd had six children herself. She could come to Scarlett now, to take care of her and this house until the Big House was repaired. Then she'd hire the women needed to run it, and she'd run them.

"You'll admit, Scarlett darling, that you've nothing in America quite like a Big House in Ireland. It needs a practiced hand. You'll need a steward, too, to manage the butler and the footmen and like that, plus a head stableman to rule the grooms, and a dozen or so gardeners with one to boss them—"

"Stop!" Scarlett was shaking her head furiously. "I'm not planning to start a kingdom here. I need a woman to help me, I grant you that, but I'll only be using a few rooms of that pile of stone up there to start with. So you'll have to ask this paragon of yours if she's willing to give up her high-and-mighty position. I doubt if she'll say yes."

"I'll ask her, then." Colum was sure she would agree, even if she had to scrub floors. Rosaleen Mary Fitzpatrick was the sister of a Fenian who'd been executed by the English, and the daughter and granddaughter of men who'd gone down in the Ballyhara coffin ships. She was the most passionate and dedicated member of his inner circle of insurgents.

Scarlett took three boiled eggs out of the bubbling water in the kettle, then poured water into the teapot. "You could have an egg or two if you're too proud to eat my porridge," she offered. "Without salt, of course."

Colum declined.

"Good, I'm hungry." She spooned porridge onto a plate, cracked the eggs and added them. The yolks were runny. Colum averted his eyes.

Scarlett ate hungrily and efficiently, talking rapidly between mouthfuls. She told him her plan for the whole family, to have all the O'Haras living in moderate luxury at Ballyhara.

Colum waited until she finished eating before he said, "They won't do it. They've been farming the land they're on for nearly two hundred years."

"Of course they will. Everybody always wants better than they've got, Colum."

He shook his head in reply.

"I'll prove you wrong. I'll ask them right now! No, that's not in my plan. I want to have everything ready first."

"Scarlett, I brought you your farmers. This morning."

"Those lazybones!"

"You didn't tell me what you were planning. I hired those men. Their wives and children are on their way here right now to move into the cottages at the end of the street. They've quit the landlords they had before."

Scarlett bit her lip. "That's all right," she said after a minute. "I'm putting the family in houses, anyhow, not cottages. These men can work for the cousins."

Colum opened his mouth, then closed it. There was no point in arguing. And he was certain that Daniel would never move.

Colum called Scarlett down from the ladder she was on, inspecting fresh plaster, in midafternoon. "I want you to see what your 'lazybones' have done," he said.

Scarlett was so overjoyed that tears came to her eyes. There was a scythed and sickled path wide enough to drive the trap where she had ridden the pony before. Now she could visit Kathleen again, and get milk for her tea and her oatmeal. She'd felt too heavy to ride for the past week and more.

"I'll go this very minute," she said.

"Then let me lace up your boots."

"No, they press on my ankles. I'll go barefoot, now that I've got a cart to ride in and a road to ride on. You can hitch up the pony, though."

Colum watched her drive off with a feeling of relief. He went back to his gate house and his books, his pipe, and his glass of good whiskey with a sense of a reward well earned. Scarlett O'Hara was the most exhausting individual of any gender, any age, any nationality he'd ever met.

And why, he wondered, does my mind always add "poor lamb" to every opinion I have of her?

She looked like a poor lamb indeed when she burst in on him just before summer's late darkness fell. The family had—very kindly and very often—turned down her invitation and then her appeals to come to Ballyhara.

Colum had come to believe that Scarlett had become almost incapable of tears. She had not cried when she'd received the notice of the divorce, nor even when the ultimate blow fell with the announcement that Rhett had married again. But on this warm rainy night in August, she sobbed and wept for hours, until she fell asleep on his comfortable couch, a luxury unknown in her Spartan two rooms. He covered her with a lightweight coverlet and went to his bedroom. He was glad that she had found release for her grief, but he feared she would not see her outburst in the same light. So he left her alone; she might prefer not to see him for a few days. Strong people didn't like witnesses to their weak moments.

He was mistaken. Again, he thought. Would he ever really get to know this woman? In the morning, he found Scarlett was sitting at his kitchen table, eating the only eggs he had. "You're right, you know, Colum. They are a lot better with salt ... And you might start thinking about good tenants for my houses. They'll have to be prosperous because everything in those houses is the best there is, and I expect a good rent."

Scarlett was profoundly hurt, even though she didn't show it again and never referred to it. She continued to ride over to Daniel's in the trap several times a week, and she worked just as hard as ever on Ballyhara, although her pregnancy was increasingly burdensome. By the end of September the town was done. Every building was clean, freshly painted inside and out, with strong doors and good chimneys and tight roofs. The population was growing by leaps and bounds.

There were two more bars, a cobbler's shop for boots and harness, the dry-goods store that had moved from Bective, an elderly priest for the small Catholic church, two teachers for the school, which would begin classes as soon as authorization came from Dublin, a nervous young lawyer who was hoping to build a practice, with an even more nervous young wife who peered from behind her lace curtains at the people on the street. The farmers' children played games in the street, their wives sat on their doorsteps and gossiped, the post rider from Trim came every day to leave the mail with the scholarly gentleman who had opened a shop with books and writing paper and ink in the one-room annex to the dry-goods store. There was a promise that an official post office would be designated after the first of the year, and a doctor had taken the lease on the largest of the houses, to begin occupancy the first week of November.

This last was the best news of all for Scarlett. The only hospital in the area was at the Work House in Dunshauglin, fourteen miles away. She'd never seen a Work House, the last refuge of the penniless, and she hoped she never would. She firmly believed in work instead of begging, but she'd rather not have to look at the unfortunates who ended up there. And it was certainly no way for a baby to start life.

Her own doctor. That was more her style. He'd be right at hand, too, for croup and chicken pox and all those things babies always got. Now all she had to do was put out word that she'd want a wet nurse in mid-November.

And get the house ready.

"Where is this perfect Fitzpatrick woman of yours, Colum? I thought you told me she'd agreed to come a month ago."

"She did agree a month ago. And gave a month's notice, like any responsible person has to do. She'll be here on October first, that's Thursday next. I've offered her the use of my house."

"Oh, have you? I thought she was supposed to housekeep me. Why doesn't she stay here?"

"Because, Scarlett darling, your house is the only building in Ballyhara that hasn't been repaired."

Scarlett looked around her kitchen-workroom in surprise. She had never paid any attention before to how it looked; it was only temporary, a convenient spot for watching the work on the town.

"It is disgusting, isn't it?" she said. "We'd best get the house done fast so I can move." She smiled, but with difficulty. "The truth is, Colum, I'm nearly worn out. I'll be glad to be done with the work so I can rest some."

What Scarlett didn't say was that the work had become just that—work—after the cousins said they wouldn't move. It had taken the joy out of rebuilding the O'Hara lands when the O'Haras wouldn't be enjoying them. She'd tried and tried to figure out why they'd turned her down. The only answer that made sense to her was that they didn't want to be too close to her, that they didn't really love her, despite all their kindnesses and warmth. She felt alone now, even when she was with them, even when she was with Colum. She'd believed he was her friend, but he'd told her they'd never come. He knew them, was one of them.

Her back hurt all the time now. Her legs, too, and her feet and ankles were so swollen that walking was agony. She wished she wasn't having the baby. It was making her ill, and it had given her the idea of buying Ballyhara in the first place. And she had six—no, six and a half—more weeks of this.

If I had the energy, I'd bawl, she thought despondently. But she found another weak smile for Colum.

He looks like he wants to say something and doesn't know what to say. Well, I can't help him. I'm clean out of conversation.

There was a knock on the street door. "I'll go," Colum said. That's right, run like a rabbit.

He came back to the kitchen with a package in his hand and an unconvincing smile on his face. "That was Mrs. Flanagan, from the store. The tobacco you ordered for Grandmother came in, she brought it over. I'll take it to her for you."

"No." Scarlett heaved herself to her feet. "She asked me to get it. It's the only thing she's ever asked for. You hitch up the pony and help me into the trap. I want to take it to her."

"I'll come with you."

"Colum, there's barely room on the seat for me, let alone the two of us. Just bring me the trap and get me in it. Please."

And how I'll get out of it, God only knows.

Scarlett wasn't very happy when her cousin Sean came out from her grandmother's cottage at the sound of her arrival. "Spooky Sean" she called him to herself, just as she always thought of her cousin Stephen in Savannah as "Spooky Stephen."

They gave her the shivers because they always watched silently while the other O'Haras were talking and laughing. She didn't care much for people who didn't talk and laugh. Or for people who seemed to be thinking secret thoughts. When Sean offered his arm to help her walk into the house, she sidestepped clumsily to avoid him.

"No need," she said gaily, "I can manage just fine." Even more than Stephen, Sean made her nervous. All failure made Scarlett nervous, and Sean was the O'Hara who had failed. He was Patrick's third son. The eldest died, Jamie worked in Trim instead of farming, so when Patrick died in 1861, Sean inherited the farm. He was "only" thirty-two at the time, and the "only" was an excuse he thought adequate for all his troubles. He mismanaged everything so badly that there was a real chance the lease would be lost.

Daniel, as the eldest, called Patrick's children together. Although he was sixty-seven, Daniel had more faith in himself than in Sean or in his own son Seamus, who was also "only" thirty-two. He'd worked beside his brother all his life; now that Patrick was gone, he wouldn't hold his tongue and watch their life's work go, too. Sean would have to go instead.

Sean went. But not away. He had lived with his grandmother for twelve years now, letting her take care of him. He refused to do any work on Daniel's farm. He made Scarlett's hackles rise. She walked away from him as fast as her bare swollen feet would carry her.

"Gerald's girl!" said her grandmother. "It's glad I am to see you, Young Katie Scarlett."

Scarlett believed her. She always believed her grandmother. "I've brought your tobacco, Old Katie Scarlett," she said with genuine cheerfulness.

"What a grand thing to do. Will you have a pipe with me?"

"No, thank you, Grandmother. I'm not quite that Irish yet."

"Ach, that's a shame. Well, I'm as Irish as God makes them. Fill a pipe for me, then."

The tiny cottage was quiet except for the sound of her grandmother's soft sucking pulls on the stem of her pipe. Scarlett put her feet up on a stool and closed her eyes. The peacefulness was balm.

When she heard shouting outside, she was furious. Couldn't she have a half hour's quiet? She hurried as best she could into the farmyard, ready to scream at whoever was making the racket.

What she saw was so terrifying that she forgot her anger, the pain in her back, the agony in her feet, everything except her fear. There were soldiers in Daniel's farmyard, and constables, and an officer on a curvetting horse with a naked saber in his hand. The soldiers were setting up a tripod of tree trunks. She hobbled across to join Kathleen, who was weeping in the doorway.

"Here's another one of them," said one of the soldiers. "Look at her. These miserable Irish breed like rabbits. Why don't they learn to wear shoes instead?"

"You don't need shoes in bed," another said, "or under a bush." The Englishman laughed. The constables looked down at the ground.

"You!" Scarlett called loudly. "You on the horse. What are you and those common creatures doing at this farm?"

"Are you addressing me, girl?" The officer looked down his long nose. She lifted her chin and stared at him with cold green eyes.

"I am not a girl, sir, and you are not a gentleman, even if you pretend to be an officer."

His mouth dropped open. Now his nose is hardly noticeable at all. I guess that's because fish don't have noses, and he looks like a landed fish. The hot joy of combat filled her with energy.

"But you're not Irish," said the officer. "Are you that American?"

"What I am is none of your concern. What you're doing here is my concern. Explain yourself."

The officer remembered who he was. His mouth closed and his back stiffened. Scarlett noticed that the soldiers were stiff all over, and staring, first at her, then at their officer. The constables were looking from the corners of their eyes.

"I am executing an order of Her Majesty's Government to evict the people resident on this farm for nonpayment of rent." He waved a scrolled paper.

Scarlett's heart was in her throat. She lifted her chin higher. Beyond the soldiers she could see Daniel and his sons running from the fields with pitchforks and cudgels, ready to fight.

"There's obviously been a mistake," Scarlett said. "What amount is supposed to be unpaid?" Hurry, she thought, for God's sake hurry, you long-nosed fool. If any O'Hara man—or men—hit a soldier, they'd be sent to prison, or worse.

Everything seemed to slow down. The officer took forever to open the scroll. Daniel and Seamus and Thomas and Patrick and Timothy moved as if they were under water. Scarlett unbuttoned her shirt. Her fingers felt like sausages, the buttons like uncontrollable lumps of suet.

"Thirty-one pounds eight shillings and nine pence," said the officer. It was taking him an hour to say every word, Scarlett was sure. Then she heard the shouting from the field, saw the big O'Hara men running, waving fists and weapons. She clawed frantically at the string around her neck, at the pouch of money when it appeared, at its tightly closed neck.

Her fingers felt the coins, the folded bank notes, and she breathed a silent prayer of thanks. She was carrying the wages of all the workers at Ballyhara. More than fifty pounds. Now she was as cool and unhurried as melting ice cream.

She lifted the cord from her neck, over her head, and she jingled the pouch in her hand. "There's extra for your trouble, you ill-bred cad," she said. Her arm was strong and her aim true. The pouch struck the officer in the mouth. Shillings and pence scattered down the front of his tunic and onto the ground. "Clean up the mess you've made," said Scarlett, "and take away that trash you brought with you!"

She turned her back on the soldiers. "For the love of God, Kathleen," she whispered, "get over in the field and stop the men before there's real trouble."

Later Scarlett confronted Old Daniel. She was livid. Suppose she hadn't brought the tobacco? Suppose it hadn't come in today? She glared at her uncle, then burst out, "Why didn't you tell me you needed money? I'd have been glad to give it to you."

"The O'Haras don't take charity," said Daniel.

"'Charity'? It's not charity when it's your own family, Uncle Daniel."

Daniel looked at her with old, old eyes. "What isn't earned by your own hands is charity," he said. "We've heard your history, Young Scarlett O'Hara. When my brother Gerald lost his wits, why did you not call upon his brothers in Savannah? They're all your own family."

Scarlett's lips trembled. He was right. She hadn't asked or accepted help from anyone. She had had to carry the burden alone. Her pride wouldn't permit any yielding, any weakness.

"And in the Famine?" She had to know. "Pa would have sent you all he had. Uncle James and Uncle Andrew too."

"We were wrong. We thought it would end. When we learned what it was, we'd left it too late."

She looked at her uncle's thin straight shoulders, the proud tilt of his head. And she understood. She would have done the same. She understood, too, why she'd been wrong to offer Ballyhara as a substitute for land he'd farmed all his life. It made all his work meaningless, and the work of his sons, his brothers, his father, his father's father.

"Robert raised the rent, didn't he? Because I made that smart remark about his gloves. He was going to pay me back through you."

"Robert's a greedy man. There's no saying that it's anything to do with you."

"Will you allow me to help? It would be an honor."

Scarlett saw approval in Old Daniel's eyes. Then a glint of humor. "There's Patrick's boy Michael. He works in the stables at the Big House. He has grand ideas about breeding horses. He could apprentice in the Curragh did he have the fee."

"I thank you," said Scarlett formally.

"Will anybody be wanting supper or should I throw it to the pigs?" Kathleen said with pretended anger.

"I'm so hungry I could cry," said Scarlett. "I'm a truly terrible cook, you should know." I'm happy, she thought. I hurt from head to toe, but I'm happy. If this baby isn't proud to be an O'Hara, I'll wring its neck.

61

"$\mathcal{Y}$ou need a cook," said Mrs. Fitzpatrick. "I do not myself cook well."

"Me neither," said Scarlett. Mrs. Fitzpatrick looked at her. "I don't cook well either," Scarlett said hastily. She didn't think she was going to like this woman, no matter what Colum said. Right off the bat when I asked her what her name was, she answered "Mrs. Fitzpatrick." She knew I meant her first name. I've never called a servant "Mrs." or "Mr." or "Miss." But then I've never had a white servant. Kathleen as lady's maid doesn't count, or Bridie. They're my cousins. I'm glad Mrs. Fitzpatrick is no kin of mine.

Mrs. Fitzpatrick was a tall woman, at least half a head taller than Scarlett. She was not thin, but there was no fat on her; she looked solid as a tree. It was impossible to tell how old she was. Her skin was flawless, like the skin of most Irish women, product of the constant soft moisture in the air. It had the look of heavy cream. The color in her cheeks was dramatic, a streak of deep rose rather than an all-over blush. Her nose was thick, a peasant's nose, but with prominent bone, and her lips were a thin wide slash. Most startling and distinctive of all were her dark, surprisingly delicate eyebrows. They formed a perfect thin feathered arch above her blue eyes, strange contrast to her snow-white hair. She was wearing a severe gray gown with plain white linen collar and cuffs. Her strong capable hands were folded in her lap. Scarlett felt like sitting on her own roughened hands. Mrs. Fitzgerald's were smooth, her short nails buffed, her cuticles perfect white half-moons.

There was an English seasoning in her Irish voice. Still soft, but it had lost some music to clipped consonants.

I know what she is, Scarlett realized, she's businesslike. The thought made her feel better. She could deal with a businesswoman whether she liked her or not.

"I am confident that you will find my services useful, Mrs. O'Hara," said Mrs. Fitzpatrick, and there was no possible doubt that Mrs. Fitzpatrick was confident about everything she did or said. Scarlett felt irritated. Was this woman challenging her? Did she intend to run things?

Mrs. Fitzpatrick was still speaking: "I would like to express my pleasure at meeting you and in working for you. I shall be honored to be housekeeper for The O'Hara."

What did she mean?

The dark brows arched. "Do you not know? Everyone is talking of nothing else." Mrs. Fitzgerald's thin wide mouth parted in a gleaming smile. "No woman in our lifetime has ever done it, perhaps no woman in many hundreds of years. They're calling you The O'Hara, head of the family O'Hara, in all its branches and ramifications. In the days of the High Kings, each family had its leader, representative, champion. Some distant ancestor of yours was The O'Hara who stood for all the valor and pride of all other O'Haras. Today that designation has been reborn for you."

"I don't understand. What do I have to do?"

"You've already done it. You're respected and admired, trusted and honored. The title's awarded, not inherited. You have only to be what you are. You are The O'Hara."

"I think I'll have a cup of tea," said Scarlett weakly. She didn't know what Mrs. Fitzpatrick was talking about. Was she joking? Mocking? No, she could tell this was not a woman who made jokes. What did it mean, "The" O'Hara? Scarlett tried it silently on her tongue. The O'Hara. It was like a drumbeat. Deep, hidden, buried, primitive, something within her kindled. The O'Hara. A light grew in her pale tired eyes, making them glow green, fire emerald. The O'Hara.

I'll have to think about that tomorrow ... and every day for the rest of my life. Oh, I feel so different, so strong. ". . . only be what you are . . ." she said. What does that mean? The O'Hara.

"Your tea, Mrs. O'Hara."

"Thank you, Mrs. Fitzpatrick." Somehow the intimidating self-confidence of the older woman had become admirable, not irritating. Scarlett took the cup and looked into the other woman's eyes. "Please have some tea with me," she said. "We need to talk about a cook and other things. We have only six weeks, and a lot to do."

* * *

Scarlett had never been in the Big House. Mrs. Fitzpatrick hid her astonishment and her own curiosity about it. She'd been housekeeper to a prominent family, directress of a very big house, but it had not approached the Big House at Ballyhara in magnificence. She helped Scarlett turn the huge tarnished brass key in the great rusted lock and threw her weight against the door. "Mildew," she said when the smell hit them. "We'll need an army of women with pails and scrubbing brushes. Let's have a look at the kitchen first. No cook worth having is going to come to a house without a first-class kitchen. This part of the house can be done later. Just ignore the paper falling off the walls and the animal droppings on the floor. The cook won't even see these rooms."

Curved colonnades connected two large wing buildings to the main block of the house. They followed the one to the east first and found themselves in a large corner room. Doors opened onto interior corridors that led to more rooms and a staircase to yet more rooms. "You'll put your steward to work here," said Mrs. Fitzpatrick when they returned to the large corner room. "The other rooms will do for servants and storerooms. Stewards do not live in the Big House; you'll have to give him a dwelling in the town, a large one, in keeping with his position as manager of the estate. This is obviously the Estate Office."

Scarlett didn't reply at once. She was seeing another office in her mind, and the wing of another Big House. "Bachelor guests" had used the wing at Dunmore Landing, Rhett had said. Well, she didn't plan to have a dozen rooms' worth of bachelor guests, or any other kind of guests. But she could certainly use an office, just like Rhett's. She'd get the carpenter to make her a big desk, twice as big as Rhett's, and she'd hang the estate maps on the walls, and she'd look out the window just the way he did. But she would see the clean-cut stones of Ballyhara, not a pile of burnt bricks, and she'd have fields of wheat, not a passel of flower bushes.

"I'll be the steward at Ballyhara, Mrs. Fitzpatrick. I don't intend to have a stranger manage my place."

"I mean no disrespect, Mrs. O'Hara, but you don't know what you're saying. It's a full-time occupation. Not only maintaining the stores and supplies, but also listening to complaints and settling disputes between workers and farmers and the people of the town."

"I'll do it. We'll put benches along that hallway for people to sit on, and I'll see anyone with a problem on the first Sunday of every month after Mass." Scarlett's firm jaw told the housekeeper that there was no point in arguing.

"And Mrs. Fitzpatrick—there will be no spittoons, is that clear?"

Mrs. Fitzpatrick nodded, even though she had never heard the word before. In Ireland, tobacco was smoked in a pipe, not chewed.

"Good," said Scarlett. "Now let's find this kitchen you're so worried about. It must be in the other wing."

"Do you feel up to walking all that way?" asked Mrs. Fitzpatrick.

"It has to be done," said Scarlett. Walking was torture for her feet and her back, but there was no question about doing it. She was appalled by the condition of the house. How would it ever be done in six weeks? It has to be, that's all. The baby must be born in the Big House.

"Magnificent," was Mrs. Fitzpatrick's pronouncement about the kitchen. The room was cavernous and two stories high, with broken sky-lights in the roof. Scarlett was sure she'd never been in a ballroom half as large. A tremendous stone chimney nearly covered the wall at the far end of the room. Doors on each side of it led to a stone-sinked scullery on the north side, an empty room on the south. "The cook can sleep here, that's good and that"—Mrs. Fitzpatrick pointed upward—"is the most intelligent arrangement I've ever seen." A balustraded gallery ran the length of the kitchen wall at the second-story level. "The rooms above the cook's and the scullery will be mine. The kitchen maids and the cook will never know when I might be watching them. That should keep them alert. The gallery must connect to the second floor of the house itself. You can come over, too, to see what's going on in the kitchen below. They'll keep working all the time."

"Why couldn't I just go in the kitchen and see?"

"Because they'd stop working to curtsey and wait for orders while the food scorched."

"You keep talking about 'they' and 'maids,' Mrs. Fitzpatrick. What happened to the cook? I thought we were going to get one woman."

Mrs. Fitzpatrick's hand gestured to the expanses of floor and wall and windows. "One woman couldn't manage all this. No competent woman would try. I'd like to see the storerooms and laundry, probably in the base-ment. Do you want to come down?"

"Not really. I'll sit outside, away from the smell." She found a door. It led out into an overgrown walled garden. Scarlett backed into the kitchen. A second door opened onto the colonnade. She lowered herself to the paved floor and leaned against a column. A heavy fatigue pressed on her. She'd no idea the house would need so much work. From the outside it looked as if it was almost intact.

The baby kicked and she absentmindedly pushed the foot or whatever back down. "Hey, little baby," she murmured, "what do you think of this?

They're calling your mother 'The O'Hara.' I hope you're impressed. I sure am." Scarlett closed her eyes to take it all in.

Mrs. Fitzpatrick came out, brushing cobwebs from her clothes. "It will do," she said succinctly. "Now what we both need is a good meal. We'll go to Kennedy's bar."

"The bar? Ladies don't go unescorted to bars."

Mrs. Fitzpatrick smiled. "It's your bar, Mrs. O'Hara. You can go there whenever you please. You can go anywhere at all, whenever you like. You are The O'Hara."

Scarlett turned the thought over in her mind. This wasn't Charleston or Atlanta. Why shouldn't she go to the bar? Hadn't she nailed down half the floorboards herself? And didn't everyone say that Mrs. Kennedy, the barkeeper's wife, made a pastry for her meat pies that would melt in your mouth?

The weather turned rainy, not the brief showers or misty days that Scarlett had gotten used to, but real torrents of rain that lasted sometimes for three to four hours. The farmers complained about the soil compacting if they walked on the newly cleared fields to spread the cart-loads of manure Scarlett had bought. But Scarlett, forcing herself to walk daily to check the progress at the Big House, blessed the mud on the ungravelled drive because it cushioned her swollen feet. She gave up boots altogether and kept a bucket of water inside her front door to rinse her feet when she came in. Colum laughed when he saw it. "The Irish in you is strengthening every day, Scarlett darling. Did you learn that from Kathleen?"

"From the cousins when they came in from the fields. They always washed the earth off their feet. I figured it was because Kathleen would be mad if they tracked up her clean floor."

"Not a bit of it. They did it because Irishmen—and women too—have done it as long as anyone's great-grandfather can remember. Do you shout '*seachain*' before you throw the water out?"

"Don't be silly, of course not. I don't put a bowl of milk on the door-step every night either. I don't believe I'm likely to drench any fairies or give them supper. That's all childish superstition."

"So you say. But one day a pooka's going to get you for your insolence." He looked nervously under her bed and pillow.

Scarlett had to laugh. "All right, I'll bite, Colum. What's a pooka? Second cousin to a leprechaun, I suppose."

"The leprechauns would shudder at the suggestion. A pooka is a fearful creature, malicious and sly. He'll curdle your cream in an instant or tangle your hair with your own brush."

"Or swell my ankles, I guess. That's as malicious as anything I've ever been through."

"Poor lamb. How much longer?"

"About three weeks. I've told Mrs. Fitzpatrick to clean out a room for me and order in a bed."

"Are you finding her helpful, Scarlett?"

She had to admit she was. Mrs. Fitzpatrick wasn't so taken with her position that she minded working hard herself. Plenty of times Scarlett had found her scrubbing the stone floor and stone sinks in the kitchen herself to show the maids how to do it.

"But Colum, she's been spending money like there's no end to it. Three maids I've got up there already, just to get things nice enough so that a cook will be willing to come. And a stove the likes of which I've never seen, all kinds of burners and ovens and a well thing for hot water. It cost almost a hundred pounds, and ten more to haul it from the railroad. Then, after all that, nothing would do but to have the smith make all kinds of cranes and spits and hooks for the fireplace. Just in case the cook doesn't like stove ovens for some things. Cooks must be more spoiled than the Queen."

"More useful, too. You'll be glad when you sit down to your first good meal in your own dining room."

"So you say. I'm happy enough with Mrs. Kennedy's meat pies. I ate three last night. One for me and two for this elephant inside me. Oh, I'll be so happy when this is over . . . Colum?" He'd been away, and Scarlett didn't feel as easy with him as she used to, but she needed to ask him anyhow. "Have you heard about this 'The O'Hara' business?"

He had and he was proud of her and he thought it was deserved. "You're a remarkable woman, Scarlett O'Hara. No one who knows you thinks otherwise. You've ridden over blows that would fell a lesser woman—or a man as well. And you've never moaned or asked pity." He smiled roguishly. "You've done what's near miraculous, too, getting all these Irish to work the way they have. And spitting in the eyes of the English officer—well, they say you put out the sight in one of them from a hundred paces."

"That's not true!"

"And why should a grand tale be tarnished by the truth? Old Daniel himself was the first who called you The O'Hara, and he was there."

Old Daniel? Scarlett flushed with pleasure.

"You'll be swapping stories with Finn MacCool's ghost one day soon, to hear the talk. The whole countryside's richer for having you here." Colum's light tone darkened. "There's one thing I want to caution you about, Scarlett. Don't turn up your nose at people's beliefs; it's insulting to them."

"I never do! I go to Mass every Sunday, even though Father Flynn looks like he might fall asleep any minute."

"I'm not speaking of the Church. I'm talking about the fairies and the pookas and that. One of the mighty deeds you're praised for is moving back to the O'Hara land when everyone knows it's haunted by the ghost of the young lord."

"You can't be serious."

"I can, and I am. It matters not whether you believe or not. The Irish people do. If you mock what they believe in, you're spitting in their eyes."

Scarlett could see that, silly as it all was. "I'll hold my tongue, and I won't laugh, unless it's at you, but I'm not going to holler before I empty the bucket."

"You don't have to. They're saying you're so respectful you whisper real soft."

Scarlett laughed until she disturbed the baby and was kicked mightily. "Now look what you did, Colum. My insides are black and blue. But it's worth it. I haven't laughed like that since you went away. Stay home for a while, will you?"

"That I will. I want to be one of the first to see this elephant child of yours. I'm hoping you'll name me a godfather."

"Can you do that? I'm counting on you to baptize him or her or them."

Colum's smile vanished. "I cannot do that, Scarlett darling. Anything else you ask me, though it be to fetch you the moon for a bauble. I do not perform the sacraments."

"Whyever not? That's your job."

"No, Scarlett, that's the job of a parish priest or on special occasions a bishop or archbishop or more. I'm a missionary priest, working to ease the sufferings of the poor. I perform no sacraments."

"You could make an exception."

"That I could not, and that's an end of it. But the grandest of godfathers I'll be, if asked, and see to it that Father Flynn doesn't drop the babe in the font or on the floor, and I'll teach him his catechism with such eloquence that he'll think he's learning a limerick instead. Do ask me, Scarlett darling, or you'll break my yearning heart."

"Of course I'll ask you."

"Then I've got what I came for. Now I can go beg a meal in a house that adds salt."

"Go on, then. I'm going to rest until the rain stops then go see Grandmother and Kathleen while I can. The Boyne's almost too high to ford already."

"One more promise, and I'll stop fussing you. Stay in your house Saturday evening with your door shut tight and your curtains drawn. It's All Hallows' Eve, and the Irish believe all the fairies are out from all the time since the world began. And, as well, goblins and ghosts and spirits carrying their heads under their arms and all manner of unnatural things. Pay heed to the customs and close yourself in safe from seeing them. None of Mrs. Kennedy's meat pies. Boil some eggs. Or, if you're really feeling Irish, have a supper of whiskey washed down with ale."

"No wonder they see spooks! But I'll do as you say. Why don't you come over?"

"And be in the house all night with a seductive lass like you? I'd have me collar taken away."

Scarlett stuck out her tongue at him. Seductive, indeed. To an elephant maybe.

The trap wobbled alarmingly when she crossed the ford and she decided not to stay long at Daniel's. Her grandmother was looking drowsy, so Scarlett didn't sit down. "I just stopped in for a second, Grandmother, I won't keep you from your nap."

"Come kiss me goodbye, then, Young Katie Scarlett. You're a lovely girl to be sure." Scarlett embraced the tough tiny body gently, kissed the old cheek firmly. Almost at once her Grandmother's chin dropped on her chest.

"Kathleen, I can't stay long, the river's rising so. By the time it's down I doubt I'll be able to get in the trap at all. Have you ever seen such a giant baby?"

"Yes, I have, but you don't want to hear it. Every baby's the only baby is my observation of mothers. You'll have a minute for a bite and a cup of tea?"

"I shouldn't but I will. May I take Daniel's chair? It's the biggest."

"You're welcome to it. Daniel's never been so warm towards any of us as he is to you."

The O'Hara, thought Scarlett. It warmed her even more than the tea and the smoke-smelling clean fire.

"Have you the time to see Grandmother, Scarlett?" Kathleen put a stool beside Daniel's chair with tea and cake on it.

"I went there first. She's napping now."

"That's grand, then. It would be a pity if she missed telling you goodbye. She's taken out her shroud from the box where she keeps her treasures. She'll be dead ere long."

Scarlett stared at Kathleen's serene face. How can she say things like that in the same tone of voice as talking about the weather or something? And then drink tea and eat cake as calm as you please?

"We're all hoping for a few dry days first," Kathleen went on. "The roads are that deep in mud people will have trouble getting to the wake. But we'll have to take what comes." She noticed Scarlett's horror and misinterpreted it.

"We'll all miss her, Scarlett, but she's ready to go, and those that live as long as Old Katie Scarlett have a way of knowing when their time is on them. Let me fill your cup, what's left must be cold."

It clattered in its saucer as Scarlett put it down. "I really can't, Kathleen, I've got to cross the ford, I have to go."

"You'll send word when the pains start? I'll be happy to stay with you."

"I will, and thank you. Will you give me a hand up in the trap?"

"Will you take a bit of cake for later? I can wrap it in no time."

"No, no, thank you, truly, but I'm worried about the water."

I'm more fretful about going crazy, Scarlett thought when she drove off. Colum was right, the Irish are all spook-minded. Who'd have thought it of Kathleen? And my own grandmother having a shroud all ready. Heaven only knows what they get up to on Halloween. I'm going to lock the door and nail it shut, too. This stuff is giving me the shivers.

The pony lost its footing for a long terrifying moment crossing the ford.

Might as well face it, no more travel for me until after the baby. I wish I'd accepted the cake.

62

*T*he three country girls stood in the wide doorway of the Big House bedroom Scarlett had chosen for her own. All were wearing big homespun aprons and wide-ruffled mobcaps, but that was the only thing about them that was the same. Annie Doyle was as small and round as a puppy, Mary Moran as tall and ungainly as a scarecrow, Peggy Quinn as neat and pretty as an expensive doll. They were holding hands and crowded together. "We'll be going now if it's all the same to you, Mrs. Fitzpatrick, before the heavy rain starts in," said Peggy. The other girls nodded vigorously.

"Very well," said Mrs. Fitzpatrick, "but come in early Monday to make up the time."

"Oh, yes, miss," they chorused, dropping clumsy curtseys. Their shoes made a racket on the stairs.

"Sometimes I despair," sighed Mrs. Fitzpatrick, "but I've made good maids out of sorrier material than that. At least they're willing. Even the rain wouldn't have bothered them if today wasn't Halloween. I suppose they think if clouds darken the sky it's the same as nightfall." She looked at the gold watch pinned on her bosom. "It's only a little after two . . . Let's get back where we were. I'm afraid that all this wet will keep us from finishing, Mrs. O'Hara. I wish it weren't so, but I'm not going to lie to you. We've got all the old paper off the walls and everything scrubbed and fresh. But you need new plaster in some spots, and that means dry walls. Then time for the plaster to dry afterwards before the wall is painted or papered. Two weeks just isn't enough."

Scarlett's jaw hardened. "I am going to have my baby in this house, Mrs. Fitzpatrick. I told you that from the beginning."

Her anger flowed right off Mrs. Fitzpatrick's sleekness. "I have a suggestion—" said the housekeeper.

"As long as it's not to go someplace else."

"On the contrary. I believe with a good fire on the hearth and some cheerful thick curtains at the windows, the bare walls won't be offensive at all."

Scarlett looked at the gray, waterstained, cracked plaster with gloom. "It looks horrible," she said.

"A rug and furniture will make a great difference. I've got a surprise for you. We found it in the attic. Come look." She opened the door to an adjoining room.

Scarlett walked heavily to the door, then burst out laughing. "God's nightgown! What is it?"

"It's called a State Bed. Isn't it remarkable?" She laughed with Scarlett while they stared at the extraordinary object in the center of the room. It was immense, at least ten feet long and eight wide. Four enormously thick dark oak posts carved to look like Greek goddesses supported a tester frame on their laurel-wreathed heads. The head and footboards were carved in deep relief with scenes of toga-clad men in heroic postures beneath bowers of intertwined grapes and flowers. At the rounded peak of the tall head-board there was a flaking, gold-leafed crown.

"What kind of giant do you reckon slept in it?" asked Scarlett.

"It was probably made especially for a visit from the Viceroy."

"Who's that?"

"The head of the government in Ireland."

"Well, I'll say this for it, it's big enough for this giant baby I'm having. If the doctor can reach far enough to catch it when it comes."

"Then shall I order the mattress made? There's a man in Trim who can do it in two days."

"Yes, do. Sheets, too, or else sew some together. My grief, I could sleep for a week in that thing and never hit the same spot twice."

"With a tester and curtains on it, it will be like a room in itself."

"Room? It'll be like a house. And you're right, once I'm in it I won't notice the nasty walls at all. You're a marvel, Mrs. Fitzpatrick. I feel better than I have in months. Can you imagine what it'll do to a baby to enter the world in that? It'll probably grow to be ten feet tall!"

Their laughter was companionable as they walked slowly down the scrubbed granite staircase to the ground floor. This'll have to be carpeted first thing, Scarlett thought. Or maybe I'll just close up the second floor altogether. These rooms are so big I'd have a huge house on the one floor alone. If Mrs. Fitzpatrick and the cook will allow it. Why not? No sense being The O'Hara if I can't have things my way. Scarlett stood aside to let Mrs. Fitzpatrick open the heavy front door.

They looked out into a sheet of water. "Damn," said Scarlett.

"This is a downpour, not a rain," the housekeeper said. "It can't last at this rate. Would you like a cup of tea? The kitchen's warm and dry; I've had the stove going all day to test it."

"Might as well." She followed Mrs. Fitzpatrick's thoughtfully slow steps to the kitchen.

"This is all new," said Scarlett suspiciously. She didn't like any spending without her approval. And the cushioned chairs by the stove looked too cozy altogether for cooks and maids who were supposed to be working. "What did this cost?" She tapped the big heavy wood table.

"A few bars of soap. It was in the tack room, filthy dirty. The chairs are from Colum's house. He suggested we woo the cook into comfort before she sees the rest of the house. I've made a list of furniture for her room. It's on the table there for your approval."

Scarlett felt guilty. Then she suspected that she was supposed to feel guilty, and she felt cross. "What about all those lists I approved last week? When are those things coming?"

"Most of them are here, in the scullery. I was planning to unpack them next week, with the cook. Most of them have their own systems for arranging utensils and such."

Scarlett felt cross again. Her back was hurting worse than usual. She put her hands over the pain. Then a new pain ripped through her side and down her leg, shoving the back pain into insignificance. She grabbed the side of the table for support and stared dumbly at the liquid streaming down her legs and across her bare feet to pool on the scrubbed stone floor.

"The water broke," she said at last, "and it's red." She looked at the window and the heavy rain outside. "Sorry, Mrs. Fitzpatrick, you're going to get very wet. Get me up on this table and give me something to soak up the water . . . or the blood. Then high-tail it to the bar or the store and tell somebody to ride hell for leather for a doctor. I'm about to have a baby."

The ripping pain was not repeated. With the chair cushions under her head and the small of her back, Scarlett was quite comfortable. She wished she had something to drink, but she decided she'd better not get off the table. If the pain came back she might fall and hurt herself.

I probably shouldn't have sent Mrs. Fitzpatrick off to scare people to death like that. I've only had three pains since she left, and they were hardly anything. I'd really feel fine if there wasn't so much blood. Every pain and every time the baby kicks it just gushes out. That's never happened before. When the water breaks, it's clear, not bloody.

Something's wrong.

Where is the doctor? Another week and there'd have been one right on the doorstep. Now it'll be some stranger from Trim, I guess. How do, Doctor, you'd never know it but it wasn't supposed to be like this, I was going to be in a bed with a gold crown on it, not on a table from the tack room. What kind of start is this for a baby? I'll have to name it "Foal" or "Jumper" or something else horsey.

There's the blood again. I don't like this. Why isn't Mrs. Fitzpatrick back—at least I could have a cup of water for pity's sake, I'm dry as a bone. Stop that kicking, baby, you don't have to act like a horse just because we're on a tack table. Stop it! You just make me bleed. Wait till the doctor comes, then you can get out. Truth to tell, I'll be glad to be rid of you.

It sure was easier starting you than it is finishing you . . . No, I mustn't think about Rhett, I'll go crazy if I do.

Why doesn't it stop raining? Pouring, more like it. Wind's rising, too. This is an honest to goodness storm. Fine time I picked to have a baby, to have my water break . . . why is it red? Am I going to bleed to death on a tack table, for God's sake, without so much as a cup of tea? Oh, how I'd love some coffee. Sometimes I miss it so much I want to scream . . . or cry . . . oh Lord, more gushing. At least it doesn't hurt. Hardly a contraction at all, more a twitch or something . . . Then why does so much blood gush out? What's going to happen when the real labor starts? Dear God, there'll be a river of blood, all over the floor. Everybody'll have to wash their feet. I wonder if Mrs. Fitzpatrick has a bucket of feet water. I wonder if she hollers before she throws it out? I wonder where the hell she is? As soon as this is over I'm going to fire her—no references, either, at least nothing she'll want to show anybody. Running off and leaving me dying of thirst here all by myself.

Don't kick like that. You're more like a mule than a horse. Oh, God, the blood . . . I'm not going to lose hold of myself, I'm not. I won't. The O'Hara doesn't do that kind of thing. The O'Hara. I like that a lot . . . What was that? The doctor?

Mrs. Fitzpatrick came in. "Are you doing all right, Mrs. O'Hara?"

"Just fine," said The O'Hara.

"I've brought sheets and blankets and soft pillows. Some men are coming with a mattress. Can I do anything for you?"

"I'd like some water."

"Right away."

Scarlett propped herself on an elbow and drank thirstily. "Who's getting the doctor?"

"Colum. He tried to cross the river for the doctor in Adamstown, but he couldn't make it. He's gone to Trim."

"I figured. I'd like some more water please, and a fresh sopper. This one's soaked through."

Mrs. Fitzpatrick tried to hide the horror on her face when she saw the blood-soaked towel between Scarlett's legs. She wadded it up and hurried to one of the stone sinks with it. Scarlett looked at the trail of bright red drops on the floor. That's part of me, she told herself, but she couldn't believe it. She'd had lots of cuts in her life, as a child playing, when she was hoeing cotton at Tara, even when she pulled up the nettles. Put them all together and they'd never bled as much as that towel had in it. Her abdomen contracted and blood gushed onto the table.

Stupid woman, I told her I needed another towel.

"What time does your watch say, Mrs. Fitzpatrick?"

"Five-sixteen."

"I reckon the storm's making travel slow. I'd like some water and another towel, please. No, come to think of it, I'd like some tea, with plenty of sugar." Give the woman something to do and maybe she'll quit hanging over me like an umbrella. I'm sick and tired of making conversation and brave smiles. I'm scared half-witted if truth be known. The contractions aren't any stronger, or closer together, either. I'm not getting anywhere at all. At least the mattress feels better than the table, but what's going to happen when it gets soaked through, too? Is the storm getting worse or am I just spooked?

Rain was buffeting the windows now, propelled by a mighty wind. Colum O'Hara was nearly knocked down by a branch torn from a tree in the wood near the house. He climbed over it and moved on, bent against the wind. Then he remembered, turned around, was blown onto the limb, fought for a foothold in the quagmire mud of the drive, dragged the limb to one side, fought against the wind again towards the house.

"What time is it?" said Scarlett.

"Almost seven."

"Towel, please."

* * *

"Scarlett darling, is it very bad?"

"Oh, Colum!" Scarlett pushed herself to half sitting. "Is the doctor with you? The baby's not kicking as much as before."

"I found a midwife in Dunshaughlin. There's no getting to Trim, the river's over the road. Lie back, now, like a good mother. Don't tire yourself more than you have to."

"Where is she?"

"On the way. My horse was faster, but she's close behind. She's brought hundreds of babies, you'll be in good hands."

"I've had babies before, Colum. This is different. There's something bad wrong."

"She'll know what to do, lamb. Try not to fret."

The midwife bustled in just after eight. Her starched uniform was limp with wet, but her competent manner was as crisp as if she hadn't been rushed on an emergency at all.

"A baby, is it? Ease your mind, missus, I know everything there is to know about helping the little dear things into this vale of tears." She took off her cape and handed it to Colum. "Spread that out near the fire so it can dry," she said in a voice accustomed to command. "Soap and warm water, missus, for me to wash my hands. This will do over here." She walked briskly to the stone sink. At the sight of the blood-soaked towels she wilted, gestured frantically to summon Mrs. Fitzpatrick. They had a whispered conference.

The brightness that had come to Scarlett's eyes faded. She lowered the lids over her sudden tears.

"Let's just see what we have here," said the midwife with false cheer. She lifted Scarlett's skirts, felt her abdomen. "A fine strong baby. He just greeted me with a kick. We'll see about inviting him to come out now and give his Ma a little rest." She turned to Colum. "You'd better leave us to our women's work, sir. I'll call you when your son is born."

Scarlett giggled.

Colum removed his Balmacaan overcoat. His collar gleamed in the lamplight. "Oh," said the midwife. "Forgive me, Father."

"For I have sinned," Scarlett said in a shrill voice.

"Scarlett," Colum said quietly.

The midwife pulled him towards the sink. "It may be you should stay, Father," she said, "for the last rites."

She spoke too loudly. Scarlett heard her. "Oh, dear God," she cried.

"Help me," the midwife ordered Mrs. Fitzpatrick. "I'll show you how to hold her legs."

Scarlett screamed when the woman's hand thrust into her womb. "Stop! Jesus, the pain, make it stop." When the examination was over she was moaning from the hurt. Blood covered the mattress and her thighs, was spattered on Mrs. Fitzpatrick's dress, the midwife's uniform, the floor for three feet on each side of the table. The midwife pushed up the sleeve on her left arm. Her right arm was red halfway to the elbow.

"I'll have to try it with both hands," she said.

Scarlett groaned. Mrs. Fitzpatrick stepped in front of the woman. "I have six children," she said. "Get out of here. Colum, get this butcher out of this house before she kills Mrs. O'Hara and I kill her. So help me God, that's what will happen."

The room was lit suddenly by a flash of brilliance through skylight and windows, and a heavier torrent of rain slashed against the glass.

"I'm not going out in that," the midwife howled. "It's full dark."

"Put her in another room, then, but get her out of here. And when she's away, Colum, go bring the smith. He doctors animals; a woman can't be that different."

Colum had the cringing midwife by the upper arm. Lightning scored the sky above, and she screamed. He shook her like a rag. "Quiet yourself, woman." He looked at Mrs. Fitzpatrick with dull hopeless eyes. "He'll not come, Rosaleen, no one will come now it's dark. Have you forgot what night this is?"

Mrs. Fitzpatrick wiped Scarlett's temples and cheeks with a cool damp cloth. "If you don't bring him, Colum, I'll do it. I've a knife and a pistol in the desk at your house. It only needs showing him there's more certain things to fear than ghosts."

Colum nodded. "I'll go."

Joseph O'Neill, the blacksmith, crossed himself. His face glistened with sweat. His black hair was plastered to his head from walking through the storm, but the sweat was fresh. "I've doctored a horse once, same as this, but a woman I cannot do such violence to." He looked down at Scarlett and shook his head. "It's against nature, I cannot."

There were lamps along the edges of all the sinks, and lightning flashing one jagged bolt after another. The huge kitchen was brighter than day, save for the shadowed corners. The storm raging outside seemed to be attacking the thick stone walls of the house.

"You've got to do it, man, else she'll die."

"She will that, and the babe too, if it's not dead some time past. There's no movement."

"Don't wait, then, Joseph. For the love of God, man, it's her only hope." Colum kept his voice steady, commanding.

Scarlett stirred feverishly on the bloody mattress. Rosaleen Fitzpatrick sponged her lips with water, squeezed a few drops between them. Scarlett's eyelids quivered then opened. Her eyes were glazed with fever. She moaned piteously.

"Joseph! I order you."

The smith shuddered. He raised his thick muscled arm over Scarlett's mounded belly. Lightning glittered on the blade of the knife in his hand.

"Who is that?" said Scarlett distinctly.

"Saint Patrick preserve me!" cried the smith.

"Who's that lovely lady, Colum, in the beautiful white gown?"

The smith dropped the knife on the floor and backed away. His hands were stretched in front of him, palms outward, fending off his terror.

The wind swirled, caught a branch, hurled it crashing through the window above the sink. Shards of glass cut Joseph O'Neill's arms, now crossed over his head. He fell to the floor, screaming, and through the open window the wind screamed in above him. Shrieking noise was everywhere—outside, inside, within the smith's screaming, around and on the howling wind, in the storm, in the distance beyond the storm, a wailing in the wind.

The flames in the lamps jumped and wavered and some went out. Quietly in the midst of the storm's intrusion the kitchen door was opened and closed again. A wide shawled figure walked across the kitchen, among the terrorized people, to the window. It was a woman with a creased round face. She reached into the sink and twisted one of the towels, wringing out the blood.

"What are you doing?" Rosaleen Fitzpatrick snapped out of her terror, stepped toward the woman. Colum's outstretched arm halted her. He recognized the *cailleach*, the wise woman who lived near the tower.

One by one the wise woman piled blood-stained towels atop one another until the hole in the window was filled. Then she turned. "Light the lamps again," she said. Her voice was hoarse, as if she had rust in her throat.

She took off her wet black shawl, folded it neatly, placed it on a chair. Beneath it she was wearing a brown shawl. That, too, came off and was folded, put on the chair. Then a dark blue one with a hole on one shoulder. And a red one with more holes than wool. "You haven't done as I told you," she scolded Colum. Then she walked to the smith and kicked him sharply in the side. "You're in the way, smith, go back to your forge." She looked at Colum again. He lit a lamp, looked for another, lit it, until a steady flame burned in each.

"Thank you, Father," she said politely. "Send O'Neill home, the storm is passing. Then come hold two lamps high by the table. You," she turned to Mrs. Fitzpatrick, "do the same. I'll ready The O'Hara."

A cord around her waist held a dozen or more pouches made of different-colored rags. She reached into one and withdrew a vial of dark liquid. Lifting Scarlett's head with her left hand, she poured the liquid into her mouth with her right. Scarlett's tongue reached out, licked her lips. The *cailleach* chuckled and lowered the head onto the pillow.

The rusty voice began to hum a tune that was no tune. Gnarled stained fingers touched Scarlett's throat, then her forehead, then pulled up and released her eyelids. The old woman took a folded leaf from one of her pouches and put it on Scarlett's belly. Then she extracted a tin snuff box from another and put it beside the leaf. Colum and Mrs. Fitzpatrick stood like statues with the lamps, but their eyes followed every move.

The leaf, unfolded, contained a powder. The woman sprinkled it over Scarlett's belly. Then she took a paste from the snuff box and rubbed it over the powder and into Scarlett's skin.

"I'm going to tie her down lest she injure herself," the woman said, and she lashed ropes from around her waist below Scarlett's knees, across her shoulders, around the sturdy table legs.

Her small old eyes looked first at Mrs. Fitzpatrick, then at Colum. "She will scream, but she will not feel pain. You will not move. The light is vital."

Before they could reply she took a thin knife, wiped it with something from one of her pouches, and stroked it the length of Scarlett's belly. Scarlett's scream was like the cry of a lost soul.

Before the sound was gone the *cailleach* was holding a blood-covered baby in her two hands. She spit something she was holding in her mouth onto the floor, then blew into the baby's mouth, once, twice, thrice. The baby's arms jerked, then its legs.

Colum whispered the Hail Mary.

A whisk of the knife cut the cord, the baby was laid on the folded sheets and the woman was back beside Scarlett. "Hold the lamps closer," she said.

Her hands and fingers moved quickly, sometimes with a flash of the knife, and bloody bits of membrane fell to the floor beside her feet. She poured more dark fluid between Scarlett's lips, then a colorless one into the horrible wound in her belly. Her cracked humming accompanied the small precise movements as she sewed the wound together.

"Wrap her in linen then in wool while I wash the babe," she said. Her knife slashed through the ropes binding Scarlett.

When Colum and Mrs. Fitzpatrick were finished, the woman returned with Scarlett's baby swaddled in a soft white blanket. "The midwife forgot this," the *cailleach* said. Her chuckle brought an answering throaty sound from the baby, and the infant girl opened her eyes. The blue irises looked like pale tinted rings around the black, unfocused pupils. She had long black lashes and two tiny lines for eyebrows. She was not red and misshapen like most newborns because she had not passed through the birth canal. Her tiny nose and ears and mouth and soft pulsing skull were perfect. Her olive skin was very dark against the white blanket.

63

Scarlett struggled towards the voices and the light her sedated mind vaguely perceived. There was something . . . something important . . . a question . . . Firm hands held her head, gentle fingers parted her lips, a cooling sweet liquid bathed her tongue, trickled down her throat, and she slept again.

The next time she fought for consciousness she remembered what the question was, the vital, the all-important question. The baby. Was it dead? Her hands fumbled to her abdomen, and burning pain leapt at her touch. Her teeth bruised her lips, her hands pressed harder, fell away. There was no kicking, no firm rounded lumpiness that was a questing foot. The baby had died. Scarlett uttered a weak cry of misery, no louder than a mew, and the releasing sweet draught poured into her mouth. Throughout her drugged sleep slow weak tears seeped from her closed eyes.

Semiconscious for the third time, she tried to hold on to the darkness, to stay asleep, to push the world away. But the pain grew, tore at her, made her move to flee it, and the moving gave it such strength that she whimpered helplessly. The cool glass vial tipped, and she was freed. Later, when she floated again to the edges of consciousness, she opened her mouth in readiness, eager for the dreamless darkness. Instead there was a cold wet cloth wiping her lips, and a voice she knew but couldn't remember. "Scarlett darling . . . Katie Scarlett O'Hara . . . open your eyes . . ."

Her mind searched, faded, strengthened—Colum. It was Colum. Her cousin. Her friend . . . Why didn't he let her sleep if he was her friend? Why didn't he give her the medicine before the pain came back?

"Katie Scarlett . . ."

She opened her eyes halfway. Light hurt them, and she closed the lids.

"That's a good girl, Scarlett darling. Open your eyes, I've something for you." His coaxing tone was insistent. Scarlett's eyes opened. Someone had moved the lamp, and the dimness was easy.

There's my friend Colum. She tried to smile, but memory flooded her mind, and her lips crumpled into childlike bubbling sobs. "The baby's dead, Colum. Put me to sleep again. Help me forget. Please. Please, Colum."

The wet cloth stroked her cheeks, wiped her mouth. "No, no, no, Scarlett, no, no, the baby's here, the baby's not dead."

Slowly the meaning became clear. Not dead, said her mind. "Not dead?" said Scarlett.

She could see Colum's face, Colum's smile. "Not dead, mavourneen, not dead. Here. Look."

Scarlett turned her head on the pillow. Why was it so hard, just to turn her head? A pale bundle in someone's hands was there. "Your daughter, Katie Scarlett," said Colum. He parted the folds of the blanket, and she saw the tiny sleeping face.

"Oh," Scarlett breathed. So small and so perfect and so helpless. Look at the skin, like rose petals, like cream—no, she's browner than cream, the rose is only a hint of rose. She looks sun-browned, like . . . like a baby pirate. She looks exactly like Rhett!

Rhett! Why aren't you here to see your baby? Your beautiful dark baby.

My beautiful dark baby. Let me look at you.

Scarlett felt a strange and frightening weakness, a warmth that washed through her body like a strong, low, enveloping wave of painless burning.

The baby opened her eyes. They stared directly into Scarlett's. And Scarlett felt love. Without conditions, without demands, without reasons, without questions, without bounds, without reserve, without self.

"Hey, little baby," she said.

"Now drink your medicine," said Colum. The tiny dark face was gone.

"No! No, I want my baby. Where is she?"

"You'll have her next time you wake up. Open your mouth, Scarlett darling."

"I won't," she tried to say, but the drops were on her tongue, and in a moment the darkness closed over her. She slept, smiling, a glow of life under her deathly paleness.

Perhaps it was because the baby looked like Rhett; perhaps it was because Scarlett always valued most what she fought hardest for; or perhaps it was because she'd had so many months with the Irish, who adored children. More likely it was one of the wonders that life gives for no cause at all. Whatever the origin, pure consuming love had come to Scarlett O'Hara after a lifetime of emptiness, not knowing what she lacked.

Scarlett refused to take any more pain-killer. The long red scar on her body was like a streak of white-hot steel, but it was forgotten in the overwhelming joy she felt whenever she touched her baby or even looked at her.

"Send her away!" Scarlett said when the healthy young wet nurse was brought in. "Time after time I had to bind my breasts and suffer agonies while the milk dried up, all to be a lady and keep my figure. I'm going to nurse this baby, have her close to me. I'll feed her and make her strong and see her grow."

When the baby found her nipple the first time and nursed greedily with a tiny wrinkle of concentration on her brow, Scarlett smiled down at her with triumph. "You're a Momma's girl, all right, hungry as a wolf and fixed on getting what you want."

The baby was baptized in Scarlett's bedroom, because Scarlett was too weak to walk. Father Flynn stood near the Viceregal bed where she was propped up against lace-trimmed pillows holding the baby in her arms until she had to give her over to Colum, who was godfather; Kathleen and Mrs. Fitzpatrick were godmothers. The baby wore an embroidered linen gown, thin from washings, that had been worn by hundreds of O'Hara babies for generation after generation. She was named Katie Colum O'Hara. She waved her arms and kicked her legs when the water touched her, but she didn't cry.

Kathleen wore her best blue frock with a lace collar, although she should have been in mourning. Old Katie Scarlett was dead. However, everyone agreed that Scarlett should not be told until she was stronger.

Rosaleen Fitzpatrick watched Father Flynn from hawk-like eyes, poised to snatch the baby if he faltered for a second. She'd been speechless for a long minute after Scarlett asked her to serve as godmother. "How did you guess how I feel about this baby?" she asked when her voice returned.

"I didn't," said Scarlett, "but I know I wouldn't have a baby if you hadn't stopped that monster woman from killing her. I remember a good bit about that night."

Colum took Katie from Father Flynn when the ceremony was over and put her in Scarlett's outstretched hands. Then he poured a tot of whiskey for the priest and the godparents and made a toast: "To the health and happiness of mother and child, The O'Hara and the newest of the O'Haras." After that, he escorted the doddering saintly old man to Kennedy's bar where he bought a few rounds for all there in honor of the occasion. He hoped against hope that it would stop the rumors that were already flying all over County Meath.

Joe O'Neill, the blacksmith, had cowered in a corner of Ballyhara's kitchen until daylight, then scuttled to his smithy to drink himself brave. "Though Saint Patrick himself would have needed more than all the prayers at his beckoning on that night," he told anyone who would listen, and there were many.

"Ready was I to save the life of The O'Hara when the witch come through the stone wall and throws me with terrible force onto the floor. Then kicks me—and I could feel in my flesh that the foot was no human foot but a cloven hoof. She cast a spell on The O'Hara then and ripped the babe from the womb. All bloody was the babe, and blood on the floors and the walls and in the air. A lesser man would have sheltered his eyes from such a fearful sight. But Joseph O'Neill saw the babe's fine strong form beneath the blood, and I'm telling you it was a manchild, with manhood plain between its limbs.

" 'I'll wash the blood away,' says the demon, and she turns her back, then presents to Father O'Hara a spindly frail near-lifeless creature—female and brown as the earth of the grave. Now who will tell me? If I didn't see a changeling, what was it I saw that terrible night? There's no good will come of it, not to The O'Hara nor any man who's touched by the shadow of the fairy babe left in place of The O'Hara's stolen boy."

The story from Dunshaughlin got to Ballyhara after a week. The O'Hara was dying, said the midwife, and could only be saved by ridding her of the dead babe in her womb. Who would know these things, pitiful though they were, better than a midwife who'd seen all there was to see of childbirth? Of a sudden the suffering mother sat up on her bed of pain. "I see it," says she, "the banshee! Tall and clad all in white with the fairy beauty on its face." Then the devils drove a spear from Hell through the window and the banshee flew out to wail the call to death. It was calling the soul of the lost babe, but the dead babe was restored among the living by sucking out the soul of the good old woman who was grandmother to The O'Hara. It was the devil's work and no mistaking and the babe The O'Hara takes for her own is nought but a ghoul.

"I feel that I should warn Scarlett," Colum said to Rosaleen Fitzpatrick, "but what can I tell her? That people are superstitious? That All

Hallows' Eve is a dangerous birth date for a baby? I cannot find any advice to give her, there's no way to protect the baby from talk."

"I'll see to Katie's safety," Mrs. Fitzpatrick said. "No one and nothing enters this house unless I say so, and no harm will come near that tiny child. Talk will be forgotten in time, Colum, you know that. Something else will come along to weave tales about and everyone will see that Katie's only a little girl like any other little girl."

A week later Mrs. Fitzpatrick took a tray of tea and sandwiches to Scarlett's room and stood patiently while Scarlett bombarded her with the same plaint she'd been making for days.

"I don't see why I have to stay stuck up here in this room forever. I feel plenty well enough to be up and about. Look at the lovely sunshine today, I want to take Katie out for a ride in the trap, but the best I can do is sit by the window and look out at the leaves falling. I'm sure she's watching. Her eyes look up and then follow them floating down— Oh, look! Come look! Look at Katie's eyes here in the light. They're changing from blue. I thought they'd turn brown like Rhett's because she's the spit of him. But I can see the first little specks, and they're green. She's going to have my eyes!"

Scarlett nuzzled the baby's neck. "You're Momma's girl, aren't you, Katie O'Hara? No, not Katie. Anybody can be a Katie. I'm going to call you Kitty Cat, with your green eyes." She lifted the solemn baby up to face the housekeeper.

"Mrs. Fitzpatrick, I'd like to introduce you to Cat O'Hara." Scarlett's smile was like sunlight.

Rosaleen Fitzpatrick felt more frightened than at any time in her life.

64

The enforced idleness of her convalescence gave Scarlett many hours to think, since her baby spent most of the day and the night sleeping, exactly like all other infants. Scarlett tried reading, but she had never cared for it, and she had not changed in that way.

What had changed was what she thought about.

First and foremost, there was her love for Cat. Only weeks old, the baby was too young to be responsive, except in reacting to her own hunger and the satisfaction of Scarlett's warm breast and milk. It's loving that's making me so happy, Scarlett realized. It has nothing to do with being loved. I like to think Cat loves me, but the truth is she loves to eat.

Scarlett was able to laugh at the joke on herself. Scarlett O'Hara, who'd made men fall in love with her as a sport, as an amusement, was nothing more than a source of food to the one person she loved more than she'd ever loved in her life.

Because she hadn't really loved Ashley; she'd known that for a long time. She'd only wanted what she couldn't have and called that love.

I threw away over ten years on the false love, too, and I lost Rhett, the man I really loved.

. . . Or did I?

She searched her memory, in spite of the pain. It always hurt to think about Rhett, about losing him, about her failure. It eased the pain some when she thought about the way he'd treated her and hatred burned away the hurt. But for the most part, she managed to keep him out of her mind; it was less disturbing.

During these long days with nothing to do, however, her mind kept going back over her life, and she couldn't avoid remembering him.

Had she loved him?

I must have, she thought, I must love him still, or my heart wouldn't ache the way it does when I see his smile in my mind, hear his voice.

But for ten years she had conjured up Ashley in the same way, imagining his smile and his voice.

And I wanted Rhett most after he left me, Scarlett's deep core of honesty reminded her.

It was too confusing. It made her head ache, even more than her heart. She wouldn't think about it. It was much better to think about Cat, to think about how happy she was.

To think about happiness?

I was happy even before Cat came. I was happy from the day I went to Jamie's house. Not like now, I didn't dream anybody could ever feel as happy as I do every time I look at Cat, every time I hold her, or feed her. But I was happy, all the same, because the O'Haras took me just the way I was. They never expected me to be just like them, they never made me feel I had to change, they never made me feel I was wrong.

Even when I was wrong. I had no call to expect Kathleen to do my hair and mend my clothes and make my bed. I was putting on airs. With people who never did anything so tacky as put on airs themselves. But they never said, "Oh, stop putting on airs, Scarlett." No, they just let me do what I was doing and accepted me, airs and all. Just like I was.

I was awful wrong about Daniel and all moving to Ballyhara. I was trying to make them be a credit to me. I wanted them to live in grand houses and be grand farmers with lots of land and hired hands to do most of the work. I wanted to change them. I never wondered what they wanted. I didn't take them just the way they were.

Oh, I'm never going to do that to Cat. I'm never going to make her different from what she is. I'm always going to love her like I do now—with my whole heart, no matter what.

Mother never loved me like I love Cat. Or Suellen or Carreen, either. She wanted me to be different from me, she wanted me to be just like her. All of us, that's what she wanted from all three of us. She was wrong.

Scarlett recoiled from what was in her head. She'd always believed her mother was perfect. It was unthinkable that Ellen O'Hara could ever be wrong about anything.

But the thought would not go away. It returned again and again when she was unprepared to shut it out. It returned in different guises, with different embellishments. It would not leave her alone.

Mother was wrong. Being a lady like her isn't the only way to be. It isn't even always the best way to be. Not if it doesn't make you happy. Happy is the best way to be because then you can let other people be happy, too. Their own way.

Mother wasn't happy. She was kind and patient and caring—for us children, for Pa, for the darkies. But not loving. Not happy. Oh, poor Mother. I wish you could have felt the way I feel now, I wish you could have been happy.

What was it Grandfather had said? That his daughter Ellen had married Gerald O'Hara to run away from a disappointment in love. Was that why she was never happy? Was she pining over someone she couldn't have the way I pined over Ashley? The way I pine now over Rhett when I can't help it.

What a waste! What a horrible, senseless waste. When happiness was so wonderful, how could anyone cling to a love that made them unhappy? Scarlett vowed that she wouldn't do it. She knew what it was to be happy, and she would not ruin it.

She caught her sleeping baby up in her arms and hugged her. Cat woke and waved her helpless hands in protest. "Oh, Kitty Cat, I'm sorry. I just had to hug you some."

They were all wrong! The idea was so explosive that it woke Scarlett from a sound sleep. They were wrong! All of them—the people who cut me dead in Atlanta, Aunt Eulalie and Aunt Pauline, and just about everybody in Charleston. They wanted me to be just like them, and because I'm not, they disapproved of me, made me feel like there was something terribly wrong with me, made me think I was a bad person, that I deserved to be looked down on.

And there was nothing I did that was as terrible as all that. What they punished me for was that I wasn't minding their rules. I worked harder than any field hand—at making money, and caring about money isn't ladylike. Never mind that I was keeping Tara going and holding the aunts' heads above water and supporting Ashley and his family and paying for almost every piece of food on the table at Aunt Pitty's plus keeping the roof fixed and the coal bin filled. They all thought I shouldn't have dirtied my hands with the ledgers from the store or put on a smile when I sold lumber to the Yankees. There were plenty enough things I did that I shouldn't have done, but working for money wasn't one of them, and that's what they blamed me for most. No, that's not quite it. They blamed me for being successful at it.

That and pulling Ashley back from breaking his neck flinging himself into the grave after Melly. If it had been the other way around, and I'd saved her at Ashley's burial, it would have been all right. Hypocrites!

What gives people whose whole life is a lie the right to judge me? What's wrong with working as hard as you can, and then more besides? Why is it so terrible to push in and stop disaster from happening to anyone, especially a friend?

They were wrong. Here in Ballyhara I worked as hard as I could, and I was admired for it. I kept Uncle Daniel from losing his farm, and they started calling me The O'Hara.

That's why being The O'Hara makes me feel so strange and so happy all at the same time. It's because The O'Hara is honored for all the same things that I've been thinking were bad all these years. The O'Hara would have stayed up late doing the books for the store. The O'Hara would have grabbed Ashley away from the grave.

What was it Mrs. Fitzpatrick said? "You don't have to do anything, you only have to be what you are." What I am is Scarlett O'Hara, who makes mistakes sometimes and does things right sometimes, but who never pretends any more to be what she's not. I'm The O'Hara, and I'd never be called that if I was as bad as they make me out to be in Atlanta. I'm not bad at all. I'm not a saint, either, God knows. But I'm willing to be different, I'm willing to be who I am, not pretend to be what I'm not.

I'm The O'Hara, and I'm proud of it. It makes me happy and whole.

Cat made a gurgling noise to indicate that she was awake, too, and ready to be fed. Scarlett lifted her from her basket and settled the two of them in the bed. She cupped the tiny unprotected head in one hand and guided Cat to her breast.

"I promise you on my word of honor, Cat O'Hara. You can grow up to be whatever you are, even if it's as different from me as day from night. If you have a leaning towards being a lady, I'll even show you how, never mind what I think about it. After all, I know all the rules even if I can't abide them."

65

I'm going out, and there's no more to be said about it." Scarlett glowered mulishly at Mrs. Fitzpatrick.

The housekeeper stood in the open doorway like an immovable mountain. "No, you are not."

Scarlett changed her tactics. "Please do let me," she coaxed, with the sweetest smile in her arsenal. "The fresh air will do me a world of good. It'll perk up my appetite, too, and you know how you've been after me about not eating enough."

"That will improve. The cook has arrived."

Scarlett forgot that she was being beguiling. "And high time, too! Is her high-and-mightiness bothering to say what took her so long?"

Mrs. Fitzpatrick smiled. "She started out on time, but her piles bothered her so badly she had to stop overnight every ten miles on the way here. It seems we won't have to worry about her lazing in a rocking chair when she should be on her feet working."

Scarlett tried not to laugh, but she couldn't help it. And she couldn't really stay mad at Mrs. Fitzpatrick; they had grown too close for that. The older woman had moved into the housekeeper's apartment the day after Cat was born. She was Scarlett's constant companion while she was ill. And readily available afterwards.

Many people came to visit Scarlett in the long convalescent weeks after Cat was born. Colum almost daily, Kathleen almost every other day, her big O'Hara men cousins after Mass each Sunday, Molly more often than

Scarlett liked. But Mrs. Fitzpatrick was always there. She brought tea and cakes to the visitors, whiskey and cakes to the men, and after the visitors left she stayed with Scarlett to hear the news the visitors had brought and finish off the refreshments. She brought news herself—about the happenings in the town of Ballyhara and in Trim—and gossip she'd heard in the shops. She kept Scarlett from being too lonely.

Scarlett invited Mrs. Fitzpatrick to call her "Scarlett" and asked, "What's your first name?"

Mrs. Fitzpatrick never told her. It wouldn't do for any informality to develop, she said firmly, and she explained the strict hierarchy of an Irish Big House. Her position as housekeeper would be undermined if the respect accorded to it was diminished by familiarity on anyone's part, even the mistress's. Perhaps especially the mistress's.

It was all too subtle for Scarlett, but Mrs. Fitzpatrick's pleasant unyieldingness made it clear to her that it was important. She settled for the names the housekeeper suggested. Scarlett could call her "Mrs. Fitz," and she would call Scarlett "Mrs. O." But only when they were alone together. In front of other people, full formality had to be maintained.

"Even Colum?" Scarlett wanted to know. Mrs. Fitz considered, then yielded. Colum was a special case.

Scarlett tried to take advantage now of Mrs. Fitz's partiality to him. "I'll only walk down to Colum's," she said. "He hasn't been to see me for ages, and I miss him."

"He's away on business and you know it. I heard him tell you he was going."

"Bother!" Scarlett muttered. "You win." She went back to her chair by the window and sat down. "Go talk to Miss Piles."

Mrs. Fitz laughed aloud. "By the way," she said as she left, "her name is Mrs. Keane. But you can call her Miss Piles if you like. You'll likely never meet her. That's my job."

Scarlett waited until she was sure Mrs. Fitz wouldn't catch her and then she got ready to go out. She'd been obedient long enough. It was an accepted fact that after childbirth a woman recuperated for a month, most of the time in bed, and she'd done that. She didn't see why she should have to add three more weeks to it just because Cat's birth hadn't been normal. The doctor at Ballyhara struck her as a good man, even reminded her a little of Dr. Meade. But Dr. Devlin himself admitted that he had no experience of babies brought by knife. Why should she listen to him? Particularly when there was something she really had to do.

Mrs. Fitz had told her about the old woman who had appeared, as if by magic, to deliver Cat in the middle of the Halloween tempest. Colum had told her who the woman was—the *cailleach* from the tower. Scarlett owed the wise woman her life, and Cat's. She had to thank her.

The cold took Scarlett by surprise. October had been warm enough, how could one month make so much difference? She wrapped the folds of her cloak around the well-blanketed baby. Cat was awake. Her large eyes looked at Scarlett's face. "You darling thing," said Scarlett softly. "You're so good, Cat, you never cry, do you?" She walked through the bricked stableyard to the route she'd used so often in the trap.

"I know you're there someplace," Scarlett shouted at the thicket of undergrowth beneath the trees that bordered the tower's clearing. "You might as well come on out and talk to me, because I'm going to stand right here freezing to death until you do. The baby, too, if that matters to you." She waited confidently. The woman who had brought Cat into the world would never let her be exposed for long to the cold damp in the shadow of the tower.

Cat's eyes left Scarlett's face to move from side to side as if she were looking for something. A few minutes later Scarlett heard a rustling in the thick growth of holly bushes to her right. The wise woman stepped out between two of them. "This way," she said, and stepped back.

There was a path, Scarlett saw when she got near. She'd never have found it if the wise woman hadn't held back the spiny holly branches with one of her shawls. Scarlett followed the path until it disappeared in a grove of low-branched trees. "I give up," she said, "where to now?"

There was a rusty laugh behind her. "This way," said the wise woman. She walked around Scarlett and bent low under the branches. Scarlett did the same. After a few steps she could straighten. The clearing in the center of the grove held a small mud hut thatched with reeds. A thin plume of gray smoke curled upward from its chimney. "Come in," said the woman. She opened the door.

"She's a fine child," said the wise woman. She had examined every aspect of Cat's body, down to the nails on her smallest toes. "What have you named her?"

"Katie Colum O'Hara." It was only the second time Scarlett had spoken. Once inside the door, she'd begun thanking the wise woman for what she'd done, but the woman had stopped her.

"Let me have the babe," she'd said, hands outstretched. Scarlett had passed Cat over at once, then kept silent during the detailed examination.

" 'Katie Colum,' " the woman repeated. " 'Tis a weak soft sound for this strong child. My name is Grainne. A strong name."

Her rough voice made the Gaelic name sound like a challenge. Scarlett shifted on her stool. She didn't know how she should reply.

The woman wrapped Cat in her napkin and blankets. Then she lifted her and whispered so quietly in her little ear that Scarlett couldn't hear, even though she strained for the words. Cat's fingers caught hold of Grainne's hair. The wise woman held Cat against her shoulder.

"You would not have understood even if you had heard, O'Hara. I spoke in the old Irish. It was a charm. You have heard that I know magic as well as herbs."

Scarlett admitted she had.

"Perhaps I do. I have some knowledge of the old words and the old ways, but I do not say they are magic. I look and I listen and I learn. To some it may be like magic that another sees, where he is blind, or hears, when he is deaf. It lies largely in the believing. Do not hope that I can do magic for you."

"I never said I came here for that."

"Only to speak thanks? Is that the all of it?"

"Yes, it is, and now I've done it and I must go before I'm missed at the house."

"I ask your forgiveness," the wise woman said. "There are few feel thankful when I enter their lives. I wonder you don't feel anger at what I did to your body."

"You saved my life and my baby's too."

"But I took life away from all other babes. A doctor might have known how to do more."

"Well, I couldn't get a doctor, or I would have had one!" Scarlett closed her lips firmly over her quick tongue. She'd come to say thank you, not to insult the wise woman. But why was she talking riddles in her raspy scary voice? It gave a person gooseflesh.

"I'm sorry," said Scarlett, "that was rude of me. I'm sure no doctor could have done any better. More likely not even half as well. And I don't know what you mean about other babies. Are you saying I was having twins and the other one died?" It was certainly a possibility, Scarlett thought. She'd been so big when she was pregnant. But surely Mrs. Fitz or Colum would have told her. Maybe not. They hadn't told her about Old Katie Scarlett dying until two weeks after it happened.

A feeling of unbearable loss squeezed Scarlett's heart. "Was there another baby? You've got to tell me!"

"Shhh, you're bothering Katie Colum," said Grainne the wise woman. "There was no second child in the womb. I did not know you would mistake my words. The woman with white hair looked knowledgeable, I believed she understood and would tell you. I lifted the womb with the baby, and I had not the skills to restore it. You will never have another child."

There was a terrible finality in the woman's words and the way she said them, and Scarlett knew absolutely that they were true. But she couldn't believe them, she wouldn't. No more babies? Now, when she'd finally discovered the encompassing joy of being a mother, when she'd learned—so late—what it was to love? It couldn't be. It was too cruel.

Scarlett had never understood how Melanie could have knowingly risked her life to have another baby, but she did now. She would do the same. She'd go through the pain and the fear and the blood again and again to have that moment of seeing her baby's face for the first time.

Cat made a soft mewing sound. It was her warning that she was getting hungry. Scarlett felt her milk begin to flow in response. What am I taking on so for? Don't I already have the most wonderful baby in the whole world? I'm not going to lose my milk fretting about imaginary babies when my Cat is real and wants her mother.

"I've got to go," said Scarlett. "It's close to time to feed the baby." She held out her hands for Cat.

"One more word," said Grainne. "A warning."

Scarlett felt afraid. She wished she hadn't brought Cat. Why didn't the woman give her back?

"Keep your babe close, there are those who say she was brought by a witch and must be bewitched therefrom."

Scarlett shivered.

Grainne's stained fingers gently undid Cat's grasp. She brushed her soft wisp-covered head with a kiss and a murmur. "Go well, Dara." Then she gave the baby to Scarlett. "I will call her 'Dara' in my memory. It means oak tree. I am grateful for the gift of seeing her, and for your thanks. But do not bring her again. It is not wise for her to have aught to do with me. Go now. Someone is coming and you should not be seen ... No, the path the other takes is not yours. It is the one from the north used by foolish women who buy potions for love or beauty or harm to those they hate. Go. Guard the babe."

Scarlett was glad to obey. She plodded doggedly through the cold rain that had begun to fall. Her head and back were bent to protect her baby from harm. Cat made sucking noises beneath the shelter of Scarlett's cloak.

* * *

Mrs. Fitzpatrick eyed the wet cloak on the floor by the fire, but she made no comment. "Miss Piles seems to have a nice light hand with a batter," she said. "I've brought scones with your tea."

"Good, I'm starving." She'd fed Cat and had a nap and the sun was shining again. Scarlett was confident now that the walk had done her a world of good. She wouldn't take no for an answer the next time she wanted to go out.

Mrs. Fitz didn't attempt to stop her. She recognized futility when she met it.

When Colum came home Scarlett walked down to his house for tea. And advice.

"I want to buy a small closed buggy, Colum. It's too cold to go around in the trap, and I need to do things. Will you pick one out for me?"

He'd be willing, said Colum, but she could do her own choosing if she'd prefer. The buggy makers would bring their wares to her. As would the makers of anything else she fancied. She was the lady of the Big House.

"Now why didn't I think of that?" said Scarlett.

Within a week she was driving a neat black buggy with a thin yellow stripe on its side, behind a neat gray horse that lived up to the seller's promise that it had good go in it with hardly a mention of the whip ever needed.

She also had a "parlor suite" of green-upholstered shiny oak furniture with ten extra chairs that could be pulled near the hearth, and a marble-topped round table large enough to seat six for a meal. All these sat on a Wilton carpet in the room adjoining her bedroom. No matter what outrageous tales Colum might tell about French women entertaining crowds while they lounged in their beds, she was going to have a proper place to see her visitors. And no matter what Mrs. Fitz said, she saw no reason at all to use the downstairs rooms for entertaining when there were plenty of empty rooms upstairs and handy.

She didn't have her big desk and chair yet because the carpenter in Ballyhara was making them. What point was there in having a town of your own if you weren't smart enough to support the businesses in it? You could be sure of getting your rent if they were earning money.

Cat's padded basket was beside her on the buggy seat everywhere Scarlett went. She made baby noises and blew bubbles and Scarlett was sure that they were singing duets when she drove along the road. She showed Cat off at every shop and house in Ballyhara. People crossed themselves when they saw the dark-skinned baby with the green eyes and Scarlett was pleased. She thought they were blessing the baby.

As Christmas came nearer, Scarlett lost much of the elation she'd felt when she was freed from the captivity of convalescence. "I wouldn't be in Atlanta for all the tea in China, even if I was invited to all the parties, or in Charleston, either, with their silly dance cards and receiving lines," she told Cat, "but I'd like to be somewhere that's not so damp all the time."

Scarlett thought it would be nice to be living in a cottage so that she could whitewash it and paint the trim the way Kathleen and the cousins were doing. And all the other cottagers too, in Adamstown and beside the roads. When she walked over to Kennedy's bar on December 22 and saw the shops and houses being limed and painted over the almost-new jobs done in the autumn, she pranced with delight. Her pleasure in the neat prosperity of her town took away the slight sadness that she often felt when she went to her own bar for companionship. It sometimes seemed as if the conversation turned stiff as soon as she entered.

"We've got to decorate the house for Christmas," she announced to Mrs. Fitz. "What do the Irish do?"

Holly branches on mantels and over doors and windows, said the housekeeper. And a big candle, usually red, in one window to light the Christ Child's way. We'll have one in every window, Scarlett declared, but Mrs. Fitz was firm. One window. Scarlett could have all the candles she wanted on tables—or the floor, if it made her happy—but only one window should have a candle. And that one could only be lighted on Christmas Eve when the Angelus rang.

The housekeeper smiled. "The tradition is that the youngest child in the house lights a rush from the coals on the hearth as soon as the Angelus is heard, then lights the candle with the flame from the rush. You might have to help her a bit."

Scarlett and Cat spent Christmas at Daniel's house. There was nearly enough admiration for Cat to satisfy even Scarlett. And enough people coming through the open door to keep her mind off the Christmases at Tara in the old days when the family and house servants went out onto the wide porch after breakfast in response to the cry, "Christmas Gift." When Gerald O'Hara gave a drink of whiskey and a plug of tobacco to every field hand as he handed him his new coat and new boots. When Ellen O'Hara said a brief prayer for each woman and child as she gave them lengths of calico and flannel together with oranges and stick candy. Sometimes Scarlett missed the warm slurrings of black voices and the flashing smiles on black faces almost more than she could bear.

* * *

"I need to go home, Colum," Scarlett said.

"And aren't you home now, on the land of your people that you made O'Hara land again?"

"Oh, Colum, don't be Irish at me! You know what I mean. I'm homesick for Southern voices and Southern sunshine and Southern food. I want some corn bread and fried chicken and grits. Nobody in Ireland even knows what corn is. That's just a word for any kind of grain to them."

"I do know, Scarlett, and I'm sorry for the heartache you're feeling. Why not go for a visit when good sailing weather comes? You can leave Cat here. Mrs. Fitzpatrick and I will take care of her."

"Never! I'll never leave Cat."

There was nothing to be said. But from time to time the thought popped up in Scarlett's head: it's only two weeks and a day to cross the ocean, and sometimes the dolphins play alongside for hours on end.

On New Year's Day, Scarlett got her first hint of what it really meant to be The O'Hara. Mrs. Fitz came to her room with morning tea instead of sending Peggy Quinn with the breakfast tray. "The blessings of all the saints on mother and daughter in the new year to come," she said cheerily. "I must tell you about the duty you have to do before your breakfast."

"Happy New Year to you, too, Mrs. Fitz, and what on earth are you talking about?"

A tradition, a ritual, a requirement, said Mrs. Fitz. Without it there'd be no luck all year. Scarlett might have a taste of tea first, but that was all. The first food eaten in the house must be the special New Year's barm brack on the tray. Three bites had to be eaten, in the name of the Trinity.

"Before you start, though," Mrs. Fitz said, "come into the room I've got ready. Because after you have the Trinity bites you have to throw the cake with all your might against a wall so that it breaks into pieces. I had the wall scrubbed yesterday, and the floor."

"That's the craziest thing I ever heard. Why should I ruin a perfectly good cake? And why eat cake for breakfast anyhow?"

"Because that's the way it's done. Come do your duty, The O'Hara, before the rest of the people in this house die of hunger. No one can eat before the barm brack is broken."

Scarlett put on her wool wrapper and obeyed. She had a swallow of tea to moisten her mouth, then bit three times into the edge of the rich fruited cake as Mrs. Fitz directed. She had to hold it in both hands because it was so big. Then she repeated the prayer against hunger during the year that Mrs. Fitz taught her and heaved with both arms, sending the cake flying and crashing against the wall. Bits flew all over the room.

Scarlett laughed. "What an awful mess. But the throwing part was fun."

"I'm glad you liked it," said the housekeeper. "You've got five more to do. Every man, woman, and child in Ballyhara has to get a little piece for good luck. They're waiting outside. The maids will take the pieces down on trays after you finish."

"My grief," said Scarlett. "I should have taken littler bites."

After breakfast Colum accompanied her through the town for her next ritual. It was good luck for the whole year if a dark-haired person visited a house on New Year's Day. But the tradition required that the person enter, then be escorted out, then be escorted back in again.

"And don't you dare laugh," Colum ordered. "Any dark-haired person is good luck. The head of a clan is ten times over good luck."

Scarlett was staggering when it was over. "Thank goodness there are still so many empty buildings," she gasped. "I'm awash with tea and foundering from all the cake in my stomach. Did we really have to eat and drink in every single place?"

"Scarlett darling, how can you call it a visit if there's no hospitality offered and received? If you were a man, it would have been whiskey and not tea."

Scarlett grinned. "Cat might have loved that."

February 1 was considered the beginning of the farm year in Ireland. Accompanied by everyone who worked and lived in Ballyhara, Scarlett stood in the center of a big field and, after saying a prayer for the success of the crops, sank a spade into the earth, lifted and turned the first sod. Now the year could begin. After the feast of applecake—and milk, of course, because February 1 was also the feast day of Saint Brigid, Ireland's other patron saint, who was also patron saint of the dairy.

When everyone was eating and talking after the ceremony, Scarlett knelt by the opened earth and took up a handful of the rich loam. "This is for you, Pa," she murmured. "See, Katie Scarlett hasn't forgotten what you told her, that the land of County Meath is the best in the world, better even than the land of Georgia, of Tara. I'll do my best to tend it, Pa, and love it the way you taught me. It's O'Hara soil, and it's ours again."

* * *

The age-old progression of plowing and harrowing, planting and praying had a simple, hard-working dignity that won Scarlett's admiration and
respect for all who lived by the land. She had felt it when she lived in
Daniel's cottage and she felt it now for the farmers at Ballyhara. For herself
as well, because she was, in her own way, one of them. She hadn't the
strength to drive the plow, but she could provide it. And the horses to pull
it. And the seed to plant in the furrows it made.

The Estate Office was her home even more than her rooms in the Big
House. There was another cradle for Cat by her desk, identical to the one
in her bedroom, and she could rock it with her foot while she worked on
her record books and her accounts. The disputes that Mrs. Fitzpatrick had
been so gloomy about turned out to be simple matters to settle. Especially
if you were The O'Hara, and your word was law. Scarlett had always had
to bully people into doing what she wanted; now she had only to speak
quietly, and there was no argument. She enjoyed the first Sunday of the
month very much. She even began to realize that other people occasionally
had an opinion worth listening to. The farmers really did know more about
farming than she did, and she could learn from them. She needed to. Three
hundred acres of Ballyhara land were set aside as her own farm. The farmers worked it and paid only half the usual rent for the land they leased
from her. Scarlett understood sharecropping; it was the way things were
done in the South. Being an estate landlord was still new to her. She was
determined to be the best landlord in all Ireland.

"The farmers learn from me, too," she told Cat. "They'd never even
heard of fertilizing with phosphates until I handed out those sacks of it.
Might as well let Rhett get a few pennies of his money back if it'll mean a
better wheat crop for us."

She never used the word "father" in Cat's hearing. Who could tell
how much a tiny baby took in and remembered? Especially a baby who
was so clearly superior in every way to every other baby in the world.

As the days lengthened, breezes and rain became softer and warmer.
Cat O'Hara was becoming more and more fascinating; she was developing
individuality.

"I certainly named you right," Scarlett told her, "you're the most independent little thing I ever saw." Cat's big green eyes looked at her
mother attentively while she was talking, then returned to her absorbed
contemplation of her own fingers. The baby never fussed, she had an infinite capacity to amuse herself. Weaning her was hard on Scarlett, but not

on Cat. She enjoyed examining her porridge with fingers and mouth. She seemed to find all experience extremely interesting. She was a strong baby with a straight spine and high-held head. Scarlett adored her. And, in a special way, respected her. She liked to scoop Cat up and kiss her soft hair and neck and cheeks and hands and feet; she longed to hold Cat in her lap and rock her. But the baby would tolerate only a few minutes of cuddling before she pushed herself free with her feet and fists. And Cat's small dark-skinned face could have such an outraged expression that Scarlett was forced to laugh even when she was being forcefully rejected.

The happiest times for both of them were at the end of the day when Cat shared Scarlett's bath. She patted the water, laughing at its splashes, and Scarlett held her, jounced her up and down, and sang to her. Then there was the sweetness of drying the perfect tiny limbs, each finger and toe individually, and spreading powder over Cat's silky skin and into each baby wrinkle.

When Scarlett was twenty years old, war had forced her to give up her youth overnight. Her will and endurance had hardened and so had her face. In the spring of 1876, when she was thirty-one, the gentle softness of hope and youth and tenderness gradually returned. She was unaware of it; her preoccupation with the farm and the baby had replaced her life-long concentration on her own vanity.

"You need some clothes," Mrs. Fitz said one day. "I've heard there's a dressmaker who wants to rent the house you lived in if you'll fresh paint the inside. She's a widow and well-fixed enough to pay a fair rent. The women in the town would like it, and you need it, unless you're willing to find a woman in Trim."

"What's wrong with the way I look? I wear decent black, the way a widow should. My petticoats hardly ever peek out."

"You don't wear decent black at all. You wear earth-stained, rolled-sleeves, peasant women clothes, and you're the lady of the Big House."

"Oh, fiddle-dee-dee, Mrs. Fitz. How could I ride out to see if the timothy grass is growing if I had on lady-of-the-house clothes? Besides, I like being comfortable. As soon as I can go back into colored skirts and shirts I'll start worrying about whether they have stains on them. I've always hated mourning, I don't see any reason to try and make black look fresh. No matter what you do to it, it's still black."

"Then you aren't interested in the dressmaker?"

"Of course I'm interested. Another rent is always interesting. And one of these days I'll order some frocks. After the planting. The fields should be ready for the wheat this week."

"There's another rent possible," the housekeeper said carefully. She'd been surprised more than once by unexpected astuteness on Scarlett's part. "Brendan Kennedy thinks he could do well if he added an inn to his bar. There's the building next to him could be used."

"Who on earth would come to Ballyhara to stay at an inn? That's crazy. Besides, if Brendan Kennedy wants to rent from me, he should carry his hat in his hand and come talk to me himself, not pester you to do it."

"Ach, well. Likely it was only talk." Mrs. Fitzgerald gave Scarlett the week's household account book and abandoned talk of the inn for the moment. Colum would have to work on it; he was much more persuasive than she was.

"We're getting to have more servants than the Queen of England," said Scarlett. She said the same thing every week.

"If you're going to have cows, you're going to need hands to milk them," said the housekeeper.

Scarlett picked up the refrain ". . . and to separate the cream and make the butter—I know. And the butter's selling. I just don't like cows, I guess. I'll go over this later, Mrs. Fitz. I want to take Cat down to watch them cutting peat in the bog."

"You'd better go over it now. We're out of money in the kitchen and the girls need paying tomorrow."

"Bother! I'll have to get some cash from the bank. I'll drive in to Trim."

"If I was the banker, I'd never give money to a creature dressed like you."

Scarlett laughed. "Nag, nag, nag. Tell the dressmaker I'll order the painting done."

But not the inn opened, thought Mrs. Fitzpatrick. She'd have to talk to Colum tonight.

The Fenians had been steadily growing in strength and numbers throughout Ireland. With Ballyhara, they now had what they most needed: a secure location where leaders from every county could meet to plan strategy, and where a man who needed to flee the militia could safely go, except that strangers were too noticeable in a town that was hardly larger than a village. Militia and constabulary patrols from Trim were few, but one man with sharp eyes was enough to destroy the best-laid plans.

"We really need the inn," Rosaleen Fitzpatrick said urgently. "It makes sense that a man with business in Trim would take a room this close but cheaper than in town."

"You're right, Rosaleen," Colum soothed, "and I'll talk to Scarlett. But not right away. She's too quick-minded for that. Give it a rest for a bit. Then when I bring it up, she won't wonder why we're both pressing."

"But Colum, we mustn't waste time."

"We mustn't lose everything by hurry, either. I'll do it when I believe the moment's right." Mrs. Fitzpatrick had to settle for that. Colum was in charge. She consoled herself by remembering that at least she'd gotten Margaret Scanlon in. And she hadn't even had to make up a tale to do it. Scarlett did need some clothes. It was a shocking disgrace the way she insisted on living—the cheapest clothes, two rooms lived in out of twenty. If Colum weren't Colum, Mrs. Fitzpatrick would doubt what he'd said, that not so long ago Scarlett had been a very fashionable woman.

" '... *and if that diamond ring turns brass, Momma's gonna buy you a looking glass*,' " Scarlett sang. Cat splashed vigorously in the sudsy water of the bath. "Momma's gonna buy you some pretty frocks, too," said Scarlett, "and buy Momma some. Then we'll go on the great big ship."

There was no reason to put it off. She had to go to America. If she left soon after Easter, she could be back in plenty of time for the harvest.

Scarlett made up her mind on the day she saw the delicate haze of green on the meadow where she'd turned the first sod. A fierce surge of excitement and pride made her want to cry aloud, "This is mine, my land, my seeds burst into life." She looked at the barely visible young growth and pictured it reaching up, becoming taller, taller, stronger, then flowering, perfuming the air, intoxicating the bees until they could hardly fly. The men would cut it then, scythes flashing silver, and make tall ricks of sweet golden hay. Year after year the cycle would turn—sow and reap—the annual miracle of birth and growth. Grass would grow and become hay. Wheat would grow and become bread. Oats would grow and become meal. Cat would grow—crawl, walk, talk, eat the oatmeal and the bread and jump onto the stacked hay from the loft of the barn just as Scarlett had done when she was a child. Ballyhara was her home.

Scarlett squinted up at the sun, saw the clouds racing towards it, knew that soon it would rain, and soon after that it would clear again, and the sun would warm the fields until the next rain, followed by the next warming sunlight.

I'll feel the baking heat of Georgia sun one more time, she decided, I'm entitled to that. I miss it sometimes so terribly. But, somehow, Tara's more like a dream than a memory. It belongs in the past, like the Scarlett I used to be. That life and that person don't have anything to do with me any more. I've made my choice. Cat's Tara is the Irish Tara. Mine will be too. I'm The O'Hara of Ballyhara. I'll keep my shares of Tara for Wade and Ella's inheritance, but I'll sell everything in Atlanta and cut those ties. Ballyhara's my home now. Our roots go deep here, Cat's and mine and Pa's. I'll take some O'Hara land with me when I go, some earth to mix into the Georgia clay of Gerald O'Hara's grave.

Her mind touched briefly on the business she had to deal with. All that could wait. What she must concentrate on was the best way to tell Wade and Ella about their wonderful new home. They wouldn't believe she wanted them—why should they? In truth she never had. Until she discovered what it felt like to love a child, to be a real mother.

It's going to be hard, Scarlett told herself many times, but I can do it. I can make up for the past. I've got so much love in me that it just spills over. I want to give some to my son and my daughter. They might not like Ireland at first, it's so different, but once we go to Market Day a couple of times, and the races, and I buy them their own ponies ... Ella should look darling in skirts and petticoats, too. All little girls love to dress up ... They'll have millions of cousins, with all the O'Haras around, and the children in Ballyhara town to play with ...

66

*Y*ou cannot leave until after Easter, Scarlett darling," said Colum. "There's a ceremony on Good Friday that only The O'Hara can do."

Scarlett didn't argue. Being The O'Hara was too important to her. But she was annoyed. What difference could it possibly make who planted the first potato? It irritated her, too, that Colum wouldn't go with her. And that he was away so much lately. "On business," he said. Well, why couldn't he do his fundraising in Savannah again, instead of wherever else he went to?

The truth was that everything irritated her. Now that she had decided to go, she wanted to be gone. She was snappish with Margaret Scanlon, the dressmaker, because it took so long to have her dresses made. And because Mrs. Scanlon looked so interested when Scarlett ordered dresses in colorful silks and linens as well as mourning black.

"I'll be seeing my sister in America," Scarlett said airily, "the colors are a gift for her." And I don't care whether you believe that or not, she thought crossly. I'm not really a widow, and I'm not about to go back to Atlanta looking drab and dowdy. Suddenly her utilitarian black skirt and stockings and shirt and shawl had become unspeakably depressing to her. She could hardly wait for the moment when she could put on the green linen frock with the wide ruffles of thick creamy lace. Or the pink and navy striped silk . . . If Margaret Scanlon ever finished them.

"You'll be surprised when you see how pretty your Momma looks in her new dresses," Scarlett told Cat. "I've ordered some wonderful little frocks for you, too." The baby smiled, showing her small collection of teeth.

"You're going to love the big ship," Scarlett promised her. She had reserved the largest and best stateroom on the *Brian Boru* for departure from Galway on the Friday following Easter.

On Palm Sunday the weather turned cold, with hard slanting rain that was still falling on Good Friday. Scarlett was soaking wet and chilled to the bone after the long ceremony on the open field.

She hurried to the Big House as soon after as she could, longing for a hot bath and a pot of tea. But there was not even time for her to put on dry clothes. Kathleen was waiting for her with an urgent message. "Old Daniel is calling for you, Scarlett. He took sick in the chest, and he's dying."

Scarlett drew in her breath sharply when she saw Old Daniel. Kathleen crossed herself. "He's slipping," she said quietly.

Daniel O'Hara's eyes were sunken in their sockets, his cheeks so hollow that his face looked like a skull covered by skin. Scarlett knelt by the austere fold-out bed and took his hand. It was hot, papery dry and weak. "Uncle Daniel, it's Katie Scarlett."

Daniel opened his eyes. The tremendous effort of will it required made Scarlett want to weep. "I've a favor to ask," he said. His breathing was shallow.

"Anything."

"Bury me in O'Hara earth."

Don't be silly, you're a long way from that, Scarlett meant to say, but she couldn't lie to the old man. "I will that," she said, the Irish way of affirmation.

Daniel's eyes closed. Scarlett began to weep. Kathleen led her to a chair by the fire. "Will you help me brew the tea, Scarlett? They'll all be coming." Scarlett nodded, unable to speak. She hadn't realized until this moment how important her uncle had become in her life. He seldom spoke, she almost never talked to him, he was simply there—solid, quiet, unchanging and strong. Head of the household. In her mind Uncle Daniel was The O'Hara.

Kathleen sent Scarlett home before dark fell. "You've your baby to tend, and there's nothing more to do here. Come back tomorrow."

On Saturday everything was much the same. People came to pay their respects in a steady stream all day. Scarlett fixed pot after pot of tea, sliced the cakes people brought, buttered bread for sandwiches.

On Sunday she sat with her uncle while Kathleen and the O'Hara men went to Mass. When they returned she went to Ballyhara. The O'Hara must celebrate Easter in the Ballyhara church. She thought Father Flynn would never finish his sermon, thought she'd never get away from the townspeople, all of whom asked about her uncle and expressed their hopes for his recovery. Even after forty days of stringent fasting—there was no dispensation for O'Haras of Ballyhara—Scarlett had no appetite for the big Easter dinner.

"Take it to your uncle's house," suggested Mrs. Fitzpatrick. "There are big men there still getting the farm work done. They'll need food, and poor Kathleen that busy with Old Daniel."

Scarlett hugged and kissed Cat before she left. Cat patted her little hands on her mother's tear-stained cheeks. "What a thoughtful Kitty Cat. Thank you, my precious. Momma will be better soon, then we'll play and sing in the bath. And then we'll go for a wonderful ride on the big ship." Scarlett despised herself for having the thought, but she hoped they wouldn't miss the *Brian Boru*.

That afternoon Daniel rallied a little. He recognized people and spoke their names. "Thank God," Scarlett said to Colum. She thanked God, too, that Colum was there. Why did he have to go away so much? She'd missed him this long weekend.

It was Colum who told her Monday morning that Daniel had died during the night. "When will the funeral be? I'd like to make the sailing on Friday." It was so comfortable to have a friend like Colum; she could tell him anything without worrying that he'd misunderstand or disapprove.

Colum shook his head slowly. "That cannot be, Scarlett darling. There are many who respected Daniel and many O'Haras with distance to come over mud-mired roads. The wake will last at least three days, more likely four. After, there's the burial."

"Oh, no. Colum! Say I don't have to go to the wake; it's too morbid, I don't think I could bear it."

"You must go, Scarlett. I'll be with you."

Scarlett could hear the keening even before the house was in sight. She looked at Colum with desperation, but his face was set.

There was a crowd of people outside the low door. So many had come to mourn Daniel that there wasn't enough room for all of them. Scarlett heard the words "The O'Hara," saw a path open for her. She wished with all her heart that the honor would go away. But she walked in with her head bent, determined to do the right thing by Daniel.

"He's in the parlor," said Seamus. Scarlett steeled herself. The eerie wailing was coming from there. She walked in.

Tall thick candles burned on tables at the head and foot of the big bed. Daniel lay on top of the coverlet in a white garment trimmed in black. His work-worn hands were crossed on his chest, the beads of a rosary between them.

"Why did you leave us? Ochón!
Ochón, Ochón, Ullagón Ó!"

The woman swayed from side to side as she lamented. Scarlett recognized her cousin Peggy, who lived in the village. She knelt by the bed to say a prayer for Daniel. But the keening filled her mind with such confusion that she couldn't think.

Ochón, Ochón.

The plaintive, primitive cry twisted her heart, frightened her. She got to her feet and went into the kitchen.

She looked with disbelief at the mass of men and women that filled the room. They were eating and drinking and talking as if nothing unusual was happening at all. The air was thick with smoke from the men's clay pipes in spite of the open door and windows. Scarlett approached the group around Father Danaher. "Yes, he woke to call people by name and to make his end with a clean soul. Ah, it was a grand confession he made, I've never heard a better. A fine man Daniel O'Hara was. We'll not see his like again in our lifetimes." She edged away.

"And do you not remember, Jim, the time Daniel and his brother Patrick, God rest his soul, took the Englishman's prize pig and carried it down into the peat bog to farrow? Twelve little ones and all of them squealing, and the sow as fierce as any wild boar? The land agent was shaking and the Englishman cursing and all the rest of the world laughing at the show."

Jim O'Gorman laughed, swatted the tale teller's shoulder with his big blacksmith's hand. "I do not remember, Ted O'Hara, no more do you, and that's the truth of it. We were neither of us born when the adventure of the sow had its happening, and well you know it. You heard it from your father same as I heard it from mine."

"But wouldn't it be a fine thing to have seen, Jim? Your cousin Daniel was a grand man, and that's the truth of it."

Yes, he was, thought Scarlett. She moved around, listening to a score of stories of Daniel's life. Someone noticed her. "And tell us, if you will, Katie Scarlett, about your uncle refusing the farm with the hundred cattle you gave him."

She thought quickly. "This was the way of it," she began. A dozen eager listeners leaned toward her. Now what am I going to say? "I ... I said to him, 'Uncle Daniel' ... I said, 'I want to give you a present.' " Might as well make it good. "I said, 'I've got a farm with ... a hundred acres and ... a quick stream and a bog of its own and ... a hundred bullocks and fifty milk cows and three hundred geese and twenty-five pigs and ... six teams of horses.' " The audience sighed at the grandeur. Scarlett felt inspiration on her tongue. " 'Uncle Daniel,' I said, 'this is all for you, and a bag of gold besides.' But his voice thundered at me till I quaked. 'I'll not touch it, Katie Scarlett O'Hara.' "

Colum grabbed her arm and pulled her outside the house, through the crowd, behind the barn. Then he let himself laugh. "You're always surprising me, Scarlett darling. You've just made Daniel into a giant—but whether it's a giant fool or a giant too noble to take advantage of a fool woman, I don't know."

Scarlett laughed with him. "I was just getting the hang of it, Colum, you should have let me stay." Suddenly she put her hand over her mouth. How could she be laughing at Uncle Daniel's wake?

Colum took her wrist, lowered her hand. "It's all right," he said, "a wake's supposed to celebrate a man's life and the importance of him to all who come. Laughter's part of it, as much as lamentation."

Daniel O'Hara was buried on Thursday. The funeral was almost as big as Old Katie Scarlett's had been. Scarlett led the procession to the grave his sons had dug in the ancient walled graveyard at Ballyhara that she and Colum had found and cleaned up.

Scarlett filled a leather pouch with soil from Daniel's grave. When she spread it on her father's grave, it would be almost as if he was buried near his brother.

When the funeral was over, the family went to the Big House for refreshments. Scarlett's cook was delighted to have an occasion to show off. Long trestle tables stretched the length of the unused drawing room and library. They were covered with hams, geese, chickens, beef, mountains of breads and cakes, gallons of porter, barrels of whiskey, rivers of tea. Hundreds of O'Haras had made the trip in spite of the muddy roads.

Scarlett brought Cat down to meet her kinfolk. The admiration was all that Scarlett could have wished for, and more.

Then Colum supplied a fiddle and his drum, three cousins found pennywhistles, and the music went on for hours. Cat waved her hands to the music until she was worn out, then fell asleep in Scarlett's lap. I'm glad I missed the ship, Scarlett thought; this is wonderful. If only Daniel's death wasn't the reason for it.

Two of her cousins came over to her and bent down from their great height to speak quietly. "We have need of The O'Hara," said Daniel's son Thomas.

"Will you come to the house tomorrow after breakfast?" asked Patrick's son Joe.

"What's it about?"

"We'll tell you tomorrow when there's quiet for you to think."

The question was: who should inherit Daniel's farm? Because of the long-past crisis when Old Patrick died, two O'Hara cousins were claiming the right. Like his brother Gerald, Daniel had never made a will.

It's Tara all over again, thought Scarlett, and the decision was easy. Daniel's son Seamus had worked hard on the farm for thirty years while Patrick's son Sean lived with Old Katie Scarlett and did nothing. Scarlett gave the farm to Seamus. Like Pa should have given Tara to me.

She was The O'Hara, so there was no argument. Scarlett felt elated, confident that she had given more justice to Seamus than anyone had ever given her.

The next day a far-from-young woman left a basket of eggs on the doorstep of the Big House. Mrs. Fitz found out that she was Seamus' sweetheart. She'd been waiting for almost twenty years for him to ask her to marry him. An hour after Scarlett's decision, he had.

"That's very sweet," Scarlett said, "but I hope they don't get married real soon. I'll never get to America at the rate I'm going." She now had a cabin booked on a ship sailing April 26, a year exactly after the date she was originally supposed to have ended her "vacation" in Ireland.

The ship wasn't the luxurious *Brian Boru*. It wasn't even a proper passenger ship. But Scarlett had her own superstition—if she delayed again until after May Day, she'd somehow never leave at all. Besides, Colum knew the ship and its captain. It was a cargo ship, true, but it was carrying only bales of best Irish linen, nothing messy. And the captain's wife always travelled with him, so Scarlett would have female companionship and a chaperone. Best of all, the ship had no paddlewheel, no steam engine. She'd be under sail all the way.

67

$\mathcal{T}$he weather was beautiful for more than a week. The roads were dry, the hedgerows were full of flowers, Cat's feverish sleeplessness one night turned out to be only a new tooth coming in. On the day before she was to leave Scarlett ran, half-dancing, to Ballyhara town to pick up the last of Cat's frocks from the dressmaker. She was confident that nothing could go wrong now.

While Margaret Scanlon wrapped the frock in tissue paper Scarlett looked out at the deserted dinner-time town and saw Colum going into the abandoned Protestant Church of Ireland on the other side of the wide street.

Oh, good, she thought, he's going to do it after all. I thought he'd never listen to reason. It makes no sense at all for the whole town to be squashed into that dinky little chapel for Mass every Sunday when there's that great big church standing empty. Just because it was built by Protestants is no reason for Catholics not to take it over. I don't know why he's been so stubborn so long, but I won't fuss at him. I'll just tell him how happy it makes me that he's changed his mind.

"I'll be right back," she told Mrs. Scanlon. She hurried along the weed-ridden path that led to the small side entrance, tapped on the door and pushed it open. A loud noise sounded, then another, and Scarlett felt something sharp hit her sleeve, heard a shower of pebbles on the ground at her feet, a booming reverberation inside the church.

A shaft of light from the open door fell directly onto a strange man who had spun to face her. His stubbled face was twisted into a snarl, and his dark, shadowed eyes were like a wild animal's.

He was half crouching, and he was pointing a pistol at her, held out from his rag-clothed body in his two dirty, rock-steady hands.

He shot at me. The knowledge filled Scarlett's mind. He's already killed Colum and now he's going to kill me. Cat! I'll never see Cat again. White-hot anger freed Scarlett from the physical paralysis of shock. She raised her fists and lunged forward.

The sound of the second shot was an explosion that echoed deafeningly from the vaulted stone ceilings for a time that seemed forever. Scarlett threw herself to the floor, screaming.

"I'll ask you to be quiet, Scarlett darling," said Colum. She knew his voice, and yet it was not his voice. There was steel in this voice, and ice.

Scarlett looked up. She saw Colum's right arm around the neck of the man, Colum's left hand around the man's wrist, the pistol pointing at the ceiling. She got slowly to her feet.

"What is going on here?" she enunciated carefully.

"Close the door if you please," said Colum. "There's light enough from the windows."

"What . . . is . . . going . . . on . . . here?"

Colum gave her no answer. "Drop it, Davey boy," he said to the man. The pistol fell with a metallic crash onto the stone floor. Slowly Colum lowered the man's arm. Quickly he moved his own arm from its stranglehold around the man's neck, made two fists with his hands and clubbed the man with them. The unconscious form fell at Colum's feet.

"He'll do," Colum said. He walked briskly past Scarlett and quietly closed the door, slid the bolt across. "Now, Scarlett darling, we have to talk."

Colum's hand closed around her upper arm from behind her. Scarlett jerked away, whirled to face him. "Not 'we,' Colum. You. You tell me what is going on here."

The warmth and lilt was back in his voice. "It's an unfortunate happening to be sure, Scarlett darling . . ."

"Don't you 'Scarlett darling' me. I'm not buying any charm, Colum. That man tried to kill me. Who is he? Why are you sneaking around to meet him? What is going on here?"

Colum's face was only a pale blur in the shadows. His collar was startlingly white. "Come where we can see," he said quietly, and he walked to a place where thin slats of sunlight slanted down from the boarded-over windows.

Scarlett couldn't believe her eyes. Colum was smiling at her. "Ach, the pity of it is, if we'd had the inn this would never have happened. I wanted to keep you out of it, Scarlett darling, it's a worrisome thing once you know."

How could he smile? How did he dare? She started, too horrified to speak.

Colum told her about the Fenian Brotherhood.

When he finished, she found her voice. "Judas! You filthy, lying traitor. I trusted you. I thought you my friend."

"I said it was a worrisome thing."

She felt too heartsick to be angry at his smiling, rueful response. Everything was a betrayal, all of it. He'd been using her, deceiving her from the moment they met. They all had—Jamie and Maureen, all her cousins in Savannah and Ireland, all the farmers on Ballyhara, all the people in Ballyhara town. Even Mrs. Fitz. Her happiness was a delusion. Everything was a delusion.

"Will you listen now, Scarlett?" She hated Colum's voice, the music of it, the charm. I won't listen. Scarlett tried to close her ears, but his words crept between her fingers. "Remember your South, with the boots of the conqueror upon her, and think of Ireland, her beauty and her life's blood in the murdering hands of the enemy. They stole our language from us. Teaching a child to speak Irish is a crime in this land. Can you not see it, Scarlett, if your Yankees were speaking in words you did not know, words you learned at the point of a sword because 'stop' must be a word you knew to the very pit of your knowing, else you would be killed for not stopping. And then your child being taught her tongue by those same Yankees, and your child's tongue not your own so that she knew not what words of love you said to her, you knew not what need she told you in the Yankee tongue and could not give her her desire. The English robbed us of our language and with that robbing they took our children from us.

"They took our land, which is our mother. They left us nothing when our children and our mother were lost. We knew defeat in our souls.

"Do you but think of it now, Scarlett, when your Tara was being taken from you. You battled for it, you've told me how. With all your will, all your heart, all your wit, all your might. Were lies needed, you could lie, deceptions, you could deceive, murder, you could kill. So it is with us who battle for Ireland.

"And yet we are more fortunate than you. Because we have yet time for the sweetnesses of life. For music and dance and love. You know what it is to love, Scarlett. I watched the growth and the blossoming with your babe. Do you not see that love feeds without gluttony on itself, that love is an always brimming cup, from which drinking fills again and still more.

"So it is with our love for Ireland and her people. You are loved by me, Scarlett, by us all. You are not unloved because Ireland is our love of loves. Must you not care for your friends because you care for your child? One does not deny the other. You thought I was your friend, you say, your brother. And so I am, Scarlett, and will be until time ends. Your happiness gladdens me, your sorrow is my grief. And yet Ireland is my soul; I can hold nothing traitorous if it be done to free her from her bondage. But she does not take away the love I have for you; she makes it more."

Scarlett's hands had slid on their own volition from her ears down to where they now hung limply by her sides. Colum had enthralled her as he always did when he spoke that way, though she understood no more than half of what he was saying. She felt as if she were somehow wrapped 'round in gossamer which warmed and bound at the same time.

The unconscious man on the floor groaned. Scarlett looked at Colum with fear. "Is that man a Fenian?"

"Yes. He's on the run. A man he thought his friend denounced him to the English."

"You gave him that gun." It was not a question.

"Yes, Scarlett. You see, I keep no more secrets from you. I have concealed weapons throughout this English church. I am the armorer for the Brotherhood. When the day arrives, as soon it will, many thousands of Irishmen will be armed for the uprising, and those arms will come from this English place."

"When?" Scarlett dreaded his reply.

"There's no date set. We need five more shipments, six if it can be done."

"That's what you do in America."

"It is. I raise the money, with help from many, then others find a way to buy weapons with it, and I bring them into Ireland."

"On the *Brian Boru*."

"And others."

"You're going to shoot the English."

"Yes. We will be more merciful, though. They have killed our women and children as well as our men. We will kill soldiers. A soldier is paid to die."

"But you're a priest," she said, "you can't kill."

Colum was still for several minutes. Dust motes turned lazily in the stripes of light from the window to his bowed head. When he lifted it, Scarlett saw that his eyes were dark with sorrow.

"When I was a boy of eight," he said, "I watched the wagons of wheat and the droves of cattle on the road from Adamstown toward Dublin and the English banquet tables there. I also watched my sister die of hunger because she was but two years old and had no strength to carry her without food. Three, my brother was, and he, too, had too little strength. The smallest always were the first to die. They cried because they were hungry and were too young to understand when they were told there was no food. I understood, for I was eight and wiser. And I did not cry because I knew that crying uses strength needed to survive without food. Another brother died, he was seven, and then the six-year-old and the one who was five, and to my eternal shame I have forgot which was the girl and which the boy. My mother went then, but I have always thought she died more from the pain of her broken heart than from the pain of her empty belly.

"It takes many months to starve to death, Scarlett. It is not a merciful death. For all those months the wagons of food rolled past us." Colum's voice sounded lifeless. Then it livened.

"I was a likely lad. Once ten, and the Famine years past and with food to fill me, I was quick at my studies, good at my books. Our priest thought me full of promise and he told my father that perhaps, with diligence, I might in time be accepted in the seminary. My father gave me everything he could give. My older brothers did more than their share of work on the farm so that I need do none and could be diligent at my books. No one grudged me for 'tis a great honor to a family to have a son who is a priest. And I took from them without thought for I had pure, encompassing faith in the goodness of God and the wisdom of Holy Mother Church, which I believed to be a vocation, a call to the priesthood." His voice rose.

"Now I will learn the answer, I believed. The seminary contains many holy books and holy men and all the wisdom of the Church. I studied and I prayed and I searched. I found ecstasy in prayer, knowledge in studies. But not the knowledge I was seeking. 'Why?' I asked my teachers, 'why must little children die from hunger?' But the only answer given me was, 'Trust in God's wisdom and have faith in His love.'"

Colum raised his arms above his tortured face, raised his voice to a shout. "God, my Father, I feel Your presence and Your almighty power. But I cannot see Your face. Why have You turned away from Your people the Irish?" His arms dropped.

"There is no answer, Scarlett," he said brokenly, "there has never been an answer. But I saw a vision, and I have followed it. In my vision the starving children came together and their weakness was less weak in their numbers. They rose up in their thousands, their fleshless small arms reaching out, and they overturned the carts heaped with food, and they did not die. It is my vocation now to turn over those carts, to drive out the English from their banqueting tables, to give Ireland the love and mercy that God has denied her."

Scarlett gasped at his blasphemy. "You'll go to Hell."

"I am in Hell! When I see soldiers mocking a mother who must beg to buy food for her children, it is a vision from Hell. When I see old men pushed into the muck of the street so that soldiers will have the sidewalks, I see Hell. When I see evictions, floggings, the groaning carts of grain passing the family with a square meter of potatoes to keep them from death, I say that all Ireland is Hell, and I will gladly suffer death and then torment for all eternity to spare the Irish one hour of Hell on earth."

Scarlett was shaken by his vehemence. She groped for understanding. Suppose she hadn't been there when the English came with the battering ram to Daniel's house? Suppose all her money was gone, and Cat was hungry? Suppose the English soldiers really were like Yankees and stole her animals and burned the fields she'd watched greening?

She knew what it was to be helpless before an army. She knew the feeling of hunger. They were memories no amount of gold could ever quite erase.

"How can I help you?" she asked Colum. He was fighting for Ireland, and Ireland was the home of her people and her child.

68

The ship captain's wife was a stout, red-faced woman who took one look at Cat and held out her arms. "Will she come to me?" Cat reached out in reply. Scarlett was sure Cat was interested in the eyeglasses hanging on a chain around the woman's neck, but she didn't say so. She loved to hear Cat admired, and the captain's wife was doing just that. "What a little beauty she is—no, sweetheart, they go on your nose, not in your mouth—with such lovely olive skin. Was her father Spanish?"

Scarlett thought quickly. "Her grandmother," she said.

"How nice." She extracted the glasses from Cat's fingers and substituted a ship's biscuit.

"I'm a grandmother four times over, it's the most wonderful thing in the world. I started sailing with the captain when the children were grown because I couldn't stand the empty house. But now there's the added pleasure of the grandchildren. We'll go to Philadelphia for cargo after Savannah, and I'll have two days there with my daughter and her two."

She's going to talk me to death before we're out of the bay, Scarlett thought. I'll never be able to stand two weeks of this.

She discovered very soon that she needn't have worried. The captain's wife repeated the same things so often that Scarlett had only to nod and say "My goodness" at intervals without listening at all. And the older woman was wonderful with Cat. Scarlett could take her exercise on deck without worry about the baby.

She did her best thinking then, with the salt wind in her face. Mostly she planned. She had a lot to do. She had to find a buyer for her store. And there was the house on Peachtree Street. Rhett paid for the upkeep, but it was ridiculous to have it sitting there empty when she'd never use it again . . .

So she'd sell the Peachtree Street house and the store. And the saloon. That was sort of too bad. The saloon produced excellent income and was no trouble at all. But she'd made up her mind to cut herself free of Atlanta, and that included the saloon.

What about the houses she was building? She didn't know anything at all about that project. She had to check and make sure the builder was still using Ashley's lumber . . .

She had to make sure Ashley was all right. And Beau. She'd promised Melanie.

Then, when she was done with Atlanta, she would go to Tara. That must be last. Because once Wade and Ella learned they were going home with her, they'd be anxious to get going. It wouldn't be fair to keep them dangling. And saying goodbye to Tara would be the hardest thing she had to do. Best to do it quickly; it wouldn't hurt so much then. Oh, how she longed to see it.

The long slow miles up the Savannah River from the sea to the city seemed to go on forever. The ship had to be towed by a steam-powered tugboat through the channel. Scarlett walked restlessly from one side of the deck to the other with Cat in her arms, trying to enjoy the baby's excited reaction to the marsh birds' sudden eruption into flight. They were so close now, why couldn't they get there? She wanted to see America, hear American voices.

At last. There was the city. And the docks. "Oh, and listen, Cat, listen to the singing. Those are black folks' songs, this is the South, feel the sun? It will last for days and days. Oh, my darling, my Cat, Momma's home."

Maureen's kitchen was just as it had been, nothing had changed. The family was the same. The affection. The swarms of O'Hara children. Patricia's baby was a boy, almost a year old, and Katie was pregnant. Cat was embraced at once into the daily rhythms of the three-house home. She regarded the other children with curiosity, pulled their hair, submitted to hers being pulled, became one of them.

Scarlett was jealous. *She won't miss me at all, and I cannot bear to leave her, but I have to. Too many people in Atlanta know Rhett and might* tell him about her. I'd kill him before I'd let him take her from me. I can't take her with me. I have no choice. The sooner I go, the sooner I'll be back. And I'll bring her own brother and sister as a gift for her.

She sent telegrams to Uncle Henry Hamilton at his office, and to Pansy at the house on Peachtree Street, and took the train for Atlanta on the twelfth of May. She was both excited and nervous. She'd been gone so long—anything might have happened. She wouldn't fret about it now, she'd find out soon enough. In the meantime she'd simply enjoy the hot Georgia sun and the pleasure of being all dressed up. She'd had to wear mourning on the ship, but now she was radiant in emerald green Irish linen.

But Scarlett had forgotten how dirty American trains were. The spittoons at each end of the car were soon surrounded by evil-smelling tobacco juice. The aisle became a filthy debris trap before twenty miles were done. A drunk lurched unevenly past her seat and she suddenly realized that she should not be travelling alone. Why, anybody at all could move my little hand valise and sit next to me! We do things an awful lot better in Ireland. First Class means what it says. Nobody intrudes on you in your own little compartment. She opened the Savannah newspaper as a shield. Her pretty linen suit was already rumpled and dusty.

The hubbub at the Atlanta Depot and the shouting daredevil drivers in the maelstrom at Five Points made Scarlett's heart race with excitement, and she forgot the grime of the train. How alive it all was, and vital, and always changing. There were buildings she'd never seen before, new names above old storefronts, noise and hurry and push.

She looked eagerly out the window of her carriage at the houses on Peachtree Street, identifying the owners to herself, noting the signs of better times for them. The Merriwethers had a new roof, the Meades a new color paint. Things weren't nearly as shabby as they'd been when she left a year and a half back.

And there was her house! Oh. I don't remember it being so crowded on the lot like that. There's hardly any yard at all. Was it always so close to the street? For pity's sake, I'm just being silly. What difference does it make? I've already decided to sell it anyhow.

This was no time to sell, said Uncle Henry Hamilton. The depression was no better, business was bad everywhere. The hardest hit market of all was real estate, and the hardest hit real estate was the big places like hers. People were moving down, not up.

The little houses, now, like the ones she'd been building on the edge of town, they were selling as fast as people could put them up. She was making a fortune there. Why did she want to sell anyhow? It wasn't as if the house cost her anything, Rhett paid all the bills with money left over, too.

He's looking at me like I smelled bad or something, Scarlett thought. He blames me for the divorce. For a moment she felt like protesting, telling her side of the story, telling what had really happened. Uncle Henry was the only one left who was on my side. Without him there won't be a soul in Atlanta who doesn't look down on me.

And it doesn't matter a bit. The idea burst in her mind like a Roman candle. Henry Hamilton's wrong in judging me just like everybody else in Atlanta was wrong in judging me. I'm not like them, and I don't want to be. I'm different, I'm me. I'm The O'Hara.

"If you don't want to bother with selling my property, I won't take it against you, Henry," she said. "Just tell me so." There was a simple dignity in her manner.

"I'm an old man, Scarlett. It would probably be better for you to hook up with a younger lawyer."

Scarlett rose from her chair, held out her hand, smiled with real fondness for him.

It was only after she was gone that he could put words to the difference in her. "Scarlett's grown up. She didn't call me 'Uncle Henry.'"

"Is Mrs. Butler at home?"

Scarlett recognized Ashley's voice immediately. She hurried from the sitting room into the hall; a quick gesture of her hand dismissed the maid who'd answered the door. "Ashley, dear, I'm so happy to see you." She held out both her hands to him.

He clasped them tightly in his, looking down at her. "Scarlett, you've never looked lovelier. Foreign climates agree with you. Tell me where you've been, what you've been doing. Uncle Henry said you'd gone to Savannah, then he lost touch. We all wondered."

I'll just bet you all wondered, especially your adder-tongued old sister, she thought. "Come in and sit down," she said, "I'm dying to hear all the news."

The maid was hovering to one side. Scarlett said quietly as she passed her, "Bring us a pot of coffee and some cakes."

She led the way into the sitting room, took one corner of a settee, patted the seat beside her. "Sit here beside me, Ashley, do. I want to look at you." Thank the Lord, he's lost that hangdog look he had. Henry Hamilton must have been right when he said that Ashley was doing fine. Scarlett studied him through lowered lashes while she busied herself clearing room on a table for the coffee tray. Ashley Wilkes was still a handsome man. His thin aristocratic features had become more distinguished with age. But he looked older than his years. He can't be more than forty, Scarlett thought, and his hair's more silver than gold. He must spend a lot more time in the lumberyard than he used to, he's got a nice color to his skin, not that office gray look he had before. She looked up with a smile. It was good to see him. Especially looking so fit. Her obligation to Melanie didn't seem so burdensome now.

"How's Aunt Pitty? And India? And Beau? He must be practically a grown man!"

Pitty and India were just the same, said Ashley with a quirk of his lips. Pitty got the vapors at every passing shadow and India was very busy with committee work to improve the moral tone of Atlanta. They spoiled him abominably, two spinsters trying to see which one was the best mother hen. They tried to spoil Beau, too, but he'd have none of it. Ashley's gray eyes lit up with pride. Beau was a real little man. He'd be twelve soon, but you'd take him for almost fifteen. He was president of a sort of club the neighborhood boys had formed. They'd built a tree house in Pitty's backyard, made from the best lumber the mill turned out, too. Beau had seen to that; he already knew more about the lumber business than his father, said Ashley with a mixture of ruefulness and admiration. And, he added with intensified pride, the boy might have the makings of a scholar. He'd already won a school prize for Latin composition, and he was reading books far above his age level—

"But you must be bored by all this, Scarlett. Proud fathers can be very tedious."

"Not a bit, Ashley," Scarlett lied. Books, books, books, that was exactly what was wrong with the Wilkeses. They did all their living out of books, not life. But maybe the boy would be all right. If he knew lumber already, there was hope for him. Now, if Ashley would just not get all stiff-necked, she had one more promise to Melly that she could settle. Scarlett put her hand on Ashley's sleeve. "I've got a big favor to beg," she said. Her eyes were wide with entreaty.

"Anything, Scarlett, you should know that." Ashley covered her hand with his.

"I'd like for you to promise that you'll let me send Beau to University and then with Wade on a Grand Tour. It would mean a lot to me—after all, I think about him as practically my son, too, seeing that I was there when he was born. And I've come into really a lot of money lately, so that's no problem. You can't be so mean that you'd say no."

"Scarlett—" Ashley's smile was gone. He looked very serious.

Oh, bother, he's going to be difficult. Thank goodness, here's that slowpoke girl with the coffee. He can't talk in front of her and I'll have a chance to jump in again before he has a chance to say no.

"How many spoons of sugar, Ashley? I'll fix your cup."

Ashley took the cup from her hand, put it on the table. "Let the coffee wait for a minute, Scarlett." He took her hand in his. "Look at me, dear." His eyes were softly luminous. Scarlett's thoughts were distracted. Why, he looks almost like the old Ashley, Ashley Wilkes of Twelve Oaks.

"I know how you came into that money, Scarlett. Uncle Henry let it slip. I understand how you must feel. But there's no need. He was never worthy of you, you're well rid of Rhett, never mind how. You can put it all behind you, as if it never happened."

Great balls of fire, Ashley's going to propose!

"You're free from Rhett. Say you'll marry me, Scarlett, and I'll pledge my life to making you happy the way that you deserve to be."

There was a time when I would have traded my soul for those words, Scarlett thought, it's not fair that now I hear them and don't feel anything at all. Oh, why did Ashley have to do that? Before the question was formed in her mind, she knew the answer. It was because of the old gossip, so long ago it seemed to be now. Ashley was determined to redeem her in the eyes of Atlanta society. If that wasn't just like him! He'll do the gentlemanly thing even if it means tearing up his whole life.

And mine, too, by the way. He didn't bother to think of that, I don't suppose. Scarlett bit her tongue to keep from unleashing her anger on him. Poor Ashley. It wasn't his fault he was the way he was. Rhett said it: Ashley belonged to that time before the War. He's got no place in the world today. I can't be angry or mean. I don't want to lose anyone who was part of the glory days. All that's left of that world is the memories and the people who share them.

"Dearest Ashley," Scarlett said, "I don't want to marry you. That's the all of it. I'm not going to play belle games with you and tell lies and keep you panting after me. I'm too old for that, and I care for you too much. You've been a big piece of my life all along, and you always will be. Say you'll let me keep that."

"Of course, my dear. I'm honored you feel that way. I won't distress you by referring again to marriage." He smiled, and he looked so young, so much like the Ashley of Twelve Oaks that Scarlett's heart turned over. Dearest Ashley. He mustn't ever guess that she'd clearly heard relief in his voice. Everything was all right. No, better than all right. Now they could truly be friends. The past was neatly finished.

"What are your plans, Scarlett? Are you home for good, as I hope?"

She'd prepared for this question even before she sailed from Galway. She must make sure that no one in Atlanta could know how to find her, it made her too vulnerable to Rhett, to losing Cat. "I'm selling up, Ashley, I don't want to be tied down at all for a while. After I visited in Savannah, I paid a visit to some of Pa's family in Ireland, then I went travelling." She had to be careful what she said. Ashley had been abroad, he'd catch her out in a minute if she claimed she'd been to places she hadn't been. "Somehow or other I never got around to seeing London. I figure I might settle there for a while. Do help me out, Ashley. Do you think London's a good idea?" Scarlett knew, from Melanie, that he considered London as perfect as a city could be. He'd talk his head off, and forget to ask any more questions.

"I enjoyed the afternoon so much, Ashley. You'll come again, won't you? I'll be here for a while settling things."

"As often as I can. It's a rare pleasure." Ashley accepted his hat and gloves from the maid. "Goodbye, Scarlett."

"Goodbye. Oh—Ashley, you will grant my favor I asked, won't you? I'll be miserable if you don't."

"I don't think—"

"I swear to you, Ashley Wilkes, if you don't let me set up a little fund for Beau, I'll cry like a river over its banks. And you know as well as I do that no gentleman ever deliberately makes a lady cry."

Ashley bowed over her hand. "I was thinking how much you'd changed, Scarlett, but I was wrong. You can still wrap men around your little finger and make them like it. I'd be a bad father to deny Beau a gift from you."

"Oh, Ashley, I do love you and I always will. Thank you."

And run to the kitchen and tell that, Scarlett thought as she watched the maid close the door behind Ashley. Might as well give all the old cats something good to gossip about. Besides, I do love Ashley and always will, in a way they'd never understand.

It took much longer than she'd expected for Scarlett to accomplish her business in Atlanta. She didn't leave for Tara until June 10.

Almost a month away from Cat already! I can't bear it. She might forget me. I probably missed a new tooth, maybe two. Suppose she was fretful and nobody knew that she'd feel better if she could splash in the water? It's so hot, too. She might have prickly heat. A little Irish baby doesn't know anything about hot weather.

During her final week in Atlanta Scarlett was so jumpy with nerves that she could hardly sleep. Why wouldn't it rain? Red dust covered everything only a half hour after it had been wiped away.

But once on the train to Jonesboro she was able to relax. In spite of the delays she had done everything she'd set out to do, and done it better than both Henry Hamilton and her new lawyer said it could be done.

Naturally enough the saloon had been the easiest. The depression increased its business and its value. She was sad about the store. It was worth more for the land it was on than as a business; the new owners were going to tear it down and put up a building eight stories tall. Five Points, at least, was still Five Points, depression or no depression. She'd realized enough from those two sales to buy another fifty acres and put up another hundred houses on the edge of the city. That would keep Ashley prosperous for a couple of years. Plus the builder had told her that other builders were starting to buy only from Ashley too. They could trust him not to sell green lumber, something that couldn't be said for the other yards in Atlanta. It really looked as if he was going to be a success in spite of himself.

And she was going to make a fortune. Henry Hamilton was right about that. Her little houses sold as fast as they were finished.

They had made a profit. A lot of profit. She was downright shocked when she saw how much money had accumulated in her bank account. Enough to cover all the expenses she'd been worried about at Ballyhara all these months with everything going out and so little coming in. Now she was even. The harvest would be all income, free and clear, plus provide seed for next year. And the rent rolls from the town were bound to keep growing. Before she left, a cooper was asking about one of the empty cottages, and Colum said he had a tailor in mind for another.

She would have done the same thing even if she hadn't made so much money, but it was much easier to do since she had. The builder was instructed to send all the future profits to Stephen O'Hara in Savannah. He'd have all the money he needed to carry out Colum's instructions.

It was funny about the Peachtree Street house, Scarlett thought. You'd think it would hurt to part with it. After all, it was where I lived with Rhett, the place where Bonnie was born and spent her terribly brief life. But the only thing I felt was relief. When that girls' school made an offer I could have kissed the old prune-faced headmistress. It felt like lifting chains off me. I'm free now. No more obligations in Atlanta. Nothing binding me in.

Scarlett smiled to herself. Just like her corsets. She had never been laced up again after Colum and Kathleen cut her free in Galway. Her waist was a few inches bigger, but she was still slimmer than most of the women she saw on the street who were laced until they could hardly breathe. And she was comfortable—at any rate as comfortable as a person could be in this heat. She could dress herself, too, not be dependent on a maid. And the thick chignon she wore was no trouble to do on her own. It was wonderful to be self-sufficient. It was wonderful not to care about what other people did or did not do or what they approved or disapproved. It was most wonderful of all to be going home to one Tara and then taking her children home to another one. Soon she'd be with her precious Cat. Soon after that back again in the fresh, sweet, rain-washed cool of Ireland. Scarlett's hand stroked the soft leather pouch in her lap. She'd take the earth from Ballyhara to her father's grave first thing.

Can you see from where you are, Pa? Do you know? You'd be so proud of your Katie Scarlett, Pa. I'm The O'Hara.

69

*W*ill Benteen was waiting for her at the Jonesboro depot. Scarlett looked at his weather-worn face and deceptively slack-looking body and grinned from ear to ear. Will must be the only man God ever made who could look like he was lounging on a peg leg. She hugged him ferociously.

"Landsake, Scarlett, you ought to warn a man. Nearly knocked me off my pin. It's good to see you."

"It's good to see you, Will. I expect I'm gladder to see you than anybody else this whole trip." It was true. Will was more dear to her than even the Savannah O'Haras. Maybe because he'd been through the bad times with her, maybe because he loved Tara as much as she did. Maybe simply because he was such an honest good man.

"Where's your maid, Scarlett?"

"Oh, I don't fool with a maid any more, Will. I don't fool with a lot of things I used to fool with."

Will shifted the straw in his mouth. "I noticed," he said laconically. Scarlett laughed. She'd never thought before of what it must feel like to a man when he hugged a girl without stays.

"No more cages for me, Will, not ever, not any kind," she said. She wished she could tell him why she was so happy, tell him about Cat, about Ballyhara. If it was only Will, she'd tell him in a second, she trusted him. But he was Suellen's husband, and she wouldn't trust her sister as far as she could throw her—with an anvil tied on besides. And Will might feel duty bound to tell his wife everything. Scarlett had to hold her tongue. She climbed up onto the seat of the wagon. She'd never known Will to use their buggy. He could combine buying stores in Jonesboro with meeting the train. The wagon was loaded with sacks and boxes.

"Tell me the news, Will," Scarlett said when they were on the road. "I haven't heard anything for such a long time."

"Well, let me see. I reckon you want to hear about the kids first. Ella and our Susie are thick as thieves. Susie being a mite younger kind of gives Ella the upper hand, and that's done her a world of good. You ain't hardly going to know Wade when you see him. He started shooting up about the day he hit fourteen last January, and it don't look like he's ever going to stop. For all the weedy look, though, he's strong as a mule. Works like one, too. Thanks to him there's twenty fresh acres under crops this year."

Scarlett smiled. What a help he'd be at Ballyhara, and how he'd love it. A born farmer, she'd never have thought it. Must take after Pa. The leather pouch was warm in her lap.

"Our Martha's seven now, and Jane, the baby, was two last September. Suellen lost a baby last year, another little girl it was."

"Oh, Will, I'm so sorry."

"We decided not to try again," Will said. "It was real hard on Suellen, the doctor advised it. We've got three healthy girls and that's more than most people get to bring them happiness. 'Course I'd have liked a boy, any man would, but I'm not complaining. Besides, Wade's been all the son any man could hope for. He's a fine boy, Scarlett."

She was happy to hear it. And surprised. Will was right, she wasn't going to know Wade. Not if he was anything close to the boy Will made him out to be. She remembered a cowardly, frightened, pale little boy.

"I'm that fond of Wade, I agreed to talk to you for him, though I don't generally cotton to sticking my nose into other folks' business. He's always been kind of scared of you, Scarlett, you know that. Any road, what he wants me to tell you is he don't want no more schooling. He's done with the school 'round here this month, and the law won't make him do no more."

Scarlett shook her head. "No, Will. You can tell him or I'll do it. His daddy went to University and so will Wade. No offense, Will, but a man can't go very far without an education."

"No offense taken. And none given, but I figure you're wrong. Wade can read and write and do all the calculations a farmer's ever going to need. And that's what he wants. Farming. Farming Tara, to put a finger on it. He says his grandpa built Tara with no more schooling than he's got and he don't see why he should have to be any different. The boy's not like me, Scarlett. Hell, I can't hardly do more than write my name. He had four years at the fancy school you had him at in Atlanta and three more here in the schoolhouse and on the land. He knows all a country boy needs to know. That's what he is, Scarlett, a country boy, and he's happy at it. I'd hate to see you mess him up."

Scarlett bristled. Who did Will Benteen think he was talking to? She was Wade's mother, she knew what was best for him.

"Long as you've got your dander up, I might as well finish what I've got to say," Will continued in his slow Cracker drawl. He looked directly ahead at the dusty red road. "They showed me the new papers about Tara over to the County Court House. Seems like you done got hold of Carreen's share. I don't know what your thinking is, Scarlett, and I ain't asking. But I'm telling you this. If anybody comes up the road flapping something legal at me 'bout taking Tara, I plan to meet 'em at the end of the drive with a shotgun in my hand."

"Will, I swear on a stack of Bibles, I'm not planning to do anything to Tara." Scarlett was grateful it was the truth. Will's soft-spoken nasal drawl was more frightening than the loudest shout could ever be.

"I'm glad to hear it. My figuring is it should be Wade's. He's your pa's only grandson, and land should stay in the family. I'm hoping you'll leave him where he is, Scarlett, to be my right hand and like a son to me, just the way he is now. You'll do what you want to do. You always did. I gave Wade my word I'd talk to you, and now I have. We'll leave it there, if you don't mind. I said all I got to say."

"I'll think about it," Scarlett promised. The wagon creaked along the familiar road and she saw that the land she'd known as cultivated fields was now all gone back to scrub trees and rough weed grasses. She felt like crying. Will saw the slope of her shoulders and the droop of her mouth.

"Where you been this last couple of years, Scarlett? If it wasn't for Carreen we wouldn't have known where you'd gone to at all, but then she lost track, too."

Scarlett forced herself to smile. "I've been having adventures, Will, travelling all over the place. I visited my O'Hara kinfolks, too. A bunch of them are in Savannah, the nicest people you'd ever want to meet. I stayed with them ever so long. And then I went to Ireland to meet some more. You can't imagine how many O'Haras there are." Her throat clogged with tears. She held the leather pouch to her breast.

"Will, I brought something for Pa. Will you let me off at the graveyard and keep everybody away for a little while?"

"Glad to."

* * *

Scarlett knelt in the sun by Gerald O'Hara's grave. The black Irish soil filtered through her fingers to mix with the red clay dust of Georgia. "Ach, Pa," she murmured, and the meter of her words was Irish, "it's a grand place to be sure, County Meath. You're remembered well, Pa, by all of them. I didn't know, Pa, I'm sorry. I didn't know you should be having a fine wake and all the stories told about when you were a boy." She lifted her head and the sunlight gleamed in the flood of tears down her face. Her voice was cracked, clogged with weeping, but she did the best she could, and her grief was strong.

"Why did you leave me? Ochón!
Ochón, Ochón, Ullagón Ó!"

Scarlett was glad she hadn't told anyone in Savannah about her plan to take Wade and Ella back to Ireland with her. Now she didn't have to explain why she'd left them at Tara; it would have been so humiliating to tell the truth, that her own children didn't want her, that they were strangers to her and she to them. She couldn't admit to anyone, not even herself, how much it hurt and how much she blamed herself. She felt small and mean; she could hardly even be glad for Ella and Wade, who were so obviously happy.

Everything had hurt at Tara. She'd felt like a stranger. Except for Grandma Robillard's portrait, she hardly recognized anything in the house. Suellen had used the money every month to buy new furniture and furnishings. The unscarred wood of the tables was glaringly shiny to Scarlett's eyes, the colors in the rugs and curtains too bright. She hated it. And the baking heat she'd longed for in the Irish rains gave her a headache that lasted the whole week she was there.

She'd enjoyed visiting Alex and Sally Fontaine, but their new baby only reminded her how much she missed Cat.

It was only at the Tarletons' that she had a good time. Their farm was doing well, and Mrs. Tarleton talked nonstop about her mare in foal and her expectations for the three-year-old she insisted that Scarlett admire.

The easy, no-invitation-required visiting back and forth had always been the best thing about the County.

But she'd been glad to leave Tara, and that hurt, too. If she didn't know how much Wade loved it, it would have broken her heart that she could hardly wait to get away. At least her son was taking her place. She saw her new lawyer in Atlanta after the Tara visit, and she made a will, leaving her two-thirds share of Tara to her son. She wasn't going to do like her father, and her Uncle Daniel, and leave a mess behind her. And if Will died first, she didn't trust Suellen an inch. Scarlett signed the document with a flourish, and then she was free.

To go back to her Cat. Who healed all Scarlett's hurts in a second. The baby's face lit up when she saw her, and the little arms reached out to her, and Cat even wanted to be hugged, and tolerated being kissed a dozen times.

"She looks so brown and healthy!" Scarlett exclaimed.

"And no wonder to it," said Maureen. "She loves the sunshine that much, she takes off her bonnet the minute your back is turned. Little gypsy is what she is, and a joy every hour of the day."

"Of the day and the night," Scarlett amended, holding Cat close.

Stephen gave Scarlett her instructions for the trip back to Galway. She didn't like them. Truth to tell, she didn't much like Stephen either. But Colum had told her Stephen was in charge of all arrangements, so she donned her mourning clothes and kept her complaints to herself.

The ship was named *The Golden Fleece* and it was the latest thing in luxury. Scarlett had no quibble with the size or the comfort of her suite. But it did not make a direct crossing. It took a week longer, and she was anxious to get back to Ballyhara to see how the crops were faring.

It was not until she was actually on the gangplank that she saw the big Notice of Departure with the ship's itinerary, or she would have refused to go, no matter what Stephen said. *The Golden Fleece* loaded passengers in Savannah, Charleston, and Boston, disembarked them in Liverpool and Galway.

Scarlett turned in panic, ready to run back to the dock. She couldn't go to Charleston, she just couldn't! Rhett would know she was on the ship—Rhett always knew everything, somehow—and he'd walk right into her stateroom and take Cat away.

I'll kill him first. Anger drove away her panic, and Scarlett turned again to walk up onto the ship's deck. Rhett Butler wasn't going to make her turn tail and run. All her luggage was already on board, and she was sure that Stephen was smuggling guns to Colum in her trunks. They were depending on her. Also, she wanted to get back to Ballyhara, and she wouldn't let anything or anybody stand in her way.

By the time Scarlett reached her suite, she had built up a consuming fury against Rhett. More than a year had passed since he had divorced her, then immediately married Anne Hampton. During that year Scarlett had been so busy, had experienced such changes in her life, that she'd been able to block out the pain he had caused her. Now it tore her heart, and with the pain was a deep fear of Rhett's unpredictable power. She transformed them into rage. Rage was strengthening.

Bridie was travelling with Scarlett part way. The Boston O'Haras had found her a good position as a lady's maid. Until she learned the ship was going to stop in Charleston, Scarlett had been glad at the prospect of Bridie's company. But the thought of stopping in Charleston made Scarlett so nervous that her young cousin's constant chatter nearly drove her crazy. Why couldn't Bridie leave her alone? Under Patricia's tutelage Bridie had learned all the duties of her job, and she wanted to try them all out on Scarlett. She was loudly distressed when she learned that Scarlett had stopped wearing corsets, and vocally disappointed that none of Scarlett's gowns needed mending. Scarlett longed to tell her that the first requirement for a lady's maid was to speak only when spoken to, but she was fond of Bridie, and it wasn't the girl's fault that they were going to stop in Charleston. So she forced herself to smile and act as if nothing was bothering her.

The ship sailed up the coast during the night, entering Charleston Harbor at first light. Scarlett hadn't slept at all. She went out on deck for the sunrise. There was a rose-tinted mist on the wide waters of the harbor. Beyond it the city was blurred and insubstantial, like a city in a dream. The white steeple of Saint Michael's Church was palest pink. Scarlett imagined that she could hear its familiar chimes faintly in the distance between the slow strokes of the ship's engine. They must be unloading the fishing boats at the Market now, no it's a little early yet, they must still be coming in. She strained her eyes, but the mist hid the boats if they were there ahead.

She concentrated on remembering the different kinds of fish, the vegetables, the names of the coffee vendors, the sausage man—anything to keep her mind occupied, to fend off memories she didn't dare confront.

But as the sun cleared the horizon behind her, the tinted mist lifted and she saw the pocked walls of Fort Sumter to one side. The *Fleece* was entering the waters where she'd sailed with Rhett and laughed at the dolphins with him and been struck by the storm with him.

Damn him! I hate him—and his damned Charleston—

Scarlett told herself she should go to her stateroom, lock herself in with Cat; but she stood as if rooted to the deck. Slowly the city grew larger, more distinct, glowing white and pink and green, pastel in the shimmering morning air. She could hear Saint Michael's chimes, smell the heavy tropical sweetness of blooming flowers, see the palm trees in White Point Gardens, the opalescent glitter of crushed oyster shell paths. Then the ship was passing the promenade along East Battery. Scarlett could see above it from the ship's deck. There were the treetop-tall columns of the Butler house, the shadowed piazzas, the front door, the windows to the drawing room, her bedroom— The windows! And the telescope in the card room. She picked up her skirts and ran.

She ordered breakfast served in her suite, insisted that Bridie stay with her and Cat. The only safety was there, locked in, out of sight. Where Rhett couldn't find out about Cat and take her away.

The steward spread a glistening white cloth on the round table in Scarlett's sitting room, then rolled in a cart with two tiers of silver domed plates. Bridie giggled. While he meticulously set places and floral centerpiece he talked about Charleston. It was all Scarlett could do not to correct him, he had so many things wrong. But he was Scottish, on a Scottish ship, why should anyone expect him to know anything?

"We'll be sailing again at five o'clock," said the steward, "after cargo's loaded and the new passengers board. You ladies might want to take an excursion to see the town." He began placing platters and lifting off their covers. "There's a nice buggy with a driver who knows all the places to see. Only fifty pence or two dollars fifty American. Waiting at the foot of the gangplank. Or if you'd like some cooler air off the water there's a boat over at the next wharf south that goes up the river. There was a big civil war in America some ten years back. You can see the ruins of big mansion houses burnt by the armies fighting over them. You'd have to hurry, though, she leaves in forty minutes."

Scarlett tried to eat a piece of toast, but it stuck in her throat. The gilded clock on the desk ticked the minutes away. It sounded very loud to her. At the end of a half hour she jumped up. "I'm going out, Bridie, but don't you dare stir a step. Open the portholes, use that palmetto fan over there, but you and Cat stay in here with the door locked no matter how hot it gets. Order anything you want to eat and drink."

"Where are you going, Scarlett?"

"Never mind about that. I'll be back before the ship sails."

The excursion boat was a small rear-wheel paddle boat painted in bright red, white, and blue. Its name, in gold letters, was *Abraham Lincoln*. Scarlett remembered it well. She'd seen it passing Dunmore Landing.

July was not a month when many people toured the South. She was one of only a dozen passengers. She sat under an awning on the upper deck fanning herself and cursing mourning dress for its long-sleeved, high-necked sweltering effect in the Southern summer heat.

A man in a tall top hat striped red and white bellowed commentary through a megaphone. It made her angrier by the minute.

Look at all those fat-faced Yankees, she thought with hatred, they're just lapping this up. Cruel slave owners, indeed! Sold down the river, my foot! We loved our darkies just like family, and some of them owned us more than we owned them. *Uncle Tom's Cabin.* Fiddle-dee-dee! No decent person would read that kind of trash.

She wished she hadn't given in to the impulse to come. It was only going to upset her. It was already upsetting her, and they weren't even out of the harbor and into the Ashley River yet.

Mercifully, the commentator ran out of things to say and for a long while the only sound was the thunk-thunk of the pistons and the splash of water as it fell from the wheel. Marsh grass was green and gold on both sides with wide moss-hung oaks on the riverbank behind it. Dragonflies darted through the midge-dancing air above the grass; occasionally a fish leapt from the water, then flopped back in. Scarlett sat quietly, removed from the other passengers, nursing her rancor. Rhett's plantation was ruined, and he was doing nothing to save it. Camellias! At Ballyhara, she had hundreds of acres of healthy crops where she had found rank weeds. And she had rebuilt an entire town, while he just sat and stared at his burnt chimneys.

That's why she had come on the paddleboat, she told herself. It would make her feel good to see how far she was outstripping him. Scarlett tensed before each bend, relaxed when it was past and Rhett's house had not appeared.

She'd forgotten Ashley Barony. Julia Ashley's big square brick house looked magnificently forbidding in the center of its unadorned lawn. "This is the only plantation the heroic Union forces did not destroy," bawled the man in the absurd hat. "It was not in the tender heart of their commander to injure the frail spinster woman who lay ill inside."

Scarlett laughed aloud. "Frail spinster," indeed! Miss Julia must have scared the pants off him! The other passengers looked at her curiously, but Scarlett was unaware of their scrutiny. The Landing would be next ...

Yes, there was the phosphate mine. So much bigger! There were five barges being loaded. She searched under the wide-brimmed hat of the man on the dock. It was that white-trash soldier—she couldn't remember his name, something like Hawkins—no matter, around that bend, past that big live oak . . .

The angle of the sunlight sculpted the great grass terraces of Dunmore Landing into green velvet giant steps and scattered sequins on the butterfly lakes beside the river. Scarlett's involuntary cry was lost in the exclamations of the Yankees crowded around her along the rail. At the top of the terraces the scorched chimneys were tall sentinels against the painfully bright blue sky; an alligator was sunning itself on the grass between the lakes. Dunmore Landing was like its owner: cultivated, damaged, dangerous. And unreachable. The shutters were closed on the wing that remained, the place that Rhett used for his office and his home.

Her eyes darted avidly from spot to spot, comparing her memory to what she saw. Much more of the garden was cleared and everything looked as if it was thriving. Some building was going up behind the house; she could smell raw lumber, see the top of a roof. The shutters of the house were fixed, or maybe new. They didn't sag at all, and they glistened with green paint. He'd done a lot of work over the fall and winter.

Or they had. Scarlett tried to look away. She didn't want to see the newly cleared gardens. Anne loves those flowers as much as Rhett does. And the fixed-up shutters must mean a fixed-up house where the two of them live together. Does Rhett fix breakfast for Anne?

"Are you all right, miss?" Scarlett pushed past the concerned stranger.

"The heat—" she said. "I'll go over there, deeper in the shade." For the remainder of the excursion she looked only at the unevenly painted deck. The day seemed to last forever.

70

*F*ive o'clock was striking when Scarlett ran pell-mell down the ramp from the *Abraham Lincoln*. Damn fool boat. She stopped to catch her breath on the dock. She could see that the gangplank of *The Golden Fleece* was still in place. No harm done. But still, the master of the excursion boat should be horsewhipped. She'd been half out of her mind ever since four o'clock.

"Thank you for waiting for me," she said to the ship's officer at the head of the gangplank.

"Oh, there are more to come," he said, and Scarlett transferred her anger to the captain of the *Fleece*. If he said five o'clock, he should sail at five o'clock. The sooner she got away from Charleston, the happier she would be. This must be the hottest place on the face of the earth. She shaded her eyes with her hand to look at the sky. Not a cloud in sight. No rain, no wind. Just heat. She started along deck towards her rooms. Poor baby Cat must be practically cooked. As soon as they got out of the harbor she'd bring her up on deck for whatever breeze the ship's movement might cause.

Clattering hoofbeats and feminine laughter caught her attention. Maybe this was who they were waiting for. She glanced down at an open victoria. With three fabulous hats on the women in it. They weren't like any hats she'd ever seen, and even from a distance she could tell they were very expensive. Wide brimmed, decorated with clusters of feathers or plumes held by sparkling jewels and swirled with airy tulle netting, from

Scarlett's perspective the hats were like wonderful parasols or fantastic confections of pastry on big trays.

I'd look simply wonderful in a hat like that. She leaned slightly over the rail to look at the women. They were elegant, even in the heat, wearing pale organdy or voile trimmed with—it looked like wide silk ribbon or was it ruching?—on cuirass fronts and—Scarlett blinked—no bustle at all, not even a hint of one, and no train either. She hadn't seen anything like that in Savannah or Atlanta. Who were these people? Her eyes devoured the pale kid gloves and folded parasols, lace, she thought, but she couldn't be sure. Whoever they were, they certainly were having a good time laughing their heads off and not hurrying to get on the ship they were holding up either.

The Panama-hatted man with them stepped down into the street. With his left hand he took off his hat. His right hand reached upward to hand the first woman down.

Scarlett's hands clutched the railing. Dear God, it's Rhett. I've got to run inside. No. No. If he's on this ship I've got to get Cat off, find a place to hide, find another ship. But I can't do that. I've got two trunks in the hold with frilly dresses and Colum's rifles in them. What in the name of God am I going to do? Her mind raced from one impossible idea to another while she stared blindly at the group below her.

Slowly her brain registered what she was seeing: Rhett was bowing, kissing one gracefully extended hand after another. Her ears opened to the repeated "goodbye and thank you" of the women. Cat was safe.

But Scarlett was not. Her protective rage had disappeared, and her heart was exposed.

He doesn't see me. I can look at him all I want. Please, please don't put your hat back on, Rhett.

How well he looked. His skin was brown, his smile as white as his linen suit. He was the only man in the world who didn't wrinkle linen. Ah, that lock of hair that annoyed him so was falling down on his forehead again. Rhett flicked it back with two fingers in a gesture that Scarlett knew so well she felt weak-kneed with possessive memory. What was he saying? Something outrageously charming, she was sure, but he was using that low intimate voice he saved for women. Curse him. And curse those women. She wanted that voice murmuring to her, only her.

The ship's captain walked down the gangplank, adjusting the set of his gold epauletted jacket. Don't make them hurry, Scarlett wanted to shout. Stay, stay just a little longer. It's my last chance. I'll never see him again. Let me store up the sight of him.

He must have just had his hair cut, there's the tiniest pale line above his ears. Is that more gray at the temples? It looks so elegant, the silver streaking his crow-black hair. I remember how it felt under my fingers, crisp and shockingly soft at the same time. And the muscles in his shoulders and his arms, sliding so smoothly under the skin, stretching the skin when they hardened. I want—

The ship's whistle shrieked loudly. Scarlett jumped. She could hear rapid footsteps, the rumble of the gangplank, but she kept her eyes fixed on Rhett. He was smiling, looking over there to her right, looking up. She could see his dark eyes and slashing brows and impeccably groomed mustache. His entire strong, masculine, unforgettable pirate's face. "My beloved," she whispered, "my love."

Rhett bowed once again. The ship was moving away from the dock. He put his hat on and turned away. His thumb tilted the hat to the back of his head.

Don't go, cried Scarlett's heart.

Rhett glanced over his shoulder as if there had been a sound. His eyes met hers, and surprise stiffened his lithe body. For a long, immeasurable moment the two of them looked at each other while the space between them widened. Then blandness smoothed Rhett's face as he touched two fingers to his hat brim in salute. Scarlett lifted her hand.

He was still standing there on the dock when the ship turned into the channel to the sea. When Scarlett could see him no longer, she sank numbly into a deck chair.

"Don't be silly, Bridie, the steward will sit right outside the door. He'll come get us if Cat so much as turns over. There's no reason for you not to come to the dining saloon. You can't have your dinner in here every night."

"There's reason enough for me, Scarlett. I don't feel easy among fancy gentlemen and ladies, pretending to be one of them."

"You're just as good as they are, I told you that."

"And I heard you say it, Scarlett, but you don't hear me. I prefer to have me meal in here with all the silver hats on the dishes and my manners my own business. 'Tis soon enough I'll have to go where the lady I'm maiding tells me to go and do what I'm told to do. It's certain that having a grand meal in private comfort won't be one of my instructions. I'll take it now while I can."

Scarlett had to agree with Bridie. But she couldn't possibly have dinner in the suite herself. Not tonight. She had to find out who those women were and why they were with Rhett, or she'd go mad.

They were English, she learned as soon as she entered the dining saloon. The distinctive accent was dominating the captain's table.

Scarlett told the steward that she would like to change her seating to the small table near the wall. The table near the wall was also near the captain's table.

There were fourteen at his table: a dozen English passengers, the captain, and his first officer. Scarlett had a keen ear and could tell almost at once that the passengers' accents were different from the ship's officers, although to her they were all English and therefore to be despised by anyone with a drop of Irish blood.

They were talking about Charleston. Scarlett gathered that they didn't think much of it. "My dears," one of the women trumpeted, "I've never seen anything as dreary in my life. How my darling Mama could have told me that it was the only civilized place in America! It simply makes me worry that she's gone dotty without our noticing."

"Now, Sarah," said the man to her left, "you do have to take that war of theirs into consideration. I found the men to be very decent. Down to their last shilling, I'm sure, but never a mention, and the liquor was first rate. Single malt at the club bar."

"Geoffrey, my love, you'd think the Sahara was civilized if there was a club with drinkable whiskey. Heaven only knows it couldn't be any hotter. Beastly climate."

There was a chorus of agreement.

"On the other hand," said a youthful female voice, "that terribly attractive Butler man said the winters are quite delightful. He invited us back."

"I'm sure he invited you back, Felicity," said an older woman. "You behaved disgracefully."

"Frances, I did no such thing," protested Felicity. "I was only having some fun for the first time on this dreary trip. I cannot credit why Papa sent me to America. It's a wretched place."

A man laughed. "He sent you, sister dear, to get you out of the clutches of that fortune hunter."

"But he was so attractive. I don't see any point in having a fortune if you have to fend off every attractive man in England simply because he's not rich."

"At least you're supposed to fend them off, Felicity," said a girl. "That's easy enough to do. Think of our poor brother. Roger's supposed to draw American heiresses like flies, and marry a fortune to refill the family coffers." Roger groaned and everyone laughed.

Talk about Rhett, Scarlett implored silently.

"There's simply no market for Honourables," Roger said. "I can't get it through Papa's head. Heiresses want tiaras."

The older woman they called Frances said that she thought they were all disgraceful and that she couldn't understand young people today. "When I was a gel—" she began.

Felicity giggled. "Frances, dear, when you were a 'gel' there were no young people. Your generation were born forty years old and disapproving of everything."

"Your impertinence is intolerable, Felicity. I shall speak to your father."

A brief silence fell. *Why on earth doesn't that Felicity person say something more about Rhett?* Scarlett thought.

It was Roger who brought up the name. Butler, he said, offered some good shooting if he came back in the autumn. Seems he had rice fields gone to grass and the ducks practically landed on the barrel of your gun.

Scarlett tore a roll into fragments. *Who gave two cents about ducks?* The other Englishmen did, it seemed. They talked about shooting throughout the main course of dinner. She was thinking she'd have done better to stay with Bridie when her ears picked up a low-toned private conversation between Felicity and her sister, whose name turned out to be Marjorie. Both of them thought Rhett one of the most intriguing men they'd ever met. Scarlett listened with mixed feelings of curiosity and pride.

"A shame he's so devoted to his wife," Marjorie said and Scarlett's heart sank.

"Such a colorless little thing, too," Felicity said. Scarlett felt a little bit better.

"Out and out rebound, I heard. Didn't anyone tell you? He was married before, to an absolute tearing beauty. She ran off with another man and left Rhett Butler flat. He's never gotten over it."

"Gracious, Marjorie, can you imagine what the other man must be like if she'd leave the Butler man for him?"

Scarlett smiled to herself. She was enormously gratified to know that gossip had her leaving Rhett and not the other way around.

She felt much better than when she'd sat down. She might even have some dessert.

The following day the English discovered Scarlett. The three young people agreed that she was a superbly romantic figure, a mysterious young widow. "Damned nice looking, too," Roger added. His sisters told him he must be going blind. With her pale skin and dark hair and those green eyes, she was fantastically beautiful. The only thing she needed was some decent clothes and she'd turn heads wherever she went. They decided they'd "take her up." Marjorie made the approach by admiring Cat when Scarlett had her on deck for an airing.

Scarlett was more than willing to be "taken up." She wanted to hear every detail of every hour they'd spent in Charleston. It wasn't difficult for her to invent a tragic story of her marriage and bereavement that satisfied all their cravings for melodrama. Roger fell in love with her within the first hour.

Scarlett had been taught by her mother that genteel discretion about family matters was one of the hallmarks of a lady. Felicity and Marjorie Cowperthwaite shocked her with their casual unveiling of family skeletons. Their mother, they said, was a pretty and clever woman who had trapped their father into marriage. She managed to be run down by his horse when he was out riding. "Poor Papa is so dim," Marjorie laughed, "that he thought he'd probably ruined her because her frock was torn and he saw her bare breasts. We're certain that she tore it herself before she ever left the vicarage. She married him like a shot before he could puzzle out what she was up to."

To add to Scarlett's confusion, Felicity and Marjorie were ladies. Not simply "ladies" as opposed to "women." They were Lady Felicity and Lady Marjorie and their "dim papa" was an earl.

Frances Sturbridge, their disapproving chaperone, was also a "Lady," they explained, but she was Lady Sturbridge, not Lady Frances, because she wasn't born a "Lady" and she'd married a man who was "only a baronet."

"Whereas I could marry one of the footmen and Marjorie could run off with the boot boy, and we'd still be Lady Felicity and Lady Marjorie in the foul sinks of Bristol where our husbands robbed poor boxes to support us."

Scarlett could only laugh. "It's too complicated for me," she admitted.

"Oh, but my dear, it can be ever so much more complicated than our boring little family. When you get into widows and horrid little viscounts and third son's wives and so on, it's like a labyrinth. Mama has to hire advice every time she gives a dinner or she'd be guaranteed to insult someone fearfully important. You simply must not seat the daughter of an earl's younger son, like Roger, below somebody like poor Frances. It's all too foolish for words."

The Cowperthwaite Ladies were more than a little giddy and rattlebrained, and Roger seemed to have inherited some of Papa's dimness, but they were a cheerful and warmhearted trio who genuinely liked Scarlett.

They made the trip fun for her, and she was sorry when they left the ship at Liverpool.

Now she had almost two full days before she got to Galway, and she wouldn't be able to delay any longer thinking about the meeting with Rhett in Charleston, that was really no meeting at all.

Had he felt the same shock of recognition she had when their eyes met? It was, for her, as if the rest of the world disappeared and they were alone in some place and time separate from everything and everyone that existed. It wasn't possible that she could feel so bound to him by a look and that he would not feel the same way. Was it?

She worried and relived the moment until she began to think she'd dreamed it or even imagined it.

When the *Fleece* entered Galway Bay she was able to store the memory with her other prized memories of Rhett. Ballyhara was waiting, and harvest time was near.

But first she had to smile and whisk her trunks past the customs inspectors. Colum was expecting the weapons.

It was hard to remember that the English were all such bad people when the Cowperthwaites were so charming.

71

*C*olum was waiting at the end of the gangplank when Scarlett left *The Golden Fleece*. She hadn't expected him, she'd known only that someone would meet her and take care of her trunks. At the sight of his stocky figure in worn black clericals and smiling Irish face, Scarlett felt that she'd come home. Her luggage went past customs without any questions other than, "And how are things in America?" to which she answered, "Awful hot," and, "How old is that grand beautiful baby, then?" to which Scarlett replied proudly "Three months shy of a year, and already trying to walk."

It took nearly an hour to drive the short distance from the port to the train station. Scarlett had never seen such traffic snarls, not even at Five Points.

It was because of the Galway Races, said Colum. Before Scarlett could remember what had happened to her the previous year in Galway, he quickly added details. Steeplechase and flat racing, five days' worth every July. It meant that the militia and constabulary were too busy in the city to be wasting time idling around the docks. It also meant that there was not a hotel room to be had at any price. They'd be taking the afternoon train to Ballinasloe and spending the night there. Scarlett wished there was a train all the way to Mullingar. She wanted to get home.

"How are the fields, Colum? Is the wheat nearly ripe? Is the hay cut yet? Has there been plenty of sun? And what about the peat that was cut? Was there enough? Did it dry out like it was supposed to? Is it good? Does it burn hot?"

"Wait and see, Scarlett darling. You'll be pleased with your Ballyhara, I'm certain of it."

Scarlett was much more than pleased. She was overcome. The townspeople had erected arches covered with fresh greenery and gold ribbon over her route through Ballyhara town. They stood outside the arches waving handkerchiefs and hats, cheering her return. "Oh, thank you, thank you, thank you," she cried over and over, with tears brimming from her eyes.

At the Big House Mrs. Fitzpatrick and the three ill-assorted maids and the four dairymaids and the stablemen were lined up to greet her. Scarlett could barely keep herself from hugging Mrs. Fitz, but she obeyed the housekeeper's rules and maintained her dignity. Cat was bound by no rules. She laughed and held out her arms to Mrs. Fitzpatrick and was immediately caught up in an emotion-ridden embrace.

Less than an hour later Scarlett was dressed in her Galway peasant clothes striding quickly over her fields, Cat in her arms. It felt so good to be moving, stretching her legs. There'd been too many hours, days, weeks of sitting. On trains, and ships, in offices and armchairs. Now she wanted to walk, ride, bend, reach, run, dance. She was The O'Hara, home again, and the sun was warm between gentle, cooling, swiftly passing Irish rains.

Fragrant mounds of golden hay stood in field cocks seven feet tall on the meadows. Scarlett made a cave in one and crawled inside it with Cat to play house. Cat shrieked with delight when she pulled part of the "roof" down on them. And then when the dust made her sneeze. She picked off dried blossoms and put them in her mouth. Her expression of disgust when she spat them out made Scarlett laugh. Scarlett's laughter made Cat frown. Which made Scarlett laugh all the more. "Better get used to being laughed at, Miss Cat O'Hara," she said, "because you're a wonderfully silly little girl and you make your Momma very, very happy, and when people are happy they laugh a lot."

Scarlett took Cat back to the house when she started yawning. "Pick the hay out of her hair while she naps," she told Peggy Quinn. "I'll be back in time to give her supper and a bath." She interrupted the slow, chewing contemplation of one of the plow horses in the stable to ride him, bareback and astride, over Ballyhara in the lingering, slowly dimming twilight. The wheat fields were richly yellow, even in the blue-hued light. There would be a bounteous harvest. Scarlett rode home, content. Ballyhara would probably never deliver the kind of profit she'd earned from building and selling cheap houses, but there were satisfactions beyond earning money. The land of the O'Haras was fruitful again; she had brought it back, at least in part, and next year there'd be more acres tilled; the year after, still more.

* * *

"It's so good to be back," Scarlett said to Kathleen next morning. "I have about a million messages from everybody in Savannah." She settled herself happily beside the hearth and put Cat down to explore the floor. Before long the heads began to appear above the half door, everyone eager to hear about America and Bridie and all the rest.

At the Angelus the women hurried back down the boreen to the village, and the O'Hara men came in from the fields for their dinner.

Everyone except Seamus, and, of course, Sean who'd always taken his meals in the small cottage with Old Katie Scarlett O'Hara. Scarlett didn't notice at the time. She was too busy greeting Thomas and Patrick and Timothy and persuading Cat to give up the big spoon she was trying to eat.

It was only after the men had gone back to their work that Kathleen told her how much things had changed while she was away.

"It's sorry I am to say it, Scarlett, but Seamus took it hard that you didn't stay for his wedding."

"I wish I could have, but I couldn't. He must have known that. I had business in America."

"I've a feeling it's more Pegeen who bears the bad will. Did you not remark that she wasn't in the visitors this morning?"

The truth was, Scarlett admitted, that she hadn't noticed at all. She'd only met Pegeen once, she didn't really know her. What was she like? Kathleen chose her words carefully. Pegeen was a dutiful woman, she said, who kept a clean house and set a good table and saw to every comfort for Seamus and Sean in the small cottage. It would be a kindness to the whole family if Scarlett would go to call on her and admire the home she was making. She was that tender of her dignity that she was waiting to be visited before she'd do any visiting herself.

"My grief," Scarlett said, "how silly. I'll have to wake Cat up from her nap."

"Leave her, I'll keep watch while I do the mending. It's better I don't go with you."

So Kathleen didn't much like her cousin's new wife, thought Scarlett, that was interesting. And Pegeen was keeping house separately instead of going in with Kathleen in the larger cottage, at least for dinner. Tender of her dignity indeed! What a waste of energy to fix two meals instead of one. She had an idea she wasn't likely to take to Pegeen, but she made up her mind to be nice. It couldn't be easy coming into a family that had so many shared years, and she knew all too well what it felt like to be the outsider.

Pegeen made it hard for Scarlett to stay sympathetic. Seamus' wife had a prickly disposition. And she looks like she's been drinking vinegar, Scarlett thought. Pegeen poured out tea that had been stewed so long it was almost undrinkable. Wants me to know I kept her waiting, I reckon. "I wish I'd been here for the wedding," said Scarlett bravely. Might as well take the bull by the horns. "I've brought best wishes from all the O'Haras in America to add to mine. I hope you and Seamus will be very happy." She was pleased with herself. Gracefully said, she thought.

Pegeen nodded stiffly. "I'll tell Seamus about your kindness," she said. "He's wanting to have a word with you. I told him to stay nearby. I'll call him now."

Well! Scarlett said to herself, I've felt more welcome in my life. She wasn't sure at all that she wanted Seamus to "have a word" with her. She'd hardly exchanged ten words with Daniel's oldest son in all the time she'd been in Ireland.

After she heard Seamus' "word," Scarlett was quite sure she wished she hadn't. He expected her to pay the rent that was coming due on the farm and he believed it was only just that he and Pegeen have the bigger cottage because he was now in Daniel's place as owner. "Mary Margaret's proper willing to do the cooking and washing for my brothers as well as me. Kathleen can do for Sean over here, seeing she's his sister."

"I'll be glad to pay the rent," said Scarlett. But she'd have liked to be asked, not told. "But I don't see why you're talking to me about who lives where. You and Pegeen—I mean, Mary Margaret—should discuss that with your brothers and Kathleen."

"You're The O'Hara," Pegeen nearly shouted, "you've got the say."

"She's got the truth of it, Scarlett," said Kathleen when Scarlett complained to her. "You are The O'Hara." Before Scarlett could say anything, Kathleen smiled and told her it made no difference anyhow. She was going to be leaving Daniel's cottage soon; she was going to marry a boy from Dunsany. He'd asked her only the Saturday before, Market Day in Trim. "I haven't told the others yet, I wanted to wait for you."

Scarlett hugged Kathleen. "How exciting! You'll let me give the wedding, won't you? We'll have a wonderful party."

"So I got off the hook," she told Mrs. Fitz that night. "But only by the skin of my teeth. I'm not so sure being The O'Hara is exactly what I thought it would be."

"And what was that, exactly, Mrs. O?"

"I don't know. More fun, I guess."

* * *

In August the potatoes were harvested. It was the best crop they'd ever had, the farmers said. Then they began to reap the wheat. Scarlett loved to watch them. The shiny sickles flashed in the sun and the golden stalks fell like rippling silk. Sometimes she took the place of the man who followed the reaper. She'd borrow the staff with a curved end that the farmers called the loghter-hook and draw up the fallen wheat into small sheaves. She couldn't master the quick twisting movement the man made to tie each sheaf with a stalk of wheat, but she became very handy with the loghter-hook.

It sure beats picking cotton, she told Colum. Yet there were still moments when sharp pangs of homesickness caught her off guard. He understood her feelings, he said, and Scarlett was sure he did. He truly was the brother she'd always wanted.

Colum seemed preoccupied, but he said it was nothing more than his impatience that the wheat took precedence over finishing the work on the inn that Brendon Kennedy was making in the building next to his bar. Scarlett remembered the desperate man in the church, the man Colum had said was "on the run." She wondered if there were more of them, what Colum did for them. But she'd really rather not know, and she didn't ask.

She preferred to think about happy things, like Kathleen's wedding. Kevin O'Connor wasn't the man Scarlett would have picked for her, but he was clearly head over heels in love, and he had a good farm with twenty cows at grass, so he was considered a very good catch. Kathleen had a substantial dowry, in cash saved up from selling butter and eggs, and in her owning all the kitchen implements of Daniel's house. She sensibly accepted a gift of a hundred pounds from Scarlett. It wasn't necessary to add it to her dowry, she said with a conspiratorial wink.

The great disappointment for Scarlett was that she couldn't hold the wedding party at the Big House. Tradition demanded that the wedding take place in the house the couple would live in. The best Scarlett could do was contribute several geese and a half dozen barrels of porter to the wedding feast. Even that was going over the edge a bit, Colum warned her. The groom's family were the hosts.

"Well, if I'm going to go over the edge, I might as well go way over," Scarlett told him. She warned Kathleen, too, in case she wanted to object. "I'm coming out of mourning. I'm sick to death of wearing black."

She danced every reel at the wedding party, wearing bright blue and red petticoats under a dark green skirt, and stockings striped in yellow and green.

Then she cried all the way home to Ballyhara. "I'm going to miss her so much, Colum. I'll miss the cottage, too, and all the visitors. I'll never go there again, not with nasty Pegeen handing out her nasty old tea."

"Twelve miles isn't the end of the earth, Scarlett darling. Get yourself a good riding horse instead of driving your buggy, and you'll be in Dunsany in no time at all."

Scarlett could see the sense to that, although twelve miles was still a long way. What she refused to consider at all was Colum's quiet suggestion that she start thinking about marrying again.

She woke up in the night sometimes, and the darkness in her room was like the dark mystery of Rhett's eyes meeting hers when her ship was leaving Charleston. What had he been feeling?

Alone in the silence of the night, alone in the vastness of the ornate bed, alone in the black blankness of the unlit room, Scarlett wondered, and dreamed of impossible things, and sometimes wept from the ache of wanting him.

"Cat," said Cat clearly when she saw her reflection in the mirror.

"Oh, thank God," Scarlett cried aloud. She'd been afraid her baby was never going to talk. Cat had rarely gurgled and cooed like other babies, and she looked at people who talked baby talk to her with an expression of profound astonishment. She walked at ten months, which was early, Scarlett knew, but a month later she was still practically mute except for her laughter. "Say 'ma-ma,'" Scarlett begged. To no avail.

"Say 'ma-ma,'" she tried again after Cat spoke, but the little girl wriggled out of her grasp and plunged recklessly across the floor. Her walking was more enthusiastic than skillful.

"Conceited little monster," Scarlett called after her. "All babies say 'ma-ma' for their first word, not their own name."

Cat staggered to a halt. She looked back at Scarlett with a smile that Scarlett said later was "positively diabolical." "Mama," she said casually. Then she lurched off again.

"She probably could have said it all along if she'd wanted to," Scarlett bragged to Father Flynn. "She tossed it to me like a bone to a dog."

The old priest smiled tolerantly. He had listened to many proud mothers in his long years. "It's a grand day," he offered pleasantly.

"A grand day in every way, Father!" exclaimed Tommy Doyle, the youngest of Ballyhara's farmers. "It's sure that we've made the harvest of harvests." He refilled his glass, and Father Flynn's. A man was entitled to relax and enjoy himself at the Harvest Home celebration.

Scarlett allowed him to give her a glass of porter, too. The toasts would be starting soon and it would be bad luck if she didn't share them with at least a sip. After the good luck that had blessed Ballyhara all year, she wasn't about to risk inviting any bad.

She looked at the long, laden tables set up the length of Ballyhara's wide street. Each was decorated with a ribbon-tied sheaf of wheat. Each was surrounded by smiling people enjoying themselves. This was the best part of being The O'Hara. They had all worked, each in his or her own way, and now they were all together, the whole population of the town, to celebrate the results of that work.

There was food and drink, sweets and a small carousel for the children, a wooden platform for dancing later in front of the unfinished inn. The air was golden with afternoon light, the wheat was golden on the table, a golden feeling of happiness bathed everyone in shared repletion. It was exactly what Harvest Home was meant to be.

The sound of horses coming made mothers look for their younger children. Scarlett's heart stopped for a moment when she couldn't find Cat. Then she saw her sitting on Colum's knee at the end of the table. He was talking to the man beside him. Cat was nodding as if she understood every word. Scarlett grinned. What a funny little girl her daughter was.

A group of militia rode into the end of the street. Three men, three officers, their polished brass buttons more golden than the wheat. They slowed their horses to a walk, and the noise around the tables died away. Some of the men rose to their feet.

"At least the soldiers have the decency not to gallop past, stirring up dust," said Scarlett to Father Flynn. But when the men reined in before the deserted church she fell silent, too.

"Which way to the Big House?" said one of the officers. "I'm here to talk to the owner."

Scarlett stood up. "I am the owner," she said. She was amazed that her suddenly dry mouth could make any sound at all.

The officer looked at her tumbled hair and bright peasant clothes. His lips curled in a sneer. "Very amusing, girl, but we're not here to play games."

Scarlett felt an emotion that had become almost a stranger to her, a wild, elated anger. She stepped up onto the bench she'd been sitting on and put her hands on her hips. She looked insolent and she knew it.

"No one invited you here—soldier—to play games or anything else. Now what do you want? I am Mrs. O'Hara."

A second officer walked his horse forward a few steps. He dismounted and came on foot to stand in front of and below Scarlett's position on the bench. "We're to deliver this, Mrs. O'Hara." He removed his hat and one of his white gauntlets and handed a scrolled paper up to Scarlett. "The garrison is going to second a detachment to Ballyhara for its protection."

Scarlett could feel tension, like a storm, in the warm end-of-summer atmosphere. She unrolled the paper and read it slowly, twice. She could feel the knots in her shoulders relax when the full meaning of the document was clear to her. She lifted her head and smiled so everyone could see her. Then she turned the full force of her smile on the officer looking up at her. "That's mighty sweet of the colonel," she said, "but I'm really not interested, and he can't send any soldiers to my town without my agreement. Will you tell him for me? I don't have any unrest here in Ballyhara at all. We get along real fine." She held the vellum sheet down to the officer. "Youall look a mite parched, would you like a glass of ale?" The admiring expression on her face had enchanted men just like this officer from the day she turned fifteen. He blushed and stammered exactly like dozens of young men she'd beguiled in Clayton County, Georgia.

"Thank you, Mrs. O'Hara, but—uh—regulations—that is, personally I'd like nothing better—but the colonel wouldn't—um—he'd think—"

"I understand," said Scarlett kindly. "Maybe some other time?"

The first toast of Harvest Home was to The O'Hara. It would have been the first toast anyway, but now the salute was a loud roar.

72

*W*inter made Scarlett restless. Except for riding there was nothing active to do, and she needed to be busy. The new fields were cleared and manured by the middle of November, and then what did she have to think about? There weren't even many complaints or disputes brought to her office on First Sundays. True, Cat could walk across the room herself to light the Christmas candle and there were the New Year's Day ceremonies of barm brack against the wall and being the dark-haired visitor in town, but even so the short days seemed too long to her. She was warmly welcomed in Kennedy's bar now that she was known to be supporting the Fenians, but she quickly tired of the songs about the blessed martyrs to Irish freedom and the loud-voiced threats to run the English out. She went down to the bar only when she was starved for company. She was overjoyed when Saint Brigid's Day arrived on February 1 and the growing year had begun again. She turned the first sod with such enthusiasm that soil flew out in a wide circle around her. "This year will be even better than last," she predicted rashly.

But the new fields put an impossible burden on the farmers. There was never enough time to do everything that needed doing. Scarlett nagged at Colum to move some more laborers into the town. There were still plenty of vacant cottages. He wouldn't agree to let strangers in. Scarlett backed down. She understood the need for secrecy about the Fenians. Finally Colum found a compromise. She could hire men just for the summer. He'd take her to the hiring fair at Drogheda. The horse fair would be on, too, and she could buy the horses she thought she needed.

" 'Thought,' my foot, Colum O'Hara. I must have been blind and half-witted too when I paid good money for the plow horses we've got. They don't go any faster than a box turtle on a rocky road. I'm not going to be cheated again that way."

Colum smiled to himself. Scarlett was an astonishing woman, amazingly competent at many things. But she was never going to best an Irish horse trader, he was sure of that.

"Scarlett darling, you look like a village lass, not landed gentry. No one will believe you can pay for a merry-go-round ride, let alone a horse."

Her frown was meant to intimidate. She didn't understand that she really did look like a girl dressed up for a fair. Her green shirt made her eyes even greener and her blue skirt was the color of the spring sky. "Will you please do me the kindness, *Father* Colum O'Hara, to get this buggy moving? I know what I'm doing. If I look rich, the dealer will think he can stick me with any old broken-down thing he has. I'll do much better in village clothes. Now come on. I've been waiting for weeks and weeks. I don't see any reason why the hiring fair can't be on Saint Brigid's Day when the work starts."

Colum smiled at her. "Some of the lads go to school, Scarlett darling." He flicked the reins and they were on their way.

"A fat lot of good that'll do them, ruining their eyes on books when they could be out in the air earning a good wage besides." She was cranky with impatience.

The miles rolled by, and the hedgerows were sweet with blackthorn blossoms. Once they were really on their way Scarlett began to enjoy herself. "I've never been to Drogheda, Colum. Will I like it?"

"I believe you will. It's a very big fair, this, much bigger than any you've seen." He knew that Scarlett didn't mean the city when she asked about Drogheda. She liked the excitement of fairs. The intriguing possibilities in a crooked old city street were incomprehensible to her. Scarlett liked things to be obvious and easily understood. It was a trait that often made him uneasy. He knew she had no real understanding of what danger she courted with her involvement in the Fenian Brotherhood, and ignorance could lead to disaster.

But today he was on her business, not his. He intended to enjoy the fair as much as Scarlett.

* * *

"Look, Colum, it's enormous!"

"Too big, I fear. Will you choose the lads first or the horses? They're at different ends."

"Oh, bother! The best ones will get snapped up in the beginning, they always do. I'll tell you what—you pick out the boys and I'll go straight for the horses. You come to me when you finish. You're sure the boys will go to Ballyhara on their own?"

"They're here for hiring and they're used to walking. Some of them likely walked a hundred miles to be here."

Scarlett smiled. "Better look at their feet, then, before you sign anything. I'll be looking at teeth. Which way do I go?"

"Back in that corner, where the banners are. You'll see some of the best horses in Ireland at Drogheda Fair. I've heard of a hundred guineas and more paid."

"Fiddle-dee-dee! What a tale teller you are, Colum. I'll get three pair for under that, you'll see."

There were big canvas tents that served as temporary stables for the horses. Ha! thought Scarlett, nobody's going to sell me an animal in bad light. She pushed into the noisy crowd that was milling around inside the tent.

My grief, I've never seen so many horses in one place in my life! How smart of Colum to bring me here. I'll have all the choice I need. She elbowed her way from one place to another, looked over one horse after another. "Not yet," she said to the traders. She didn't like the system in Ireland at all. You couldn't just walk up to the owner and ask him what he wanted for his animal. No, that was too easy. The minute there was any interest one of the traders jumped in to name a price that was way out of line one end or another and then badger buyer and seller into an agreement in the end. She'd learned the hard way about some of their tricks. They'd grab your hand and slap down on it so sharp it hurt, and that meant you might have bought yourself a horse if you weren't careful.

She liked the looks of a pair of roans that the dealer shouted were perfectly matched three-year-olds and only seventy pounds the pair. Scarlett put her hands behind her back. "Walk them out in the light where I can see them," she said.

Owner and dealer and people nearby all protested furiously. "Takes all the sport out," said a small man in riding breeches and a sweater.

Scarlett insisted, but very sweetly. Catch more flies with honey, she reminded herself. She looked at the horses' gleaming coats, rubbed her hand over them and looked at the pomade on her palm. Then she caught expert hold of one horse's head and examined his teeth. She burst out laughing. Three-year-old, my maiden aunt! "Take 'em in," she said, with a wink at the dealer. "I've got a grandfather younger than them." She was enjoying herself very much.

After an hour, though, she'd only found three horses that she liked both as animal and as a good buy. Every single time she had to coax and charm the owner into letting her examine the horse in the light. She looked enviously at the people buying hunters. There were jumps set up in the open, and they could get a good look at what they were buying, doing what they were buying it to do. They were such beautiful horses, too. For a plow horse, looks weren't important. She turned away from the view of the jumping. She needed three more plow horses. While her eyes accustomed themselves to the shaded interior of the tent, Scarlett leaned against one of the thick tent supports. She was starting to get tired. And she was only half done.

"Where is this Pegasus of yours, Bart? I don't see anything flying over the jumps."

Scarlett's hands reached for the thick support. I'm losing my mind. That sounded like Rhett's voice.

"If you brought me on a wild goose chase—"

It is! It is! I can't be mistaken. No one else in the world sounds like Rhett. She turned quickly, looking into the sunlit square, blinking.

That's his back. Isn't it? It is, I'm sure it is. If only he'd say something else, turn his head. It can't be Rhett. He's got no reason to be in Ireland. But I couldn't be wrong about that voice.

He turned to speak to the slightly built fair-haired man beside him. It was Rhett. Her knuckles were white against her hands, so tightly was she holding on to the post. She was trembling.

The other man said something, pointed with his crop, and Rhett nodded. Then the fair-haired man walked away, out of her sight, and Rhett was there alone. Scarlett stood in the shadow, looking out to the light.

Don't move, she ordered herself when he started to walk away. But she couldn't obey. She burst from the shadows and ran after him. "Rhett!"

He stopped awkwardly, Rhett who was never clumsy, and he spun around. An expression she couldn't recognize flickered on his face, and his dark eyes seemed very bright beneath the shading bill of his cap. Then he smiled the mocking smile she knew so well. "You do turn up in the most unexpected places, Scarlett," he said.

He's laughing at me, and I don't care. I don't care about anything as long as he'll say my name and stand near me. She could hear her own heart beating.

"Hello, Rhett," she said, "how are you?" She knew it was a foolish, inadequate thing to say, but she had to say something.

Rhett's mouth twitched. "I'm remarkably well for a dead man," he drawled, "or was I mistaken? I thought I glimpsed a widow at the dock in Charleston."

"Well, yes. I had to say something. I wasn't married, I mean I didn't have a husband—"

"Don't try to explain, Scarlett. It's not your forte."

"Forty? What are you talking about?" Was he being mean? Please don't be mean, Rhett.

"It's not important. What brings you to Ireland? I thought you were in England."

"What made you think that?" Why are we standing here making conversation about nothing at all? Why can't I think? Why am I saying these stupid things?

"You didn't get off the ship in Boston."

Scarlett's heart leapt to the meaning of what he'd said. He'd taken the trouble to find out where she was going, he cared about her, he wanted to keep her from disappearing. Happiness flooded her heart.

"May I assume from your cheerful attire that you're no longer mourning my death?" said Rhett. "Shame on you, Scarlett, I'm not yet cold in my grave."

She looked down in horror at her peasant clothes, then up at his impeccably tailored hacking jacket and perfectly tied white stock. Why did he always have to make her feel like a fool? Why couldn't she at least feel angry?

Because she loved him. Whether he believed it or didn't, it was the truth.

Without planning or thought of consequences, Scarlett looked at the man who had been her husband for so many years of lies. "I love you, Rhett," she said with simple dignity.

"How unfortunate for you, Scarlett. You always seem to be in love with another woman's husband." He lifted his cap politely. "I have another commitment, please excuse me if I leave you now. Goodbye." He turned his back on her and walked away. Scarlett looked after him. She felt as if he had slapped her face.

For no reason. She'd made no demands on him, she'd made a gift of the greatest thing she'd learned to give. And he'd trampled it into the muck. He'd made a fool of her.

No, she'd made a fool of herself.

Scarlett stood there, a brightly colored, small isolated figure amid the noise and movement of the horse fair, for a measureless time. Then the world came back into focus, and she saw Rhett and his friend near another tent, in a circle of intent spectators. A different tweed-clad man was holding a restless bay by the bridle, and a red-faced man wearing a plaid vest was swooping his right arm down, in the familiar motions of the horse trade. Scarlett imagined she could hear the slapping palms as he exhorted Rhett's friend, and the horse's owner, to come to a deal.

Her feet moved by themselves, marching across the space separating her from them. There must have been people in her way, but she was unconscious of them, and somehow they melted away.

The dealer's voice was like some ritual chant, cadenced and hypnotic: "... a hundred and twenty, sir, you know that's a handsome price, even for a beast as grand as this one ... and you, sir, you can go twenty-five, isn't that the fact of it, to add a noble animal like this to your stables ... one-forty? Sure, you must add a little reasonableness to your thinking, the gentleman's come up to one twenty-five, it's only the way of the world for you to take a small step to meet him; say one-forty's your price down from forty-two and we'll be making a deal before the day's out ... One-forty it is, now see the generous nature of the man, you'll prove you can match him, won't you now? Say one-thirty instead of one twenty-five and there's only a breath between you, no more than can be managed for the cost of a pint or two ..."

Scarlett stepped into the triangle of seller, buyer, and dealer. Her face was shockingly white above her green shirt, her eyes greener than emeralds. "One-forty," she said clearly. The dealer stared confused, his rhythm broken. Scarlett spit into her right hand and slapped it loudly against his. Then she spit again, looking at the seller. He lifted his hand and spat into the palm, then slapped once, twice against hers in the age-old seal of deal made. The dealer could only spit and seal in acquiescence.

Scarlett looked at Rhett's friend. "I hope you're not too disappointed," she said in a honeyed tone.

"Why, of course not, that is to say—"

Rhett broke in. "Bart, I'd like you to meet ..." he paused.

Scarlett did not look at him. "Mrs. O'Hara," she said to Rhett's bewildered companion. She held out her spit-wet right hand. "I'm a widow."

"John Morland," he said, and took her grimy hand. He bowed, kissed it, then smiled ruefully into her blazing eyes. "You must be something to see taking a fence, Mrs. O'Hara. Talk about leaving the field behind! Do you hunt around here?"

"I . . . um . . ." Dear heaven, what had she done? What could she say? What was she going to do with a thoroughbred hunter in Ballyhara's stable? "I confess, Mr. Morland, I just gave in to a woman's impulse. I had to have this horse."

"I felt the same way. But not quickly enough, it seems," said the cultivated English voice. "I'd be honored if you'd join me some time, join the hunt from my place, that is. It's near Dunsany, if you're familiar with that part of the County."

Scarlett smiled. She'd been in that part of the County not so long ago, at Kathleen's wedding. No wonder the name John Morland was familiar. She'd heard all about "Sir John Morland" from Kathleen's husband. "He's a grand man, for all that he's a landlord," said Kevin O'Connor a dozen times. "Didn't he tell me himself to drop five pounds from the rent as a gift for my wedding?"

Five pounds, she thought. How very generous. From a man who'll pay thirty times that for a horse. "I'm familiar with Dunsany," Scarlett said. "It's not far from the friends I'm visiting. I'd dearly love to hunt with you sometime. I can hack over any day you name."

"Saturday next?"

Scarlett smiled wickedly. She spit in her palm and lifted her hand. "Done!"

John Morland laughed. He spit in his, slapped hers once, twice. "Done! Stirrup cup at seven and breakfast after."

For the first time since she'd pushed in on them, Scarlett looked at Rhett. He was looking at her as if he'd been looking for a long time. There was amusement in his eyes and something else that she couldn't define. Great balls of fire, you'd think he'd never met me before or something. "Mr. Butler, a pleasure to see you," she said graciously. She dangled her dirty hand elegantly in front of him.

Rhett removed his glove to take it. "Mrs. O'Hara," he said with a bow.

Scarlett nodded to the staring dealer and the grinning former owner of her horse. "My groom will be here shortly to make the necessary arrangements," she said airily, and she hiked up her skirts to take a bundle of banknotes from the garter above her red-and-green striped knee. "Guineas, is that right?" She counted the money into the seller's hand.

Her skirts swirled when she turned and walked away.

"What a remarkable woman," said John Morland.

Rhett smiled with his lips. "Astonishing," he said in agreement.

* * *

"Colum! I was afraid you'd got lost," said Scarlett when her cousin emerged from the crowds near the tents.

"Not a bit of it, Scarlett. I got hungry. Have you eaten?"

"No, I forgot."

"Are you pleased with your horses?"

Scarlett looked down at him from her perch on the rail of the jumping ring. She began to laugh. "I think I bought an elephant. You've never seen such a big horse in your life. I had to, but I don't know why." Colum put a steadying hand on her arm. Her laughter was ragged and her eyes were bright with pain.

73

*C*at will go out," said the little voice.

"No, sweetheart, not today. Soon, but not today." Scarlett felt a terrifying vulnerability. How could she have been so reckless? How could she have ignored the danger to Cat? Dunsany was not that far away, not nearly far enough to be sure that people wouldn't know about The O'Hara and her dark-skinned child. She kept Cat with her day and night, upstairs in their two rooms while she looked worriedly out the window above the drive.

Mrs. Fitz was her go-between for the things that had to be done, and done faster than fast. The dressmaker raced back and forth for fittings of Scarlett's riding habit, the cobbler worked like a leprechaun far into the night on her boots, the stableman labored with rags and oil over the cracked and dry sidesaddle that had been left in the tack room thirty years before Scarlett arrived, and one of the boys from the hiring fair who had quiet hands and an easy seat exercised the powerful big bay hunter. When Saturday dawned, Scarlett was as ready as she'd ever be.

Her horse was a bay gelding named Half Moon. He was, as she'd told Colum, very big, nearly seventeen hands, with a deep chest and long back and powerfully muscled thighs. He was a horse for a big man; Scarlett looked tiny and fragile and very feminine on him. She was afraid she looked ridiculous.

And she was quite certain that she'd make a fool of herself. She didn't know Half Moon's temperament or peculiarities, and there was no chance to get to know them because she was riding sidesaddle, as all ladies did. When she was a girl, Scarlett had loved riding sidesaddle. It produced a graceful fall of skirts that emphasized her tiny waist. Also, in those days she seldom went faster than a walk, the better to flirt with men riding alongside.

But now the sidesaddle was a serious handicap. She couldn't communicate with the horse through pressure of her knees because one knee was hooked around the sidesaddle's pommel, the other one rigid because only by pressing on the one stirrup could a lady counterbalance her unbalanced position. I'll probably fall off before I even get to Dunsany, she thought with despair, and I'll certainly break my neck if I get as far as the first fence. She knew from her father that jumping fences and ditches and hedges and stiles and walls was the thrilling part of hunting. Colum had made things no better when he told her that ladies frequently avoided active hunting altogether. The breakfast was the social part and riding clothes were very becoming. Serious accidents were much more likely when riding sidesaddle and no one blamed the ladies for being sensible.

Rhett would be glad to see her cowardly and weak, she was convinced. And she'd much prefer to break her neck than to give him that satisfaction. Scarlett touched her crop to Half Moon's neck. "Let's try a trot and see if I can balance on this stupid saddle," she sighed aloud.

Colum had described a fox hunt to Scarlett, but she wasn't prepared for the first impact of it. Morland Hall was an amalgamation of building over more than two centuries, with wings and chimneys and windows and walls attached higgledy-piggledy to one another around the stone-walled courtyard that had been the keep of the fortified castle erected by the first Morland baronet in 1615. The square courtyard was filled with mounted riders and excited hounds. Scarlett forgot her apprehensions at the sight. Colum had omitted to mention that the men wore "pinks," misnamed bright red jackets. She had never seen anything so glamorous in her life.

"Mrs. O'Hara!" Sir John Morland rode over to her, his gleaming top hat in his hand. "Welcome. I didn't believe you'd come."

Scarlett's eyes narrowed. "Did Rhett say that?"

"On the contrary. He said wild horses wouldn't keep you away." There was no guile in Morland. "How do you like Half Moon?" The Baronet stroked the big hunter's sleek neck. "What a beauty he is."

"Um? Yes, isn't he?" said Scarlett. Her eyes were moving quickly, searching for Rhett. What a lot of people! Damn this veil anyhow, every-thing looks blurred. She was wearing the most conservative riding clothes fashion allowed. Unrelieved black wool with a high neck, and low black top hat with a face veil pulled tight and tied over the netted thick knot of hair at the nape of her neck. It was worse than mourning, she thought, but respectable as all get-out, a real antidote to bright-colored skirts and striped stockings. Scarlett was rebellious in only one matter: she would not wear a corset under her habit. The sidesaddle was torture enough.

Rhett was looking at her. She looked away quickly when she finally saw him. He's counting on me to make a spectacle of myself. I'll show Mr. Rhett Butler. I might break every bone in my body, but nobody's going to laugh at me, especially not him.

"Ride along easy, well back, and watch what the others do," Colum had said. Scarlett began as he advised. She felt her palms sweating inside her gloves. Up ahead the pace was picking up, then beside her a woman laughed and whipped her horse, breaking into a gallop. Scarlett looked briefly at the panorama of red and black backs streaming down the slope in front of her, at the horses jumping effortlessly over the low stone wall at the base of the hill.

This is it, she thought, it's too late now to worry about it. She shifted her weight without knowing she should and felt Half Moon moving faster, faster, sure-footed veteran of a hundred hunts. The wall was behind her and she had hardly noticed the jump. No wonder John Morland wanted Half Moon so much. Scarlett laughed aloud. It made no difference that she'd never hunted in her life, that she hadn't sat sidesaddle for more than fifteen years. She was all right, better than all right. She was having fun. No wonder Pa never opened a gate. Why bother when you could go over the fence?

The specters of her father and Bonnie that had plagued her were gone. Her fear was gone. There was only the excitement of the misty air streaking past her skin and the power of the animal that she controlled.

That and the new determination to overtake and pass and leave Rhett Butler far behind.

Scarlett stood with the muddy train of her habit looped over her left arm and a glass of champagne in her right hand. The paw of the fox that she'd been awarded would be mounted on a silver base, if she'd allow it, said John Morland.

"I'd love it, Sir John."

"Please call me Bart. All my friends do."

"Please call me Scarlett. Everybody does, whether they're friends or not." She was giddy and pink-cheeked from the exhilaration of the hunt and her success. "I've never had a better day," she told Bart. It was almost true. Other riders had congratulated her, she saw the unmistakable admiration in the men's eyes, jealousy in the women's. Everywhere she looked there were handsome men and beautiful women, silver trays of champagne, servants, wealth; people having a good time, a good life. It was like life before the War, only now she was grown up, she could do and say what she liked, and she was Scarlett O'Hara, country girl from North Georgia, in a baronet's castle partying with Lady this and Lord that and even a countess. It was like a story in a book, and Scarlett's head was turned.

She could almost forget that Rhett was there, almost erase the memory of being insulted and despised.

But only almost. And her treacherous mind kept remembering things she had seen and heard as she rode back to the house after the hurt: Rhett acting like it didn't matter that she'd beaten him to the kill . . . teasing the Countess as if she were just anybody at all . . . looking so damned at ease and comfortable and not impressed . . . being so . . . so Rhett. Damn him, anyhow.

"Congratulations, Scarlett." Rhett was at her side, and she hadn't seen him approaching. Scarlett's arm jerked, and champagne spilled on her skirts.

"Dammit, Rhett, do you have to sneak up on people like that?"

"I'm sorry." Rhett offered her a handkerchief. "And I'm sorry for my boorish behavior at the horse fair. My only excuse is that I was shocked to see you there."

Scarlett took the handkerchief and bent over to wipe at the dampness on her skirts. There was no point to it; her habit was already spattered with mud from the wild cross-country chase. But it gave her a chance to collect her thoughts and to hide her face for a moment. I will not show how much I care, she vowed silently. I will not show how much he hurt me.

She looked up, and her eyes were sparkling, her lips curved in a smile. "You were shocked," she said. "Imagine what I was. What on earth are you doing in Ireland?"

"Buying horses. I'm determined to win at the races next year. John Morland's stables have a reputation for producing likely yearlings. I go to Paris Tuesday to look at some more. What brought you to Drogheda in local costume?"

Scarlett laughed. "Oh, Rhett, you know how I love to dress up. I borrowed those clothes from one of the maids at the house I'm visiting." She looked from side to side, searching for John Morland. "I've got to make my manners and get going," she said over her shoulder. "My friends will be furious if I'm not back pretty soon." She looked at Rhett for an instant, then hurried off. She didn't dare stay. Not close to him like that. Not even in the same room ... the same house.

The rain began when she was a little more than five miles from Ballyhara. Scarlett blamed it for the wetness on her cheeks.

On Wednesday she took Cat to Tara. The ancient mounds were just high enough for Cat to feel triumphant when she climbed them. Scarlett watched Cat's recklessness on the run down the mound and forced herself not to warn her that she might fall.

She told Cat about Tara, and her family, and the banquets of the High Kings. Before they left she held the little girl as high as she could to look out over the country of her birth. "You're a little Irish Cat, your roots go deep here ... Do you understand anything I'm saying?"

"No," said Cat.

Scarlett put her down so she could run. The strong little legs never walked now, always ran. Cat fell often. There were ancient hidden irregularities under the grass. But she never cried. She got to her feet and ran some more.

Watching her was healing for Scarlett. It made her whole again.

"Colum, who's this man Parnell? People were talking about him at the hunt breakfast, but I couldn't make any sense out of what they were saying."

A Protestant, said Colum, and an Anglo. Nobody to concern them.

Scarlett wanted to argue but she'd learned it was a waste of time. Colum never discussed the English, especially not the English landowners in Ireland, who were known as the Anglo-Irish. He would manage to change the subject before she knew he was doing it. It bothered her that he wouldn't even admit that some of the English might be nice people. She'd liked the sisters on the ship from America, and everyone had been nice to her at the hunt. Colum's intransigence made her feel a distance between them. If he'd only talk about it instead of snapping her head off.

She asked Mrs. Fitz the other question that had been on her mind. Who were the Irish Butlers that everyone hated so much?

The housekeeper brought her a map of Ireland. "Do you see this?"

She swept her hand over an entire county, as big as County Meath. "That's Kilkenny. Butler country. The Dukes of Ormonde they are. They're probably the strongest Anglo family in Ireland." Scarlett looked closely at the map. Not far from the city of Kilkenny she saw the name Dunmore Cave. And Rhett's plantation was called Dunmore Landing. There had to be a connection.

Scarlett started to laugh. She'd been feeling so superior because the O'Haras were rulers of twelve hundred acres, and here were the Butlers with their own county. Without lifting a finger Rhett had won again. He always won. How could any woman be blamed for loving a man like that?

"And what's so amusing, Mrs. O?"

"I am, Mrs. Fitz. Thank God I can laugh about it."

Mary Moran poked her head around the door without knocking. Scarlett didn't bother to say anything. The gangly, nervous girl would be even worse for weeks if anyone criticized her. Servants. A problem even when you hardly had any. "What is it, Mary?"

"A gentleman to see ye." The maid held out a card. Her eyes were even rounder than usual.

Sir John Morland, Bart.

Scarlett ran down the stairs. "Bart! What a surprise. Come in, we can sit on the steps. I don't have any furniture." She was genuinely pleased to see him, but she couldn't take him up to her sitting room. Cat was having her nap next door.

Bart Morland sat down on the stone steps as if it were the most natural thing in the world to have no furniture. He'd had the devil of a time finding her, he said, until he ran into the postman in the bar. That was his only excuse for being so late delivering her trophy from the hunt.

Scarlett looked at the silver plaque with her name and the date of the hunt. The fox pad was no longer bloody, that was something, but it was not a thing of beauty.

"Disgusting, isn't it?" said Bart cheerfully.

Scarlett laughed. No matter what Colum said, she liked John Morland. "Would you like to say hello to Half Moon?"

"Thought you'd never suggest it. I was wondering how to drop a really weighty hint. How is he?"

Scarlett made a face. "Underexercised, I'm afraid. I feel guilty about it, but I've been very busy. It's haying time."

"How's your crop?"

"So far, so good. If we don't get a real rain."

They walked through the colonnade and out to the stable. Scarlett was going to pass it on the way to the pasture and Half Moon, but Bart stopped her. Could he go inside? Her stables were famous, and he'd never seen them. Scarlett was puzzled, but she agreed readily. The horses were at work or pasture, so there was nothing to see except empty stalls, but if he wanted to see them—

The stalls were separated by granite columns with Doric capitals. Tall vaulting sprang up from the columns to meet and cross and create a ceiling of stone that looked as light and weightless as air and sky.

John Morland cracked his knuckles, then apologized. When he was really excited, he said, he did it without thinking. "You don't find it extraordinary to have a stable that looks like a cathedral? I'd put an organ in it and play Bach to the horses all day."

"Probably give them strangles."

Morland's whooping laugh made Scarlett laugh, too; he sounded so comic. She filled a small bag with oats for him to feed Half Moon.

Walking beside Morland, Scarlett searched her mind for some way to interrupt his admiring chatter about her stables, something casual she could say to start him talking about Rhett.

There was no need. "I say, what luck for me that you're friends with Rhett Butler," Bart exclaimed. "If he hadn't introduced us, I'd never have gotten a look at those stables of yours."

"I was so surprised to run into him like that," Scarlett said quickly. "How do you happen to know him?"

He didn't really know Rhett at all, Bart replied. Some old friends had written to him a month ago, saying that they were sending Rhett to look at his horses. Then Rhett had arrived, bearing a letter of introduction from them. "He's a remarkable fellow, really serious about horses. Knows a lot, too. I wish he could have stayed longer. Are you old friends? He never quite got around to telling me."

Thank goodness, thought Scarlett. "I have some family in Charleston," she said. "I met him when I was visiting there."

"Then you must have met my friends the Brewtons! When I was at Cambridge I'd go down to London for the Season just in hopes that Sally Brewton might have come over. I was mad for her, just like everybody else."

"Sally Brewton! That monkey face?" Scarlett blurted before she thought.

Bart grinned. "The very same. Isn't she marvelous? She's such an original."

Scarlett nodded enthusiastically, and smiled. But in truth she'd never understand how men could be mad for anyone that ugly.

John Morland assumed that everyone who knew Sally must certainly adore her, and he talked about her for the next half hour while he leaned on the pasture fence and tried to entice Half Moon to come get the oats he held in his palm.

Scarlett half-listened while she thought her own thoughts. Then Rhett's name captured her full attention. Bart chuckled as he recounted the gossip Sally had included in her letter. Rhett had fallen into the oldest snare in history, it seemed. Some orphanage was having an outing at his country place, and one of the orphans turned up missing when it was time to leave. So what did he do but go off with the schoolteacher to search for it. All ended well, the child was found, but not until after dark. Which meant, of course, that the spinster teacher was compromised, and Rhett had to marry her.

The best part was that he'd been run out of town years before when he refused to make an honest woman out of another girl he'd been indiscreet with.

"You'd think he would have learned to be careful after the first time," Bart chortled. "He must be a lot more absentminded than he appears. Don't you find that hilarious, Scarlett? Scarlett?"

She gathered her wits. "Speaking as a female, I'd say it serves Mr. Butler right. He has the look of a man who's caused a lot of girls a lot of trouble when he wasn't being absentminded."

John Morland whooped with laughter. The sound attracted Half Moon, who approached the fence warily. Bart shook the bag of oats.

Scarlett was elated, and yet she felt like crying. So that was why Rhett had been so quick to divorce and remarry. What a sly boots Anne Hampton is. She had me fooled good and proper. Or maybe not. Maybe it was just wretched luck for me that it took so long to find the stray orphan. And that Anne is Miss Eleanor's special favorite. And that she looks so much like Melly.

Half Moon backed away from the oats. John Morland reached into a pocket of his jacket and found an apple. The horse nickered in anticipation.

"Look here, Scarlett," Bart said as he broke the apple. "I've got something a bit ticklish to talk to you about." He extended his open palm with one quarter of the apple on it for Half Moon.

"A bit ticklish!" If he only knew how ticklish his conversation had already been. Scarlett laughed. "I don't mind you spoiling that animal rotten, if that's what you mean," she said.

Heavens no! Bart's gray eyes widened. What could have put such a thought in her head?

It was something truly delicate, he explained. Alice Harrington— she was the stoutish one at the hunt who'd ended up in the ditch —was having a house party at Midsummer Night, and she wanted to invite Scarlett but didn't have the nerve. He'd been appointed diplomat to sound her out about it.

Scarlett had a hundred questions. Essentially they boiled down to when, where, and what to wear. Colum would be furious, she was sure, but she didn't care. She wanted to get dressed up and drink champagne and ride like the wind again over streams and fences following the hounds and the fox.

74

*H*arrington House was a huge block of a house made of Portland stone. It wasn't far from Ballyhara, just past a crossroads village named Pike Corner. The entrance was hard to find; there were no gates and no gatehouse, only a pair of unadorned and unmarked stone columns. The gravel drive skirted a broad lake then turned into a plain gravelled area in front of the stone house.

A footman came out of the front door at the sound of the buggy's wheels. He handed Scarlett down, then turned her over to a maid who was waiting in the hallway. "My name is Wilson, miss," she said with a curtsey. "Will you be wanting to rest a bit after your journey or will you be joining the others?" Scarlett chose to join the others, and the footman led her the length of the hall to an open door onto a lawn.

"Mrs. O'Hara!" shouted Alice Harrington. Now Scarlett remembered her vividly. "Ended up in a ditch" hadn't been much of a description, nor had "stout." Fat and loud would have identified Alice Harrington for her at once. She moved toward Scarlett with a surprisingly light step and bellowed that she was happy to see her. "I do hope you like croquet, I'm terrible, and my team would adore to lose me."

"I've never played," Scarlett said.

"All the better! You'll have beginner's luck." She held out her mallet. "Green stripes, it's perfect for you. You have such unusual eyes. Let me introduce everyone, then you can take my place and give my team a chance."

Alice's team—now Scarlett's—was made up of an elderly man in tweeds introduced as General Smyth-Burns, and a couple in their early twenties who both wore spectacles, Emma and Chizzie Fulwich. The General presented the opponents to her, Charlotte Montague, a tall, thin woman with beautifully dressed gray hair, Alice's cousin Desmond Grantley, who was as rotund as she, and an elegant pair named Genevieve and Ronald Bennet. "Watch out for Ronald," said Emma Fulwich, "he cheats."

The game was fun, Scarlett thought, and the scent of freshly mowed lawn was better than flowers. Her competitive instincts were at their full height before her third turn came around, and she earned a "Well done!" and a pat on the shoulder from the General when she whacked Ronald Bennet's ball far out onto the lawn.

When the game was over Alice Harrington halloed them an invitation to tea. The table was set up under a tremendous beech tree; its shade was welcome. So was the sight of John Morland. He was listening attentively to the young woman sitting beside him on the bench, but he waggled his fingers at Scarlett in greeting. The rest of the house party was there, too. Scarlett met Sir Francis Kinsman, a handsome rakehell type, and his wife, and she pretended convincingly that she remembered Alice's husband Henry, from the hunt at Bart's.

Bart's companion was clearly not pleased to be interrupted for introductions, but she was icily gracious. "This is Louisa Ferncliff," said Alice with determined cheerfulness. "She's an Honourable," Alice whispered to Scarlett.

Scarlett smiled, said, "How do you do," and let it go at that. She had a pretty good idea that the frosty young woman wouldn't take kindly to being called Louisa right off the bat, and surely you didn't call people Honourable. Especially when they looked like they hoped John Morland would suggest a little dishonorable kissing behind a bush.

Desmond Grantley held a chair for Scarlett and asked if she would permit him to bring her an assortment of sandwiches and cakes. Scarlett generously said she would. She looked at the circle of what Colum scornfully called "gentry" and thought again that he shouldn't be so pigheaded. These people were really very nice. She was sure she was going to have a good time.

Alice Harrington took Scarlett up to her bedroom after tea. It was a long way, through rather shabby reception rooms, up a wide staircase with a worn runner and along a broad hall with no rug at all. The room was big, but sparsely furnished, Scarlett thought, and the wallpaper was definitely faded. "Sarah has unpacked for you. She'll be up to do your bath and help you dress at seven, if that's all right. Dinner's at eight."

Scarlett assured Alice that the arrangements were fine.

"There's writing material in the desk, and some books on that table, but if you'd rather have something different—"

"Heavens no, Alice. Now don't let me take up your time, when you have guests and all." She snatched up a book at random. "I can hardly wait to read this. I've been wanting to for ages."

What she'd really been wanting was escape from Alice's incessant noisy recital of the virtues of her fat cousin Desmond. No wonder she was nervous about inviting me, Scarlett thought; she must know that Desmond's nothing to make a girl's heart beat faster. I guess she found out I'm a rich widow and she wants to help him get his licks in first, before anybody else finds out about me. Too bad, Alice, there's not a chance, not in a million years.

As soon as Alice was gone, the maid assigned to Scarlett tapped on the door and entered. She curtseyed, smiling eagerly. "Me name is Sarah," she said. "I'm honored to be dressing The O'Hara. When will the trunks be arriving, then?"

"Trunks? What trunks?" Scarlett asked.

The maid covered her mouth with her hand and moaned through her fingers.

"You'd better sit down," Scarlett said. "I have an idea I need to ask you a bunch of questions."

The girl was happy to oblige. Scarlett's heart grew heavier by the minute as she learned how much she didn't know.

The worst thing was there'd be no hunt. Hunting was for autumn and winter. The only reason Sir John Morland had arranged one was to show off his horses to his rich American guest.

Almost as bad was the news that ladies dressed for breakfast, changed for lunch, changed for afternoon, changed for dinner, never wore the same thing twice. Scarlett had two daytime frocks, one dinner gown, and her riding habit. There was no point in sending to Ballyhara for any more, either. Mrs. Scanlon, the dressmaker, had gone without sleep to finish the things she had with her. All her clothes made new for the trip to America were hopelessly out of fashion.

"I think I'll leave first thing in the morning," said Scarlett.

"Oh, no," Sarah cried, "you mustn't do that, The O'Hara. What do you care what the others do? They're only Anglos."

Scarlett smiled at the girl. "So it's us against them, Sarah, is that what you're telling me? How did you know I was The O'Hara?"

"Everyone in County Meath knows about The O'Hara," said the girl proudly, "everyone Irish."

Scarlett smiled. She felt better already. "Now, Sarah," she said, "tell me all about the Anglos who are here." Scarlett was sure the servants in the house must know everything about everybody. They always did.

Sarah didn't disappoint her. When Scarlett went downstairs for dinner, she was armored against any snobbishness she might meet. She knew more about the other guests than their own mothers did.

Even so, she felt like a backwoods Cracker. And she was furious at John Morland. All he'd said was "light frocks in the daytime and something rather naked for dinner at night." The other women were gowned and jewelled like queens, she thought, and she'd left her pearls and her diamond earbobs at home. Also, she was sure that her gown fairly screamed aloud that a village dressmaker had made it.

She gritted her teeth and made up her mind that she was going to have a good time anyhow. Might as well, I'll never get invited any place else.

In fact there were many things she enjoyed. In addition to croquet, there was boating on the lake, plus contests shooting at targets with bow and arrows and a game called tennis, both of them quite the latest rage, she was told.

After dinner Saturday everyone rummaged through big boxes of costumes that had been brought to the drawing room. There was buffoonery and uninhibited laughter and a lack of self-consciousness that Scarlett envied. Henry Harrington draped Scarlett in a long-trained silk cloak glittering with tinsel and put a crown of fake jewels on her head. "That makes you tonight's Titania," he said. Other men and women draped or clothed themselves from the boxes, shouting out who they were and racing through the big room in a free-for-all game of hiding behind chairs and chasing one another.

"I know it's all very silly," John Morland said apologetically through a huge papier-mâché lion's head. "But it is Midsummer Night, we're all allowed to go a bit mad."

"I'm mighty put out with you, Bart," Scarlett told him. "You're no help to a lady at all. Why didn't you tell me I needed dozens of dresses?"

"Oh, Lord, do you? I never notice what ladies have on. I don't understand why they fuss so."

By the time everyone tired of the game they were playing, the long, long Irish twilight was done.

"It's dark," Alice shouted. "Let's go look at the fires."

Scarlett felt a wave of guilt. She should be at Ballyhara. Midsummer

Night was almost as important as Saint Brigid's Day in farming tradition. Bonfires marked the turning point in the year, its shortest night, and gave mystical protection for the cattle and the crops.

When the house party went out onto the dark lawn they could see the glow of a distant fire, hear the sound of an Irish reel. Scarlett knew she should be at Ballyhara. The O'Hara should be at the bonfire ceremony. And there, too, when the sun rose and the cattle were run through the dying coals of the fire. Colum had told her she shouldn't go to an Anglo house party. Whether she believed in them or not, the ancient traditions were important to the Irish. She'd gotten angry with him. Superstitions couldn't run her life. But now she suspected she was wrong.

"Why aren't you at the Ballyhara fire?" asked Bart.

"Why aren't you at yours?" Scarlett snapped angrily.

"Because I'm not wanted there," said John Morland. His voice in the darkness sounded very sad. "I did go once. I thought there might be one of those folk wisdom things behind running the cattle through the ashes. Good for the hooves or something. I wanted to try it on the horses."

"Did it work?"

"I never found out. All the joy went out of the celebration when I arrived, so I left."

"I should have left here," Scarlett blurted.

"What an absurd thing to say. You're the only real person here. An American, too. You're the exotic bloom in the patch of weeds, Scarlett."

She hadn't thought of it that way. It made sense, too. People always made much over guests from far away. She felt much better, until she heard The Honourable Louisa say, "Aren't they entertaining? I do adore the Irish when they go all pagan and primitive like this. If only they weren't so lazy and stupid, I wouldn't mind living in Ireland."

Scarlett vowed silently to apologize to Colum the minute she got back home. She should never have left her own place and her own people.

"And hasn't any other living soul ever made a mistake, Scarlett darling? You had to learn the way of them for yourself else how would you know? Dry your eyes, now, and ride out to see the fields. The hired lads have started building the haycocks."

Scarlett kissed her cousin's cheek. He hadn't said, "I told you so."

In the weeks that followed, Scarlett was invited to two more house parties, by people she had met at Alice Harrington's. She wrote stilted, proper refusals for both. When the haycocks were finished she had the hired lads start working on the ruined lawn behind the house. It could be back in good grass by next summer, and Cat would love to play croquet. That part had been fun.

The wheat was ripe yellow, almost ready to harvest, when a rider brought a note to her and invited himself into the kitchen for a cup of tea "or something more manly" while he waited for her to write a reply for him to take back.

Charlotte Montague would like to call on her if it was convenient.

Who on earth was Charlotte Montague? Scarlett had to rack her brain for nearly ten minutes before she recalled the pleasant, unobtrusive older woman at the Harringtons'. Mrs. Montague, she remembered, had not raced around like a wild Indian on Midsummer Night. She'd sort of disappeared after dinner. Not that it made her any less English.

But what could she want? Scarlett's curiosity was piqued. The note said "a matter of considerable interest to us both."

She went to the kitchen herself to give Mrs. Montague's messenger the note inviting her to tea that afternoon. She knew she was trespassing on Mrs. Fitz's territory. The kitchen was supposed to be viewed only from the bridge-like gallery above. But it was her kitchen, wasn't it? And Cat had started spending hours there every day, why couldn't she?

Scarlett nearly put on her pink frock for Mrs. Montague's call. It was cooler than her Galway skirts and the afternoon was very warm, for Ireland. Then she put it back in the wardrobe. She wouldn't pretend to be what she was not.

She ordered barm brack for tea instead of the scones she usually had.

Charlotte Montague was wearing a gray linen jacket and skirt with a lace jabot that Scarlett's fingers itched to touch. She'd never seen lace so thick and elaborate.

The older woman took off her gray kid gloves and gray feathered hat before she sat in the plush-covered chair next to the tea table.

"Thank you for receiving me, Mrs. O'Hara. I doubt that you want to waste time talking about the weather; you'd prefer to know why I'm here, is that correct?" Mrs. Montague had an interesting wryness in her voice and her smile.

"I've been dying of curiosity," said Scarlett. She liked this beginning.

"I have learned that you're a successful businesswoman, both here and in America ... Don't be alarmed. What I know, I keep to myself; it's one of my most valuable assets. Another, as you can imagine, is that I have means of learning things that others do not. I'm a businesswoman, too. I would like to tell you about my business, if I may."

Scarlett could only nod dumbly. What did this woman know about her? And how?

To put it at its most basic level, she arranged things, said Mrs. Montague. She was born the youngest daughter of a younger son of a good family, and she had married a younger son of another. Even before he died in a hunting accident she had grown tired of being always on the edge of things, always trying to keep up appearances and lead the life expected of well-bred ladies and gentlemen, always in need of money. After she was widowed she found herself in the position of poor relation, a position that was intolerable.

What she had was intelligence, education, taste, and entrée to all the best houses in Ireland. She built on them, adding discretion and information to the attributes she began with.

"I am—in a manner of speaking—a professional houseguest and friend. I give generously of advice—in clothing, in entertaining, in decorating houses, in arranging marriages or assignations. And I am paid generous commissions by dressmakers and tailors, bootmakers and jewelers, furniture dealers and rug merchants. I am skillful and tactful, and it is doubtful that anyone suspects that I am being paid. Even if they do suspect, either they don't want to know or they are so satisfied with the outcome that they don't care, particularly since it costs them nothing."

Scarlett was shocked and fascinated. Why was the woman confessing all of this, to her of all people?

"I'm telling you this because I am sure you're no fool, Mrs. O'Hara. You would wonder—and rightly—if I offered to help you, as the saying goes, out of the goodness of my heart. There is no goodness in my heart, except insofar as it adds to my personal well-being. I have a business proposal for you. You deserve better than a shabby little party given by a shabby little woman like Alice Harrington. You have beauty and brains and money. You can be an original. If you put yourself in my hands, under my tutelage, I will make you the most admired, the most sought-after woman in Ireland. It will take two to three years. Then the whole world will be open to you, to do with as you will. You will be famous. And I will have enough money to retire in luxury."

Mrs. Montague smiled. "I've been waiting nearly twenty years for someone like you to come along."

75

Scarlett hurried across the kitchen bridge to Mrs. Fitzpatrick's rooms as soon as Charlotte Montague left. She didn't care that she was supposed to send for the housekeeper to come to her; she had to talk to someone.

Mrs. Fitz came out of her room before Scarlett could knock on the door. "You should have sent for me, Mrs. O'Hara," she said in a low voice.

"I know, I know, but it takes so long, and what I have to tell you just won't wait!" Scarlett was extremely agitated.

Mrs. Fitzpatrick's cold look calmed her down rapidly. "It will have to wait," she said. "The kitchen maids will hear every word you say and repeat it with embellishments. Walk slowly with me, and follow my lead."

Scarlett felt like a chastised child. She did as she was told.

Halfway across the gallery above the kitchen Mrs. Fitzpatrick stopped. Scarlett stopped with her and contained her impatience while Mrs. Fitz talked about improvements that had been made in the kitchen. The wide balustrade was plenty big enough to sit on, Scarlett thought idly, but she stood as erect as Mrs. Fitz, looking down at the kitchen and the exceedingly busy-looking maids far below.

Mrs. Fitzpatrick's progress was stately, but she did move. When they reached the house, Scarlett started talking as soon as the door to the bridge closed behind them.

"Of course it's ridiculous," she said after she reported what Mrs. Montague had said. "I told her so, too. 'I'm Irish,' I said, 'I don't want to be sought after by the English.' " Scarlett was talking very fast, and her color was high.

"Quite right you were, too, Mrs. O. The woman's no better than a thief, by the words out of her own mouth."

Mrs. Fitzpatrick's vehemence silenced Scarlett. She didn't repeat Mrs. Montague's response. "Your Irishness is one of the intriguing things about you. Striped stockings and boiled potatoes one day, partridge and silks the next. You can have both; it will only add to your legend. Write to me when you decide."

Rosaleen Fitzpatrick's account of Scarlett's visitor infuriated Colum. "Why did Scarlett even let her in the door?" he raged.

Rosaleen tried to calm him. "She's lonely, Colum. No friends save you and me. A child is all the world to its mother, but not much company. I'm thinking some fancy socializing might be good for her. And for us, if you put your mind on it. Kennedy's Inn is nearly finished. We'll have men coming and going soon. What better than to have other comings and goings to distract the eyes of the English?

"I took this Montague woman's measure at a glance. She's a cold, greedy sort. Mark my words, the first thing she will do is tell Scarlett that the Big House must be furnished and furbished. This Montague will play games with the cost of everything, but Scarlett can well afford it. And there will be strangers coming through Trim to Ballyhara every day of the year with their paints and velvets and French fashions. No one will pay heed to one or two more travelling this way.

"There's wonder already about the pretty American widow. Why isn't she looking for a husband? I say we'll do better to send her out to the English at their parties. Otherwise, the English officers may start coming here to court her."

Colum promised to "put his mind on it." He went out that night and walked for miles, trying to decide what was best for Scarlett, what was best for the Brotherhood, how they could be reconciled.

He'd been so worried of late that he didn't always think clearly. There had been reports of some men losing their commitment to the Fenian movement. Good harvests for two years in a row were making men comfortable, and comfort made it harder to risk everything. Also, Fenians who had infiltrated the constabulary were hearing rumors about an informer in the Brotherhood. Underground groups were perpetually in danger from informants. Twice in the past an uprising had been destroyed by treachery. But this one had been so carefully, so slowly planned. Every precaution taken. Nothing left to chance. It mustn't go wrong now. They were so close. The highest councils had planned to give the signal for action in the coming winter, when three-fourths of the English militia would be away from their garrisons for fox hunting. Instead the word had come down: delay until the informer is identified and disposed of. The waiting was eating away at him.

When the sunrise came, he walked through the rose-tinted ground mist to the Big House, let himself in with a key, and went to Rosaleen's room. "I believe you're right," he told her. "Does that earn me a cup of tea?"

Mrs. Fitzpatrick made a graceful apology to Scarlett later that day, admitting that she had been too hasty and too prejudiced. She urged Scarlett to start creating a social life for herself with Charlotte Montague's help.

"I've decided it's a silly idea," Scarlett replied. "I'm too busy."

When Rosaleen told Colum, he laughed. She slammed the door when she left his house.

Harvest, Harvest Home celebration, golden autumn days, golden leaves beginning to fall. Scarlett rejoiced in the rich crops, mourned the end of the growing year. September was the time for the half-yearly rents, and she knew her tenants would have profit left over. It was a grand thing, being The O'Hara.

She gave a big party for Cat's second birthday. All the Ballyhara children ten and under played in the big empty rooms on the ground floor, tasted ice cream for probably the first time, ate barm brack with tiny favors baked in it as well as currants and raisins. Every one of them went home with a shiny coin. Scarlett made sure they went home early because of all the superstitions about Halloween. Then she took Cat upstairs for her nap.

"Did you like your birthday, darling?"

Cat smiled drowsily. "Yes. Sleepy, Momma."

"I know you are, angel. It's way past your nap time. Come on . . . into bed . . . you can nap in Momma's big bed because this is a big birthday."

Cat sat up as soon as Scarlett laid her down. "Where's Cat's present?"

"I'll get it, darling." Scarlett brought the big china dollbaby from its box where Cat had left it.

Cat shook her head. "The other one." She turned on her stomach and slid down under the eiderdown to the floor, landing with a thump. Then she crawled under the bed. She backed out with a yellow tabby cat in her arms.

"For pity's sake, Cat, where did that come from? Give it to me before it scratches you."

"Will you give it back?"

"Of course, if you want it. But it's a barn cat, baby, it might not want to stay in the house."

"It likes me."

Scarlett gave in. The cat hadn't scratched Cat, and she looked so happy with it. What harm could it possibly do to let her keep it? She put the two of them in her bed. I'll probably end up sleeping with a hundred fleas, but a birthday is a birthday.

Cat nestled into the pillows. Her drooping eyes opened suddenly. "When Annie brings my milk," she said, "my friend can drink mine." Her green eyes closed and she went limp with sleep.

Annie tapped on the door, came in with a cup of warm milk. She told them when she got back to the kitchen that Mrs. O'Hara had laughed and laughed, she couldn't think why. She'd said something about cats and milk. If anybody wanted to know what she thought, said Mary Moran, she thought it would be a lot more seemly for that baby to have a decent Christian name, may the saints protect her. All three maids and the cook crossed themselves three times.

Mrs. Fitzpatrick saw and heard from the bridge. She crossed herself, too, and said a silent prayer. Cat would soon be too big to keep protected all the time. People were afraid of fairy changelings, and what people feared, they tried to destroy.

Down in Ballyhara town, mothers were scrubbing their children with water in which angelica root had steeped all day. It was a known protection against witches and spirits.

The horn did it. Scarlett was exercising Half Moon when both of them heard the horn and then the hounds. Somewhere close by in the countryside people were hunting. For all she knew, Rhett might even be with them. She put Half Moon over three ditches and four hedges on Ballyhara, but it wasn't the same. She wrote to Charlotte Montague the next day.

Two weeks later three wagons rolled heavily up the drive. The furniture for Mrs. Montague's rooms had arrived. The lady followed in a smart carriage, along with her maid.

She directed the disposition of the furniture in a bedroom and sitting room near Scarlett's, then left her maid to see to her unpacking. "Now we begin," she said to Scarlett.

"I might just as well not be here at all," Scarlett complained. "The only thing I'm allowed to do is sign bank drafts for scandalous amounts of money." She was talking to Ocras, Cat's tabby. The name meant "hungry" in Irish and had been given by the cook in an exasperated moment. Ocras ignored Scarlett, but she had no one else to talk to. Charlotte Montague and Mrs. Fitzpatrick seldom asked her opinion about anything. Both of them knew what a Big House should be, and she didn't.

Nor was she very interested. For most of her life the house she lived in had simply been there, already as it was, and she'd never thought about it. Tara was Tara, Aunt Pittypat's was Aunt Pitty's, even though half of it belonged to her. Scarlett had involved herself only with the house Rhett built for her. She'd bought the newest and most expensive furnishings and decorations, and she'd been pleased with them because they proved how rich she was. The house itself never gave her pleasure; she hardly saw it. Just as she didn't really see the Big House at Ballyhara. Eighteenth-century Palladian, Charlotte said, and what, pray tell, was so important about that? What mattered to Scarlett was the land, for its richness and its crops, and the town, for its rents and services and because no one, not even Rhett, owned his own town.

However, she understood perfectly well that accepting invitations placed an obligation on her to return them, and she couldn't invite people to a place that had furniture in only two rooms. She was lucky, she supposed, that Charlotte Montague wanted to transform the Big House for her. She had more interesting things to do with her time.

Scarlett was firm about the points that mattered to her: Cat must have a room next to her own, not in some nursery wing with a nanny; and Scarlett would do her own accounts, not turn all her business over to a bailiff. Other than that, Charlotte and Mrs. Fitz could do whatever they liked. The costs made her wince, but she had agreed to give Charlotte a free hand and it was too late to back out once she'd shaken hands on it. Besides, money just didn't matter to her now the way it used to.

So Scarlett took refuge in the Estate office and Cat made the kitchen her own while workmen did unknown, expensive, noisy, smelly things to her house for months on end. At least she had the farm to run, and her duties as The O'Hara. Also she was buying horses.

"I know little or nothing about horses," said Charlotte Montague. It was a statement that made Scarlett's eyebrows skid upwards. She'd come to believe that there was nothing on earth Charlotte didn't claim to be an expert on. "You'll need at least four saddle horses and six hunters, eight would be better, and you must ask Sir John Morland to assist you in selecting them."

"Six hunters! God's nightgown, Charlotte, you're talking about more than five hundred pounds!" Scarlett shouted. "You're crazy." She brought her voice down to normal sound, she'd learned that shouting at Mrs. Montague was a waste of energy; nothing bothered the woman. "I'll educate you a little about horses," she said with venomous sweetness. "You can only ride one. Teams are for carriages and plows."

She lost the argument. As usual. That was why she didn't bother to argue about John Morland's help, she told herself. But Scarlett knew that really she had been hoping to have a reason to see Bart. He might have some news of Rhett. She rode over to Dunsany the next day. Morland was delighted by her request. Of course he'd help her find the best hunters in all Ireland . . .

"Do you ever hear from your American friend, Bart?" She hoped the question sounded casual, she'd waited long enough to get it in. John Morland could talk about horses even longer than Pa and Beatrice Tarleton.

"Rhett, do you mean?" Scarlett's heart turned over at the sound of his name. "Yes, he's much more responsible about his correspondence than I am." John gestured towards the untidy pile of letters and bills on his desk.

Would the man just get on with it? What about Rhett?

Bart shrugged, turned his back to the desk. "He's determined to enter the filly he bought from me in the Charleston races. I told him she was bred for hurdles and not for the flat, but he's sure her speed will compensate. I'm afraid he's going to be disappointed. In another three or four years, perhaps he might prove right, but when you remember that her dam was out of . . ."

Scarlett stopped listening. John Morland would talk bloodlines all the way back to the Flood! Why couldn't he tell her what she wanted to know? Was Rhett happy? Had he mentioned her?

She looked at the young Baronet's animated, intense face and forgave him. In his own eccentric way, he was one of the most charming men in the world.

John Morland's life was built around horses. He was a conscientious landlord, interested in his estate and his tenants. But breeding and training race horses was his true passion, followed closely by fox hunting in the winter on the magnificent hunters he kept for himself.

Possibly they compensated for the romantic tragedy of Bart's absolute devotion to the woman who had gained possession of his heart when they were both not much more than children. Her name was Grace Hastings. She'd been married to Julian Hastings for nearly twenty years. John Morland and Scarlett shared a bond of hopeless love.

Charlotte had told her what "everyone in Ireland" knew—John was relatively immune to husband-hunting women because he had little money. His title and his property were old—impressively old—but he had no income except his rents, and he spent almost every shilling of that on his horses. Even so, he was very handsome in an absentminded way, tall and fair with warm, interested gray eyes and a breathtakingly sweet smile that accurately reflected his goodhearted nature. He was strangely innocent for a man who had spent all of his forty-some years in the worldly circles of British society. Occasionally a woman with money of her own, like the Honourable Louisa, fell in love with him and made a determined pursuit that embarrassed Morland and amused everyone else. His eccentricities became more pronounced then; his absentmindedness bordered on vacancy, his waistcoats were often buttoned wrong, his contagious whooping laughter became sometimes inappropriate, and he rearranged his collection of paintings by George Stubbs so often that the walls of his house became peppered with holes.

A beautiful portrait of the famous horse Eclipse was balanced perilously on a stack of books, Scarlett noticed. It made no difference to her, she wanted to know about Rhett. I'll go ahead and ask, she decided. Bart won't remember anyhow. "Did Rhett say anything about me?"

Morland blinked, his mind on the filly's forebears. Then her question registered. "Oh, yes, he asked me if you might possibly sell Half Moon. He's thinking about starting up the Dunmore Hunt again. He wants me to keep my eye open for any more like Half Moon, too."

"He'll have to come back to buy them, I guess," Scarlett said, praying for affirmation. Bart's answer sunk her in despair.

"No, he'll have to trust me. His wife's expecting, you see, and he won't leave her side. But now that I'll be aiming you at the cream of the crop, I couldn't help Rhett anyhow. I'll write and tell him so as soon as I find the time."

Scarlett was so preoccupied with Bart's news that he had to shake her arm to get her attention. When did she want to start the search for her hunters, he asked.

Today, she answered.

Throughout the winter she went every Saturday with John Morland to one hunt or another in County Meath, trying out hunters that were for sale. It wasn't easy to find mounts that suited her, for she demanded that the horse be as fearless as she was. She rode as if demons were chasing her, and the riding eventually made it possible for her to stop imagining Rhett as father to any child but Cat.

When she was home, she tried to give the little girl extra attention and affection. As usual, Cat scorned embraces. But she would listen to stories about the horses for as long as Scarlett would talk.

When February came, Scarlett turned the first sod with the same happy excitement as in earlier years. She had succeeded in relegating Rhett to the past and seldom thought of him at all.

It was a new year, full of good things to come. If Charlotte and Mrs. Fitz ever got finished with whatever they were doing to her house, she might even be able to give a party. She missed Kathleen, and the rest of the family. Pegeen made visits so uncomfortable that she almost never saw her cousins any more.

That could wait, it would have to. There was planting to be done.

In June Scarlett spent a long, exhausting day being measured by the dressmaker Charlotte Montague had brought over from Dublin. Mrs. Sims was merciless. Scarlett had to hold her arms up, out, in front, at her sides, one up one down, one forward one back, in every imaginable position and some she would never have imagined. For what seemed like hours. Then the same thing sitting. Then in every position of the quadrille, the waltz, the cotillion. "The only thing she didn't measure me for was my shroud," Scarlett groaned.

Charlotte Montague gave one of her infrequent smiles. "She probably did, without your knowing it. Daisy Sims is very thorough."

"I refuse to believe that terrifying woman's name is Daisy," Scarlett said.

"Don't you ever call her that, unless she invites you to. No one below the rank of Duchess is ever allowed to be familiar with Daisy. She's the best at her trade; they wouldn't dare risk offending her."

"You called her Daisy."

"I'm the best at my trade, too."

Scarlett laughed. She liked Charlotte Montague, and respected her as well. Though she wouldn't call her exactly cozy to have for a friend.

She put on her peasant clothes then and had supper—Charlotte reminded her it was dinner—before she went out to the hill near Knightsbrook River for the lighting of the Midsummer Night bonfire. When she was dancing to the familiar music of the fiddles and pipes and Colum's *bodhran*, she thought how lucky she was. If what Charlotte had promised was true, she was going to have both worlds, Irish and Anglo. Poor Bart, she remembered, wasn't welcome at his own estate's bonfire.

Scarlett thought of her good fortune again, when she presided at the Harvest Home banquet. Ballyhara had another good crop, not as good as the two previous years, but still enough to make every man's pocket jingle.

Everyone in Ballyhara celebrated their good fortune. Everyone except Colum, Scarlett noticed. He looked as if he hadn't slept in a week. She wished she could ask him what was wrong, but he'd been cross as a bear with her for weeks. And he never seemed to go to the bar any more, according to Mrs. Fitz.

Well, she wasn't going to let his gloom ruin her good mood. Harvest Home was a party.

Also, the hunting season would be starting any day now, and her new riding habit was the most enchanting design Scarlett had ever seen. Mrs. Sims was everything Charlotte had said she was.

"If you're ready we will take a tour," said Charlotte Montague. Scarlett put down her teacup. She was more eager than she wanted to admit.

"Mighty kind of you, Charlotte, seeing as how every door except my rooms has been locked for practically a year." She sounded as cranky as she could, but she suspected that Charlotte was too smart to be fooled. "I'll just find Cat to go with us."

"If you like, Scarlett, but she saw everything as it was done. She's a remarkable child, just appears when a door or window is left open. It made some of the painters quite nervous when they found her on top of their scaffolding."

"Don't tell me things like that, I'll have a seizure. Little monkey, she climbs everything." Scarlett called for Cat and looked for Cat to no avail. Sometimes the little girl's independence annoyed her, like now. Usually she was proud. "I guess she'll catch up with us if she's interested," she said at last. "Let's go, I'm dying to see." Might as well admit it. She wasn't fooling anybody.

Charlotte led the way upstairs first to long corridors lined with bedrooms for guests, then back down again to what Scarlett still had trouble calling the first floor instead of, in American usage, the second. Charlotte took her to the end of the house away from the rooms she'd been using. "Your bedroom, your bath, your boudoir, your dressing room, Cat's playroom, bedroom, nursery." The doors flew open as Charlotte unveiled her labors. Scarlett was enchanted with the feminine pale-green-and-gilt furniture in her rooms and the frieze of alphabet animal paintings in Cat's playroom. The child-size chairs and tables made her clap her hands. Why hadn't she thought of it? There was even a child-size tea set on Cat's table and a child-size chair by the hearth.

"Your private rooms are French," said Charlotte, "Louis Sixteenth, if you care. They represent your Robillard self. Your O'Hara self dominates the reception rooms on the ground floor."

The only ground floor room that Scarlett knew was the marble-floored hall. She used its door to the drive and the broad stone staircase to the upper floors. Charlotte Montague led her quickly through it. She opened tall double doors on one side of it and ushered Scarlett into the dining room. "My stars," Scarlett exclaimed, "I don't know enough people to fill up all those chairs."

"You will," said Charlotte. She led Scarlett through the long room to another tall door. "Now this is your breakfast room and morning room. You may want to have dinner in here as well when you are a small number." She walked across the room to more doors. "The great salon and ballroom," she announced. "I admit to being very pleased with this."

One long wall was made up of widely spaced French doors with tall gilt mirrors between them. The wall opposite was centered by a fireplace surmounted by another gilt-framed mirror. All the mirrors were infinitesimally tilted so that they reflected not only the room but also the high ceiling. It was painted with scenes from the heroic legends of Irish history. The High Kings' buildings on the hill of Tara looked rather like Roman temples. Scarlett loved it.

"The furniture throughout this floor is Irish-made, so are the fabrics —all wools and linens—and the silver, china, glass, almost everything. This is where The O'Hara is hostess. Come, there's only the library still to see."

Scarlett liked the leather-covered chairs and Chesterfield, and she recognized that the leather-backed books were very handsome. "You've done a wonderful job, Charlotte," she said sincerely.

"Yes, well it wasn't as difficult as at first I feared. The people who lived here must have used a Capability Brown design for the gardens, so there was only pruning and cleaning to do. The kitchen garden will be very productive next year, though it may be two years before the wall fruits come back. They had to be pruned back to leaders."

Scarlett hadn't the remotest idea what Charlotte was talking about, nor the faintest interest. She was wishing Gerald O'Hara could see the ceiling in the ballroom and Ellen O'Hara could admire the furniture in her boudoir.

Charlotte opened more doors. "Here we are in the hall again," she said. "Excellent circular movement for large parties. The Georgian architects knew precisely what they were doing . . . Come through to the entrance door, Scarlett."

She escorted Scarlett onto the top of the steps that led down to the freshly gravelled drive. "Your staff, Mrs. O'Hara."

"My grief," Scarlett said weakly.

Two long rows of uniformed servants were facing her. To her right Mrs. Fitzpatrick stood slightly in front of the cook, four kitchen maids, two parlor maids, four upstairs maids, three dairymaids, the head laundress, and three laundry maids.

To her left she saw a haughty-looking man who could only be a butler, eight footmen, two nervous-footed boys, the stableman she knew and six grooms, and five men she guessed were gardeners by their earth-stained hands.

"I believe I need to sit down," she whispered.

"First you smile and welcome them to Ballyhara," Charlotte said. Her tone would permit no remonstrance. Scarlett did as she was told.

Back inside the house—which had now become an establishment—Scarlett began to giggle. "They're all better dressed than I am," she said. She looked at Charlotte Montague's expressionless face. "You're about to bust out laughing, Charlotte, you can't fool me. You and Mrs. Fitz must have had a high old time planning this."

"We did rather," Charlotte admitted. A smile was the nearest thing to "bust out laughing" that Scarlett could get from her.

Scarlett invited all the people from Ballyhara and Adamstown to come up to see the revived Big House. The long dining room table was spread with refreshments, and she darted from room to room, urging everyone to help themselves, dragging them to see the High Kings. Charlotte Montague stood quietly to one side of the big staircase, quietly disapproving. Scarlett ignored her. She tried to ignore the discomfort and embarrassment of her cousins and villagers, but within a half hour of their arrival, she was close to tears.

"It goes against tradition, Mrs. O," Rosaleen Fitzpatrick murmured to her, "it's naught to do with you. No farmer's boot has ever crossed the threshold of a Big House in Ireland. We're a people ruled by the old ways, and we're not ready for change."

"But I thought the Fenians wanted to change everything."

Mrs. Fitz sighed. "That is so. But the change is for a return to even older ways than the ones that keep the boots out of a Big House. I wish I could explain more clearly."

"Don't bother, Mrs. Fitz. I've just made a mistake, that's all. I won't do it again."

"It was the error of a generous heart. Take credit for that."

Scarlett forced a smile. But she was bewildered and upset. What was the point of having all these Irish-decorated rooms if the Irish didn't feel comfortable in them? And why did her own cousins treat her like a stranger in her own house?

After everyone left and the servants removed all traces of the party, Scarlett went from room to room alone.

Well, I like it, she decided. I like it a lot. It was, she thought, a damn sight prettier than Dunmore Landing would ever be, or ever was.

She stood in the midst of the reflected images of the High Kings and imagined Rhett there with her, full of envy and admiration. It would be years from now, when Cat was grown, and he would be heartsick that he had missed seeing his daughter grow up to become the beautiful heiress of the home of the O'Haras.

Scarlett ran to the stairs and up them and through the corridor to Cat's room. "Hello," said Cat. She was sitting at her little table, carefully pouring milk into a cup for her big tabby. Ocras was watching attentively from his commanding position in the center of the table. "Sit down, Momma," Cat invited. Scarlett lowered herself onto a small chair.

If only Rhett were there to join the tea party. But he wasn't, and he never would be, and she had to accept it. He would have tea parties with his other child, his other children—by Anne. Scarlett resisted the impulse to grab Cat in her arms. "I'd like two lumps of sugar, please, Miss O'Hara," she said.

That night Scarlett couldn't sleep. She sat upright in the center of her exquisite French bed with her silk-covered eiderdown wrapped closely around her for warmth. But the warmth and comfort she wanted was to feel Rhett's arms around her, to hear his deep voice mocking the disastrous party until she could laugh at it and at the error of giving it.

She wanted comfort for her disappointment. She wanted love, grown-up caring and understanding. Her heart had learned to love, it was over-flowing with love, and she had nowhere to spend it.

Damn Rhett for getting in the way! Why couldn't she love Bart Morland? He was kind, he was attractive, Scarlett enjoyed being with him. If she really wanted him, she didn't doubt for a minute that she could make him forget Grace Hastings.

But she didn't want him, that was the problem. She didn't want anybody except Rhett.

It's not fair! she thought, like a child. And, like a child, eventually she cried herself to sleep.

When she woke, she was in control of herself once more. So what if everyone had hated her party? So what if Colum hadn't stayed more than ten minutes? She had other friends, and she was going to make lots more. Now that the house was finally done, Charlotte was busy as a spider spinning a web with plans about the future. And in the meantime, the weather was perfect for hunting, and Mrs. Sims had made a tremendously becoming riding habit for her.

76

$\mathcal{S}$carlett rode to Sir John Morland's hunt in style. She was riding a saddle horse and was accompanied by two grooms leading Half Moon and Comet, one of her new hunters. The skirts of her new habit flowed elegantly over her new sidesaddle, and she was very pleased with herself. She had had to fight Mrs. Sims like a tiger, but she had won. No corsets. Charlotte had been amazed. No one, she said, ever argued with Daisy Sims and won. No one till me, maybe, Scarlett thought. I won the argument with Charlotte, too.

Bart Morland's hunt was no place for Scarlett to make her emergence into the world of Irish society, said Charlotte. He himself was beyond reproach and, except for his lack of money, one of the most eligible bachelors around. But he didn't keep a grand household at all. The footmen at his breakfasts were really stable grooms in livery for a few hours. Charlotte had secured a much more important invitation for Scarlett. It would do exactly what was needed to prepare for her real debut. Scarlett couldn't possibly go first to Morland Hall instead of Charlotte's selection.

"I can and I will," Scarlett said firmly. "Bart is my friend." She repeated it until Charlotte gave in. She didn't tell Charlotte the rest. She needed to go someplace where she felt at least a little bit comfortable. Now that it was getting close, the prospect of "Society" scared her even more than it enticed her. She kept thinking of what Mammy had said about her once: "Just a mule in horse's harness." As the Paris-inspired wardrobe from Mrs. Sims came into the house Scarlett thought of the saying more and more often. She could imagine hundreds of lords and ladies and earls and countesses whispering it when she went to her first important party.

"Bart, I'm glad to see you."

"I'm glad to see you, too, Scarlett. Half Moon is looking ready for a good run. Come along over here and have a stirrup cup with my special guest. I've been lion-hunting. I'm proud as Lucifer."

Scarlett smiled graciously at the young Member of Parliament for County Meath. He was very handsome, she thought, even though usually she didn't much like men who wore beards, even well-trimmed ones like this Mr. Parnell. She'd heard the name before—oh, yes, at Bart's breakfast. She remembered now. Colum really detested this Parnell. She'd have to pay attention so she could tell Colum all about him. After the hunt. For now Half Moon was eager to go and so was she.

"I can't for the life of me understand how you can be so stubborn, Colum." Scarlett had passed from enthusiasm to explanation to rage. "You've never even bothered to go hear the man speak, for pity's sake. Well, I heard him, he was fascinating, everybody was hanging on his every word. And he wants exactly what you always talked about—Ireland for the Irish, and no evictions, and even no rent and no landlords. What more can you ask?"

Colum's patience cracked. "I can ask that you not be such a trusting fool! Do you not know that your Mr. Parnell is a landlord himself? And a Protestant. And educated at the English Oxford University. He's looking for votes, not justice. The man's a politician, and his Home Rule policy, that you've swallowed for the sugar coating of his earnest manner and handsome face, is nothing more nor less than a stick for him to shake at the English and a carrot to tempt the poor ignorant Irish donkey."

"There's simply no talking to you! Why, he said right out that he supports the Fenians."

Colum grabbed Scarlett's arm. "Did you say anything?"

She jerked away from him. "Of course not. You take me for a fool and lecture me like I'm a fool, but I am not a fool. And I know this much. There's no reason to smuggle in guns and start a war if you can get what you want without it. I lived through a war that a bunch of hotheads started because of some high-faluting principles. All it did was kill most of my friends and ruin everything. For nothing. I'm telling you right now, Colum O'Hara, there's a way to get Ireland back for the Irish without killing and burning, and that's what I'm for. No more money for Stephen to buy guns with, do you hear? And no more guns hidden away in my town. I want them out of that church. I don't care what you do with them, sink them in the bog for all it matters to me. But I want to be rid of them. Right away."

"And rid of me as well, are you saying?"

"If you insist, then—" Scarlett's eyes filled with tears. "What am I saying? What are you saying? Oh, Colum, don't let this happen. You're my best friend, my almost brother. Please, please, please Colum, don't be so hardheaded. I don't want to fight." The tears spilled over.

Colum took her hand in his and held it very tight. "Ach, Scarlett darling, it's the Irish temper in the two of us talking, not Colum and Scarlett. The fearful pity of it, the two of us scowling and shouting. Forgive me, *aroon*."

"What does that mean, '*aroon*'?" she asked between sobs.

"It means 'darling' like Scarlett darling in English. In Irish you're my Scarlett *aroon*."

"That's pretty."

"All the better as a name for you, then."

"Colum, you're charming the birds from the trees again, but I'm not going to let you charm me into forgetting. Promise me you'll get rid of those guns. I'm not asking you to vote for Charles Parnell, just promise me you won't start a war."

"I promise you, Scarlett *aroon*."

"Thank you. I feel worlds better. Now I've got to go. Will you come up to the house for dinner in my fancy morning room though it's at night?"

"I cannot, Scarlett *aroon*. I'm meeting a friend."

"Bring him, too. With the cook fixing food for those nine million servants I've got all of a sudden, I'm sure there'll be enough to feed you and your friend."

"Not tonight. Another time."

Scarlett didn't press him, she had gotten what she wanted. Before she went home she detoured to the little chapel and made her confession to Father Flynn. Losing her temper with Colum was part of it, but not the main part. She was there to be absolved of the sin that made her own blood run cold. She had thanked God when John Morland told her that six months earlier Rhett's wife had lost her baby.

Not long after Scarlett left, Colum O'Hara entered the confessional. He had lied to her, a heavy sin. After doing his penance he went to the arsenal in the Anglican church to make sure the arms were sufficiently well concealed in the event she decided to investigate.

Charlotte Montague and Scarlett left for the house party that was Scarlett's debut after she went to early Mass on Sunday. The party was to last a week. Scarlett didn't like being away from Cat for so long, but the birthday party was only just over—Mrs. Fitz was still in a tight-lipped fury about the damage all the running children had done to the parquet in the ballroom—and she was certain that Cat wouldn't miss her. With all the new furnishings to inspect and new servants to investigate, Cat was a very busy little girl.

Scarlett, Charlotte, and Evans, Charlotte's maid, rode in Scarlett's elegant brougham to the train station in Trim. The house party was in County Monaghan, too far to go by road.

Scarlett was more excited than nervous. Going to John Morland's first had been a good idea. Charlotte was nervous enough for both of them, although it didn't show; Scarlett's future in the fashionable world would be decided by the way she impressed people this week. Charlotte's future, also. She glanced at Scarlett to reassure herself. Yes, she looked lovely in her green merino travelling costume. Those eyes of hers were a gift from God, so distinctive and memorable. And her slim uncorseted body was sure to set tongues wagging and the pulses of men racing. She looked precisely like what Charlotte had insinuated to chosen friends: a beautiful, not-too-young American widow with fresh Colonial looks and charm; somewhat gauche, but refreshing as a result; romantically Irish, as only a foreigner could be; substantially, perhaps even phenomenally wealthy, so much so that she could afford to be a free spirit; well bred, with an aristocratic French bloodline, but vigorous and exuberant from her American background; unpredictable but well-mannered, naive yet experienced; all in all an intriguing and amusing addition to the circles of people who knew too much about one another and were avid for someone new to talk about.

"Perhaps I should tell you again who is likely to be at the party," Charlotte suggested.

"Please don't, Charlotte, I'll forget again anyhow. Besides, I know the important part. A duke is more important than a marquess, then comes an earl, and after that viscount, baron, and baronet. I may call all the men 'sir' just like in the South, so I needn't worry about that 'milord' and 'your grace' business, but I must never call the ladies 'ma'am' the way we do in America, because that's reserved for Queen Victoria, and she's definitely not going to be there. So, unless I'm asked to use the Christian name, I just smile and avoid using anything. A plain old 'mister' or 'miss' is hardly worth bothering with at all unless they're 'honourable.' I do think that's funny. Why not 'respectable' or something else like that?"

Charlotte shuddered inside. Scarlett was too confident, too breezy. "You haven't paid attention, Scarlett. There are some names with no title at all, not even 'honourable,' that are equally as important as any non-royal dukes. The Herberts, Burkes, Clarkes, Lefroys, Blennerhassetts—"

Scarlett giggled. Charlotte stopped. What would be, would be.

The house was an immense Gothic-style structure with turrets and towers, stained-glass windows as tall as a cathedral's, corridors that extended for more than a hundred yards. Scarlett's confidence ebbed when she saw it. "You're The O'Hara," she reminded herself and she marched up the stone entrance steps with her chin at an angle that dared anyone to challenge her.

By the end of dinner that night she was smiling at everyone, even the footman behind her tall-backed chair. The food was excellent, copious, exquisitely presented, but Scarlett barely tasted it. She was feasting on admiration. There were forty-six guests in the house party, and they all wanted to know her.

"... and on New Year's Day, I have to knock on every single door in the town, go in, go out, go in again and drink a cup of tea. I declare, I don't know why I don't turn yellow as a Chinaman, drinking half the tea in China the way I do," she said gaily to the man on her left. He was fascinated by the duties of The O'Hara.

When the hostess "turned" the table, Scarlett enchanted the retired general on her right with a day-by-day account of the siege of Atlanta. Her Southern accent was not at all what one expected an American to sound like, they reported later to anyone who'd listen, and she's a damn'd intelligent woman.

She was also a "damn'd attractive woman." The excessively big diamond-and-emerald engagement ring she'd received from Rhett sparkled impressively on her bare-but-not-too-bare bosom. Charlotte had ordered it remade into a pendant that hung from a white gold chain so fine that it was nearly invisible.

After dinner Scarlett played whist with her customary skill. Her partner won enough money to cover her losses at three previous house parties, and Scarlett became a sought-after companion among ladies as well as gentlemen.

The following morning, and for five mornings after, there was a hunt.

Even on a mount from her host's stables Scarlett was adept and fearless. Her success was assured. The Anglo-Irish gentry as a whole admired nothing quite as much as they did a fine rider.

Charlotte Montague had to be vigilant, or she'd be caught looking like a cat who'd just finished a bowl of thick cream.

"Did you enjoy yourself?" she asked Scarlett on the way back to Ballyhara.

"Every minute, Charlotte! Bless you for getting me invited. Everything was perfect. It's so thoughtful having those sandwiches in the bedroom. I always get hungry late at night, I guess everybody does."

Charlotte laughed until her eyes were streaming with tears. It made Scarlett huffy. "I don't see what's so funny about a healthy appetite. With the card game lasting until all hours, it's a long time after dinner when you go to bed."

When Charlotte could speak, she explained. At the more sophisticated houses the ladies' bedrooms were supplied with a plate of sandwiches that could be used as a signal to admirers. Set on the floor of the corridor outside a lady's room, the sandwiches were an invitation for a man to come in.

Scarlett blushed crimson. "My grief, Charlotte, I ate every crumb. What must the maids think?"

"Not just the maids, Scarlett. Everyone in the house party must be wondering who the fortunate man was. Or men. Naturally no gentleman would claim the title, or he wouldn't be a gentleman."

"I'll never be able to look anyone in the face again. That's the most scandalous thing I ever heard. It's disgusting! And I thought they were all such nice people."

"But my dear child, it's precisely the nice people who devise these discretions. Everyone knows the rules, and no one refers to them. People's amusements are their own secrets, unless they choose to tell."

Scarlett was about to say that where she came from people were honest and decent. Then she remembered Sally Brewton in Charleston. Sally had talked the same way, all about "discretion" and "amusements" as if infidelity and promiscuity were a normal, accepted thing.

Charlotte Montague smiled complacently. If any one thing had been needed to create a legend for Scarlett O'Hara, the mistake about the sandwiches had accomplished it. Now she'd be known as refreshingly Colonial, but satisfactorily sophisticated.

Charlotte began to make preliminary schedules in her mind for her retirement. Only a few more months to go, and she'd never again suffer through boredom at a fashionable party of any kind.

"I shall arrange for delivery of the *Irish Times* every day," she said to Scarlett, "and you must study every word in it. Everyone you will meet in Dublin will expect you to be familiar with the news it reports."

"Dublin? You didn't tell me we were going to Dublin."

"Didn't I? I thought surely I had. I do apologize, Scarlett. Dublin is the center of everything, you will love it. It's a real city, not an overgrown country town like Drogheda or Galway. And the Castle is the most thrilling thing you will ever experience in your entire life."

"A Castle? Not a ruin? I didn't know there was such a thing. Does the Queen live there?"

"No, thank heaven. The Queen is a fine ruler but an extremely dull woman. No, the Castle in Dublin is ruled by Her Majesty's representative, the Viceroy. You will be presented to him and to the Vicereine in the Throne Room ..." Mrs. Montague painted a word picture for Scarlett of pomp and splendor beyond anything she'd ever heard of. It made Charleston's Saint Cecilia sound like nothing at all. And it made Scarlett want success in Dublin society with all her heart. That would put Rhett Butler in his place. He wouldn't be important to her at all.

It was safe to tell her now, Charlotte thought. After this week's success the invitation will surely come. There's no longer a chance that I'll lose the deposit on the suite at the Shelbourne that I booked for the Season when I got Scarlett's note last year.

"Where's my precious Cat?" Scarlett called when she ran into the house. "Momma's home, sweetheart." She found Cat, after a half hour's search, in the stables sitting atop Half Moon. She looked frighteningly small on the big horse. Scarlett muted her voice, so that she wouldn't spook Half Moon. "Come to Momma, darling, and give me a hug." Her heart thumped out of rhythm while she watched her child jump down into the straw near the powerful, metal-shod hooves. Cat was out of Scarlett's sight until her small dark face popped up over the half door to the stall. She was climbing it, not opening it. Scarlett knelt to catch her in an embrace. "Oh, I'm so happy to see you, angel. I missed you a lot. Did you miss me?"

"Yes." Cat wriggled out of her arms. Well, at least she missed me, she's never said that before. Scarlett stood up when the warm surge of love for Cat subsided into the total devotion that was her habitual emotion.

"I didn't know you liked horses, Kitty Cat."

"I do. I like animals."

Scarlett forced herself to sound cheerful. "Would you like to have a pony of your own? The right size for a little girl?" I won't let myself think of Bonnie, I won't. I promised that I wouldn't hobble Cat or wrap her in cottonwool because I lost Bonnie in the accident. I promised Cat when she was fresh born that I'd let her be whoever she turned out to be, that I'd give her all the freedom a free spirit needs to have. I didn't know it would be so hard, that I'd want to protect her every single minute. But I've got to keep my promise. I know it was right. She'll have a pony if she wants one, and she'll learn to jump, and I'll make myself watch if it kills me. I love Cat too much to hem her in.

Scarlett had no way of knowing that Cat had walked down to Bally-hara town while she was away. Three now, Cat was becoming interested in other children and games. She went looking for some of the playmates who'd been at her birthday party. A group of four or five little boys were playing in the wide street. When she walked toward them, they ran away. Two stopped long enough to scoop up rocks and throw them at her. "*Cailleach! Cailleach!*" they screamed in terror. They'd learned the word from their mothers, the Gaelic for witch.

Cat looked up at her mother. "Yes, I'd like a pony," she said. Ponies didn't throw things. She considered telling her mother about the boys, asking her about the word. Cat liked to learn new words. But she didn't like that word. She wouldn't ask. "I'd like a pony today."

"I can't find a pony today, baby. I'll start looking tomorrow. I promise. Let's go home now and have tea."

"With cakes?"

"Definitely with cakes."

Up in their rooms Scarlett got out of her beautiful travelling suit as quickly as she could. She felt an undefined need to wear her shirt and skirt and bright peasant stockings.

By mid-December Scarlett was pacing the long hallways of the Big House like a caged animal. She had forgotten how much she hated the dark, short, wet days of winter. She thought about going down to Kennedy's several times, but ever since her unfortunate party for all the townspeople, she no longer felt as easy with them as once she had. She rode a little bit. It wasn't necessary, the grooms kept all the horses exercised. But she needed to be out, even in the ice-filled rain. When there were a few hours of sun she watched while Cat rode her Shetland pony in great joyful loops across the frozen meadow. Scarlett knew it was bad for next summer's grass, but Cat was as restless as she was. It was all Scarlett could do to persuade her to stay indoors, even in the kitchen or the stables.

On Christmas Eve Cat lit the Christ Child candle and then all the candles she could reach on the Christmas tree. Colum held her up to reach the higher ones. "Outlandish English custom," he said. "You'll probably burn your house to the ground."

Scarlett looked at the bright decorations and glowing candles on the tree. "I think it's very pretty even if the Queen of England did start the fashion," she said. "Besides, I've got holly over all the windows and doors, too, Colum, so it's Irish everywhere in Ballyhara except this room. Don't be such a grumpy."

Colum laughed. "Cat O'Hara, did you know your godfather was a grumpy?"

"Today yes," said Cat.

This time Colum's laugh wasn't forced. "Out of the mouths of babes," he said. "It's my fault for asking."

He helped Scarlett bring out Cat's present after she fell asleep. It was a full-size stuffed toy pony on rockers.

On Christmas morning Cat looked at it with scorn. "It's not real."

"It's a toy, darling, for indoors in this nasty weather."

Cat climbed on it and rocked. She conceded that for a pony that wasn't real it was not a bad toy.

Scarlett breathed a sigh of relief. She wouldn't feel quite so guilty now when she went to Dublin. She was to meet Charlotte at the Gresham Hotel there the day after New Year's barm brack and tea.

$\mathcal{S}$carlett had no idea Dublin was so near. It seemed she was barely settled in the train at Trim before Dublin was announced. Evans, Charlotte Montague's maid, met her and directed a porter to take her cases. Then, "Follow me, if you please, Mrs. O'Hara," Evans said, and walked off. Scarlett had trouble keeping up with her because of the hurrying crowds in the station. It was the biggest building Scarlett had ever seen, and the busiest.

But nothing like as busy as Dublin's streets. Scarlett pressed her nose to the window of the hackney in her excitement. Charlotte was right, she was going to love Dublin.

All too soon the hackney stopped. Scarlett stepped down, helped by a lavishly uniformed attendant. She was staring at a passing horse-drawn tram when Evans touched her arm. "This way, please."

Charlotte was waiting for her behind a tea table in the sitting room of their suite of rooms. "Charlotte!" Scarlett exclaimed, "I saw a streetcar with an upstairs and a downstairs, and both of them packed full."

"Good afternoon to you, too, Scarlett. I'm pleased that Dublin pleases you. Give Evans your wraps and come and have tea. We have a great deal to do."

That evening Mrs. Sims arrived with three assistants carrying muslin-wrapped gowns and dresses. Scarlett stood and moved as ordered while Mrs. Sims and Mrs. Montague discussed every detail of every garment. Each evening gown was more elegant than the one that preceded it. Scarlett preened before the pier glass when she wasn't being prodded and pinched by Mrs. Sims.

When the dressmaker and her woman left Scarlett discovered suddenly that she was exhausted. She was happy to agree when Charlotte suggested they dine in the suite, and she ate ravenously.

"Do not gain so much as a millimeter around the middle, Scarlett, or you'll have to be fitted all over again," Charlotte warned.

"I'll run it all off shopping," Scarlett said. She buttered another piece of bread. "I saw at least eight shop windows that looked wonderful on the drive from the station."

Charlotte smiled indulgently. She'd receive a very welcome commission from every shop Scarlett patronized. "You'll have all the shopping your heart desires, I can promise you that. But only in the afternoons. In the mornings, you'll be sitting for your portrait."

"That's nonsense, Charlotte. What do I want with a portrait of myself? I had one done once, and I hated it. I looked mean as a snake."

"You will not look mean in this one, take my word. Monsieur Hervé is an expert at ladies. And the portrait is important. It must be done."

"I'll do it, because I do everything you say, but I won't like it, take my word."

The next morning Scarlett was awakened by the sound of traffic. It was still dark, but street lamps showed her four lines of wagons and drays and carriages of every description moving along the street below her bedroom window. No wonder Dublin has such wide streets, she thought happily, almost everything in Ireland with wheels on it is here. She sniffed, sniffed again. I must be going crazy. I could swear I smell coffee.

Fingers tapped gently on her door. "Breakfast is in the sitting room when you're ready," said Charlotte. "I've sent the waiter away, all you need is a wrapper."

Scarlett nearly knocked Mrs. Montague down opening the door. "Coffee! If you knew how much I've missed coffee. Oh, Charlotte, why didn't you tell me they drink coffee in Dublin? I'd have taken the train every morning just for breakfast."

The coffee tasted even better than it smelled. Luckily Charlotte preferred tea, because Scarlett drank the entire pot.

Then she obediently put on the silk stockings and combinations Charlotte unpacked from a box. She felt quite wicked. The light slippery undergarments were altogether different from the batiste or muslin she'd worn all her life. She tied her wool dressing gown tightly around her when Evans came in with a woman she'd never seen before. "This is Serafina," said Charlotte. "She's Italian, so don't be concerned if you don't understand a word she says. She's going to do your hair. All you have to do is sit still and let her talk to herself."

She's having a one-way conversation with every hair on my head, thought Scarlett after nearly an hour. Her neck was getting stiff, and she hadn't the faintest idea what the woman was doing to her. Charlotte had seated her near the window in the sitting room where the morning light was strongest.

Mrs. Sims and one assistant looked as impatient as Scarlett felt. They'd arrived twenty minutes earlier.

"*Ecco!*" said Serafina.

"*Benissimo*," said Mrs. Montague.

"Now," said Mrs. Sims.

Her assistant lifted the muslin wrap from the gown Mrs. Sims was holding. Scarlett drew in her breath. The white satin glistened in the light, and the light made the silver embroidery shine as if it were a living thing. It was a fantasy of a gown. Scarlett stood, her hands reached out to touch it.

"Gloves first," Mrs. Sims commanded. "Every finger would leave a mark." Scarlett saw that the dressmaker was wearing white kid gloves. She took the pristine long gloves Charlotte was holding out to her. They were already folded back and powdered for her to get them on without stretching.

When she had smoothed them all the way up, Charlotte used a small silver buttonhook with rapid competence, Serafina dropped a silk handkerchief over her head and removed her wrapper, and then Mrs. Sims lowered the dress onto Scarlett's upraised arms and onto her body. While she fastened the back, Serafina deftly removed the handkerchief and made a few delicate touches to Scarlett's hair.

There was a knock at the door. "Well timed," said Mrs. Montague. "That will be Monsieur Hervé. We'll want Mrs. O'Hara over here, Mrs. Sims." Charlotte led Scarlett to the center of the room. Scarlett could hear her opening the door and speaking in a low voice. I suppose she's talking French and expects me to. No, Charlotte must know me better than that by now. I wish I had a looking glass, I want to see the gown on me.

She lifted one foot, then the other when Mrs. Sims' assistant tapped her toes. She couldn't see the slippers the woman slipped onto her feet, Mrs. Sims was poking her in the shoulder blades and hissing at her about standing up straight. The assistant fiddled with the bottom of her skirt.

"Mrs. O'Hara," said Charlotte Montague, "please allow me to present Monsieur François Hervé."

Scarlett looked at the rotund bald man who walked in front of her and bowed. "How do you do," she said. Was she supposed to shake hands with a painter?

"*Fantastique*," said the painter. He snapped his fingers. Two men carried the enormous pier glass to a spot between the windows. When they stepped away Scarlett saw herself.

The white satin gown was more décolleté than she'd realized. She stared at the daring expanse of bosom and shoulder. Then at the reflection of a woman she hardly recognized. Her hair was piled high on her head in a mass of curls and tendrils so artful that they looked almost happenstance. The white satin glimmered the narrow length of her body, and a silver-encrusted white satin train spread in a sinuous semicircle around the white satin slippers, with silver heels.

Why, I look like Grandma Robillard's portrait more than I look like me.

The years of habitual girlishness fell away. She was looking at a woman, not the flirtatious belle of Clayton County. And she liked what she saw very much. She was mystified and excited by this stranger. Her soft lips quivered faintly at the corners, and her tilted eyes took on a deeper, more mysterious sheen. Her chin lifted in supreme self-confidence, and she looked directly into her own eyes with challenge and approval.

"That's it," whispered Charlotte Montague to herself. "That's the woman to take all Ireland by storm. The whole world, if she wants it."

"Easel," murmured the artist. "Quickly, you cretins. I shall do a portrait that will make me famous."

"I don't understand it," Scarlett said to Charlotte after the sitting. "It's like I never saw that person before in my life, yet I knew her ... I'm confused, Charlotte."

"My dear child, that is the beginning of wisdom."

"Charlotte, do let's ride one of those darling trams," Scarlett begged. "I deserve a reward after standing like a statue for hours on end."

It had been a long sitting, Charlotte agreed; future ones would probably be shorter. For one thing it would likely rain, and without good light M. Hervé wouldn't be able to paint.

"Then you agree? We'll take the tram?" Charlotte nodded. Scarlett felt like hugging her, but Charlotte Montague wasn't that kind of person. And, in an undefined way, neither was she any longer, Scarlett felt. The view of herself as a woman, no longer a girl, had thrilled her but unsettled her, too. It was going to take some getting used to.

They climbed the iron spiral to the upper level of the tram. It was exposed and very cold, but the view was superb. Scarlett looked on all sides at the city, the crowded wide streets, the swarming wide sidewalks. Dublin was the first real city she'd ever seen. It had a population of more than a quarter million people. Atlanta was a boomtown of twenty thousand.

The tram moved on its tracks through the traffic with inexorable right of way. Pedestrians and vehicles scattered hastily at the last minute as it approached. Frenzied and noisy, the narrow escapes delighted Scarlett.

Then she saw the river. The tram stopped on the bridge and she could see along the Liffey. Bridge after bridge after bridge, all different, all teeming with traffic. The quays enticing with shop fronts and crowds. The water bright in the sunlight.

The Liffey was left behind, the tram was suddenly in shadow, tall buildings were near on both sides. Scarlett felt the chill.

"We'd better go down at the next stop," said Charlotte. "We get off at the following one." She led the way. After they crossed a bedlam intersection Charlotte gestured toward the street that curved ahead of them. "Grafton Street," she said, as if she were making an introduction. "We'll want to take a hackney back to the Gresham, but on foot is the only way to see the shops. Would you like coffee before we begin? You should become acquainted with Bewley's."

"I don't know, Charlotte. I might just take a look inside this shop first. That fan in the window—see the one in that back corner, with the pink tassels—it's the most adorable thing. Oh, and that Chinesey one, I didn't see that at first. And that precious pomander! Look Charlotte, at the embroidery on those gloves. Have you ever? Oh, my goodness."

Charlotte nodded at the liveried door attendant. He pulled the door wide and bowed.

She didn't mention that there were at least four more shops on Grafton Street with hundreds of fans and gloves. Charlotte was quite sure that Scarlett would discover for herself that a major attribute of a major city is an infinite spectrum of temptation.

After ten days of sittings and fittings and shopping Scarlett went home to Ballyhara with dozens of presents for Cat, several gifts for Mrs. Fitz and Colum, ten pounds of coffee and a coffee maker for herself. She was in love with Dublin and could hardly wait to return.

At Ballyhara her Cat was waiting. As soon as the train left the city, Scarlett was in a fever to get home. She had so many things to tell Cat, so many plans for the time when she'd take her funny little monkey of a country child to the city. She had to hold her after-Mass office hours, too. She'd delayed them for a week already. And soon it would be Saint Brigid's Day. Scarlett thought that was the best of all, the moment when the year really began with the turning of the first sod. How very, very lucky she was. She had both—country and city, The O'Hara and that still unknown woman in the pier glass.

Scarlett left Cat engrossed in a picture book of animals, her other presents still unwrapped. She ran down the drive to Colum's gatehouse with the cashmere muffler she'd brought him and all her impressions of Dublin to share.

"Oh, I'm sorry," she said when she saw that he had a guest. The well-dressed man was a stranger to her.

"Not at all, not at all," said Colum. "Come meet John Devoy. He's just in from America."

Devoy was polite but clearly not pleased to be interrupted. Scarlett made her excuses, left Colum's gift, and walked home briskly. Now what kind of American comes to an out-of-the-way place like Ballyhara and isn't pleased to meet another American? He must be one of Colum's Fenians, that's it! And he's annoyed because Colum isn't part of that crazy revolution thing any more.

The reverse was the truth. John Devoy was seriously leaning towards support for Parnell, and he was one of the most influential American Fenians. If he abandoned support for the revolution, the blow would be nearly mortal. Colum argued passionately against Home Rule long into the night.

"The man wants power and will use any treachery to get it," he said about Parnell.

"What about you, Colum?" Devoy retorted. "Sounds to me like you can't stand a better man getting your job done, and done better."

Colum's reply was immediate. "He'll make speeches in London till Hell freezes, and he'll win headlines in all the newspapers, but we'll still be left with starving Irish under the boots of the English. The Irish people will win nothing at all. And when they tire of Mr. Parnell's headlines they'll revolt. With no organization and no hope of success. I tell you, Devoy, we're waiting too long. Parnell talks, you talk, I talk—and all the while the Irish suffer."

After Devoy went to Kennedy's Inn for the night Colum paced his small sitting room until the oil in the lamp burned out. Then he sat in the cold darkness on a stool by the dying embers on the hearth. Brooding on

Devoy's angry outburst. Could the man be right? Was power the motive, and not love for Ireland? How could a man know the truth of his own soul?

Thin watery sunlight shone briefly as Scarlett drove a spade into the earth on Saint Brigid's Day. It was a good omen for the year to come. To celebrate, she treated everyone in Ballyhara town to porter and meat pies at Kennedy's. It was going to be the best year of all, she was sure of it. The next day she went to Dublin for the six weeks known as the Castle Season.

78

She and Charlotte had a suite of rooms at the Shelbourne Hotel this time, not the Gresham. The Shelbourne was THE place to stay in Dublin for the Season. Scarlett hadn't gone inside the imposing brick building on her previous visit to Dublin. "We choose the occasion to be seen," Charlotte told her. Now she gazed around the huge hall inside the entrance and understood why Charlotte wanted them to be here. Everything was imposingly grand—the space, the staff, the guests, the controlled hushed busyness. She lifted her chin, then followed the porter up the half-flight to the first floor, the most desirable of desirables. Though Scarlett did not know it, she looked exactly like Charlotte's description to the doorman. "You will know her at once. She is extremely beautiful, and she carries her head like an empress."

In addition to the suite, a private drawing room was reserved for Scarlett's use. Charlotte showed it to her before they went down for tea. The finished portrait stood on a brass easel in a corner of the green brocaded room. Scarlett looked at it with wonder. Did she really look like that? That woman wasn't afraid of anything, and she felt as nervous as a cat. She followed Charlotte downstairs in a daze.

Charlotte identified some of the people at other tables in the sumptuous lounge. "You'll meet them all eventually. After you're presented, you'll serve tea and coffee in your drawing room every afternoon. People will bring people to meet you."

Who? Scarlett wanted to ask. Who will bring people, and who are the people they'll bring? But she didn't bother. Charlotte always knew what she was doing. The only thing Scarlett needed to be responsible for was not getting tangled up in her train when she backed away after her presentation. Charlotte and Mrs. Sims were going to coach her with a practice presentation gown every day until The Day.

The heavy white envelope bearing the Chamberlain's seal was delivered to the hotel the day after Scarlett arrived. Charlotte's expression gave no hint of how relieved she was. One never knew for sure about best-laid plans. She opened it with steady fingers. "First Drawing Room," she said, "as expected. Day after tomorrow."

Scarlett waited in a group of white-gowned girls and women on the landing outside the closed double doors to the Throne Room. It seemed to her she'd been doing nothing but waiting for a hundred years. Why on earth had she agreed to do this? Scarlett couldn't answer her own question, it was too complex. In part she was The O'Hara, determined to conquer the English. In part she was an American girl dazzled by the grandeur of the British Empire's royal panoply. At bottom, Scarlett had never in her life backed down from a challenge and never would.

Another name was called. Not hers. God's nightgown! Were they going to make her be last? Charlotte hadn't warned her about that. Charlotte hadn't even told her until the last minute that she'd be alone all the way. "I'll find you in the supper room after the Drawing Room is over." That was a fine way to treat her, throwing her to the wolves like that. She stole another glance down her front. She was terrified that she might just fall right out of the scandalously low-cut gown. That would really make this—what had Charlotte said? "An experience to remember."

"Madam The O'Hara of Ballyhara."

Oh, Lord, that's me. She repeated Charlotte Montague's coaching litany to herself. Walk forward, stop outside the door. A footman will lift the train you have looped over your left arm and arrange it behind you. The Gentleman Usher will open the doors. Wait for him to announce you.

"Madam The O'Hara of Ballyhara."

Scarlett looked at the Throne Room. Well, Pa, what do you think of your Katie Scarlett now? she thought. I'm going to stroll along that fifty miles or so of red carpet runner and kiss the Viceroy of Ireland, cousin of the Queen of England. She glanced at the majestically dressed Gentleman Usher, and her right eyelid quivered in what might almost have been a conspiratorial wink.

The O'Hara walked like an empress to face the Viceroy's red-bearded magnificence and present her cheek for the ceremonial kiss of welcome.

Turn to the Vicereine now and curtsey. Back straight. Not too low. Stand up. Now back, back, back, three steps, don't worry, the weight of the train holds it away from your body. Now extend your left arm. Wait. Let the footman have plenty of time to arrange the train over your arm. Now turn. Walk out.

Scarlett's knees obligingly waited until she was seated at one of the supper tables before they started trembling.

Charlotte made no attempt to hide her satisfaction. She entered Scarlett's bedroom with the stiff squares of white cardboard fanned in her hand. "My dear Scarlett, you were a dazzling success. These invitations arrived before even I was up and dressed. State Ball, that's quite special. Saint Patrick's Ball, that was to be expected. Second Drawing Room, you'll be able to watch other people running the gauntlet. And a small dance in the Throne Room. Three-fourths of the peers in Ireland have never been invited to one of the small dances."

Scarlett giggled. The terror of being presented was behind her, and she was a success! "I guess I won't mind now that I spent last year's wheat crop on all those new clothes. Let's go shopping today and spend this year's crop."

"You won't have time. Eleven gentlemen, including the Gentleman Usher, have written to ask permission to call on you. Plus fourteen ladies, with their daughters. Tea time won't be long enough. You'll have to serve coffee and tea in the mornings, too. The maids are opening your drawing room right now. I ordered pink flowers, so wear your brown and rose plaid taffeta for the morning and the green velvet faced in pink for the afternoon. Evans will be here to do your hair as soon as you're up."

Scarlett was the Season's hit. Gentlemen flocked to meet the rich widow who was also—*mirabile dictu*—fantastically beautiful. Mothers swarmed her private reception room with daughters in tow to meet the gentlemen. After the first day, Charlotte never ordered flowers again. Admirers sent so many that there wasn't room for all of them. Many of the bouquets contained leather cases from Dublin's finest jeweler, but Scarlett reluctantly returned all the brooches, bracelets, rings, earrings. "Even an American from Clayton County, Georgia, knows that you're expected to pay back favors," she told Charlotte. "I won't be obligated to anybody, not that way."

Her goings and comings were reported faithfully and sometimes even accurately in the gossip column of the daily *Irish Times*. Shop owners in morning coats came themselves to show her choice items they hoped she might like, and she defiantly bought herself many of the jewelry pieces she had refused to accept. The Viceroy danced with her twice at the State Ball.

All the guests at her coffees and teas admired her portrait. Scarlett looked at it every morning and every afternoon before the first visitors arrived. She was learning herself. Charlotte Montague observed the metamorphosis with interest. The practiced flirt vanished, replaced by a serene, somewhat amused woman who had only to turn her smoky green eyes on man, woman, or child to draw them, mesmerized, to her side.

I used to work like a mule to be charming, Scarlett thought, now I don't do anything at all. She couldn't understand it at all, but she accepted the gift of it with simple gratitude.

"Did you say two hundred people, Charlotte? That's what you call a small dance?"

"Relatively. There are always five or six hundred at the State and Saint Patrick's balls and more than a thousand at the Drawing Rooms. You certainly already know at least half the people who'll be there, probably many more than half."

"I still think it's tacky that you weren't invited."

"It's the way things are. I'm not offended." Charlotte was anticipating the evening with pleasure. She planned to go over her account book. Scarlett's success and Scarlett's extravagance had greatly exceeded even Charlotte's most optimistic expectations. She felt like a nabob, and she liked to gloat over her wealth. Admission to the coffee hour alone was bringing in "gifts" of almost a hundred pounds a week. And there were still two weeks left in the Season. She would see Scarlett off to her privileged evening with a light heart.

Scarlett paused in the doorway of the Throne Room to enjoy the spectacle. "You know, Jeffrey, I never get used to this place," she said to the Gentleman Usher. "I'm like Cinderella at the ball."

"I'd never associate you with Cinderella, Scarlett," he said adoringly. Scarlett's wink had put his heart in her pocket when she entered the First Drawing Room.

"You'd be surprised," Scarlett said. She nodded absentmindedly in response to bows and smiles from familiar faces nearby. How lovely it was.

It couldn't be real, she couldn't really be here. Everything had happened so fast; she needed time to absorb it.

The great room shimmered gold. Gilded columns supported the ceiling, gilded flat column pilasters filled the walls between the tall windows draped in gold-fringed crimson velvet. Gilt armchairs upholstered in crimson surrounded the supper tables along the walls, each table centered with a gold candelabrum. Gilt covered the intricately carved gaslit chandeliers and the massive canopy above the gold and red thrones. Gold lace trimmed men's court dress of brocaded silk skirted coats and white satin knee breeches. Gold buckles decorated their satin dancing pumps. Gold buttons, gold epaulets, gold frogging, gold braid gleamed on the dress uniforms of regimental officers and the court uniforms of Viceregal officials.

Many of the men wore bright sashes slashed across their chests, pinned with jewelled orders; the Viceroy's knee breeches touched the Garter around his leg. The men were almost more splendid than the women.

Almost, but not quite, for the women were jewelled at neck, breast, ears, and wrists; many wore tiaras as well. Their gowns were made of rich materials—satin, velvet, brocade, silk—embroidered often in glowing silks or gold and silver threads.

A body could get blinded just looking, I'd better go on in and make my manners. Scarlett made her way across the room to curtsey to the Viceregal host and hostess. The music started as she finished.

"May I?" A gold-braided red arm crooked to offer support for her hand. Scarlett smiled. It was Charles Ragland. She'd met him at a house party, and he had called on her every day since her arrival in Dublin. He made no secret of his admiration. Charles' handsome face blushed every time she spoke to him. He was awfully sweet and attractive, even though he was an English soldier. They weren't at all like Yankees, no matter what Colum said. For one thing, they were infinitely better dressed. She rested her hand lightly on Ragland's arm, and he escorted her into the pattern of the quadrille.

"You are very beautiful tonight, Scarlett."

"So are you, Charles. I was just thinking that the men are more dressed up than the ladies."

"Thank heaven for uniforms. Knee breeches are the devil to wear. A man feels a perfect fool in satin shoes."

"Serves them right. They've been peeking at ladies' ankles for ages, let them see what it feels like when we ogle their legs."

"Scarlett, you shock me." The pattern shifted and he was gone.

I probably do, Scarlett thought. Charles was as innocent as a schoolboy sometimes. She looked up at her new partner.

"My God!" she said aloud. It was Rhett.

"How flattering," he said with his twisty half smile. No one else smiled like that. Scarlett was filled with light, with lightness. She felt as if she were floating above the polished floor, buoyant with happiness.

And then, before she could speak again, the quadrille took him away. She smiled automatically at her new partner. The love burning in her eyes took his breath away. Her mind was racing: Why is Rhett here? Could it be because he wanted to see me? Because he had to see me, because he couldn't keep away?

The quadrille moved at its stately tempo, making Scarlett frantic with impatience. When it ended, she was facing Charles Ragland. It took all her self-control to smile and thank him and murmur a hasty excuse before she turned to search for Rhett.

Her eyes met his almost immediately. He was standing only an arm's length away.

Scarlett's pride kept her from reaching out to him. He knew I'd be looking for him, she thought angrily. Who does he think he is, anyhow, to come strolling into my world and just stand there and expect me to fall into his arms? There are plenty of men in Dublin—in this room, even—who've been smothering me with attention, hanging around my drawing room, sending flowers every day, and notes, and even jewelry. What makes Mister High and Mighty Rhett Butler think that all he has to do is lift his little finger and I'll come running?

"What a pleasant surprise," she said, and the cool tone of her voice pleased her.

Rhett held out his hand, and she put hers in it without thinking. "May I have this dance, Mrs. . . . er . . . O'Hara?"

Scarlett caught her breath in alarm. "Rhett, you're not going to tell on me? Everybody believes I'm a widow!"

He smiled and took her into his arms as the music began. "Your secret is safe with me, Scarlett." She could feel the rasp of his voice on her skin, and his warm breath. It made her weak.

"What the devil are you doing here?" she asked. She had to know. His hand was warm at her waist, strong, supporting, directing her body as they turned. Unconsciously Scarlett revelled in his strength and rebelled against his control over her even as she remembered the joy of following his steps in the giddying swirling motion of the waltz.

Rhett chuckled. "I couldn't resist my curiosity," he said. "I was in London on business, and everyone was talking about an American who was taking Dublin Castle by storm. 'Could that be Scarlett of the striped stockings?' I asked myself. I had to find out. Bart Morland confirmed my suspicions. Then I couldn't get him to stop talking about you. He even made me ride with him through your town. According to him, you rebuilt it with your own hands."

His eyes raked over her from head to toe. "You've changed, Scarlett," he said quietly. "The charming girl has become an elegant, grown-up woman. I salute you, I really do."

The unvarnished honesty and warmth of his voice made Scarlett forget her resentments. "Thank you, Rhett," she said.

"Are you happy in Ireland, Scarlett?"

"Yes, I am."

"I'm glad." His words were rich with deeper meaning.

For the first time in all the years she'd known him, Scarlett understood Rhett, at least in part. *He did come to see me,* she understood, *he's been thinking about me all this time, worrying about where I'd gone and how I was. He never stopped caring, no matter what he said. He loves me and always will, just as I'll always love him.*

The realization filled her with happiness, and she tasted it, like champagne; sipped it, to make it last. *Rhett was here, with her, and they were, in this moment, closer than they had ever been.*

An aide-de-camp approached them when the waltz ended. "His Excellency requests the honor of the next dance, Mrs. O'Hara."

Rhett raised his eyebrows in the quizzical mockery Scarlett remembered so well. Her lips curved in a smile for him alone. "Tell His Excellency that I will be delighted," she said. She looked at Rhett before she took the aide's arm. "In Clayton County," she murmured to Rhett, "we'd say that I was in high cotton." She heard his laughter follow her as she walked away.

I'm allowed, she told herself, and she looked back over her shoulder to see him laughing. *It's really too much,* she thought, *it's not fair at all. He even looks good in those silly satin britches and shoes.* Her green eyes sparkled with laughter when she curtseyed to the Viceroy before they began to dance.

Scarlett felt no real surprise that Rhett was no longer there when she looked for him again. For as long as she had known him, Rhett had appeared and disappeared without explanation. *I shouldn't have been surprised to see him here tonight,* she thought. *I was feeling like Cinderella, why shouldn't the only Prince Charming I want be here?* She could feel his arms around her as if he had left a mark; otherwise it would be easy to believe that she had made it all up—the gilded room, the music, his presence, even hers.

When she returned to her rooms at the Shelbourne, Scarlett turned up the gas and stood before a long looking glass in the bright light to look at herself and see what Rhett had seen. She looked beautiful and sure of herself, like her portrait, like the portrait of her grandmother.

Her heart began to ache. Why couldn't she be like the other portrait of Grandma Robillard? The one in which she was soft and flushed with love given and received.

For in Rhett's caring words, she knew, there had also been sadness and farewell.

In the middle of the night Scarlett O'Hara woke in her luxurious scented room on the best floor of the best hotel in Dublin and wept with racking convulsive sobs. "If only . . ." repeated again and again in her head like a battering ram.

79

The night's anguish left no visible marks on Scarlett. Her face was smoothly serene the next morning, and her smiles were as lovely as ever when she poured out coffee and tea for the men and women who crowded her drawing room. Sometime during the dark hours of the night she had found the courage to let Rhett go.

If I love him, she understood, I must not try to hold on to him. I have to learn to give him his freedom, just the way I try to give Cat hers because I love her.

I wish I could have told Rhett about her, he'd be so proud of her.

I wish the Castle Season was over. I miss Cat dreadfully. I wonder what she's up to.

Cat was running with the strength of desperation through the woods at Ballyhara. The ground mists of morning still clung in places, and she couldn't see where she was going. She stumbled and fell, but she got up right away. She had to keep running, even though she was short of breath from running so much already. She sensed another stone coming and ducked behind the protection of a tree trunk. The boys chasing her shouted and jeered. They had almost caught up with her, even though they'd never ventured into the woods near the Big House before. It was safe now. They knew The O'Hara was in Dublin with the English. Their parents talked about nothing else.

"There she is!" one shouted, and the others lifted their hands to throw. But the figure stepping from behind a tree was not Cat. It was the *cailleach*, with a gnarled finger pointing. The boys howled with fear and ran.

"Come with me," said Grainne. "I will give you some tea."

Cat put her hand in the old woman's. Grainne came out from hiding and walked very slowly, and Cat had no trouble keeping pace with her. "Will there be cakes?" Cat asked.

"There will," said the *cailleach*.

Although Scarlett grew homesick for Ballyhara, she lasted the Castle Season out. She'd given Charlotte Montague her word. It's exactly like the Season in Charleston, she thought. Why is it, I wonder, that fashionable people work so hard at having fun for so long at a time? She soared from success to even greater success, and Mrs. Fitz shrewdly took advantage of the rapturous paragraphs in the *Irish Times* that described them. Every evening she took the newspaper down to Kennedy's bar to show the people of Ballyhara how famous The O'Hara was. Day by day, grumbling about Scarlett's fondness for the English gave way to pride that The O'Hara was more admired than any of the Anglo women.

Colum did not applaud Rosaleen Fitzpatrick's cleverness. His mood was too somber for him to see the humor in it. "The Anglos will seduce her just as they're doing John Devoy," he said.

Colum was both wrong and right. No one in Dublin wanted Scarlett to be less Irish. It was a large part of her attractiveness. The O'Hara was an original. But Scarlett had discovered an unsettling truth. The Anglo-Irish thought of themselves as being just as Irish as the O'Haras of Adamstown. "These families were living in Ireland before America was even settled," Charlotte Montague said one day in irritation. "How can you call them anything but Irish?"

Scarlett couldn't unravel the complexities, so she stopped trying. She didn't really have to, she decided. She could have both worlds—the Ireland of Ballyhara's farms and the Ireland of Dublin Castle. Cat would have them, too, when she grew up. And that's much better than she would have had if I'd stayed in Charleston, Scarlett told herself firmly.

When the Saint Patrick's Ball ended at four in the morning, the Castle Season was over. The next event was some miles away in County Kildare. Everyone would be at the Punchestown Races, Charlotte told her. She'd be expected to be there.

Scarlett declined. "I love racing and horses, Charlotte, but I'm ready to go home now. I'm late already with this month's office hours. I'll pay for the hotel reservations you made."

No need, said Charlotte. She could sell them for four times their cost. And she herself had no interest in horses.

She thanked Scarlett for making her an independent woman. "You are independent now as well, Scarlett. You don't need me any more. Stay on Mrs. Sims' good side and let her dress you. The Shelbourne has reserved your rooms for next year's Season. Your house will accommodate all the guests you ever want to have, and your housekeeper is the most professional woman I've ever met in that position. You are in the world now. Do with it what you will."

"What will you do, Charlotte?"

"I will have what I always wanted. A small apartment in a Roman palazzo. Good food, good wine, and day after day of sunlight. I abhor rain."

Even Charlotte couldn't complain about this weather, Scarlett thought. The spring was sunnier than anyone could remember a spring ever being. The grass was tall and rich, and the wheat planted three weeks before on Saint Patrick's Day had already hazed the fields with tender fresh green. The harvest this year should make up for last year's disappointment and then some. It was wonderful to be home.

"How is Ree doing?" she asked Cat. It was just like her daughter to name the small Shetland pony "King," Scarlett thought indulgently. Cat valued her loves high. It was nice, too, that Cat used the Gaelic word. She liked to think of Cat as a true Irish child. Even though she did look like a gypsy. Her black hair would not stay neatly in its braids, and the sunny weather had browned her even more. Cat took off hat and shoes the moment she got outside.

"He doesn't like it when I ride him with a saddle. I don't like it either. Bareback is better."

"No you don't, my precious. You've got to learn to ride with a saddle and so does Ree. Be thankful it's not a sidesaddle."

"The one you have for hunting?"

"Yes. You'll have one some day, but not for a long, long time." Cat would be four in October, not all that much younger than Bonnie was when she had her fall. The sidesaddle could wait for a very long time. If only Bonnie had been astride instead of still learning to ride sidesaddle—no, she mustn't think like that. "If only" could break your heart.

"Let's ride down to the town, Cat, would you like that? We could go see Colum." Scarlett was worried about him, he was so moody these days.

"Cat doesn't like town. Can we ride to the river?"

"All right. I haven't been to the river in a long time, that's a good idea."

"May I climb up in the tower?"

"You may not. The door's too high, and it's more than likely full of bats."

"Will we go see Grainne?"

Scarlett's hands tightened on her reins. "How do you know Grainne?" The wise woman had told her to keep Cat away, to guard her close to home. Who had taken Cat there? And why?

"She gave Cat some milk."

Scarlett didn't care for the sound of it. Cat only referred to herself in the third person when something made her nervous or angry. "What didn't you like about Grainne, Cat?"

"She thinks Cat is another little girl named Dara. Cat told her, but she didn't hear."

"Oh, honey, she knows it's you. That's a very special name she gave you when you were just a little baby. It's Gaelic, like the names you gave Ree and Ocras. Dara means oak tree, the best and strongest tree of all."

"That's silly. A girl can't be a tree. She doesn't have leaves."

Scarlett sighed. She was overjoyed when Cat wanted to talk, the child was so often quiet, but it wasn't always easy to talk to her. She's such an opinionated little thing, and she always can tell when you're fudging a little. The truth, the whole truth, or she gives you a look that could kill.

"Look, Cat, there's the tower. Did I tell you the story about how old it is?"

"Yes."

Scarlett wanted to laugh. It would be wrong to tell a child to lie, but sometimes a polite fib would be welcome.

"I like the tower," said Cat.

"I do too, sweetheart." Scarlett wondered why she hadn't come here for so long. She'd almost forgotten how strange the old stones made her feel. It was eerie and peaceful at the same time. She made a promise to herself not to let so many months slip away before her next visit. This was, after all, the real heart of Ballyhara, where it had begun.

The blackthorn was already blooming in the hedges and it was still April. What a season they were having! Scarlett slowed the buggy for a long sniff. There was no real need to hurry, the dresses would wait. She was driving into Trim for a package of summer clothes Mrs. Sims had sent. There were six invitations to June house parties on her desk. She wasn't sure she was ready to start partying so soon, but she was ready to see some grown-ups. Cat was her heart of hearts, but ... And Mrs. Fitz was so busy running the big household that she never had time for a friendly cup of tea. Colum had gone to Galway to meet Stephen. She didn't know how she felt about Stephen coming to Ballyhara. Spooky Stephen. Maybe he wouldn't be so spooky in Ireland. Maybe he'd just been so strange and silent in Savannah because he was mixed up in the gun business. At least that was over! The extra income she was getting now from the little houses in Atlanta was pleasant, too. She must have given the Fenians a fortune. Much better spent on frocks; frocks didn't hurt anyone.

Stephen would have all the news from Savannah, too. She was longing to know how everyone was. Maureen was just as bad about writing letters as she was. She hadn't heard anything about the Savannah O'Haras in months. Or about anyone else. It made sense that when she'd made the decision to sell up in Atlanta she'd decided to put everything in America behind her and never look back.

Still, it would be nice to hear about Atlanta folks. She knew, from the profits she was making, that the little houses were selling, so Ashley's business must be good. What about Aunt Pittypat, though? And India? Had she dried up so much she was dust? And all those people who had once been so important to her so long ago? I wish I'd kept in touch with the aunts myself instead of leaving money with my lawyer to send them their allowance from. I was right not letting them know where I was, I was right to protect Cat from Rhett. But maybe he wouldn't do anything now; look at the way he was at the Castle. If I write to Eulalie, I'll get all the Charleston news from her. I'll hear about Rhett. Could I bear it to hear that he and Anne are blissfully happy, raising racehorses and Butler babies? I don't believe I want to know. I'll let the aunts stay like they are.

All I'd get anyhow is a million crossed pages of lecturing, and I get enough lecturing from Mrs. Fitz to fill that hole. Maybe she's right about giving some parties; it is a shame to have that house and all those servants standing idle. But she's dead wrong about Cat. I don't give a fig what Anglo mothers do, I'm not going to have a nanny running Cat's life. I see little enough of her now, the way she's always off at the stables or in the kitchen or wandering over the place or up a tree somewhere. And the idea of sending her away to some convent school is just plain crazy! When she's old enough, the school in Ballyhara will do just fine. She'll have friends there, too. It's worrisome to me sometimes that she never wants to play with any other children ... What on earth is going on? It's not Market Day. Why's the bridge all jammed up with people like this?

Scarlett leaned down from the buggy and touched a hurrying woman on the shoulder. "What's happening?" The woman looked up. Her eyes were bright, her whole face excited.

"It's a flogging. Better hurry, or you'll miss it."

A flogging. Scarlett didn't want to see some poor devil of a soldier being whipped. She had an idea that flogging was punishment in the military. She tried to turn the buggy around, but the pushing, hurrying mass of people avid to see the spectacle caught her up in their press. Her horse was buffeted, her buggy rocked and pushed. The only thing she could do was get down and hold the bridle, soothe the horse with strokes and soft sounds, walking at the pace of the people around her.

When forward motion stopped, Scarlett could hear the whistling of the lash and the dreadful liquid sound it made when it landed. She wanted to cover her ears, but she needed her hands to gentle the frightened horse. It seemed to her that the ghastly noises went on forever.

". . . one hundred. That's it," she heard, then the groaning disappointment of the mob. She held tightly on to the bridle; the pushing and shoving was worse than before as the crowd dispersed.

She didn't shut her eyes until too late. She'd already seen the mutilated body, and the picture was burned on her brain. He was tied onto an upright spoked wheel, his wrists and ankles bound with leather thongs. A purple-stained blue shirt hung over his rough woolen pants from the waist, baring what must have once been a broad back. Now it was a giant red wound with loose red strips of flesh and skin hanging from it.

Scarlett turned her head into the horse's mane. She felt sick. Her horse tossed his head nervously, throwing her away. There was a terrible sweet smell in the air.

She heard someone vomiting, and her stomach heaved. She leaned over as best she could without releasing the bridle and was sick onto the cobbles.

"All right then, lad, there's no shame to losing your breakfast after a flogging. Go along to the pub and have a large whiskey. Marbury'll help me cut him down." Scarlett raised her head to look at the speaker, a British soldier in the uniform of a sergeant in the Guards. He was talking to an ashen-faced private. The private stumbled away. Another came forward to assist the sergeant. They cut the leather from behind the wheel, and the body fell into the blood-soaked mud beneath it.

That was green grass last week, Scarlett thought. This can't be. That's meant to be soft green grass.

"What about the wife, Sergeant?" A pair of soldiers were holding the arms of a silent, straining woman in a hooded black cloak.

"Let her go. It's over. Let's go. The cart will come later to take him away."

The woman ran after the men. She caught the sergeant's gold-striped sleeve. "Your officer promised I could bury him," she cried. "He gave me his word."

The sergeant shoved her away. "I only had orders for the flogging, the rest is none of my business. Leave me be, woman."

The black-cloaked figure stood alone on the street, watching the soldiers walk into the bar. She made one sound, a shuddering sob. Then she turned and ran to the wheel, the blood-covered body. "Danny, oh Danny, oh my dear." She crouched, then kneeled in the ghastly mud, trying to lift torn shoulders and lolling head into her lap. Her hood fell away, revealing a pale fine-boned face, neatly chignoned golden hair, blue eyes in shadowed circles of grief. Scarlett was frozen in place. To move, to clatter wheels over cobbles would be an obscene intrusion on the woman's tragedy.

A dirty little boy ran barefoot across the square. "Can I have a button or something, lady? My ma wants a keepsake." He shook the woman's shoulder.

Scarlett raced over the cobbles, the blood-spattered grass, the edge of the churned mud. She grabbed the boy's arm. He looked up, startled, mouth gaping. Scarlett slapped his face with all the strength in her arm. The sound of it was like the crack of a rifle shot. "Get out of here, you filthy little devil! Get out of here." The boy ran, bawling with fear.

"Thank you," said the wife of the man who had been beaten to death.

She was in it now, Scarlett knew. She had to do what little could be done. "I know a doctor in Trim," she said. "I'll go get him."

"A doctor? Will he want to bleed him, do you think?" Her bitter, desperate words were English-accented, like the voices at the Castle balls.

"He'll prepare your husband for burial," said Scarlett quietly.

The woman's bloody hand seized the hem of Scarlett's skirt. She lifted it to her lips, an abject kiss of gratitude. Scarlett's eyes clouded with tears. My God, I don't deserve this. I would have turned the buggy if I could. "Don't," she said, "please don't."

The woman's name was Harriet Stewart, her husband's Daniel Kelly. That was all Scarlett knew until Daniel Kelly was in the closed coffin inside the Catholic Chapel. Then the widow, who had spoken only to answer the priest's questions, looked around her with wild, darting eyes. "Billy, where's Billy? He should be here." The priest found out that there was a son, locked in a room at the hotel to keep him away from the flogging. "They were very kind," said the woman, "they let me pay with my wedding ring, though it's not gold."

"I'll bring him," Scarlett said. "Father? You'll take care of Mrs. Kelly?"

"That I will. Bring a bottle of brandy, too, Mrs. O'Hara. The poor lady's near breaking."

"I will not break down," Harriet Kelly said. "I cannot. I must take care of my boy. He's such a little boy, only eight." Her voice was thin and brittle as new ice.

Scarlett hurried. Billy Kelly was a sturdy blond boy, big for his age, loud with anger. At his captivity behind the thick locked door. At the British soldiers. "I'll get a rod of iron from a smithy and smash their heads till they shoot me," he shouted. The innkeeper needed all his burly strength to hold the boy.

"Don't be a fool, Billy Kelly!" Scarlett's sharp words were like cold water thrown in the child's face. "Your mother needs you, and you want to add to her grief. What kind of man are you?"

The innkeeper could release him then. The boy was still. "Where is my mother?" he said, and he sounded as young and frightened as he was.

"Come with me," said Scarlett.

80

*H*arriet Stewart Kelly's story was revealed slowly. She and her son had been at Ballyhara for more than a week before Scarlett learned even the bare bones of it. Daughter of an English clergyman, Harriet had taken a post as assistant governess in the family of Lord Witley. She was well educated, for a woman, nineteen, and completely ignorant of the world.

One of her duties was to accompany the children of the house on their rides before breakfast. She fell in love with the white smile and playful lilting voice of the groom who also accompanied them. When he asked her to run away with him, she thought it the most romantic adventure in the world.

The adventure ended on the small farm of Daniel Kelly's father. There were no references and so no jobs for a runaway groom or governess. Danny worked the stony fields with his father and brothers, Harriet did what his mother told her to do, for the most part scrubbing and darning. She had mastered fine embroidery as one of the accomplishments necessary to a lady. That Billy was her only child was testimony to the death of the romance. Danny Kelly missed the world of fine horses in grand stables and the dashing striped waistcoat, top hat, and tall leather boots that were a groom's dress livery. He blamed Harriet for his fall from grace, consoled himself with whiskey. His family hated her because she was English, and Protestant.

Danny was arrested when he attacked an English officer in a bar. His family gave him up for dead when he was sentenced to a hundred stripes of the whip. They were already holding the wake when Harriet took Billy's hand and a loaf of bread and set out to walk the twenty miles to Trim, the site of the insulted officer's regimental barracks. She pled for her husband's life. She was granted his body for burial.

"I'll take my son to England, Mrs. O'Hara, if you will lend me the fare. My parents are dead, but I have cousins who might give us a home. I'll repay you from my wages. I'll find some kind of work."

"What nonsense," said Scarlett. "Haven't you noticed that I have a little girl running wild as a woods colt? Cat needs a governess. Besides, she's already attached herself to Billy like a shadow. She needs a friend even more. You'd be doing me a mighty big favor if you'd stay, Mrs. Kelly."

It was true, as far as it went. What Scarlett didn't say was that she had no confidence at all in Harriet's ability to get herself on the right boat to England, much less earn a living once she got there. She's got plenty of spine but no smarts, was Scarlett's summing-up. The only things she knows are things she learned out of books. Scarlett's opinion of bookish people had never been very high.

Despite her scorn for Harriet's lack of practical sense, Scarlett was pleased to have her in the house. Ever since she'd returned from Dublin, Scarlett had found the big house disturbingly empty. She hadn't expected to miss Charlotte Montague, but she had. Harriet filled the gap nicely. In many ways she was even better company than Charlotte, because Harriet was fascinated by even the smallest thing the children did, and Scarlett heard about small adventures that Cat would not have thought worth reporting.

Billy Kelly was company for Cat, too, and Scarlett's uneasiness about Cat's isolation was laid to rest. The only drawback to Harriet's presence was Mrs. Fitzpatrick's hostility. "We don't want English at Ballyhara, Mrs. O," she had said when Scarlett brought Harriet and her son from Trim. "It was bad enough having the Montague woman here but at least she did something useful to you."

"Well, maybe you don't want Mrs. Kelly, but I do, and it's my house!" Scarlett was tired of being told what she should and shouldn't do. Charlotte had done it, and now Mrs. Fitz. Harriet never criticized her at all. On the contrary. She was so grateful for the roof over her head and Scarlett's hand-me-down clothes that sometimes Scarlett felt like shouting at her not to be so all-fired meek and mild.

Scarlett felt like shouting at everybody, and she was ashamed of herself, because there was absolutely no reason for her ill temper. Never in memory had there been such a growing season, everyone said. The grain was already half again as tall as normal, and the potato fields were thick with strong green growth. One glorious sunny day followed another, and the celebrations at weekly Market Day in Trim lasted long into the soft warm night. Scarlett danced until her shoes and stockings had holes in them, but the music and laughter failed to raise her spirits for long. When Harriet sighed romantically about the young couples walking along the river with their arms entwined, Scarlett turned away from her with an impatient shrug of the shoulders. Thank goodness for the invitations that were coming daily in the mail, she thought. The house parties were beginning soon. It seemed that the elegant festivities in Dublin and the temptations of the shops had made Trim Market Day lose most of its appeal.

By the end of May the waters of the Boyne were so low that one could see the stones laid centuries before as footing for the ford. The farmers were looking anxiously at the clouds blown by the west wind across the beautiful low sky. The fields needed rain. The brief showers that refreshed the air wet the soil only enough to draw the roots of wheat and timothy grass toward the surface, weakening the stalks.

Cat reported that the north track to Grainne's cottage was turning into a beaten path. "She has more butter than she can eat," Cat said, spreading her own butter on a muffin. "People are buying spells for rain."

"You've decided to be friends with Grainne?"

"Yes. Billy likes her."

Scarlett smiled. Whatever Billy said was law to Cat. It was lucky the boy was so good natured; Cat's adoration could have been a terrible trial. Instead he was as patient as a saint. Billy had inherited his father's "way with horses." He was teaching Cat to be an expert rider, far beyond anything that Scarlett could have done. As soon as Cat was a few years older, she'd be on a horse, not a pony. She mentioned at least twice a day that ponies were for little girls and Cat was a big girl. Fortunately it was Billy who said "not big enough." Cat would never have accepted it from Scarlett.

Scarlett went to a house party in Roscommon in early June, confident that she was in no way deserting her daughter. *She probably won't even notice that I'm not there. How humbling.*

"Isn't the weather splendid?" said everyone at the party. They played tennis on the lawn after dinner in the soft clear light that lasted until after ten o'clock.

Scarlett was pleased to be with so many of the people she'd liked most in Dublin. The only one she didn't greet with real enthusiasm was Charles Ragland. "It was your regiment that flogged that pitiful man to death, Charles. I'll never forget, and I'll never forgive. Wearing regular clothes doesn't change the fact that you're an English soldier, and that the military are monsters."

Charles was surprisingly unapologetic. "I'm truly sorry that you saw it, Scarlett. Flogging's a filthy business. But we're seeing things that are even worse, and they must be stopped."

He declined to give examples, but Scarlett heard from general conversation about the violence against landlords that was cropping up all over Ireland. Fields were torched, cows had their throats cut, an agent for a big estate near Galway was ambushed and hacked to pieces. There was hushed, anxious talk about a resurgence of the Whiteboys, organized bands of marauders that had terrified landowners more than a hundred years before. It couldn't be, said wiser heads. These latest incidents were scattered and sporadic and usually the work of known troublemakers. But they did tend to make one a bit uncomfortable when the tenants stared in the carriage as one drove past.

Scarlett forgave Charles. But, she said, he mustn't expect her to forget. "I'll even take the blame for the flogging if it will make you remember me," he said ardently. Then he blushed like a boy. "Dammit, I invent speeches worthy of Lord Byron when I'm in the barracks thinking of you, then I blurt out some rubbish when I'm in your presence. You know, don't you, that I'm most abominably in love with you?"

"Yes, I know. It's all right, Charles. I don't believe I would have liked Lord Byron, and I like you very much."

"Do you, my angel? Might I hope that—"

"I don't think so, Charles. Don't look so desperate. It's not you. I don't think so with anybody." The sandwiches in Scarlett's room slowly curled up their edges during the night.

"It's so good to be home! I'm afraid I'm an awful kind of person, Harriet. When I'm away I always get an itch to be home, no matter how much fun I'm having. But I'll bet you I start thinking about the next party I've accepted before this week's out. Tell me all about what happened while I was gone. Did Cat pester Billy half to death?"

"Not too much. They've invented a new game they call 'sink the Vikings.' I don't know where the name comes from. Cat said you could explain, she only remembered enough to make up the name. They've put a rope ladder on the tower. Billy hauls rocks up it, then they throw them through the slits into the river."

Scarlett laughed. "That minx. She's been nagging me about getting up in the tower for ages. And I notice she's got Billy doing the heavy work. Before she's even four years old. She's going to be a terror by the time she's six. You'll have to beat her with a stick to make her learn her letters."

"Probably not. She's already curious about the animal alphabet in her room."

Scarlett smiled at the implied suggestion that her daughter was probably a near-genius. She was willing to believe that Cat could do everything earlier and better than any child in the history of mankind.

"Will you tell me about the house party, Scarlett?" Harriet asked wistfully. Experience hadn't caused her to lose her romantic dreaminess.

"It was lovely," said Scarlett. "We were—oh, about two dozen, I guess—and for once there was no boring old retired general to talk about what he'd learned from the Duke of Wellington. We had a knock-down-drag-out croquet tournament with someone taking bets and giving odds like a horse race. I was on a team with—"

"Mrs. O'Hara!" The words were screamed, not spoken. Scarlett jumped up from her chair. A maid ran in, panting and red-faced. "Kitchen . . ." she gasped. "Cat . . . burned . . ." Scarlett almost knocked her down when she tore past her.

She could hear Cat wailing when she was only halfway through the colonnade from house to kitchen wing. Scarlett ran even faster. Cat never cried.

"She didn't know the pan was hot" . . . "already buttered her hand" . . . "dropped it soon as she picked it up" . . . "Momma . . . Momma . . ." The voices were all around her. Scarlett heard only Cat's.

"Momma's here, darling. We'll fix Cat up quick as a wink." She scooped the crying child up in her arms and hastened to the door. She'd seen the furious red weal across Cat's palm. It was so swollen her little fingers were spread wide.

The drive had doubled its length, she'd swear it. She was running as fast as she could without risking a fall. If Dr. Devlin's not at his house, he won't have a roof over his head when he comes back. I'll throw out every stick of furniture he owns, and his family with it.

But the doctor was there. "Now, now, there's no need to be in such a state, Mrs. O'Hara. Aren't children having accidents all the time? Let me take a look at it."

Cat screamed when he pressed her hand. It tore Scarlett like a knife.

"It's a bad burn, and that's a fact," said Dr. Devlin. "We'll keep it greased till the blister fills, then cut and drain the liquid."

"She's hurting now, Doctor. Can't you do something?" Cat's tears were soaking Scarlett's shoulder.

"Butter's best. It will cool it in time."

"In time?" Scarlett turned and ran. She thought of the liquid on her tongue when Cat was born, the blessed quick release from pain.

She'd take her baby to the wise woman.

So far—she'd forgotten the river and the tower were so far. Her legs were getting tired, that mustn't be. Scarlett ran as if the hounds of Hell were in pursuit. "Grainne!" she cried when she reached the hollies. "Help! For God's sake, help."

The wise woman stepped out from a shadow. "We'll sit here," she said quietly. "There's no more running needed." She sat on the ground and held up her arms. "Come to Grainne, Dara. I'll make the hurt go away."

Scarlett put Cat into the wise woman's lap. Then she crouched on the ground, poised to snatch her child and run again. To wherever there might be help. If she could think of any place or anyone.

"I want you to put your hand in mine, Dara. I won't touch it. Lay it in my hand yourself. I will talk to the burn and it will heed me. It will go away." Grainne's voice was calm, certain. Cat's green eyes looked into Grainne's placid wrinkled face. She placed the back of her injured small hand against Grainne's herb-stained leathery palm.

"You have a big, strong burn, Dara. I will have to persuade it. It will take a long time, but it will begin to feel better soon." Grainne blew gently on the burned flesh. Once, twice, three times. She put her lips close to their two hands and began to whisper into Cat's palm.

Her words were inaudible, her voice like the whisper of soft young leaves or clear shallow water running over pebbles in sunlight. After a few minutes, no more than three, Cat's crying stopped, and Scarlett sank onto the ground, slack-muscled from relief. The whispering continued, low, monotonous, relaxing. Cat's head nodded, then dropped onto Grainne's breast. The whispers went on. Scarlett leaned back on her elbows. Later her head drooped and she slid onto the ground, supine and soon sleeping. And still Grainne whispered to the burn, on and on, while Cat slept and Scarlett slept, and slowly, slowly the swelling subsided and the red receded until Cat's skin was as if she had never burned it at all. Grainne lifted her head then and licked her cracked lips. She laid Cat's hand over the other, then folded her two arms around the sleeping child and rocked gently forth and back, humming under her breath. After a long while she stopped.

"Dara." Cat opened her eyes. "It's time to go. You tell your mother. Grainne is tired and will sleep now. You must take your mother home." The wise woman stood Cat on her feet. Then she turned and went into the holly thicket on her hands and knees.

"Momma. It's time to go."

"Cat? How could I fall asleep like that? Oh, my angel, I'm so sorry. What happened? How do you feel, baby?"

"I had my nap. My hand is well. May I go up in the tower?"

Scarlett looked at her little girl's unblemished palm. "Oh, Kitty Cat, your Momma really needs a hug and a kiss, please." She held Cat to her for a moment, then let her go. It was her gift to Cat.

Cat pressed her lips to Scarlett's cheek. "I think I'd rather have tea and cakes than go in the tower right now," she said. It was her gift to her mother. "Let's go home."

"The O'Hara was under a spell and the witch and her changeling were talking in a tongue known to no man." Nell Garrity had seen it with her own eyes, she said, and that frightened she was she turned on her heel into the Boyne, forgetting altogether she needed to go back to the ford. She would have drowned for certain sure had the river been its usual deep self.

"Casting spells on the clouds to make them pass us by they were."

"And didn't Annie McGinty's cow go dry that very day and her one of the best milkers in all Trim?"

"Dan Houlihan in Navan has the affliction of warts on his feet so bad he can't put them to the floor."

"The changeling rides a wolf disguised as a pony by day."

"Her shadow fell on my churn and the butter never came."

"Those who know say she sees in the dark, her eyes glowing like fire for her prowling."

"And did you never hear the tale of her birthing, Mr. Reilly? It was on All Hallows' Eve, and the sky fairly torn to shreddings with comets . . ."

The stories were carried from hearth to hearth throughout the district.

It was Mrs. Fitzpatrick who found Cat's tabby on the doorstep of the Big House. Ocras had been strangled, then disembowelled. She rolled the remains into a cloth and hid it in her room until she could go unobserved to the river to dispose of it.

Rosaleen Fitzpatrick burst into Colum's house without knocking. He looked up at her, but he remained seated in his chair.

"Just what I thought I'd be finding!" she exclaimed. "You can't do your drinking in the bar like an honest man, you've got to hide your weakness here with that sorry excuse for a man." Her voice was rich with contempt, as was her gesture when she prodded Stephen O'Hara's limp legs with her booted foot. He was snoring unevenly through his slack open mouth. The smell of whiskey clung to his clothes, saturated his breath.

"Leave me be, Rosaleen," Colum said wearily. "My cousin and myself are mourning the death of Ireland's hopes."

Mrs. Fitzpatrick put her hands on her hips. "And what about the hopes of your other cousin, then, Colum O'Hara? Will you drown yourself in another bottle when Scarlett is mourning the death of her darling babe? Will you sorrow with her when your godchild is dead? Because I tell you, Colum, the child is in mortal danger."

Rosaleen fell on her knees before his chair. She shook his arm. "For the love of Christ and His Blessed Mother, Colum, you've got to do something! I've tried every way I know how, but the people won't listen to me. Mayhap it's even too late for them to listen to you, but you've got to make the try. You cannot hide away from the world like this. The people feel your desertion, and so does your cousin Scarlett."

"Katie Colum O'Hara," mumbled Colum.

"Her blood will be on your hands," said Rosaleen with cold clarity.

Colum made a leisurely round of visits to every house, cottage, and bar in Ballyhara and Adamstown the following day and night. The first visit was to Scarlett's office, where he found her studying the estate ledgers. Her frown smoothed out when she saw him at the door, reappeared when he suggested she give a party to welcome her cousin Stephen back to Ireland.

She capitulated at last, as he'd known she would, and then Colum was able to use the invitation to the party as his reason for all the other visits. He listened keenly for indications that Rosaleen's warning had a basis, but he heard nothing, to his great relief.

After Sunday Mass, all the villagers and O'Haras from all County Meath came to Ballyhara to welcome Stephen home and to hear about America. There were long trestle tables on the lawn with steaming platters of boiled salt beef and cabbage, baskets piled with hot boiled potatoes, and foamy pitchers of porter. The French doors were open to the drawing room with its ceiling of Irish heroes, as invitation into the Big House for any who cared to enter.

It was almost a good party.

Scarlett consoled herself afterwards with the thought that she'd done her best, and she'd had a long time with Kathleen. "I've missed you so, Kathleen," she'd told her cousin. "Nothing's the same since you left. The ford might be under ten feet of water for all the good it does me, I can't stand to go to Pegeen's house."

"And if things always stayed the same, Scarlett, what would be the reason for bothering to draw breath?" Kathleen replied. She was mother to a healthy boy and expecting a brother for him, she hoped, in six months.

She hasn't missed me at all, Scarlett realized sadly.

Stephen talked no more in Ireland than he had in America, but the family didn't seem to mind. "He's a silent man, and that's the all of it." Scarlett avoided him. He was still Spooky Stephen to her. He had brought back one delicious piece of news. Grandfather Robillard had died and left his estate to Pauline and Eulalie. They were in the pink house together, took their constitutionals every day, and were reputed to be even richer than the Telfair sisters.

They heard thunder in the distance at the O'Hara party. Everyone stopped talking, stopped eating, stopped laughing to look up in hope at the mocking bright blue sky. Father Flynn added a special Mass every day and people lit candles with private prayers for rain.

On Midsummer Day the clouds borne on the west wind began to pile together instead of scudding past. By late afternoon they filled the horizon, half-black and heavy. The men and women who were building the bonfire for the night's celebration lifted their heads into the staccato gusts of wind, smelling rain. It would be a celebration indeed if the rains returned and the crops were saved.

The storm broke at first dark, in a cannonade of deafening cracks of lightning that lit up the sky brighter than day, and a deluge of rain. People fell to the ground and covered their heads. Hail peppered them with stones of ice as big as walnuts. Cries of pain and fear filled the moments of silence between lightning cracks.

Scarlett was leaving the Big House for the music and dancing at the bonfire. She ducked back inside, soaked to the skin in only seconds, and ran upstairs to find Cat. She was looking out the window, her green eyes wide, her ears covered by her hands. Harriet Kelly huddled in a corner holding Billy close for protection. Scarlett kneeled beside Cat to watch the rampage of nature.

It lasted a half hour, then the sky was clear, star-studded, with a gleaming three-quarter moon. The bonfire was sodden and scattered; it would not be lighted this night. And the fields of grass and wheat were flattened by the hail that covered them in gray-white misshapen balls. A keening rose from the throats of the Irish of Ballyhara. Its piercing sound cut through the stone walls and glass panes into Cat's room. Scarlett shuddered and drew her dark child close. Cat whimpered softly. Her hands were not enough to hold back the sound.

"We've lost our harvest," Scarlett said. She was standing on a table in the middle of Ballyhara's wide street, facing the people of the town. "But there's plenty to be saved. The grass will still dry to hay, and we'll have straw from the wheat stalks even though there'll be no kernels to grind for flour. I'm going now to Trim and Navan and Drogheda to buy supplies for the winter. There'll be no hunger in Ballyhara. That I promise you, my word as The O'Hara."

They cheered her then.

But at night by their hearths they talked about the witch and the changeling and the tower where the changeling had stirred the ghost of the hanged lord to vengeance.

81

The clear skies and relentless heat returned, and lasted. The front page of the *Times* was made up entirely of reports and speculations on the weather. Pages two and three had more and more items about outrages against landlords' property and agents.

Scarlett glanced at the newspaper every day, then threw it aside. At least she didn't have to worry about her tenants, thank God for that. They knew she'd take care of them.

But it wasn't easy. Too often, when she arrived in a town or city that was supposed to have stockpiles of flour and meal, she discovered that the supplies were only rumors, or were all gone. In the beginning she haggled with vigor about the inflated prices, but as supplies became more scarce, she was so happy to find anything at all that she paid whatever was asked, often for inferior goods.

It's as bad as it was in Georgia after the War, she thought. No, it's worse. Because then we were fighting the Yankees, who stole or burned everything. Now I'm fighting for the lives of more people than I ever had depending on me at Tara. And I don't even know who the enemy is. I can't believe God's put a curse on Ireland.

But she bought a hundred dollars' worth of candles for the people of Ballyhara to light in supplication when they prayed in the chapel. And she rode her horse or drove her wagon carefully around the piles of stones that had begun to appear beside roads or in fields. She didn't know what older deities were being appeased, but if they'd bring rain she was willing to give them every stone in County Meath. She'd carry them with her own hands if she had to.

Scarlett felt helpless, and it was a new and frightening experience. She had thought she understood farming because she'd grown up on a plantation. The good years at Ballyhara had, in fact, been no more than she expected, because she had worked hard and demanded hard work from others. But what was she to do, now that willingness to work wasn't enough?

She continued to go to the parties she had accepted in such high spirits. Now she was looking for information from other landowners, not for entertainment.

Scarlett arrived a day late at Kilbawney Abbey for the Giffords' house party. "I'm terribly sorry, Florence," she said to Lady Gifford, "if I had any manners at all I would have thought to send a telegram. But the truth is, I was going from pillar to post looking for flour and meal contracts and I completely lost track of what day it was."

Lady Gifford was so relieved that Scarlett was there that she forgot to be offended. Everyone else at the house party had accepted her invitation instead of another because she'd held out the bait that Scarlett was coming.

"I've been waiting for the opportunity to shake your hand, young woman." The knickerbockered gentleman pumped Scarlett's hand vigorously. He was a vigorous old man, the Marquess of Trevanne, with an undisciplined white beard and an alarmingly purple-veined beak of a nose.

"Thank you, sir," said Scarlett. What for? she wondered.

The marquess told her, in the loud voice of the deaf. He told the entire house party, whether they wanted to listen or not. His bellows reached all the way out to the croquet lawn.

She deserved congratulations, he roared, for rescuing Ballyhara. He'd told Arthur not to be such a fool, not to waste his money buying ships from the thieves who robbed him, claiming the timbers were sound. But Arthur wouldn't listen, he was determined to ruin himself. Eighty thousand pounds he'd paid, more than half his patrimony, enough to buy all the land in County Meath. He was a fool, he'd always been a fool, the man never had any sense at all, even when they were boys together he'd known it. But demme, he'd loved Arthur like a brother even if he was a fool. No man ever had a truer friend than Arthur was to him. He had wept, yes, ma'am, actually wept when Arthur hanged himself. He'd always known he was a fool, but who could have dreamed he'd be such a fool as that? Arthur loved that place, he gave his heart to it, and in the end his life. It was criminal that Constance abandoned it the way she did. She should have preserved it as a memorial to Arthur.

The marquess was grateful to Scarlett for doing what Arthur's own widow didn't have the decency to do.

"I'd like to shake your hand again, Mistress O'Hara."

Scarlett surrendered it to him. What was this old man telling her? The young lord of Ballyhara hadn't hanged himself, a man from the town had dragged him to the tower and hung him. Colum said so. The marquess must be wrong. Old people got things mixed up in their memories ... Or Colum was wrong. He'd only been a child, he only knew what people said, he wasn't even in Ballyhara then, the family was at Adamstown ... The marquess wasn't in Ballyhara either, he only knew what people said. It's all too complicated.

"Scarlett, hello." It was John Morland. Scarlett smiled sweetly at the marquess and retrieved her hand. She tucked it in Morland's elbow.

"Bart, I'm so glad to see you. I looked for you at every single party of the Season and never found you."

"I passed this year. Two mares in foal outrank a viceroy every time. How have you been?"

It had been an aeon since she'd last seen him, and so much had happened. Scarlett hardly knew where to begin. "I know what interests you, Bart," she said. "One of the hunters you helped me buy is outjumping Half Moon. Her name is Comet. It's as if one day she looked up and decided it was fun instead of work ..." They strolled off to a quiet corner to talk. In due time Scarlett learned that Bart had no news of Rhett at all. She also learned more than she wanted to know about delivering a foal when it was turned in the mare's womb. It didn't matter. Bart was one of her favorite people and always would be.

All the talk was of the weather. Ireland had never before in its history had a drought, and what else could this succession of sunny days be called? There was almost no corner of the country that didn't need rain. There'd be trouble for sure when rents were due in September.

She hadn't thought of that. Scarlett's heart felt like lead. Of course the farmers wouldn't be able to pay their rents. And if she didn't make them pay, how could she expect the town tenants to pay? The shops and bars, even the doctor, depended on the money the farmers spent with them. She was going to have no income at all.

It was horribly difficult to keep up the appearance of cheerfulness, but she had to. Oh, she'd be glad when the weekend was over.

The final night of the party was July 14, Bastille Day. Guests had been told to bring fancy dress. Scarlett wore her best and brightest Galway clothes, with four petticoats of different colors beneath a red skirt. Her striped stockings were scratchy in the heat, but they caused such a sensation that it was worth the discomfort.

"I never dreamed the peasants were so charmingly dressed under their dirt," Lady Gifford exclaimed. "I'm going to buy some of everything to take to London next year. People will be begging for the name of my dressmaker."

What a stupid woman, thought Scarlett. Thank goodness this is the last night.

Charles Ragland came in for the dancing after dinner. The party he'd been to had broken up that morning. "I would have left anyhow," he told Scarlett later. "When I heard that you were so near, I had to come."

"So near? You were fifty miles away."

"A hundred would be the same."

Scarlett let Charles kiss her in the shadow of the great oak tree. It had been so terribly long since she'd been kissed, or felt a man's strong arms tighten protectively around her. She felt herself melting in his embrace. It felt wonderful.

"Beloved," Charles said hoarsely.

"Shhh. Just kiss me till I'm dizzy, Charles."

Dizzy she became. She held on to his broad muscular shoulders to keep from falling. But when he said he'd come to her room, Scarlett drew away from him, her head clear. Kisses were one thing, sharing her bed was out of the question.

She burned the contrite note he slid under her door during the night, and she left too early in the morning to need to say goodbye.

When she got home, she went at once to find Cat. It came as no surprise to learn that she and Billy had gone to the tower. It was the only cool place on Ballyhara. What was a surprise was to find Colum and Mrs. Fitzpatrick waiting for her under a big tree at the rear of the house, with a lavish tea spread on a shadowed table.

Scarlett was delighted. Colum had been such a stranger for so long, so stand-offish about coming up to the Big House. It was wonderful to have her almost-brother back.

"I've got the strangest story to tell you," she said. "It drove me half-crazy with curiosity when I heard it. What do you think, Colum? Is it possible that the young lord really hanged himself in the tower?" Scarlett described the Marquess of Trevanne with laughing, wicked accuracy and mimicked his speech as she repeated it.

Colum set down his teacup with tightly controlled precision. "I have no opinion, Scarlett darling," he said, and his voice was as light and laughing as Scarlett liked to remember it. "Anything is possible in Ireland, else we would be plagued with snakes like the rest of the world." He smiled as he stood up. "And now I must go. I tarried from my day's duties only to see your beautiful self. Disregard anything this woman may tell you about my fondness for the cakes I ate with my tea."

He walked away so rapidly that Scarlett had no time to wrap some cakes in a napkin for him to take along.

"I'll return shortly," said Mrs. Fitz, and she hurried after Colum.

"Well!" said Scarlett. She saw Harriet Kelly in the distance, at the end of the browned lawn, and waved at her. "Come have tea," Scarlett shouted. There was plenty left.

Rosaleen Fitzpatrick had to lift up her skirt and run to catch up with Colum halfway down the long drive. She walked silently at his side until she caught her breath sufficiently so that she could speak. "And what happens now?" she asked. "You're rushing to your bottle, is that the truth of it?"

Colum stopped, turned to face her. "There is no truth of anything, and that is what scours my heart. Did you hear her, then? Quoting the Englishman's lies, believing them. Just as Devoy and the others believe the shining English lies of Parnell. I could stay no longer, Rosaleen, for fear of smashing her English teacups and howling protest like a chained dog."

Rosaleen looked at the anguish in Colum's eyes and hardened her expression. Too long had she poured sympathy on his wounded spirit; it had not helped. He was tortured by his sense of failure and betrayal. After more than twenty years of working for Ireland's freedom, after success at his assigned task, after filling the arsenal in the Protestant church at Ballyhara, Colum had been told it was all valueless. Parnell's political actions had more meaning. Colum had always been willing to die for his country; he could not bear to live without believing that he was helping her.

Rosaleen Fitzpatrick shared Colum's distrust of Parnell; she shared his frustration that his work, and hers, had been discarded by the Fenian leaders. But she could put her own feelings aside to follow orders. Her commitment was as great as his, perhaps greater, for she lusted for personal revenge even more than justice.

Now, however, Rosaleen put aside her allegiance to Fenianism. Colum's suffering meant more to her than Ireland's, for she loved him in a way that no woman should permit herself to love a priest, and she could not let him destroy himself through doubt and anger.

"What kind of Irishman are you then, Colum O'Hara?" she said harshly. "Will you let Devoy and the others rule alone and wrongly? You hear what's happening. The people are fighting on their own, and paying a fearful price for lack of a leader. They do not want Parnell, no more than you. You created the means for an army. Why don't you go now and build the army to use the means instead of drinking yourself to blindness like any bravery-spouting layabout in a corner bar?"

Colum looked at her, then beyond her, and his eyes slowly filled with hope.

Rosaleen dropped her gaze to the ground. She couldn't chance letting him see the emotion burning in her eyes.

"I don't know how you can bear this heat," said Harriet Kelly. Under her parasol, there was a sheen of perspiration on her delicate face.

"I love it," Scarlett said. "It's just like home. Have I ever told you about the South, Harriet?"

She had not, Harriet said.

"Summer was my favorite time," said Scarlett. "The heat and the dry days were just what was wanted. It was so beautiful, the cotton plants green and fixing to bust open, all in row after row, stretching as far as your eye could see. The field hands would sing when they hoed, you could hear the music in the distance, kind of hanging there in the air." She heard her own words and was horrified. What was she saying? "Home?" This was her home now. Ireland.

Harriet's eyes were dreamy. "How lovely," she sighed.

Scarlett looked at her with disgust, then turned it on herself. Romantic dreaminess had gotten Harriet Kelly into more trouble than she knew what to do with, and she still didn't know any better.

But I do. I didn't have to put the South behind me, General Sherman did it for me, and I'm too old to pretend it never happened.

I don't know what's wrong with me, I'm all at sixes and sevens. Maybe it's the heat, maybe I've lost the knack of it.

"I'm going to go work on the accounts, Harriet," said Scarlett. The neat rows of numbers were always calming for her, and she felt like she was about to jump out of her skin.

The account books were terribly depressing. The only money she had coming in was the profit from the little houses she was building on the edge of Atlanta. Well, at least that money was no longer going to that revolutionary movement Colum used to belong to. It would help some—a lot, really. But not nearly enough. She'd spent incredible sums on the house and the village. And Dublin. She couldn't believe how extravagant she'd been in Dublin, although the orderly columns of numbers proved it beyond question.

If only Joe Colleton would shave a little in building those houses. They'd still sell like hotcakes, but the profit would be much bigger. She wouldn't let him buy cheaper lumber—the whole reason for building them in the first place was to keep Ashley in business. There were plenty of other ways to cut expenses. Foundations . . . chimneys . . . brick didn't have to be top quality.

Scarlett shook her head impatiently. Joe Colleton would never do it on his own. He was just like Ashley, bone honest and full of unbusinesslike ideals. She remembered them talking together at the site. If ever there were birds of a feather, it was those two. She wouldn't be surprised if they stopped in the middle of talking lumber prices to start talking about some fool book they'd read.

Scarlett's eyes grew thoughtful.

She ought to send Harriet Kelly to Atlanta.

She'd be a perfect wife for Ashley. They were another two of a kind, living out of books, hopeless in the real world. Harriet was a ninny in lots of ways, but she stuck by her obligations—she'd stayed with her no-good husband for nearly ten years—and she had her own kind of gumption. It took a lot of sand to walk in to the commanding officer in broken shoes and beg for Danny Kelly's life. Ashley needed that kind of steel behind him. He needed somebody to take care of, too. It couldn't be doing him any good having India and Aunt Pitty fussing over him all the time. What it was likely doing to Beau was too awful to think about. Billy Kelly would teach him a thing or three. Scarlett grinned. She'd better send a box of smelling salts for Aunt Pitty along with Billy Kelly.

Her grin faded. No, it wouldn't do. Cat would be heartbroken without Billy. She'd drooped for a week when Ocras ran away, and the tabby hadn't been one-tenth of what Billy was in her life.

Besides, Harriet couldn't stand the heat.

No, it wouldn't do at all. Not at all.

Scarlett bent her head to the account books again.

82

We've got to stop spending so much money," Scarlett said angrily. She shook the account book at Mrs. Fitzpatrick. "There's no reason on earth for feeding this army of servants when flour for bread costs a fortune. At least half of them will have to be let go. What good do they do, anyhow? And don't sing me that old song about having to churn the cream to make the butter, because if there's one thing that there's too much of these days, it's butter. You can't sell it for hapenny a pound."

Mrs. Fitzpatrick waited for Scarlett's tirade to end. Then she calmly took the book from her and put it on a table. "You'd turn them out onto the road, then?" she said. "They'll find plenty of company, for many of the Big Houses in Ireland are doing just what you're proposing. Not a day goes by we don't have a dozen or more poor souls begging a bowl of soup at the kitchen door. Will you add to their number?"

Scarlett strode impatiently to the window. "No, of course not, don't be ridiculous. But there must be some way we can cut expenses."

"It's more costly to feed your fine horses than your servants." Mrs. Fitzpatrick's voice was cold.

Scarlett turned on her. "That will be all," she said furiously. "Leave me alone." She picked up the book and went to her desk. But she was too upset to concentrate on the accounts. How could Mrs. Fitz be so mean? She must know that I enjoy hunting more than anything else in my life. The only thing that's getting me through this horrible summer is knowing that come fall, the hunting will begin again.

Scarlett closed her eyes and tried to remember the crisp cold mornings, with the night's light frost turned to trailing mist, and the sound of the horn signalling the beginning of the chase. A tiny muscle jumped involuntarily in the soft flesh over her clenched jaw. She wasn't good at imagining, she was good at doing.

She opened her eyes and worked doggedly on the accounts. With no grain to sell and no rents to collect, she was going to lose money this year. The knowledge bothered her, because she had always made money in business and losing it was a highly disagreeable change.

But Scarlett had grown up in a world where it was accepted that sometimes a crop failed or a storm wrought havoc. She knew that next year would be different, and certainly better. She was not a failure because of the disaster of the drought and the hail. It wasn't like the lumber business or the store where she would have been responsible if there had been no profit.

Besides, the losses would barely make a dent in her fortune. She could be extravagant for the rest of her life, and the crops at Ballyhara could fail every year, and she would still have plenty of money.

Scarlett sighed unconsciously. For so many years she had worked and scrimped and saved, thinking that if only she could have enough money, she would be happy. Now she had it, thanks to Rhett, and somehow it didn't mean anything at all. Except that there was no longer anything to work for, to scheme and strive for.

She wasn't foolish enough to want to be poor and desperate again, but she needed to be challenged, to use her quick intelligence, to conquer obstacles. And so she thought with longing about jumping fences and ditches and taking chances on a powerful horse that she controlled by force of will.

When the accounts were done, Scarlett turned to the pile of personal mail with a silent groan. She hated writing letters. She already knew what was in the mail. Many were invitations. She put them in a stack. Harriet could pen the polite refusals for her, no one would know she hadn't written them herself, and Harriet loved being useful.

There were two more proposals. Scarlett received at least one a week. They pretended to be love letters, but she knew very well that they wouldn't be there if she wasn't a rich widow. Most of them, anyhow.

She replied to the first one with the convenient phrases about "honored by your regard" and "unable to return your affection to the degree you merit" and "place incalculable value on your friendship" that protocol demanded and supplied.

The second was not so easy. It was from Charles Ragland. Of all the men she had met in Ireland, Charles was the most truly eligible to her. His adoration was convincing, not at all like the elaborate fawning over her that so many men did. He wasn't after her money, she was sure of that. He came from money himself, his people were big landowners in England. He was a younger son, and he'd chosen the army instead of the Church. But he must have some money of his own. His dress uniform cost more than all her ball gowns put together, she was sure.

What else? Charles was handsome. He was as big as Rhett, only blond instead of dark. Not washed-out blond, though, like so many fair people. His hair was gold, with just a touch of red in it, startling against his tanned skin. He was really very good looking. Women looked at him like they could eat him with a spoon.

So why didn't she love him? She had thought about it, she'd thought often and long. But she couldn't, she didn't care enough.

I want to love somebody. I know how it feels to love, it's the best feeling in the world. I can't bear the unfairness, that I learned about loving too late. Charles loves me, and I want to be loved, I need it. I'm lonely by myself without it. Why can't I love him?

Because I love Rhett, that's why. That's why for Charles and for every other man in the world. They're none of them Rhett.

You will never have Rhett, her mind told her.

And her heart cried out in anguish: Do you think I don't know that? Do you think I can ever completely forget it? Do you think that it doesn't haunt me every time I see him in Cat? Do you think it doesn't spring on me from nowhere just when I believe that my life is my own?

Scarlett wrote carefully, looking for the kindest words she knew to say no to Charles Ragland. He would never understand if she told him that she truly liked him, that in a very small way perhaps she even loved him because he loved her, and that her affection for him made it impossible for her to marry him. She wished better for him than a wife who would forever belong to another man.

The year's final house party was not far from Kilbride, which was not far from Trim. Scarlett could drive herself instead of all the complications of taking the train. She left very early in the morning when it was still cool. Her horses were suffering from the heat, despite being sponged down four times a day. Even she had started to feel it; she felt twitchy and sweaty almost all night when she was trying to sleep. Thank heaven it was August. The summer was almost done, if it would only admit it.

The sky was still tinged with pink, but there was already a haze of heat in the distance. Scarlett hoped she'd calculated the time right for the trip. She'd like to have her horse and herself in the shade when the sun was full up.

I wonder if Nan Sutcliffe will be up? She never looked like an early riser to me. No matter. I wouldn't mind having a cool bath and changing my clothes before I see anybody. I do hope there's a decent maid for me here, not like that ham-handed idiot at the Giffords'. She practically tore the sleeves off my frocks hanging them up. Maybe Mrs. Fitz is right, she usually is. But I don't want a personal maid hanging around me every minute of my life. Peggy Quinn does all I need at home, and if people want me to come visit they'll just have to put up with me not bringing my maid. I really should give a house party myself, to pay back all the hospitality I owe. Everyone has been so kind … But not yet. Next summer will do. I can say this year was just too hot, plus I was worried about the farms …

Two men stepped from shadows on each side of the road. One caught the horse's bridle; the other was pointing a rifle. Scarlett's mind raced, her heart did too. Why hadn't she thought to bring the revolver with her? Maybe they'd just take her rig and her cases and let her walk back to Trim if she swore not to tell what they looked like. Idiots! Why couldn't they at least be wearing those masks, like she'd read about in the newspaper?

For the love of God! They were in uniform, they weren't Whiteboys at all.

"Damn your eyes, you scared me half to death!" She could still barely see the men. The green uniforms of the Royal Irish Constabulary blended into the shadowy hedgerows.

"I'll have to ask you for some identification, madam," said the man holding her horse. "Kevin, you look in the back there."

"Don't you dare touch my things. Who do you think you are? I am Mrs. O'Hara of Ballyhara, on my way to the Sutcliffes' at Kilbride. Mr. Sutcliffe is a magistrate, and he'll see to it that both of you end up in the dock!" She didn't really know that Ernest Sutcliffe was a magistrate, but he looked like one with his bushy ginger mustache.

"Mrs. O'Hara is it?" The Kevin who'd been told to search her buggy came forward beside her. He took off his hat. "We heard tell of you in barracks, ma'am. I was asking Johnny here only a couple of weeks ago should we go over and make ourselves known to you?"

Scarlett stared incredulously. "Whatever for?" she said.

"They're saying you're from America, Mrs. O'Hara, a fact I can tell the truth of myself after hearing you speak. They're also saying you come from the grand state called Georgia. It's a place we two hold a fondness for in our hearts, seeing we both fought in the army there back in 'sixty-three and more."

Scarlett smiled. "You did?" Think of meeting someone from home on the road to Kilbride. "Where were you? What part of Georgia? Were you with General Hood?"

"No, ma'am, I was one of Sherman's boys. Johnny there, he was with the Confederates, that's where he got the name, for Johnny Reb and all that."

Scarlett shook her head to clear it. She couldn't be hearing right. But more questions and more answers confirmed it. The two men, both Irish, were now the best of friends. With happy shared memories of being on opposite sides in a savage war.

"I don't understand," she admitted at last. "You were trying to kill each other fifteen years ago, and you're friends now. Don't you even argue about the North and the South and who was right?"

"Johnny Reb" laughed. "What's it to a soldier the right and the wrong of it all? He's there for the fighting, that's what he likes. Doesn't matter who you're fighting, long as he gives you a good fight."

When Scarlett reached the Sutcliffes' house she shocked their butler almost out of his professional composure by asking for a brandy with her coffee. She was more confused than she could handle.

Afterwards she bathed and put on a fresh frock and came downstairs, her composure restored. Until she saw Charles Ragland. He shouldn't be at this party! She acted as if she hadn't noticed him.

"Nan, how lovely you look. And I just love your house. My room's so pretty I might stay forever."

"Nothing would please me more, Scarlett. You know John Graham, don't you?"

"Only by reputation. I've been angling for an introduction. How do you do, Mr. Graham?"

"Mrs. O'Hara." John Graham was a tall slender man with the loose-limbed ease of the natural athlete. He was the Master of Hounds of the Galway Blazers, perhaps the most famous hunt in all Ireland. Every fox hunter in Great Britain hoped to be invited to join one of the Blazers' hunts. Graham knew it, and Scarlett knew that he knew it. There was no point in being coy.

"Mr. Graham, are you open to bribery?" Why didn't Charles quit staring at her like that? What was he doing here anyhow?

John Graham threw back his silvered head in laughter. His eyes were lively with it when he looked back down at Scarlett. "I have always heard that you Americans come straight to the point, Mrs. O'Hara. Now I see it's true. Tell me, what precisely did you have in mind?"

"Would an arm and a leg do? I can stay on a sidesaddle with one leg —it's the only good thing about a sidesaddle that I can think of—and I only need one hand for the reins."

The Master smiled. "Such an extravagant offer. I've heard that about Americans, too, that they tend to extravagance."

Scarlett was tiring of banter. And Charles' presence made her edgy. "What you may not have heard, Mr. Graham, is that Americans take fences where the Irish go through gates and the English go back home. If you'll let me ride with the Blazers, I'll take at least a pad or I'll eat a flock of crows in front of you all—without salt."

"By God, madam, with style like yours, you'll be welcome any time you say."

Scarlett smiled. "I'll take you up on that." She spit in her hand. Graham smiled broadly and spit in his. The slap they gave each other's palm resounded throughout the long gallery.

Then Scarlett strode over to Charles Ragland. "I told you in my letter, Charles, that this was the one house party in the whole country you should stay away from. It's mean of you to come."

"I'm not here to embarrass you, Scarlett. I wanted to tell you myself, not in a letter. You needn't worry about my pressing you or importuning you. I understand that no means no. The regiment's going to Donegal next week; it was my last chance to say what I wanted to say. And, I confess, to see you again. I promise not to lurk or gaze with soulful eyes." He smiled with rueful humor. "I practiced that speech, too. How did it sound?"

"Pretty fair. What's in Donegal?"

"Whiteboy trouble. It seems to be more concentrated there than any other county."

"Two constables stopped me to search my buggy."

"All the patrols are out now. With rents coming due soon—but I don't want to talk military. What did you say to John Graham? I haven't seen him laugh like that in years."

"Do you know him?"

"Very well. He's my uncle."

Scarlett laughed until her sides ached. "You English. Is that what 'diffident' means? If you'd only brag a little, Charles, you could have saved me a lot of trouble. I've been trying to get with the Blazers for a year, but I didn't know anybody."

"The one you'll really like is my Aunt Letitia. She can ride Uncle John into the ground and never look back. Come on, I'll introduce you."

* * *

There were promising rumbles of thunder, but no rain. By midday the air was stifling. Ernest Sutcliffe rang the dinner gong to get everyone's attention. He and his wife had planned something different for the afternoon, he said nervously. "There is the usual croquet and archery, what? Or the library and billiards in the house, what? Or whatever one does customarily. What?"

"Do get on with it Ernest," said his wife.

With many starts and stops and sputters Ernest got on with it. There were bathing costumes for anyone who wanted one and ropes strung across the river for the adventurous to hold on to while cooling off in the rushing water.

"Hardly 'rushing,'" amended Nan Sutcliffe, "but a decent little current. Footmen will be there with iced champagne."

Scarlett was one of the first to accept. It sounded like being in a cool tub all afternoon.

It was immensely more enjoyable than a cool tub, even though the water was warmer than she'd hoped it would be. Scarlett moved along the rope hand over hand towards the center and deeper water. Suddenly she found herself in the grip of the current. It was colder, so much colder that gooseflesh rose on her arms, and very swift. It pushed her up against the rope then knocked her feet out from under her. She was holding on for her life. Her legs gyrated out of control and the current twisted her body in half circles. She felt a dangerous temptation to let go of the rope and ride swirling in the current to wherever it would take her. Free of the earth under her feet, free of walls or roads or anything controlled and controlling. For long heart-racing moments she imagined herself letting go, just letting go.

She was shaking from the effort she had to make to keep her grip fast on the rope. Slowly, with intense concentration and determination, she moved on, hand over hand, until she was free of the current's pull. She turned her head away from the others splashing and shouting in the water, and she cried, she didn't know why.

There were slow eddies, like fingers from the current, in the warmer water outside it. Scarlett slowly became aware of their caresses, then she let herself float among them. Warm tendrils of movement stroked her legs, her thighs, her body, her breasts, twined around her waist and her knees beneath the wool tunic and bloomers. She felt longings she could not name, an emptiness that cried out to be filled within her. "Rhett," she whispered against the rope, bruising her lips, inviting the roughness and the hurt.

"Isn't this splendid fun?" cried Nan Sutcliffe. "Who wants champagne?"

Scarlett forced herself to look around. "Scarlett, you brave thing, you went right through the frightening part. You'll have to come back. None of us has the nerve to bring your champagne to you."

Yes, thought Scarlett, I have to go back.

After dinner she made her way to Charles Ragland's side. Her cheeks were very pale, her eyes very bright.

"May I offer you a sandwich tonight?" she asked quietly.

Charles was an experienced, skillful lover. His hands were gentle, his lips firm and warm. Scarlett closed her eyes and let her skin receive his touch the way it had received the caresses of the river. Then he spoke her name, and she felt the ecstatic sensations slipping away. No, she thought, no, I don't want to lose it, I mustn't. She closed her eyes tighter, thought of Rhett, pretended that the hands were Rhett's hands, the lips Rhett's lips, that the warm, strong thrusting filling her aching emptiness was Rhett's.

It was no good. It was not Rhett. The sorrow of it made her want to die. She turned her face away from Charles' questing mouth and wept until he was at rest.

"My darling," he said, "I love you so."

"Please," Scarlett sobbed, "oh, please go away."

"What is it, darling, what's wrong?"

"Me. Me. I was wrong. Please leave me alone." Her voice was so small, so poignant with despair that Charles reached out to comfort her, then drew back in full knowledge that there was only one comfort he could give. He moved quietly as he gathered his clothes, and he shut the door behind him with only the slightest sound.

I have gone to join my regiment. I will love you forever. Yours, Charles.

Scarlett folded the note carefully, tucked it beneath the pearls in her jewel case. If only . . .

But there was little room in her heart for anyone. Rhett was there. Laughing at her, outwitting her, challenging her, surpassing her, dominating her, sheltering her.

She went down to breakfast with bruise-like dark shadows under her eyes, imprint of the desolate weeping that had replaced sleep for her. She looked cool in her mint-green linen frock. She felt encased in ice.

She was obliged to smile, talk, listen, laugh. Guests had a duty to make a house party a success. She looked at the people seated along the sides of the long table. Smiling, talking, listening, laughing. How many of them, she wondered, have wounds inside them, too? How many feel dead, and grateful for it? How brave people are.

She nodded at the footman who was holding a plate for her at the long sideboard. At her signal he opened the big silver serving dishes one after another for her approval. Scarlett accepted some rashers of bacon and a spoonful of salt and scrambled eggs. "Yes, a grilled tomato," she said, "no, nothing cold." Ham, preserved goose, jellied quail eggs, spiced beef, salted fish, aspics, ices, fruits, cheeses, breads, relishes, jams, sauces, wines, ale, cider, coffee—all no. "I'll have tea," she said.

She was sure she could swallow some tea. Then she'd be able to go back to her room. Luckily this was a big party, and mostly for shooting. Most of the men would already be out with their guns. There would be luncheon in the house and somewhere on the grounds, wherever the shoot was. There would be tea served indoors and out. Everyone could choose amusements. No one was required to be any special place at any special time until dinner was served. The guest card in her room said to gather in the drawing room after the first dinner gong at seven forty-five. Processing into dinner at eight.

She indicated a chair beside a woman she hadn't met before. The footman deposited her plate and the small tray with individual tea service. Then he pulled out the chair, seated her, shook out the folds of her napkin, and draped it across her lap. Scarlett nodded to the woman. "Good morning," she said, "my name is Scarlett O'Hara."

The woman had a lovely smile. "Good morning. I've been looking forward to meeting you. My cousin Lucy Fane told me that she'd met you at Bart Morland's. When Parnell was there. Tell me, don't you find it delectably seditious to admit that one supports Home Rule? My name's May Taplow, by the way."

"A cousin of mine said he was sure I wouldn't be for Home Rule at all if Parnell was short and fat and had warts," Scarlett said. She poured her tea while May Taplow laughed. "Lady May Taplow" to be exact, Scarlett knew. May's father was a duke, her husband the son of a viscount. Funny how one picked up these things as time and parties went by. Funnier still how a country girl from Georgia got used to thinking about "one" doing this and that. Next thing you know, I'll be saying "toe-mah-toe" so that the footmen will know what it is I want. Guess it's no different really from telling a darky you want goobers so he'll know you'd like a handful of peanuts.

"I'm afraid your cousin would be dead on the nose if he accused me of the same thing," May confided. "I lost all interest in the succession when Bertie started to put on weight."

It was Scarlett's turn to confess. "I don't know who Bertie is."

"Stupid of me," said May, "of course you don't. You don't do the London Season, do you? Lucy said you run your own estate all alone. I do think that's wonderful. Makes the men who can't cope without a bailiff look as pouffish as they are, half of them. Bertie's the Prince of Wales. A dear, really, so enjoys being naughty, but it's beginning to show. You would adore his wife, Alexandra. Deaf as a post, you can't possibly tell her a secret unless you write it down, but beautiful past measuring and as sweet as she is pretty."

Scarlett laughed. "If you had any idea, May, what I feel like, you'd die laughing. Back home when I was growing up, the most high-toned gossip going was about the man who owned the new railroad. Everybody wondered when he'd started wearing shoes. I can hardly believe I'm chatting about the King of England to be."

"Lucy told me I'd be mad about you, and she was dead on the nose. Promise me you'll stay with us if you ever decide to do London. What did you decide about the railway man? What kind of shoes did he have? Did he limp when he walked? I'm sure I would adore America."

Scarlett discovered with surprise that she'd eaten all her breakfast. And that she was still hungry. She lifted her hand and the footman behind her chair stepped forward. "Excuse me, May, I'm going to ask for seconds," she said. "Some kedgeree, please, and some coffee, lots of cream."

Life goes on. A mighty good life, too. I made up my mind I was going to be happy and I guess I am. I've just got to notice it.

She smiled at her new friend. "The railroad man was as Cracker as they come—"

May looked confused.

"Oh. Well, Cracker is what we call a white man who likely never wore shoes. That's not the same as poor white . . ." She enthralled the Duke's daughter.

It rained that evening during dinner. All the house party ran outside and capered for joy. The impossible summer would soon be over.

Scarlett drove home at midday. It was cool, the dusty hedgerows had been washed clean, and soon the hunting season would begin. *The Galway Blazers! I'll definitely want my own horses. I'll have to see about sending them ahead by rail. The best thing, I suppose, would be to load them at Trim, then to Dublin, then back across to Galway. Otherwise it's the long road to Mullingar, then rest them, then train to Galway. I wonder if I should send feed, too? I'll have to find out about stabling. I'll write to John Graham tomorrow . . .*

She was home before she knew it.

"Such good news, Scarlett!" She'd never seen Harriet looking so excited. *Why, she's much prettier than I thought. With the right clothes—*

"While you were gone a letter came from one of my cousins in England. I told you, did I not, that I'd written of my good fortune and your kindness? This cousin, his name is Reginald Parsons but the family always called him Reggie, has arranged for Billy to be admitted to the school his son attends, Reggie's son, that is. His name is—"

"Wait a minute, Harriet. What are you talking about? Billy's going to the school in Ballyhara, I thought."

"Naturally he'd have had to if there was no alternative. That's what I wrote to Reggie."

Scarlett's jaw set. "What's wrong with the school here, I'd like to know."

"Nothing is wrong with it, Scarlett. It's a good Irish village school. I want something better for Billy, surely you understand that."

"Surely I do no such thing." She was prepared to defend Ballyhara's school, Irish schools, Ireland itself, at the top of her lungs if need be. Then she took a good look at Harriet Kelly's soft, defenseless face. It was no longer soft, there was no weakness. Harriet's gray eyes were normally hazy with dreams; now they looked like steel. She was ready to fight anyone, anything for her son. Scarlett had seen the same kind of thing before, the lamb turned lion, when Melanie Wilkes took a stand about something she believed in.

"What about Cat? She'll be so lonely without Billy."

"I'm sorry, Scarlett, but I have to think of what's best for Billy."

Scarlett sighed. "I'd like to suggest a different alternative, Harriet. You and I both know that in England Billy will always be branded the Irish son of an Irish stable groom. In America he can become anything you want him to be . . ."

Early in September Scarlett held a stoically silent Cat in her arms to wave goodbye to Billy and his mother as their ship left Kingstown Harbor for America. Billy was crying; Harriet's face had the radiance of resolve and hope. Her eyes were cloudy with dreams. Scarlett hoped at least part of the dreams would come true. She had written to Ashley and Uncle Henry Hamilton, telling them about Harriet and asking them to watch out for her and help her find a place to stay and work as a teacher. She was sure they'd do that much at least. The rest was up to Harriet and circumstances.

"Let's go to the zoo, Kitty Cat. There are giraffes and lions and bears and a big, big elephant."

"Cat likes lions best."

"You might change your mind when you see the baby bears."

They stayed in Dublin for a week, going to the zoo every day, eating cream buns in Bewley's coffee shop afterwards, then the puppet theater followed by high tea at the Shelbourne with silver tiers of sandwiches and scones, silver bowls of whipped cream, silver trays of éclairs. Scarlett learned that her daughter was indefatigable and had a digestive system of cast iron.

Back at Ballyhara she helped Cat turn the tower into Cat's private place, to be visited only by invitation. Cat swept the dried cobwebs and droppings of centuries out of the high doorway, then Scarlett pulled up bucket after bucket of water from the river and the two of them scrubbed the walls and floor of the room. Cat laughed and splashed and blew soap bubbles while she scrubbed. It reminded Scarlett of the baths when Cat was a baby. She didn't mind at all that it took them over a week to get the place clean. Nor did she mind that the stone steps to upper levels were missing. Cat would have liked to wash the tower all the way to the top.

They finished just in time for what would have been Harvest Home in a normal year. Colum had advised her not to try and make a celebration when there was nothing to celebrate. He helped her distribute the sacks of flour and meal, salt and sugar, potatoes and cabbages that came to the town on wide wagons from all the suppliers Scarlett had found.

"They didn't even say 'thank you,'" she said bitterly when the ordeal was over. "Or if they did, they sure didn't act like they meant it. You'd think it might just dawn on a few people that I'm hurting from the drought, too. My wheat and grass were ruined the same as theirs, and I'm losing all my rents, and I bought all that stuff."

She couldn't verbalize the deepest hurt of all. The land, the O'Hara land, had turned against her, and the people, her people, of Ballyhara.

She poured all of her energies into Cat's tower. The same woman who hadn't so much as peered through a window to see what was happening to her house now spent hours going through all the rooms, scrutinizing each piece of furniture, each rug, every blanket, quilt, pillow, selecting the best. Cat was the final arbiter. She looked over her mother's choices and picked a bright flowered bathmat, three patchwork quilts, and a Sevres vase, the vase for her paintbrushes. The mat and quilts went into a deep wide indentation in the massively thick wall of the tower. For her nap, said Cat. Then she patiently went back and forth, house to tower, with her favorite picture books, her paint box, her leaf collection, and a box containing stale crumbs saved from cakes that she had especially liked. She was planning to lure birds and animals to her room. Then she'd paint their pictures on her wall.

Scarlett listened to Cat's plans and watched her laborious preparations with pride in Cat's determination to create a world that would satisfy her even without Billy in it. She could learn from her four-year-old daughter, she thought sadly. On Halloween she gave Cat the birthday party that the little girl designed for herself. There were four small cakes, each with four candles. They ate one of the cakes themselves, sitting on the clean floor of Cat's tower sanctuary. They gave the second one to Grainne, eating it with her. Then they went home, leaving the other two cakes for the birds and animals.

The next day not a crumb was left, Cat reported with excitement. She didn't invite her mother to come see. The tower was all hers now.

Like everyone else in Ireland, Scarlett read the newspapers that autumn with alarm that grew into outrage. For her, the alarm was caused by the number of evictions reported. The farmers' efforts to fight back were perfectly understandable as far as she was concerned. Attacking a bailiff or a pair of constables with fists or pitchfork was only a normal human reaction, and she was sorry that it stopped none of the evictions. It wasn't the fault of the farmer that crops had failed and there was no money from sale of the grain. She knew all about that herself.

At nearby hunts the talk was always about the same thing, and the landowners were much less tolerant than Scarlett. They were worried by the instances of resistance by farmers. "Dammit, what do they expect? If they don't pay their rents, they don't keep their houses. They know that, it's always been like that. Bloody insurgence, that's what's going on . . ."

But Scarlett's reactions became the same as her neighboring estate owners' when the Whiteboys entered in. There had been scattered incidents during the summer. The Whiteboys were more organized now, and more brutal. Night after night barns and hayricks were torched. Cattle and sheep were killed, pigs slaughtered, donkeys and plow horses had legs broken or tendons cut. Shop windows were smashed, and manure or burning torches thrown inside. And more and more as autumn turned to winter there were attacks from concealment against military men, English soldiers and Irish constables, and gentry in carriages or on horseback. Scarlett took two grooms along on the roads to the meets.

And she worried constantly about Cat. Losing Billy seemed to have upset Cat much less than she had feared. Cat never moped, and she never whined. She was always occupied with some project or some game she invented for herself. But she was only four, it made Scarlett nervous now that Cat went off by herself so much. Scarlett was determined not to cage her child, but she began to wish that Cat were less agile, less independent, less fearless. Cat visited stables and barns, stillroom and dairy, garden and gardensheds. She wandered through woods and fields like a wild creature at home there, and the house was a land of opportunity for play in rooms that were cleaned but not used, attics full of boxes and trunks, basements with wine racks, barrels of foodstuffs, rooms for servants, for silver, for milk, butter, cheese, ice, ironing, washing, sewing, carpenter's repairs, bootblacking, the myriad activities that maintained the Big House.

There was never any point in looking for Cat. She might be anywhere. She always came home for her meals and bath time. Scarlett couldn't figure out how the child knew what time it was, but Cat was never late.

Mother and daughter went riding together every day after breakfast. But Scarlett grew afraid to go out on the roads because of the Whiteboys, and she didn't want to spoil the intimacy of their rides by taking grooms along, so their route became the path she had first used, past the tower and through the ford and into the boreen that led to Daniel's cottage. Pegeen O'Hara might not like it, she thought, but she'll have to put up with Cat and me if she wants me to keep on paying Seamus' rent. She wished Daniel's youngest son, Timothy, wasn't taking such a long time about finding a bride. He would have the little cottage when he did, and the girl could only be an improvement on Pegeen. Scarlett missed the easy intimacy she had known with her family before Pegeen joined it.

Every time she left for a hunt Scarlett asked Cat if she minded being left. The little brown forehead wrinkled with perplexity above Cat's clear green eyes. "Why do people mind?" she asked. It made Scarlett feel better. In December she explained to Cat that she'd be gone for a longer time because she was going a long way, on the train. Cat's response was the same.

Scarlett set off for the long-awaited hunt with the Galway Blazers on a Tuesday. She wanted a day of rest for herself as well as her horses before Thursday's hunt. She wasn't tired; on the contrary, she was almost too excited to sit still. But she wasn't about to take any chances. She had to be better than her best. If Thursday was a triumph, she'd stay for Friday and Saturday as well. Her best would be good enough then.

At the end of the first day's hunting, John Graham presented Scarlett with the gore-gummed pad that she had won. She accepted it with a court curtsey. "Thank you, Your Excellency." Everyone applauded.

The applause was even louder when two stewards came in bearing a huge platter that held a steaming pie. "I've been telling everyone about your sporting bet, Mrs. O'Hara," said Graham, "and we'd devised a small joke for you. This is a pie of minced crow meat. I will now take the first bite. The rest of the Blazers will follow. I had expected you to be doing it unaccompanied."

Scarlett smiled her sweetest smile. "I'll sprinkle some salt on it for you, sir."

She first noticed the hawk-faced man on the black horse on Friday when he made an impossible jump ahead of her and she reined in abruptly to watch, nearly losing her seat. He rode with an arrogant fearlessness that made her own recklessness seem tame.

Afterwards, people surrounded him at the hunt breakfast, all of them talking, the man saying little. He was tall enough for her to see his aquiline face and dark eyes and hair almost blue it was so black.

"Who is that bored-looking tall man?" she asked a woman she knew.

"My dear!" The woman said with excitement. "Isn't he too fascinating for words?" She sighed happily. "Everyone says he's the most wicked man in Britain. His name is Fenton."

"Fenton what?"

"Just Fenton. He's the Earl of Fenton."

"You mean he doesn't have any name of his own at all?" She'd never understand all this English title rigmarole, Scarlett thought. It made no sense at all.

Her companion smiled. A superior smile, it seemed to Scarlett, and she became angry. But the woman quickly disarmed her. "Isn't it silly?" she said. "His Christian name is Luke; I don't know what the family name is. I just think of him as Lord Fenton. No one in my circle of friends is important enough to address him any other way, except 'Milord' or 'Lord Fenton' or 'Fenton.' " She sighed again. "He's terribly grand. And so outrageously attractive."

Scarlett made no comment aloud. Privately she thought he looked like he needed taking down a peg or two.

Returning from the kill on Saturday, Fenton walked his horse alongside Scarlett's. She was glad she was on Half Moon; it put her almost at eye level. "Good morning," said Fenton, touching the brim of his top hat. "I understand we're neighbors, Mistress O'Hara. I'd like to call and pay my respects, if I may."

"That would be very pleasant. Where is your place?"

Fenton raised his thick black eyebrows. "Don't you know? I'm on the opposite side of the Boyne, Adamstown."

Scarlett was glad she hadn't known. Obviously he'd expected her to. What conceit.

"I know Adamstown well," she said, "I have some O'Hara cousins who are tenants of yours."

"Indeed? I've never known my tenants' names." He smiled. His teeth were brilliantly white. "It is quite charming, that American candor about your humble origins. It was mentioned in London, even, so you see it's serving your purposes very well." He touched his crop to his hat and moved off.

The nerve of the man! And the bad manners—he didn't even tell me his name. As if he was sure I must have asked someone. Oh, I do wish I hadn't!

When she got home she told Mrs. Fitz to give instructions to the butler: she was not at home to the Earl of Fenton the first two times he called.

Then she concentrated on decorating the house for Christmas. She decided they really should have a bigger tree this year.

Scarlett opened the parcel from Atlanta as soon as it was delivered to her office. Harriet Kelly had sent her some cornmeal, bless her heart. I guess I talk about missing corn bread more than I know I do. And a present for Cat from Billy. I'll let her have it when she comes home for tea. Ah, here it is, a nice fat letter. Scarlett settled herself comfortably with a pot of coffee to read it. Harriet's letters were always full of surprises.

The first one she wrote when she arrived in Atlanta had brought— among eight tightly written pages of rhapsodic thanks—the unbelievable story that India Wilkes had a serious beau. A Yankee, no less, who was the new minister at the Methodist church. Scarlett relished the idea. India Wilkes—Miss Confederacy Noble Cause herself. Let a Yankee in britches come along and give her the time of day and she'll forget there ever was a war.

Scarlett skimmed the pages about Billy's accomplishments. Cat might be interested, she'd read them aloud later. Then she found what she was looking for. Ashley had asked Harriet to marry him.

It's what I wanted, isn't it? It's silly for me to feel a twinge of jealousy. When's the wedding? I'll send a magnificent present. Oh, for heaven's sake! Aunt Pitty can't live alone in the house with Ashley after India's wedding because it wouldn't be proper. I do not believe it. Yes, I do. It's just what Aunt Pitty would swoon over, worrying about how it would look for her, the oldest spinster in the world, to be living with a single man. At least that gets Harriet married pretty soon. Not exactly the most passionate proposal in the world, but I'm sure Harriet can do it up with lace and rosebuds in her mind. Too bad the wedding's in February. I'd have been tempted to go, but not tempted enough to miss the Castle Season. It hardly seems possible that I once thought Atlanta was a big city. I'll see if Cat would like to go to Dublin with me after New Year's. Mrs. Sims said the fittings would only take a few hours in the mornings. I wonder what they do with those poor zoo animals in the winter?

"Have you another cup in that pot, Mistress O'Hara? It was a chilly ride over here."

Scarlett stared up at the Earl of Fenton, her mouth gaping in surprise. Oh, Lord, I must look a sight, I hardly even brushed my hair this morning. "I told my butler to say I'm not at home," she blurted.

Fenton smiled. "But I came the back way. May I sit down?"

"I'm amazed you wait to be asked. Please do. Ring the bell first, though. I've only got one cup, seeing I wasn't at home to visitors."

Fenton tugged the bellpull, took a chair close to hers. "I'll use your cup if you don't mind. It will take a week for another to get here."

"I do mind. So there!" Scarlett blurted. Then she burst out laughing. "I haven't said 'so there' in twenty years. I'm surprised I didn't stick out my tongue, too. You're a very irritating man, Milord."

"Luke."

"Scarlett."

"May I have some coffee?"

"The pot's empty . . . so there."

Fenton looked a little less overbearing when he laughed as he did then.

84

$\mathcal{S}$carlett visited her cousin Molly that afternoon, throwing that socially ambitious creature into such a frenzy of gentility that Scarlett's offhand questions about the Earl of Fenton were barely noticed. The visit was very short. Molly didn't know anything at all, save that the Earl's decision to spend some time at his Adamstown estate had shocked his servants and his agent. They kept the house and stables ready at all times, just in case he might choose to come there, but this was the first time in nearly five years that he had arrived.

The staff were now all preparing for a house party, said Molly. There had been forty guests when the Earl last came, all with servants of their own, and horses. The Earl's hounds and their attendants had come, too. There had been two weeks of hunting, and a Hunt Ball.

At Daniel's cottage, the O'Hara men commented on the Earl's arrival with bitter humor. Fenton had picked his time badly, they said. The fields were too dry and hard to be ruined by the hunters, like last time. The drought had been there before him and his friends.

Scarlett returned to Ballyhara no wiser than she'd left it. Fenton had said nothing to her about a hunt, or about a house party. If he gave one, and she wasn't invited, it would be a terrible slap in the face. After dinner she wrote a half dozen notes to friends she'd made during the Season. "Such a fuss in these parts," she scribbled, "about Lord Fenton popping up at his place near here. He's been absentee for so many years that even the shop-keepers don't have any good gossip about him."

She smiled as she sealed the notes. If that doesn't bring out all the skeletons in his closet, I don't know what will.

The next morning she dressed with care in one of the gowns she'd worn at her drawing rooms in Dublin. I don't care a fig about looking attractive for that irritating man, she told herself, but I will not let him sneak up on me again when I'm not ready for guests.

The coffee grew cold in the pot.

Fenton found her in the fields exercising Comet that afternoon. Scarlett was wearing her Irish clothes and cloak, riding astride.

"How sensible you are, Scarlett," he said. "I've always been convinced that sidesaddles are ruinous to a good horse, and that looks like a fine one. Would you care to match him against mine in a short race?"

"I'd be delighted," Scarlett said, with honeyed sweetness. "But the drought left everything so parched that the dust behind me will probably choke you half to death."

Fenton raised his eyebrows. "Loser provides champagne to lay the dust in the throat of both," he challenged.

"Done. To Trim?"

"To Trim." Fenton wheeled his horse and began the race before Scarlett knew what was happening. She was coated with dust before she caught up with him on the road, choking as she urged Comet alongside, coughing when they thundered across the bridge into town in a tie.

They reined in on the green beside the castle walls. "You owe me a drink," said Fenton.

"The devil you say! It was a tie."

"Then I owe you one as well. Shall we have two bottles, or would you prefer to break the tie by racing back?"

Scarlett kicked Comet sharply and took a head start. She could hear Luke laughing behind her.

The race ended in the forecourt of Ballyhara. Scarlett won, but barely. She grinned happily, pleased with herself, pleased with Comet, pleased with Luke for the fun she'd had.

He touched the brim of his dusty hat with his crop. "I'll bring the champagne for dinner," he said. "Expect me at eight." Then he galloped off.

Scarlett stared after him. The nerve of the man! Comet sidestepped skittishly, and she realized that she had let the reins go slack. She gathered them up and patted Comet's lathered neck. "You're right," she said aloud. "You need a cool-down and a good grooming. So do I. I think I've just been tricked good and proper." She began to laugh.

* * *

"What's that for?" asked Cat. She watched her mother inserting the diamonds in her earlobes with fascination.

"For decoration," said Scarlett. She tossed her head and the diamonds swayed and sparkled beside her face.

"Like the Christmas tree," said Cat.

Scarlett laughed. "Sort of, I guess. I never thought of that."

"Will you decorate me for Christmas, too?"

"Not until you're much, much older, Kitty Cat. Little girls can have tiny pearl necklaces or plain gold bracelets, but diamonds are for grown-up ladies. Would you like to have some jewelry for Christmas?"

"No. Not if it's for little girls. Why are you decorating you? It's not Christmas yet for days and days."

Scarlett was startled to realize that Cat had never seen her in evening dress before. When they had been in Dublin, they'd always dined in their rooms at the hotel. "There's a guest coming for dinner," she said, "a dress-up guest." The first one at Ballyhara, she thought. Mrs. Fitz was right all along, I should have done this sooner. It's fun to have company and get dressed up.

The Earl of Fenton was an entertaining and polished dinner companion. Scarlett found herself talking much more than she had intended—about hunting, about learning to ride as a child, about Gerald O'Hara and his Irish love of horses. Fenton was very easy to talk to.

So easy that she forgot what she wanted to ask him until the end of the meal. "I suppose your guests will be arriving any minute," she said as the dessert was served.

"What guests?" Luke held his glass of champagne up to examine the color.

"Why, for your hunting party," said Scarlett.

Fenton tasted the wine and nodded approval to the butler. "Where did you get that idea? I'm not having a hunt, nor any guests."

"Then what are you doing in Adamstown? They say you never come here."

The glasses were both filled. Luke lifted his in a toast to Scarlett. "Shall we drink to amusing ourselves?" he said.

Scarlett could feel herself blushing. She was almost certain she had just been propositioned. She raised her glass in response. "Let's drink to you being a good loser of very good champagne," she said with a smile, looking at him through lowered lashes.

* * *

Later, when she was getting ready for bed, she turned Luke's words over and over in her mind. Had he come to Adamstown just to see her? And did he intend to seduce her? If he did, he was in for the surprise of his life. She'd beat him at that game just like she had beat him in the race.

It would be fun, too, to make such an arrogant self-satisfied man fall hopelessly in love with her. Men shouldn't be that handsome and that rich; it made them think they could have everything their own way.

Scarlett climbed into bed and nestled under the covers. She was looking forward to going riding with Fenton in the morning as she'd promised.

They raced again, this time to Pike Corner, and Fenton won. Then back to Adamstown, and Fenton won again. Scarlett wanted to get fresh horses and try again, but Luke declined with a laugh. "You might break your neck in your determination, and I'd never collect my winnings."

"What winnings? We had no bet on this race."

He smiled and said nothing more, but his glance roved over her body.

"You're insufferable, Lord Fenton!"

"So I've been told, more than once. But never with quite so much vehemence. Do all American women have such passionate natures?"

You'll never find out from me, Scarlett thought, but she curbed her tongue as she curbed her horse. It had been a mistake to let him goad her into losing her temper, and she was even more annoyed with herself than she was with him. I know better than that. Rhett always used to make me fly off the handle, and it gave him the upper hand every time.

. . . Rhett . . . Scarlett looked at Fenton's black hair and dark mocking eyes and superbly tailored clothes. No wonder her eyes had sought him out in the crowded field at the Galway Blazers. He did have a look of Rhett about him. But only at first. There was something very different, she didn't know exactly what.

"I thank you for the race, Luke, even if I didn't win," she said. "Now I've got to be going, I have work to do."

A momentary look of surprise showed on his face, then he smiled. "I expected you to have breakfast with me."

Scarlett returned his smile. "I expect you did." She could feel his eyes on her as she rode away. When a groom rode over to Ballyhara in the afternoon with a bouquet of hothouse flowers and Luke's invitation to dinner at Adamstown, she wasn't surprised. She wrote a note of refusal for the groom to take back.

Then she ran upstairs, giggling, to put on her riding habit again. She was arranging his flowers in a vase when Luke strode through the door into the long drawing room.

"You wanted another race to Pike Corner, if I'm not mistaken," he said.

Scarlett's laughter was in her eyes only. "You're not mistaken about that," she said.

Colum climbed up onto the bar in Kennedy's. "Now stop your yawping, all of you. What more could the poor woman do, I ask you? Did she forgive your rents or did she not? And did she not give you food for the winter? And more grain and meal in the storehouse waiting for when you run out of what you've got. It's ashamed I am to see grown men pulling their mouths into a baby's pout and inventing grievances as excuse for having another pint. Drink yourselves into the floor if you want to—it's a man's right to poison his stomach and addle his head—but don't be blaming your weakness on The O'Hara."

"She's gone over to the landlords" . . . "prancing off to the lords and ladies all summer" . . . "hardly a day goes by she's not tearing down the road racing the black devil lord of Adamstown" . . . The bar was aroar with angry shouts.

Colum shouted them all down. "What kind of men are they that gossip like a bunch of women about another woman's clothes and parties and romances? You make me sick, the lot of you." He spit on the top of the bar. "Who wants to lick that up? You're not men, it should suit you fine."

The sudden silence could have produced any kind of reaction. Colum spread his feet apart and held his hands loosely in front of him ready to form fists.

"Ach, Colum, it's that restless we are with no reason to do a little burning and shooting like the lads we hear about in other towns," said the oldest of the farmers. "Get down from there and get out your *bodhran* and I'll be the whistle and Kennedy the fiddle with you. Let's sing some songs about the rising and get drunk together like good Fenian men."

Colum literally jumped at the chance to calm things down. He was already singing when his boots hit the floor.

> *There beside the singing river, that dark mass of men were seen*
> *Far above the shining weapons hung their own beloved green.*
> *"Death to every foe and traitor! Forward! strike the marching tune*
> *And hurrah my boys, for freedom, 'tis the risin' of the moon!"*

It was true that Scarlett and Luke raced their horses on the roads around Ballyhara and Adamstown. Also over fences, ditches, hedges, and the Boyne. Almost every morning for a week he forded the cold river and strode into the morning room with a demand for coffee and challenge to a race. Scarlett was always waiting for him with seeming composure, but in fact Fenton kept her constantly on edge. His mind was quick, his conversation unpredictable, and she could not relax her attention or her defenses for a minute. Luke made her laugh, made her angry, made her feel alive to the ends of her fingertips and toes.

The all-out racing across the countryside released some of the tension she felt when he was around. The battle between them was clearer, their common ruthlessness undisguised. But the excitement she always felt when she forced her courage to its reckless limits was threatening as well as thrilling. Scarlett sensed something powerful and unknown, hidden deep within her, that was in danger of breaking free of her control.

Mrs. Fitz warned her that the townspeople were disturbed by her behavior. "The O'Hara is losing their respect," she said sternly. "Your social life with the Anglos is different, it's distant. This racketing around with the Earl of Fenton rubs their noses in your preference for the enemy."

"I don't care if their damn noses are rubbed bloody. My life is my own business."

Scarlett's vehemence startled Mrs. Fitzpatrick. "Is it like that, then?" she said, and her tone wasn't stern at all. "Are you in love with him?"

"No, I'm not. And I'm not going to be. So leave me alone, and tell all of them to leave me alone, too."

Rosaleen Fitzpatrick kept her thoughts to herself after that. But her instincts as a woman saw trouble in the feverish brightness of Scarlett's eyes.

Am I in love with Luke? Mrs. Fitzpatrick's question forced Scarlett to question herself. No, she answered at once.

Then why am I out of sorts all day on the mornings he doesn't show up?

She could find no convincing answer.

She thought about what she'd learned from the letters of friends responding to her mention of him. The Earl of Fenton was notorious, they all said. He possessed one of the greatest fortunes in Britain, owned properties in England and Scotland as well as his estate in Ireland. He was an intimate of the Prince of Wales, maintained a huge town house in London where rumored bacchanals alternated with famously elaborate entertainments to which all Society schemed for invitations. He had been the favored target of matchmaking parents for over twenty years, ever since he had inherited his title and wealth at the age of eighteen, but he had escaped capture by anyone, even several noted beauties with fortunes of their own. There were whispered stories about broken hearts, shattered reputations, even suicides. And more than one husband had met him on the duelling field. He was immoral, cruel, dangerous, some said evil. Therefore, of course, the most mysterious and fascinating man in the world.

Scarlett imagined the sensation it would cause if an Irish-American widow in her thirties succeeded where all the titled English beauties had failed, and her lips curved in a small, secret smile that faded at once.

Fenton showed none of the signs of a man desperately in love. He intended to possess her, not marry her.

Her eyes narrowed. I'm not about to let him add my name to the long list of his conquests.

But she couldn't help wondering what it would be like to be kissed by him.

85

Fenton whipped his horse into a burst of speed and passed Scarlett, laughing aloud. She bent forward, crying aloud to Half Moon to go faster. Almost immediately she had to pull back on the reins. The road curved between high stone walls, and Luke had stopped up ahead, with his horse turned to block the way.

"What are you playing at?" she demanded. "I could have crashed right into you."

"Exactly what I had in mind," said Fenton. Before Scarlett understood what was happening, he had caught hold of Half Moon's mane and drawn the two horses close. His other hand closed over the back of Scarlett's neck and held her head immobile while his mouth fastened over hers. His kiss was bruising, commanding her lips to open, drawing her tongue between his teeth. His hand forced her to succumb. Scarlett's heart pounded with surprise, fear, and—as the kiss lasted on and on—a thrill of surrender to his strength. When he released her she was shaken and weak.

"Now you'll stop refusing my invitations to dinner," said Luke. His dark eyes glittered with satisfaction.

Scarlett gathered her wits. "You presume too much," she said, hating her breathlessness.

"Do I? I doubt it." Luke's arm curved along her back and held her against his chest while he kissed her again. His hand found her breast and squeezed it to the border of pain. Scarlett felt a surging response, a longing for his hands on all her body, and his brutal lips against her skin.

The nervous horses moved, breaking the embrace, and Scarlett was nearly unseated. She fought for balance on the saddle and in her thoughts. She mustn't do this, she mustn't give herself to him, give in to him. If she did, he'd lose interest as soon as he conquered her, she knew it.

And she didn't want to lose him. She wanted him. This was no love-sick boy like Charles Ragland, this was a man. She could even fall in love with a man like this.

Scarlett stroked Half Moon, calming him, thanking him in her heart for saving her from folly. When she turned to face Fenton, her swollen lips were stretched in a smile.

"Why don't you put on an animal's pelt and drag me to your house by my hair?" she said. There was precisely the right blend of humor and contempt in her voice. "Then you wouldn't frighten the horses." She urged Half Moon into a walk, then a trot, heading back the way they had come.

She turned her head and spoke over her shoulder. "I won't come to dinner, Luke, but you may follow me to Ballyhara for coffee. If you want more than that, I can offer you early luncheon or late breakfast."

Scarlett murmured softly to Half Moon, urging hurry. She couldn't read the meaning of the scowl on Fenton's face, and she felt something very like fear.

She had already dismounted when Luke rode into the stableyard. He swung a leg over and slid down from his horse, throwing the reins to a groom.

Scarlett pretended not to notice that Luke had commandeered the only groom in sight. She led Half Moon inside the stable herself to find another boy.

When her eyes adjusted to the dim light, she stopped in her tracks, afraid to move. Cat was in the stall directly in front of her, standing barefoot and bare-legged atop Comet, with her small arms outstretched for balance. She had on a heavy Aran jersey, borrowed from one of the stable-boys. It bunched over her tucked-up skirts, and the sleeves hung past the ends of her fingers. As usual her black hair had escaped its braids and was a mass of tangles. She looked like an urchin, or a gypsy child.

"What are you doing, Cat?" said Scarlett quietly. She knew the big horse's edgy disposition. A loud noise could spook him.

"I'm starting to practice circus," said Cat. "Like the picture in my book of the lady on the horse. When I go in the ring I'll need a parasol please."

Scarlett kept her voice even. This was more frightening even than

Bonnie. Comet could shy Cat off, then crush her. "It would be more fair if you waited to start next summer. Your feet must feel very cold on Comet's back."

"Oh." Cat slid onto the floor at once, next to the metal-shod hooves. "I didn't think of that." Her voice came from deep in the gated stall. Scarlett held her breath. Then Cat climbed over the gate with her boots and wool stockings in her hand. "I knew the boots would hurt."

Scarlett willed herself not to grab her child in her arms and hold her safe. Cat would resent her relief. She looked to her right for a groom to take Half Moon. She saw Luke, standing quietly and staring at Cat.

"This is my daughter, Katie Colum O'Hara," she said. And make of it what you will, Fenton, she thought.

Cat looked up from her concentration on tying her boot laces. She studied Fenton's face before she spoke. "My name is Cat," she said. "What is your name?"

"Luke," said the Earl of Fenton.

"Good morning, Luke. Would you like the yellow of my egg? I'm going to eat my breakfast now."

"I would like that very much," he said.

They made a strange procession; Cat led the way to the house, with Fenton walking beside her, adjusting his long stride to her short legs. "I had my breakfast before," Cat told him, "but I'm hungry again, so I will have breakfast again."

"That strikes me as eminently sensible," he said. There was no mockery in his thoughtful tone of voice.

Scarlett followed the two of them. She was still unsettled by the fright Cat had given her, and she had not yet quite recovered from the moments of passionate emotion when Luke kissed her. She felt dazed and confused. Fenton was the last man on earth she would have expected to love children, and yet he seemed to be fascinated by Cat. He was treating her exactly right, too, taking her seriously, not condescending to her because she was so small. Cat had no patience with people who tried to baby her. Somehow Luke seemed to sense that and respect it.

Scarlett felt tears fill her eyes. Oh, yes, she could love this man. What a father he could be to her beloved child. She blinked rapidly. This was not the time for sentimentality. For Cat's sake as well as for her own, she had to be strong and clear headed.

She looked at Fenton's sleek dark head, inclined toward Cat. He looked very tall and broad and powerful. Invincible.

She shivered inwardly, then rejected her cowardice. She would win. She had to, now. She wanted him for herself and for Cat.

Scarlett nearly laughed at the scene Luke and Cat presented. Cat was totally absorbed in the delicate business of cutting off the top of her boiled egg without shattering it; Fenton was watching Cat with equal concentration.

Suddenly, without warning, desperate grief drove Scarlett's amusement away. Those dark eyes watching Cat should be Rhett's, not Luke's! Rhett should be the one fascinated by his daughter, Rhett the one to share her breakfast egg, Rhett the one to walk beside her, matching his pace to her small steps.

Painful longing carved a hollow in Scarlett's breast where her heart should be, and anguish—so long held at bay—flooded in to fill it. She ached for Rhett's presence, for his voice, for his love.

If only I'd told him about Cat before it was too late . . . If only I'd stayed in Charleston . . . If only . . .

Cat tugged at Scarlett's sleeve. "Are you going to eat your egg, Momma? I'll open it for you."

"Thank you, darling," said Scarlett to her child. Don't be a fool, she said to herself. She smiled at Cat, and at the Earl of Fenton. What was past was past, and she had to think about the future. "I have a suspicion you're going to have another yolk to eat, Luke," Scarlett laughed.

Cat said goodbye and ran outdoors after breakfast, but Fenton stayed. "Bring more coffee," he told the maid, without looking at her. "Tell me about your daughter," he said to Scarlett.

"She only likes the white of the egg," Scarlett answered, smiling to mask her worry. What should she tell him about Cat's father? Suppose Luke asked his name, how he died, who he was.

But Fenton asked only about Cat. "How old is this remarkable daughter of yours, Scarlett?"

He professed astonishment when told that Cat was barely four, asked if she was always so self-possessed, if she had always been precocious, if she was very high-strung . . . Scarlett warmed to his genuine interest and talked until her throat was raw about the marvels of Cat O'Hara. "You should see her on her pony, Luke, she rides better than I do—or you . . . And she climbs everything like a monkey. The painters had to pluck her off their ladders . . . She knows the woods as well as any fox, and she has a built-in compass, she never gets lost . . . 'High-strung'? There's not a nervous bone in her body. She's so fearless that it terrifies me sometimes. And she never carries on when she gets a bump or a bruise. Even when she was a baby she hardly ever cried, and when she started walking, she'd just look surprised when she fell, then got right back up again . . . Of course she's healthy! Didn't you see how straight and strong she is? She eats like a horse, too, and never gets sick. You wouldn't believe the number of éclairs and cream buns she can tuck away without turning a hair . . ."

When Scarlett heard the hoarseness in her voice, she looked at the clock and laughed. "My grief, I've been bragging for an age. It's all your fault, Luke, for egging me on so. You should have shut me up."

"Not at all. I'm interested."

"Watch out or you'll make me jealous. You act like you're falling in love with my daughter."

Fenton raised his eyebrows. "Love is for shopkeepers and penny romances. I'm interested in her." He stood and bowed, lifted Scarlett's hand from her lap and brushed it with a light kiss. "I leave for London in the morning, so I'll take leave of you now."

Scarlett stood up, close to him. "I'll miss our races," she said, meaning every word. "Will you be back soon?"

"I'll call on you and Cat when I return."

Well! thought Scarlett after he was gone. He didn't even try to kiss me goodbye. She didn't know whether it was a compliment or an insult. He must regret the way he acted when he kissed me before, she decided. I guess he lost control of himself. And he sure is scared of the word "love."

She concluded that Luke showed all the symptoms of a man who was falling in love against his will. It made her very happy. He'd be a wonderful father for Cat . . . Scarlett touched her bruised lips gently with the tip of a finger. And he was a very exciting man.

86

*L*uke was very much on Scarlett's mind during the following weeks. She was restless, and on bright mornings she raced alone over the routes they'd followed together. When she and Cat decorated the tree, she remembered the pleasure of dressing up for dinner the night he first came to Ballyhara. And when she pulled the wishbone of the Christmas goose with Cat, she wished that he would return from London soon.

Sometimes she closed her eyes and tried to remember the way it felt to have his arms around her, but every attempt made her tearfully angry, because Rhett's face and Rhett's embrace and Rhett's laughter always filled her memory instead. That was because she'd known Luke such a short time, she told herself. In time his presence would blot out the memories of Rhett, that was only logical.

On New Year's Eve there was a great racket, and Colum marched in beating the *bodhran* followed by two fiddlers and Rosaleen Fitzpatrick playing the bones. Scarlett screeched with joyful surprise and ran to hug him. "I'd given up hope that you'd ever come home, Colum. Now it's bound to be a good year, with a beginning like this." She got Cat up from her sleep, and they saw in the first moments of 1880 with music and love all around them.

New Year's Day began with laughter as the barm brack shattered against the wall, showering crumbs and currants all over Cat's dancing body and upturned, open-mouthed face. But afterwards the sky darkened with clouds, and an icy wind tore at Scarlett's shawl when she made the rounds of New Year's visits in her town. Colum took a drink in every house, liquor, not tea, and talked politics with the men until Scarlett thought she would scream.

"Will you not come to the bar, then, Scarlett darling, and raise a glass to a brave New Year and new hope for the Irish?" said Colum after the last cottage had been visited.

Scarlett's nostrils flared at the smell of whiskey on him. "No, I'm tired and cold and I'm going home. Come with me and we'll have a quiet time by the fire."

"A quiet time is what I dread most, Scarlett *aroon*. Quiet lets the darkness creep into a man's soul." Colum walked unsteadily through the door of Kennedy's bar, and Scarlett trudged slowly up the drive to the Big House, holding her shawl close around her. Her red skirt and the blue and yellow stripes on her stockings looked drab in the cold gray light.

Hot coffee and a hot bath, she promised herself as she pushed open the heavy front door. She heard a stifled giggle when she entered the hall, and her heart tightened. Cat must be playing hide and seek. Scarlett pretended to suspect nothing. She closed the door behind her, dropped her shawl on a chair, then looked around.

"Happy New Year, The O'Hara," said the Earl of Fenton. "Or is it Marie Antoinette? Is this the peasant costume all the best dressmakers in London are creating for costume balls this year?" He was on the landing of the staircase.

Scarlett stared up at him. He was back. Oh, why had he caught her looking this way? It wasn't what she'd planned at all. But it didn't matter. Luke was back, and so soon, and she no longer felt tired at all. "Happy New Year," she said. And it was.

Fenton stepped to one side, and Scarlett saw Cat on the stairs behind him. Both Cat's arms were held up for her two hands to steady the gleaming jewelled tiara on her tousled head. She walked down the steps to Scarlett, her green eyes laughing, her mouth twitching to keep from grinning. Behind her trailed a long, wide slash of color, a crimson velvet robe bordered with a wide band of ermine.

"Cat's wearing your regalia, Countess," Luke said. "I've come to arrange our marriage."

Scarlett's knees gave way and she sat on the marble floor in a circle of red, with green and blue petticoats spilling from beneath. A flicker of anger mixed with her shocked thrill of triumph. This couldn't be true. It was too easy. It took all the fun out of everything.

* * *

"It seems our surprise was a success, Cat," said Luke. He untied the heavy silk cords at her neck and took the tiara from her hands. "You may go now. I have to talk to your mother."

"Can I open my box?"

"Yes. It's in your room."

Cat looked at Scarlett, smiled, then ran giggling up the stairs. Luke gathered the robe over his left arm, held the tiara in his left hand, and walked down to stand near Scarlett with his right hand reaching down to her. He looked very tall, very big, his eyes very dark. She gave him her hand, and he lifted her to her feet.

"We'll go into the library," said Fenton. "There's a fire, and a bottle of champagne for a toast to seal the bargain."

Scarlett allowed him to lead the way. He wanted to marry her. She couldn't believe it. She was numb, speechless with shock. While Luke poured the wine she warmed herself at the fire.

Luke held a glass out to her. Scarlett took it. Her mind was beginning to register what was happening, and she found her voice.

"Why did you say 'bargain,' Luke?" Why hadn't he said he loved her and wanted her to be his wife?

Fenton touched the rim of his glass to hers. "What else is marriage but a bargain, Scarlett? Our respective solicitors will draw up the contracts, but that's just a matter of form. You know, surely, what to expect. You're not a girl or an innocent."

Scarlett set her glass carefully on a table. Then she lowered herself carefully into a chair. Something was horribly wrong. There was no warmth in his face, in his words. He wasn't even looking at her. "I would like for you to tell me, please," she said slowly, "what to expect."

Fenton shrugged impatiently. "Very well. You'll find me quite generous. I assume that is your chief concern." He was, he said, one of the wealthiest men in England, although he expected she had found that out for herself. He genuinely admired her astuteness at social climbing. She could keep her own money. He would naturally provide her with all her clothing, carriages, jewels, servants, et cetera. He expected her to be a credit to him. He had observed that she had the ability.

She could also keep Ballyhara for her lifetime. It seemed to amuse her. For that matter, she could play with Adamstown, too, when she wanted to muddy her boots. After her death Ballyhara would go to their son, even as Adamstown would be his upon Luke's death. The joining of contiguous lands had always been one of the chief causes for marriage.

"For, of course, the essential feature of the bargain is that you provide me with an heir. I'm the last of my line, and it's my duty to continue it. Once I get a son on you, your life is your own, with the usual attention to maintaining a semblance of discretion."

He refilled his glass, then drained it. Scarlett could thank Cat for her tiara, said Luke. "I had, needless to say, no thought of making you the Countess of Fenton. You're the kind of woman I enjoy playing with. The stronger the spirit, the greater the pleasure in breaking it to my will. It would have been interesting. But not as interesting as that child of yours. I want my son to be like her—fearless, with indestructible rude health. The Fenton blood has been thinned by inbreeding. Infusing your peasant vitality will remedy that. I note that my tenant O'Haras, your family, live to a great age. You are a valuable possession, Scarlett. You will give me an heir to be proud of, and you won't disgrace him or me in society."

Scarlett had been staring at him like an animal mesmerized by a serpent. But now she broke the spell. She took her glass from the table. "I will when Hell freezes over!" she cried, then she threw the glass into the fire. The alcohol flared in an explosion of flame. "There's your toast to seal your bargain, Lord Fenton. Get out of my house. You make my flesh crawl."

Fenton laughed. Scarlett tensed, poised to spring at him, to batter his laughing face. "I thought you cared for your child," he said with a sneer. "I must have been mistaken." The words kept Scarlett from moving.

"You disappoint me, Scarlett," he said, "you really do. I attributed more shrewdness to you than you are demonstrating. Forget your injured vanity and consider what you have in your grasp. An impregnable position in the world for yourself and your daughter. It's unprecedented but I have the power to overthrow precedent, even law, if I choose. I shall arrange an adoption, and Cat will become the Lady Catherine. 'Katie' is, of course, out of the question, it's a kitchen maid's name. As my daughter she will have immediate and unquestioned access to the best of everything she will ever need, or want. Friends, ultimately marriage—she will have only to choose. I will never harm her; she's too valuable to me as a model for my son to follow. Can you deny all that to her because your lower-class yearning for romance is unfulfilled? I don't think so."

"Cat doesn't need your precious titles and 'best of everything,' Milord, and neither do I. We've done very well without you, and we'll keep on the way we are."

"For how long, Scarlett? Don't rely on your success in Dublin too much. You were a novelty, and novelties have short spans of life. An orangutan could be the toast of a provincial setting like Dublin if it were well dressed. You have one more Season, two at the most, and then you will be forgotten. Cat needs the protection of a name and a father. I'm one of a very few men with the power to remove the taint from a bastard child— no, save your protests, I don't care what tale you concoct. You would not be in this godforsaken corner of Ireland if you and your child were welcome in America.

"Enough of this. It's beginning to bore me, and I detest being bored. Send word when you've come to your senses, Scarlett. You'll agree to my bargain. I always get what I want." Fenton began to walk to the door.

Scarlett called to him to stop. There was one thing she had to know. "You can't force everything in the world to do what you want, Fenton. Did it ever cross your mind that your brood mare wife might give birth to a girl-child and not a boy?"

Fenton turned to face her. "You're a strong, healthy woman. I should get a male child eventually. But even at the worst, if you give me only girls, I'll arrange that one of them marry a man willing to give up his name and take hers. Then my blood will still inherit the title and continue the line. My obligation will be satisfied."

Scarlett's coldness was the equal of his. "You think of everything, don't you? Suppose I was barren? Or you couldn't father a child?"

Fenton smiled. "My manhood is proven by the bastards I've scattered through all the cities of Europe, so your attempted insult doesn't touch me. As for you, there's Cat." A look of surprise crossed his face, and he strode back toward Scarlett, making her shrink from his sudden approach.

"Come now, Scarlett, don't be dramatic. Haven't I just told you I only break mistresses, not wives? I have no desire to touch you now. I was forgetting the tiara, and I must put it in safekeeping until the wedding. It's a family treasure. You'll wear it in due time. Send word when you capitulate. I am going to Dublin to open my house there and prepare for the Season. A letter will find me on Merrion Square." He bowed to her with full courtly flourishes and left, laughing.

Scarlett held her head proudly high until she heard the front door close behind him. Then she ran to shut and lock the library doors. Safe from the eyes of the servants, she threw herself onto the thick carpet and sobbed wildly. How could she have been so wrong about everything? How could she have told herself that she could learn to love a man who had no love in him? And what was she going to do now? Her mind was filled with the picture of Cat on the stairs, crowned and laughing with delight. What should she do?

"Rhett," Scarlett cried brokenly, "Rhett, we need you so much."

87

Scarlett gave no outward sign of her shame, but she condemned herself savagely for the emotions she'd felt for Luke. When she was alone, she picked at the memory like a half-healed scab, punishing herself with the pain of it.

What a fool she'd been to imagine a happy life as a family, to build a future on that one breakfast when Cat divided the eggs on their three plates. And what laughable conceit, to think she could make him love her. The whole world would ridicule her if it was known.

She had fantasies of revenge: she would tell everyone in Ireland that he had asked her to marry him and been refused; she would write to Rhett and he would come kill Fenton for calling his child a bastard; she would laugh in Fenton's face before the altar and tell him that she could never bear another child, that he'd made a fool of himself by marrying her; she would invite him to dinner and poison his food . . .

Hatred burned in her heart. Scarlett extended it to all the English, and she threw herself passionately into renewed support of Colum's Fenian Brotherhood.

"But I have no use for your money, Scarlett darling," he told her. "The work now is in planning the moves of the Land League. You heard us talking on New Year's, do you not remember?"

"Tell me again, Colum. There must be something I can do to help."

There was nothing. Land League membership was open only to tenant farmers, and there would be no action until rents came due in the spring.

One farmer on each estate would pay, all the others would refuse, and if the landlord evicted, all would go to live at the cottage where the rent was paid up.

Scarlett couldn't see the reason for that. The landlord would just rent to someone else.

Ah, no, said Colum, that's where the League came in. They'd force everyone else to stay away, and, without farmers, the landlord would lose his rents and also his newly planted crops because there'd be no one to tend them. It was the idea of a genius; he was only sorry he hadn't thought of it himself.

Scarlett went to her cousins and pressured them to join the Land League. They could come to Ballyhara if they were evicted, she promised.

Without exception every O'Hara refused.

Scarlett complained bitterly to Colum.

"Don't be blaming yourself for the blindness of others, Scarlett darling. You're doing all that's needed to make up for their failings. Aren't you The O'Hara and a credit to the name? Do you not know that every house in Ballyhara and half of them in Trim have cuttings from the Dublin papers about The O'Hara being the shining Irish star in the Castle of the English Viceroy? They keep them in the Bible, with the prayer cards and pictures of the saints."

On Saint Brigid's Day there was a light rain. Scarlett said the ritual prayers for a good farm year with a fervor no other prayer had ever held, and she had tears on her cheeks when she turned the first sod. Father Flynn blessed it with holy water, then the chalice of water was passed from hand to hand for everyone to drink and share. The farmers left the field quietly, with bowed heads. Only God could save them. No one could stand another year like the last one.

Scarlett returned to the house and removed her muddy boots. Then she invited Cat to have cocoa in her room while she got her things organized to be packed for Dublin. She would be leaving in less than a week. She didn't want to go—Luke would be there, and how could she face him? With her head held high, it was the only way. Her people expected it of her.

Scarlett's second Season in Dublin was an even greater triumph than her first. Invitations awaited her at the Shelbourne for all the Castle events, plus five small dances and two late-night suppers in the Viceregal private apartments. She also found in a sealed envelope the most coveted invitation of all: her carriage would be admitted through the special entrance behind the Castle. There'd be no more waiting in line for hours on Dame Street while carriages were allowed into the Castle yard four at a time to put down guests.

There were also cards requesting her presence at parties and dinners in private houses. These were reputed to be much more entertaining than the Castle events with their hundreds of people. Scarlett laughed, deep in her throat. An orangutan in fine clothes, was she? No, she was not, and the pile of invitations proved it. She was The O'Hara of Ballyhara, Irish and proud of it. She was an original! It made no difference that Luke was in Dublin. Let him sneer all he liked. She could look him in the eye without fear or shame, and be damned to him.

She sorted through the pile, picking and choosing, and a tiny bubble of excitement rose in her heart. It was nice to be wanted, nice to wear pretty gowns and dance in pretty rooms. So what if the social world of Dublin was Anglo? She knew enough now to recognize that Society's smiles and frowns, rules and transgressions, honors and ostracisms, triumphs and losses, were all part of a game. None of it was important, none of it mattered to the world of reality outside the gilded ballrooms. But games were made to be played, and she was a good player. She was glad, after all, that she'd come to Dublin. She liked to win.

Scarlett learned immediately that the Earl of Fenton's presence in Dublin had set off a frenzy of excitement and speculation.

"My dear," said May Taplow, "even in London people can talk of nothing else. Everyone knows Fenton considers Dublin a third-rate provincial outpost. His house hasn't been opened for decades. Why in the world is he here?"

"I can't imagine," Scarlett replied, relishing the thought of May's reaction if she told her.

Fenton seemed to turn up every place she went. Scarlett greeted him with cool good manners and ignored the expression of contemptuous confidence in his eyes. After the first encounter she didn't even fill with anger when she chanced to meet his gaze. He had no power to hurt her any more.

Not as himself. But she was pierced by pain again and again when she glimpsed the back of a tall dark-haired man clad in velvet or brocade, and it turned out to be Fenton. For Scarlett looked for Rhett in every crowd.

He'd been at the Castle the year before, why not this year ... this night ... this room?

But it was always Fenton. Everywhere she looked, in the talk of everyone around her, in the columns of every newspaper she read. She could at least be thankful that he paid no special attention to her; then the gossips would have pursued her as well. But she wished to heaven that his name was not on every tongue every day.

Rumors gradually coalesced into two theories: he had readied his neglected house for a surreptitious, unofficial visit from the Prince of Wales; or he had fallen under the spell of Lady Sophia Dudley, who had been the talk of London's Season in May and was repeating her success now in Dublin. It was the oldest story in the world—a man sows his wild oats and resists the snares of women for years and years until bang!—when he's forty, he loses his head and his heart to beauty and innocence.

Lady Sophia Dudley was seventeen. She had hair the gold of ripe hay and eyes as blue as the summer sky and a pink-and-white complexion that put porcelain to shame. At least so said the ballads that were written about her and sold on all the street corners for a penny.

She was, in fact, a beautiful, shy girl who was very much under her ambitious mother's control and who blushed often and attractively because of all the attention and gallantries paid her. Scarlett saw quite a bit of her. Sophia's private drawing room was next to Scarlett's. It was second best in terms of furnishings and the view of Saint Stephen's Green, but first in terms of people vying for admission. Not that Scarlett's was by any means unattended; a rich and well-received widow with fascinating green eyes would always be in demand.

Why should I be surprised, thought Scarlett. I'm twice her age, and I had my turn last year. But sometimes she had trouble holding her tongue when Sophia's name was linked with Luke's. It was common knowledge that a duke had asked for Sophia's hand, but everyone agreed that she'd do better to take Fenton. A duke had precedence over an earl, but Fenton was forty times richer and a hundred times handsomer than the Duke. "And he's mine if I want him," Scarlett longed to say. Who'd they be writing ballads about then?

She scolded herself for her pettiness. She told herself she was a fool for thinking of Fenton's prediction that she would be forgotten after a year or two. And she tried not to worry about the little lines in the skin beside her eyes.

Scarlett returned to Ballyhara for her First Sunday office hours, thankful to get away from Dublin. The final weeks of the Season seemed endless.

It was good to be home, good to be thinking about something real, like Paddy O'Faolain's request for a bigger allocation of peat, instead of what to wear to the next party. And it was pure heaven to have Cat's strong little arms nearly strangle her with a fierce hug of welcome.

When the last dispute had been settled, the last request granted, Scarlett went to the morning room for tea with Cat.

"I saved your half," Cat said. Her mouth was smeared with chocolate from the éclairs Scarlett had brought from Dublin.

"It's a funny thing, Kitty Cat, but I'm not real hungry. Would you like some more?"

"Yes."

"Yes, thank you."

"Yes, thank you. May I eat them now?"

"Yes, you may, Miss Pig."

The éclairs were gone before Scarlett's cup was empty. Cat was dedicated when it came to éclairs.

"Where shall we go for our walk?" Scarlett asked her. Cat said she'd like to go visit Grainne.

"She likes you, Momma. She likes me more, but she likes you a lot."

"That would be nice," said Scarlett. She'd be glad to go to the tower. It gave her a feeling of serenity, and there was little serenity in her heart.

Scarlett closed her eyes and rested her cheek on the ancient smooth stones for a long moment. Cat fidgeted.

Then Scarlett pulled on the rope ladder to the high door to test it. It was weathered and stained. It felt strong enough. Still, she thought she'd better see about having a new one made. If it broke, and Cat fell—she couldn't bear to think of it. She did so wish that Cat would invite her up into her room. She tugged at the ladder again, hinting.

"Grainne will be expecting us, Momma. We made a lot of noise."

"All right, honey, I'm coming."

The wise woman looked no older, no different from the first time Scarlett had seen her. I'd even be willing to bet those are the same shawls she was wearing, Scarlett thought. Cat busied herself in the small dark cottage, getting cups from their shelf, raking the ancient-smelling burning peat into a mound of glowing embers for the kettle. She was very much at home. "I'll fill the kettle at the spring," she said as she carried it outside. Grainne watched her lovingly.

"Dara visits me often," said the wise woman. "It's her kindness to a lonely soul. I haven't the heart to send her away, for she sees the right of it. Lonely knows lonely."

Scarlett bristled. "She likes to be alone, she doesn't have to be lonely. I've asked her time and again if she'd like to have children come play, and she always says no."

"It's a wise child. They try to stone her, but Dara is too quick for them."

Scarlett couldn't believe she'd heard right. "They do what?" The children from the town, Grainne said placidly, hunted through the woods for Dara, like a beast. She heard them, though, long before they got to her. Only the biggest ever came near enough to throw the stones they carried. And those came near only because they could run faster than Dara on longer, older legs. She knew how to escape even them. They wouldn't dare chase her into her tower, they were afraid of it, haunted as it was by the ghost of the young hanged lord.

Scarlett was aghast. Her precious Cat tormented by the children of Ballyhara! She'd whip every single one of them with her own hands, she'd evict their parents and break every stick of their furniture into splinters! She started up out of her chair.

"You will burden the child with the ruin of Ballyhara?" said Grainne. "Sit you down, woman. Others would be the same. They fear anyone different to themselves. What they fear they try to drive away."

Scarlett sank back onto the chair. She knew the wise woman was right. She'd paid the price for being different herself, again and again. Her stones had been coldness, criticism, ostracism. But she had brought it on herself. Cat was only a little girl. She was innocent. And she was in danger! "I can't just do nothing!" Scarlett cried. "It's intolerable. I've got to make them stop."

"Ach, there's no stopping ignorance. Dara has found her own way, and it is enough for her. The stones do not wound her soul. She is safe in her tower room."

"It's not enough. Suppose a stone hit her? Suppose she got hurt? Why didn't she tell me she was lonely? I can't bear that she's unhappy."

"Listen to an old woman, The O'Hara. Listen from your heart. There is a land that men know of only from the songs of the *seachain*. Its name is Tir na nOg, and it lies beneath the hills. Men there are, and women too, who have found the way to that land and have never been seen again. There is no death in Tir na nOg, and no decay. There is no sorrow and no pain, nor hatred, nor hunger. All live in peace with one another, and there is plenty without labor.

"This is what you would give your child, you would say. But listen well. In Tir na nOg, because there is no sorrow, there is no joy.

"Do you hear the meaning of the *seachain*'s song?"

Scarlett shook her head.

Grainne sighed. "Then I cannot ease your heart. Dara has more wisdom. Leave her be." As if the old woman had called her, Cat came through the door. She was concentrating on the heavy, water-filled kettle, and she didn't look at her mother and Grainne. The two of them watched silently while Cat methodically set the kettle on the iron hook over the coals, then raked more coals into a heap below it.

Scarlett had to turn her head. If she continued to look at her child, she knew she wouldn't be able to stop herself from grabbing Cat in her arms and holding her tightly in a protective embrace. Cat would hate that. I mustn't cry, either, Scarlett told herself. It might frighten her. She'd sense how frightened I am.

"Watch me, Momma," said Cat. She was carefully pouring steaming water into an old brown china teapot. A sweet smell rose from the steam, and Cat smiled. "I put in all the right leaves, Grainne," she chortled. She looked proud and happy.

Scarlett caught hold of the wise woman's shawl. "Tell me what to do," she begged.

"You must do what's given you to do. God will guard Dara."

I don't understand anything she says, thought Scarlett. But somehow her terror was relieved. She drank Cat's brew in the companionable silence and warmth of the herb-scented shadowy room, glad that Cat had this place to come to. And the tower. Before she returned to Dublin, Scarlett gave orders for a new, stronger rope ladder.

88

*S*carlett went to Punchestown for the races this year. She'd been invited to Bishopscourt, the seat of the Earl of Clonmel, who was known as Earlie. To her delight, Sir John Morland was also a guest. To her dismay, the Earl of Fenton was there.

Scarlett rushed over to Morland as soon as she could. "Bart! How are you? You're the biggest stay-at-home I've ever heard of in my life. I look for you all the time, but you're never anywhere."

Morland was gleaming with happiness and cracking his knuckles loudly. "I've been busy, the most splendid kind of busy, Scarlett. I've got a winner, I'm sure of it, after all these years."

He'd talked like this before. Bart so loved his horses that he was always "sure" each foal was the next Grand National champion. Scarlett felt like hugging him. She'd have loved John Morland even if he had no connection at all to Rhett.

"... named her Diana, fleet of foot and all that sort of thing, you know, plus John for me. Hang it all, I'm practically her father except for the biology part. It came out Dijon when I put it together. Mustard, I thought, that won't do at all. Too damn French for an Irish horse. But then I thought again. Hot and peppery, so strong it makes your eyes water. That's not a bad profile. Sort of 'get out of my way, I'm coming through' and all that. So Dijon it is. She's going to make my fortune. Better lay a fiver on her, Scarlett, she's a sure thing."

"I'll make it ten pounds, Bart." Scarlett was trying to think of some way to mention Rhett. What John Morland was saying didn't register at first.

"... be really sunk if I'm wrong. My tenants are doing that rent strike thing the Land League dreamed up. Leaves me without money for oats. I wonder now how I could have thought so highly of Charles Parnell. Never thought the fellow would end up hand in glove with those barbarian Fenians."

Scarlett was horrified. She'd never dreamed the Land League would be used against anyone like Bart.

"I can't believe it, Bart. What are you going to do?"

"If she wins here, even places, then I suppose the next big one is Galway and after that Phoenix Park, but maybe I'll sort of tuck in one or two smaller races in May and June, to keep her mind on what's expected of her, so to speak."

"No, no, Bart, not about Dijon. What are you going to do about the rent strike?"

Morland's face lost some of its glow. "I don't know," he said. "All I've got are my rents. I've never evicted, never even thought of it. But now I'm up against it, I might have to. Be a bloody shame."

Scarlett was thinking about Ballyhara. At least she was safe from any trouble. She'd forgiven all rents until the harvest was in.

"I say, Scarlett, I forgot to mention it. I received some very good news from our American friend Rhett Butler."

Scarlett's heart leapt. "Is he coming over?"

"No. I was expecting him. Wrote to him about Dijon, you see. But he wrote back that he couldn't come. He's to be a father in June. They took extra care this time, kept the wife in bed for months until there wasn't any danger of what happened last time. But everything's splendid now. She's up and happy as a lark, he says. He is too, of course. Never saw a man in my life cared as much about being a proud father as Rhett."

Scarlett caught hold of a chair for support. Whatever unrealistic daydreams and hidden hopes she might have had were over.

Earlie had reserved a complete section of the white iron grille-work stands for his party. Scarlett stood with the others, scanning the course through mother-of-pearl opera glasses. The turf track was brilliant green, the infield of the long oval was a mass of movement and color. People stood on wagons, on the seats and roofs of their carriages, walked around singly and in groups, massed at the interior rail.

It began to rain and Scarlett was grateful for the second tier of grandstand overhead. It made a roof for the privileged seat-holders below.

"Good show," Bart Morland chortled. "Dijon is a great little mudder."

"Do you fancy anything, Scarlett?" said a smooth voice in her ear. It was Fenton.

"I haven't decided yet, Luke."

When the riders came onto the track, Scarlett cheered and applauded with the rest. She agreed twenty times with John Morland that even the naked eye could pick out Dijon as the handsomest horse there. All the time she was talking and smiling her mind was methodically making its way through the options, the plusses and the minuses of her life. It would be highly dishonorable to marry Luke. He wanted a child, and she could not give him one. Except Cat, who would be safe and secure. No one would ever question who her real father was. Not quite true, they would wonder but it would make no difference. She would eventually be The O'Hara of Ballyhara, and the Countess of Fenton.

What kind of honor do I owe Luke? He has none himself, why should I feel he's entitled to it from me?

Dijon won. John Morland was in transports. Everyone crowded around him, shouting and pounding on his back.

Under cover of the happy rowdiness, Scarlett turned to Luke Fenton. "Tell your solicitor to see mine about the contracts," she said. "I choose late September for the wedding date. After Harvest Home."

"Colum, I'm going to marry the Earl of Fenton," said Scarlett.

He laughed. "And I'll take Lilith for a bride. Such merrymaking there'll be, with the legions of Satan for guests at the wedding feast."

"It's not a joke, Colum."

His laughter stopped as if severed by a blade, and he stared at Scarlett's pale, determined face. "I'll not allow it," he shouted. "The man's a devil and an Anglo."

Patches of red blotched Scarlett's cheeks. "You ... will ... not ... *allow?*" she said slowly. "You ... will ... not ... allow? Who do you think you are, Colum? God?" She walked to him, eyes blazing, and thrust her face close to his. "Listen to me, Colum O'Hara, and listen good. Not you or anybody else on earth can talk to me like that. I won't take it!"

His stare matched hers, and his anger, and they stood in stony confrontation for a timeless moment. Then Colum tilted his head to one side and smiled. "Ah, Scarlett darling, if it isn't the O'Hara temper in the both of us, putting words we don't mean in our two mouths. I'm begging your forgiveness, now; let's talk this thing over."

Scarlett stepped back. "Don't charm me, Colum," she said sadly, "I don't believe it. I came to talk to my closest friend, and he's not here. Maybe he never was."

"Not so, Scarlett darling, not so!"

Her shoulders hunched in a brief, dejected shrug. "It doesn't matter. I've made up my mind. I'm going to marry Fenton and move to London in September."

"You're a disgrace to your people, Scarlett O'Hara." Colum's voice was like steel.

"That's a lie," said Scarlett wearily. "Say that to Daniel, who's buried in O'Hara land that was lost for hundreds of years. Or to your precious Fenians, who've been using me all this time. Don't worry, Colum, I'm not going to give you away. Ballyhara will stay just as it is, with the inn for the men on the run, and the bars for you all to talk against the English in. I'll make you bailiff for me, and Mrs. Fitz will keep the Big House going just the way it is. That's really what you care about, not me."

"No!" The cry burst from Colum's lips. "Ach, Scarlett, you're grievous wrong. You're my pride and my delight, and Katie Colum holds my heart in her tiny hands. 'Tis only that Ireland is my soul and must be first." He held out his hands to her in supplication. "Say you believe me, for I'm speaking the plain truth of it."

Scarlett tried to smile. "I do believe you. And you have to believe me. The wise woman said, 'You'll do what's given you to do.' That's what you're doing with your life, Colum, and it's what I'm doing with mine."

Scarlett's steps dragged as she walked to the Big House. It was as if the heaviness of her heart had travelled to her feet. The scene with Colum had cut deep. She had gone to him before anyone else, expecting understanding and compassion, hoping against hope that he might tell her some way out of the path she had chosen. He had failed her, and she felt very alone. She dreaded telling Cat that she was going to be married, that they'd have to leave Ballyhara's woods that Cat so loved and the tower that was her special place.

Cat's reaction lifted her heart. "I like cities," said Cat. "That's where the zoo is." I am doing the right thing, thought Scarlett. Now I know it without a doubt. She sent to Dublin for picture books of London and wrote to Mrs. Sims asking for an appointment. She had to order a wedding gown.

A few days later a messenger from Fenton came with a letter and a package. In the letter he said that he would be in England until the week of the wedding. The announcement would not appear until after the London Season. And Scarlett should have her gown designed to complement the jewels sent by the same messenger as the letter. She still had three months to herself! No one would press her with questions or invitations until the news of the engagement was released.

Inside the package she found a square shallow box of oxblood leather, finely tooled in gold. The hinged top lifted and Scarlett gasped. The case was lined in padded gray velvet, shaped and compartmented to display a necklace, two bracelets, and a pair of earrings.

The settings were fashioned of heavy old gold with a dull, almost bronze finish. The jewels were pigeon's blood rubies, matched stones, each as large as her thumb nail. The earrings were single oval ruby drops from an intricately shaped boss. Bracelets held a dozen stones each, and the necklace was made up of two rows of stones linked by swagged thick chains. For the first time Scarlett understood the difference between jewelry and jewels. No one would ever refer to these rubies as jewelry. They were too exceptional and too valuable. They were, without doubt, jewels. Her fingers were trembling when she clasped the bracelets on her wrists. She couldn't do the necklace by herself, she had to ring for Peggy Quinn. When she saw herself in the looking glass, Scarlett drew in a long breath. Her skin looked like alabaster with the dark richness of the rubies against it. Her hair was in some way darker and more lustrous. She tried to remember what the tiara looked like. It, too, was set with rubies. She would look like a queen when she was presented to the Queen. Her green eyes narrowed slightly. London was going to be a much more challenging game than Dublin. She might even learn to like London very much.

Peggy Quinn lost no time telling the news to the other servants and her family in Ballyhara town. The magnificent parure plus the ermine-trimmed robe plus the weeks of morning coffee could only mean one thing. The O'Hara was going to wed the rack-renting villain Earl of Fenton.

And what will become of us? The question and apprehension spread from hearth to hearth like a brushfire.

Scarlett and Cat rode together through the wheat fields in April. The child wrinkled her nose at the strong smell of freshly spread manure. The stables and barns never reeked this way; they were mucked out daily. Scarlett laughed at her. "Don't you ever make faces at manured land, Cat O'Hara. It's sweet perfume to a farmer, and you've got farmers' blood in your veins. I don't want you ever to forget it." She looked over the plowed and planted and enriched acres with pride. This is mine. I brought it back life. She knew she'd miss this part of her life most of all when they moved to London. But she'd always have the memory and the satisfaction. In her heart, she would forever be The O'Hara. And someday Cat could return, when she was grown and could protect herself. Then she would earn the name "The O'Hara" for herself. "Never, ever forget where you come from," Scarlett told her child. "Be proud."

"You'll have to swear on a stack of Bibles not to tell a soul," Scarlett warned Mrs. Sims.

Dublin's most exclusive dressmaker gave Scarlett her most freezing stare. "No one has ever had cause to question my discretion, Mrs. O'Hara."

"I'm to be married, Mrs. Sims, and I want you to create my gown." She held out the jewel case in front of her and opened it. "These will be worn with it."

Mrs. Sims' eyes and mouth made O's. Scarlett felt repaid for all the hours of torture she'd spent in the dressmaker's dictatorial fittings. She must have shocked ten years off the woman's life.

"There's a tiara also," Scarlett said in an off-handed manner, "and I'll want my train edged in ermine."

Mrs. Sims shook her head vigorously. "You cannot do that, Mrs. O'Hara. Tiaras and ermine are only for the grandest ceremonies at Court. Most particularly ermine. In all likelihood, it hasn't been worn since Her Majesty's wedding."

Scarlett's eyes glittered. "But I don't know all that, do I, Mrs. Sims? I'm only an ignorant American who will become a countess overnight. People are going to cluck-cluck and shake their heads no matter what I do. So I'm going to do what I want, the way I want it!" The misery in her heart became cutting imperiousness in her voice.

Mrs. Sims cringed inwardly. Her agile mind swiftly sorted through Society gossip to identify Scarlett's future husband. They'll be a well-matched pair, she thought. Trample all decent tradition and be admired the more for it. What was the world coming to? Still, a woman had to make her way in it, and people would be talking about the wedding for years to come. Her handiwork would be on display as never before. It must be magnificent.

Mrs. Sims' habitual haughty certainty returned. "There's only one gown that will do justice to ermine and these rubies," she said. "White silk velvet with overlaid lace, Galway would be best. How long do I have? The lace must be made, then sewn onto the velvet around each petal of each flower. It takes time."

"Will five months do?"

Mrs. Sims' well-kept hands dishevelled her well-groomed hair. "So short . . . Let me think . . . If I get two extra needlewomen . . . if the nuns will do only this . . . It will be the most talked-about wedding in Ireland, in Britain . . . It must be done, no matter what." She realized she was talking aloud, and her fingers covered her mouth. Too late.

Scarlett took pity on her. She stood and held out her hand. "I leave the gown in your care, Mrs. Sims. I have every confidence in you. Let me know when you need me to come to Dublin for the first fitting."

Mrs. Sims took her hand and squeezed it. "Oh, I'll come to you, Mrs. O'Hara. And it would please me if you called me Daisy."

In County Meath the sunny day made no one happy. Farmers worried about another year like the year before. At Ballyhara they shook their heads and predicted doom. Wasn't the changeling seen coming from the witch's cottage by Molly Keenan? And another time by Paddy Conroy, though what he was doing going there himself he wouldn't say outside the confessional. They did say, too, that there'd been owls heard in daylight over to Pike Corner, and Mrs. MacGruder's prize calf had died in the night for no cause at all. Rain, when it came the next day, did nothing to stop the rumors.

Colum went with Scarlett to the hiring fair in Drogheda in May. The wheat was well begun, the meadow grass very nearly ready for cutting, the rows of potatoes bright green with healthy foliage. Both of them were unusually quiet, each of them preoccupied with private concerns. For Colum the worry came from the increase in militia and constabulary troops all over County Meath. An entire regiment was coming to Navan, said his informants. The Land League's work was good; he'd be the last to deny the good of reduced rents. But the rent strikes had stirred up the landlords. Now evictions were done without prior warning and the thatch burned before the people could drag their furnishings out of the house. It was said two children had burned to death. Two soldiers were wounded the next day. Three Fenians had been arrested in Mullingar, including Jim Daly. Inciting violence was the charge although he'd been serving drinks in his bar day and night all the week.

Scarlett remembered the hiring fair for only one thing. Rhett had been with Bart Morland there. She avoided even looking in the direction of the horse sales; when Colum suggested they walk around and enjoy the fair, she all but shouted when she told him no, she wanted to get home. There'd been a distance between them ever since she told Colum she was going to marry Fenton. He didn't say anything harsh, but he didn't have to. Anger and accusation were hot in his eyes.

It was the same with Mrs. Fitz. Who did they think they were anyhow, judging her like that? What did they know about her sorrows and her fears? Wasn't it enough that they'd have Ballyhara to themselves after she left? That was all they had ever really wanted. No, that wasn't fair. Colum was her almost-brother, Mrs. Fitz her friend. All the more reason they should be sympathetic. It wasn't fair. Scarlett began to think she saw disapproval everywhere, even on the faces of Ballyhara's shopkeepers when she made the special effort to think of things to buy from them in these lean months before the harvest. Don't be a fool, she told herself, you're imagining things because you're not really sure yourself about what you're going to do. It's the right thing, it is, for Cat and for me. And it's nobody else's business what I do. She was irritable with everyone except Cat, and she saw little of her. One time she even climbed several rungs of the new rope ladder, but then she backed down. I'm a grown woman, I can't go boohooing to a little child for comfort. She worked in the hayfields day after day, glad to be busy, grateful for the ache in her arms and legs after the labor. Grateful, most of all, for the rich crop. Her fears about another bad harvest gradually went away.

Midsummer Night, June 24, completed the cure. The bonfire was the biggest ever, the music and dancing were what she'd been needing to relax her tense nerves and restore her spirits. When, as timeless tradition demanded, the toast to The O'Hara was shouted over the fields of Ballyhara, Scarlett felt that all was right with the world.

Still, she was a little sorry she'd refused all the house party invitations for the summer. She had to, she was afraid to leave Cat. But she was lonely, and she had too much time on her hands, too much time to think and worry. She was almost happy when she received the semi-hysterical telegram from Mrs. Sims, saying that the lace had not arrived from the convent in Galway, nor had she had any reply to her letters and telegrams.

Scarlett was smiling when she drove her buggy to the train depot in Trim. She was an old hand at battling with Mother Superiors, and she was glad to have a clear-cut reason for a fight.

89

There was just time enough in the morning to dash to Mrs. Sims' workshop, calm her down, gather the specifics of yardage and pattern of lace ordered, and race to the station for the early train to Galway. Scarlett settled herself comfortably and opened the newspaper.

My grief, there it is. *The Irish Times* had printed the announcement of the wedding plans on the front page. Scarlett darted looks at the other passengers in the compartment to see if any of them were reading the paper. The tweed-suited sportsman was engrossed in a sporting magazine; the nicely dressed mother and son were playing cribbage. She read about herself again. The *Times* had added a great deal of its own commentary to the formal announcement. Scarlett smiled at the part about "The O'Hara of Ballyhara, a beautiful ornament to the innermost circles of Viceregal society" and "exquisite and dashing equestrienne."

She had brought only a single small case with her for her stay in Dublin and Galway, so she needed only one porter to accompany her from the station to the nearby hotel.

The reception area was jammed with people. "What the devil?" said Scarlett.

"The races," said the porter. "You didn't do something so foolish as to come to Galway not knowing, did you? You'll find no room to sleep in here."

Impertinent, thought Scarlett, see if you get a tip. "Wait here," she said. She weaved her way to the reception desk. "I'd like to speak to the manager."

The harassed desk clerk looked her up and down, then said, "Yes, of course, madam, one moment," and vanished behind an etched-glass screen. He returned with a balding man in a black frock coat and striped trousers.

"Is there some complaint, madam? I'm afraid that the hotel's service does become less, ah, flawless, shall we say, when the races are in progress. Whatever inconvenience—"

Scarlett interrupted him. "I remember the service as flawless." She smiled winningly. "That's why I like to stay at the Railway. I'll need a room tonight. I am Mrs. O'Hara of Ballyhara."

The manager's unctuousness evaporated like August dew. "A room tonight? It's quite out of—" The desk clerk was pulling at his arm. The manager glared at him. The clerk murmured in his ear, jabbed his finger at a *Times* on the desk.

The hotel manager bowed to Scarlett. His smile was quivering with the will to please. "Such an honor for us, Mrs. O'Hara. I trust you'll accept a very particular suite, the finest in Galway, as the guest of the management. Do you have baggage? A man will take it up."

Scarlett gestured to the porter. There was really a lot to be said for marrying an earl. "Send this to my rooms. I'll be back later."

"At once, Mrs. O'Hara."

In truth Scarlett didn't expect to need the rooms at all. She hoped she'd be able to get the afternoon train back to Dublin, maybe even the early afternoon train, then she'd have time to connect for the evening journey back up to Trim. Thank heavens for the long days. I'll have until ten tonight if I need it. Now let's see if the nuns are as impressed by the Earl of Fenton as the hotel manager was. Too bad he's Protestant. I guess I shouldn't have made Daisy Sims swear to keep everything a secret.

Scarlett started toward the door to the square. Phew, what a smelly crowd. It must be raining on their tweeds at the track. Scarlett edged between two gesticulating, red-faced men. She bumped headlong into Sir John Morland and hardly recognized him. He looked as if he were extremely ill. There was no color in his normally ruddy face and no light in his usually warm, interested eyes. "Bart, my dear. Are you all right?"

He seemed to have trouble bringing her face into focus. "Oh, sorry Scarlett. Not quite myself. One too many and all that kind of thing."

At this hour of the day? It wasn't like John Morland to drink too much at any time, and certainly not before luncheon. She took firm hold of his arm. "Come along, Bart. You're going to have coffee with me and then something to eat." Scarlett walked him to the dining room. Morland's steps were unsteady. I guess I'll be needing my room after all, she thought, but Bart's a lot more important than rushing off after some lace. What on earth could have happened to him?

After a great deal of coffee she found out. John Morland broke down and cried when he told her.

"They burned my stables, Scarlett, they burned my stables. I'd taken Dijon to race at Balbriggan, not a big race at all, I thought she might like a run on the sands, and when we came home the stables were just black ruins. My God, the smell! My God! I hear the horses screaming in my dreams, in my head even when I don't sleep."

Scarlett felt herself gagging. She put down her cup. It couldn't be. No one would do such a horrible thing. It had to be an accident.

"It was my tenants. Because of the rents, you see. How could they hate me so much? I tried to be a good landlord, I always tried. Why couldn't they burn the house? At Edmund Barrows' place they burned the house. They could have burned me in it, I wouldn't care. Not if they'd spared the horses. Name of God, Scarlett! What had my poor burned horses ever done to them?"

There was nothing she could say. All Bart's heart was in his stables . . . Wait, he'd been away with Dijon. His special pride and joy.

"You've got Dijon, Bart. You can start over, breed her. She's such a wonderful horse, the most beautiful I've ever seen. You can have the stables at Ballyhara. Don't you remember? You told me they were like a cathedral. We'll put in an organ. You can raise your new foals on Bach. You can't let things beat you, Bart, you've got to keep going on. I know, I've been down to the bottom myself. You can't give up, you just can't."

John Morland's eyes were like cold embers. "I'm going to England tonight on the eight o'clock boat. I never want to see an Irish face or hear an Irish voice again. I put Dijon in a safe place while I sold up. She's entered in the claiming race this afternoon, and when it's over, so is Ireland for me." His tragic eyes were at least steady. And dry. Scarlett almost wished he would begin to cry again. At least he'd felt something then. Now he looked as if he would never be able to feel anything ever again. He looked dead.

Then, as she watched, a transformation took place. Sir John Morland, Baronet, came back to life by effort of will. His shoulders firmed, and his mouth curved in a smile. His eyes even had a hint of laughter in them. "Poor Scarlett, I fear I rather put you through the wringer. It was beastly of me. Do forgive me. I'll soldier on. One does. Finish your coffee, there's a good girl, and come along to the track with me. I'll put a fiver on Dijon for you, and you can buy the champagne with your winnings when she shows her heels to the rest of the field."

Scarlett had never in her life respected anyone as much as she did Bart Morland at that moment. She found a smile to meet his.

"I'll match your fiver with one of my own, Bart, and we'll have champagne, too. Done?" She spit in her palm, held it out. Morland spat, slapped, smiled.

"Good girl," he said.

On the way to the race course Scarlett tried to dredge up from her memory what she'd heard about "claiming races." All the horses running were for sale, their prices set by their owners. At the end of the race anyone could "claim" any one of the horses, and the owner was obliged to sell for the price he'd set. Unlike every other horse sale in Ireland, there was no bargaining. Unclaimed horses had to be reclaimed by their owners.

Scarlett didn't believe for a minute that horses couldn't be bought before the race began, no matter what the rules were. When they reached the race course, she asked Bart for the number of his box. She wanted, she said, to tidy up.

As soon as he was gone she found a steward and got directions to the officials' office where the claiming would take place. She hoped Bart had put a whopping big price on Dijon. She intended to buy her and send her to him later when he was settled in England.

"What do you mean Dijon's already been claimed? That's not supposed to happen until after the race."

The top-hatted official was careful not to smile. "You're not the only one with foresight, madam. It must be an American trait. The gentleman who put in the claim was American, too."

"I'll double it."

"It cannot be done, Mrs. O'Hara."

"Suppose I bought Dijon from the Baronet before the race began?"

"Impossible."

Scarlett felt desperate. She had to have that horse for Bart.

"I might suggest one thing . . ."

"Oh, please. What can I do? It's really awfully important."

"You might ask the new owner if he would be willing to sell."

"Yes. I'll do that." She'd pay the man a king's ransom if need be. American, the official said. Good. Money talks in America. "Will you point him out to me?"

The top-hatted man consulted a sheet of paper. "You might find him at Jury's Hotel. He's listed that as his address. His name is Butler."

Scarlett had half-turned to leave. She stumbled to get her balance. Her voice was strangely thin when she spoke. "That wouldn't by any chance be Mr. Rhett Butler?"

It seemed to take an eternity for the man's eyes to return to the page in his hand, for him to read, for him to speak. "Yes, that is the name."

Rhett! Here! Bart must have written him about the stables, about selling up, about Dijon. He must be doing what I was going to do. He came all the way from America to help a friend.

Or to get a winner for the next Charleston races. It doesn't matter. Even poor, dear, tragic Bart doesn't matter, may God forgive me. I'm going to see Rhett. Scarlett realized that she was running, running, pushing people aside without apology. To the devil with everyone, everything. Rhett was here, only a few hundred yards away.

"Box eight," she gasped at a steward. He gestured. Scarlett forced herself to breathe slowly until she thought she must appear normal. No one could see her heart pounding, could they? She climbed the two steps into the bunting-trimmed box. Out on the great turfed oval twelve brightly shirted riders were whipping their horses towards the finish. All around Scarlett people were shouting, urging on the horses. She didn't hear a thing. Rhett was watching the race through field glasses. Even ten feet away she could smell the whiskey on him. He was rocking on his feet. Drunk? Not Rhett. He could always hold his liquor. Had Bart's disaster upset him that much?

Look at me, her heart begged. Put the glasses down and look at me. Say my name. Let me see your eyes when you say my name. Let me see something for me in your eyes. You loved me once.

Cheering and groans hailed the end of the race. Rhett lowered the glasses with a shaky hand. "Damn, Bart, that's my fourth loser in a row," he laughed.

"Hello, Rhett," she said.

His head snapped, and she saw his dark eyes. They held nothing for her, nothing but anger. "Why hello, Countess." His eyes raked her from her kidskin boots to her egret-plumed hat. "You are certainly looking—expensive." He turned abruptly towards John Morland. "You should have warned me, Bart, so I could stay in the bar. Let me by." And he sent Morland staggering as he pushed out of the box on the side away from Scarlett.

Her eyes followed him hopelessly as he plunged into the crowds. Then they filled with tears.

John Morland patted her shoulder clumsily. "I say, Scarlett, I apologize for Rhett. He's had too much to drink. That's two of us you've had to deal with today. Not much fun for you."

"Not much fun." Is that what Bart called it? "Not much fun" to be trampled on? I wasn't asking for much. Just to say hello, say my name. What gives Rhett the right to be angry and insulting? Can't I marry again after he threw me out like trash? Damn him. Damn him straight to Hell! Why is it fine and dandy for him to divorce me so he can marry a proper Charleston girl and have proper Charleston babies to grow up into more proper Charlestonians, but it's oh-so-disgraceful for me to marry again and give his child all the things that he should be the one to give her.

"I hope he falls over his own drunken feet and breaks his neck," she said to Bart Morland.

"Don't be too hard on Rhett, Scarlett. He had a real tragedy last spring. I'm ashamed to feel so sorry for myself about the stables when there are people like Rhett with troubles like his. I told you about the baby, didn't I? Beastly awful thing happened. His wife died having it, then the baby only lived for four days."

"What? What? Say that again." She shook his arm so fiercely that Morland's hat fell off. He looked at her with confused dismay, almost fear. There was something so savage about her, something stronger than anything in his experience. He repeated that Rhett's wife and child were dead.

"Where did he go?" Scarlett cried. "Bart, you must know, you must have some idea, where would Rhett be likely to go?"

"I don't know, Scarlett. The bar—his hotel—any bar—anywhere."

"Is he going with you tonight to England?"

"No. He said he had some friends he wanted to look up. He's a really astonishing fellow, has friends everywhere. Did you know he was on safari with the Viceroy once? Some maharajah fellow was host. I must say I'm surprised he got so drunk. I don't remember him even keeping up with me. He took me to my hotel last night, put me to bed and all that. Was in fine fettle, a strong arm to lean on. I was counting on him, actually, to get me through the day. But when I came downstairs this morning, the porter fellow told me Rhett had ordered coffee and a newspaper while he waited for me, then suddenly bolted without even paying. I went in the bar to wait for him—Scarlett, what is it? I can't fathom you today. What are you crying for? Was it something I did? Did I say something wrong?"

Scarlett's eyes were flooded. "Oh, no, no, no, dearest, darlingest John Morland, Bart. You didn't say anything wrong at all. He loves me. He loves me. That's the rightest, most perfect thing I could ever hear."

Rhett came after me. That's why he came to Ireland. Not for Bart's horse, he could have bought her and all the rest of it by mail. He came for me as soon as he was free again. He must have been wanting me as much as I've been wanting him. I've got to go home. I don't know where to find him, but he can find me. The wedding announcement shocked him, and I'm glad. But it won't stop him. Nothing stops Rhett from going after what he wants. Rhett Butler's not impressed by titles and ermine and tiaras. He wants me and he'll come to get me. I know it. I knew he loved me, and I was right all the time. I know he'll come to Ballyhara. I've got to be there when he comes.

"Goodbye, Bart, I've got to go now," said Scarlett.

"Don't you want to see Dijon win? What about our fivers?" John Morland shook his head. She was gone. Americans! Fascinating types, but he'd never understand them.

She'd missed the through train to Dublin by ten minutes. The next one wouldn't leave until four. Scarlett bit her lip in frustration. "When is the next train east to anywhere?" The man behind the brass grille was maddeningly slow.

"You could go to Ennis, now, if you had a mind to. That's east to Athenry, then south. Two new carriages that train has, very nicely done they are too, say the ladies . . . or there's the Kildare train, but you'll not be able to take that one, the whistle's already sounded . . . Tuam, now, it's a short trip and more north than east, but the engine's the finest of all on the Great Western line . . . madam?"

Scarlett was shedding tears all over the uniform of the man at the barrier to the track. ". . . I only got the telegram two minutes ago, my husband's been run over by a milk dray, I've got to get that train to Kildare!" It would take her more than halfway to Trim and Ballyhara. She'd walk the rest of the way if she had to.

Every stop was torture. Why couldn't they hurry? Hurry, hurry, hurry, said her mind with the clack-clack of the wheels. Her case was in the best suite in Galway's Railway Hotel, in the convent sore-eyed nuns were putting the final tiny stitches into exquisite lace. None of it mattered. She must be home, waiting, when Rhett arrived. If only John Morland hadn't taken so long to tell her about everything, she could have been on the Dublin train. Rhett might even be on it, he could have been going anywhere when he left Bart's box.

It took nearly three and a half hours to get to Moate, where Scarlett got out of the train. It was after four, but at least she was on her way, instead of on the train that was just leaving Galway. "Where can I buy a good horse?" she asked the station master. "I don't care what it costs, as long as it has a saddle and bridle and speed." She had almost fifty miles still to go.

The owner of the horse wanted to bargain. Wasn't that half the pleasure of the selling? he asked his friends in the King's Coach bar after he bought a pint for every man there. The crazy woman had thrown gold sovereigns at him and gone off like the devil was on her trail. Astride! He didn't want to say how much lace she was showing nor how much leg with no decent covering to it at all, only a silk stocking and some boots not thick enough to walk on a floor with, never even to imagine resting in a stirrup.

Scarlett led the limping horse across the bridge into Mullingar just before seven o'clock. At the livery stable she handed the reins to a groom. "He's not lame, just winded and with a weakness," she said. "Cool him down slowly and he'll be as good as he ever was, not that he was ever much. I'll give him to you if you'll sell me one of the hunters you keep for the officers at the fort. Don't tell me you don't have any, I've hunted with some of the officers, and I know where they rented their mounts. Change over this saddle in under five minutes and there's an extra guinea for you." By ten after seven she was on her way, with twenty-six miles ahead and directions for a shortcut if she went cross-country instead of following the road.

She rode past Trim Castle and onto the road to Ballyhara at nine o'clock. Every muscle in her body ached, and her bones felt splintered. But she was only a little over three miles from home, and the misty twilight was gentle and soft on eyes and skin. A gentle rain began to fall. Scarlett leaned forward, patted the horse's neck. "A good walkaround and rubdown and the best hot mash in County Meath for you, whatever your name is. You took those jumps like a champion. Now we'll trot home easy, you deserve the rest." She half-closed her eyes and let her head loll. She'd sleep tonight like she'd never slept before. Hard to believe she'd been in Dublin this morning and crossed Ireland twice since breakfast.

There was the wooden bridge over the Knightsbrook. Once over the bridge I'm on Ballyhara. Only a mile to the town, a half-mile through it to the crossroad, then up the drive and I've made it. Five minutes, not much more than that. She sat up straight, clicked her tongue against her teeth, urged the horse with her heels.

Something's wrong. Ballyhara town's up ahead, and there are no lights in the windows. Usually the bars are glowing like moons by now. Scarlett kicked with the heels of her battered, delicate city boots. She had passed the first five dark houses before she saw the group of men at the crossroads in front of the Big House drive. Redcoats. Militia. What did they think they were doing in her town? She'd told them before, she didn't want them here. How bothersome, tonight of all nights, when she was about to drop from fatigue. Of course, that's why the windows are dark, they don't want to have to pull any pints for the English. I'll get rid of them and then things can get back to normal. I wish I didn't look so bedraggled. It's hard to order people around when your underclothes are hanging out all over the place. I'd better be walking. At least my skirts won't be up around my knees.

She reined in. It was hard not to groan when she swung her leg over the back of the horse. She could see a soldier—no, an officer—walking towards her from the group at the crossroad. Well, good! She'd give him a piece of her mind, she was just in the mood to do it. His men were in her town, in her way, keeping her from getting home.

He stopped in front of the post office. He could, at the very least, have the manners to come all the way to her. Scarlett walked stiffly down the center of her town's wide street.

"You there, with the horse. Halt, or I'll fire." Scarlett stopped short. Not because of the officer's command; it was his voice. She knew that voice. God in heaven, that was the one voice in all the world she'd hoped never to hear again as long as she lived. She had to be wrong, she was so tired, that was it, she was imagining things, inventing nightmares.

"The rest of you, in your houses, there'll be no trouble if you send out the priest Colum O'Hara. I have a warrant for his arrest. No one will be hurt if he gives himself up."

Scarlett had a mad impulse to laugh. This couldn't be happening. She'd heard right, she did know the voice, she'd last heard it next to her ear speaking words of love. It was Charles Ragland. Once, only once in her entire life, she had gone to bed with a man who wasn't her husband, and now he had come from the far end of Ireland to her town to arrest her cousin. It was insane, absurd, impossible. Well, at least she could be sure of one thing—if she didn't die of shame when she looked at him, Charles Ragland was the one officer in the entire British army who would do what she wanted him to do. Go away and leave her and her cousin and her town alone.

She dropped the horse's reins and strode forward. "Charles?"

Just as she called his name, Charles Ragland shouted, "Halt!" He fired his revolver into the air.

Scarlett winced. "Charles Ragland, have you gone crazy?" she shouted.

There was the crack of a second shot, drowning out her words, and Ragland seemed to jump into the air, then fall sprawling. Scarlett started to run. "Charles, Charles!" She heard more shots, heard shouting, ignored it all. "Charles!"

"Scarlett!" she heard, and "Scarlett!" from another direction, and "Scarlett," weakly, from Charles when she knelt by him. He was bleeding horribly from his neck, red blood spurting onto, staining his red tunic.

"Scarlett darling, get down, Scarlett *aroon*." Colum was somewhere nearby, but she couldn't look at him now.

"Charles, oh, Charles, I'll get a doctor, I'll get Grainne, she can help you." Charles raised his hand, and she took it between hers. She felt the tears on her face, but she had no knowledge of crying. He mustn't die, not Charles, he was so dear and loving, he'd been so tender with her. He mustn't die. He was a good, gentle man.

There was terrible noise all around. Something whined past her head. Dear God, what was happening? Those were shots, people were shooting, the British were trying to kill her people. She would not allow it. But she had to get help for Charles, and there were boots running, and Colum was shouting, and oh, God, please help, what can I do to stop this, oh, God, Charles' hand is getting cold. "Charles! Charles, don't die!"

"There's the priest!" someone shouted. Shots fusilladed from the dark windows of the houses of Ballyhara. A soldier staggered and fell.

An arm closed around Scarlett from behind, she threw up her arms to defend herself from the unseen attack. "Later, my dear, no fighting now," said Rhett. "This is the best chance we'll ever have. I'll carry you, just go limp." He threw her across his shoulder, his arm behind her knees, and ran crouching into the shadows. "What's the back way out of here?" he demanded.

"Put me down and I'll show you," said Scarlett. Rhett lowered her to her feet. His big hands closed on her shoulders, and he pulled her to him impatiently, then kissed her, briefly, firmly, and let her go.

"I'd hate to be shot without getting what I came for," he said. She could hear the laughter in his voice. "Now, Scarlett, get us out of here."

She took his hand and ducked into a narrow dark passageway between two houses. "Follow me; this goes to a boreen. We can't be seen once we're in it."

"Lead on," Rhett said. He freed his hand and gave her a light push. Scarlett wanted to keep hold of his hand, never let go. But the firing was loud, and close, and she ran for the safety of the boreen.

The hedgerows were high and thick. As soon as Scarlett and Rhett ran four paces into the boreen, the sound of battle became muffled and indistinct. Scarlett stopped to catch her breath, to look at Rhett, to comprehend that at last they were together. Her heart was swelling with happiness.

But the seemingly distant sound of shooting demanded her attention, and she remembered. Charles Ragland was dead. She'd seen a soldier wounded, maybe killed. The militia was after Colum, was shooting at the people of her town, maybe killing them. She could have been shot—Rhett, too.

"We've got to get to the house," she said. "We'll be safe there. I've got to warn the servants to stay away from town until this is over. Hurry, Rhett, we've got to hurry."

He caught her by the arm as she started to move. "Wait, Scarlett. Maybe you shouldn't go to the house. I've just come from there. It's dark and empty, darling, with all the doors left open. The servants are gone."

Scarlett wrenched her arm from his clasp. She moaned with terror as she grabbed up her skirts and ran, faster than she had ever run in her life. Cat. Where was Cat? Rhett's voice was speaking, but she paid no attention. She had to get to Cat.

Behind the boreen, in the wide street of Ballyhara, there were five red-coated bodies and three wearing the rough clothing of farmers. The book-seller lay across the sill of his shattered window, blood-streaked bubbles falling from his lips with the whispered words of prayer. Colum O'Hara prayed with him, then traced a cross on his forehead as the man died. The broken glass refracted the thin light from the moon that was becoming visible in the rapidly darkening sky. The rain had stopped.

Colum crossed the small room in three long steps. He seized the twig broom on the hearth by its handle and thrust it into the bed of coals. It made a crackling sound for a moment, then burst into flame.

A shower of sparks flew from the torch onto Colum's dark cassock when he ran into the street. His white hair was brighter than the moon. "Follow me, you English butchers," he shouted as he plunged toward the deserted Anglo church, "and we'll die together for the freedom of Ireland."

Two bullets tore into his broad chest, and he fell to his knees. But he staggered to his feet and forward for seven uneven steps more until another three shots spun him right, then left, then right again and to the ground.

Scarlett raced up the wide front steps and into the dark great hall, Rhett one stride behind her. "Cat!" she screamed. "Cat!" The word echoed from the stone stairs and marble floor. "Cat!"

Rhett grabbed her upper arms. Only her white face and pale eyes were visible in the shadows. "Scarlett!" he said loudly, "Scarlett, get hold of yourself. Come with me. We've got to get away. The servants must have known something. The house isn't safe."

"Cat!"

Rhett shook her. "Stop that. The cat's not important. Where are the stables, Scarlett? We need horses."

"Oh, you fool," said Scarlett. Her strained voice was heavy with loving pity. "You don't know what you're saying. Let me go. I've got to find Cat—Katie O'Hara, called Cat. She's your daughter."

Rhett's hands closed painfully on Scarlett's arms. "What the devil are you talking about?" He looked down into her face, but he couldn't make out her expression in the darkness. "Answer me, Scarlett," he demanded, and he shook her.

"Let go of me, damn you! There's no time for explanations now. Cat must be here someplace, but it's dark, and she's all alone. Let go, Rhett, and ask your questions later. All that isn't important now." Scarlett tried to break free, but he was too strong.

"It's important to me." His voice was rough with urgency.

"All right, all right. It happened when we went sailing and the storm came. You remember. I found out I was pregnant in Savannah, but you hadn't come for me, and I was angry, so I didn't tell you right away. How was I to know you would be married to Anne before you could hear about the baby?"

"Oh, dear God," Rhett groaned, and he released Scarlett. "Where is she?" he said. "We've got to find her."

"We will, Rhett. There's a lamp on the table by the door. Strike a match so we can find it."

The yellow flame of the match lasted long enough to locate a brass lamp and light it. Rhett held it up. "Where do we look first?"

"She could be anywhere. Let's start." She led him at a rapid pace through the dining room and morning room. "Cat," she called, "Kitty Cat, where are you?" Her voice was strong but no longer hysterical. It would not frighten a little girl. "Cat . . ."

"Colum!" screamed Rosaleen Fitzpatrick. She ran from Kennedy's bar into the middle of the British troops, pushing, shoving to get through, then down the center of the wide street toward Colum's sprawled body.

"Don't shoot," shouted an officer. "It's a woman."

Rosaleen threw herself on her knees and put her hands over Colum's wounds. "*Ochón*," she wailed. She rocked from side to side, keening. The firing stopped; the intensity of her grief commanded respect, and men looked away.

She closed the lids over his dead eyes with gentle fingers stained with his blood and whispered goodbye in Gaelic. Then she caught up the smouldering torch and leapt to her feet, waving it to bring the flame back to life. Her face was terrible in its light. So quick was she that not a shot was fired until she reached the passageway that led to the church. "For Ireland and her martyr Colum O'Hara!" she cried triumphantly, and she ran into the arsenal, brandishing the torch. For a moment there was a silence. Then the stone wall of the church exploded into the wide street in a tower of flame and a deafening blast of sound.

The sky was lit brighter than day. "My God!" Scarlett gasped. The breath was knocked out of her body. She covered her ears with her hands and ran, calling to Cat, as one explosion followed another, then another and another, and the town of Ballyhara burst into flame.

She ran upstairs, with Rhett at her side, and along the corridor to Cat's rooms. "Cat," she called, again and again, trying to keep the fear from sounding in her voice. "Cat." The animals were orange-lit on the wall, the tea set on a freshly ironed cloth, the coverlet smooth on Cat's bed.

"Kitchen," said Scarlett, "she loves the kitchen. We can call down." She raced through the corridor again, Rhett at her heels. Through the sitting room with the menu books, account books, the list she'd been making of friends to invite to the wedding. Through the door onto the gallery to Mrs. Fitzpatrick's room. Scarlett stopped in the center. She leaned across the balustrade. "Kitty Cat," she called softly, "please answer Momma if you're down there. It's important, sweetheart." She kept her voice calm.

Orange light flickered in the copper pans on the wall beside the stove. Red coals glowed on the hearth. The enormous room was still, filled with shadows. Scarlett strained her ears and her eyes. She was just about to turn away when the very small voice spoke. "Cat's ears hurt." Oh, thank God! Scarlett rejoiced. Calm, now, and quiet.

"I know, baby, that was an awfully loud noise. You hold Cat's ears. I'll come around and down. Will you wait for me?" She spoke as casually as if there was nothing to be afraid of. The balustrade vibrated under her clenched hands.

"Yes."

Scarlett gestured. Rhett followed her quietly along the gallery and through the door. She closed it carefully behind them. Then she began to shake. "I was so frightened. I was afraid they'd taken her away. Or hurt her."

"Scarlett, look," said Rhett. "We must hurry." The open windows above the drive framed a distant cluster of lights, torches, moving towards the house.

"Run!" said Scarlett. She saw Rhett's face in the orange light of the fire-filled sky, capable and strong. Now she could look at him, lean on him. Cat was safe. He put his hand beneath her arm, supporting her even as he hurried her.

Down the stairs they ran and through the ballroom. The firelit heroes of Tara were life-like above their heads. The colonnade to the kitchen wing was glaringly bright, and they could hear a blurred roaring of far-off angry shouts. Scarlett slammed the kitchen door behind them. "Help me bolt it," she gasped. Rhett took the iron bar from her, dropped it into its slots.

"What is your name?" said Cat. She walked out from the shadows near the hearth.

"Rhett." There was a frog in his throat.

"You two can make friends later," said Scarlett. "We've got to get to the stables. There's a door to the kitchen garden, it's got high walls, though, I don't know if there's another door out of it. Do you know, Cat?"

"Are we running away?"

"Yes, Kitty Cat, the people who made the awful noise want to hurt us."

"Do they have stones?"

"Very big ones."

Rhett found the door to the kitchen garden, looked out. "I can lift you onto my shoulders, Scarlett, then you can reach the top of the wall. I'll hand Cat up to you."

"Fine, but maybe there's a door. Cat, we have to hurry now. Is there a door in the wall?"

"Yes."

"Good. Give Momma your hand, and let's go."

"To the stables?"

"Yes, come on, Cat."

"The tunnel would be faster."

"What tunnel?" There was an uneven quality to Scarlett's voice. Rhett came back across the kitchen, put his arm around her shoulders.

"The tunnel to the servants' wing. The footmen have to use it so they can't look in the window when we're having breakfast."

"That's horrible," said Scarlett, "if I'd known—"

"Cat, take your mother and me to the tunnel, please," Rhett said. "Would you mind if I carried you, or would you rather run?"

"If we have to hurry, you'd better carry me. I can't run as fast as you."

Rhett knelt, held out his arms, and his daughter walked trustingly into them. He was careful not to clasp her too tight in the brief embrace he could not withhold. "Onto my back, then, Cat, and hold around my neck. Tell me where to go."

"Past the fireplace. That door that's open. That's the scullery. The door to the tunnel is open, too. I opened it in case I had to run. Momma was in Dublin."

"Come on, Scarlett, you can bawl your eyes out later. Cat is going to save our unworthy necks."

The tunnel had high grated windows. There was barely enough light to see, but Rhett moved at a steady speed, never stumbling. His arms were bent, his hands under Cat's knees. He jounced her in a gallop, and she shrieked with delight.

My lord, our lives are in terrible danger, and the man's playing horsie! Scarlett didn't know whether to laugh or cry. Was there ever in the history of the world a man who was as crazy about babies as Rhett Butler?

From the servants' wing Cat directed them through a door into the stable yard. The horses were maddened with fright. Rearing, neighing, kicking at the gates to the stalls. "Hold Cat tight while I let them out," Scarlett said urgently. Bart Morland's story was vivid in her memory.

"You take her. I'll do it." Rhett put Cat in Scarlett's arms.

She moved to the safety of the tunnel. "Kitty Cat, can you stay here for a little while by yourself while Momma helps with the horses?"

"Yes. A little while. I don't want Ree to be hurt."

"I'll send him to the good pasture. You're a brave girl."

"Yes," said Cat.

Scarlett ran to Rhett's side, and together they released all the horses except Comet and Half Moon. "Bareback will do," said Scarlett. "I'll get Cat." They could see torches moving inside the house now. Suddenly a ladder of flame raced up a curtain. Scarlett raced to the tunnel while Rhett calmed the horses. When she ran back with Cat in her arms, he was on Comet's back, holding Half Moon by the mane with one hand to keep him steady. "Give Cat to me," he said. Scarlett handed his daughter up to him and climbed the mounting block then onto Half Moon.

"Cat, you show Rhett the way to the ford. We'll go to Pegeen's, the way we always do, remember? Then we can take the Adamstown road to Trim. It's not far. There'll be tea and cakes at the hotel. Just don't dawdle. You show Rhett the way. I'll keep up. Now go."

They stopped at the tower. "Cat says she'll invite us to her room," said Rhett evenly. Over his broad shoulder Scarlett could see flames licking into the sky beyond. Adamstown was on fire, too. Their escape was cut off. She jumped from the back of her horse.

"They're not far behind," she said. She was steady now. The danger was too close for nerves. "Hop down, Cat, and run up that ladder like a monkey." She and Rhett sent the horses running along the riverbank, then followed.

"Pull up the ladder. They can't get to us then," Scarlett told Rhett.

"But they'll know we're here," he said. "I can keep anyone from getting in; only one can come up at a time. Quiet, now, I hear them."

Scarlett crawled into Cat's cubbyhole and drew her little girl into her embrace.

"Cat's not afraid."

"Shhh, precious. Momma's scared silly."

Cat covered her giggling with her hand.

The voices and the torches came nearer. Scarlett recognized the boasting of Joe O'Neill, the blacksmith. "And didn't I say we'd kill the English to a man if they ever dared to march into Ballyhara? Did you see it, then, the face of him when I raised my arm? 'If you have a God,' says I, 'which I doubt, make your peace with him now,' and then I drove the pike into him, like spitting a grand fat pig." Scarlett held her hands over Cat's ears. How frightened she must be, my fearless little Cat. She's never nestled close to me this way in her life. Scarlett blew softly on Cat's neck, *aroon, aroon,* and rocked her baby in her lap from side to side as if her arms were the safe tall sides of a sturdy cradle.

Other voices overlapped O'Neill's. "The O'Hara'd gone over to the English, did I not say it long ago?" . . . "Aye, that you did Brendan, and fool I was to argue" . . . "Did you see her, now, down on her knees by the redcoat?" . . . "Shooting's too good for her, I say we hang her with a choking rope" . . . "Burning's better, burning's what we want" . . . "The changeling's what we've to burn, the dark one that brought the afflictions, I say the changeling spelled The O'Hara" . . . "spelled the fields . . . spelled the rain from the clouds themselves" . . . "changeling" . . . "changeling" . . . "changeling" . . . Scarlett held her breath. The voices were so close, so inhuman, so like the yowling of wild beasts. She looked at the outline of Rhett's shadow in the darkness beside the opening to the ladder. She sensed his controlled alertness. He could kill any man who dared to climb the ladder, but what could stop a bullet if he showed himself? Rhett. Oh, Rhett, be careful. Scarlett felt a flooding, tingling happiness in every part of her. Rhett had come. He loved her.

The mob reached the tower and stopped. "The tower . . . they're in the tower." The shouts were like the baying of hounds at the death of the fox. Scarlett's heart hammered in her ears. Then O'Neill's voice cut through the others.

". . . not there, see the rope still hanging down?". . . "The O'Hara's clever, she'd be tricking us that way," another argued, and then all joined in. "You go up and see, Denny, you made the rope, you know its strength" . . . "Sure, go see for yourself, Dave Kennedy, since it's your idea" . . . "The changeling talks with the ghost up there, they do be saying" . . . "He's hanging still, his eyes open cutting right through you like a knife" . . . "Me old mother saw him walking on All Hallows', the rope was dragging behind blighting all it touched to shrivelled backness" . . . "I feel a cold wind down my back, I'm leaving this haunted place" . . . "But if they're up there, The O'Hara and the changeling? We need to kill them for the ill they've done us" . . . "Ach, isn't slow starving a death as good as burning? Put your torches to the ropes, then, lads. They'll not get down without breaking their necks!"

Scarlett smelled the rope burning, and she wanted to shout in jubilation. They were safe! No one could come up now. Tomorrow she could make a rope from strips of the quilts on the floor beneath her. It was over. They'd make their way to Trim somehow, when daylight came. They were safe! She bit her lips to stop herself from laughing, from crying, from calling Rhett's name so she could feel it in her throat, hear it in the air, hear his deep, sure, laughing response, hear his voice speak her name.

It was a long time before the voices and the sound of trampling boots faded completely away. Even then Rhett did not speak. He came to her, and to Cat, and held them both in his strong embrace. It was enough. Scarlett rested her head against him, and it was all she wanted.

Much later, when Cat's heavy looseness told of deep sleep, Scarlett laid her down and covered her with a quilt. Then she turned to Rhett. Her arms circled his neck, and his lips found hers.

"So that's what it means," she whispered shakily when the kiss ended. "Why, Mr. Butler, you fairly take my breath away."

Muted laughter rumbled in his chest. He unlocked her embrace and gently separated them. "Come away from the baby. We have to talk."

His low, quiet words did not make Cat stir. Rhett tucked the quilt closely around her. "Over here, Scarlett," he said. He backed out of the niche and walked to a window. His profile was like a hawk's against the fire-lit sky. Scarlett followed him. She felt as if she could follow him to the ends of the earth. He had only to call her name. No one had ever said her name quite the way Rhett did.

"We'll get away," she said confidently when she was beside him. "There's a hidden path from the witch's cottage."

"From what?"

"She's not really a witch, at least I don't think so, and it doesn't matter anyhow. She'll show us the path. Or Cat will know one, she's in the woods all the time."

"Is there anything Cat doesn't know?"

"She doesn't know you're her father." Scarlett saw the muscles tighten in his jaw.

"Some day I'll beat you black and blue for not telling me."

"I was going to, but you fixed it so I couldn't!" Scarlett said hotly. "You divorced me when it was supposed to be impossible, and then before I could turn around you had gone and gotten married. What was I supposed to do? Hang around your front door with my baby wrapped in my shawl like some kind of fallen woman? How could you do such a thing? That was rotten of you, Rhett."

"Rotten of me? After you went charging off to God knows where without a word to anybody? My mother was worried sick, literally ill, until your Aunt Eulalie told her you were in Savannah."

"But I left her a note. I wouldn't upset your mother for the world. I love Miss Eleanor."

Rhett caught her chin in his hand, turned and held her face in the uneven garish light from the window. Suddenly he kissed her, then he put his arms around her and held her to him. "It happened again," he said. "My darling, hot-tempered, pigheaded, wonderful, infuriating Scarlett, do you realize we've been through this before? Missed signals, missed chances, misunderstandings that need never have happened. We've got to stop it. I'm too old for all this drama."

He buried his lips and his laughter in her tangled hair. Scarlett closed her eyes and rested against his broad chest. Safe in the tower, safe in Rhett's embrace, she could afford her fatigue and relief. Luxurious weak tears of exhaustion ran down her cheeks, and her shoulders slumped. Rhett held her close and stroked her back.

After a long time, his arms tightened with demand, and Scarlett felt new, thrilling energy race through her veins. She lifted her face to his, and there was neither rest nor safety in the blinding ecstasy she felt when their lips met. Her fingers combed his thick hair, grabbed, held his head down and his mouth on hers until she felt faint and at the same time strong and fully alive. Only the fear of waking Cat kept the wild cry of joy from bursting out of her throat.

When their kisses grew too urgent, Rhett broke away. He gripped the stone sill of the window with corded, white-knuckled hands. His breathing was ragged. "There are limits to a man's control, my pet," he said, "and the one thing I can think of that's more uncomfortable than a wet beach is a stone floor."

"Tell me you love me," Scarlett demanded.

Rhett grinned. "What makes you think that? I come to Ireland on those damned clanking chugging steamships so often because I like the climate here so much."

She laughed. Then she hit him on the shoulder with both fists. "Tell me you love me."

Rhett trapped her wrists in a circle of his fingers. "I love you, you abusive wench." His expression hardened. "And I'll kill that bastard Fenton if he tries to take you from me."

"Oh, Rhett, don't be silly. I don't even like Luke. He's a horrible, cold-blooded monster. I was only going to marry him because I couldn't have you." Rhett's skeptical raised eyebrows forced Scarlett to continue. "Well, I did sort of like the idea of London . . . and being a countess . . . and paying him back for insulting me by marrying him and getting all his money for Cat."

Rhett's black eyes glinted with amusement. He kissed Scarlett's imprisoned hands. "I've missed you," he said.

They talked through the night, sitting close together on the cold floor with their hands clasped. Rhett could not get enough of learning about Cat, and Scarlett delighted in telling him, delighted in his pride in what he learned. "I'll do my best to make her love me more than you," he warned.

"You don't stand a chance," Scarlett said confidently. "We understand each other, Cat and I, and she won't put up with babying and spoiling from you."

"How about adoring?"

"Oh, she's used to that. She's always had it from me."

"We'll see. I have a way with women, I've been told."

"And she has a way with men. She'll have you jumping through hoops before a week's out. There was a little boy named Billy Kelly—oh, Rhett, guess what? Ashley's married. I did the matchmaking. I sent Billy's mother to Atlanta . . ." The story of Harriet Kelly led to the news that India Wilkes had finally found a husband, which led to the news that Rosemary was still a spinster.

"And likely to stay one," Rhett said. "She is at Dunmore Landing, plowing money into restoring the rice fields and getting to be more like Julia Ashley every day."

"Is she happy?"

"She glows with it. She would have packed my things herself if it would have hurried my departure."

Scarlett's eyes questioned him. Yes, Rhett said, he had left Charleston. It had been a mistake to think that he could ever be content there. "I'll go back. Charleston never gets out of the blood of a Charlestonian, but I'll go to visit, not to stay." He had tried, he'd told himself that he wanted the stability of family and tradition. But in the end, he began to feel the nagging pain where his wings had been clipped. He couldn't fly. He was earthbound, ancestor-bound, Saint Cecilia–bound, Charleston-bound. He loved Charleston—God, how he loved it—its beauty and its grace and its soft-scented salt breezes and its courage in the face of loss and ruin. But it wasn't enough. He needed challenge, risk, some kind of blockade to be run.

Scarlett breathed a quiet sigh. She hated Charleston, and she was sure Cat would, too. Thank heaven Rhett wasn't going to take them back there.

In a quiet voice, she asked about Anne. Rhett was silent for what seemed to her a very long time. Then he spoke, and his voice was heavy with sorrow. "She deserved better than me, better than life granted her. Anne had a quiet bravery and strength that puts every so-called hero to shame . . . I was more than half crazy about that time. You'd gone, and no one knew where you were. I believed you were punishing me, so to punish you, and to prove that I didn't care about your leaving, I got the divorce. An amputation."

Rhett stared into space, unseeing. Scarlett waited. He prayed he hadn't hurt Anne, he said. He'd searched his memory and his soul, and he could find no willful hurt. She was too young, and she loved him too much, to suspect that tenderness and affection were only the shadows of a man's loving. He would never know what blame he should take for marrying her. She'd been happy. One of the injustices of the world was that it was so easy to make the innocent and caring ones happy with so little.

Scarlett put her head on his shoulder. "It's a lot, making somebody happy," she said. "I didn't understand that until Cat was born. I didn't understand a lot of things. Somehow, I learned from her."

Rhett rested his cheek on her head. "You've changed, Scarlett. You've grown up. I have to get to know you all over again."

"I have to get to know you, period. I never did, even when we were together. I'll do better this time, I promise."

"Don't try too hard, you'll wear me out." Rhett chuckled, then kissed her forehead.

"Stop laughing at me, Rhett Butler—no, don't. I like it, even when it makes me mad." She sniffed the air. "It's raining. That should finish off the fires. When the sun comes up, we'll be able to see if anything's left. We should try and get some sleep. We're going to be very busy in a few hours." She nestled her head into the hollow of his neck and yawned.

While she slept, Rhett moved her, lifted her into his arms and sat down again, holding her as she had held Cat. The gentle Irish rain made a curtain of soft silence around the old stone tower.

At sunrise, Scarlett stirred and woke. When she opened her eyes, the first thing she saw was Rhett's beard-shadowed, hollow-eyed face, and she smiled contentedly. Then she stretched, moaning softly. "I hurt all over," Scarlett complained. Her brow wrinkled. "And I'm starving to death."

"Consistency, thy name is woman," murmured Rhett. "Get up, my love, you're breaking my legs."

They walked carefully to Cat's hideaway. It was dark, but they could hear her soft snoring. "She sleeps with her mouth open if she turns over onto her back," Scarlett whispered.

"A child of many talents," Rhett said.

Scarlett stifled her laughter. She took Rhett's hand and drew him with her to a window. The sight that met their eyes was sobering. Dozens of dark fingers of smoke reached up from every direction, making dirty stains on the tender rose color of the sky. Scarlett's eyes filled with tears.

Rhett put his arm around her shoulders. "We can build it all back, darling."

Scarlett blinked away the tears. "No, Rhett, I don't want to. Cat's not safe in Ballyhara, and I guess I'm not either. I won't sell up, this is O'Hara land, and I won't let it go. But I don't want another Big House, or another town. My cousins can find some farmers to work the land. No matter how much shooting and burning, the Irish will always love the land. Pa used to tell me it was like his mother to an Irishman.

"But I don't belong here, not any more. Maybe I never did really, or I wouldn't have been so ready to go off to Dublin and house parties and hunts ... I don't know where I belong, Rhett. I don't even feel at home any more when I go to Tara."

To Scarlett's surprise, Rhett laughed, and the laughter was rich with joy. "You belong with me, Scarlett, haven't you figured that out? And the world is where we belong, all of it. We're not home-and-hearth people. We're the adventurers, the buccaneers, the blockade runners. Without challenge, we're only half alive. We can go anywhere, and as long as we're together, it will belong to us. But, my pet, we'll never belong to it. That's for other people, not for us."

He looked down at her, the corners of his mouth quivering with amusement. "Tell me the truth on this first morning of our new life together, Scarlett. Do you love me with your whole heart, or did you simply want me because you couldn't have me?"

"Why, Rhett, what a nasty thing to say! I love you with all my heart and I always will."

The pause before Scarlett answered his question was so infinitesimal that only Rhett could have heard it. He threw his head back and roared with laughter. "My beloved," he said, "I can see that our lives are never going to be dull. I can hardly wait to get started."

A small grimy hand tugged on his trousers. Rhett looked down.

"Cat will go with you," said his daughter.

He lifted her to his shoulder, his eyes glistening with emotion. "Are you ready, Mrs. Butler?" he asked Scarlett. "The blockades are waiting for us."

Cat laughed gleefully. She looked at Scarlett with eyes that were bright with shared secrets. "The old ladder is under my quilts, Momma. Grainne told me to save it."